THE BOY IN WINTER'S GRASP

JOHN D. SCOTCHER

WWW.JOHN-D-SCOTCHER.CO.UK

For my parents.
They dragged me around castles from an unfairly young age.
Because of them, I fell in love with the past years before
I went to a single history lesson.

And for my friend Ryan.
I started this book the year I met him. I finished it the year he left us.
If he were still here, he would have no qualms about telling me which bits
need improvement. Half the time, he'd be right.

TABLE OF CONTENTS

CHAPTER ONE

The Master of Cragtop

Albert hated Friday mornings. It wasn't that his paper round was any harder, and he didn't spend any more time tramping over the wet Derbyshire moors. Though the winter chill seemed particularly harsh this morning — it had been getting steadily worse all December — that was nothing compared to the clutching in his stomach.

Friday was the day that he delivered the papers to Cragtop.

Albert's round was long. Sometimes if he was lucky, his father, who owned the general store, took pity on him and ordered his brother to help. On those days, he could be finished in time to get to Mrs Lane's reading lessons in the church school. Even on the slowest rounds, when he dangled his eleven-year-old legs into the brook for an hour, or took a mug of tea with Thomas the shepherd, he'd still be back in time to join his friends on the school wall at break time. There they would talk in excited voices about the war, how they would join up and beat their way to Germany.

'We'll teach the Kaiser!' his friend Harry had said yesterday, then gone on to tell the boys exactly how. Mrs Lane eventually came out to see what all the laughing had been about, scolding them and telling them they sounded like monkeys. Albert hadn't been laughing, though. He had already realised that Friday was just around the corner and his feet felt like lead weights.

Now Friday was here, Albert just wanted it to be over. He took his bag, pulled his coat over a thick jumper, and crashed out into the winter morning. He sped through the first part of the round, pushing papers with careless determination through people's doors, his feet turning almost before the flaps snapped shut.

When the bag was finally empty he raced back to the shop, trying not to think too much. It was only when he found himself staring at the irregular pile of papers for Cragtop House that his butterflies returned.

Thankfully, Cragtop didn't take a daily paper, but the Friday delivery filled a whole bag. There would be about forty items, sometimes many more. The delivery was made up of such a variety of papers, magazines and more, that Albert often found himself stopping to look as he packed them.

Some were regulars. From Fleet Street came every issue of the Times. From Scotland came the Herald, Monday, Wednesday, and Friday. From Manchester the Manchester City News. Occasionally the front pages of these newspapers with stories of the situation in Europe caught his attention, but he was too jittery to stay distracted for long.

Along with the nationals, there were many local papers with articles about lads joining up, gossip about members of the parish, and notices that surely had meaning to no one but the people who lived there. Albert had often wondered what it was that made these papers so interesting to the solitary owner of Cragtop.

However, it was the odd assortment of magazines and pamphlets that unnerved him. Each week there would be a handful, their subject matter hinting at mysterious things quite out of place with Albert's world. Archaeological journals detailed discoveries of ancient tombs. Badly printed newsletters from obscure societies with articles that were even stranger. Some were so worn by their journeys that they were falling apart.

Most Albert could not open, as they were sealed in brown paper, but many of these had the name of the sender on their reverse. Even the names seemed scary; 'The Society of Light from the Silver Dagger', 'Journal of the Flowered Knife'. They made him think about folk tales that he had occasionally heard from the old men of the village.

Once, in late November a small white booklet had arrived that was not in an envelope. Instead the pages were glued together, needing a paper knife to separate them. The booklet's title was fixed to the front cover, just below an address label; 'On Controlling Fiends and Monsters'.

He'd shown his father, who had smirked and cuffed him on the back of the head. All that mattered as far as his father was concerned was that a man paid his bills and kept a civil tongue in his head. There, the Master of Cragtop was faultless.

Albert glanced across at his father as he stuffed the last of the papers into the bag. The stern-faced man was busy with an early customer. It wouldn't do to be here when he was done. His father was very free with his cuffs.

Albert pulled the bag up on to his shoulder and headed back out into the cold. He turned left and began to trudge through the snow towards the outskirts of the village.

He didn't know very much about the owner. Cragtop was perched high on the rocks a few miles from the village. It had always seemed to attract strangers.

Like his predecessors, the current owner had been the subject of village gossip when he arrived in 1911. He lived alone, apart from an elderly manservant, and had made no attempt to befriend the locals in the three years since.

There had been wild stories about him from the villagers. 'I hear he mined in Africa,' Thomas had said, buying tobacco in the crowded shop one morning. 'Got rich finding diamonds on land he stole from the Boers.'

'He's the mark of a slave trader, if you ask me,' Old Clem had replied. Old Clem had once been to sea and so considered himself an authority on most things beyond the village. 'It's in the eyes. I saw 'em all over in the old days. 'Orrible buggers.'

Like anything fresh, though, eventually he had become old news and the villagers had found other things to talk about. On the rare occasions he was seen in the village, people would nod politely and perhaps say that they saw him, but other than that no one much cared.

Albert thought differently: The owner of Cragtop was a wizard.

Albert lingered by the entrance to Cragtop, summoning the courage to walk through the rusty iron gates. From the gates there was a half-mile walk through a steep-sided valley. If those gates closed behind him, Albert knew he was trapped. Nothing, not the nagging weight of the bag or even the dirty sleet soaking through his coat and chilling him so much it was hard to breathe, would make him take another step until he was ready.

From here everything became a tried and tested plan that he'd used and constantly improved since he first delivered to Cragtop. The plan had a simple goal, to be in and out of the grounds in the shortest amount of time and draw as little attention as possible whilst there. That way he would be as safe as he could be, though he didn't think that was safe at all. He closed his eyes and muttered a few words of encouragement to himself. Then he started forward through the gateway.

Tall trees grew tightly together, struggling for the light, before the sides of the valley climbed too high and cast the grounds beyond into shadow. Branches crept over the driveway, creating a gloomy tunnel that bent around to the west. Albert followed the bend, walking briskly and keeping tight to where the light was dimmest and he felt least exposed.

A single bird whistled a lonely song in the otherwise silent wood. Animals seemed to shy away from this place. Albert had seen no signs of life here. In fact, the only thing he had once seen was the body of a cat, just in from the gates. It had been stretched out with its paws up, as if trying to ward off something, its eyes wide open in terror. He had bent and looked, but had been unable to see any reason for the cat to be dead.

The drive opened out into a slim valley. Grass grew in thick clumps and occasional heathers sprouted up. At the far end, the valley began to rise beyond a second copse. Above the trees, Cragtop lurched into the grey morning. The angles of its tall rock-built chimneys and high-arched windows gave it the constant feel that it was about to crash to the ground.

The whole building just looked precarious. Dark stone carvings of lions and wolves clung to the walls, shadowing the doors and windows they surrounded. From one side of the house a cold, moss-covered wall ran out to the ruins of an outhouse, a grim shell with a caved-in roof that could hide all sorts of dangers. Albert had never gone near it.

He crept out from the hood of trees into the valley and quickened his step, fixing his eyes firmly on the drive in the distance. He knew if he picked up his pace he could get across, leave the papers, and be back by the entrance in less than five minutes.

Even in the brief time he had been under the trees the morning had darkened. The drops of sleet had become fatter and colder, turning to snow. He pulled the collar of his sopping coat tighter with his free arm and pushed on across the grass, his heart pounding.

As he marched he began to recite under his breath in a hollow reedy voice. 'Her eyes are as bright as they were the first night, when we danced to an old fashioned tune. In a dusty old schoolhouse on Saturday night, how we laughed as we waltzed round the room.'

The song always made him feel better. He knew if he marched in time he would have delivered the post after the fourth time he had sung it.

'You came from the valleys to the dark city alleys, to care for the young and the poor. And me a young soldier with medals galore, that I'd won in the African war.'

He sang the rest of it as he tramped over the grass. The wind rocked the trees audibly. It whistled against his ears, making his voice sound very small. When he reached the end of the song, he counted eight steps in his head then began again, clicking wet fingers to mark the time.

He reached the far end of the drive by his third recitation, and began to feel some relief. He was getting close to the house.

He began again. 'Her eyes are as bright as they were the first night, when we danced to an old fashioned …'

4

Then he saw them.

There were three of them, standing off by the furthest trees to his right, just where the valley side began to rise sharply. They stood motionless, watching. Two were men in simple white shirts that were soaked to the skin, not that they seemed to have noticed. The third was a woman, a step or two ahead of the others, one leg tensed as if ready to spring forward and rush him.

The woman was the clearest to him. Weathered skin stretched painfully tight over a bony face that looked desperately hungry. Her eyes bore straight into him, her mouth hung open, as if she were trying to suck in his scent and taste it on her tongue. Her face seemed somehow wrong, too pinched up and sharp to be entirely human. Albert remembered the title of the pamphlet 'Controlling Fiends and Monsters' and a rush of adrenaline pumped into his body, making his legs and arms tingle.

The woman took a step forward. One of the men behind her reached and grabbed her arm, yanking her back. She snarled at him but didn't try to free herself. After a moment all three of them turned and walked into the darkness of the woods. The woman looked back once, just before she disappeared.

Albert gasped, rooted to the spot. He thought about dropping the papers where he stood and leaving, but if there was a complaint to his father, he'd be beaten so hard he wouldn't be able to sit on the wooden school seats for a week. That prospect forced him to be brave.

He willed his legs onward up the drive, wiping away tears of fear. A person in the trees could get from where those three had been to the house almost without being seen at all. Albert picked up his pace until he was nearly running. His eyes stayed firmly on the trees. He was ready to drop his burden at any time and turn for home. The canvas bag swung heavily, threatening to overbalance him. So he loped along, the effort he was making out of all proportion to the speed he was going.

Finally, he reached the porch. He gripped on the bell rope and pulled hard three times. Somewhere deep in the house a bell rang. Albert began to pull out the papers, dumping them in a messy pile on the door step. He stole desperate glances into the woods. Nothing seemed to be approaching.

The papers took ages to pull from the bag. Eventually they were all on the pile. All that remained was to be sure that someone was coming to get them. Albert listened at the door, shifting his weight from one foot to the other. He strained his ears for the creak of a floorboard that would tell him he could escape.

'Boy.' A whisper that sounded like tearing paper froze him.

He turned back toward the dingy woods. A short distance beyond the tree line three figures crept towards him, black silhouettes against a grey background.

'Boy,' the voice repeated, all silk and poison. 'Boy, come to us.'

Albert's legs were jelly. His feet below felt glued to the ground. He stared into the woods. The creatures began to edge nearer. A tiny voice in the back of his head was calling out to him, reminding him about something, but he couldn't for the life of him make it out. All he could focus on were the dark shadows growing closer to the edge of the trees.

There was a sudden click. The entrance door to Cragtop unlatched. At the noise the three figures in the wood shrank back and disappeared. Albert gasped aloud, his senses coming back to him.

Run! That's what the little voice had been saying. Run! Albert grabbed his discarded bag from the porch entrance and, summoning all the strength his young legs could muster, he raced back down the drive.

As he ran, crashes and cracks of wood being crushed underfoot followed him from within the trees. He shot a look into the darkness and caught a brief glimpse of three shapes racing along at the side of him, then he burst into the valley leaving the woods and house behind. He didn't dare look back again as he tore across the grass.

When he reached the comparative safety of the gates, he stopped and glanced back. Everything was still again. He leaned forward, resting his weight on a tree trunk and struggled to catch his breath.

'Now, what did you see to make you so scared?' A thin hand with long elegant fingers clamped on to his shoulder and pulled him around.

Albert stared up into the cold merciless face of the Master of Cragtop. Eyes, with irises so dark they were almost black, bore into him.

He came nearer; Albert could feel hot breath on his face.

'Answer me, boy.'

Then Albert knew he was doomed. With a sob he screwed his eyes shut, fear making him wet himself. It ran down his leg and on to the slush below, blossoming into a little yellow puddle.

The man looked at the puddle and shoved Albert away from him. He fell into the road and bashed his head on the rough stone. Blood dripped into his eyes, stinging them and making it hard to see. He raised his arms to ward off blows, whimpering, but none came.

'Your father will hear about this, boy. I imagine you will be soundly beaten.' The pitiless voice was further away now.

Albert looked up, wiping blood from his eyes.

The Master of Cragtop stood looking at him, his angular face unmoved. Then he turned, as if he had lost interest, and walked off into his grounds. A black walking stick clicked by his side as he took full confident strides. His long coat, which reached from his bony shoulders to the ground dragged through the sludge underfoot. He disappeared around the bend in the track without turning back again.

Albert sobbed with relief. A beating from his father, though painful, was suddenly preferable to any of the other fears that he turned around in his mind. As the click of the cane quietened into the distance, he clambered to his feet and limped away towards the village.

The Master of Cragtop could sense them watching him as he strode across to the house, three pairs of eyes from the darkness. He stopped and faced the trees.

'Whoever that child saw,' he said in a sharp voice, 'remember this. The next time I find someone other than me has seen you, there will be consequences. You still have families that you could put in danger.'

A single howl came from the darkness, a howl so full of hatred that the Master smiled to himself. They still had fire, for all the good it would do them. He would miss his gypsies when they were gone.

He reached his study ten minutes later. The room was dim with the only light seeping through the open hallway door. His butler, Pope, had already placed the pile of papers by his favourite leather chair and was building a fire in the great stone hearth.

Next to the papers, on a small single-legged table stood a mug of steaming mulled wine. Its rich smell was enticing. He lowered himself into the chair, listening to the satisfying creak as its arms took his weight. Then he reached for the mug of wine and sat back for a moment savouring the dark fruity aroma.

'How is he?' the Master asked Pope.

Pope carried on with his task, placing the last logs in a pyramid around a pile of kindling. 'No change, sir.'

The Master nodded. 'Leave me.'

Pope struck a match against the hearth and touched its flame to some scrunched-up newspaper at the very centre of the fire. Once sure it was lit, he rose silently to his feet and left the room, shutting the door behind him. The

Master closed his eyes, listening to the soft crackles as the flames caught on the dry wood.

It was not long before the firelight was bright enough that he could detect its flickering behind his eyelids. He sighed. It was time to start work. He opened his eyes and glanced around.

The study was full. Every space, every table, every bookshelf was packed. Books battled for space with piles of periodicals and papers. Squashed amongst them were collections of letters, bundles of drawings, maps and boxes.

To his left a series of shelves were filled with books of science, from the earliest ideas of the ancients, to those of more recent authors such as Darwin and Freud. Another pile of books on languages towered to the ceiling from one side of a large oak desk in the centre of the room.

On the other side of the desk were piles of books claiming to explain magic. Of the whole room, these seemed to be the least read. A layer of dust had settled on them. Under the desk, the periodicals that the paper boy had found so disturbing lay looking almost as underused.

The Master's red leather armchair was clearly the centre of activity. The books within reach were the most thumbed, some left open on particular pages. Close by also was a pile of storybooks and legends from the ages nestled among penny dreadfuls and adventure magazines for boys. Next to them another pile seemed mainly concerned with artists' visions of hell and terror.

In front of the leather chair, just to the left of the giant fire where the light would illuminate it the most, was a vast wooden board. Loosely pinned folders covered it from top to bottom. From many of them newspaper clippings and other bits of paper stuck out. On each folder, there was a photo or drawing of a child.

By the pictures, each child's name and age was written in the Master's flowing script. 'Harold Bonnard. Eleven. Baker's son. Northampton.' 'Claire Albiston. Thirteen. Dressmaker's daughter. Glasgow.' 'Alfred Frumpton. Nine. Orphan. London.' And so it went on.

The children ranged in age from nine years to sixteen. All sections of society were represented. The children of thieves were placed next to the children of lords.

Some folders had other notes on them scrawled in red ink. Angry exclamations such as 'the doctor's treatments are working' and 'her grandmother still won't die!' ran across them in large accusing letters. On others, a dark blue ink seemed to show a more positive reaction; 'looking at having her committed', 'won school prize for creative writing'.

A handful of the second kind were marked in their top right corners with stars. These folders were the most thumbed, with creases and tears where they had been regularly examined.

The Master sipped his mulled wine, cooled enough for him to drink now, and calmly watched the pictures. He allowed the young faces staring back to wash over him, their features seeping in and refreshing his memory as they did each Friday. Then he drained the rest of the drink, took the top paper from the morning's pile and began to read.

For the next few hours he pored over the papers. He scanned the contents on every page thoroughly. Occasionally he would sit up as a story caught his attention, gripping the item he was reading with tightened hands. Most of the time he would read part of the article and then dismiss it. Then he would settle back down into his chair.

Twice though, he found something that he was looking for. Once at eleven o'clock, just after Pope had brought in a pot of steaming tea and some fine Derbyshire sponge from the village, and again at three o'clock, when his mind was beginning to wander from the task at hand. In both cases he pulled out a handsome little pair of ivory handled scissors from a drawer in the table and cut out the article. Then he got up from his chair and walked to the folders on the wall, slipping the article into one.

The first time the folder was that of a girl, 'Edna Palmer. Ten. Butler's daughter. Malham.' The girl had a single star on the corner of the folder. For a second the Master hovered his pen over that corner, considering whether he should add another star, then he shook his head and sat back down.

The second time was far less exciting. The article was dropped into a virtually empty folder, with the face of a smiling eleven year old boy called Billy on the front. The Master didn't even glance at the photo, as though the boy hadn't begun to register properly in the league that he had set up on the wall. He reached for the servant's bell by the door, thirsty again.

By the time Pope had brought a new tray of tea, the Master was reading Thursday's Times. He could feel his attention waning and sat higher in his seat, willing himself to keep concentration on the front page.

The articles meandered around domestic politics and the war. Pages two and three were much the same. There was nothing that attracted his attention. The Master felt his eyes drooping. He rested the paper on his lap and poured himself a cup of the hot tea. He turned the page and lifted the tea to his mouth.

He saw the article straight away and his heart missed a beat. It was small, in the top corner of page five, the society page. Many people would probably have glanced at the headline and turned over. The Master though, leaned forward, his mouth slightly ajar, reading the words with wide eyes.

Son Of Novelist Returns Home Disgraced.

Lieutenant Frederick Flyte, eldest son of the late renowned novelist Sarah Flyte, has been returned to England from Belgium. During an action in Ypres, Lieutenant Flyte attempted to lead his men from the field after suffering some kind of episode.

Before being returned home Lieutenant Flyte stood in front of a military tribunal. It was reported that he was confused and unaware of his circumstances. Lieutenant Flyte's father, General Sir Robert Flyte sent a statement from his post in Northern France, in which he asked the court to take into account his son's distinguished service record including the earlier awards of two commendations for bravery within the past two months.

He also asked the tribunal to take into account the death by suicide of Lieutenant Flyte's mother. Mrs Flyte had suffered terribly with melancholia over some years. Since her death, doctors have warned that the latest research indicates such conditions could be hereditary. Mrs Flyte, famous for her popular series of children's books on King Arthur and the Round Table, walked into the sea at Brighton three and a half years ago and drowned herself.

No formal decision was reached at the tribunal. A postponement was settled upon, and it is expected that the trial will continue should Lieutenant Flyte become fit enough.

The Master re-read the story twice, the teacup frozen in his hand, until at last he set it down with a crash. He leapt up, clutching the paper, and strode to the desk. With his free hand, he swept the books on to the floor. They landed with a great cloud of dust.

He dropped the paper on to the desk, then turned and raced for the board. He began to pull folders off, glancing quickly at the images before discarding them on to the floor.

'Where are you?' he said out loud, his movements becoming more urgent.

His eyes flashed. There was his goal, hidden behind another folder. He reached up and pulled it from the wall. A photo of a pale, slight boy with sensitive eyes and dark unruly hair shyly smiled back at him. In the corner, there were already four stars marked, and all over the folder notes had been scribbled – *'His mother has killed herself.'* *'Deeply imaginative child.'* *'Disappeared for five days and won't say where!'*

Next to the photo was the boy's name. 'Christopher Flyte. Fifteen years old. Alton.'

The Master walked back to the desk and set the folder next to the article. He picked up his pen. He leaned forward and made a fifth mark in the corner, then stood quietly and smiled down at the picture.

Behind him, the door opened and Pope looked into the room. 'Is everything all right, sir? I heard a crash.'

The Master nodded without turning around. 'The waiting is over.'

He lifted the folder to where Pope could see it. 'Christopher Flyte has just received his fifth point of attention. We move tonight.'

Pope nodded. 'Very good, sir.'

The Master scribbled an address on to a scrap of paper and thrust it towards his servant. 'Set the gypsies moving. They will need to be there as soon as they can. And they'll need to take the child.'

Pope frowned. 'He may not survive a journey.'

The Master was unconcerned. 'He'll not need to survive for long.'

He glanced down again at the self-conscious eyes of Christopher Flyte staring from the photo. 'Before the boy goes, bring me what he holds.'

Pope looked wary. 'Are you sure that I can, sir?'

'There are charms to protect you. Put it into the box and bring it to me.'

Pope returned a few minutes later. His complexion had gone ashen and he trembled slightly as he set down a slim, plain wooden box.

The Master noted his colour with amusement and walked up to the box. He lifted it, feeling the warmth of barely contained energy from within, and slipped it into his inside pocket. 'The old things will be gone soon, Pope. I can draw on this no more.'

'Until the cycle is completed, sir,' Pope said.

The Master nodded. 'Traces of us will need to be gone tonight. In the downstairs cupboard, you will find two bags. Leave the larger of the two for me and take the smaller. In it you will find a little money for accommodation.'

'Very good, sir.' Pope nodded and made to leave the room then stopped, looking a little embarrassed. 'Best of luck, sir.'

The Master turned back to the paper and placed the folder next to it once again. He smiled to himself and seemed to stand straighter, as if a great worry had been taken from his shoulders, then he turned and strode to the door.

It took about three hours in all to get everything set. The few of his gypsies that remained at the house had disappeared off on the road whilst it had still been light. Pope had made his farewells by bringing in a final pot of tea that was now cold. The Master looked around the hallway, glancing at some of the great, beautiful things he had put there. Then he turned and walked out of the front door, leaving it open behind him.

He trudged across the valley, keeping to the path, dipping in and out of black, moon-cast shadows of the trees. His breath misted out in front of him as he walked. He felt free once again. There was nothing more exciting than to be at the start of a great adventure with no one to be responsible to and nothing to come back to.

He stopped, closed his eyes and whispered an incantation.

The Master didn't like to use power in this way. Spells were of course useful, but he preferred the ones that were not so showy. In this case, though, using more mundane ways to get the same result would take time he didn't want to waste.

He had been saving the incantation for this very moment and he was aware of how its loss would feel. Still that didn't prepare him. The rush of loss was a physical pain, starting in his throat as he mouthed the words. It was as if the very air was being sucked from his body. The wrenching feeling spread down into his lungs, his stomach, his guts, his muscles until it seemed that every part of him was being sucked at, an essence ripped away. His sight dimmed and for a long moment he could see nothing.

Then, as quickly as it had begun, it was over. The wrenching stopped so suddenly he stumbled forward where his weight had been counterbalancing against it. He dropped to one knee, laying his arms across each other. He bent down his head and listened.

Behind him, from within Cragtop a dull whump sounded, and then suddenly the entire building was ablaze. Flames licked every wall, burst from every window and door and spread out towards the woods around. The heat was so intense, the Master could feel it from where he knelt. The glow in the sky would be seen for miles. He needed to be away.

Summoning his strength, he pushed himself up and shuffled onwards towards the gate. With each step, he felt a little more able to continue, and by the time he reached the road he felt almost normal again. It would be like this now, each trick, each spell would drain him until he had a new source of power. Until the cycle was complete.

He turned southwards and strode down to the main highway some miles ahead. There he would turn towards Birmingham with its great chimneys and smoke and then onwards to the south and his goal.

CHAPTER TWO

Christopher

Christopher stepped out of the gymnasium door. He glanced unenthusiastically at the sky. At Marlo School for boys, whatever the weather, games were on Saturday morning. The morning's cold unrelenting drizzle that could seep through a meagre sports kit and sting the skin in minutes had done nothing to deter the games masters of Marlo. Of course, they were wrapped in coats and hats against the chill.

They had already marched most of the boys over to the large playing fields behind the main school building, shouting rallying words of encouragement like, 'Do you think this would stop our chaps in France?' and 'The Germans don't stop attacking Belgium because it's raining!' The boys for their part understood that their masters knew what they were talking about. They threw themselves into games with enthusiasm.

The largest groups of boys were engaged in frenzied games of rugby. The two school rugby pitches, affectionately known as 'Rose Waters' and 'The Stinker', based on their proximity to the grounds men's large compost heap had been split into four smaller pitches for the morning, each containing its own game. There brave young heroes fought to best one another, imagining their abilities on the rugby field would serve them well in other fields of combat.

In the past few months an ambitious spirit had swept the staff rooms and dormitories of Marlo. The passion for the war that had filled the country had filled the school too. It was felt most keenly in the pitched Saturday battles on the rugby fields. Boys who dreamed of being old enough to follow elder brothers and cousins in the stampede to join the army, acted out their own fantasies of victory in the games. Bravado and belief inspired the young combatants to run that little bit faster, kick that little harder and show themselves to be outstanding. At the touch lines the masters sucked at pipes and cigars. The smoke from their lungs mixed with icy morning breath as they hurled tight-lipped bellows of encouragement across the frozen ground.

Christopher trudged past the nearest game, hugging himself to keep warm and keeping his head down. With any luck he would be able to get past the pitch without attracting attention.

'Pick up that pace, Flyte!' Mr Shipway's voice bellowed across the frozen ground. 'An Englishman does not shuffle about. Show some backbone!'

'Yes sir,' Christopher automatically responded, straightening and picking up his pace before Mr Shipway could say more.

For once Christopher envied the rugby players. Normally, the prospect of a bloody nose, grazed knees, or the host of other minor injuries that older boys would inflict on younger put him off the game. There was plenty of opportunity for them to find ways to do that in normal school life, without giving them open excuse. However, the freezing morning made running around to keep up some kind of body warmth seem more appealing.

It wasn't up to the boys what activities they got to play in games. The masters chose. A boy would only be at Marlo for a few days, barely enough time to find his way about, before his first games morning. He would be lined up in the courtyard, dressed in shorts and vest to await his fate.

Mr Shipway was actually a history teacher but also the unofficial head of games. He would march down the line glaring at the boys, assessing physical abilities and strength of character, before splitting them up, propelling them roughly into loose groups based on his decision.

Most boys played rugby at first. Eventually, those who turned out to be of a less able nature would find themselves moved off the pitches in favour of other activities. Christopher had endured a full year of being hurled into the mud before he had been told to report to the gymnasium. He had done so with some trepidation.

Fortunately the masters had seen that his size and wiry frame would be of no use to them in the boxing ring, either. Then his own house master, Mr Whitestone, had handed him a short, tightly strung bow and led him out to the three wooden targets to the north of Rose Waters. With his back to the cries and screams of the rugby pitch, Christopher had watched as Mr Whitestone explained how to hold the bow and how to aim, then had let fly to strike the nearest target with a shot that was just off bull's-eye. When it came to Christopher's turn to make his first attempt he felt more at home with the bow in his hands than he thought possible with any game.

Since then he had become quite good. He was regularly in the top five boys. He had even represented the school. He had found that the masters had begun to notice him in a positive light. Even Mr Shipway had exclaimed, 'So you are a Flyte boy, after all,' after one successful match against another school. That was a compliment indeed.

Whilst he never blamed Freddie, Christopher often wished his big brother had not been quite so good at everything when he was at Marlo. He had also been popular with his easy way and equally easy laugh. Christopher, who was shy at the best of times, struggled to fill the void his brother had left. So seeing anything other than faint disappointment in school masters' faces was a welcome change.

Ahead, Mr Whitestone waved a friendly arm at him. There was one master, at least, who simply took him for who he was. Smiling, Christopher waved back and broke into a light jog, crossing the remainder of the distance to the archery practice targets with enthusiasm.

From the touchline by the posts of Old Stinker, Daniel Corbyne watched Christopher with a cruel smirk on his face. He had been particularly looking out for the slight boy. Now he could see his quarry was going to be conveniently close he was delighted.

In some ways Daniel and Christopher were very similar. They were both quite naturally shy. Both lived in the shadow of an elder brother who had been in the school. But that was where the similarity ended. From a very early age, Daniel had found that the best way to hide his own failings was to root them out in others.

In this respect Daniel was a copy of his own brother. The only difference was that his brother was gifted, whereas Daniel was not. His brother could hurt with both brain and brawn. Daniel had suffered both more than most. Still, he had convinced himself years ago that he loved his brother. That was why he was so proud when he received a letter from him.

In the letter, Daniel's brother had told him all about Frederick Flyte and the article in the Times. Newspapers were strictly forbidden to the pupils in the school, so without the letter Daniel might never have known of the outrage. His brother had even enclosed the clipping.

The letter itself savoured the story with relish. An observant eye would perhaps wonder whether Daniel's brother had been at school at the same time as Freddie; whether they had actually been enemies. However, Daniel didn't have an observant eye, so the letter left him with no questions. Lieutenant Frederick Flyte was not just mad; he was a coward.

He told his friends that night and word had spread. Freddie Flyte's cowardice was Christopher Flyte's cowardice and he should be punished. Now the boy had appeared it was just a case of waiting for the right moment.

Christopher hugged himself to try to keep warm. Though archery was far less active than rugby there was no concession to the cold; the boys still wore shorts and a thin school sporting top. The line of archers waiting their turn hopped and jumped about, wrapping arms tight to their bodies, jogging on the spot and breathing fast to get the blood pumping.

Practice was simple. Each boy would take three shots, then return to the back of the queue to await another go. This would continue until each had taken five turns.

Christopher had been off form that morning. The best he had achieved was a single arrow in the bull. Cold, and the conversations around him, had put him off and he was glad he would soon take his final turn at the firing line.

Philip Swann stood ahead of Christopher, his bow raised with his eyes half closed on his final shot. He was almost a full head taller than Christopher. To his left Bernard Miller slouched against the stump of a tree watching Philip intently, his podgy arms gripping his own bow tightly. When they had their bows Swann and Miller never seemed to feel the cold, the rain, or anything for that matter. They were the two best archers in the school. They were also the nearest thing to friends that Christopher had.

Swann let loose his final arrow. It flew perfectly through the air to thump lightly into the centre of the bull's-eye.

'Well done, Swann!' Miller grinned. 'You'll be beating my score soon, if I'm not careful.'

Swann looked back with a grin and stepped out of the way for Christopher to take the position.

From a vantage point about thirty feet behind the archers, Mr Whitestone watched the proceedings. Despite the ribbing he took good-naturedly from the other masters, the young teacher took the sport very seriously.

'Come on now, Christopher,' he called, his voice missing the harsh edge that was common in the other masters. 'Let's see you hit that bull again.'

Christopher lifted his bow and pulled back on the bowstring with a stiff, cold hand. It cut tight into his fingers until their tips throbbed fat with blood. Finally, he released. The arrow flew toward the target, lodging itself into the outside ring.

'Bad luck, boy! Try again,' Mr Whitestone called.

'Yes bad luck, old fellow,' Miller said quietly enough that only the boys at the front of the queue could hear him. 'Still, I'm sure you could still beat my Aunt Elizabeth.'

Swann stifled a laugh. 'Has she lost her false arm then, Miller?'

The front of the queue erupted into laughter, Christopher included. Mr Whitestone smiled at the boys and walked toward them.

'All right, now. Do try to stay in control. If you don't get these shots in soon there is a good chance that we will all freeze before we ever get a chance to show Winchester what we're made of!'

The mention of the imminent contest with the old school rivals brought a respectful silence over the giggling boys.

'Go on, Flyte.' A voice came from somewhere in the back of the line. Christopher lifted his second arrow, took aim trying to ignore the shivers running through him, and let loose. The arrow followed the path of the first, landing only fractionally closer to the bull.

The final arrow proved marginally better for him, lodging just inside the middle ring. The bull's-eye remained defiantly free of arrows. Christopher sighed and turned to where Miller and Swann waited. Behind him one of the younger boys ran to the target and pulled the arrows from the straw face.

'Never mind, Flyte. There's another practice on Tuesday,' Swann said, flashing him a commiserate smile.

Mr Whitestone gestured at the three of them. 'Right, gentlemen. You may return to the gym.' He turned his attention back to the line of remaining archers.

Christopher fell in next to Miller and Swann. The three of them started across the field in silence. As the sound of their feet crunched into the frosty grass they fell into rhythm until it seemed that there were not three boys but one heavy footed man. Boys always seemed to fall into pace when walking together at Marlo school. Christopher supposed it was all the drilling and marching that was so often a part of their school activities.

Ahead, on the Stinker, a school master signalled the end of a game to a group of older boys. The boys ran dutifully to the touch lines, gathering around the master in a tight semi-circle. Their breath rose above them in little steam clouds.

'They looked on good form,' Miller noted, always the first to break a silence. He glanced at Christopher quickly. 'All right, old man?'

'Yes, absolutely,' Christopher said, then trailed off, not really sure how else to reassure his friend. He actually felt rather useless, but the position of being the least able of them was something he'd grown accustomed to. There was little point in dwelling on it.

'He'll be happier when he gets back to his books,' Swann said, grinning and punching Christopher lightly in the arm.

Miller raised his brow. 'Oh yes. That reminds me! We have a question for you. Wondered if you'd settle an argument.

'Swann here was telling me that your old chum King Arthur had a couple of swords, the Sword in the Stone being one, and Excalibur being the other. Now I say that they're both the same, and you being the expert in this we thought you'd be able to tell us. There's a good size tin of jam resting on the outcome.'

Christopher didn't doubt for a moment that there had been an argument. Most subjects that the two happened upon would be used to fuel their well-established rivalry. Of course, they probably had no need for him to help them prove the answer. It would have been very simple for them to look it up in the vast school library and neither boy was afraid of books. However, they were generous friends and this was a subject that Christopher knew well. They would often find ways to let him use it.

Christopher smiled at him. 'Sorry, Miller, Swann's right.'

Miller frowned. 'Really?'

'Actually, I may have something of an advantage over you here, Miller,' Swann said. He glanced across, a sheepish grin on his face. 'I'm reading a book on Camelot.'

'That's cheating!'

'Well yes, I suppose, but it's funny to see your face!'

Miller did indeed look a little red for a moment before he saw the joke.

Christopher's interest had been caught. 'Which book are you reading?'

Swann stopped, looking guilty. 'Hope you don't mind, Flyte. It's your mother's. "*The Little Knight*".'

Christopher felt his skin tingle at her mention. 'Of course not. She wrote them to be read.'

'Well, that's as may be, but you're still a rotten cheater,' Miller said. 'I think I might have to look in your tuck box and take your jam anyway as punishment.'

With that he took off down the side of Old Stinker in the direction of the gymnasium as fast as his chubby legs could go. Finally, when Swann decided he had allowed him enough of a head start, he leant forward on the balls of his feet and took off.

He pulled up suddenly a few paces later and turned back. 'My sister sent it to me. I should have told you.'

'I'm glad you're reading it.' Christopher smiled broadly in order to leave Swann in no confusion that he was completely fine.

'It really is very good, Christopher,' Swann said, then turned and sprinted after Miller.

Christopher nodded. 'Yes it is, isn't it?'

Michael Stone, the thick-necked scrum half, spotted Flyte was alone. He slapped Daniel's shoulder and nodded in the direction of the boy. Daniel smiled with anticipation.

As if on cue the master dismissed the boys and turned away, relighting his pipe and stomping to the other end of the field, where pupils still battled for mud-soaked victory. Some boys followed suit, keen to be seen to be showing an interest for the school. Others jogged off toward the gym. Soon Daniel Corbyne stood with just Michael Stone.

'What about the others?' Stone asked, looking around him.

'What about them? We can't put off our duty because we haven't got a full company,' Daniel said, feeling that morally he had the might of the entire British Army behind him. 'Come on.'

Daniel strode toward Christopher, his sense of right bolstering the other sense of thrill he felt at the opportunity to dominate. Behind him Stone stayed close to his shoulder, his second in command, ready to move at the leader's word.

As they approached, Christopher looked up. Immediately Daniel saw the fear in his face. Just like his brother, scared at a hint of danger. Daniel drew himself up, puffing out his already wide chest.

'Flyte!'

The boy stopped walking and visibly shrank back a little.

'Can you hear me, Flyte?' It was obvious to Daniel that the boy could hear him, but it was something his brother used to shout at him when he was hiding from a beating back at home. He remembered how scared it made him feel. It felt good to shout it now.

They reached Flyte. To his credit he didn't try to run. He just stood there, fear in his eyes but prepared to see what the matter was.

'What do you want, Corbyne?' the boy asked, the tremor in his voice kept barely in check.

'You're a dirty little coward, Flyte. Just like your brother.'

To Daniel's surprise, the personal insult fell on deaf ears.

'My brother is not a coward!'

Daniel stepped forward and grabbed the boy before he could shy away, pulling him close until their faces were almost touching. Behind him, Stone glanced backwards, but everyone was involved with the games still in play. The three of them were unnoticed.

'Don't answer me back,' Daniel snapped, pleased with the way little drops of spittle sprayed into the boy's face, making him blink. 'If I say you're cowards then you're cowards.'

'Why?' the boy asked.

Daniel hadn't expected a question and it confused him a little. He imagined that the boy's fear would make him accept whatever he was told. 'Because I say so,' he said, expecting this would make the boy see the sense of agreeing.

Christopher's face, though scared, remained confused.

'And because your brother ran away from the Hun, and went mad,' Daniel added, feeling that now would be a good time to put weight to his words.

'What?' At the mention of madness, Flyte's face took on a different look altogether. It suddenly seemed to Daniel that the grip he had on him might have been the touch of the school nurse for all the effect it was having. He considered maybe twisting the boy's wrist to actually cause pain.

'What do you mean?' the boy asked again before he could act on the thought.

'He went mad at the front and tried to lead his men away from the battle. My brother wrote to me and told me about it.'

'Freddie!' The anguish in the boy's voice had completely taken over the fear. This wasn't going at all how Daniel had imagined.

'They're going to court martial him, as soon as he's sane enough to understand.' Daniel spat again, but the moment was lost.

'Get off me.' Flyte pulled out of his grip, actually sounding annoyed with him. 'When did you hear about this?'

'Don't ask me questions!' Daniel said, feeling completely ineffectual.

The boy glanced at him, well, through him actually, then turned away and started hurrying toward the gym. Behind Daniel, Stone made a noise that could have been a giggle. This wouldn't do at all.

'Do you know what they do to cowards?' Daniel called after him. 'When they court martial him, they'll shoot him stone dead. Just like your mad mother!'

The boy stopped and turned around. Any look of fear or anguish was gone, replaced by one of pure anger and hate.

All of a sudden Daniel remembered what it was like to be the scared one.

Afterwards, Christopher tried to remember what had happened. No matter how hard he tried, he could recall nothing. That scared him more than any punishment that might be meted out.

When Corbyne had mentioned his mother's death in that gloating voice he used, Christopher had felt a rush of blood to his head. When he turned and saw the look of fear on Corbyne's face, even though he was a full two years older and a good half foot taller, the rushing had become deafening. As he had run back and leapt at the elder boy, hands stretched out like talons ready to rip at the face before him, his vision had blurred to white-hot blindness.

When he came to his senses, he was being marched across the quadrangle, towards the headmaster's house, a full three hundred yards and two buildings away from the playing fields. How he had gotten there or what had happened was a mystery to him.

His mother had once told him in one of her more lucid moments towards the end that she had suffered sudden memory losses. If he could go blank like this then it could mean that he could also suffer from the madness.

And, if Christopher was honest with himself, over all the things that he feared, madness was the scariest of all.

CHAPTER THREE

Being a Gentleman

It seemed to Christopher that Colonel Horton, the headmaster of Marlo, was already aware of the situation with his brother. Mr Shipway and Mr Whitestone had brought him from the playing fields and stood him against the wall outside the headmaster's office. Mr Shipway had rammed his shoulders forcefully against the cold white plasterwork with a painful thud, and ordered him to 'Stand to attention and don't move!' When Mr Shipway had knocked on the headmaster's door and entered, Christopher had heard the school's leader exclaim at the sound of his name. It was as if the old man had been expecting to see him imminently, under quite different circumstances. However, no matter what the truth of his brother's fate, the grim face in front of him now showed no sympathy.

He stood before the headmaster's large oak desk. It was bare but for a bible, a black ink pen on a stand, and a pile of blank writing paper, lightly bound with black ribbon.

'Sir, I heard a scream,' Mr Shipway began. 'I turned from where I was on the top field and saw Flyte on top of Daniel Corbyne, beating him about the head quite ferociously. Of course, I got over there as soon as I was able, by which time Michael Stone, who was nearby, had pulled Flyte off.

'Flyte was still struggling to get at Corbyne. In fact, it was only after we had forced him off the field and a good way to here that he started to calm down.'

'I see.' The headmaster nodded. 'And Corbyne?'

'Scratches all over his face, Headmaster. Quite a lot of blood drawn.' Mr Shipway paused and shifted his weight from one foot to the other. 'And it looks like his left hand has been bitten, sir. Quite badly.'

The headmaster looked at Christopher for a very long time, saying nothing, rubbing his grey moustache. Then he walked to the tall narrow window and looked out into the snowy morning.

'Thank you. You may return to your duties,' he murmured without turning back.

Mr Shipway hurried to the door, opened it and went through. Mr Whitestone flashed Christopher an unsure smile and followed. The door shut behind them with a click.

Christopher tried to stay at attention. He was in for it. That was for sure. The headmaster was a veteran of a number of military campaigns. He didn't tolerate even the hint of undisciplined behaviour.

'A gentleman doesn't scratch another gentleman,' the headmaster finally said, voice shaking with anger. He spun away from the window and walked to his desk, leaning on it with both hands and looming toward Christopher. 'A gentleman doesn't bite another gentleman!'

Christopher looked to the floor, heart pounding. The headmaster's stare made his cheeks burn with shame. His eyes stung with the beginning of tears. He clenched his teeth together and concentrated on remaining absolutely still.

'Well? Explain yourself.'

Christopher didn't move a muscle. Hundreds of thoughts flew through his head. His brother's situation, his mother, what he should say first. Suddenly in his mind he saw Corbyne's face as a hand he knew was his own scratched down a cheek, drawing blood and eliciting a scream that raised the heads of masters and boys a pitch away. The thought made him feel suddenly sick. He swallowed hard at the pool of saliva that blossomed on his tongue.

'Look at me, Flyte!' The headmaster's voice had raised a notch now. It was only a matter of time before he lost control. 'Say something, boy.'

Christopher looked up. The headmaster's face was thunder.

'I ... I ...' Christopher struggled. 'I don't remember.' The words came out more as a sob.

The headmaster moved around the desk in a flash. Somehow his cane, light and thin, with a permanent kink from so many uses, was in his hand.

The cane flew down on to the backs of his bare legs with a sharp thwack. A red hot line of pain exploded across his flesh, then spread out like a ripple of boiling water. There was no time to recover before the next blow. The headmaster brought the cane down again and again. After the sixth blow he stepped back, breathing heavily. Christopher fell forward against the desk, sobbing and gasping.

For long, agonizing minutes he was unaware of anything other than the intense burning on the backs of his legs. Slowly though, he started to gather his thoughts. The pain began to ebb away. Eventually he was able to stand and look up.

The headmaster had resumed his place by the window, looking out on to the quadrangle below. He didn't turn, but somehow knew Christopher's attention was back with him.

'Four of our old boys died in the last two weeks. Four officers,' he said in a tired voice. 'All leading their men against the Hun. All doing what they trained to do. Four. Doesn't that seem like a lot?'

He came back to his desk, sitting heavily in the high-backed chair behind it. The dull winter light from the window cast grey shadows over his face.

From a drawer he lifted a newspaper. 'Your brother has had an episode whilst on duty, Flyte. He was in the middle of a battle and suddenly tried to get his men to retreat, even though no order had been given. I know no more than what was printed here, but that is enough.

'To any matter, he is being sent home. The influence of your father, no doubt.'

'Corbyne told me, Headmaster,' Christopher stammered. The pain in his legs made his voice high and broken. 'Then he told me my brother would be dead soon, like my mother.'

'Corbyne is a blunt boy, Flyte,' the headmaster said, 'but not wholly inaccurate. Besides, that does not excuse your behaviour. As far as I am concerned, these two matters are unrelated. The behaviour of a gentleman must remain constant, no matter what the adversity.'

He lowered the paper, dropping it back into a drawer. 'Go to your dorm and remain there until I send for you. There will be no lunch or supper for you today. You are forbidden to talk to other boys.'

Christopher limped to the door, trying hard not to show the fresh throb of agony each step caused. He pushed through and quietly shut the door behind him. Only then did he buckle, his hands reaching to rub at the hot bruised meat of his legs.

The headmaster stood and watched Christopher limp slowly across the quadrangle from his window. In the covered bridge that linked the library to the Old Building, a group of boys also watched, pointing and talking with animated gestures, until one of them noticed the headmaster. They melted away in a second. He sighed. There was no illusion then; the pupils of Marlo School knew that one of their ex-boys was branded a coward and a lunatic.

The boy finished his painful journey across the quad then disappeared off down beyond a long hedge of holly bushes. The headmaster sighed. The boy couldn't stay here, it simply wouldn't do. Not only would he prove a distraction to the other pupils, he would undermine the reputation of the school.

There was still a week before the start of the Christmas holidays and that was simply too long. The boy needed to be gone as soon as was possible.

Pulling on his gown, then reaching for his pipe and matches, the headmaster opened the door to his study. He walked the length of the corridor, down to three dull grey stone stairs and outside. As he walked across the cobbles, he struck a match, pausing for a second to light his pipe. He suddenly jerked up his head toward the bridge to see if any pupils were again staring out. None were so foolhardy. Satisfied in his authority and feeling a little better, he strode through an arch wide enough to fit a carriage and out into the grounds of the school.

The main telephone in Marlo was in the school secretaries' offices. The headmaster hated their insistent ringing and refused to have one in his office. The offices were in a small whitewashed building that had originally been the gatehouse before the School acquired more land and moved its borders outward.

The building was divided into two rooms. One was a functional reception with light blue painted walls. It was dominated by a large painting of the school's founder. A long wooden bar ran its width. A secretary would be standing behind it from seven thirty in the morning until seven at night every day that there were pupils in the school, bar Sundays.

The second room was smaller. It was crammed with three desks, four filing cabinets, and the remainder of the secretaries. This room tended to be a little too frivolous for the headmaster's tastes. He was uncomfortable with the company of so many women in one place. As their work was exemplary, however, he had no reason to complain. The telephone was there on the largest of the desks.

The secretaries predictably went into a flurry at the unusual sight of the headmaster at their door. He greeted them, ignoring their flapping, and curtly explained his needs. Within a few moments Mrs Clayton, the senior secretary, found a telephone number for the Flyte household and was reciting it to the operator.

'Just connecting us now, Headmaster.' Mrs Clayton smiled and nodded. She glanced at the other girls with her eyebrows raised. They understood immediately and bustled out of the room to leave her and the headmaster in privacy.

'Hello?' Mrs Clayton returned her attention to the phone. 'Hello. I have Colonel Horton, headmaster at Marlo here to talk to ...' She glanced down at the small card in her hand, 'to Mr E. Welstone.' Then she nodded and lifted the phone toward him.

He took it, glancing at its black stem with distaste. 'Thank you Mrs Clayton.' She hovered for a moment at the door until he glanced at her and she scurried out.

He put the receiver to his ear and lifted the phone to his mouth. 'Hello?'

'Mr Horton?'

The well-spoken voice at the other end of the phone had a syrupy quality that the headmaster took an immediate dislike to. 'It's Colonel Horton, but Headmaster will do. This is Mr Welstone?'

'Indeed, Headmaster.' Welstone's voice showed no hint of remorse at the mistake. In fact, the headmaster could almost detect a pleasure at the slight in the sickly-sweet tone. 'This is he.'

'Mr Welstone, you must excuse my ignorance.' The headmaster ignored his feelings of revulsion at the voice. Not a voice, he wagered, that had seen any military service. 'I am calling regarding Christopher Flyte. I'd hoped to talk to a member of his family.'

'Ah. Alas, there is no such member to talk to, Headmaster,' Welstone said. 'I am the family lawyer. I look after all the family affairs whilst General Flyte is at the front, including the well-being of the boy.'

'I see.' The headmaster understood now. The simpering creature on the other end of the line was used to dealing with his own kind. Lawyers were men of too many words, all deals and bargains. For them an outcome was the only important thing, rather than how it was achieved. The headmaster had very little time for lawyers. No wonder Flyte had so easily attacked Corbyne, with this sort of moral example. 'Well, there has been an incident here, Welstone. The boy has attacked another in the most ungentlemanly of fashions, with very little provocation.'

'How awful.' Welstone sounded like he couldn't be less interested. 'The other boy is hurt?'

'Nothing he cannot bear,' the headmaster replied. 'He's one of our full backs.'

'A full back? Yet little Christopher attacked him? That sounds quite brave to me, Headmaster. Not ungentlemanly at all.'

The headmaster resisted the urge to ask the man at the other end how he would know. 'Well, Mr Welstone, I am afraid the methods that he used were inappropriate, not to mention the idea of two Marlo boys fighting at all. However, that is of no matter. I am telephoning to tell you that I will be sending the boy home early, on the Monday morning train in fact.'

Now Welstone's voice took on some interest. 'Oh no, Headmaster, I am afraid that won't do at all. We have had some trouble with Christopher's elder brother. There is no possibility of you asking to send Christopher home early. We've far too much to do. In fact, I had been considering having him stay at Marlo throughout the holidays.'

'Mr Welstone.' The headmaster controlled his temper. Later he would write letters of condolence to the families of the dead. That was so much more important than negotiating with Flyte's guardian. 'I am quite informed on Lieutenant Flyte. However, it remains that Christopher Flyte today attacked a boy in a manner unbefitting of a Marlo pupil. The alleged conduct of his brother simply adds to the problem. Boys here can read newspapers, Mr Welstone. Boys here can talk. At this time, Marlo does not require a Flyte boy at the school.

'Christopher will be placed on the train. You will expect him to be home on Monday evening and that is the end of the matter. I suggest that you make plans to have him educated locally until this trouble with his brother is over. These are very important times, Mr Welstone. We all have our duty.'

Welstone didn't speak. The headmaster waited calmly. He took a pull on his pipe, letting the smoke escape from the side of his mouth in small puffs. He had looked down the barrel of a Boer rifle and lived to tell the tale. He would not allow the lawyer of a family of cowards to stop him from keeping the reputation of Marlo intact.

'Very well, Headmaster.' Welstone's voice had lost its syrupy edge now. 'I'll have a man wait at the station. Good day to you.'

The headmaster smiled and took another pull from his pipe.

Edwin Welstone slammed down the telephone receiver and pushed back on General Robert Flyte's favourite study chair. He lifted his feet up on to General Flyte's seventeenth-century teak desk and swore. He gripped the handles of the chair tightly, waiting for his irritation to subside. Having Christopher home early was a damn inconvenience.

Welstone was quite young for a lawyer in his position, only twenty-nine, but he dressed and acted far older. Wispy streaks of unusually blonde hair framed a face with small, mean eyes and a high, upward pointing nose that made him look as though he was turning it up at everything. Perhaps to compensate, he constantly hunched his shoulders and bent his head forward when with clients to look up at them with a fixed smile on his face. It made him look like some kind of rodent.

He narrowed his eyes and glanced at the ledger on the desk. The detailed plans of all the Flyte investments were contained within. He sighed, but sat straight again and pulled the ledger towards him.

Robert Flyte had employed him just after his wife's death and then simply left. His explanation was that he did not want his two boys to see him upset, but Welstone didn't believe people did things for others. No, the general wanted to deal with his grief without distraction. That suited Welstone fine. Slowly, he had taken more control of the finances, of course making sure the general knew he was 'happy to help shoulder the burden'.

If he happened to run into the boys in those first few months, he would always stop and exchange a moment with Freddie. He'd pretend interest in the conversation for the least possible amount of time he could get away with. He hardly spoke to Christopher at all. Once Freddie had joined the army, he had convinced the general he would be far more help if he took up permanent residence at Fox Grange. Then he found Christopher even easier to ignore.

He nodded to himself. The boy's coming home, an inconvenience, yes, but it should not be a problem. Most of the staff had been fired — he claimed it was a money saving decision to the general — so the boy had almost no friends here. He'd stay out of his way most of the time, Welstone was sure.

Before he could resume concentration properly, he heard the click of footsteps in the hallway. He glanced up. The replacement housekeeper he had employed only a few days before stood at the door.

'Brodie.' His voice was harsh now, with none of the simpering tones he reserved for his clients and those he needed something from.

Molly Brodie looked at him. 'Yes Mr Welstone?'

'On Monday, Christopher Flyte will be home. Make sure his room is prepared,' he said, then looked back down at the ledger in front of him.

'Yes Mr Welstone,' Brodie replied, her voice emotionless.

If Welstone had looked up again at that moment, he might have seen Molly Brodie's eyes light up in her plain face, her thin lips parted in anticipation. However, he was a man obsessed with his own plans and rarely observed things in others, no matter how clever and cunning he thought himself.

He paid no more attention as she walked to a small table, where he had taken his cup of coffee earlier, and picked up the tray. Perhaps if he had observed any of that, then there would have been a chance he'd have noticed her glance out of the window. There she locked eyes with a shabbily dressed man, who skulked outside by the bushes. A man who, despite the cold, wore a dirty white shirt, soaking wet, and open all the way to his navel.

What he could not have noticed was the understanding that passed between Molly Brodie and the man. That had no outward sign.

It was only when she said, 'Monday,' that he looked up once again.

'Yes, yes. Monday,' he said impatiently. The woman was facing the window. 'And when you're speaking to me, Brodie, please have the common decency to face me.'

She turned. 'I'm sorry, Mr Welstone. Will there be anything else?'

Welstone waved the back of his hand at her. 'No. You may go.'

As she walked away from the window, a sudden movement out in the bushes caught his eye. He glanced across, but now there was nothing. He rubbed at his eyes, wondering how long he had been sitting there, staring at the ledger. A good many hours, he was sure. He shrugged and bent his head to the figures again.

Christopher learned about his fate the following morning. His evening had been cold and lonely. The other boys, quite aware that he was not to be spoken to, had avoided going anywhere near him, instead congregating in the junior common room at the far end of the sparse dormitory.

At lights out, Swann had clambered up on to his bunk above Christopher's, whispering, 'Chin up, Flyte.' He flashed him a secret smile of sympathy.

That had been Christopher's only communication with another soul. He closed his eyes, ignoring the pain of hunger and the heat from his legs, and forced himself to sleep.

On Sunday, as the other boys filed into the school chapel to take their places on the hard, uncomfortable pews, Mr Whitestone walked him back to the headmaster's office.

The headmaster was dressed in his best suit as he always did for service, with his master's robe on top. Instead of his usual purple school tie, he had chosen a black tie. On his arm, he was pulling on a black armband of mourning.

'Flyte,' he said, not looking up, 'I have spoken with your guardian, Welstone. We have agreed that you should return home to Alton. You will take the morning train tomorrow.'

He glanced up, the armband now pulled into place. 'After service today, you will return to your dormitory and pack. The staff will move them to the car. Then you will go to a room in the kitchen staff quarters. You will stay there until you leave. You will take your meals there today. You will continue to refrain from speaking with any other pupils. Only speak to staff when they speak to you. Is that clear?'

Christopher nodded, taking in the new development.

'Is that clear?' The headmaster raised his voice a little and stared directly at Christopher.

'Yes, Headmaster,' Christopher replied quickly, dropping his eyes to avoid meeting the gaze that bore into him.

'Very well.' The headmaster nodded to Mr Whitestone. 'Take him to the gallery. He can take part in the service from there.'

The gallery had traditionally been a place where any boy in trouble attended the Sunday service. It was a small, high chamber, in the gloom above the main chapel. Its balcony gave a view of the altar and the first couple of pews, whilst hiding the rest from sight underneath it. A boy placed here could watch the service with little chance of distracting other pupils. A single pew was nailed to the floor, most of its length covered in thick dust. In two places, the backsides of previous occupants had brushed the wood clean.

Christopher sat in one of the clean spaces. He leaned forward to rest his arms on the rail that ran along the balcony's edge. It creaked dubiously. A small cloud of dust dislodged and floated down towards the nave. The chaplain, who stood just before the altar with an open bible in his hands, looked up sharply. Christopher shrank back, pressing his spine against the pew. He was in enough trouble without disrupting the morning reading. The chaplain looked at his bible and cleared his throat. 'This morning's reading is from Ephesians Six.'

Christopher wasn't yet sure about this latest turn of events. He certainly wouldn't miss the atmosphere of Marlo, which would likely only become more unfriendly. Plus, being at home would be the best place to find out about Freddie. However, the unpleasant prospect of sharing the house with Mr Welstone was something he was not looking forward to. Since the horrid little man had moved in permanently the house felt very little like home.

From below, the chapel organ played a note. Christopher glanced down and saw the front rows of pupils standing, hymn books open and held high. He looked about, but there was no book in the gallery.

The pupils began to sing. It was 'Jerusalem'. He knew most of the words. In the past few months, this hymn had been sung more and more. Its words were rousing and patriotic. It stirred boys' hearts and minds to understand what duty was. It told them God would support them unflinchingly if they carried out that duty. The boys below sung it out with the gusto they understood was expected.

Christopher stayed quiet, though. Singing the stirring words would just make him feel guilty. Corbyne was there somewhere, his face covered in cuts, scratches, and a bite mark on his hand. Signs for everyone that Christopher had not done his duty.

He looked at the chaplain to see if he was being watched. The man had his head buried in his own hymn book. Satisfied that he wouldn't be noticed, Christopher sat down quietly to listen to the rest of the hymn with his head in his hands.

CHAPTER FOUR

Alton

Just after eight on Sunday evening, the Master of Cragtop walked to the edge of the village green in Alton and glanced around. Christopher's home was a sleepy little place. There were barely a dozen houses clustered about its centre. The Master smiled, relieved.

He'd been worried the village might be larger, or perhaps closer to the bustle of Henley-On-Thames, but there was a mile and a half of river between them. Smaller, out of the way places meant fewer people. That was good. The more eyes to see him, the harder he would have to work to carry out his plans without arousing suspicion.

He started down the lane along the eastern edge of the green. It sloped gently, passing two cottages. He glanced through a window, yet to have had its curtains drawn. A couple sat at a kitchen table, deep in conversation, their faces caught in the flickering light of a fire. They looked warm and comfortable and he briefly envied them.

It had been a long and tiring day. He had been very strict with himself on how much of the remaining magic he used. He would be much happier if he could get to the transition with tricks remaining up his sleeve. Whilst his resources were finite and few, everything had to be accounted for.

He wished he had kept more of the mead. Those who drank it became extremely suggestible. He'd used it far too liberally in the previous few years. Now there was not much more than a draught left. Still, at least he had that.

There had been some expenditures he could not do without. Communicating with his gypsies had warned him he would not have the rest of the school term to prepare for Christopher's arrival. The boy was being sent home early. Even though hearing them over such long distances was particularly draining, it was essential.

He needed to use another enchantment when he realised his plan to take a few days to reach Alton would be impossible. Part of him was sorry he would not be carefully picking a route through back roads, with time to consider all possibilities for when he arrived. Fortunately, he had something that he had been saving for exactly this sort of eventuality.

The enchantment simply made him unremarkable to others. Most of the time they would not notice him, and even if they happened to, they would immediately forget him. He had boarded a train in Birmingham and travelled the rest of his journey in speed and comfort. The only slight annoyance was that the charm did its job so well that twice fellow travellers sat on him.

The village green was quite small. To his left a stream bubbled alongside the lane, passing under a wooden bridge further down. Past the cottages, three houses each larger than the previous, were built up with four or five steps to front doors set in clean white walls and brushed stonework. The houses cost good money. The village was not just local tradesmen.

Over the little bridge, a smaller lane turned left. It cut straight up the other side of the green, where it forked. One fork passed through a gate into a well-kept churchyard. Beyond, a medieval church with a square tower at one end was picked out by the moonlight. Next to the churchyard stood three thatched cottages, light spilling from lower windows, outlining the tiny gardens before them. In one, the Master could see the blossom of a winter rose bush, still and quiet as the night around it.

The front door of the second cottage opened. Three men blundered out, laughing and jostling. They started across the green in great spirits. The Master watched them calmly. Their path would cross his at the junction ahead. That was good. The enchantment was still working. It would cause him no problem to get close to the men and besides, getting a sense of the locals could only help him in the coming days.

It was obvious where the men were heading. Beyond the junction stood an inn. Warm light from its windows cast orange rectangles on to the snowy ground. Occasional shadows crossed as the residents moved past the windows. A steady stream of smoke puffed out of a tall chimney. From inside, the chatter of drinkers was quite audible. Two large oak trees stood in front of the inn, like two moonlit giants keeping watch over the little village.

One of the men pointed down at the inn and the other two laughed. From the way that two of them were walking, it seemed that they had sampled a good deal of alcohol already.

The Master crossed over to the nearest of the two oaks, then stopped, waiting for the men to come near. He glanced at the name painted over the doorway, 'The Stumblepot Inn.' He smiled, then glanced back at the three men. An apt name for such a place.

'Unless I'm very wrong—' one of the men ahead said to his companions in lubricated tones, '—it'll be the turn of the good doctor here to buy the drinks.'

Another, the doctor, laughed. 'Why is it that whenever we take a drink with you on a Sunday, it seems to be my turn?'

'Whilst we drink on a Sunday, Conrad, I'd say it was your civic duty to buy the local police force a drink,' the first man replied.

'Really? You're a police force now, are you? I thought you were a policeman.' Dr Conrad laughed.

'I'll be buying tonight,' the third man said, less slurred than his companions. 'If the lads are in there, I want to buy them a drink before they go to join my Len and the others at training.'

'Well, I'm all for sending them off to fight with whiskey in their blood, but we have a few days to do that,' the doctor agreed. 'If we start tonight, they may not be sober enough to walk by the time they go.'

'Well, as long as I'm not buying, I'm happy,' the policeman noted.

The doctor punched him lightly on the arm and he lurched forward, nearly stumbling into the Master before he righted himself. The Master deftly stepped around the drunken men and slipped amongst them.

Not a single one of them even looked at the tall, gaunt figure passing through their midst. He passed so close that the doctor raised his hand and brushed at the air.

'It's certainly December. I should have put on a thicker coat.' He frowned and pulled the coat he did have tight around his neck.

'Well, let's get ourselves warmed then before my wife misses me.' The policeman grasped the doctor's shoulder and propelled him towards the door of the Stumblepot Inn.

The doctor grasped the handle, pulling the door open with a slight creak. In a flash, the Master was past him, slipping into the warmth of the saloon bar beyond.

He looked around the room. Cream stone walls on three sides, with the bar taking up the length of most of the fourth. On the walls hung about fifteen paintings of different sizes, far too many for the modest room.

The pictures followed a common theme. In boats, or on the bank, each picture showed scenes of men fishing. There were men calmly sitting with rods by wide, slow moving rivers, men in water up to their waists casting flies into white foamy streams, and even men painted holding the fish they had just caught.

The theme continued in three display cases on the longest wall above the mantle of a blazing fire. Each contained an impressively sized fish with a tiny plaque proclaiming the name of the fisherman that had caught it.

The Master strolled to a space at the end of the bar and leaned against it. The room and its layout held less interest for him than the inhabitants. He had allowed himself this detour for a reason. He turned his attention to the men drinking.

The men were mostly middle-aged. Most of the village's young men would have left to volunteer for the war, he imagined. That was another good thing. Older men were so much easier to manipulate with their vanity and closing minds. This war had proven to be a great ally to him in so many ways.

A younger group stood at the bar with the doctor and his companions. Three lads, all bright-eyed and laughing, heads held high as though they had the world at their feet. The tallest of the three was a giant, at least six-foot-six. He laughed at a joke with a deep booming laugh.

The older men around the bar occasionally looked at them and, if they caught their eye, would smile or raise a glass respectfully. The young men would smile back, a little embarrassed by the attention. If they saw the occasional hint of sadness and worry in the older men's eyes, as the Master did, they took no notice and instead returned to their conversation.

The Master crossed the room, sitting in a spare seat at a table of three men. For a while he leaned in, listening to their conversations, taking in their details, then he got up again, and moved to another group.

For an hour, he sat with the men, group by group, learning their names, watching their faces. He saw how they animated themselves as they spoke or listened. He learned who made the others smile, who was the butt of the jokes, who had friends, who did not. He looked at the flushed, well-fed faces, with groomed moustaches and listened to the naive bravado and patriotism with which they spoke. When he grew thirsty, he helped himself to a freshly bought pint of ale, smiling as its previous owner grew suddenly confused looking for it.

He ended his observations at the bar again, standing amongst the young men. He listened to the doctor, then the policeman, then the doctor again passing on drunken pearls of wisdom to take to war with them. He saw the good natured way the three lads, Jim, Mike and the giant, Joe, took the advice in the spirit with which it was given.

He knew their names now. He would know their faces when he saw them tomorrow. He would know who they were and what their relationships were. He would fit in. Satisfied, he turned back to the door.

His eyes had begun to ache. The extra hour had only made him feel more tired. There was one more important task to complete before he could rest. He opened the door and stepped through. Then, without bothering to shut it behind him, he strode on down the lane.

A moment later the doctor appeared at the open doorway. He looked out to see if anyone had opened it. Seeing no one, he shrugged his shoulders and shut it again.

The doctor turned back to the patrons of the bar. As a man, they looked toward him and the door, each with disconcerted faces; as if they had just remembered something really important and then forgotten it again.

'Smile, lads, for heaven's sake,' the doctor said, quite taken aback by their faces. 'You look as though you've seen a devil!'

Bailey dug his little penknife into the wood and gouged out another tiny piece. Carving like this was slow going, but he wanted to be sure that the end result, a replica of the cottage he sat in, would be perfect. It was all going well, but it never did to rush these things.

He looked at the carriage clock on the mantle, one of Joe's prized possessions. It was a quarter past nine. That was good. It would be at least another hour before Joe heaved his huge frame back from the pub. That would give Bailey plenty more time to work on the gift and still be able to clear the tell-tale wood chippings from the stone floor. Bailey wanted to keep the gift hidden from Joe right up until the point he went away.

It was a fairly easy cottage to carve. It was not as well-to-do as the larger houses around the green. Nor was it as plainly functional as the boat builders' cottages further out from the village. It was, however, pretty and inviting. Bailey was confident he could capture that.

Of course, he was only carving the cottage. The neat little path that ran up though a market garden stocked with winter vegetables to the blue painted front door would have to stay in Joe's memory.

He had thought about a second piece to carve the workshop behind the cottage. The mess of boats, farm equipment and other broken items waiting for repair in a loosely constructed line would have proved too hard in the time.

The old man grinned to himself as he imagined even trying. There were so many things out there. Only earlier a plough, the main shaft splintered, had arrived and been placed next to a little row boat with a hole on its base. Worn equipment, waiting to be mended.

He did love it out there, though. Nothing went to waste. Joe could find a use for everything. A workbench stood against the old shed, and from the shed a makeshift wooden roof stretched over the bench, supported by two mismatched old columns of timber that had originally been masts from boats. On the bench, a mower waited for its blades to be replaced on the ground in front of the bench. Next to it, the wheel from a long-forgotten bicycle lay, until some new and ingenious use could be found for it.

Everyone brought their repairs to Joe. It didn't end there, either. For the big houses up along the top road between Henley and here, Joe was the first port of call when an extra pair of hands was needed. Tomorrow, for instance, he had been asked by that nasty little man at General Flyte's house to pick up the youngest boy in his cart from the station. Joe was a little worried about that. The family had troubles and he wasn't looking forward to seeing the boy's mood. He'd cheer the boy up though, of that Bailey was sure. Joe could do no wrong in Bailey's opinion.

He would be sorely missed whilst he was fighting the war. Bailey sighed. It was a lot of responsibility Joe was entrusting him with after only a month of being friends, and he appreciated the trust more than he could say.

When the loud knock on the door came, Bailey almost dropped the carving. He caught it at the last minute, swore, and placed it carefully on the floor next to the worn old armchair. The knock came again, insistent. Desperate, even. He frowned at the noise, but clambered to his feet and stumbled over. He unlatched the door and pulled it open.

The man standing at the step stopped his heart cold. Tall and still, like some stone statue, the only movement was the slight rise and fall of his long coat, in time with his deep breathing.

The man smiled. 'Perfect.' He stepped forwards.

'Excuse me!' Bailey exclaimed, recovering his senses and raising a hand to stop the man. 'You can't just walk in here!'

'Shh.' The man raised a finger to just below his mouth. His breath carried over the short space between them, wafting into Bailey's face. There was a faint smell of ale on it.

That would not do at all. He'd been left in charge of the little three room cottage whilst Joe was with his friends. He wasn't going to let some half-cut stranger come bounding in, no matter how tall and imposing he looked, and he was going to damn well tell him. He opened his mouth to speak.

No words came out.

Bailey's throat tightened in fear. No words? He tried again, straining to speak, but nothing.

He made to back away from the man and give himself a moment to think. Like his voice, his body did not respond. He struggled again to move. Nothing. He was completely and utterly paralysed.

'That's better.' The man smiled and gently moved him out of the way of the door, then stepped fully into the room. Beyond the door, three shadowy figures lurked, moving and grunting like animals. Their faces were impossible to make out, but now and again a light from within would reflect off eyes that were too brown and inhuman. Worse yet, when one of them leaned into the doorway a little further, Bailey caught the glisten of a short pointed tooth.

The man looked around the room. 'This will do nicely.' He turned back to the door and addressed the shadowy figures beyond. 'You're sure about this man? No family? Few friends?'

'Yes, master,' one replied. Bailey felt his heart pounding. No human voice should sound that husky. It was as if the figure was missing a normal voice box.

'A relative stranger here? You're sure.'

'Yes, a stranger,' came the growled reply.

'Very well.' He turned to face Bailey. 'Then we should get to know each other a little better, my friend.'

Bailey knew his heart hadn't pounded this fast in decades. Fear gripped him absolutely. Sweat beaded on his forehead, running down into his eyebrows, where it collected and dripped down into eyes that he could not blink, stinging them and blurring his vision.

He strained in his mind to move his body. He desperately searched through memories of which parts of his brain he could feel working in the past, when he had moved. Of course, that was so second nature to him that it had worked unnoticed. As the man got closer, he prayed in his head that he would regain the ability to move, gain the strength to fight him. The prayer went unanswered.

The man lifted his right hand and gently touched Bailey's left cheek. His skin tingled at the touch. He could certainly still feel. The man held it there for a moment, looking into his eyes, his face utterly impassive. Bailey felt like a fox caught in a trap faced with the huntsman's return. The man glanced over Bailey's face, his eyes examining every pock mark, every crevice, every line.

He slowly passed his hand over Bailey's forehead. And suddenly, to accompany the tingling of his skin, images began to flash through his mind; unbidden memories dragged up from his unconscious.

The memory came of a stone hitting his head, so real it felt as if the stone was striking him now, when he had been chased out of Henley by those boys a few weeks back. His knee blossomed in pain as the memory of stumbling away from them hit him.

Then came a memory of being younger. Days when a travelling man could still go around the country in search of casual work without being menaced. A time before the hysteria of the papers had started claiming every stranger could be a German spy.

His brow tingled just as his cheek had done as the man's hand passed over it. The sweat under his hands dried instantly. The moisture of the skin itself seemed to be sucked up towards those fingers.

Still the memories came. It was as if the man was drawing them from him as he drew the sweat from his skin. Now he was walking past Joe's house after a night sleeping in cold bushes, surprised when the huge young man wished him a friendly good morning. Even more surprised when he was offered a cup of tea and told he looked as if he needed a sit down.

The man dropped his hand down to Bailey's right cheek and slowly ran his fingers over Bailey's eyes and nose. The same tingling drying sensation followed the fingers. Bailey could feel the moisture draining from his eyes, leaving them dry.

In his head, the weeks that he had ended up staying flashed by. Helping Joe in the workshop. Enjoying their burgeoning friendship. Teaching the younger man some of his own crafts. Gladly accepting the spare upstairs room in the cottage.

As the hand passed down to his mouth and chin his eyes began to stream with water. Tear ducts struggled to replace the moisture this strange examination had taken.

When the hand moved over his mouth, Bailey felt his lips parting. From his throat a dryness blossomed, as moisture and breath were sucked from his body. His voice box began to vibrate as the breath was sucked through it. Involuntarily, he groaned.

Bailey's consciousness began to swim as the last air in his lungs was sucked up into this man's desiccating touch. In his mind, he was hammering at the plough outside. Each hammer blow sounded as though it was from further and further away.

Suddenly, just as it had started, it was over. Bailey fell to the floor, his body and mind restored to him. He briefly struggled to rise and resist, but the effort was too much. He curled into a ball and gasped at the air, staring up at his attacker.

Above him, the man had stepped back and leaned against the door frame, panting heavily. He lifted the hand he had examined Bailey with. Then slowly, deliberately, he ran it over his own face.

'Well,' he said. 'Let's see if this works, shall we?' He dropped his hand to his side and leaned his head back, breathing regularly, then stood still.

The man's face seemed suddenly to blur. Bailey rubbed his eyes, ignoring the pain, and trying to regain his focus. The man's face seemed, if anything, to get more blurred. Features that a moment ago had been angular and defined seemed to be flowing. Bailey shook his head, not able to believe what he was seeing. He rubbed at his eyes again and looked up.

The man seemed a little shorter now, and stockier! His face was changing into something altogether different. Bailey clambered up, fear giving his limbs strength, and shrank back against the wall.

'Oh dear Jesus, protect me in this time of need,' he muttered to himself, closing his eyes.

His heart leapt. He had heard himself speak! He had his voice back. He sucked in a big breath to shout for help, opening his eyes.

The breath caught in his lungs.

The man had gone. Instead, it was like looking into a mirror. Bailey stared at an exact replica of himself and gasped. The hair, the little cut he'd got when Joe had thrown that useless screw over his shoulder and caught him by accident, the same day's growth of beard, everything was the same.

The replica smiled. 'Good. From your face, I would guess this looks exactly how I hoped.'

It passed him and sat in his chair, pushing the cushions around to achieve a more comfortable position.

'Now that has been a very good day's work,' it said. It looked at Bailey and frowned at him with his own face. 'Unfortunately though, I can't have your young landlord finding us both here, can I?'

The replica motioned to the door. Two of the creatures outside surged forward. As the light hit them, Bailey saw their faces properly. For the second time of the night, he drew in a breath to scream.

The air never got a chance to leave his lungs. A strong hand, with thick hard fingers bunched into a fist, struck down on his head, knocking the sense from his mind. He collapsed down, finally, mercifully, unconscious.

The Master felt exhausted. Now there would be a continual drain on his powers to hold himself in this shape, like a tap that dripped steady and constant.

The need for raw power, however, he could at least feed, though it would still require a sacrifice of other resources. He looked at his gypsies, struggling to lift the body of the man.

They looked back, immediately aware of his eyes on them. One growled in a low guttural hum. He wondered for a moment how their hatred of him must feel, knowing it was an impossibility that they could ever raise a finger against him. Hatred and frustration were a terrible combination. No wonder they could be so ferocious when he allowed them an outlet.

'Take him back to your camp,' he said, marvelling at the way he sounded with the old man's voice. 'Keep him with the boy. No one must see him.'

The first grunted and started to back out of the door, one muscular arm holding Bailey upright. The other two, supporting the old man from the back, followed.

'You,' the Master said quietly at the third. 'You must stay here with me.'

Immediately the three knew what this meant. They started whimpering, reaching across the old man to touch each other in fear. The two at the back, next to one another, clutched and nuzzled at each other.

'Stop that,' he said. 'There's no time for this. Do your duties now.'

Whimpering still, the first two dragged the unconscious man out into the night. The third stared after them balefully, then moaned a high, bestial, note of despair.

'Come here,' the Master commanded.

The creature edged slowly toward him. 'Master, please,' it entreated.

'There's no point crying at me. I am afraid I need your strength,' the Master said. 'You would have been gone soon anyway, burst apart and reborn as a thousand other things, with no memory of this life. You should thank me, really. I'm saving you from a few more days of sadness.'

The gypsy bared its teeth at him and hissed.

'Yes, very scary,' he said with an eyebrow raised. 'Now come here.' He patted a spot before him.

Obediently the creature came and sat down, fear in its eyes. 'Please,' it began to plead again. 'Don't take me, Master ...'

Consuming the energy that the creatures were created from was not unlike the action of taking in a sharp breath. The difference, of course, was that the one did not draw in with the lungs, but rather with one's own essence. He would have struggled to explain it. Over the past twenty-two years it had become instinctual.

The result was the same as always. In the blink of an eye, the gypsy, its clothing, a little knife that it had worn tucked into its belt, every part of it, were all gone, transformed into immeasurable tiny sparks of bright blue energy.

For the briefest of seconds, the energy kept the shape of the creature it was before. It was as if a perfect sculpture had been formed from countless grains of glowing blue sand. The creature's expression of shock could even be seen in the pricks of light where its face had been. Then, as the sparks moved apart, it was gone.

The sparks zipped across the short distance between where the creature had been and where the Master sat. They slammed into his body and sunk beneath his skin. The hair on the back of his neck stood up, then those on his arms. His skin tingled all over as the hair on his head rose too. He closed his eyes, savouring the feeling as the power recharged him.

As the last of the light entered his body, he sat back in the chair, drunk on the energy that coursed around inside him, feeding his essence again. For a time, it was hard to concentrate. Slowly, however, the static sensation began to ease off.

He opened his eyes. There was no trace of the gypsy that had been before him. Just memory of its final plea.

'It's not Master, now,' he said, though the creature would never hear. 'It's Bailey.'

CHAPTER FIVE

Homecoming

'Christopher!'

Christopher struggled down from the last step of the train, dragging his book-laden bag behind him and crunched on to the snow-flecked platform. He got a few paces between himself and the carriage, then glanced in the direction of the voice. Ahead of him, Joe Litmus strode up Henley station's little platform. His face was red from the icy wind. His rough workman's hands were stuck deep in the pockets of a thick woollen overcoat. He grinned at Christopher with dancing eyes.

'Christopher! Hello there!'

Christopher smiled and waved. An overweight porter appeared next to him, putting a dark leather suitcase straining to contain its contents on to the platform. The man puffed loudly with the effort. 'There's your case, young master.'

'Thank you,' Christopher muttered, barely noticing the porter in his excitement. Joe was the first genuine friend he had seen in what seemed like ages. He reached down to the suitcase handle, preparing for the struggle to lift it.

Ahead, Joe broke into a light run. 'Wait up. I'll take those for you,' he called, covering the distance. He reached down and grabbed Christopher's hand, shaking it vigorously. 'I'll bet you've had enough of moving bags about for one day.'

'Hello, Joe. You're looking very well,' Christopher said, stepping back to give him room.

His grin growing wider, Joe lifted both the case and bag with ease and swung them over his shoulder. They looked quite uncomfortable, but he didn't seem to notice. 'Come on, I've got the cart outside. If we get on quickly, we might have you home before the snow comes down again.'

Christopher found himself having to break into a jog to keep up with Joe's enormous stride. On Joe's back, the bags bounced up and down like they were tiny sacks. The only other passenger who had been on the early evening train moved out of the way to let this mammoth of a man and his comparatively tiny companion through.

'How was the journey? Not too much bother I hope.' Joe glanced down at him, as if suddenly remembering why Christopher was home early.

Christopher put on his bravest face. 'Not too bad. I'm just glad to be home. I can find out what's what and hopefully I can see Freddie.'

Joe stepped out of the way, allowing Christopher to get down a narrow alley that connected the platform to the road outside. He slowed his pace so as not to catch Christopher's heels and followed him out. 'I was ever so sorry to hear about Freddie,' he mumbled.

'Oh, I'm sure everything will be all right, Joe. Freddie will be fine,' Christopher said back, forcing his voice to sound positive. 'You know what he's like; always getting into scrapes then getting out of them. You don't need to worry.'

'Yes, you're right. He is, isn't he?'

Christopher was glad he couldn't see Joe's face. Knowing Joe, he would be having trouble maintaining an expression that would make it look like he believed what he was saying. One of the reasons that he always did so well was that people knew he couldn't do a shoddy repair job even if he wanted to. His face would give it away.

They reached the end of the alley and came out on to the road. On the other side, shops festooned with holly and decorations made warm contrast with the snow. With the snow and the trappings of Christmas, Henley looked quite different from when he had last seen it at the end of the summer.

They were not the only difference. A large billboard had been erected across the road so it would be immediately seen by anyone who came out of the station. It proclaimed, 'Recruiting office this way!' Next to the words was a large arrow that pointed up the street, the way they were heading. Underneath, a second line read, 'Join up now! Do your bit!'

Ahead the road bent around towards the wide bridge. All along the river, snow-covered boats and barges pulled hard on moorings, tightly tied against the river's heavy flow. The cobbled street had almost completely disappeared. There were just a few bare places amongst the white frosting where one could see the stones of the street under a glaze of clear ice, as though they were trapped beneath, drowning.

A shop on the other side of the road had taken inspiration from the recruitment sign outside the station. In the window was a large poster. In it, a pretty woman and her son watched a formation of soldiers marching proudly off into the distance. Above their heads were the words, 'Women of Britain say "Go!"'

The town was busy. People, laden with goods, moved as fast as safety allowed, picking their way carefully along the street to avoid the worst snow and ice. Above the bridge, an ominous cloud seemed ready to shed its white bounty at any moment.

'That cloud is moving a lot faster than I thought it would,' Joe said. He almost seemed annoyed that the cloud should be doing anything that went against his own knowledge of the weather. 'Oh well, all the more reason to be on our way.'

He pointed down toward the river. 'There's the cart. I put two blankets in there in case we get caught, so it shouldn't be too much bother.'

Joe's neat little cart always seemed to be entirely too small for his huge frame. Mary, Joe's old horse, stood patiently in the cold. She had a blanket thrown over her and her face deep in a nosebag of oats. By her side, an old but vigorous looking man stoked her mane. He watched calmly as Joe and Christopher came close.

'Who's that?' asked Christopher. The old man's face wasn't familiar. Christopher frowned. He was sure that apart from a couple of babies that hadn't started looking like anything but babies, he knew the faces of everyone in the village.

'Oh, that's Bailey.' Joe smiled. 'He helps me with the mending now. He's a great fellow. Lots of stories. He's been everywhere! You're going to like him, Christopher.'

As they reached the cart, Bailey stepped forward and took Christopher's bag from Joe, lifting it into the cart. He looked down and nodded amiably. 'You'll be Master Flyte then. Pleased to meet you. I'm Bailey,' he said in a warm, rich voice that made Christopher want to hear him speak again.

Joe was climbing on to the little bench at the front of the cart. He sat down and pulled at the reins. Mary shook her head and gave a reproachful glance back before trying to delve back down into her bag of oats. 'Come on now, girl, you can have some more when we're back home in the warm,' Joe said, tugging at the reins again.

Bailey walked around and unhooked the bag strap from Mary's head. She whinnied mournfully as he walked to the back of the cart, then immediately forgot what she was worrying about. She glanced up the snowy road, drumming a hoof against the cobbles in anticipation.

'Why not sit in the back with Christopher?' Joe said to Bailey. 'Get to know each other.'

'Why not?' Bailey nodded and vaulted up. He turned back and extended a helping hand. 'Come on then, Master Flyte.' Christopher hesitated a moment, shy as he always was in the company of someone new, then reached out and allowed the old man to help him up.

He was almost lifted from his feet by the old man's strength. He sat in the corner opposite his bags. He pulled one of the blankets Joe had mentioned over his legs. Bailey sat down next to the bags and regarded him with intense blue eyes.

With a shake of the reins, Joe urged Mary forward. The little cart began to clatter along the road. Christopher glanced up at the sky nervously trying to think of something to say to the old man. Above, the far reaches of the cloud started to blur from vision. In the distance, the first flurries of snow had begun to fall.

The cart struggled its way along the road. No encouragement Joe could call would convince Mary to walk the icy route any less gingerly, and he would not dream of using violence against her. Christopher looked out at the people making their way along the pavement, still at a loss of how to speak with the old man.

They passed a shop. In its window, another poster for the war nestled among the decorations. As he looked, the hairs on the back of his neck rose. He felt a shiver of discomfort.

'Remember Belgium!' The poster exclaimed in sharp orange letters with jagged edges. Below them, a great hairy beast stood on two muscular legs. Its wild red eyes glared out. The eyes seemed to stare directly at whoever was looking at the poster. In its open mouth great tusks protruded, each tinged with red at its tips, as if the beast had been savaging a person.

Christopher was transfixed by the horror on the poster. Upon its head, it wore a lopsided Picklehaulbe; the helmet of the German army. Its hairy body was a mass of muscle. It was barely contained within its German officer's uniform, which was actually split open in places. Where the splits were, thick brown tufts of hair sprouted through the gaps. In its right hand, the beast carried a rifle almost as large as it was. A cruel looking bayonet was fixed to its barrel.

In the beast's left hand, draped as if in a swoon of horror, lay a woman. Her clothes were tattered. The front of her top had been ripped open completely, exposing her breasts. Christopher felt his face redden as he noticed. Along the length of her skirt the word Belgium was written once again.

Below the beast more red lines mingled with brown as if to indicate blood and mud. Above the mud, the poster repeated the regular call to 'Join up now! Do your bit!'

Christopher turned away, at once excited and ashamed and not sure why. He shuddered and pushed back against the side of the cart.

'Are you warm enough there lad?' Bailey asked, still looking at him intently.

Christopher smiled at him. 'Yes thank you Mr Bailey.'

In the front, Joe stifled a giggle. The old man himself lifted his head and laughed aloud. 'Bless me, Master Flyte, there's no "mister." It's just Bailey. No one calls me mister.' He leaned forward, quite theatrical. Slowly and deliberately he looked to his left, then his right. 'I used to have a first name, but I left it somewhere on my travels. And you know, it's a funny thing, but sometimes I can hear it calling to me from somewhere far away. Whenever I've looked for it, though, I've never had any luck finding it.' He grinned and sat back.

Christopher began to feel his shyness melt away. The old man's easy way was oddly informal considering what he was used to, but like his voice it was reassuring. He sat up slightly, almost taking himself by surprise and stuck out his hand. 'Well, if you're just Bailey, then I'm just Christopher.'

Bailey stared at his hand for a second, then clasped it with both of his and laughed again. 'I suppose you are, Christopher. I suppose you are.'

The cart continued steadily over the bridge and soon turned left, leaving the town and heading down a long narrow lane that followed the river's course back towards Alton. Houses were replaced with snow-covered fields, white trees beyond their edges. Soon flakes from the cloud above began to land all over the cart. Some flakes blew off as quickly as they landed. Some melted on to the wood of the structure. An icy flake landed on Christopher's cheek, just below his eye. It melted immediately on to his skin and ran down his face. He reached up and wiped it away. Bailey glanced at him again.

'All right?' he said.

'Oh yes,' said Christopher. 'Just some snow.'

Bailey nodded wisely and closed his eyes, leaning his head back against the side of the cart. 'I think we'll be seeing a lot more snow in the next few weeks.'

'Are you going to be living in the village then, Bailey?' Christopher asked.

'Bailey's going to look after things for me, Christopher,' Joe said from the front. 'Selling the veg, doing the mends. You know.'

'Why, Joe?'

'Why? The war of course! You didn't think that I wasn't going to go and lend a hand did you!' Joe exclaimed. 'I can hardly let Len bloomin' Archer and his farm cronies get all the glory! They've been off to basic training for over two months now.'

He pulled up the horse for a second and turned to Christopher with his big honest eyes glistening. 'I'll tell you, Christopher, it'd be a hard time for a man who didn't want to go. Only last week Michael Brophy and I were in town and a group of young ladies came up to us and handed us white feathers! As if we're bloody cowards!' His face went suddenly red. 'I'm sorry, Christopher, I didn't mean to swear. It's just … Well, it makes me angry that people don't think about why a man hasn't gone in. I couldn't just drop my livelihood and go. And Mike, he had his old Ma to think about, and Jim, he had to get his father's permission and be sure that he could run the pub on his own.' He turned back and pulled gently on the reins again. 'I just wish these girls going about with their white feathers and their ideas would stop to think a bit more, that's all.'

Bailey laid a hand on Joe's back. 'Never mind, lad. A few days and you'll be off won't you? All's well that ends well. '

'I suppose,' Joe muttered from the front.

'Of course it is,' Bailey continued, 'And you know that I'll be keeping things nicely in order here for when you get back.'

Joe said nothing.

'And when you do get back, I'm sure that girl you're so sweet on in Henley will have forgotten all about white feathers and such. She'll welcome you with an embrace fit for a returning hero.' Bailey winked at Christopher.

'Well,' Joe said, affront still quite apparent in his voice, 'Even if I was sweet on her, I'm not any more. She can take her feathers and give them to some other fellow, because she won't get the chance with me again.'

'Quite right. Quite right.' Bailey patted Joe on the back again, grimacing comically at Christopher.

They rode on in silence. Christopher glanced over at Bailey. Once again the old man seemed lost in his own thoughts, eyes closed and face turned up toward the snowy skies. Joe sat hunched over the reins. He was still contemplating the deep hurt that had been meted out.

Christopher wondered what Joe would see once he got to France. The papers were full of how well the army was doing, but a few times Christopher had heard the school masters talking. The way they spoke seemed far less optimistic than the papers.

'I'm glad you're going a bit later, Joe,' Christopher said finally.

Both men started, Bailey opening his eyes.

'Oh. Why's that, then?' Joe asked.

'Well, when Freddie gets better and goes back, it'll probably be around the same time that you are going. He'll like it if he knows his friends are out there.'

'Well, I don't think—' Joe started, then stopped. He glanced back and smiled just a little. 'Actually, yes you're right. He will like that, won't he?'

The fall of snow grew thicker, silently mirroring the bleak mood that had taken over the little cart. The river, only a stone's throw to their left, became harder to see through the flakes and late afternoon light. Somewhere, Freddie was lying strapped to a hospital bed, or in a cell hugging himself in a corner, just as Christopher had watched his mother do in her last months. Christopher shuddered, whether the reason was the war or something deeper. Something inherited.

Christopher shook the thought away and craned his neck to look over the seat on the side, where Joe's huge body didn't totally block the view. To their right, just ahead, a smaller track twisted between two hedges and on into the woods that lined the hill beyond. If a person were to follow the track, eventually they would end up in the upper meadow. There they would be able to puzzle over the oddness of the Pickering Tower. It was a local folly built years ago by an eccentric landowner. He had apparently claimed it was to lock his daughter in from the advances of men. Christopher had no idea whether the landowner had ever carried out his threat. In the summer months, he had spent many hours wondering at how he could get the door open and climb to its highest reaches. Now he knew where they were, Christopher sat back against the side of the cart. It would still take another twenty or so minutes to reach home from here, maybe more in this weather.

Bailey smiled at him. 'So in answer to your question, yes I'm going to be living in the village. And with Joe off, I won't have that many friends, so you'll have to come down and visit me if your guardian allows it.'

'Oh, I'm sure he wouldn't even notice,' Christopher answered.

'Good.' Bailey paused a second then looked at him, with the slightest of glints in his eye. 'I was almost on my way home. If it hadn't have been for Joe here, I probably would have gone.'

'Where's that?'

Bailey leaned forward again. 'Cornwall. Where your King Arthur started.'

'My King Arthur!' Christopher said, sitting up. A little quiver of excited interest ran up the back of his neck.

The old man smiled at his reaction. 'Well, lad, I must admit I only found out today, but you and I have an interest in common. Well, that's if you have the same interests as your wonderful mother, God rest her soul.'

'I do!' Christopher answered, more animated than he had been for days.

'Well, I never knew until this morning when I mentioned to Chops at the store that I was coming with Joe today to get you and she told me that you were the lad of Sarah Flyte. Great writer your mother was, knew her subject.'

Joe turned, dumbfounded. 'You've read them?'

'Not all, but some. I was working at a farm a while back and the farmer's children took a shine to me. Ended up I was almost part of the family. Sometimes of an evening, I used to read them Mrs Flyte's stories from a book they had.'

'Well, I never!' Joe exclaimed, 'You never said a word. All that journey to the station and you never said a word.'

Bailey looked to the sky, his eyes narrowing as he thought. 'You know, Joe, I didn't. What with all the talk of getting that plough mended and back up to Mr Woods before you go, it slipped from my mind.'

Joe shook his head. 'I didn't even know you could read.'

Bailey ignored Joe and looked at Christopher. 'When I was your age I lived no further than a mile along the coast from Tintagel. There's where Arthur was conceived.'

'I'm not sure that you should use such words around Christopher,' Joe said stiffly.

'I don't mind, Joe,' Christopher answered, really wanting Joe to be quiet and let the old man speak. 'What was it like?'

'Well, it's a great heap of a place these days.' Bailey smiled. 'Most of it fell into the sea years ago. It's still quite the thrill to see it, mind you. You can see why Arthur's father had such a hard time getting in!'

'What did he want to get in for?' Joe asked, from the front.

Christopher answered before Bailey could speak, finding himself surprisingly irritated with Joe's interruptions. 'Uthur loved Igraine, but she was married to The Duke of Cornwall and they lived at Tintagel. So Uthur took his army, killed the duke, then laid siege to Tintagel, but whatever he tried he couldn't get in. So Merlin helped him make himself look exactly like the duke and he got in, then he got to lie with Igraine and then later Arthur was born.' He turned back to Bailey. 'So can you walk around the castle?'

'What's left of it. Two parts the castle has, one on the mainland and one on the point. They were connected by a bridge. Hundreds of people lived in the parts, lords and ladies and knights and magicians. Serfs and soldiers and beggars and thieves.' Bailey smiled slowly, his voice gliding down a note, making Christopher feel warm and comfortable. 'And you can still find a thing or two around there if you know where to look. A sword, a lady's ring. If you know where to look.'

Christopher laid his head back against the side of the cart, shifting his weight to make himself more comfortable. This was exciting stuff. Dimly he wondered why he wasn't full of questions. Just listening was so relaxing. He somehow knew that Bailey would tell him all the things that he wanted to know without asking.

'There's a silver gauntlet named "Winter's Grasp" that a young man claimed as his, when he was about your age,' Bailey continued, his voice beguiling. 'The gauntlet has been many things to many people in its long life, but once it was a gift from the great knight Lancelot that never reached its intended. I can tell you if you want.'

Christopher nodded his head and smiled. Joe sat silently forward, staring into the distance with hunched shoulders and the reins held in loose distracted hands.

'There's a story they tell about Camelot. How a beautiful lady, known as the Lady of Shallot, fell in love with Lancelot and begged him to marry her. But Lancelot was in love with the Queen and refused. The lady was said to have died of a broken heart. She was supposed to have been buried at Camelot and it was her death that made the Queen realise Lancelot still loved her. And that went on to cause all manner of troubles.'

As the gentle strumming of Bailey's voice continued, Christopher closed his eyes. Immediately his mind's eye was filled with images of a mighty walled city. White walls glistened in the spring air. Throngs of people lined up to watch solemn knights ride ahead of an ornate funeral carriage.

'But we in Cornwall know a different story, and I'll tell you the truth of it,' Bailey continued. 'Lancelot met the Lady of Shallot many years earlier and her name was Abigail. For a time he had been mad, roaming the country like a beggar, without weapons or colours, shouting at the land and fighting with the weather. Everywhere he went the people shunned him.

'Now after some time he came upon the edge of England, with its great walls and castles. He crossed into the borderlands between it and Cornwall, where no king held rule and chaos reigned. In this godless place, he was set upon by thieves. They stripped him of what little he had and left him for dead.

'After he had lain bleeding of his wounds and battling the demons of his mind for three moonless nights, a lady happened along. The Lady Abigail. Seeing this poor naked man, she took pity on him.

'As she knelt by his side, tending to his wounds and calming him with her words, she looked down into his face. Despite the scars and blood, and despite the madness in his eyes, she recognized him as a knight of good and pure heart. She fell instantly in love with him.

'The lady made a litter and placed him upon it. She struggled for a day and a night to drag the litter back to her home, avoiding bands of outlaws and many other dangers on the way.

'Finally they reached her home, a high walled Keep, deep in a forest. There she placed him in her bed and tended to his wounds. Then, exhausted from her efforts, she fell on to the bed at his side into a deep sleep.

'And in the morning Lancelot awoke and turned to see the woman beside him. And in his eyes the woman beside him was Guinevere the Queen, who he loved and had gone mad for through that love. And he turned to her and held her in his embrace. The lady, who was so in love with him, yielded to his embrace. And later Lancelot fell back into a deep sleep.

'Now the Lady of Shallot spent many weeks administering to Lancelot. She fed him and tended his wounds. She lent him her father's sword, so he could once again become strong. And throughout this time, though she loved him, she never spoke of the first morning he had arrived. After a time, the Lady of Shallot discovered that she was with child. Yet still she said nothing of the first morning he had arrived.

'Through her care Lancelot became strong again in both body and mind. There came a time when he was ready to leave. So he came to the lady and said to her, "Good lady, you have tended me and I am well. I must now take my leave of you, for I am a knight of Camelot and I must return to my King and Queen."

'And the Lady of Shallot began to cry, and Lancelot felt very sorry for her. "My lady, don't weep. You have been my saviour. I will not leave you here in this godless place. You shall come to Camelot and serve the Queen."

'And the Lady of Shallot turned to Lancelot and said to him. "I will gladly come with you if you tell me that you love me."

'But Lancelot shook his head. "My lady, I cannot tell you that I love you for my heart belongs to another, though that can cause me nothing but pain."

'And the Lady of Shallot turned her face away from him. "Sir Knight, without your love I have no wish to see that place, but will remain here alone."

'And no matter how Lancelot pleaded he could not convince the Lady of Shallot to leave the borderlands. So he took his leave of her and returned to Camelot.

'Some time later, Sir Tristan of Cornwall arrived at Camelot. Though Cornwall and Camelot were always enemies, Tristan was a friend to both of the Kings and welcome at their courts. And through Tristan, King Arthur and King Mark could talk to each other.

'As the court sat down to eat, Tristan saw that Lancelot was deeply troubled. He came to his good friend and asked him why. Lancelot told Tristan that he had left a fair lady who had tended to his needs and brought him to recovery in the borderlands and was sore worried for her safety.

'Tristan said. "Fear not my friend, for I shall be passing through that place soon as I return home. I will look to her and see if she is well."

'And so Lancelot went to Merlin, who was very old, and said to him. "Merlin, I am sorely worried for a lady who has no knights to defend her. Grant me a gift that I can send her so she may be safe."

'And Merlin searched through his bags and looked at his potions. He opened his chests and emptied his cupboards. And finally he gave Lancelot a beautiful silver gauntlet.

'Merlin said, "This gauntlet is called Winter's Grasp. If your lady is in danger, she need only place the gauntlet on her hand and reach for where she wishes to be and it will take her there."

'Lancelot took Winter's Grasp and gave it to Tristan. And Tristan bade the court farewell and set off.

'Now the Lady of Shallot was heavy with child and took to her bed. "Oh, poor me," she cried, "that I have to bring my child into this world alone, with no midwife or priest."

'And her cries were so strong that the thieves who lived in the forest came to her door to listen. And after many hours the cries stopped and the keep was silent. The thieves turned to one another and said, "What shall we do? For we do not want to enter her house, for she has been a light in this darkness, but we cannot leave until we hear her speak." So they waited some more, but still the keep was silent.

'The thieves, though sorry, entered the keep and soon came across the Lady of Shallot in her room. She was quite dead. On her breast was lain a sleeping baby girl.

'And the thieves said, "We cannot leave this child here, for she will die. Let us take her with us and raise her as our own child." And they took the baby and, before they left, they washed the body of the Lady of Shallot and clothed it in clean clothes and left it gently lain on her bed as though sleeping.

'Tristan happened upon the keep and found the lady and was deeply sorry. He placed her body on a litter and took it to a castle on the border. And he took Winter's Grasp with him, because he did not know that there was a child who should have it instead.

'Tristan said, "Here is the body of the Lady of Shallot, who has died for the love of Lancelot and must be borne to the King." But he did not give them Winter's Grasp, because that was too valuable. So he kept it and continued to Tintagel, saying, "I will return this to Lancelot when I am next with the King."

'And so the body of the Lady of Shallot was borne to the King and there was a great disturbance. When Lancelot heard that the lady had died alone he was greatly saddened, but the Queen, hearing that this lady had died for love of Lancelot, rejoiced, as then she knew that Lancelot loved her and no other with all his heart. And there would come a time when they would embrace one another, but that is a different story.

'So the lady was buried at Camelot. On her tomb, it read, "Here lies a lady who died for love of Lancelot."

'And in time Tristan, who had not been back to the court of King Arthur for a great time, fell out with his uncle King Mark for love and was murdered, but that is a different story. And in his rooms at Tintagel, where the gauntlet called Winter's Grasp lay waiting, there was a great groaning and straining as the building mourned for his loss, and fell from the side of the castle down on to the rocks below.

'And the baby whom the thieves saved and named Eleila, grew up strong and tall. She was as well versed in fighting with the sword and bow as any of her adopted brothers and fathers. And when she stopped being a child and became a young woman, she yearned for adventure and so set off for Camelot. She never knew that her father was the knight, Lancelot Du Lac, nor of the gift that he had sent her mother nineteen springs before. And when she reached Camelot, she found that the court was far from what she imagined, but that too is another story.'

The jolt of the cart stopping banged Christopher's head suddenly against the side. He opened his eyes. He felt disorientated. It was hard to decide when Bailey had stopped talking. It could have been a minute or twenty for all

Christopher knew. Even when the words had stopped, his head had been filled with the sights and feelings of the story. Images of Sir Tristan and the litter with the lady on it, respectfully travelling through the borderlands. Images of the tomb with her epitaph cut deep in the rock, of the girl, growing among the thieves, without any knowledge of who she was. Most of all, images of the silver gauntlet, Winter's Grasp, that never reached its intended.

'Here we are, then. Fox Grange.' Bailey was watching him carefully. Christopher moved a little more, his sense of the now returning to him. Bailey nodded to himself and climbed down over the side of the cart.

'But what happened to the girl? And who found the gauntlet? You said someone found Winter's Grasp!' Christopher suddenly found himself full of the questions he had been too relaxed to ask before. 'And tell me more about the borderlands. Bailey!'

Bailey laughed. 'All in time, Christopher. You come down and see me and I'll tell you all in time. Now look, you best catch Joe up and greet your guardian.'

Sure enough, Joe had already walked a fair distance up the well-kept driveway, almost to the front door of Fox Grange.

'Thank you, Bailey! I had never heard that version before.'

'Well, just you remember to come and hear the rest. And maybe see something special, too.'

Christopher stared at the old man, at the glint in his eye. 'What do you mean?'

'You come down and hear the rest and you'll find out.' Bailey nodded at him. 'Now you get off to your business.'

Full of divided desires, Christopher turned and chased down the path after Joe.

Joe was full of questions at his return to the carriage, but the Master, tired of his prattle, whispered a small incantation, wincing as another part of his powers left him. Joe became as docile as the horse, quietly driving the cart home.

The Master was happy. The boy had felt nothing of the charms to enhance and excite his imagination with the story around him. All he had felt was a great thrill at the adventure and a deep desire to hear more.

'Seeds have been set, Joe,' he said, looking at the huge man with a half-smile. Joe stared ahead with glazed eyes, occasionally flicking at the reins in slow, trance-like movements.

CHAPTER SIX

Sama

Sama rubbed the dish towel impatiently over the plate she was drying, glanced out of the window and sighed. Her father, Stanley, grinned at her back as he strolled past towards the direction of the bar.

'Buck up, Sama,' he said, trying to keep the amusement out of his voice. 'Staring out of the window won't get them plates dry. Sooner you get done, the sooner you get to sit down.'

'I know, Dad. I'll have them done in a bit,' Sama said in her most obedient voice possible. She turned and flashed her father the smile she knew he loved. The corners of his mouth struggled not to wrinkle up again in response.

'It'll take more than a cheeky grin to get out of your chores, Sama Neeley,' he said, as much to himself as to her. 'You've been running around me and your brother all week.'

He disappeared into the bar. Sama crashed the dried plate on to a pile and reached into the sink for another. It was so unfair!

Sama wasn't like other girls of her age. At seventeen, she was really supposed to be a demure young woman, fitting into a role that everyone expected and understood. So far, however, she had successfully resisted all attempts to turn her into one. Whilst the other girls she knew seemed to spend countless boring hours finding ways to appear more feminine, Sama couldn't care less. And as for capering around the floor of numbingly polite church dances with some idiot farm hand, all stares and boasts, the very idea made her want to throw a plate at the wall.

Instead, she added the plate to the pile with another crash, then reached into the sink, feeling through the hot cloudy water for another plate. Empty. Sama's heart leapt. She rubbed her hands on the towel to dry them and hurled it over to the corner where it was kept. She nearly tripped over herself in her rush to get the dishes into the cupboard. She set them down with more crashes.

'Sama!' her father called through from the bar. 'Be careful!'

'All finished, Dad!' she called back before a telling off followed.

She ducked through to the bar. Her father was kneeling at the hearth, building a fire to welcome the evening's visitors. Above him, the three fish in their display cabinets stared into the room with three beady glass eyes.

'I'm going to get the whites ironed for Auntie Violet,' Sama blurted, and then bolted back into the kitchen, leaving her father staring bemusedly.

She dragged the large basket of washing out of the pantry entrance. She frowned at the sheer amount of sheets and tablecloths. Then, steeling herself to the boredom, she fetched the little iron and placed it on top of the stove to heat up.

It was all Auntie Violet's fault, really, though Sama couldn't resent her. It was impossible to feel anything but love for the red-faced little woman. It was her own true wish to be seen as a real lady that put so much pressure on her niece. They argued like cat and dog, but when they had both said their piece, they were quick to calm and move on.

Most people in the village referred to her aunt affectionately as 'Chops', a name she had been given by her late husband when they had worked together in the grand meat markets of London. There the sight of a tiny woman wielding a great knife on the carcasses of cows and pigs and bellowing across the hall at potential customers was an unusual spectacle. Her nickname had followed her to the village.

When her husband passed away, she had a good amount of money behind her, no children of her own, and a wish to take a more feminine role now she was older. So, she had taken over the local store. She moved into a room in the Stumblepot, occasionally helping her brother behind the bar in the evenings.

Once her aunt lived with them, Sama found herself under increasing scrutiny. Firstly it had just been the simple observations, delivered in her deep, blunt tones. 'Sama, look at your hair! You look as if you've been drinking gin in a gutter!' she would cry, grabbing a comb and raking it through Sama's thick brown hair, or, 'Sama, come down from that wall, climbing is for boys and monkeys, not young ladies.'

Now Sama never had drunk gin nor anything else for that matter. As to climbing being for boys and monkeys, well, it would be far easier to do it without the difficulties presented by the long skirts she had to wear.

Soon Chops had decided that good hard work would be the only answer to help Sama become marriageable material. So the evening tasks had begun; helping with a host of chores that never seemed to end. Then as soon as she was old enough to leave school, she began to work full time at the store.

This left very little time for getting into adventures, but Sama still managed it. She took long walks alone on her afternoons off, climbing trees, paddling in the shallow streams that supplied the river. Most weeks, she would come home with her clothes dishevelled to her aunt's disapproving eye.

Sometimes Sama would tag along with her brother Jim and his friends, Joe and Mike. They would tolerate her and tease her mercilessly, but at least they let her be as involved in their scrapes as she wanted.

Her favourite person to spend time with, though, was Christopher. He was a year younger than she was, but funny and kind, if a bit shy. When he was back, he would always be a good sport and tag along on her adventures. Plus he would fuel her imagination with the stories and histories he had learned at that school he went to.

At the thought of Christopher, she remembered the job in hand. If she was to successfully sneak away later, she mustn't let anything indicate this wasn't just a usual Monday night. The iron was hot enough. In fact, she had been daydreaming so long that it was probably too hot. She pulled it off the heat and set about readying the first sheet.

All this sneaking off to see her friend was fun, but it was quite an inconvenience. It had started back in the summer when Chops told her father in no uncertain terms that Sama was too old to be alone with a boy of Christopher's age now. Apparently people were beginning to talk.

Stanley said he didn't much care whether people were talking. Chops, however, knew how to wear her brother down in their ongoing war of attrition. Eventually, all it had taken was mention of Sama's mother, long ago estranged from Stanley and only invoked in the most extreme of circumstances in the Neeley household. Anything that might make Sama turn out like 'that damn woman' would make Stanley react against it immediately. It was decided that Sama should not go out alone with Christopher any more.

Sama was a resourceful girl, though, and this hadn't stopped her from finding ways to see her friend. Even the outbreak of war with its extra pressures to 'do your duty,' or the added responsibility that was about to fall on her with Jim leaving for training didn't put Sama off her adventures.

She glanced at the clock above the stove and estimated the time this last job of the day would take her. Then, grabbing a cloth to protect her hand, she lifted the iron and started to smooth the first sheet.

Christopher sat at the dining room table, feeling small amongst his father's imposing collection of military paintings. In the past, dinner for the family had felt more informal and friendly. Then the room had had everyone in. Now he was alone.

It wasn't the loneliness that made him feel out of sorts. He had grown used to that in previous holidays. Something else was different. From the moment Crawford, the long serving Flyte butler, had politely greeted him at the front door, he had sensed it.

His own room had been how he left it. His collection of lead soldiers was still as he had set them; engaged in a pitched battle with swords, bows and lances on the table. His vast collection of books in the tall bookcase seemed undisturbed. Here at least, surrounded by his own things, he felt at home.

His dark leather suitcase had been placed against one of the oak panels that stretched halfway up across three of the room's walls. Christopher dragged the case to the centre of the room and undid the tightly fastened belts. The case popped open immediately. It spewed socks, vests, hankies and a host of other small clothes over the cold wooden floor. Glad of something to do, Christopher began to put things away.

When he had finished, he lay quietly on his bed by the window and reached for a book to read whilst he waited for the dinner bell. It wasn't long before his eyes were feeling heavy and began to droop.

When the dinner bell roused him, he had been snoozing fitfully through a nightmare. In it, he'd been chased through the school corridors by what started as a gang of boys, headed by Daniel Corbyne, jeering at him with taunts about his brother and his mother. At some point however they had changed. Instead of a group of schoolboys, he had found himself pursued by a great hairy beast, a Picklehaulbe perched on its head and bloody tusks protruding from its mouth. No matter where he had run, the beast had been close behind, relentless in its pursuit.

He clutched at the blankets as he regained his senses. He frowned, surprised that the war poster he had seen had stuck so vividly in his mind. He sat on the edge of his bed and rubbed his eyes, pushing the dream from his thoughts. Mr Welstone would be around somewhere and he would have answers. Christopher stumbled down to the dining room with his stomach rumbling and a host of questions about Freddie in his mind.

He glanced around the room. Perhaps there would be something that gave him a clue as to why things felt different. Before he had even studied beyond the ornate settings on the table, a connecting door to his father's study swung open.

Edwin Welstone walked in. He scurried to the seat at the head of the table and sat down. He glanced at Christopher quickly and then poured himself a large glass of red wine from a cut crystal decanter. He took a long sip and moved it around in his mouth audibly. The sound was revolting, but Christopher showed nothing on his face. There was no way he would allow this nasty little man to know he was having an unpleasant effect.

Welstone set down the glass and looked at Christopher again. 'So, Christopher, how was your journey?' he simpered eventually, a fixed smile coming to his lips.

'Very good, thank you, Mr Welstone,' Christopher muttered.

'Well, that's capital.' Welstone reached for his wine. He took another long, gurgling sip. 'Terrible business, this thing with that boy,' he continued after he had swallowed, sounding bored. 'Still, I'm sure that you felt you were defending your honour or suchlike.' He glanced at his place, fingering at his knife with thin, restless fingers.

'Well, they said that Freddie was a coward,' Christopher replied, watching Welstone for a reaction.

The little man looked up and met his gaze. For a moment a flash of irritation at the mention of Freddie's name passed across his face, quickly replaced by a dry, professional smile. 'Did they, indeed?'

Christopher nodded and went to speak again, but the main door opened and Crawford entered carrying two plates.

'Ah, marvellous.' Welstone sat forward, rubbing his hands together. 'I hope you don't object, Christopher, I had Mrs Brodie serve the food on to plates in the kitchen.' He leaned forward conspiratorially. 'No need for all that formality when it's just two good friends like you and me, eh?'

'Who's Mrs Brodie?' Christopher asked as Crawford set down his plate. A meagre portion of grey beef and boiled potatoes had been placed in its centre. Welstone's plate, by comparison, was far more generously loaded.

'Ah yes. An excellent find.' Welstone smiled to himself. 'She does both the housekeeping and the cooking, and she costs less than the cook did alone.'

'You've dismissed Cook? And Miss Chanters?' Christopher exclaimed.

'Indeed I have. Your father will be pleased with the money I have saved for him, I'm sure.'

Christopher could hardly believe his ears. 'But they've been here since I was little. Mother employed them!'

Then suddenly it dawned on Christopher what was different. So subtle but so much of a change. It was the smell. The light, fresh smell of the polish his mother had insisted the staff use was gone, replaced by something unfamiliar and cloying.

'And that is a great shame, Christopher, but all the same they had to go,' Welstone said sharply. His simpering smile had disappeared. Without it, his face was predatory and calculating. 'There are difficult times upon us. There's the war, and Freddie's treatment may cost a good deal. We all have to tighten our belts.'

'But what about all the money from the sale of mother's books?' Christopher felt a sudden emptiness. Neither the cook nor the housekeeper had been particularly close to him, but they were familiar and something of his mother.

'Actually, I don't think that I will go into the affairs of the house with you, Christopher. That is a matter for your father and myself.' The little man's voice was sharp. After he had finished speaking, he glared at his plate. He shovelled in two mouthfuls of food in quick succession, grinding his teeth over the meat as he chewed.

'I should like to see Freddie as soon as possible, Mr Welstone,' Christopher said.

Welstone swallowed his food loudly. 'Oh, I am afraid that won't be possible Christopher. Freddie is being kept under observation.'

'Where?'

'I find your manner inappropriate,' Welstone said, banging his knife down on to the linen covered table. 'Your headmaster mentioned that your behaviour had been somewhat off, but I am surprised at you, Christopher.'

The little man glared down the length of the table at him. Christopher bowed his head, fixing his own gaze on the dry slices of beef on his plate.

'Freddie is being treated at one of the best hospitals there are,' Welstone finally said. 'He isn't far out of Oxford. That is all you need to know. However, I will tell you this, Christopher. I don't know what you have been getting away with at your school, but I will not be interrogated by a boy who is under my charge. Do you hear me?'

He leaned forward in his chair, his pointy nose catching the light from the lamp, making him look suddenly like a crow staring down at a worm. 'Do you hear me, I say?'

'Yes Mr Welstone.'

Welstone nodded, satisfied. 'Good.' The mask of paternal friendliness slipped back on to his face. 'Now, I know that you must be worried about your brother, heaven knows we all are, but you must leave the care and attention to me, Christopher.

'The hospital does not encourage visits, but I call each day, as per your father's instructions. If there is anything that I think you should know, dear boy, I assure you I will tell you. You need to think about your studies and how you propose to learn to be a man when you are denied entry to school until further notice.

'If it weren't for the respect I hold your dear father in,' he continued, rubbing his hands and looking toward the heavens in an over-dramatic gesture of humility, 'I would have returned to my offices in London many months ago.'

He rose to his feet and lifted his plate. 'Now, if you will excuse me, I intend to finish this in the study whilst I look over some papers.'

With his spare hand, he placed his knife and fork on the plate and stretched out for his wine glass. He glanced at the table for a moment, deep in thought, then placed the wineglass against his side, trapping the stem tight with his forearm. His hand now free again, he took the decanter from the table and scurried out of the room without another word.

Christopher finished his meal in silence. The old house creaked. In the hall, the grandfather clock ticked steadily. From the direction of the kitchen, he could hear the sounds of someone moving about. Still the house felt empty and oppressive. It was such stark contrast to when the rooms were filled with the sounds of his mother's laughter.

The clock struck seven-thirty in crisp metallic chimes and he stirred. With a sigh, he got up, making sure that he left his plate tidy and walked out into the dark hall. There was nothing to do. There was no one to talk to. He briefly considered going to find Crawford, but the butler was rarely anything but a poor distraction. Feeling like the loneliest boy in the world, he started up the stairs to his room. At least there he could immerse himself in a book.

'Dinner was to your liking?'

The voice was so close that Christopher gasped. By the foot of the stairs where he had passed a moment before a shape moved. A hand reached toward the switch for the electric lamps and flooded the hall in yellow light.

The woman who stood by the switch was in all ways severe. She wore a drab grey dress with a white pinafore on top of it. Her hair was stretched tightly into a dense black bun high on the back of her head. Her skin was so sallow it was almost tinted yellow. Grey eyes stared out from under thick, dark brows and thin lips stretched out in a resemblance of a smile.

'I didn't mean to startle you,' she said, in a voice almost too low to be heard. 'I just wanted to say hello.'

Christopher took a step backwards up the stairs. 'That's all right. Really, you didn't.'

'Good.' The thin smile stretched wider, opening to reveal dark uneven-looking teeth. 'I just wanted to say hello,' she repeated.

'Yes. Well, hello.'

She took a step forward. 'My name is Molly Brodie. I'm going to be looking after you.'

Christopher nodded, forcing a smile to his face. He backed up one more step. 'Well, thank you very much, but I think I shan't need much looking after. '

'No. You're almost a man,' she said, looking at him steadily. 'You're welcome to come to my kitchen whenever you want. If you're hungry or just want to talk.'

'Yes. Thank you. That's very kind,' Christopher said. 'Now I think you'd better go back downstairs. I'd hate for you to get into trouble on my account.'

Brodie glanced at the door to the study and chuckled. 'I won't, Christopher.' She looked back and stretched out her hand. 'I just wanted to say hello,' she said again, looking at his hand expectantly.

Christopher reached down, manners outweighing the sense of distaste he was feeling. Her hand was cold and clammy as if she had a fever. He snatched his hand away, revolted, and climbed three more stairs before turning back to look down at her.

'Well, thank you, Mrs Brodie. I'll be sure to come and find you if I need anything.' He nodded down at her unremitting gaze. 'Good night.'

With that, he bolted up the rest of the stairs. Once out of her sight, he ran to his room, closing the door and turning the big iron key in the lock with relief. He tore off his clothes, leaving them in a heap on the floor, put on his pyjamas and climbed into bed. Only then, as he reached for the book on his bedside table, did he begin to feel the sense of revulsion slowly ebb away.

The ironing was taking an age. Sama hopped from foot to foot in impatience. Once the sheets were done, she would be able to start her plan of escape.

It was all Sama could do not to swear out loud when her aunt walked in. She had finally put the final sheet, perfectly folded, on to the completed pile. She gritted her teeth. Of all her habits, it was her insistent use of bad language that grated on her aunt the most. If she had any hope of escaping, an extended lecture on her faults needed to be avoided.

Instead, she smiled sweetly at the little woman and poured her a cup of hot tea. Then she sat next to her at the small kitchen table. A few minutes of conversation, then she would claim tiredness and slip upstairs.

Unfortunately, Chops' day had been alive with information from the village. She liked nothing better than to pass on the gossip to Sama. How any of the gossip could ever be interesting was quite beyond Sama. However, she listened and nodded at all the right points.

Eventually, the conversation actually worked in Sama's favour. After an excruciating hour, she couldn't hide her boredom any more. She yawned behind a hastily raised hand. Chops shook her head with exasperation, realising how little of the conversation her niece cared about.

'Oh, just get off to bed, young lady,' Chops said, waving her away with the back of her hand.

Sama bounced into the bar to her father. She wrapped her arms around him and planted a wet kiss on his cheek.

'Night, dad.' She grinned. Then she turned and slipped back into the kitchen.

Chops had left the room, probably in exasperation. Sama grinned and opened a cupboard. She pilfered a couple of the good biscuits that were only supposed to be for guests. She dropped them into her pocket, covered her tracks, then turned and strolled nonchalantly through the side door. There, thin, steep wooden back stairs led up to the family bedrooms. On the other side of the inn, there was a far more ostentatious set of stairs that led to the seven rooms available to guests. Sama only used those stairs when she was forced to clean them.

Once she was safely in her room, Sama stripped down to her undergarments and slipped into bed. Now she just had to lie quietly and wait for the inevitable visit that would come.

Once, a few months before, she had slipped out to watch the moonrise from one of her favourite spots up by Pickering Tower. As she returned, she had been spotted from a distance by her arch-enemy, Sergeant Dench. It had been a race to get back to the Stumblepot before him. Of course, she had managed it. She'd been back in her bed, in her nightclothes, before Chops had burst in to check on her. However, it had left her under considerable suspicion.

Since then Chops, or on rare occasions her father, had taken to slipping a head through the door each night. They would quietly wait until she moved or let out a heavy breath. Then, presumably satisfied it was her and not a pillow, they would leave.

Sama accepted this was the price of freedom and limited her night time activities to special occasions. Tonight, though, was definitely one of those nights. She fidgeted impatiently, willing the visit to come soon.

After an age, she heard the creak of the door. Chops stood and waited, listening to her niece. Sama, who had practiced many times, regulated her breathing, making it deep and slow, like a person asleep until she heard the door click shut.

She still waited a further twenty minutes to slip out of bed, just in case. Once up, she opened her cupboard. Hidden behind a tedious amount of dresses was a pair of threadbare riding britches. She slipped them on and dropped the now broken biscuits into the pocket.

She had stolen the britches from a washing line in Remenham in late autumn. She hadn't felt a single pang of guilt. They were really past their time of use to the owner. Besides, anyone who lived in such a large house really didn't need them.

Ready, she sneaked out on to the flat roof by her window. At the side of the roof was a drainpipe that led down to an overgrown part of the inn's garden. There Sama knew she would be very hard to spot. There was one point, however, as she slipped over the side of the wall, she was very easy to see. She crawled over the roof, keeping her body as flat to the light gravelled surface as possible.

She peeped over the top of the wall, held her breath and glanced down to the left. From here, she could see the whole left hand side of the village green up to the church and the little row of cottages by its side. The white sheet of snow that covered everything shone blue in the bright clear moonlight. There was no one in sight.

Sama vaulted over the top of the wall and swung down on to the drainpipe, lowering herself steadily with strong arms. Her legs dangled below, feet stretched down towards the floor. Once she had lowered herself a few feet, she let go. She dropped the remainder of the way toward the ground, feeling a secret thrill at the silence of her landing.

Sama was not one to read books, but she did have a vivid imagination. When she heard a story that grabbed her, she would spend weeks afterwards imagining herself cast in its most dangerous and exciting role. Recently it had all been about spying. The week before, she had overheard a conversation between her father and Dr Conrad. They had been reliving stories from the penny dreadfuls of their youth. The conversation had set her imagination on fire. Ever since she had pretended everything that she did was a cover for her real activities as a spy.

Sama took one more peep from her hiding place out toward the church, more because it was in keeping with the spy she was being, than out of any real concern for her own safety. There was still no one there. She burst into a light, low run. Keeping to the shadows, she dashed fifty or so yards along the road. There, well out of sight of the Stumblepot, she crossed to the shadows on the other side.

Keeping low, Sama sped through the dark on the edge of the green. She made an open fist with her right hand, imagining herself to be carrying a revolver as she sped through a German village, documents stolen from the Kaiser himself secreted about her person. If she could just reach the safe house that was her destination, she knew that the entire fate of the war would be decided in the favour of the British.

At the top end, she joined the upper spur of the lane. Eventually, it would pass the larger houses on the outskirts of Alton on its way towards Henley. This was also nearly the point of safety. Sama knew she was much less likely to be spotted once away from the green. She just had to get past Roger.

Roger, whose kennel was behind the last cottage, was a very excitable young Scottish terrier. Unfortunately his owner, Mrs McGuirk, never tired of her dog's reaction to anything that passed his way outside. She would come out to have a nose, no matter what the time or the weather. Mrs McGuirk was Officer Dench's mother-in-law. She tended to side with him on many matters, especially those concerning Sama. Thus, Roger presented something of a problem. Sama, however, was unconcerned. It took more than a dog and a nosy old woman to stop her.

She crossed the track to the white wall of the end cottage. Immediately four sets of claws scuffled loudly into action from the yard behind the cottage. She reached into her pocket. Roger's brown head pushed out of the side gate. His happy eyes stared up at the approaching girl. He sucked air into his little lungs ready to shout his greeting.

Sama threw the first bit of biscuit to him and Roger forgot his urge to bark. He jumped, snapping at the titbit in mid-air. He landed and danced around looking for more crumbs on the ground.

'Shh!' she whispered, kneeling next to the dog and rubbing behind his ears. Roger bounced from one side to another, delighted at the sudden attention. Sama fished out the next bit of biscuit and passed it to the dog. He snatched it from her fingers greedily.

Sama stoked Roger for a good five minutes, whispering quietly to him, and slowing down the action of her strokes. Soon the little dog had settled down next to her and was breathing evenly and contentedly.

It was now or never. Patting Roger, Sama rose lightly to her feet and stepped away. The dog immediately lifted his head, again a picture of alertness. Sama stalked away, not looking back. Behind her, the scraping of Roger's paws on the yard told her he was up on his feet again.

'Good boy,' Sama hissed back over her shoulder. 'Stay quiet!'

Roger took this to be an invitation to talk and immediately began to bark at the top of his voice. Cursing, Sama broke into a run and raced down the slope.

Behind her, a light came on. The back door to Mrs McGuirk's cottage opened.

'What is it, Roger? Who's there?' The woman's voice carried out into the night. Roger's bark sounded ecstatic at having the attention of not one, but two people in the space of a few minutes.

Sama ran faster. A moment before the old lady craned her birdlike neck over the gate, she burst around the corner at the bottom of the slope. As soon as she was out of sight, she slowed to a standstill.

She crouched, resting her elbows on her knees and allowing her head to hang down as she panted, catching her breath. Roger still barked in the distance. Soon she was breathing normally. She pushed back up on to her feet.

The trees along the stretch of lane grew higher, casting deep moon shadows along the rough snow-covered earth. It was almost impossible to see which way to go. Sama strolled on, both sure of her route and fearless in the gloom. The dark had never been a place to fear.

In no more than five minutes, Sama stood at the entrance to Fox Grange. She nestled against one tall gatepost as she scanned to see that her route was clear. A light shone out over the well-kept garden from the study. The little lawyer working late. Still it was to the other side of the property that she needed to go. There, Christopher's bedroom could be reached by climbing a young ash tree that grew just below his window.

She quickly covered the distance. She jumped up to grasp at the lowest of the tree's stronger branches, feeling it bend in protest at her weight. She pulled herself on to the branch and stood. The entire tree shifted slightly, bending toward the house, more so than the last time she had used this method of seeing her friend. She was definitely growing more than the young tree was.

Sama grasped the trunk where it was slim enough to get two hands around it and pulled herself higher. She was almost level with the bottom of

Christopher's window. There was a hint of light from behind the curtains. He was still awake.

She focused on the window ledge, avoiding glancing downward. If she did, she knew she'd be looking at a straight drop to the ground. It wasn't something she liked to admit to herself, but this was the moment that she felt most vulnerable. Feeling vulnerable was actually something that made her quite annoyed.

With one more pull up she was able to reach out to the wide windowsill. She vaulted up on to it, sitting comfortably on a good foot of whitewashed wood. The tree sprang back into place, suddenly the length of a good jump away. Fortunately, Sama had never had to leave the way she arrived, always managing to sneak away through the house.

She glanced in through a crack in the thick velvet curtains. Christopher was tucked in his bed, his head in a book, all concentration. She grinned and knocked quietly on the window.

Immediately his head shot up, a sudden smile of recognition erupting on his face. Sama felt a flash of pride. There was no one else who could get to Christopher's room this way.

He slipped out of bed and padded over to the window. The catch released and he slid the heavy wooden frame upwards with some effort. 'Sama!'

'Who else?' Sama answered, dropping on to the floor of the room. She stood and punched him playfully on the arm. Then she grabbed him and squeezed him in an enthusiastic hug.

CHAPTER SEVEN

The Weasel's Secret

Listening to Sama made everything in Christopher's life seem less of a worry. That was a good thing, as from the moment she had flopped on to the end of his bed, she hadn't shut up. Though she spent such effort to tell him about how bored she was by her aunt's constant gossip about the village, Christopher noticed that it didn't stop her from doing the same sort of thing.

Sama filtered out anything that she didn't consider exciting. Thus, Christopher was treated to stories of her adventures rather than village gossip. The time in autumn she discovered a new route through the woods that enabled one to reach Henley almost completely unseen. How she had been allowed to go with her brother Joe and Michael Brophy into the fields to fire Michael's old shotgun at a scarecrow, a homemade German helmet on its grinning head.

'When Jim took his go, it blew the bugger's head clean off!' Sama finished. Her voice had risen as she grew excited. He shushed her, frowning and listening for footsteps coming up the stairs at the noise.

She shook her head and looked at him. 'Always so worried! If someone comes, I can hide. You'll never get into trouble because of me.'

'I suppose,' Christopher said. It was true that Sama and he had never been caught in their various escapades.

'Besides,' Sama continued, 'the Weasel will be going out soon.'

'The weasel?'

Sama laughed. 'It's what dad and the men at the pub call Mr Welstone. He's not very popular around here.'

'Good.' Christopher thought of the way the little man had tried to seem so friendly earlier.

'He was coming down to the pub for a while a month or so back, but no one wanted to talk to him no matter how many rounds he stood. So he gave up and started going to Henley for a drink,' Sama said. 'Same thing every night it is. We see your dad's car going off with Mr Crawford driving and the Weasel sitting in the back as if he owned the whole world!'

'I wonder if my father knows he's doing that.' Christopher frowned.

'Dunno,' Sama said, glancing around the room, her mind already moving on to new subjects.

Sure enough, less than a quarter hour later the sound of a car interrupted Sama's stream of conversation. Christopher went to the window. On the gravel drive outside, his father's huge Austin Shooting Brake moved smoothly towards the gate. Through the back window, Christopher saw the lawyer's greasy head and then a flash of orange. He was lighting a cigar. One of Christopher's father's, he bet.

'Blooming cheek, I think.' Sama came up next to him.

Christopher looked at the retreating car and sighed quietly. Its bright lights disappeared out of the gate and the driveway dimmed back into darkness again.

'What is it?' Sama asked.

Christopher looked at her, wondering for a moment whether it was entirely proper to discuss family matters with anyone, no matter how close a friend.

'Stop kneeling there with that sheep face and tell me.' Sama gave him an impatient stare. 'Christopher?'

'Well,' Christopher said, realising that she wouldn't let up until he told her. 'It's just that he told me that we have to be careful with spending too much. He's dismissed cook and the housekeeper. There's some horrid new woman called Brodie instead.'

'Well, it doesn't look like he's doing what he said if you ask me.' Sama looked back out towards where the car had disappeared.

'I don't know,' Christopher said. 'Freddie needs looking after. I bet that is quite expensive, but he's got that all organised.'

'Oh yes? What's he done?'

'Well, Freddie's over at some hospital in Oxford. It's one of the best, apparently.'

'Oh, Oxford!' Sama exclaimed, a smile lighting her face. 'I went to Oxford with Jim in October. We went around the shops and then we went to the music hall in the evening! They were wearing the brightest costumes I've ever seen. I didn't think I'd like it, but Jim told me I would and he was right!'

Her eyes glazed over for a moment at the memory. Then just as quickly it was gone. She turned to Christopher. 'Freddie will be right as rain soon as you like if he's in Oxford. When are you going to see him?'

'I'm not,' Christopher muttered. 'Mr Welstone doesn't think it's a good idea.'

'Not a good idea!' Sama shifted on the bed. 'What does the Weasel know? 'Course it's a good idea! I bet as soon as Freddie saw you he'd start feeling better!'

She clutched Christopher's shoulders. 'You should go and see him anyway! Bugger what the Weasel thinks.'

'I don't think that I should go against his wishes,' Christopher said, recognising the tone of her voice. 'After all it may be …'

'Why are you sticking up for him? There he is driving around in your car for all the world to see him like he's lord of the manner and telling you that you've got no money.'

'Well, I didn't say …'

'And he won't let you go and see your own brother.' Sama drew close to him, her face screwed up with indignation. 'That's criminal!'

She shook his shoulders, making his head nod against the movement. 'We'll go! We'll go tomorrow! I'll come up with a plan.'

'Sama, I don't know where he is.'

That stopped her. She opened and closed her mouth as if she were about to say something more. No words came. She sighed and looked out of the window, a little frown clouding her brow.

'It's probably for the best, Sama,' Christopher said. 'After all, you've got to work in the shop and Oxford is quite a long way to get there and back without being missed.'

Sama said nothing. Her frown deepened. The grip that she had on Christopher's shoulders slowly grew softer.

'Besides,' he continued, 'even if we could get there I am sure they wouldn't just let us walk in without an adult.'

Suddenly Sama turned her head toward him. 'We'll worry about that when we get there.' She jumped up and walked to the door. 'Come on!'

'What? Where?' He turned to watch her.

'The Weasel's out, isn't he?' Sama said, her eyes glinting with excitement. 'I'll bet that we can find out where Freddie is if we look through his things.'

Without another word, she opened the bedroom door. She looked to the left and then to the right.

'Sama wait!' Christopher climbed off the bed and stepped towards her.

It was too late. Sama glanced back once and grinned, then disappeared into the dark corridor beyond.

'Bugger!' Sama's favourite curse sounded strange in his mouth. He ran to the door and peered out. Sama was already at the top of the stairs. She looked back at him, grinning in the darkness.

'I knew you couldn't stay there.'

'Sama, if we get caught …' Christopher hissed, scuttling after her.

'What?' She cut him off loudly, making him cringe. 'What will they do? Besides, who's here to catch us?'

'Mrs Brodie is here,' he answered with exaggerated quiet, remembering the way the new housekeeper had just appeared earlier, as if from nowhere.

'Then we should get ourselves moving rather than crouching here and arguing,' Sama said.

She started downwards, stepping tentatively from stair to stair, testing each for tell-tale creaks. Each time an oak floorboard started to groan she lifted her foot back, finding a different spot to place her weight on to. 'Step where I step,' she whispered up at him, obviously enjoying herself.

The lights were out again in the hall. Another change. When his mother had been alive, the house had been a blaze of light in the evenings. There had not been a single corner without some lamp illuminating its hidden places. Now, however, any respect for his mother's love of the light had gone with the old staff.

The moon cast a melancholy glow into the hall, shining coolly through the great bay window on the halfway landing. Exaggerated shadows fell across the hall. Alcoves where the moonlight could not reach stood in pitch black.

On the far side of the room, a beam from one of the long panes cut across a great painting of the battle of Agincourt. In the light, a small group of English archers loosed arrows from longbows into a distance that remained hidden in the dark, whilst before them others restrung their bows preparing for another volley. Christopher knew the darkness contained a host of French knights with horses rearing against the rain of missiles. Now though, the painting was strange and the dark section seemed unknown, hiding any one of a host of foes. Christopher shuddered, hating the unexpected mystery of the familiar room.

In front of him, Sama disappeared down into a dark shadow. 'Come on. Stop standing around or we will get caught!'

Christopher quickly tiptoed down the four stairs that were between them until he was covered in shadow, too.

'Which room is he using for his work then?' Sama asked in low tones.

'He's taken over the study.' Christopher pointed toward a door on the other side of the hallway. The moonlight caught his hand in its glow, casting a long bony finger on to the door. It was flanked on either side by pedestals upon which stood figurines of King Arthur and Queen Guinevere. His mother had commissioned them as a celebration for the success of her first book.

The door to the dining room creaked. Christopher froze. Next to him Sama drew a sharp intake of breath. The creak continued, a high-pitched groan of rusty hinges desperately needing attention. The door swung open.

Sama grabbed at his hand, pulling it back into the shadows. She wrapped her other arm around his waist to draw him near. 'Keep quiet. We can't be seen,' she whispered, her head inches away from him.

Molly Brodie walked into the hall. Christopher held his breath. The beating of his heart suddenly seemed so loud that anyone within the village, let alone the house, would hear it. Beside him, Sama's grip on his waist grew tighter. Her other hand clutched his with a grip of fear. As one, they drew back further, trying to reduce themselves as far into the blackness as they could.

Almost as soon as the woman had stepped through, Christopher sensed that there was something different about her. When she had stopped him in the corridor before, she had seemed strange. If he was honest with himself, she had been quite disturbing, with her clammy hands and the way she had kept repeating herself whilst staring so much. Now, however, her movements had strength and purpose to them he had not noticed before. She even seemed taller, even though Christopher was far higher than she was.

She walked toward the centre of the hall, darting glances in every direction to see if she was alone. Once convinced, she stole to the front door, deftly pulled the bolts, and then heaved it open. She stuck her head outside and sniffed the air. Again her head darted around as she looked out into the night, quickly checking this way and that. Then she dropped on to her haunches, looking like she would be able to spring out at the first sign of something she didn't like.

Sama's grip on Christopher loosened. Her expression had lost its fearful edge. Now she looked curious. She stepped forward to look over the banister, staying careful to remain in the shadow.

Sama was well practiced in moving quietly. Christopher was sure that she hadn't made a sound. Yet as soon as she moved Molly Brodie's head whipped around to their direction. In a moment, the housekeeper's body had turned. She sprang back on to her feet. With three quick steps, she was in the middle of the hall, staring up at the middle stair landing, absolutely still.

Her face was caught in the moonlight, her thin lips and angular face turning his stomach. This time though, it was her eyes that he noticed. The dull grey of before had been replaced by a darkness so black that it was impossible to distinguish between iris and pupil. She stared into the shadows, a frown creeping across her thick hairy brow, and sucked at the air with her teeth with a hissing sound.

Sama took a slow, measured step backwards, her movement eerily calm. She clutched his waist and buried her head in the crook of his neck. Her breath came in rapid shallow movements.

Molly Brodie stalked forward and raised her hand in front of her. Her nails were long and dark, like talons in the moonlight. They glinted with the sheen of a black, highly polished boot.

She was looking directly at them now. Christopher held his breath. Surely she must be able to see them, or hear them, or something. She had turned around at nothing. Now she was so much closer. Her strange dark eyes seemed to bore right into him. He felt sick with fear.

She smiled with those thin, measly lips, and her long misshapen teeth flashed for a moment in the blue moonlight. As though she did indeed know exactly what was concealed in the dark before her. Then she cocked her head to one side. To Christopher the gesture was unmistakable. It was saying, 'I know you're there.' It was saying, 'I have the power to expose you if I wish.'

Instead, however, she spun on her heel without another sound and covered the distance to the front door. Then she was gone, leaving the door swinging to a close behind her.

It took a moment before Christopher felt that it was safe enough to relax. He let out a long breath and the tenseness in his body receded a little.

Sama lifted her head and glanced down into the hall. 'Bloody hell, that was scary! I thought we were caught for sure then! That would have been both of us in trouble for days!'

She broke her tight grasp around him and stepped down another stair. 'Where did she go, then?'

'In trouble? It was worse than that! I thought she was going to kill us,' Christopher said in a small voice. 'Did you see her eyes?'

Amazingly, she laughed. 'I don't think a good beating could be thought of as murder. Though the extra chores I would have got might have killed me.'

She looked around, then skipped down the last few stairs. 'Come on. We might not have much time.'

'Sama, listen!' Christopher couldn't believe how quickly she had regained her composure. 'That was really strange. There was something about her. As if she wasn't even human.'

Sama had her back to him now and was pushing at the study door. 'Sounds like you've been reading too many fairy stories! The only strange thing was that she was stupid enough to sneak out of the front. If she got caught, she would lose her position in a minute.'

She disappeared into the study. A moment later, there were loud sounds of drawers being wrenched open. Christopher hesitated, looking at the front door, expecting it to open at any moment and Molly Brodie return with her black eyes and dark intentions.

There was a loud crash, followed by one of Sama's more colourful expressions. He sighed and shook his head, amazed how she could be so quiet one moment and so loud the next. Then he jumped down the final steps and jogged into the study to join her.

From where the Master stood watching, nestled in the shadows of the old ruined gatehouse, left to rot many years before, Molly Brodie looked free. She lifted her head to the cold night air. Her face twisted into a grimace of delight. She bent down and slipped off her shoes, then, holding them in one hand, crossed the garden toward him. Feet that were far too long squelched through the snow. The imprints they left behind looked more bestial than human, with distinct claw indentations at the end of the toe prints.

He stepped out from the shadows of the gateway, stopping in its broken doorway. As she saw him, her shoulders slumped and the spring in her step disappeared. He beckoned over to her, noting the change in her aspect.

He watched her calmly. Judging by her look of hatred, she was not fooled by the way he now looked.

'Well, Molly,' he said. 'Why don't you tell me how have things been getting on?'

With effort Molly was struggling to stay quiet. Sometimes they tried to defy him, desperately searching for willpower they had no idea they could not possess. She dug her thick black nails into the soft meat of her palms, immediately drawing dark blood from eight gouges. She gritted her teeth in silence.

'I don't have the time for games tonight.' He brushed a hand over her palms. Immediately the holes healed. 'Now stop trying to resist and tell me what you have found out.'

With the simple words, he denied her any choice of resistance. Her eyes went dull as she conceded defeat.

'The boy has settled in as you had hoped. The lawyer has taken no more notice of him than he does of anyone. He is a distraction.'

The Master nodded. 'Good, and the boy himself?'

'Sad. Lonely,' she answered. 'I could feel his pain at the changes you had me make. He misses the atmosphere of his mother's home.'

'Boys must grow,' the Master said. 'What else?'

'You were right about the lawyer. He's stealing from them.'

'Don't bore me. I know I was right. Tell me what I want to know about. The brother and the house.'

'Frederick Flyte is in Oxford, at Hartington Hospital, under the care of a Dr Blanchard,' she said.

'Good. You have removed the details?'

Molly reached into a small pocket in her dress and pulled out some sheaves of paper. 'Yes.'

'Excellent. And there are no other details in the house? You are sure? I don't want the boy finding anything out about where his brother is.'

'No. This is the only information. The lawyer won't tell him, either. He has already asked.'

'The boy was satisfied with the answer?' The Master looked at her closely.

'No, he's trying to find information in the study as we speak. He was hiding in the hall as I left.'

'Damn!' The Master crashed his hand into the side of the ruined gatehouse wall. 'He saw you?'

'He did.'

The Master stared into space, narrowing his eyes. Then he smiled. Perhaps that could be a good thing. No harm in opening the boy up to a little horror. 'If that happens again, don't be afraid of showing him your true self. After all, there's no one that he'll be able to turn to in order to discuss it with. Now, what of the house?'

'Yes, the civil war passage you mentioned is still open,' Molly replied. 'It leads to a small cellar, then on to an exit in the woods.'

'Good.' The Master nodded. 'That may be useful.' He turned and looked at Molly calmly. 'Anything else?'

She shook her head.

'Say it, then.'

'No, there is not anything else,' Molly answered, her voice thick with hatred.

'Then I release you to return to your duties.' He savoured the word release, just to remind her that he never would. 'Go.'

At his word, it was as if a physical force pushed her away. She stumbled as she retreated. It was only when she had gotten halfway across the garden that she began to steady.

He watched her move across the lawn. From the road, the sound of a car reached his ears, growing close. The butler returned. If she did not pick up her pace, the car would be here before she was gone.

'Go now!' he whispered across the grass. 'Fly!'

From her reaction, it was as if he had shouted it. She raced across the remainder of grass just as the light of the headlamps swung into the drive. A fraction before they turned to catch her in their glare, two huge black shapes unfolded from her back and flexed in the dark, just once. The Master's eyes flicked upwards toward the roof, following her path. She had disappeared over the roof tiles.

The Master turned and made his way through the undergrowth. As he reached the road, he hunched his shoulders lightly, adjusting his gait to that of Bailey's. Now, just an old man taking a night stroll before bed, he headed towards the centre of the village.

Sama's foot was still throbbing when Christopher pointed to the lights in the drive. The pile of papers was still all over the floor. The order from which they fell so heavily on her foot was a mystery. All in all, this had been an unsuccessful search. She had found nothing.

'It's Crawford!' Christopher exclaimed, staring through the window. 'Hurry Sama, we've got to get back upstairs.'

'You can go.' Sama wondered why he hadn't simply waited upstairs, for all the use he had been. 'I'm not finished yet.'

She pulled open another drawer. To be honest, she didn't really know what it was she should be looking for, but being here and stealing through the Weasel's things was a fun adventure in itself.

'Sama! He's parking the car in the garage!' Christopher hopped impatiently from foot to foot by the window.

'Yes, then he'll go in through the servants' entrance. Then I'll bet he sits down with a cup of tea before he even thinks to come into the house,' Sama said, flicking through yet another set of papers.

She was looking for an address. She checked the top of each letter, hoping for something obvious like 'hospital' in big bold letters, but so far there had been nothing. It was getting to the point that she was prepared to give up. Despite her best intentions, the search itself was getting a bit boring. The little lawyer had everything filed to a system, but Sama had never had to learn about such things and frankly, she was searching blind.

She finished leafing through the papers in her hand and glanced up. 'Go on. I'll be with you in a moment. Get upstairs in case he comes in. I can always hide.'

In the moonlight, Christopher looked as white as a sheet. Sama felt a wave of concern. With all the things that had happened to him recently, perhaps it had been unfair of her to think that he would be ready for this kind of an adventure. Still, a few escapades with her and he'd be right as rain. She'd make sure of it.

'Really, Christopher, go. I'll clear the mess and be up in a jiffy.'

Christopher looked relieved. 'Well, if you're sure,' he said, already moving towards the door.

Sama started to lift the papers back on to the desk in a rough pile she hoped would look similar to their original resting place. It only took moments, but suddenly being alone in the room made her heart beat faster. Doubling her efforts she picked up the last few piles and added them to the precarious tower.

It was atop the second to last pile that she saw the name. 'Hodder, Henty and Roché, Investment brokers.' Without thinking, she ripped the paper from the pile and stuffed it into her britches' pocket. Then she popped the last pile on top of it and ran out to the hall.

Beyond the door to the dining room, Sama heard the sound of footsteps. She swore under her breath, cursing that her assumption about Crawford had been wrong. She raced across the hall, bounding up the stairs to the sound of creaking hinges.

In a moment, she was in Christopher's room. 'Read your book,' she mouthed at his startled face, and then dove under the bed.

With effort, she shallowed her breathing and lay still. Soon there was a polite knock at the door.

'Master Flyte? Everything all right?' Crawford's voice came from the other side.

'Yes, thank you, Crawford,' Christopher answered. 'I'm just reading my book.'

'Very well then, sir,' the butler said, muffled through the thick wood. 'Sleep well.'

Sama waited a good two minutes before sidling out. Christopher had climbed under his bedclothes. Only his face and arms were showing. He looked quite miserable, dwarfed by the large bed.

'Never mind,' Sama said with quiet gusto. 'We'll get another chance to find Freddie. I promise we will.'

Christopher nodded.

Sama wished she could think of something that would bring a smile to his face. Perhaps the paper stuffed into her pocket. She pulled it out and opened it up. 'And I found this.'

Of course, it could have been anything. Just a random letter from one of the many investors working on the Flyte fortune. Sama's hopes were low. But as she read, she felt excitement welling up.

'Listen to this!' Her eyes grew wide. 'Dear Mr Welstone, It was with great surprise that we received your letter requesting that we sell Flyte concerns in the Perry and Perkin Gold Company. We have complied with your wishes and transferred the proceeds to the bank account that you instructed accordingly. However, we again wish to warn you that your actions may well be jeopardizing the long-term safety of the Flyte estate. This is the fourth such sale you have instructed us to make. All have been investments that we consider have not reached their full potential. Again, we would politely ask you if there is a reason why such liquid capital is being generated? Then we can attempt to offer you a more efficient method for your endeavours on behalf of the Flyte family.'

Sama looked up at Christopher, her eyes wide. 'He's selling off your family's stuff. I'll bet he's got all the money stashed somewhere. We should look.'

Christopher shook his head, his brow furrowed. 'Let me see that.'

Sama passed him the letter. He studied it intently, reading, then re-reading the few lines.

She sat on the end of the bed, then wriggled impatiently. 'We should definitely look. If we find it we can expose him to Crawford and tell my dad and my brother and everyone. He'll have to admit what he's up to. Then he'll have to go, along with that horrid housekeeper.'

Christopher put down the letter, still frowning in thought. 'I don't know, Sama. Would they believe us? Besides, we don't know that for sure. This could mean he was telling the truth earlier. Maybe he knows more than these people.' He waved the letter.

'Then all the more reason to look for more things,' Sama said.

'Well, if there is, we're not going to do it again tonight,' he said. 'I'd like to think about this a little bit if you don't mind.'

Sama looked at him. His tone had changed just slightly. Most people probably wouldn't even notice, but Sama knew him well. When he spoke like that, there wasn't any point in trying to convince him of something else. His mind was made up.

She still waited quietly on the end of his bed, in case he did look like he might change his mind. Soon enough though, she decided that she was sure she had been right the first time and got up.

'Well, I best be getting back. I got another early start in the morning. Not like some.'

Christopher smiled at her. 'No, not like some. I might stay in bed all morning and read a book.'

'Bugger that. I think I'd rather be in the store, and that's saying something.'

'Be careful on your way out,' Christopher said. 'Don't go getting caught.'

Sama looked at him with disdain, raising her eyebrows, then turned and tiptoed to the door. Once more she opened it just a crack and glanced outside. Sure there was no one out there she turned her head and winked at the boy dwarfed in the bed then slipped out.

She was very proud of her journey home, quite convinced that she had never managed to move as silently. Even Roger didn't stir this time as she passed his gate. She congratulated herself as she shinned up the drainpipe and into her room. Even as she climbed through the window she was feeling full of her own abilities. In fact, she felt proud right up until the moment that she heard her aunt's voice quietly in the darkness.

'Now my girl, where have you been?'

CHAPTER EIGHT

The Cave in the Cliff

As it turned out, Sama was not the only one to have to answer questions after that night's events. The following morning Christopher had only just finished dressing and was sitting in his room wondering what sort of meagre breakfast would be served, when Edwin Welstone bellowed up the stairs.

'Christopher! Come down here this instant!'

Christopher stiffened, immediately guessing the reason for the lawyer's raised voice. The pile of papers! Swallowing, he walked into the hall.

'Coming, Mr Welstone.'

'Be quick about it, boy,' Welstone shouted again. His high, reedy voice sounded quite silly when raised in anger. Christopher still felt a tremor in his step as he went into the study.

'I know that you were in here last night, Christopher. I know you were.' He glared with little beady eyes. 'All my papers have been moved.'

Christopher hated to lie. 'I read a book last night, Mr Welstone. In my room.'

'Really?' said Welstone. 'All night?'

That had him, Christopher thought. There was probably no point in trying to out think the little man. After all, he was a professional when it came to negotiation and discussion. He'd probably spot a lie.

'Well ...' Christopher started.

'Mr Welstone.'

Welstone looked up past Christopher's shoulder. 'Not now Brodie.'

Christopher moved away as the plain woman stepped into the room. In the daylight, she seemed somewhat less imposing. It suddenly seemed foolish that he had felt so strange about her before.

'I'm sorry, Mr Welstone, but I must say something. I was just coming to apologise to you, because I was the one who knocked over your papers. So I must tell you before you punish Master Christopher.'

Christopher stared over at her in shock.

'I came in here looking for my dusters. I mislaid them in all the activity getting ready for his return yesterday. I thought that it would be best to look for them last night whilst I wasn't disturbing anyone.'

Welstone glanced between the two of them. His eyes narrowed as he tried to spot any collusion between the pair.

'Very well,' he said. 'Thank you, Brodie. We will speak about this later. You can go.'

As Brodie left, the lawyer turned back to Christopher with the fixed smile that he wore when trying to appear friendly. 'Well, that's all cleared up. So tell me, my boy, what do you have planned today?'

'I hadn't really thought about it sir,' Christopher answered truthfully.

'Well, my suggestion is to get yourself outside. It's a lovely crisp day and I'm sure you'll want to say hello to a few people.' Welstone gestured at his desk. 'Better than being cooped up all day with me and these boring old papers, eh?'

Christopher nodded, thinking that it was probably better for the Weasel's privacy than it was for him. Still, he found himself completely in agreement. 'Yes sir, that's a capital idea.'

'Good, good.' The lawyer nodded and turned to his desk. 'Well, I am afraid I must ask you to breakfast without me. I'll be most of the morning sorting these papers again, I'll wager. Brodie will have something in the dining room for you.'

Sure enough, there was a steaming bowl of hot porridge waiting for him when he sat down in the dining room. He took a tentative spoonful and found it much to his liking.

Brodie came in once to replace his soon emptied bowl with some hot toast smothered in damson jam. When she was satisfied no one would come into the room, she glanced at him.

'Don't you worry, Christopher,' she hissed and bent to get closer to him. 'I'll keep your secrets for you. No harm in a little adventure at night, eh?'

Her breath smelled. Christopher fought against wrinkling his nose. The smell reminded him of the compost behind Old Stinker in the autumn, when the rains had fallen on it and the final warmth left from summer just started to rot it. He shifted away.

'No, none,' he said quickly. This close to him, Brodie seemed much more like she had during the night.

'I'm glad.' She lifted her head and swapped the bowl and plate in one fluid movement. Without another word, she turned her back and headed to the door.

It felt good to be out in the crisp bright morning. Once he had been left to finish his toast, he had been so keen to get himself ready and out that he hadn't thought any more about what he might do.

He had thought to take the letter with him, though. Christopher was sure that as soon as he was out of the door there would be someone looking through his room. So he stuffed it into the pocket of his overcoat and marched out of the front door.

By the time Christopher had strolled up to the edge of the green he decided to go and see Sama. It also occurred to him that it was the first day since the start of term that he had nothing to do. Despite all the things that he had to think about, he felt a lot more contented. For a while at least, he was free.

'Well, Master Flyte,' a slightly muffled voice broke his thoughts. 'Joe said in the pub last night you were back. Back to the village for Christmas, eh?'

Christopher looked over to see Officer Dench leaning against the fence of his mother-in-law's house. In his hand were the remains of a piece of toasted bread with a hunk of cheese on top. In his mouth was another fair portion.

Dench swallowed loudly. 'Well, as long as you remember that you behave yourself. Don't you forget there's a war on. We've all got to work together now.'

Christopher nodded and flashed a polite smile at the policeman. He took a half step away, concerned that the meeting was about to turn into a lecture. Fortunately, the policeman waved him off with his free hand and turned his attention back to the food. Christopher turned toward the Stumblepot.

Sama wouldn't be at the pub, of course. She'd be suffering at the shop. He reached the bottom of the green and turned down toward the river, passing Joe's house. From behind the house there came the sound of a steady hammering.

The general store was at the end of the village. Its inconvenient location had been something that villagers had complained about in one form or another for over fifty years. A succession of owners had fielded complaints, explaining the convenience for the deliveries with both the river and a track to Henley so nearby.

That had all changed when Chops had taken over the store. It took a brave person to argue with her on any matter. These days the villagers were careful to make their complaints to one another, far away from the shop and her ears.

Christopher opened the gleaming white door. The little bell above it rang insistently. Chops stood behind the counter. When she saw who it was, she stared, thin lipped, in his direction.

'Well, I see you met with no misfortune after your activities last night.'

'Hello, Chops,' Christopher said.

'Don't "hello Chops" me, Christopher Flyte.' Chops narrowed her eyes at him. 'I thought I'd explained to you that it's improper to be spending time alone with Sama. She is not a child any more, and you're nearly a young man. I won't have people talking.'

From the back of the shop, there came a cry of exasperation. 'Auntie!' Sama stormed out from behind the curtain. 'I didn't see Christopher last night, I told you!'

Sama looked miserable. She was dressed in a light blue dress with a high frilly collar. On her feet were matching blue shoes, fastened by little metal buckles on either side. Her hair was tied back in a blue ribbon and she wore a neat apron. She came around the counter and grabbed Christopher in a big hug.

'This is the first time we've met, get it?' she whispered into his ear.

'Sama, get back here!' Chops was nearly beside herself, glancing quickly between the window and Sama. 'Stop that at once.'

Sama let go of Christopher and winked before sauntering back behind the counter. 'I just wanted to say hello to him. He's my friend.'

'Well, that's as may be, but that's not the proper way to behave,' Chops said, shaking her head. 'You've got to learn. How I can be thinking about going to London tomorrow is quite beyond me.'

Sama murmured something under her breath.

'And that's most certainly not going to help you either, young lady,' Chops said. She stared at Sama for a moment and then, deciding that silence showed that Sama knew she was right, turned to Christopher. 'Well, anyway, enough nonsense. Was there something that you came in for?'

Christopher nodded. 'Well, to say hello, and to see Sama, actually.'

'Well, that's very polite of you, paying us a call.' Chops sounded only slightly convinced. 'And now you seen us both.'

'I was wondering if Sama would like to come to tea,' Christopher said.

'And who would be there as well as you two? Anyone? It seems like there's a lot of opportunities for you to be on your own at your home, Christopher. That wouldn't do at all.'

'What on earth do you think might happen, Auntie?' Sama exclaimed, rolling her eyes skywards.

'Never mind what I think might happen. It's just that there comes a time when young men and young women should not be left alone.'

Sama made to speak again.

'No, young lady. You've said quite enough today already.' Chops turned to Christopher. 'Thank you for your invitation, Christopher, but I am afraid that Sama is not allowed to go anywhere. She sneaked out of her room late last night and went heavens knows where.' Once again, her eyes narrowed on his face looking for clues he had been a part of the crime. 'She won't be accepting any invitations of any sorts for a few weeks.'

'Auntie!' Sama said again, sounding angry.

'Still it would be very rude to simply decline the invitation. Once Sama has learned the error of her ways she would be happy to accept your invitation, and I'll be happy to come along and chaperone her.'

'Oh, bugger!' Sama said and stormed through the curtain.

'Samantha Neeley!' Chops exclaimed. 'Heavens above, girl!'

A second later Sama was back. She set her shoulders and held her head high. 'And there's gypsies up at Pickering Tower. Jim told me. I guess you'll have to go and take a look for both of us, because I can't blooming go!'

'Right, that's it!' Chops said, grabbing Sama about the waist and swinging her around. 'In the back with you, right now!'

Sama disappeared through the curtain once again. Chops came around the counter. 'And I am afraid that's the shop closed for a few minutes whilst I deal with her. I'm sorry, Christopher. Out you go.'

She loomed over Christopher and grabbed the door, pulling it open. With her strong bulk between him and the entire shop, Christopher had no choice but to retreat the way she intended. As soon as he was out, Chops shut the door and turned the sign from open to closed. That done, she turned and stormed into the back room. Immediately there were raised voices.

Christopher waited for a moment, looking at his feet. Knowing there wasn't really any point, he sighed and walked down the path to the river. It rushed along, bloated with winter flow, but at its edges, in little inlets and curves of the bank, thin sheets of ice had formed.

The sound of hammering from Joe's workshop carried along the water more clearly than it had from the track. It had a quite metallic ring. Christopher smiled to himself and turned.

As he rounded the side of the house, it wasn't Joe's giant frame that he saw hammering, but rather Bailey's. Smaller by a long way, the old man still had the steady strength of someone used to labour. His blows fell on to a rusty old plough blade that burned orange in the light of the morning sun. Christopher had to call loudly between the rings of the hammer.

The old man turned around. 'Oh hello. Come to take over, have you?' He offered the large hammer to Christopher. 'I could do with a rest.'

Laughing, Christopher took the hammer, straining against its weight. 'What should I do?'

Bailey leaned against the shed, which creaked and shifted a little. 'Well, see that dent there?' He pointed at a substantial bend in the plough blade. 'We're trying to straighten that out so she'll fit back into where she's from.'

'She?' Christopher asked, eyeing the dent whilst getting used to the feel of the hammer in his hands.

'Oh yes. All machinery is "she".' Bailey smiled. 'Especially when it's not doing what it's supposed to. Go on.'

Christopher lifted the hammer and brought it down on to the dent. There was a loud clang in response. The shock wave ran all the way up his arm. He snatched it back, struggling to keep hold of the hammer, and rubbed his elbow.

Bailey laughed. 'Seems like you clanged louder than she did.' He took the hammer and set it on the ground. 'Best you leave that down to me, lad.'

He indicated a broken bench just under the shelter of the makeshift roof. 'Have a seat.'

As Christopher sat down, Bailey picked up a large screw from a pile of bits of the plough and with an oily rag and started to clean it.

'So you're walking around the village with nothing to do with yourself, and you thought that you might come in and see what Joe and Bailey were doing, eh? Well, I can tell you that Joe's off on his rounds this morning, and I'm left here with this stubborn old plough.' He glanced up. 'So what do you think of that?'

'Well, I think that I'd better keep you company, then,' Christopher answered, happy with the way Bailey just slipped into conversation without really needing any of the normal formalities. 'I very much doubt if the plough has much conversation.'

Bailey's laughter boomed out into the morning. 'Now there you are absolutely right. I suppose I better get us a good hot cup of tea, then. You stay here a moment and see if she says anything whilst I'm gone.'

He passed Christopher the screw and rag, then walked off into the house. Christopher set about running the rag through the little screw's thread, pressing down with the edges of his nails to get in as deeply as he could. Occasionally he glanced up with anticipation to see if there was any sign of the old man.

Soon enough Bailey appeared with two steaming mugs and set one down next to him. 'So then, all settled in at home?'

'I suppose,' Christopher answered.

'Oh?' Bailey sat down on a stump of log on the other side of the shelter. 'That doesn't sound very good. Don't sound like you're settled in at all.'

'It's just, everything seems different,' Christopher said without thinking. He suddenly caught himself, realising how easily he could say that to Bailey, whom he had known less than a day.

'What kind of different?' the old man said after a while.

'Well, things have just changed.' Christopher found himself speaking again. 'Cook is gone, so is Miss Chanters. There's this horrid new housekeeper, and Mr Welstone says we haven't much money, but we found a letter that says he's selling stocks that he shouldn't be. Now Sama wants to tell everyone, but I thought we needed more proof and so we need to go and get some. But Sama got caught being out last night and now she's not allowed to do anything and I'm on my own.' He paused, breathless, and glanced up. Bailey's eyebrows had risen and he shifted in his seat. 'And he's told me that I can't go and see Freddie,' he finished lamely.

'You have got troubles, haven't you?' Bailey said.

He looked almost annoyed. Then a moment later the look was gone. Bailey grinned, then glanced around surreptitiously. When he was sure that no one was watching, he turned back his grin even wider. Christopher smiled back. Bailey couldn't have been annoyed, he must have imagined it.

Bailey pulled out a small flask from his pocket. 'Tell you what, pass me your mug over here, lad. This will help everything feel a lot calmer.'

Christopher looked at the flask with suspicion. 'What is it?'

'Ha ha. It's a bit of mead. Recipe is older than you and me and a hundred other villagers added together. You try a bit in there and we'll sit here and talk about the sort of things you should on a bright winter morning this close to Christmas.'

Christopher passed over his mug. Bailey poured in a splash then passed it back.

'There you go, lad.' He smiled. 'Take a sip.'

Dutiful, Christopher lifted the mug and let the hot sweet liquid pour into his mouth. His senses were filled with a delicious heavy sensation that was neither entirely taste nor entirely smell. He swallowed. Warmth spread up from his stomach, through his spine and into the back of his neck and head. He felt himself sinking backwards into the warmth, as if a giant blanket had been spontaneously placed behind him. All around, the world seemed to soften.

Christopher blinked against the sensation, but it was too potent. His head began to swim and his eyes saw stars.

'Better?' Bailey asked. He was standing at the plough rubbing away some of the rust from the top with glass paper. 'Funny stuff, that mead. Quite takes you out of yourself sometimes.'

Christopher looked down at his mug. It was quite empty. 'How long have we been here?'

'Oh, not long,' Bailey answered, concentrating on a particularly stubborn piece of rust. 'You went a bit quiet and it never does to disturb another man's thinking.'

'Anyway,' he continued, 'a bit of quiet is good for the soul. I bet you feel better.'

Christopher did feel better. He couldn't for the life of himself think why the idea of home and Mr Welstone had been worrying him at all. The concerns all seemed a lot less worrying. In fact, everything seemed a lot more relaxed. He was suddenly sure that he had been worrying himself needlessly. 'Yes, actually.'

'Good,' Bailey said and set down his work once more. 'In that case, perhaps it's time to tell you a bit more about that silver gauntlet.'

'Winter's Grasp?' Christopher said dreamily. 'I'd like to know more about Tristan.'

'Well,' Bailey said, once more taking his place on the stump. 'I've got a story to tell you that isn't strictly about him, though of course his fate was entwined in Winter's Grasp. This story is much more recent, though. Less than a hundred years!'

'That sounds nice,' Christopher said, not really because he wanted to, but more because he didn't want to offend Bailey by looking like he wasn't paying attention. Bailey's voice sounded like it was in a great hall and wispy echoes floated back to Christopher's ears from far away.

Bailey reached forward and touched his forehead. The touch tingled, cutting through the pleasant haze. 'Now you just sit there and relax, lad.' The old man's whisper was a sudden focus. 'Relax and listen to the story.

'After Tristan was killed, no one remembered the gauntlet. Merlin died a score of years later. Lancelot and the Queen became lovers and neither thought of the Lady of Shallot again. The world moved on.

'Winter's Grasp lay under the rubble of Tintagel, which was lashed smooth by the sea and the wind. As time went on more of the castle and the rock that it was built upon fell down into the water below. After hundreds of years,

Winter's Grasp was deep beneath the ruins and the ruins were deep within the water.

'Winter's Grasp, though, was no ordinary gauntlet. It wasn't heavy like other, less gifted gauntlets. As the sea moved in, it floated round in little spaces between the rocks it lay in, up and down and all around.

'But everywhere it floated rocks slowed its path. It stayed there for years more, knocking away at the old rocks, moving in and out with the tides. Occasionally it slipped through one space to another, travelling through submerged caves into the cliff itself. And eventually, after hundreds of lifetimes had passed and Arthur and his knights had become characters in books, it finally freed itself.

'It came up in a cavern. A great tall thing with sheer sides that rose high into the hill, empty of water at low tide and filled with a deep pool at high. And being a light and magical object it rose and fell with the tides, until it eventually floated on to a natural shelf hidden high in the cavern wall. There, it caught on some seaweed, and its journey with nature ended.'

Bailey stopped. Christopher looked up. 'Go on,' he said. 'Why did you stop?'

The old man grinned. 'Just making sure you were listening to me and not the mead.'

'I am!' Christopher said, sitting up and shaking his head. 'What happened then?'

'Well, you need to remember that the coast is always changing. Sometimes it takes a very long time, like the rounding of a pebble, and sometimes it happens in seconds.

'There came a night, about a century ago, when the castle and the village and the whole area were struck by a storm of which they had never seen the like. They still talk about it today. The waves were so big that they were reaching the tops of the cliffs. The rain was so heavy that it was hard to tell where it stopped and the sea began. The people left their houses and hid inland, until it was over.

'When it was over, they came back to Tintagel and walked up on the cliffs. There they found a great hole where the coast had simply collapsed away with the water. In the hole, the rocks were exposed, and within those rocks was an entrance to the caves below.

'Now, in those days many visitors came to Tintagel to see the castle where King Arthur had been born. Most of 'em were too rich, with too much time on their hands. Some of these rich people saw the cave entrance and thought it'd be a great adventure to go and see where it led. So seven of them put on miners helmets, took strong rope and food, and climbed down into the entrance early one morning at mid tide. They planned to go as far as they could before they reached the water.

'They climbed down through the caves and found a long tunnel. From there, they had to clamber past many rock falls and step over many crevices. And as they went they laughed and congratulated themselves at how easy the journey down had been with all their lights and ropes and tools. At the end of the tunnel, there was a hole in the roof. They climbed up through it and there was the little cavern where Winter's Grasp lay hidden above them.

'The people didn't realise how long the climb down had taken, though. In their arrogance, they supposed that the tide had been going out. No one had bothered to check. They had gone far lower than was safe. By the time the water started lapping at the hole in the floor, they realised their mistake. By then they didn't have a chance.

'They ran around the cavern trying to find a way out, but there was none. The water filled up in the cavern and they swam in it, trying to keep afloat, but one by one they grew tired. Then each in his turn sank down into the dark. And the last to drown, who was the strongest swimmer, looked up into the distant roof and saw the moonlight dimly shining through from an unreachable fissure in the rock, high and far away. Then his strength left him and he too sank down into the dark.

'When the adventurers didn't return, the people in Tintagel decided that the cave was too dangerous to ever go into again. They held a ceremony at the entrance. Then they put a fence around the entrance and banned anyone from ever going in there again.

'So, Winter's Grasp stayed where it was for another twenty years. Moss and weeds grew up over the entrance and birds made their nests in the fences around it. The rich people that had drowned became a story mothers would tell their children to explain why the sea could be dangerous.

'And the children themselves would make up scary stories about the skeletons in the cave that no one could visit. And, as they played in the fields above the cliffs, they would stray and visit the entrance, daring each other to stand closer and closer to it.

'Now the children of the village grew older, as children do. The boys became young men, strong and full of the joys of the world, yearning to see what adventures would befall them. The girls became young women and laughed at the way the boys would fall over themselves to get their attention.

'There was in Tintagel, a girl called Elizabeth Lanyon. She was tall and proud, with long blonde curls that reached to her waist. Of all the girls of the village, she was the one that the young men tried hardest with. If you asked many of them who they would marry, they would turn to you with fire in their eyes and cry, "Elizabeth Lanyon will be my wife!"

'Elizabeth Lanyon knew that she could have the pick of the men for her husband. Whenever she was asked by one of the young men who she loved, she would say, "I'll love the man who proves he loves me most."

'Well, being as she was the prettiest girl in the village, this question was asked many times. Yet Elizabeth Lanyon still wouldn't say who it was she would love. So the young men of the village got together and decided that they would show her once and for all who loved her most. They remembered the cave that they had been forbidden to enter, with the skeletons that they believed were within, and they decided. The man who deserved Elizabeth Lanyon's hand in marriage would be the one who could get to that cavern and bring her back a gift from what they found there.

'Five of the young men said they would try to reach the cavern. The strongest and the fastest and the most brave. All were good swimmers, living as they did by the sea, and good climbers, living as they did by the rocks. So, on five nights they waited until the tide was at its highest. Then, one by one, they took their turn to climb down into the cavern.

'The first didn't get very far. When he got into the cave, he found that he was too big to fit through the gaps to the lower chambers and gave up.

'The second and third didn't fare much better. Though they both got deeper, they moved too slowly and did not reach the cavern. The rising tide forced them to go back.

'It was the fourth of the young men that reached the cavern. He climbed through the entrance and there he saw the washed bones, stripped of all flesh by the tides. He snatched a broken watch that he found on the ground, then made his way out again. He reached the surface with very little time to spare, soaked to the skin and claimed that to take longer would be suicide.

'Now by this time Elizabeth Lanyon had heard what the young men were doing and, being a good person for all of her pride, she was very troubled. She had no wish for anyone to lose their life for her. On the final night, she went to the entrance to the cave where the young men had gathered.

'The fifth of the men was preparing to climb down into the cave. His name was Ben Bailey and he was the strongest and the best of them.'

'Ben Bailey!' Christopher said, his eyes wide.

Bailey glanced at him and smiled. 'Yes. Ben Bailey.'

Christopher felt light headed and confused. Bailey was now the only thing that his mind could focus on. Around him things seemed to be melting into each other, a dull swirl of shapes and colours.

'When Elizabeth Lanyon saw him, she was even more distressed. Of all the men in the village, Ben Bailey was the one that she hoped would love her the most.

'She called out to the men, telling them they were foolish. They looked around at the floor and felt foolish. All except Ben Bailey.

'He looked at the entrance of the cave. As she chided the men for risking their lives, Ben started down towards it.

'Elizabeth Lanyon saw him going and called "Ben Bailey, where are you going?"

"To the cave, my girl," he called back, "I will not stay when the others have gone."

'Elizabeth Lanyon knew that he was proud like she, and knew that he would not stay without good reason, so she called to him again. "Ben Bailey! You have no need to go down there. You're the one I love and it's you I'll marry."

'And he turned to her and smiled a sad smile. "Then that is even more reason why I must go." And with that, he disappeared into the mouth of the cave.

'Now Ben Bailey was fast and determined. His frame was a little slimmer than the others. His limbs were a little more agile. He climbed down and reached the cavern a good few minutes quicker than anyone ever had. It was still free of water. He walked about looking for something to take back.

'Nothing that he found made him happy, until eventually at the back of the cavern he found a bone sticking out of the sand that had gathered on the floor. He dug around the bone and discovered that it was an arm. On that arm was still a jacket. "In this jacket I'll find what I am looking for!" he exclaimed and began to dig.

'And whilst he scrabbled around in the sand, the sea rose. As he pulled at the jacket, it began to lap around the edges of the hole behind him. As he rifled through the pockets, finding nothing and swearing aloud, the first puddles began to swell out on to the cavern floor.

'When Ben Bailey turned around, still with nothing to take back, he saw his fate had been sealed. He sighed and laughed quietly, cursing himself for a fool.

"Bailey," he said. "If you had listened before you started this climb, you could be setting your wedding day in front of a warm fire. Instead, you will die alone and become another skeleton for foolish friends to compete for."

'Ben Bailey didn't run around the cavern crying and weeping. He sat quietly against the back wall, watching the water rise. He thought about all the things he had done and seen. Not that he had seen anything that people thought were fantastic, just the day to day things that are magic in themselves.

'The water rose and Ben Bailey did with them. And he paddled for as long as he could before exhaustion got the better of him. And at the last, high above him, he saw a distant fissure in the rock and through it how the moonlight shone dimly. Then he heaved a sigh and sank down into the darkness.

'As he sank, a glint caught his eye. In a hidden shelf next to him, something shone. He reached out to it. His hand touched metal, smooth to the touch. His fingers clasped against it and he pulled. As lightly as cloth, Winter's Grasp freed from its long resting place and came out to him.

'Such was its beauty that Ben Bailey quite forgot the pain in his lungs and the fear in his heart. He drew it to him and marvelled at the way it glistened, even in the dark.

"That I should find something to show my love now." Ben Bailey thought to himself in the darkness. "There is a lesson for my pride." With that, he pulled Winter's Grasp on to his hand.

'Then the burning in his chest became too much to bear. He let out his breath and gasped again, but only water filled his lungs. And as his mind began to dim, he reached out with his hands toward the light from the fissure and grasped.

'At the entrance to the cave, Elizabeth Lanyon begged the other young men to go down and find him. Knowing what they would see, the young men climbed down into the cave, heads bowed. Below them the water still rose, blocking their way and telling Ben Bailey's fate. They climbed back up and came to Elizabeth Lanyon. None of them could meet her eye. "Where is he?" she cried.

"The waters have risen, but he has not," one of the men said quietly.

'Then Elizabeth Lanyon let out a wail that was louder than the wind around the cliffs. "He could be setting his wedding day in front of a warm fire. Instead, he has died alone and become another skeleton for foolish friends to compete for."

'Elizabeth Lanyon gathered her coat around her and turned from the other young men. She walked away proudly, with tears in her eyes. She didn't turn back.

'As she came to the top of the cliffs, there was a rock. On this rock sat Ben Bailey, warm and dry and smiling. He lifted Winter's Grasp to show her, and said, "I have proven my love for you. In the rocks, I found this gauntlet and it is for you."

'But Elizabeth Lanyon was so pleased to see him alive, she said, "I need nothing from you, but promise you will never do anything so foolish again."

'And Ben Bailey kept that promise. He kept the gauntlet too. He wrapped it in a cloth and put it in a special box, because he knew that it was something magical and it had saved his life. It had pulled him up to the light that he had grasped for and he had found a hidden way out.

'And though the others asked him how he had come out from the cavern, he never told them. In a short time, he married Elizabeth Lanyon and they loved each other as much as two people could.

'So that is how Winter's Grasp came to be in the world again.'

Bailey reached down to the ground by Christopher's feet. He picked up the screw and cloth that lay discarded and set again to cleaning them. Christopher shivered and blinked. The day suddenly seemed colder and the white of the snow sharp on his eyes.

'There you go, lad,' Bailey said without looking up from the screw. 'I hope that was good enough for you.'

'Yes. Thank you.' Christopher nodded.

Bailey glanced up. 'Aha, that mead gone through you already? Here, let's have another.'

His flask was again in his hand. Christopher frowned and looked down. The screw was still with the cloth by his feet. 'I'm not sure that I should.'

'The best cure for one is another,' Bailey said. He poured the liquid into the empty mug.

'Will you tell me more about Ben Bailey?' Christopher said, eyeing the mug suspiciously. 'Why you have the same name?'

'I will,' Bailey said and passed the mug across. 'But now I want to tell you other things. Drink.'

Christopher lifted the mug to his lips and once again drank.

CHAPTER NINE

The Master Moves

As the dusk sun drooped towards the horizon, painting the snow orange, the Master put down his work tools and went into the cottage. Joe was still out at one of the big houses, repairing an old door or window or something equally mundane. Alone, he relaxed Bailey's form and flowed back into his own. He slumped in Bailey's chair and closed his eyes. It felt good to be himself for a while. The effort of constantly holding himself in the guise of Bailey was both tiring and uncomfortable.

Clearing the boy's mind from the petty distractions of the lawyer's actions had been an unexpected chore that he could have done without. Of course, he had managed it, but he had still had to use most of the mead. There was just one draught left and now, there was only one use for that. He grimaced.

Admittedly things were moving along nicely. The boy's head was once again filled with thoughts of Winter's Grasp. Plus, now Christopher was marked. Should he come close to any of the Master's creatures, the aura from the mead would single him out.

The Master had no wish to meddle in the affairs of the Flyte family, but the boy must not be distracted again. The illusion had to be complete, and until the boy had joined with the gauntlet it would not be.

The Master smirked at himself. The gauntlet indeed. He was believing his own stories. It had only been a few days since it had been a tiny wooden crucifix, blessed to ward away the bites of vampires. He reached into his coat pocket, feeling for the solid wooden box he kept within.

His fingers closed around it, warm to the touch as always, and he pulled it out. Not particularly large, about the size of a cigar box, it took a moment to work it through the opening of his pocket. He lifted it up, turning its plain wood sides around until the little black metal clasp faced him. By the clasp was a keyhole set in a black metal plate. Actually, the box was unlocked. It never left his pocket anyway. He even slept with it. He would until its contents were joined with Christopher.

Around the cracks of the box tiny sparkles of blue light danced and crackled.

It was more than warm now. Its contents awoke, somehow aware it was the focus of someone's attention, and it had begun to generate heat. The Master lifted it to his eye level and carefully opened the lid just a hint.

There was no longer the crucifix in there. Instead, an effervescent amorphous blue lump lay within. Sparks fizzed around it. A blue light glowed from its core. He squinted. It was always hard to look at that light. Such intense power, like a tiny sun. However, if a person managed to stare into the light for long enough, the hints of images, ghosts of people and places, would slip in and out of their consciousness like distant memories.

It had been many things over the years it had been his. Some had been small, like the crucifix, others far larger. Yet until released from the box, somehow they always fitted inside.

The Master lifted the lid a little more and the mass inside became alive! Its whole shape twisted and changed, tiny ridges rising and falling like waves on a tiny sea. It suddenly lurched forward toward the opening. Quick as a flash, the Master shut the box tight and slipped it back into his pocket. He smiled to himself, suddenly aware of how fast his excited heart was beating.

By the time Joe arrived home an hour or so later, night had drawn. The Master had lit all the lamps and drawn the curtains, all the while debating whether a visit to Edwin Welstone was the best course of action. Eventually, he concluded it was the only course of action. As the door clicked open, he took a deep breath and pushed his form into that of Bailey's.

'Hello, Joe. Kettle's on,' he said.

Joe pulled off his huge coat and scarf and hung them on the back of the door. 'Good. I haven't had a cup of tea since this morning. Do you know, not even old Hettie at the farm offered me a cup today! And after I made a special point of going out of my way to take that new tablecloth to her.'

'Now Joe, I'm just going to take a walk up to Mrs Clements. I did say to her that one of us would look at her stove today.' The Master hoped that Joe was too tired to question. He did not want to be forced to use another charm on the big man.

Joe raised his eyebrows. 'Tonight? I don't know why you would bother. I doubt she'll expect you now.'

'That's not like you to say such a thing. You must be tired,' the Master replied.

Joe looked slightly guilty. 'You're right. If you said we would go, then we should.' He got up. 'Let me get my coat on, then.'

'No, Joe,' the Master said slightly too sharply. Joe looked at up at him, surprised.

'Really,' he continued, forcing a smile out of Bailey's weathered face. 'I'll do it. It was me she spoke to and you've been out all day. Let me go.'

'Well, I would like to sit down for a spell.' Joe glanced at his armchair, a look of pure longing on his face. 'As long as you are sure that you don't mind.'

'I am.' He stood up before Joe could change his mind. 'If I get off now, it shouldn't take me more than an hour.'

At the entrance to Fox Grange, out of sight of the road behind, the Master slipped into his own form again. Instead of his usual clothes though, a smart town overcoat replaced his long coat. Beneath he wore a dark suit and white silk shirt. Around his neck was a deep blood red neck tie. He started up the drive, keeping to one side where a car's tires had cut a convenient path through the dirty snow.

It was an imposing house. Welstone had been clever to get himself so ensconced with the Flyte family. The Master frowned, hoping that the lawyer would not prove difficult to deal with. At the door, he reached up and yanked the iron bell pull with two sharp jerks.

There was no danger of seeing the boy. The charms that he had given him earlier would not wear off fully until late the next afternoon. Christopher would likely be in his room sleeping deeply, in a magical sleep where dreams would continue the Master's work.

The butler opened the door. Crawford. That was the name Molly Brodie had mentioned. 'May I help you?' the butler said, barring the way, professionalism masking any surprise he might feel at the lateness of the hour.

'You may,' the Master said, his voice sounding clipped and business-like. 'I am here to see Mr Welstone on a matter of business. My name is Reedy.'

'Well, sir, we weren't expecting anyone,' Crawford said, still barring his way.

'Indeed.' The Master nodded, lifting his hand and glancing nonchalantly at his fingers. 'I was not expecting to be here. Please tell Mr Welstone that I bring news which may be to his advantage.'

The butler stepped back. 'If you would care to wait here, I'll let Mr Welstone know of your arrival.'

Crawford took his coat silently and disappeared off through a door. A few moments later, the door opened and Welstone came through, wiping his mouth with a white napkin. He glanced at the Master blankly.

'Mr Reedy?' he said.

'Mr Welstone,' the Master said. 'Please do excuse the unannounced nature of this visit. I have come straight from London on the afternoon train.'

'I see,' the little lawyer said, suspicious. 'Well, you will have to take us as you find us, Mr Reedy, which I hope is very well, but it is you who must excuse me. I am afraid I am not familiar with you or the reason for your visit.'

'I am here to explain a situation to you, Mr Welstone. One that you may well find to be to your advantage.'

'And what would that be?' Welstone's interest had been aroused.

'It is of a somewhat private and, um, lucrative nature,' the Master answered, flashing the little lawyer a conspiratorial smile.

'Is it indeed?' Welstone asked, setting the white napkin on to a small dark oak table. 'Then perhaps you should follow me into the study.'

'Thank you,' the Master said.

Welstone opened a large door between the figurines of Arthur and Guinevere on plinths. The Master followed him in, glancing at the figurines, recognising them immediately and smiling.

Welstone shut the door and turned to the Master. 'Can I offer you a drink?'

'That would be most kind, Mr Welstone.' The Master smiled. 'The journey here is not the most direct. I must say I found it most exhausting.'

The little lawyer frowned across at him, obviously intrigued as to what would bring a man on such a journey unannounced. Nevertheless he held his tongue and turned to a silver tray on a sideboard, upon which rested a decanter of deep golden liquor. 'A brandy, then?'

'Well, I don't usually,' the Master said. 'But in the circumstances, that would be capital.'

As Welstone poured two brandies, the Master glanced around the room, quickly spotting the papers upon the desk. He smiled, skimming the topmost ones, noting the names and the companies. This would be all he needed.

It was, as it turned out, quite easy. The lawyer's greed made him so quick to manipulate that any concerns the Master might have had melted away. He spun a simple story, hinting at mutual clients that he could not divulge and a sure fire investment. As soon as he sprinkled in the name of one of the companies he had seen in the papers on the desk, then pretended to forget the details of their address, Welstone was up eager to help. As the little man crossed to his papers, the Master slipped the remaining mead into his brandy.

'I must say, Mr Welstone,' the Master lifted his own glass as the lawyer sat back down. 'I am so delighted to find you in such good spirits. I think this will be a very beneficial meeting for us both. Let's drink on it.'

Welstone dutifully lifted his own glass and took a sip. As the liquid slid into his mouth he lifted the glass higher, at once caught in the mead's grip, and drained it in one.

It was much easier with the lawyer than it was with Christopher. There was no need to get him to focus on any particular thing. Instead, all the Master needed was to instil the urge to return to London as soon as possible. Once the little man was there, as far as the Master was concerned, he could carry on with whatever machinations he was engaged in. That was frankly of absolutely no interest, as long as he did it away from Christopher.

Once the thought was planted, the little lawyer slumped down into the armchair, a long line of dribble hanging from the side of his mouth. The Master decided to take a closer look around. He had to admit, he was impressed. The most interesting papers were locked in the bottom most drawer, opened by a key found in Welstone's pocket. The story they told showed the lawyer as a very clever fellow. He was amassing himself a small fortune.

The Master slipped out fifteen minutes later in a very good mood. Everything was back on track. In fact, he thought to himself as he strolled through the dark, it was better than that. In many ways, Welstone's conniving would be of great use. Should Christopher's family elect to try and find him in the future, any spare finances that might be used to hire professional help would quickly dry up.

The Master grinned to himself. 'Sleep well, Mr Welstone.'

It wasn't often that Sama regretted her actions, but that evening, when she was finally allowed to go to bed, she lay awake wishing she'd been more careful. Four hours! Four hours after work of sitting and listening as her aunt, then her father, then her aunt again, had lectured her for rough behaviour and improper ways. Even Jim had a crack, telling her that she was bringing shame to her good family, then smirking when he thought no one was looking.

It was made very clear to her that her adventuring days were over. Even more chores were piled on to keep her free time to a minimum. Her father even talked about nailing the window in her bedroom shut!

Still the worst thing was the worry that Chops would cancel her trip to London. If she stayed to keep an eye on Sama then that would be it, no chance of getting out again and of course, the one thing Sama wanted to do now was be outside.

The following morning, however, Sama was able to heave a sigh of relief. After a lot of fretting, Chops decided she couldn't put off her trip. She eventually left just after eleven, leaving Sama with instructions to cover every eventuality in the shop.

'And in between customers, you can use the time to think about how you're going to improve your behaviour,' she said as she left, closing the door firmly behind her.

The rest of the day dragged. Usually on the occasions Chops was absent, Sama would find it easy to pass the time in daydreams, but today she was just too agitated.

In between customers, Sama paced the shop forty-one times, counting each time she did it in her head. She sorted out the jars of sweets by colour, helping herself to a number of them on the way. She even tried to read her aunt's copy of The Lady magazine, but it didn't take long before she slammed it shut with disgust.

At four o'clock Christopher came in. Sama grinned with delight and immediately began to tell him about her dressing down the night before, right up until the moment of Chops' departure. In her haste to tell him all about what had happened to her, she didn't immediately notice that he looked a little off colour.

'Are you all right?' she asked. 'You don't look all that well.'

'Well, I am a little tired,' Christopher said. 'Though I seem to have done nothing but sleep since yesterday.'

'See! We have to do something. If we don't you'll fall into a permanent sleep and I'll probably end up burning the shop down. I'm going to be out tonight, whether they like it or not.'

At that moment, Mrs Dench walked in. She raised an eyebrow, seeing them alone in the shop together, but said nothing. Still, Sama was sure the mousy woman would have no hesitation in reporting it back to her husband.

She spent the next ten minutes fetching produce, cutting cheese, measuring out an ounce of pipe tobacco and fiddling with change before Mrs Dench left the store with another disapproving look. Finally, they were alone again.

'We should go and search the Weasel's study some more. I bet we can find where Freddie is,' she said as soon as the door shut.

'Oh, we don't need to.' Christopher beamed. 'The Weasel relented. He's going to take me to see Freddie next week. He told me at breakfast. And he's gone back to London. "Urgent business," he said.'

'Blimey, that's good. Who'd have thought he'd do that, eh?' Sama said, and then suddenly had a thought. 'I bet you that he's just covering up. I bet you that letter we found was about him stealing your money.'

'Oh, that,' Christopher said. 'No, that was all nothing.'

'But that letter looked pretty off to me,' she said.

'No, really. It wasn't anything. I'm not worried about it.'

'Righty ho.' Sama looked closely at him, but he really did look like he wasn't worried. 'It's up to you.'

She narrowed her eyes. 'Still, that does mean that we don't have an adventure for tonight.'

'What about we go and take a look at those gypsies?'

'What, you haven't been yet?' Sama grinned. 'Perfect!'

The atmosphere at the Stumblepot that night was more relaxed than Sama had seen it for a while. She suspected that the removal of Chops from the evening gave Jim and her father more chance to relax. Part of her was quite angry to discover they had more in common with her than either would let on. Still, there was no way she was going to bring that up whilst they were giving her a bit of space.

By the end of the night, Stan Neeley was quite the worse for wear and Jim had a constant grin on his face. Once in bed, Sama listened for her father coming to check on her. It wasn't long, quicker than usual, before she heard his footsteps lumbering up the stairs. Outside her door, he stopped. The handle turned then turned back.

''night, Sama. Don't you go out, now.' He spoke through the door, trying to sound gruff. The slurring of his words somehow ruined the effect.

''night, Dad. I won't, I promise,' Sama called back in her most tired voice. Within minutes, she could hear the rhythmic sound of his snoring.

Sama took the road by the river to Fox Grange. It took longer as she had to cut through the woods to reach the top road, but it avoided Roger and his barking. She thought the extra precaution quite wise.

By the time she reached the house, Christopher was already hidden by the gate. 'You're keen.' Sama grinned.

'Well, I'm not tired any more,' Christopher replied simply.

They fell into step together and headed along the road. Soon they came to the overgrown footpath that was their steep short-cut up to Pickering Tower. Sama took the lead, having walked the path on far darker nights than this. Christopher followed, placing his feet where she placed hers and occasionally reaching out to touch her back when it got really dark.

As they walked, Christopher told her about Winter's Grasp and the adventures it had been part of. It was quite exciting, she supposed. She did enjoy hearing about Ben Bailey, but the story wasn't anywhere near as interesting as the things she had heard about spies. The thing with the stories Christopher told her was that they were always from the past. Of course, Sama would never tell him that, what with lots of them being from his mother and all.

They reached a clearing that had been sheltered from the worst of the storms by the trees around it. A pool of moonlight lit up the centre of the clearing. Grass clumps stuck through the thin layer of snow. Sama sat down on one to catch her breath.

'So it ended with Ben Bailey and Elizabeth Lanyon getting married,' Christopher finished.

'Well, that would have been the end of her,' Sama said, tossing her head with disgust. 'Dishes and babies.'

'That's not the point though, Sama. The point was they had Winter's Grasp.'

'So?'

'That was only a hundred years ago. His name was Bailey.' Christopher knelt down next to her.

'Well, I think your friend Bailey is a rubbish storyteller if he couldn't even come up with a different name.'

'No, Sama.' Christopher sounded exasperated, 'It's because the story is true. I think that this Ben Bailey was his grandfather, or great-grandfather or something, anyway.'

'I think you're sleeping too much.' She snorted.

'Really? Well, I think it's a story about his family.'

Sama got up. 'Come on before we get cold.' She started upwards again.

Christopher jumped up and fell into step next to her. 'In fact, I'm sure it's more than just a story.'

'Do be sure to tell me when you know.' Sama glanced at him. 'Now let's stop talking about other people's adventures and enjoy our own.' She pushed him playfully and he stumbled. Giggling, she ran forward into the dark of the trees.

When she reached the end of the top field, she dropped to her stomach and looked out across the snow shrouded grass. The Pickering Tower stood just to the west of them, where the ground was at its highest. It reached up above the tops of the trees by a good way. Its sheer, white-plastered stone walls rose quite distinct in the moonlight from a compact square base. She had spent many hours wondering how to get the single black door open and discover the secrets beyond.

She rolled on to her back and looked into the night sky, waiting for

Christopher to catch her up. She could hear grumbling from twenty yards away. 'Quietly!' she hissed as he neared.

Christopher dropped down next to her. She turned on to her stomach and scanned the field beyond. 'I can't see anything. Not much of a camp,' she said after a moment.

'Wait.' Christopher pointed. 'Look.'

At the far corner, where the field sloped down out of sight, there was the slightest orange glow.

'I bet that's from their fires.'

Sama nodded. 'Let's go that way.'

They ran along the perimeter of the trees, careful to stay low in the shadows. As they drew closer, they slowed their pace, edging nearer to the glow.

It was indeed a fire. The closer that they got to it the more they could see. Three large, dark shapes stood between them and the fire's glow.

'Caravans!' said Sama. She could make out the spokes of the wheels on the nearest shape and the horse harness at one end. From the space under the caravans, the flames of the fire flickered brightly.

On the other side of the fire were two more caravans. She shifted along a little until she was looking through the gap between the two nearest. Now she could see the wooden side of one beyond. It was covered in paintings of fierce animals. They seemed to move in the shifting firelight. There were wolves and foxes and birds of prey, all looking fiercely outward into the night as if watching for some hidden threat. Sama found herself wanting to squirm closer to the ground to avoid their gaze.

Of course that was stupid, she told herself. They were just paintings. Instead, she beckoned to Christopher, then led him another fifty or so yards through the shadows.

When they stopped, they were close enough to hear the crackles of the burning wood. Now they could look down the length of the camp with no obstruction. Now the gypsies were plain to see, dotted around the camp fire in ones or twos, sitting, almost motionless. She touched Christopher's shoulder and pointed. He looked, then nodded, nestling in closer to her.

What struck Sama first was how eerily quiet the gypsies were. For five minutes as she and Christopher watched them, occasionally silently pointing out different things they noticed, the dim figures didn't even make enough noise to muffle out the sound of the burning logs. They just weren't talking. In fact, they seemed to take no notice of one another at all. Even when one gypsy moved, standing and loping across from one group to another then sitting once more, hardly any noise was made.

'I don't know why he bothered,' Sama whispered. 'It's not like they're having an interesting chat.'

The gypsies all seemed to be staring deep into the flames ahead of them. Their chests rose and fell gently in a steady rhythm. Sama's eyes widened. It was the same steady rhythm! The movement of their breathing was in perfect sync within the dull cloaks and blankets they were wrapped in.

'We need to get closer,' Sama whispered, intrigued, and began to slither forward on her belly. Ahead of them was a slight ridge made from some dense clumps of snow-smothered grass. It would give at least some cover. She started toward it.

'Don't be an idiot,' Christopher whispered back. 'Anyone will be able to see ...'

His words cut off. Sama didn't need to ask why. As he had begun to speak, three of the shadowy figures had turned toward them. A moment later others were doing the same. At the far end of the fire, one stood up, the blanket he wore falling to the floor and revealing a light white shirt over tight flesh. He stared out in their direction, his eyes glinting with the firelight.

'They heard us!' Sama whispered. 'Get back.'

'How could they have done?' Christopher whispered. 'I can hardly hear us.'

As he spoke, another two rose to their feet. The first sniffed the air, then ran forward, low and fast, to stop with sinewy grace on the nearside of the fire. There he froze, motionlessly looking outward.

'No,' Christopher said even more quietly. 'They heard me!'

At his words, more gypsies were on their feet. They sprung across to stand behind the first, each falling into place, heads bent or stretched to the side to create the maximum amount of watching space. Nine pairs of eyes stared out into the darkness. Now they were making noise. It was not words that came from their mouths, though. Instead, they were making small grunts that didn't sound at all like the sort of noises Sama had expected from gypsies.

'They couldn't have just heard you,' Sama whispered back, excited but not in the least bit scared. Still there was no harm in being on the safe side. 'Don't speak, though.'

She began to retreat in the darkness toward the tree line a few feet behind. Christopher followed her example, edging backwards as quickly as care would allow.

They managed to get into the trees without any further movements from the gypsies, though they stayed in their huddle, staring out. She put a finger to her lips. Christopher nodded vigorously, needing no reminder.

All of a sudden something gripped Sama's foot. Her heart lurched, and she tensed against the urge to cry out. Another hand grabbed above the first and dragged her backwards. To her side a shadowy figure had hold of Christopher, whilst another had reached up to put a hand over his mouth.

Sama rolled on to her back and kicked as hard as she could with her free leg. It met with something soft and solid. She heard a satisfying grunt of pain.

She tried to kick again, but this time her attacker was ready. In a moment, both of her legs were being held fast and she was dragged down into the trees. Panic hit her and she screwed her eyes shut.

'Sama, it's me!'

Sama opened her eyes to see the face of her brother, dark and shadowed, but unmistakable still. 'Stop bloody struggling.'

'You bugger!' she spat, forgetting the gypsies for a second and slapping him on the top of his head.

He grabbed her hand and forced it down. 'Stop it! Come on!'

They slid down into the gloomy darkness. Half running, half sliding down a steep slope, avoiding murky clusters of snow tipped plants and black trees as they went. When they had got down far enough that the edge of the trees was a good distance above them. Jim pulled her to a stop.

'You'll catch it when I tell dad you were here.'

'What about you?' Sama panted. 'You can't tell on me without getting it yourself. You just see.'

'We followed you.' Jim shrugged.

There was a noise from their left. Michael Brophy burst through a gap in the bushes, followed by Christopher and Joe Litmus.

'Did you see them devils?' Michael grinned, 'Like bloody wolves.' He turned to Christopher and ruffled his hair. 'They didn't like you two, did they?'

'I don't reckon they'll like any of us if we don't get out of here.' Joe sounded concerned. 'Gypsies don't take to strangers.'

Jim nodded. 'Let's get down to the road.'

They took the rest of the slope more carefully and reached the riverside road a good mile out of Alton. Jim took the lead with Sama close behind. Michael Brophy walked next to Christopher, still grinning widely, and Joe took the rear, occasionally glancing back the way they had come to make sure that they had not been followed.

Sama stepped forward and pushed at Jim. 'Anyway, if you followed us that's even worse! What will you say when dad asks why you didn't stop us, eh?'

Jim frowned in the dark. 'Listen, Sama. You've got to stop this. I can't go away knowing that you're getting yourself into trouble all the time. What would have happened if we hadn't seen you earlier?'

'Whereas with us keeping an eye on you, Sama,' Michael chipped in, his voice full of bravado, 'you had three English soldiers to stop them gypos. Eh, lads?'

He turned back toward Joe. 'What do you say, big man? Wait until we get over to France, eh? Then we'll show anyone who stands against us who's the boss!'

Joe looked uncomfortable. 'Let's just get these two home to their beds, Mike.'

'Exactly,' Jim muttered. He stomped ahead, outpacing Sama, not looking at her again.

Michael gave up on getting a smile from Joe. He jogged past Sama and caught up with Jim. He slipped an arm around his friend's shoulders. 'But I'm not wrong, am I?'

Jim tried to hold his frown. Michael squeezed his shoulders. After a second, a grudging grin slid on to Jim's face. 'No, you're not wrong.'

The pair of them fell into a gale of laughter. Moments later were reliving the night's adventure.

Sama waited for Christopher to catch up. 'Are you all right?'

He nodded and fell into step with her. From behind, Joe's giant shadow covered them both.

After they said goodbye to Michael at the edge of the village and watched him go through the front door of his mother's home, Jim swung around and looked at Sama through the darkness.

'All right,' he said. 'You promise that you won't get into any trouble when I'm gone and I'll not tell, Dad.'

Sama thought long and hard. She didn't want to get any more chores added to her list, but equally she didn't want to lie to Jim. 'I tell you what I'll promise,' she said. 'I won't start any trouble.'

Jim shook his head and strode away in the direction of the Stumblepot.

Joe spoke. 'Well, Christopher. I'll walk you back up to home, if you don't mind. Good night, Sama.'

As Christopher went to follow the enormous man, Sama caught his arm. 'Are you sure you're all right?'

Christopher looked straight at her. 'Sama, they could tell I was there. Not you. Not the lads. Me.'

'Don't be daft.' She punched him lightly on the shoulder. 'That's not possible.'

Christopher looked to the ground. 'I know.' He looked up again, a pinprick of moonlight caught in his eyes. 'But they did.'

'I better go.' Sama pursed her lips. 'Jim will never let me hear the end of it if I don't.' She grasped his arm. 'We'll have plenty of time to talk about it tomorrow. Come to the shop.'

Christopher nodded, looking dejected. He glanced over at where Joe was standing and sighed. Then he turned and went toward him. The pair of them walked off into the night.

'Sama!'

She glanced over in the direction of the voice. Jim stood a short distance away.

'Come on,' he said with a conciliatory tone. 'We best get in together, or he's twice the chance of hearing us.'

She sighed and glanced back the way Christopher had gone. He and Joe were just two black shapes against the grey darkness. Then she turned, lifted her chin haughtily, and headed towards her brother.

The Master had been waiting up when Joe got back. It had been far after the pub would have locked up, and his absence piqued the Master's interest. Joe was typically open, telling how he and the other lads had fetched Christopher and Sama from the gypsy camp. He didn't notice the way the Master sat up with excitement.

There was no time to waste. With a charm, the Master sent Joe to bed. The big man was already tired and the charm cost little. Then he was through the door and striding up the road.

No one was out in the village at this time of night. A little dog barked as he passed and he debated whether permanently silencing it would be worth the effort. Instead strode on, dimly noticing the glow of an upstairs light coming on behind him. It was of no matter. The boy had seen the gypsies. More to the point, they had reacted to him. The boy would have noticed. The boy would be scared. Now was the time. A wave of excitement sizzled through his spine.

The gypsies were around their fires, staring into the hypnotic dancing flames, probably dreaming of homes they would never see again. He stepped into their camp. As the light hit him they shrank back, growling and whimpering hatefully.

'Come now,' he said, his voice commanding and clear. 'Don't take on so. I'm not here for one of you, tonight.'

He stepped closer to the largest fire, waiting for their fretting to lessen.

'Good,' he said, once their cries died down. 'The time has come to close the cycle and start afresh.'

One of the gypsies howled, as if his heart would break.

'I know, I know,' the Master said, his voice a mask of kindness. 'But soon you will be born anew.'

Another gypsy lifted her voice to join the first.

'Enough,' the Master snapped. 'You know what to do. Go.'

For a moment they still hesitated, huddling together in little groups. He sighed. There was no time for their pantomime of resistance now.

'Go!' he said again in a voice that they would not deny.

The gypsies got up from their positions, casting hateful glances at the Master and howling mournful screams at the sky. They loped off into the darkness, swift and deadly. He watched them go, satisfied, then spun on his heel and strode back toward Joe's cottage.

CHAPTER TEN

Another World

Christopher woke in a cold sweat. Still fully clothed, he lay on top of the bed covers where he had collapsed earlier. The strange feral movements of the gypsies at the sound of his voice had so filled his mind that he had climbed to his room without a thought of discovery. He had buried his head under a pillow and tried to shut out the angular figures moving sinuously through his senses. Somehow he had fallen asleep, but sleep had been no better. The figures pervaded his subconscious. They chased him through dreams until his eyes snapped open.

He rolled upright and pulled at his clothes, separating cloth from sweaty skin. 'It isn't real.' He forced himself to say it in calm tones. 'This is your imagination.' If it was his imagination, though, it was just as terrifying. He shuddered. Was this what madness was like?

He stood up from his bed, forcing the thought from his head, and walked to the window. Deep clouds had rolled across the clear night sky, obscuring the moon. A dirty sleet had begun to smack against the glass. Outside the grounds were dim and barely penetrable. Beyond the gate, wet night completely shrouded the road.

Yet suddenly Christopher saw a movement, out by the furthest reach of the drive. Something lurched forward, from shadow to shadow. Then it was lost again to the dark.

Christopher dropped to his knees and peered carefully out of the lowest part of the window. There it was again. It was nearer now and heading toward the house. And behind it there was another! A few more feet and there would be no shadows in which to hide. Christopher gripped the sill with white knuckles, already convinced of what he was going to see.

Out on to the lawn, arms held tight and fingers spread wide, stepped one of the gypsies. Christopher gasped, the truth of his convictions still shocking him.

Immediately the gypsy turned its head and stared straight up at the window. Its eyes glinted, despite the lack of moonlight, and it opened its mouth. A moment later, it turned back to the dark and called something through the steady sleet into the shadows.

Christopher launched himself backwards across his bedroom and raced through the door. His whole body sharp with fear, he ran full pelt along the corridor, through to the back stairs that led up to the servants' quarters.

'Crawford!' he screamed, stumbling in his haste. 'Crawford!'

He burst through the door at the top of the stairs and ran to the butler's room, banging his shoulder against the wall as he turned. 'Crawford!'

The butler came to his door. His jacket was unbuttoned and his shirt was open where there would usually be a tie. He stared wide-eyed at the panicked boy before him. 'Master Flyte! What in heaven's name is the matter? Why are you dressed?'

'Crawford, there's men in the garden! I think they mean to get in!'

'Men?' Crawford took a step forward, concerned. 'What sort of men?'

'Gypsies from up by the tower!'

Crawford looked down at him. 'What have you been doing to make them come here at this time of night?'

'I … Nothing,' Christopher said. 'Crawford, they're outside now!'

'All right. Calm down, Christopher.' Crawford pushed past him with determination. 'I'll sort this out. Couple of blasts of the shotgun will see them off. We can talk about the whys and wherefores afterwards.'

He strode along to the back stairs. 'Stay here,' he said. He glanced backwards, then disappeared through the door.

Christopher hesitated for a moment, unsure of whether to follow, then thought better of it. Instead, he bolted over to the butler's window. It was no good, though. The angle was wrong and he could see nothing. He struggled for a second, trying to work out where to find the best view. In a flash, it came to him. Up one more flight of the back stairs was the uppermost servants' corridor, where Miss Chanters once had her rooms. There, he remembered, was a small window that faced the gate. From there, he could see.

The gypsies were still at the edge of the shadows when he stared desperately through the dirty square of glass. There were two of them for sure now, possibly a third. They muttered together and occasionally one stretched a head forward, craning toward the house looking for something.

A desperate urge to test his fears began to grow in Christopher. He gritted his teeth against it, tears blossoming at the sides of his eyes. His entire body tensed, but now the urge was there it was impossible to deny.

With the quietest breath he could manage, he whispered, 'I'm here.'

Immediately they looked up, straight at the window. They stepped forward, three of them for sure now. The last one was a woman, dressed in a light white smock that was soaked to the skin and offered no protection against the weather. She twisted her head in the sleet and howled up at the window with a dread mournful voice.

'This can't be happening. This can't be happening,' Christopher cried quietly into his hands. He sat down against the wall and hugged his knees tight to him.

The crack of a gunshot exploded outside. Christopher pulled himself up again, elated. Crawford was in the grounds. He was wrapped in a greatcoat. He held Christopher's father's shotgun in his arms.

'Go on with you!' Crawford shouted, his voice clear above the weather.

The gypsies retreated. They seemed to melt into the dark, once again indistinct shapes.

Crawford continued forward. 'I can still see you, my lads. There's nothing for you here.' He raised the shotgun to point above their heads and let off another blast. 'They'll hear that in the village. We'll have company in a minute. You best not be here then!'

The gypsies sank further into the dark. One shape crept off to the right, towards the gate. The others followed.

Crawford loaded another cartridge into the shotgun and stalked forward again. He was now almost into the shadows himself. Again he fired the gun.

Now that they had retreated to the gate, Christopher could only see the barest of movements. Still Crawford pushed forward; his view of them presumably that much clearer.

'Don't go so far, Crawford!' Christopher clutched the sill of the window, his knuckles white.

A moment later the butler had disappeared into the dark. Christopher felt terrifyingly alone. Once again, the only sound was the fat slaps of sleet covering the night.

Suddenly, from the left part of the grounds, the three gypsies burst back into his view. No sneaking this time, they loped across the garden towards the front door. It had been a trick!

He glanced back. There was no sign of Crawford. Anything could have befallen him in the dark. There was one thing for it. Get down the back stairs, on through the house and try to reach the kitchen before they caught him. It wasn't much of a plan and he suddenly wished he had Sama with him, but it was all he had. He stepped towards the stairs, speed tempered now by stealth.

Then he heard the noise. There was a distinct sigh. Someone in Miss

Chanters' old room to his left. He glanced at the slightly ajar door. Of course. Molly Brodie must have the room. From the dark space inside the door, a dull green glint reflected out.

'Christopher? What are you doing up here?' Molly Brodie's whisper was like wind through a graveyard. 'What can be happening?'

'Um, nothing. Sorry,' Christopher said, aware of how close the door was to the edge of the stairs. He took another tentative step forwards. At once, the crack in her door seemed to widen. 'I just wanted to see the sleet from up here, but I'll go now. I didn't mean to …'

'Disturb me?' her voice hissed again from the darkness. 'It is no matter, I was awake. Come in now you are here. We can watch the storm together.'

The door opened further. The dull glow silhouetted the black impenetrable shape of her body. She seemed larger, looser even, than seemed right.

Below there was the crash of china on cold wood floor, followed by a muffled yelp. Christopher tensed himself for action.

'There's someone in the grounds and Crawford is out there too. I had best go and see that he is all right.'

'That doesn't sound very safe, Christopher. Come to me and we can go together!'

The door whisked open, widening to let her free. Christopher bolted. He covered the first step before the door had finished its swing and shot halfway across the second as Molly Brodie sprung from her room into the dim light.

Christopher gasped in horror. Molly Brodie was completely without clothes. Her body was hideously lean. The same yellow, cadaverous skin of her face stretched tight over hard balls of muscle. Over her shoulders, arms, and legs, blue veins throbbed near the skin's surface, criss-crossing in complex patterns. Thick grey hair grew in dense clumps from her chest to her thighs, then began again on her calves, almost like socks. The hair stopped just below her ankles, below which stretched impossibly long feet that ended in sharp talons.

Christopher shrank against the wall. If the horror of her body were not enough, from her back rose two yellowed wings, jointed in three places with cruel looking hooks jutting out at the joints. Instead of feathers, great sheets of her vein-patterned skin hung lank, just waiting for a flex of the wings to billow out and catch the air.

The creature lashed forwards with an inhuman noise that was at once like the cry of a bird and the bark of a dog. She raked forward at him with her hand. Long, sharp nails ripped through the wool of his jumper and shirt beneath. His left side exploded with pain. He fell forward on to the top most stairs, crashing down to the next landing on his front.

'Christopher, wait!' Molly's voice sounded above him.

He shook his head to clear his senses. With adrenaline dulling the pain, he rolled on to his back and kicked at the wall, pushing himself away from the stairwell entrance.

'Don't be scared!' the creature above called at him, hunger in her voice unmistakable now. 'I didn't mean it.'

She loomed at the top part of the stairs. Her dull grey eyes were now a blazing green. They bore down on his prone body. She leapt forward. Her wings flexed. The membranes of skin tightened as they caught the air. Christopher tensed and raised an arm in defence. There was a great crash and splinters of wood exploded down the stairs, but the creature got no further. Her wings were caught in the doorway. Stuck fast, Molly Brodie squealed and thrashed, arms whipping at the air in front of her, her lustful eyes never leaving his.

For a second, the sight of the impossible creature above him froze Christopher. He struggled to take in the mass of muscle, skin and hair that struggled to free itself from its barriers. Part of him even wanted to laugh, to tell his brain that this was all imagination and that the best thing he could possibly do would be to simply close his eyes and concentrate on something else. He was sure he would end up back in his bed once more, realising this was just a nightmare.

Molly Brodie gasped with effort. The door frame shuddered with a screech of wood. One dreadful wing appeared almost all the way through. Christopher pushed himself up and ran to the second stairs. Behind came another scream of breaking wood, followed by the thud of something landing. Not daring to look back, he spurred himself on down the stairs, into the main house.

There was a scuttling of claw on wood, then a great whump of beaten air, as Molly's great wings found room for her to use them. She landed with a thud just behind him, at the top of the stairs. She was so quick! Christopher raced along the top corridor, past his bedroom door to the main staircase of the house.

The three gypsies were a few steps below him. The woman at their helm glared up at him. She screeched with delight. Her mouth was a mass of sharp pointed teeth. She leapt forward.

Christopher skidded to a halt, losing his balance in his effort to turn around. He pulled in his legs, blindly kicking as hard as he could in the direction of the stairs. He struck something with a thud. A howl of pain was followed by the crash of bodies falling into other bodies, rolling away downwards.

Again he clambered up and raced back the way he had come. Behind, the gypsies had already recovered. They scrabbled after him.

Suddenly, two great wings shadowed what little light there was in the corridor. For a frozen moment, they seemed fixed, suspended in mid-movement and fat with air like two black sails. Then they crashed down and a mass of hair and claw flew towards him.

Christopher bolted into his room and slammed the door shut. He grabbed the iron key in the lock, straining to turn it. It clicked into place. He sank to the floor, breathing heavily.

He stared around the room for a weapon, anything that he could use to defend himself. There was nothing. A few tin soldiers and a library of books didn't make for a good defence. Frustrated tears sprang to his eyes. This had to be a dream.

The sounds of snuffling seeped through the cracks in the door. Christopher held his breath. Something was very close, just on the other side of the door, breathing in his scent.

He stared again around the useless room, an ice-cold feeling in his heart. He stumbled over to the bed, eyes blurred through the tears of fear. He climbed up on to it and reached for his pillow, clasping it close to his face. His wide, bloodshot eyes peaked over it, back towards the door.

If this was real, he was going to be murdered in his bed by creatures that had no business being alive. If it wasn't he was going to spend the rest of his life locked away from decent people, mad like his mother and brother. He pushed his face into the pillow and screwed his eyes shut. He was mad and a coward, just like Daniel Corbyne had said.

The door thundered from a strong blow on the other side. A second later, another came. It sounded to all intents as though his pursuers were throwing their entire bodies against it with all the force they could muster.

Bizarrely in Christopher's mind, a sudden image of Daniel Corbyne shouting at him manifested, words mingling with the crashes of the doors. 'Stone dead! Just like your mad mother!'

On the fifth crash, splinters of wood flew so far into the room they reached all the way to the bed, bouncing off his body on to the blanket beneath him. Christopher sat up, wrenching open his eyes, the image of the bully disappearing. He looked at the door with a rush of sudden clarity. Cowering on a bed would not save him. He hadn't cowered when Corbyne had attacked him.

The next crash splintered the wood around the lock. From beyond there was a howl of approval, followed quickly by another impact. The door was going to give way. It would give way and they would be in here with him. Whether monsters or nightmares, they would be in. That would be it. He'd not see Freddie or Sama or Joe or anyone again.

Now his fear was infused with fire. He was not going to sit and wait for things to happen. What use was that? He leaped up. Another crash. This time, the door itself moved.

Staying quiet and timid hadn't stopped him from being attacked at school. He turned and ran over to the window, wrenching it open. Trying not to be noticed hadn't stopped him from getting into trouble, or from being stuck in this great big house with that horrible lawyer.

The door crashed again. He climbed on to the window, balancing on the sill, careful not to look down. Fear hadn't stopped Freddie from being arrested, it hadn't stopped his father from never being there to look after him. Behind him, the door burst open with a crash. The gypsies scrabbled into the room bowling over the floor towards him. The door frame filled with the black shaggy shape of the housekeeper.

Trying to keep himself safe hadn't stopped his mother from dying. He stepped up on to his haunches, fixing his gaze on the slim tree Sama had used so often to reach his room from the other way.

'And it's not going to stop me escaping,' Christopher said and leapt into the night.

The gypsies bounded over to the window to watch the boy run across the grass, a heaving mass of arms and heads as they craned to stare. For the moment, none pursued.

Molly Brodie dropped her wings, folding them neatly away on to her back with grace, and walked to the window. The gypsies shrank back, giving her plenty of room. They stared at her with fearful eyes. For one of them, it was too much. He made to jump out into the garden. Before he could, she reached forward, catching him in mid-air. She snarled, throwing him against his companions.

The female gypsy bared her teeth, braver than her male comrades and swiped at Molly with an outstretched hand. In an instant, Molly flexed her wings, engulfing the air above the three creatures. They shrank back whimpering.

She glanced out of the window. Christopher was out of sight now. She returned her gaze to the three gypsies. 'Do not catch him. Guide him to the Master.'

She gestured at the window. They leapt past her, ignoring the tree and landed almost silently on the ground below. She watched them race off after the boy. A moment later, she launched herself into the sleet-filled air.

Christopher's first instinct was Sama. If he could reach her and the Stumblepot, there would be safety. The sleet slapped against his face, cold and hard, running into his eyes, making it hard to see where he was going. He ran away from the house, to the trees at the side of the grounds. Hopefully, the darkness would lend him some shelter from his pursuers.

There was no noise of them behind him now. The sound of the weather filled his ears. A mass of tiny spatters through the howl of the wind, punctuated by the desperate splashes of his feet ploughing through the slush. He sped through the shadows, around to the gateway and on to the lane that led to Alton.

Ahead of him a crumpled shape lay on the muddy track. Crawford. He slowed, then bent to the unconscious butler. The side of Crawford's head was bleeding from a cut just above the ear. There was no sign of the shotgun.

'Crawford, wake up,' Christopher pleaded, shaking the butler by the shoulder. 'Come on, wake up.'

The butler didn't stir. Christopher grabbed his arm and pulled him with all his strength. Crawford's body moved a fraction down the lane, scraping against the slush and stones. Christopher swore and pulled again.

From the direction of the house came a great howl, a song of the hunt, high and exultant. Christopher froze. They were coming.

With a final impotent pull at Crawford, Christopher let go and turned tail towards the village. He stretched his legs, widening his pace as far as he could, ignoring the pain in his lungs. He had to keep going or he was lost.

There was a crash in the trees some way behind to his left. Something was keeping pace. As he ran, he could feel it matching his speed but staying behind. It was constant and sure, never shortening the distance, but never stretching itself. It was playing with him.

Christopher pushed it out of his mind. That was its choice. There was nothing he could do. He concentrated on the road ahead, on just getting through. There was only a stretch through the trees. Then he'd be on the slope up to the village.

He broke away and sprinted up the path. Suddenly there was no one at his side. He was free of them. Yet, he could not believe that he was faster. It was as if they had slowed.

That was of no matter now. He would take the chances he was given. He had reached the top of the village before he knew it, unaware of the distance he'd covered in his determination. He glanced to the side. Roger the dog lay in his gateway, ears were flat to his head. He stared out at Christopher with terrified eyes.

Christopher felt a pang at passing the little dog, but ran on. It wasn't Roger who was being chased. He headed down the slope, the Stumblepot was just ahead. In an upstairs window, the dim light from some room beyond caught the window frame with a brush of orange. Someone was still up! Christopher's spirits soared. He raced toward the pub, success giving him new strength.

They were by the oaks.

As he reached the junction, two gypsies stepped out. Like the others, they were soaked through their light, simple clothes through to the skin. Christopher spun around as they leapt towards him.

At the top of the lane, his pursuers had appeared. They pushed on powerful legs and sprinted towards him. Above their heads, Molly Brodie swept down in a great, graceful attack dive.

Christopher sped off down the only remaining path, down the lower road towards the river. As he rounded the corner, he saw the white walls of Joe's house, made grey by night. He burst across through the gate to the door. With all of his effort, he smashed against the door with his fists.

The Master was on his feet before the third knock. He had been waiting for what seemed like an age and his sense of anticipation was electric. He slipped into Bailey's form as he pulled open the door.

Christopher burst into the room. The boy was as white as a sheet and breathless. His eyes were open wider than the Master had seen them.

'What on earth?' the Master exclaimed in Bailey's countrified tones. 'Christopher?'

The boy pointed back at the door. 'The gypsies! Monsters!'

The Master moved Christopher aside and made to look out of the door. The gypsies had arrived and stood outside calmly. As he glanced at them, Molly Brodie swooped down and landed on a branch of a tree a short distance away. The branch shook, but her landing was measured and any sound was muffled by the sleet. The Master flicked a gesture at the window with his eyes. Immediately the gypsies started to move.

He ducked his head inside. 'Step back, lad. Behind me.' He grabbed the boy by the shoulders and positioned him away from the window.

Christopher allowed himself to be manhandled but looked up, words forming on his lips. Before the boy could speak, the main window of the cottage smashed in and a gypsy leaped on to the sill.

The Master was ready. Usually the charm he was about to use would fill him with distaste in its showiness. He considered it a cheap parlour trick, but the boy was not to know that. He shouted an incantation, nonsense words really, raising his arm dramatically, and hurled a bolt of blue light at the window. It was really no more than a slight distillation of the raw power on the artefact. No more than a light show. Inwardly he exulted at the look of amazement on the boy's face. He would be putty.

The gypsy disappeared backwards out of the window, diving perhaps a tad too dramatically. The Master grabbed Christopher by the shoulder and manhandled him into the kitchen, pushing the door shut behind them and slipping a chair under the handle.

'That should stop 'em for a moment. They won't try to come in now they know there's a real danger for them.' He turned back to Christopher with a grim smile. 'Did they hurt you, lad?'

'They … No,' Christopher said, a face full of questions. 'Bailey, what is …?'

'Going on?' the Master finished, reaching down an arm to drape around the boy's shoulders protectively. 'I am so sorry, Christopher. This is all my fault. All my fault.'

'Sit down.' He gestured at a stool next to the little kitchen table. Christopher started to protest, but he raised a hand. 'Don't worry about them. They'll not be in for a while and you'll need your legs to run again soon, I am afraid. Rest them whilst you can.'

Numb, Christopher sat down. The Master looked over at Christopher for a second, his face carefully formed into a mask of concern and guilt. Then he reached down into his pocket. His fingers found the wooden box he had placed there and pulled it out.

'Christopher, I'm going to have to tell you some things that I had hoped that I would have more time with. It's going to be a little hard to believe in places,' he said, making sure to occasionally glance towards the kitchen door, 'but I dare say that you are already having something of a time with the hard-to-believe.

'I didn't just arrive here by chance, Christopher. I came because of you.'

Christopher frowned. 'What do you mean?'

A wave of contentment washed over him. The boy was totally involved. 'You've already felt it. The reason why you don't fit in. It's because you are different. You are different the same way that I'm different.'

Christopher shook his head. 'Bailey, what are you talking about?' Through the kitchen door, there was a muffled growl. They were in the house.

'I think I should show you,' the Master answered slowly and looked down at the box.

This was the moment it all began again. In that box was the amorphous blob of energy just waiting to be believed in. The Master prised open the little catch with Bailey's calloused hands. He pulled the lid upwards, facing the box towards Christopher.

A white pulsating light, tinted with hints of the coldest blue, like a sunrise on a frozen morning, shone out in tight, clean beams. As he opened the box to its fullest, the light became blinding. Christopher raised his arm to shield his eyes.

'Give him a second,' the Master said with a hint of amusement. 'He'll stop shining so much.'

Sure enough, as the light began to pale Christopher gazed down at the contents of the box.

'Christopher,' the Master murmured, filled with anticipation. 'This is Winter's Grasp.' Then finally, he allowed himself to look down at what the boy was seeing.

Lying atop the box, far too large to have ever fitted within, lay a beautiful silver gauntlet glowing with glorious cold light. Intricate patterns etched into its surface, swirling and impossibly complex, seeming to shift in shape almost like ripples on a lake. The finger joints were so delicate it looked as though to touch them would be to destroy them. Around the wrist and running back to the guard were five bands of silver, each overlapping the previous.

In the reflections of the precious metal, it was not the room around him the Master could see but rather beautiful shimmering landscapes, forests of pine and lakes of steel blue.

He let himself marvel at its beauty for just a moment, then pressed on. 'Made when we still knew how to harness the forces of magic. The tool of many a great hero, until it was lost with Tristan at Tintagel. Found again by my grandfather who protected it and kept it away from those who would use it unwisely. Then he passed to my father, who passed it to me.'

He reached forward and picked up the gauntlet, cradling it to his chest like a child. 'Since my grandfather found it we have been bound to its protection, from father to son.'

He looked up and caught Christopher's eye. 'The old myths are all true Christopher. And the old items of power, there are those who would take them and use them to cause havoc.'

'The gypsies?' Christopher said, wide eyed.

'They're a part of it, yes.' The Master kept his voice grim. 'They're nothing more than the slaves of something far greater. So is the housekeeper from your father's house.'

'Then who is controlling them?' Christopher asked.

'I wish I had the time to tell you, but we have wasted too much already,' the Master answered. 'You will have to find that out for yourself, lad.'

He held out Winter's Grasp, his heart thudding in his chest. 'Take him, Christopher. He's yours now,' he said steadily, masking his anticipation.

'What?' Christopher's hand strayed towards the gauntlet without him even noticing. The master fought down a smile.

'Take him. He led me to you. I have failed. No children, you see. No one to pass him on to. So one day I felt an urge. He was talking to me, not through words, mind you, but the message was just as strong. I knew that I had to come here and I would find my successor,' the Master continued. 'When I got here and I met you, I just knew.'

'But the gypsies, why are they here?'

'I must have been careless.' The Master hung his head in a display of shame. 'Stupid. Stupid. I moved too quickly. People are suspicious of strangers these days. I took risks. I didn't cover my trail. Then they must have seen me with you and figured you for an easy target.'

He lifted the gauntlet just a little higher. 'We have no more time, Christopher. I am so sorry I've not been able to tell you more. Take the gauntlet. You must leave tonight. Now.'

'Leave? What do you mean "leave?"' Christopher blurted, his lip trembling. He shot a look at the back door and shuddered.

'Yes, leave. You have to get Winter's Grasp away from here before more of them come. Head to Henley, then get to a big city. You'll be harder to find in a big city, but I'll find you.'

'Can't you come now?' Christopher said with fear.

'No, lad. If we both run, we'll never shake them. I can stay here and give you enough time to get away. Put on the gauntlet, it will make it harder for them to find you and easier for me.'

Christopher reached forward, took the gauntlet. From deep below in his mind a great chime filled the Master's ears and vibrated his very body. Suddenly the gauntlet glowed blue, flooding the room with light as bright as day.

The Master laughed, his eyes wild with joy. 'See, Christopher! He's been waiting for you.'

He walked past Christopher to the back door. He clicked it open with exaggerated care and glanced outside expecting and seeing nothing.

'Good. No one.' He turned back to the boy. 'They might be scary-looking devils, but they haven't got a brain between the lot of 'em.'

He held his arm above him, creating an arch. 'Now lad. If you get into trouble remember, just reach with the glove to a place of safety and you'll be there. You just need to believe.'

'Bailey, this is all happening so fast,' Christopher said. 'It's not possible.'

The Master placed a calming hand on his shoulder. 'There'll be time, but not now. Put on the gauntlet, Christopher. Put it on and let it guide you.'

With a deep breath, Christopher pulled on the gauntlet. The Master fought back the urge to shout with joy. Already the boy's face had taken on a distant look. It would not be long now. 'Go, lad. Go.'

The Master all but shoved Christopher out of the door and watched as he stumbled off through the garden. The boy disappeared around the side of the shed and was gone.

The Master swung around and strode back into the living room. The single gypsy in the room snarled at him as he passed it and headed to the window. He leaned out. The others were waiting where he had left them.

With a flex of her wings, Molly Brodie glided over and landed next to them. They shrank back, kept in place only because of his will.

'It is time,' the Master said, a vicious grin on his face. 'Now finish it.'

Christopher ran as fast as he could down to the river. He dropped through frozen reeds to a slim mud bank. Out of sight of the road, he sneaked away from the village.

Winter's Grasp felt alive on his hand. Its presence filled his senses, pushing the world around him further outward so that he felt like he was looking at his surroundings through a very long tunnel.

Within his view of sleet and black night other shapes began to appear. A horse suddenly passed through his peripheral vision, great and white, covered with shining armour, its huge nostrils blowing out clouds of warm air. He looked over at it, but it disappeared, and a vague shimmer seemed all that remained before the dark river beyond.

His right hand tingled, as though a thousand tiny pins were resting on his skin, all ice cold. In his mind the wet noises of the night mingled with distant voices, a woman's laughter, the sound of metal on metal.

Trying to focus his thoughts Christopher stumbled on. Ahead a stream cut into the riverbank in a deep gully stretching upwards, all the way up the hill to the main road beyond that led down into Henley.

It was getting harder to move. He knew the gully well. He had hidden in it from Sama in play, used it as a short cut to the main road, and dammed it up on more than one occasion as a child with Freddie, just for the sheer enjoyment. Now it was like a strange land to him.

The gentle slopes on either side, normally covered in bushes and trees now seemed to be the start of great cliffs, shining white even in the dark night sky. Again he heard the sound of a horse. In the distance, for a moment it seemed as though there were a host of standards, raised on high poles, ragged and dirty from battle.

Somewhere behind him there was a scream, angry and bloodthirsty. His mind struggled to keep the geography of the countryside he knew from being overwhelmed. The scream was from back by Joe's house. The gypsies! Another scream joined the first, then another. Then silence.

Christopher struggled to focus against the voices and visions that tried to overwhelm him. 'Please!' he whispered at the gauntlet. 'Not now. Show me when we're safe.' The fact that he was talking to a metal glove was not entirely lost on him. 'Please, help me concentrate.'

As if it could hear him, Winter's Grasp dulled, the bluish sparks that zipped happily around it coming to a stop. A moment later the gully was as he remembered it, plain and deep, stretching slowly up and away from him.

'Thank you,' Christopher whispered and began to run up the side of the stream.

Cracks came from behind, the sound of bare feet crushing sticks, dislodging stones, spraying mud and snow in powerful thrusts of muscular legs. Christopher didn't dare stop to look back. Instead, he redoubled his efforts, desperately hoping that Bailey would somehow distract them. As long as the old man had not been hurt before he got the chance.

Another crash. They were almost upon him now. He could hear their guttural breathing, steady and measured despite the speed with which they moved. His heart sank. He would never outrun them. He leapt up on to a small island of grass, bordered on each side by gurgling rivulets, and turned to face them.

They stopped, surrounding him but keeping at a safe distance. There were too many to count, more than he had seen in the garden, or even in their camp. Some stood still, some moved around, almost flowing from one space to the next, mingling with the night.

'Stay back,' Christopher yelled at them, raising his fist. As if it knew, Winter's Grasp suddenly shone with all its power, lighting the space in which they stood with cold blue light. The gypsies shied back, all eyes on the gauntlet.

From one side the female gypsy who had been in his house appeared, her eyes fixed on the gauntlet. She glanced back at the others, then around beyond them, as if looking for something else out there in the dark. After a moment, another grunted at her and pushed her forwards, almost gently. Christopher tensed, ready for a fight.

There were tears in her eyes. Christopher was amazed. She reached toward the gauntlet, her face a picture of grief. She spoke slowly, as if the words were hard to form. 'Master, please,' she implored, her black doglike eyes flicking from the gauntlet to Christopher. 'Don't let it change.'

She stepped forward again. The others shifted in their positions, staring at her, then at him, then at the gauntlet with open fear on their bestial faces.

'Master,' she began again.

'What?' Christopher said, curiosity getting the better of fear. 'I don't understand.'

Before she got a chance to answer, a howl of anger came from above, utterly inhuman and utterly without hope. The gypsies ducked in fear, raising their arms above their heads and squealing to one another. A moment later came a great whump of vast wings filling with air.

Christopher looked up. A dim winged silhouette showed against the clouds, growing rapidly bigger. Suddenly the wings folded into a dive and Molly Brodie streaked down through the night sky.

Instinct gripped Christopher. The tingling in his hand from the gauntlet redoubled. He spun around, looking to the distant end of the gully. There he could make out a great oak tree. He reached towards it with the gauntlet, stretching his fingers, desperate. The air was filled with mournful pleas. The gypsy woman leapt on to the tuft. Her hands thrust out to touch his back. Her grip was almost gentle. 'Masster, pleasse!'

Then the air above him was filled with shadow. Molly Brodie struck down, talons stretched.

His mind full of the gauntlet, full of the stories Bailey had told him, Christopher grasped out. Immediately, there was powerful rushing all around him, drowning the cries of the gypsies. In his mind's eye, hot white steams of energy from the glove flashed into the distance.

He felt himself moving, flowing through the landscape. It was as if he were liquid. Far off, he could still hear noises from the outside, but it was nothing compared to the rushing of the glove. Then, as his vision blurred to white and his head swam, Christopher finally lost consciousness.

The boy dropped to the ground like a stone in front of Molly Brodie. The Master stepped out from behind a bush and walked towards the prone boy.

'Back to your camp,' the Master muttered to the gypsies, his eyes never leaving Christopher. 'Your work is done.'

In ones and twos the gypsies melted away, their agility and purpose departed. Some even leaned on their fellows as if they were suddenly very old.

Molly looked around. Already her face looked older, weaker, he noted.

'You can still fly?' he said dispassionately.

She lifted her wings with effort, flexing them. The pain on her face was evident, but she nodded.

'Good,' the Master said. 'Then pick him up and fly him home. I will be along shortly.'

It was pitiful to watch her as she struggled to lift the boy into her arms. The flight would take more out of her, and now she had little left, but the Master didn't care. All that he could think of was the new reserves of power he would have. His eyes glazed over for a moment dreaming about it.

He shook his head to dispel the daydream. 'Still here, Molly? Go! And I command you not to drop him.'

Molly shot him a look of pure hate. Good. There was still some fire left in her after all. He watched quietly as she turned, flexed her wings and flew off into the night.

CHAPTER ELEVEN

Strangers in Town

The steady sleet that fell in Alton fell throughout the south of England. Dirty drops of soaking snow slapped on to town and country alike. Those people still outside at such a late hour pulled coats higher or nestled further under umbrellas against the deluge, hurrying to be away from the wet.

In London, Knightsbridge was all but deserted. The streets were silent except for the relentless pitter-patter as icy drops hit wet stone. On Alfred Street the houses, innocuous and uniform, the white of their paint grey in the gloom, were quite still. The only light was from streetlamps. The windows of the houses were all black, the street's residents having retreated to their beds.

From one little window, so close to the ground that it must once have been a servant's, a sudden alarm sounded. Inside the room, the loud, insistent ringing drowned out the smack of the sleet against the glass.

Ward McCloud's eyes burst open. He pushed himself up on to his elbows, blinking bleary eyes and struggled to come to his senses. With effort, he twisted his fat body around and pressed the wooden panel behind his head. It slid open. Inside a red light pulsed on and off, flooding the room with a crimson glow. McCloud squinted against its rude insistence and punched at the button next to it. The light went off and the alarm fell silent.

He listened for a moment in the dark, straining to hear if the noise had disturbed any of the lodgers in the house. Silence once again. He sat up and rubbed his eyes, massaging life into his round face, then groaned and clambered off the bed. Pulling a dark red dressing gown over his huge chest, he reached for his walking stick. Then he pulled open his door and hurried down the corridor.

At the end, steps led up to what used to be the main family home. It hadn't been a family home for thirty years, of course. Once Ward's predecessors had bought it, they had converted it into a smart lodging house, leaving only his sleeping quarters and two others immediately above for members of the organisation.

The real lodgers had no idea that their homes were a front for a secret entrance. They were an inspired cover, even if it did make sneaking around in the night something of a chore.

To the left of the stairs was a cupboard. He unlocked it and climbed inside. It was always a struggle to turn and lock himself in, but protocols were protocols. Not for the first time he considered asking for smaller meals, but there was nothing to do about it now. He turned to the back of the cupboard and reached out into the dark.

He pressed a tiny depression hidden behind the door. The wall covered in shelves of food disappeared. Beyond, a set of stone steps disappeared down into darkness. He squeezed through, muttering as his vast belly caught against the door frame, then stepped on to a short ladder. He descended with a distinct lack of grace. Above him, the opening into the cupboard slid shut with a click.

He reached the bottom of the long staircase that led down from the landing a few minutes later, sweating and out of breath. Levert waited at the bottom of the stairs, a gaunt little man with dark rings under his eyes, grim and concerned. He fell into pace with McCloud. Together they strode along the corridor that led through the children's ward on out into the Fountain Hall.

'Well?' McCloud struggled to get the breath to speak.

'A fountain has replenished,' Levert said, trotting along next to him.

McCloud nodded. There was little other reason for them to call him back down during one of his infrequent rests. 'Do we have any more information?'

'The diviners are in the hall now,' Levert replied, which meant no. McCloud sighed. This was the last thing they needed. Everything was stretched already.

They passed the through the empty day ward without stopping. Ahead, at the entrance to the Fountain Hall, Makena stood waiting, running a worried hand through her short, curly hair.

'Ward,' the black woman said as he drew near.

'Makena,' McCloud replied, 'where is your husband?'

'John is in the chamber.' She fell into step with the two of them. 'He said we should expect to move.'

Ward nodded grimly. 'As soon as we know where the change has taken place, you will need to go.'

Makena stared straight ahead, expressionless. 'Of course.'

The Fountain Hall was vast, easily the size of a cathedral and roughly the same shape. Ward remained privately convinced that it must indeed have been a place of worship aeons ago, though the huge cavern pre-dated any religions that he had heard of. Now, however, much of the space was empty or used for storage.

Ward liked to imagine that once, perhaps when the fountains had first been built, the hall may have been a far more decorated and animated place. That the catacombs around it had perhaps bustled with an ancient people. But that was too long ago to know anything. Certainly since it had been rediscovered by his Victorian predecessors and put to use, most of the subterranean complex remained abandoned. The majority of the organisation's activity took place above, in the main building. Only the fountains, the children's wards and the more unusual research had any activity down here.

Ahead, the sounds of splashing water were audible. A tremendous circular stone plinth stood on one side of the hall, surrounded by twelve stone steps to reach it. They drew near. As they reached the first step, the sounds of the water above was like that of a fair sized waterfall.

The fountain plinth was the oldest part of the hall. Some of the historians estimated that it might be older by a thousand years. The cavern floor around the plinth was natural rock, whereas, in the rest of the hall, the walls and floor were chipped by primitive tools. It was almost impossible to comprehend the manpower and time it would have taken to enlarge the hall to its current size.

Ward knew he should not think about such things tonight. As long as the fountains were doing their job right now, history made no difference. He reached the top of the steps, walking out on to the marble flagstones of the plinth.

Twenty-four fountains stood on the plinth in a wide circle. As always, being this close to such magnificent creations touched him with a sense of awe. The giant figures reached towards the ceiling, all standing fourteen feet high.

Each fountain was in the shape of a child, the exact age and sex ambiguous, their bodies covered with carved flowing robes upon which water cascaded from those that had powerful enough flow. The great heads of the children, covered with long flowing curls, stared upwards. Their faces looked to the arm stretched above them and beyond to the high stone ceiling far above.

From the palms of their up-stretched arms, the fountains sprang. It had been noted more than once by the academics who would scurry down from the main building to stand and marvel at the great statues, that the force required to power the water up to the hands alone was a feat of engineering.

Yet of course, the usual laws of engineering did not apply here. It was not simple hydrodynamics that made these fountains flow. Each fountain spouted forth water at a different rate. There was no correlation between any of them. Some were strong and vital, spewing their water up in a powerful arc, some barely a trickle.

Draped over the feet of the immense statues was a length of shining coloured silk. Unlike the statues themselves, the origin of these was no mystery. They had been placed there as information had come to light. Ward was fairly sure that they were accurate. There were eight black-draped fountains, six white, a further three in a bright green, and the rest were individual colours.

It was in front of one of these, its drape a shining lilac, that a small group of diviners huddled together talking in low voices. A few feet away a heavily muscled man stood with his back to the approaching group, stroking his large moustache reflectively.

'One of the independents,' Ward said, reaching the man. 'That's something, at least.' He turned to him, 'Do we have any idea who, John?'

John Braddock shook his head and then glanced at the diviners. 'They've been squabbling for the past ten minutes. Not one of them has said anything useful.' He glanced back at Ward, his brow furrowed.

'They will,' Makena said, stepping to her husband, her hand reaching up to rub the back of his neck. 'This was not expected. Our time-scale predictions are out.'

'So it would appear,' Braddock muttered.

'Well, there may still be time.' Ward moved to the side. 'The fountain is replenished, but the bond isn't complete yet.' He turned, so he was facing all his subordinates.

'Stop a moment,' he called. Once the diviners had stopped muttering among themselves and all had turned to face him, he spoke again. 'One of them has used up another child and taken a successor. There will be time to mourn for the first soon, but now our focus must be on the second. For many of you, this will be the first time you have been party to the events at a transition. This tragedy can be an opportunity, but time is always of the essence. Work fast. I want to know where this has happened before sunrise. As soon as we have something, John and Makena will go.'

John Braddock looked at him for a moment. 'We'll need access to the armoury.'

McCloud sighed, then nodded. 'I know, John. Take what you need.'

The sound of children's voices rang through the morning air. Sama glanced up from where she was struggling to drag an overfilled basket of logs for the fireplace in the bar. A minute before, Jim had poked his head out from the kitchen door of the Stumblepot and laughed at her efforts. Sama didn't care. It was far better to struggle with one big load than traipse back and forth with the little bucket the way Jim always did.

At the bottom of the village green, a cluster of children were pulling a home-made sled up the slope. The sled was made of a Fry's Soapbox that Chops had almost certainly given them.

'Go on then,' Sama said quietly, a half-smile on her face. 'If she saw me with a soapbox sled she'd probably drop dead of horror.'

Still, Sama thought, that wouldn't be entirely without cause. There had been a time when she was twelve and Chops had not long been in the village that she and Christopher had tagged along with Jim, Joe, and Freddie Flyte to a steep hill above Henley. There was a long line of clear ground between the trees, thick with snow. 'The Devil's Slide,' Freddie had christened it with a grin, being as he had discovered it. They had taken it in turns to hurtle down the slope at breakneck speed on a neat little sled that Joe had made.

Sama had loved the feeling of zooming down the narrow route. So much so that each time it had come to her turn she had climbed higher and pushed off with more effort than any of the boys. Eventually, it ended in disaster. Sama had veered off course, straight into a tree trunk. She'd smashed up the sled and got a gashed head and impressive black eye. It was still a sickly shade of yellow a fortnight later. It had also earned her one of the first of Chops' exasperated lectures, with the now familiar heaping on of housekeeping tasks designed to keep her idle body out of trouble.

The children reached the top of the green. The biggest, a scruffy looking lad with unkempt, dirty brown hair called Eddie Swain, pushed his way to the front and grabbed the soapbox. He ran down toward the pub in great strides then dived forward. He flew through the air, the soapbox sled held below him, then hit the ground with a great explosion of snow. He burst through the white cloud and sailed in a graceful arc to the bottom of the green. The other children whooped and shouted, imploring him to hurry back so they could jostle for the next turn.

Eddie Swain got up and bowed. Sama laughed. He turned around and saw her with an immediate grin. 'Hello, Sama. Will you come and ride on my sled with me?'

Sama scowled at him, knowing it was common knowledge amongst the children of the village that the legendary Sama Neeley was just a shop girl these days. 'I'd rather sit with my bare bum in the snow, thank you, Eddie Swain.'

Eddie's eyes widened in shock for a moment, Sama noted with satisfaction.

Eddie was a year older than Christopher and he was forever asking her if she wanted to do such and such with him. Of course, she always said no. It wasn't because she worried that people would think badly of her. Or that they'd call her 'fast' like Chops sometimes called the independent-looking young women in the magazines she pored over. She said no because Eddie Swain had a look to him when he asked her, that was the same as the looks she sometimes caught from the men in the pub. Also, Eddie Swain smelled.

'Are you sure, Sama?' he said. 'You'd like a cuddle with me more than you'd like a cold bum, I'll bet.'

Sama smiled demurely at him and bent to the floor out of his sight. Quickly she made a snowball out of a little drift that leaned against their low fence, then stood up. Eddie Swain was dragging the sled up the hill, his back to her. She assessed the distance between them and let fly. 'Eddie!' she called as the snowball's arc began to descend.

He turned in perfect timing for the snowball, which smashed into his face with a wet smack. He spat out snow and glared at her. 'Lucky shot.'

That was no lucky shot, Sama thought to herself. She had the best throw in the village and that had been just the right time to remind people! Without another word Sama lifted her chin at Eddie, then turned back to her basket and dragged it toward the door. Eddie Swain muttered something under his breath and turned to trudge up to the cackling children, the sled dragging behind him.

Christopher never acted like that to her, or looked at her in that way, Sama thought to herself as she dragged the basket through the kitchen. Sama had heard enough talk from the bar. She was not completely ignorant of 'the way men could be,' as Chops put it in her countless lectures. Yet Christopher had never been anything other than the same shy friend she loved and trusted. Sama stopped and thought about that. Then she nodded her head and smiled. She was glad.

'Jim,' she said as she reached the fireplace. 'Have you ever kissed a girl?'

Jim sat at a table by the window. A box of brightly coloured ribbons was laid before him and next to it a small pile of holly branches. He raised his eyebrows. 'You better not let Chops or Dad hear you asking that sort of a question. If they did, the next time you'd be let out of this place would be the day they found you a boy and a church to marry him in, all properly.'

'Bugger that,' Sama grinned. 'I'll go and join the suffragettes before that happens!'

'That's a long word for a short person.' He smiled back.

131

'I'm not short,' Sama said, picking up a small stick from the basket and lifting it to throw at him. 'And you haven't answered me.'

'I'll tell you one thing,' Jim said, watching the stick warily with a hand raised to fend it off should she launch it. 'I'd have probably kissed a good deal more girls in the village if you had any as friends!'

'Eugh! If I did have any, the last thing I'd let them do is kiss you.' She tossed the stick toward him, watching him easily deflect it.

'Why all this sudden interest in kissing, anyhow?' Jim looked sharply at her. 'I hope you're not going to give me more to worry about whilst I'm away.'

Sama shook her head violently. 'Not in a thousand years.'

'We'll see. Anyway, now you're here, you can give me a hand with these.' He gestured at the box and the holly before him.

Strictly speaking, there were two days to go before Christmas decorations should go up, but Stan Neeley had been adamant. 'If my lad is going to be in soldiers' barracks over Christmas, then at least we'll send him off with the memory of decorations.' Thus, before Sama had gotten up that morning, he had gone out. He'd taken a couple of good bottles of ale and a piece of Chops' damson fruit cake that had a little brandy in it and set off to see Dr Conrad. The doctor had a holly bush right in his garden covered with scores of scarlet berries. Chops, of one mind with her brother, had pulled out the box of ribbons remaining from last year's decorating and put it in the bar.

'Sama?' she had called up the stairs. 'You'd better be dressed, my girl. Wednesday mornings aren't for loafing around. If you aren't going to get on with the cleaning, I'll have to think about having you in the shop on Wednesdays too.'

Fortunately, Sama had been dressed and had rushed down and grabbed a duster, before placing an offhand kiss on her aunt's cheek. 'Yes, Auntie.'

'Mind you get on with those decorations for your dad after.' Chops' voice had carried up the stairs to her retreating heels.

It was actually fun sitting with Jim and sharing the work. They chatted, passing little insults and jokes whilst they sorted the ribbons into colours, then tied them around the holly branches and fixed them up on the walls and corners of the bar. Jim took down one of the large stuffed fish and slid it out of its glass case. He tied a red ribbon around it and slipped a single holly leaf into its open mouth, then placed it back on the wall to Sama's delighted giggles.

Jim got bored of sorting ribbons after a while and, with a final poke in Sama's shoulder, he started upstairs to organise his packing. At the door, he turned and made little kissing noises into the air. 'You wait, Sama. You'll be kissing a boy before I get back, I'll bet. Then I'll have to come home and bloody his nose before dad gets demands for some huge dowry!'

'Never.' Sama replied firmly, but after he was gone, she frowned to herself. Was it inevitable?

She shook the thought from her mind and pulled out another ribbon. Soon she was completely engrossed in the task, and though she would deny it to anyone who asked, and probably to herself as well, she was quite enjoying it.

It was mid-morning when there was a loud knock on the bar's main door. By that time, Sama had run out of holly and was using the rest of the ribbons to wrap around anything that she could. The thin wooden columns holding the shelves for glasses above the bar were hardly visible under the swathes of red, pink, and green. Bottles of whiskey and brandy were similarly covered. It was only after that Sama had considered it may cause her father a problem, when he came to serve drinks. She had shrugged and turned away, looking for something else that she could similarly festoon.

She listened for the sounds of her father coming to see who the visitors were. Hearing nothing, she put down the ribbon, then went to the door and unbarred its sturdy iron bolt. She opened it, a polite smile on her face, ready to greet the visitors properly. When her father did appear, he'd see that she could act the young lady when required. As the door swung open, her words caught in her throat.

Standing outside were the two most unusual looking people Sama had ever seen. They were a man and a woman. He stood to the front. She stood a little behind him, almost completely hidden in a long travelling cloak with the hood pulled over her head. From within, bright green eyes stared out, the only thing piercingly visible in the shadow. Immediately Sama knew these people had more adventures in a year than she had experienced in her entire life.

The man spoke first. 'Good morning. My name is John Braddock, and this is my wife. We've driven up from London and are looking for a room to stay.' A smart looking car was parked to the side of the road behind him. Its shiny black bodywork, with gracefully arched running boards, were a striking contrast against the snow. 'They told us in Henley that you take guests.'

Sama stared at him. John Braddock just looked powerful. As if there was nothing that he couldn't try. Not just big and strong like Joe was, it was more than that. He looked determined and sharp.

He wore a long grey coat made of some fine material that looked warm and soft. It moved lightly in the wind as he gestured back to the car. On either side, it had huge pockets. They were quite possibly the largest Sama had ever seen, both stuffed to their brim. Their contents were hidden by wide flaps that reached over each and sealed with an ornate brass button. He had pulled the coat's high collars up against the cold and their tips reached almost above his ears. Wrapped around his neck was a thick, woollen, jet-black scarf.

On his feet, he wore strong black boots. The same type that Sama had seen on the soldiers who had come to the church hall back in August to talk to the men of the village about joining up and fighting the Hun. Tucked into them were dark brown britches. Sama could just see the colour under the bottom of the greatcoat.

John Braddock's mouth curled into a small smile. 'I expect you are not used to people wanting rooms at this time of year.'

The smile warmed his ruddy, angular face, but did nothing to diminish Sama's sense of him. Though his grey eyes had crinkled and his mouth twitched under his large sandy-brown moustache, Sama imagined he would still knock a man to kingdom come before the smile had even left him.

'No. Not much,' she finally blurted.

John Braddock nodded. 'That is a great shame. Still, I am sure that we could find room in Henley.'

'Oh no!' Sama cut in, anxious that these new excitements should stay exactly where they were. 'We've got rooms. I'd best get my dad.'

She spun around and took two steps to the bar, then stopped and turned back. 'Come in. I'm Sama.'

John Braddock smiled again without moving. Sama looked at him for a moment more, unaware of quite how wide her mouth had opened. 'I'd best get dad.'

Stan Neeley was in the back garden, singing to himself under his breath as he shovelled earth into a medium-sized pot holding a young Christmas tree. He turned to Sama with kind patience as she burst into the air, her words coming garbled in her excitement.

'Hold up, Sama. You're just making a noise with that chatter. I'll do better with actual words.'

'There's a man with his wife. His name is John Braddock. He's ever so big, Dad. Not like Joe, but he's got a look about him. They want a room.'

Then Stan Neeley frowned. 'A room? At this time of year? You'll be telling me they've got a donkey with them next.' He dropped his spade and walked past Sama, into the pub.

The couple had come into the bar during the time that Sama had taken to fetch her father. Their leather travelling case stood on the mat by the door, melting snow dripping off its underside.

John Braddock looked toward them from the case with the holly-eating fish he had been examining. 'Your decorations are a little unusual, and a little early.' He smiled. 'John Braddock.' He stepped forward with an outstretched palm.

Stan Neeley, clearly as impressed as his daughter, was far quicker to come to his senses. He took Braddock's hand and shook it. 'Stan Neeley. Some of our lads join up tomorrow. We wanted them to have a Christmas send off, Mr. Braddock.'

'Good idea.' Braddock nodded amiably. 'Once a Sergeant gets them marching, cleaning, and shooting, the thought of Christmas with their family will keep them warm at night.'

Stan smiled, disarmed. 'It's quite unusual to have guests at this time of year. We don't expect that many until regatta time.'

'Well, we're here looking for a house,' John Braddock replied. 'We thought if we took a few days now, we'd still be able to get to my father's in London for Christmas.'

'Oh, I see,' Stan said, as though that seemed quite proper. Sama looked at him with surprised eyes. She had never heard of guests staying whilst they looked for a place to live. Henley, maybe, but not here. 'Well, we have a room that is all made up, Mr. Braddock. You'll have to take us as you find us at this time of year, especially with my lad one of the ones going away, but you're welcome.'

'Thank you.' Braddock nodded. 'That will do us well.' He turned. 'Makena? You agree.'

The woman had not yet removed her cloak, but now she lifted her hands and slipped the hood back to her shoulders. Sama gasped. The woman's skin was deep, rich brown.

'My wife.' John Braddock smiled, though there was the tiniest edge to his voice now.

'This will do us very well,' the woman said, her voice deep and rich with an accent Sama had never heard before. 'You're very kind, Mr. Neeley, to share your home with us at such a festive time. We will do our best make the least disturbance to it we can.'

Stan Neeley nodded up and down, looking at the woman. The composure that he had regained so quickly after sizing up the husband had left him, and Sama could see why. If John Braddock had impressed, his wife stunned.

With her hood off, the bright green eyes shone out from her dark skin with even greater intensity. Below them was a wide, distinguished nose above full bowed lips. In each of her ears, she had six rings that started small and became larger along the length of her earlobe. Her hair was cut short, but there was no styling to it. Rather, it looked hacked short out of necessity. The woman was about as far away from all the photos that Sama had seen of supposedly beautiful women, and yet she was more striking than them all.

The woman smiled at them both, her eyes dancing with amusement. 'We are not your usual kind of guests.' Then she stepped forward and lifted her own hand to Stan's. 'I hope we won't cause you any inconvenience.'

'No. I'm sure,' Stan said, his words sounding anything but sure. Then his face reddened as he realised that he was still staring. 'I'm sorry,' he continued, 'You're absolutely right, you are not my usual kind of guests, but everyone is welcome here.'

John Braddock nodded. 'We appreciate that, Mr. Neeley. We will be out looking around the area for most of our stay, so I assure you we will be very little bother.'

Sama was still mesmerised by the woman. Summoning up courage, she spoke shyly, feeling frumpish and stupid in the blue dress she had thrown on this morning. 'Where are you from?'

'Sama!' her father said sharply, distracting her from the woman's eyes. 'We don't go around asking impertinent questions!'

She turned to her father. 'What? I just wanted to know.'

'Get outside now.' Her father had become quite red-faced all of a sudden. 'Finish off potting that Christmas tree.'

'But dad, I was only asking,' Sama said, watching the red turn to more of a purple. 'How can I find out things if I don't ask?'

Stan Neeley took a step towards his daughter, looking to all intents that he was going to grab her by the scruff of her dress and march her outside. Before he got another step forward though, Makena smiled and crossed in front of him.

'No impertinence, Mr. Neeley.' She looked at Sama. 'I'm from Africa. If we have the time, I'll tell you about it.' She placed a hand on her shoulder and smiled down. Sama was again lost in the intense stare.

Sama felt embarrassed under the scrutiny. 'I'm sorry if my question was impertinent. I'm not very good at being polite.'

Makena laughed. 'There's nothing to be sorry about. If you feel bad, then perhaps you'll show us where we can stay.'

Then, quite suddenly, Stan Neeley laughed.

John Braddock raised his eyebrows and Makena turned toward him.

'Sorry,' Stan Neeley said. 'If you knew my daughter, you would realise that for her to say sorry so quickly is an unusual thing to see. You have made quite an impression on her.'

The Master led Pope down into the kitchen after showing him around the upper house. Not the most comprehensive of tours, as he was still finding his own way around the Flyte family home, but Pope would soon settle in and make the best of things. That was why he was still with the Master after all these years.

Molly Brodie sat heavily at the Flyte kitchen table, her elbows on the clean brown wood and her hands supporting her head. A shaft of light stole across the room from the small single window high in the south wall and caught a line of the brick red tiles covering the kitchen floor and corridor beyond. The lights were off, leaving the rest of the room murky grey. Above, the utilitarian porcelain sink shelves held large white plates and dishes. Next to the sink, a door opened to steps that led down to the pantry.

There, behind boxes of fine smoked meats and racks of expensive wine, was another door, hardly used and all but forgotten to the Flyte family. The door opened into a further cellar that dated from the civil war. Beyond was a passage that led a short distance away from the house, coming out at a brick archway in the woods, long since covered in leaves and fallen branches. Once, when this house had been owned by royalists, the passage had provided a way to enter or exit unseen.

Molly hissed weakly as they entered. She pushed to raise up from her chair then crumpled down before she managed, the effort appearing to exhaust her.

Pope glanced at Molly Brodie. The shaft of light caught his wispy grey hair. 'She's still here, sir?'

'As are some of the gypsies, but not for long.' The Master regarded the shadow in the chair before him. 'She is diminished. Not long now, Molly, then you will join your family, reunited.'

'There is nothing to join,' Molly sneered with effort. 'You've destroyed it all.'

'Rubbish.' The Master smiled, too contented to be concerned by an old used up thing. 'There's everything. Perhaps it will not be anything that you know, or can even feel this time, but you will be part of it.'

Weakly Molly raised her hand and flexed her talons at him. 'Come closer.'

Pope looked surprised. 'She has will.'

'Some.' The Master nodded, looking at the outstretched talons with amusement. 'I am not directly linked with her now, but no matter. I will still be able to use enough of what I have left from her world to hold her to my needs one more time.'

He turned back to Pope. 'Follow me. I will show you the chamber before I leave you to commence your duties.'

With tremendous effort Molly stood. She flexed her wings high into the air and beat down with them, moving strenuously forward. She lifted her hands, aiming her still sharp talons at the Master's neck.

Pope's eyes widened. 'Sir!' he exclaimed, moving backward.

The Master simply stepped away, beyond the sharp points of her nails. Deprived of a target, Molly fell forwards. Her wings strived to rise again. One wing half extended and the vein-covered skin inflated as it caught, but the other failed her. Off balance, she landed with a dull thud on to the floor and cried out at the pain.

The Master didn't even glance down. He stepped over her crumpled body and walked across the room, silently opening the door to the pantry and walked down the steps. Only then did he call back in cheerful tones, 'Come along now, Pope.'

'What on earth happened?' Jim said, staring at the remains of Joe's window. Most of the glass from it had been collected into a large, badly frayed wicker basket that sat on the path. The glass twinkled in the cold winter sun each time Joe or Michael Brophy threw another piece into it.

Joe stood inside his house with a small hammer, knocking out the remaining shards of glass in tight, controlled taps so as not to damage the frame around it. Michael was alternately collecting the bits of knocked out glass and sorting out larger bits of wood that had once been parts of individual panes.

Sama thought it was obvious what had happened; a fight! This was turning into a very exciting day indeed. All along Joe's once tidily whitewashed walls, there was damage. Some scars were small and shallow, barely cutting through the lime whitewash to the cheap bricks beneath, but others were far deeper.

'Don't ask him what happened,' Mike Brophy said. He stomped around toward the side of the house and disappeared. 'He won't accept it.'

'Accept what?' Jim asked. 'Accept what, Joe?'

Sama shifted impatiently on her heels. This was getting too good to be true. She had to tell Christopher. As soon as she was sure that Jim was distracted with his friends completely, she would be off. Not that she really thought Jim would stop her if she just started walking away now, but it was best not to risk it.

They were still within a shout of the Stumblepot here and if she took a couple of steps backward she could easily see the front of the general store. If Chops came out, there was no chance she would see it as a good idea that Sama was out and about. Not even though her father had smiled when she insisted on going out walking with Jim as it was 'his last day as a civilian'. Jim had puffed out his chest proudly when he heard her say it.

'Let her then, Dad,' Jim had said with a smile that she thought made him look far too big for his boots. 'I'm only going to pop over to see Joe for an hour or so. I'll keep her out of trouble.'

Well, Sama would see about that. Jim was already looking like he had forgotten his promise at the sight of Joe's window.

'Joe? Accept what?'

Joe harrumphed and frowned, hitting the piece of timber he was trying to dislodge with a little too much force. It came away sharply, splitting the wood of the frame with a crack. 'Damn it.' He stood back, wiping his brow with an irritated hand. 'I'll have to replace the whole side now.'

He lifted the hammer and began to bang loudly against the frame itself. Sama immediately stepped closer to the door and glanced down the road towards the store. There was nothing like a loud disturbance to have Chops out of her door and marching down the road, the peace of the village foremost in her mind.

'Joe, stop that.' Jim reached forward to grasp his friend's wrist through the glassless pane.

Sama breathed out, relieved that the noise had stopped. Mike reappeared from the side of the house, dragging a sheet of tatty wood about the size of the window.

'This should do it, Joe. Come and have a look,' he said with effort.

Joe dropped the hammer and came outside. He glanced at Sama. 'Sorry, Sama. I didn't mean to swear in front of you.'

'Don't apologise to her.' Jim winked in Sama's direction. 'She talks like a bar full of sailors most of the time anyway. Tell me what happened.'

Joe sighed, his huge shoulders lifting, then dropping as though someone had placed a weight on to them. 'I don't know, Jim.'

'What he means is that he doesn't want to know,' Mike interrupted.

'That's not what I mean,' Joe almost shouted. 'For pity's sake, Mike, stop telling me what to think.'

He looked back at Jim. 'All I know is that when I got up this morning and came down, the window was all in pieces. It's not just that, there's these,' he continued, gesturing at the damage on the wall. 'The garden too. Things knocked over, footprints in the flowerbeds. It took me half the morning to set things straight out the back.'

'Then I came along and we got started on this,' Mike interjected. 'Tell them what else, Joe. Tell them the important bit.'

'Oh, Mike.' Joe sounded tired.

'All right, I will,' Mike said. 'Bailey's gone missing.'

'Mike, this isn't anything to do with him.' Joe looked desperately unhappy.

'Really?' Mike said, looking at Joe with almost pitiful eyes. 'I said it before, Joe. I know why he seemed like a godsend and all, but you don't just let a stranger into your house. No matter how helpful he seems.'

Joe stared at the floor. 'He did nothing but help me. And he helped you for that matter. Who re-roofed your ma's outhouse when I was stuck filling in the church ditch for Father Alistair? Wasn't you, was it? You wouldn't know how to do a proper job on anything without someone to tell you what to use.'

'All right, Joe.' Jim put a hand on his shoulder. 'There's no need to fall out.'

'All I'm saying, Joe,' Mike continued, 'is that now isn't the time to be opening your doors to strangers. There's a war on.'

Joe flashed him an angry look. 'I know, Mike.'

Jim patted his old friend on the back. 'Mike's not trying to upset you. He's just telling you what he thinks. After all, there are a lot of strangers around at the moment. Look at those gypos, for one. And you should see the pair we've had turn up to stay in one of the rooms this morning. Queer lot, let me tell you.'

Joe looked betrayed. 'I thought you liked Bailey.'

'I didn't dislike him, Joe, but I didn't know him either.'

Joe stood silent for a moment. Suddenly Sama thought he looked quite small, almost like a little boy. A wave of emotion came over her and she hurried over and hugged him. 'It'll be all right, Joe. You'll see.'

She let go and looked up. Joe half-smiled down at her and nodded. 'Well, let's hope so.'

'Come on,' Mike said, resuming his efforts to move the sheet of wood over. 'Let's get this up and worry about the other later.'

Joe looked at the wood. He sighed again. 'Yes, you're right, but we'll never get it done with that old bit of rubbish. There's another bit around the back.'

He lifted the sheet of wood out of Mike's hands and strode around the corner. Jim fell into step behind him, cuffing Mike around the head as he passed. 'Come on.' Mike shook his head and followed them around the corner.

Sama had never seen Joe look so distraught. She stood there for a while, listening to the sounds of the young men pulling at their window replacement around the corner, thinking of Joe's face and how sad his big innocent eyes had looked. It had so caught her that it was almost a minute before she realised that she was alone. Excited, she bolted off in the direction of Fox Grange.

Christopher's curtains were shut when Sama climbed the tree and leapt over to his sill. She had never seen his curtains shut in the middle of the day. It was most unlike him. She would have expected to find him nestled over a book, or arranging his soldiers in some new formation; something that she always laughed at, but he would never be sitting in darkness.

She rapped on the window loud enough to make sure that he would hear, but not to alert the rest of the house to her presence. They had actually tried it one night, testing the amount of noise her knocks made. Sama had been very proud of this level of forethought and made sure Christopher was aware of how clever it was.

Today there was no answer, though. Sama frowned, wondering where he could possibly be. If he wasn't here, then she would have expected to see him on the way into the village, or even more likely he should have been at Joe's, concerned and helping out. There was no way he would go off on an adventure without her, she decided firmly. She turned back to the tree and swore under her breath.

'Don't you bloody break,' she ordered the tree and leapt back across the divide. The tree bent at a worrying angle, spraying snow down on to the ground below, but didn't break. As it bent back towards its original position, she clambered down through its branches and dropped the last four feet, landing with a thump.

Sama glanced at the garden behind her. Her footprints made a very obvious line to the tree. She looked into the sky, but it was as clear as it could be, crisp blue stretching up to the heavens. 'A bit of snow would be nice,' she said to the sky, then turned and marched around to the front door of the house.

She reached up to the heavy door knocker and banged it three times. It was a bit forward, coming to the front door, but Crawford was all right. Besides,

Sama knew that he had definitely been one in the pub to give her 'that' look once or twice. Perhaps it was time she made use of that, especially with all the excitement of today.

A few moments later the door opened, but the butler standing there resplendent in starched white shirt and black morning suit was not Crawford.

'Who are you?' Sama blurted. 'Where's Crawford?'

The man before her raised his eyebrows. 'Trade around the back.'

'I'm not trade. I'm Sama. I'm a friend of Christopher's,' Sama replied.

The Butler stepped closer into the gap of the door and frame. 'I see.'

'I should like to see him.' Sama didn't like her chances.

The butler's face was impassive. 'Master Flyte is in his room studying. He is not to be disturbed.'

'But he's …' Sama caught herself suddenly realising what she was about to say.

The butler looked at her, waiting.

'Oh well,' Sama said quickly. 'I suppose if he is studying. Would you let him know that Sama came to see him? He'll want to know.'

The butler was already shutting the door. 'Good day to you, miss.'

'Will you?' Sama asked again, but the door was shut.

Disgruntled, Sama walked back down the drive. At the gate, she turned back. Something here wasn't at all right. If Christopher had been in his room, then he would have known her knock and answered it immediately. That man had lied to her. Who was he anyway?

There was too much going on to just walk away and forget it. There would be something she should do, Sama thought to herself. After a moment, she nodded and turned away. She would do something, though if she were caught, she knew she could give up on all hopes of freedom ever, ever again.

CHAPTER TWELVE

Strange Landscapes

In the centre of a bustling world, an Entity slept. The sights and sounds and movements of the world passed it by without disturbance, unnoticed. Though it had created everything around it, it had long since forgotten. It was dormant.

It could have been sleeping for a moment or millennia. All time was the same to it. There was nothing to allow the counting of its passing.

Sometimes wisps of memory fluttered through its consciousness. Some vague recollection that there had been something else, something more. In those moments the Entity stirred, a sense of loneliness almost waking it. Then the wisp was gone and it slumbered on.

Then there was Christopher.

The Entity felt the presence appear immediately. Suddenly where there had been one, there were two. It burst awake. Every part of its being stretched out to the new awareness that had entered its void. A childlike joy overwhelmed it. No longer alone. No longer asleep.

And as joy consumed it, the world around it was destroyed. Disintegrating into waves of blue energy that floated off into the void. In an instant, the world was gone.

The Entity didn't notice.

As it snuffed out the world, it had could only focus on its new companion. As the energy from the world scattered, hanging inert in the void, the Entity snaked Christopher's consciousness, entwining it with its own. It flowed through his thoughts, awed by the vast glut of new stimulation. And as it moved with him, the Entity grew.

It was infinitesimal at first. With each new part of Christopher it encountered, sparks of energy from the void gathered to it. They danced around in the darkness, sparkles melding together. As they grew, they were drawn to the Entity like metal to a magnet. As they reached it, they became one with it. And the Entity grew.

For a while, it didn't notice. It was consumed with the realities it was experiencing. It ploughed on, struggling to make sense of the knowledge it had found.

When it did feel the changes, it found itself bloated. Suddenly it was scared. It was too much. It had consumed everything it had encountered and now it felt as if it would burst. The energy was a storm it didn't know how to control.

Fear rose. The Entity pulled back, trying to separate itself from the other presence. It was too late. It had woven itself so completely through the other that it could not find a way to separate. Now it was panicked. Every part of its being was infected with the knowledge it had so delighted in.

In desperation, it turned inwards again, back to the other presence. Its desperation gave it purpose. It searched through the consciousness anew, struggling to find something that would stop the changes.

This time it sensed focus.

In the vast sea of the other's thoughts, it found a centre. A place where the experiences were sharper. It rushed towards them, grasping desperately at their solidity. It saw what the other dreamed. It felt what the other felt.

Still it grew. Nothing would free it from the mind it had joined with. Finally, the energy was too much to contain. The Entity shuddered.

High above the boy's consciousness the great walls of energy vomited cascades of its force downwards.

And the genesis began.

The snow was gone.

Christopher looked out across the mound where he had awoken, half under the lowest branches of a pine tree. Instead of the smooth white contours that had glinted dimly in last night's moonlight, rough grass bent at a sharp angle from the force of the wind blowing through the gully.

He rolled on to his back. It was late in the day. Dull sunlight filtered through a sky dotted with grey clouds. The previous night began to refocus in his mind as the image of a gypsy watching him from the lawn popped into his head. Then it all rushed back to him. The gypsies and the horror at the house. Crawford on the ground beyond the drive, blood dripping down into the slush beside his head. The terrifying beating of the housekeeper creature's wings. The meeting with Bailey. Finally, his escape. Somehow stretching himself away from their presence with Winter's Grasp. Just like Bailey's story.

He scrambled back further under the branches as the memories reignited his fear, and his back collided painfully with the tree trunk. Wincing, he pulled his legs close to him and lay still, listening for any sounds of danger still close.

All he could hear was the rush of the strong wind and under it the steady sound of water running down the little stream he had leapt across. The stream sounded far faster though. It was a torrent, fattened with extra water from melted snow.

Christopher frowned. If he had been out here all night and more then he felt surprisingly warm and dry. He touched his jacket. It was completely dry. His thick woollen trousers were the same. If all that snow had melted around him, surely he should be soaked. He patted all over his body, but wherever he placed his hands, it felt the same.

Both hands! Christopher's heart plunged as realisation tingled his nerves. He lifted them to his face. They both stood in front of him, small with clean, well-kept nails. Winter's Grasp was gone.

Christopher stared at his hands, a shaky guilty feeling rising in his chest. Where was it? What would Bailey say? The old man had stayed behind to hold Christopher's pursuers back, yet they had still caught up with him. If Bailey had been hurt or worse, and the gauntlet had gone anyway, then it had all been for nothing.

Perhaps they didn't get it, Christopher thought, dropping his hands and staring out urgently over the mound. Perhaps it had fallen from his hand when he had used it. He had used it, he thought, his brow furrowed. The last thing he had felt before he blacked out was a sense of tremendous movement. He had rushed away from his pursuers, he was sure.

Yet now they seemed gone and he was here without Winter's Grasp. There was a sinking feeling in his heart. He had to look. It had to be around. Christopher listened for a moment more but still there was just the howl of the wind and the rush of the stream. He rolled out from his hiding place and sat up.

He gasped out loud.

The mound he was on was not the same at all. Though it had seemed similar from where he had lain, now that he sat up he saw it was not just the lack of snow that was different. It was larger, for a start. Also, it sloped away at a far steeper angle than he remembered. As it disappeared out of his sight, the grass was mottled with thick orange gorse bushes.

Christopher ran his fingers through it. Apart from a little dew, it was as dry as his clothes. It was certainly not grass that had been covered in snow only hours earlier. He pushed up to his feet and turned around to look upstream. Less than one hundred feet away from him, above the trees, a steep rock face jutted up at least fifty feet, covered with grooves and fissures. And at the top, great white foam, as a waterfall cascaded over the edge.

He rushed to the other side of the mound and looked down. There was still a stream just like the mound from last night, but this stream was more powerful. It cut into a deep groove where it gushed through a mass of rocks and flowed away from sight.

Christopher suddenly felt tiny against the precipice behind him. Nothing about this was right. He glanced around half-heartedly to see if he noticed any glint of silver, not really expecting to see anything. Sure enough, the gauntlet was nowhere.

He flopped down on to his backside with a heavy sigh. He put his head in his hands. How could he be here?

A sudden thought occurred to him. Perhaps this was a dream. He closed his eyes, squeezed them tight shut, held his breath, and concentrated. The powerful stream was still distinctly audible. He pushed fingers into his ears, muffling it to a dull, distant rush. In his mind he counted, slow and determined. As his inner voice reached five, he flung his hands away from his head and his eyes burst open. Everything was the same, the stream, the cliff, the gorse ahead.

'Where am I?' Christopher said aloud. He felt very alone.

He was alone! The thought found resonance in his mind. Actually, no matter how unfamiliar the landscape around him seemed, at least no one appeared to be chasing him. That was something. In fact, that was a definite improvement.

To be sure, he glanced around again. The only thing moving was the landscape. Feeling more positive, he thought about what to do.

'I'm just lost,' he said, and surprised himself as to how reassuring the words sounded. Perhaps lost was not the best situation, but compared to other predicaments he had been in recently, it didn't really scare him.

Perhaps Winter's Grasp had moved him further than he had intended. He had certainly pulled with all his might when he reached out to those trees, and Bailey hadn't really had any time to explain how it actually worked. Who was to say how far the magic might have taken him?

He stopped, a dry inner voice reminding him how far his thinking had come. Only two days ago he had been on a train. The biggest concern he had then was the punishment he might receive at home for fighting Daniel Corbyne. Now his world had changed. In two days he had seen creatures that he would not have considered possible. The tales his mother had read him to sleep by were now more than just stories. For if Winter's Grasp was real and the stories Bailey had told him were real too, then surely what he had thought were just his mother's stories could also be true. He felt a shiver — half excitement, half fear — at the possibilities.

Still, that wasn't his immediate concern. What he needed to do was find out where he was and get help. He should start moving, find some people and explain that he had become lost. Of course, he decided, it would probably be wise to watch anyone that he found first and try to work out if it were safe. That's what Bailey would do. That was what Sama would do, too. Well, probably. There was always the chance that she would burst out of a hiding place and walk right up to a total stranger.

'Anyway, sitting around and waiting for something bad to happen doesn't do anyone any good,' he said aloud, reminding himself of the previous night's resolutions. It made good sense to move anyway, if this was where Winter's Grasp had put him, then perhaps there was a way for the gypsies to trace that. The longer he sat here, the more chance that they would appear.

That thought spurred him to his feet again. He looked for a route out. There was no point in going upwards. The cliff behind was far too sheer to make it a sensible escape route. It would have to be downwards.

Before he set off, he made a more thorough inspection of the mound. If Winter's Grasp had deposited him here, then perhaps it was around somewhere. He scrabbled under the branches where he had lain, pulling the dead ones out from under the tree. Soon the area was clear, but there was no sign of the gauntlet. He frowned and widened the search, with no more success.

After making sure that he had looked all over, Christopher turned his attention to the stream. What if the gauntlet had somehow ended up in there and washed downwards? Of course! Winter's Grasp was light and it could float. It had floated up into the cave where Ben Bailey had found it, he remembered.

Still, if that was the case, then there really was no point in looking here further. Christopher pulled his coat around him and walked down towards the edge of the mound. Just over the rocks at its end, the gully bent around to the right and dropped sharply. Ahead, a thick mass of pine trees blocked the way. There was no choice, then. He would have to clamber along the stream.

Getting into the deep scar the stream had cut actually turned out to be quite easy. When he looked down, a ledge of rock jutted out a few feet below and, once he lowered himself on to it and peered over again, he immediately spotted another two. The fourth proved a little more difficult as it was close to the water and covered in moss. Christopher had to grab at a hole in the rock as he stepped on to it.

On the other side of the stream, a sort of path ran along its edge, where the water probably ran even higher on really rainy days. It would do as a means to follow down. Christopher let go of the rock, sure of his footing now, and leapt across. He sailed over the heavy flow and landed perfectly on the damp silt of the path, surprising himself with his sure footedness.

He looked down at where his feet had sunk into the silt and pulled them up. They came free with a sucking noise, quite distinct against the noise of the stream's flow. Red mud covered his shoes.

There were what looked like tracks in the silt. It was hard to be sure, but there were definitely some foot-shaped indentations. So perhaps he wasn't the first to have travelled this route, then. Another thought occurred to him. Maybe someone had taken the gauntlet from him whilst he was asleep! If someone had, then escaped down here, that could also explain why he couldn't find it.

He doubted it was the gypsies. If this was a set of tracks, it was only one, and they were many. Still, it would pay to be careful. The indentations continued downwards, so he followed, carefully watching his footing to stay on the driest parts of the makeshift path.

The tracks petered out after about five minutes of walking. By this time, he had passed a couple of other streams which joined the one he followed, and the gully was wider. The little space he had walked down was almost a full path now and a good few steps away from the water.

The trees had started thinning out quite soon after he had gotten on to the path, replaced by more and more of the gorse along with red-brown brackens and long grass. Within another ten minutes, the gully had opened out into a narrow valley between two hills, empty of trees and altogether bleaker. Brown rocks rose out of the grass and low ledges topped with patches of sandy brown earth grew more frequent.

Ahead the sound of the stream mixed with something deeper and more rhythmic. Christopher stopped to listen. It sounded like waves. He stepped up his pace, pressing on. Sure enough, a short while later the valley opened up some more. The stream turned to the left, following the low ground, but the path climbed away along the sides of a hill.

The sound of waves was becoming louder. The path began to grow steeper. He struggled with the effort of the climb, panting loudly to pull more oxygen into his lungs. He pushed on as the slim track began to bend in tight turns, snaking up the slope. For a time, all he could concentrate on was his body and maintaining his pace. He clambered on to the brow of the hill, his legs protesting with the exertion, and looked out across the landscape.

The other side of the hill fell away sharply. Steep slope gave way to a cliff and beyond, as far as he could see was water. He held his sides and tried to catch his breath. Below him, white waves crashed against cliffs stretching away on either side. A winter sun lingered above the horizon, distinct now between grey clouds, reflecting distorted orange in the sea below. The refection shifted with the sea, its shape changing as the waves moved, unpredictable, like a reflection of the world as it was now for Christopher.

Below the cliffs to his left, he could make out a beach covered in rocks that had fallen on to it over time and become dulled by the waves. He watched as a great wave came in and covered the dark sand of the beach completely, then rolled back with a rush. The wet rocks caught the low sun and twinkled like the embers of a fire.

Christopher took in the scene for a few minutes. Tide was coming in and there seemed little point in heading down towards that way. He glanced to the right where the path continued to climb slowly higher. He sighed and started off again.

He had been walking for a good hour and so far he had managed to keep his spirits even by concentrating on the journey. Now though, the thought occurred to him that he had no real idea what he was going to do if he didn't find anyone. On top of the cliffs, though the path stayed mostly level, the wind came in gusts so strong that he had to lean against them with every few steps. He was becoming tired.

If he wasn't near any kind of civilization who knew how long he could be out in this unfamiliar wild countryside with no hope of food or shelter? The wind was chilling now he was exposed. His coat, which had been adequate as he had clambered down the gully, seemed to be sucking in the cold from every angle it could. Ahead, thicker, darker clouds looked set to roll in from the sea, full with rain that would inevitably start to fall once they arrived.

Sama would probably think this was a tremendous adventure, Christopher thought grimly. She would probably rush up and down the path many more times than she needed to, exploring them. Then she'd burst back to check on him and how far he had travelled, all the while grinning from ear to ear. She was probably in the warmth of the Stumblepot right now, doing some mundane chore and dreaming up more ways of getting them into trouble.

'Well, I'm in trouble this time,' Christopher said, his voice almost disappearing into the wind. He suddenly felt quite angry towards her. If he hadn't agreed to follow her to see the gypsies, then perhaps he'd be at home, reading a book and wondering what the Weasel would grudgingly be having cooked for his tea.

He stopped and shook his head. There was no point in blaming Sama. For a start, it made no sense, and also it wouldn't help. If only there had been more time. Then Bailey could have told him more things that might have helped.

He shook his head and stepped forward, determined. He knew that feeling, the one where he started to worry about what to do next, and he knew what would happen if he listened. Giving in to the fears; he needed to make sure that didn't happen. He had to keep going.

His salvation turned out to be visible from the next rise. He felt a wave of relief spread through him, briefly dulling the chill. A good distance away another beach reached across the end of a broad valley. The beach was far larger than the one he had seen before, a great swathe of sand, burning orange in the diminishing light of the low sun. Long brown shadows from rocks at its furthest end stretched across it, cutting through the glow. Beyond it, the coast rose up into another sheer cliff and there, nestled on its summit, he could make out a square tower quite distinct against the curves of nature around it. There was a roofed building as well and a stone wall that looked from here as though it reached around the whole structure. Pinpoints of light flickered at regular intervals along the wall, illuminating it with a dull glow. A further row of little lights stretched back towards him, reaching the edge of the cliff. There he could just make out the shadowy groove of a ledge that wound down the cliff side. A path down.

He glanced once more at the structure, then set off towards it. It looked old, he thought to himself. Still, the lights meant there must be someone in. Perhaps it was some kind of church. A church would at least mean shelter. Moreover, worshippers would need to reach the church and that meant a road. Roads led to towns and towns led to help.

By the time he stepped down on to the sand, the sun was almost touching the sea. The dark clouds above had thickened and joined. Soon there would be rain, he thought with worry. He was not dressed to be out in a storm. At least for the moment, here on the beach, the wind didn't blow so hard. He trudged across, making little crunching noises as his shoes sunk into the sand. His footsteps left a lonely trail behind him that had already begun to disappear as he reached the far end of the beach and looked back. Sighing, he looked up at the beginning of the stone path.

The steps upwards cut into the high rocks at the bottom of the cliff. The path was shallow at first. It was made of great wide slabs of smooth grey rock, harvested from the sea's edge and dragged here to be laid into depressions to make steps. As the pathway rose, the slabs became smaller and the height between each greater. He panted with the effort of lifting his legs higher and higher to climb onward. Once the stairway reached the cliff itself, the slabs all but disappeared. Now each step was cut into the rock itself.

The stairs ran upwards for a while along the side of the cliff. He stayed tight to the rock face. The other side was a sheer drop down on to a dangerous ridge of rocks, close to the edge of the sea and constantly lashed by the heavy waves. The sun was almost completely below the skyline now and the waves had become a dull grey. It was getting harder to see and the higher he climbed, the more exposed to the wind he was. He pressed onwards, using his hands to grip at the steps above him to add more balance.

Fortunately, it was only a short distance further before the path turned inward. It followed a huge indent in the cliff that was a little more sheltered from the wind. Almost to the exact point that Christopher's spirits lifted a little the rain started. Dark icy-cold drops beat down on to the rock steps with sudden fervour. In moments, the surface was black and slippery. His pace became agonizingly slow as he squinted to find steady footing. His jacket was soon sopping wet and the winter chill in its very seams.

He knew when he heard the noise properly that it had been going on for a short while. The reason that it became noticeable through his climbing efforts was that it had grown louder. It was a sort of deep snuffling, in the darkness off to the left somewhere. He stopped and looked, but there was nothing visible. Whatever it was, he didn't like the sound of it. He turned back and concentrated on scrabbling up the steps.

There is was again. This time the snuffling was accompanied by sounds of movement. He frowned. It was not snuffling, it was sniffing. He had the sudden sense that something out there had his scent.

He didn't dare stop to clarify his suspicions. If something had taken an interest in him, waiting around to see what it was would be a mistake. He clambered on, taking risks now to increase his speed. He grasped up, pushing with his legs before his hands had found the next grip, his concentration caught between the rock he needed to touch and the noises behind.

He heard it move again. There was a low note, perhaps a growl. It was hard to be sure in the spatter and howl of the rainfall. Christopher felt his limbs tighten and let out an involuntary squeal.

At the squeal, the noise became louder. Something big was moving fast behind him, scaling the path with far more assured movements than his. He briefly wondered if it was the gypsies having caught up with him, but the sound was too heavy to be them. This was something new.

It was gaining. He pushed up, knowing that he could move faster if he just ran. Behind him, the something made an almost human noise of delight for joy of the chase. Its feet smashed down on the wet steps, only a few feet behind.

Christopher leapt upwards, slamming his foot down where the next step should be and found nothing. Before he knew it, he had stretched down too far and his balance was gone. He fell forward. His body hit three hard rock steps at once.

Through the pain, he could sense his pursuer's triumph. It paused for a split second, watching his prone body. In the fading light, its eyes were probably far more able to see than his. Then it bounded forward.

Christopher struggled up and grabbed ahead, hoping for a hold. The creature was a step below him now. Its body was huge, blocking what little light from the wet night sky that had remained. It growled triumphantly. Christopher felt hot breath from a giant mouth blast the back of his head. The stench of rotted meat and stomach acids made him gag.

Suddenly he felt a tight grip close around his left leg. It had him! Sharp pricks of pain ran along his calf as claws dug in. He screamed, his heart racing, and kicked backwards with his right foot. It struck something terrifyingly substantial.

A realisation came to him all at once. Afterwards, he would not understand how. He knew quite distinctly there was a grip in front of him, on a rock up and just to the right. It was the strangest feeling; a sense of truth that washed over him in a second, calming and focusing him. Blindly he reached forward into the dark, ignoring the pain in his leg and the fact that his body was now being pulled backwards towards whatever had him in its grip.

He stretched and closed his hand into space and there it was! His fingers connected with a hole in the rock, completely dry and ideally sized for his hand. He gripped, feeling the perfect fistful of rock in his palm.

The creature was unperturbed. It growled and pulled harder on his leg. Christopher held fast to his grip, not sure how much use it would be. Whatever had him would surely wrench him free. He screamed out desperately, his voice lost to the wind and the louder creature at his back. Yet his grip didn't falter.

Instead, the rock moved!

It was as if the rock were perfectly balanced. It rocked like a great pendulum, just a little at first, then swaying back into place. The creature, apparently enjoying playing with its prey, allowed its hold on his leg to give a little, unaware it was the boulder above rather than the boy that pulled away.

Christopher held fast. Again the creature, grunting with delight at the game its prey was giving it, pulled at his leg. This time, he pulled at the rock too. It swayed out again. If he could just pull it over its tipping point, it would teeter, then fall. He knew as sure as he had known the grip was there. He pulled harder. Sensing the extra effort, the creature did too.

The rock was no longer teetering. Its weight no longer pulled against his hand. Now he could feel it slowly toppling toward him. He let go and allowed the creature to pull him down, rolling on to his back and facing up.

All he could see was a dark cavern of a mouth. A huge wet tongue slavered over razor sharp teeth, each the length of his thumb. The creature let out a howl of delight, spraying him with saliva. It lifted its head slightly, intent on biting down to end him there and then. Huge, surprisingly human-like eyes peered down, wide with excitement, for the briefest of seconds.

Then suddenly it noticed the boulder. Its eyes shot up at the massive rock that plunged towards it. At once, realising the danger, the creature let go of his leg and raised giant paws to ward off the rock. Christopher rolled to the side and covered his head with his hands, pressing his body tight to the wall of the path.

The rock hit the creature with a dull thud. It had just enough time to cry out in surprise and fear, but could do nothing to stop itself being carried downwards by the weight. The sounds of rock and flesh crashing against one another echoed down the path.

Christopher lay panting until silence replaced the clatter. Slowly, as his heart stopped racing, he picked himself up. He looked down at his leg, but it was too dark to see what damage the creature had inflicted. He felt the muscle of the calf. It seemed that there were no gashes, but until he reached light, he would not be able to tell.

He turned around. Ahead there was a dull glow of the building he had seen. It was not far now. In front of him, he could make out the depression where that rock had been so precariously balanced. He frowned. The convenience of it seemed impossible luck.

Before he could think too deeply about it, a gust of wind blew in a great torrent of rain and sea spray, almost washing him down the steps. He could not stay here. He clambered to his feet and took a cautious step. Finding that his leg was usable, he began to climb again

The footing became surer as he reached the final rise. A short while later, the ground levelled out. He found that he no longer needed to concentrate on every step.

He pulled his sodden coat tightly around him against the ongoing rain for all the good it did and glanced forwards. The building loomed ahead. It was quite distinct now and far larger than he had anticipated.

The upper part of the tower was quite easily visible from where he stood. It was three storeys high, the upper two visible over the impressive looking stone wall surrounding it. There were crenellations on top of the wall. The tower itself had an overhanging square roof of dark tiles. At its apex was a smaller roofed lookout point, unusual for a church, with openings in the walls. It reminded him immediately of the top of the Pickering Tower. In fact, the layout of the openings was almost identical.

Next to the tower, attached so that its corner was actually part of the same structure, was a larger building with a roof that sloped down on two sides. He could not see how far the building went. It stretched out of sight.

He reached the top of the rise and crouched low to look over it. Further along from the tower the large wall itself was bright, lit with more covered torches that flickered in between every fourth dip in the crenellations. He frowned. No church that he had heard of was lit with flaming torches. In fact, he couldn't think of any churches at all that he had seen lit with anything other than candles.

Christopher decided he had been wrong. The building was not a church. Whatever it was, it was built to protect those inside from far more than just the weather. He turned back and looked down the dark space that he had just climbed. No wonder, if there were creatures like whatever had just chased him.

'A bear,' he said quietly to himself, drowning out the voice. 'Just a bear.'

Really? His mind answered him, pointing out that bears didn't live in England. In fact, they hadn't for many years. Now didn't that make him want to stop and ask himself more questions?

Before he had time to respond to his thoughts, he heard a voice. The words were impossible to make out, but it was a man's voice. It had come from somewhere off to his right.

Christopher stole to the edge of the shadows, careful to stay out of sight.

The voice had come from around the far corner of the wall, beyond where he could see. A little way further on was a scrub of bushes and heathers. It was far enough out that he would be able to see around the corner, plus it should keep him hidden until he could see whether it was safe. He ran quickly, keeping his body low, following a wide arc that kept him away from the brightest torchlight.

As he grew nearer, he heard a second voice, higher than the first. A woman. Her tone carried across, angry, though her words remained tantalizingly indistinct.

Christopher ducked behind the scrub and looked down the length of the building. At the middle of the wall, a large wooden door stood slightly open. Around its arch, further torches lit the entrance brightly. Just in front of the entrance the woman who had spoken stood tall and straight in a nun's habit. Her face was lined and her skin looked grey even in the light of the torches. She directed her words outwards towards a group of men on horseback just beyond the glow. Behind her, half in the doorway, a man in simple brown clothes stood holding something to his shoulder, his gaze never leaving the men in the gloom.

Christopher strained his eyes. The man was pointing something like it was a weapon.

The nun spoke again. Now he was nearer, her words were clear. 'I'll tell you again. There is no Queen here. This is a place of worship, not war.'

Christopher edged forward to the thinnest part of the scrub. What was that man holding?

'Yet, you do appear to have protection, Abbess,' the man at the head of the riders said, gesturing forward. 'Unless that isn't a crossbow your man there is pointing at me.'

Christopher's eyes widened in surprise. Even though he had thought what the man held looked like a weapon, it was unexpected to find out it actually was. Before he had a moment to consider that, the man on the horse rode into the light.

Both the man and his horse were dressed in full battle armour. They both looked as if they had been in little else for a while. The man's breastplate and pauldrons were covered in mud. Underneath he wore a light chain mail equally as dull. Only the greave on the leg that Christopher could see had any kind of shine to it.

The horse was just as dishevelled. A lopsided shaffron seemed to be giving the horse considerable difficulty seeing, and there was a stump on the top where a metal spike had once risen.

The knight lifted off his helmet and rested it on the front of his saddle, revealing a nearly bald head with bushy eyebrows and a fully grown beard. 'So unless you mean to have your man loose that bolt at me, I suggest you ask him to lower his weapon. We're not here to cause trouble. We just need to see the Queen.'

'Then I tell you again …' There was almost contempt in the woman's voice. 'There's no Queen here. This is a place of peace and privacy.'

'Our message is more important than your peace and privacy,' the knight replied, climbing from his horse.

Behind him, the other men clambered off their horses with such a clatter they must have been wearing armour, too. The man at the door took a shaky step forward.

'Please don't force me to draw my sword,' the knight continued and Christopher could hear how tired his voice sounded. 'I am here at the order of my King. I shouldn't need to remind you he's your King, as well I will not leave until I have seen Guinevere.'

Christopher almost fell forward into the scrub with amazement. This simply wasn't possible, his logical mind told him. He frowned, staring down at the ground as he listened to his thoughts. It was one thing to believe the things he had thought fantasy were grounded in fact. It was quite another to be transported into the fantasy. How could he possibly be here?

Before he got a moment to think about it more, a clear voice rang out. 'There's no need to force your way in, Sir Galind. I know you don't want to.'

Christopher looked around, heart beating fast. The man at the door had disappeared. A moment later another woman, dressed from the neck down in the scapular but with her head bare, stepped through the gap. Immediately the knights dropped to their knees.

'My Queen.' Sir Galind bowed his head toward the ground.

Christopher could not take his eyes from the woman. She was beautiful even from this distance. Her hair was long, straight, and very dark, but in many places it was mingled with grey. She stood proudly, but her voice was soft. There was no mistaking who she was. Guinevere. Her resemblance to the figurine that his mother had commissioned was striking, right up to the way that she held herself. 'But that's not possible.' Christopher frowned to himself.

'I'm not your Queen, Galind,' the woman replied firmly. 'You know that.'

'You are my sister in Christ, though.' The abbess had a tone of disapproval in her voice. 'Yet you are not veiled.'

Guinevere turned to the abbess. 'Forgive me, Mother. My pride is my shame. I thought it was fitting they should see the woman they remembered.'

The abbess sighed and looked flat-lipped at Guinevere. 'It was not long ago that this place was a quiet house of God.'

Guinevere nodded. 'It will be again.' She looked back to the men, still kneeling. 'Galind, you can see that your presence is causing discomfort. Tell me what you came to.'

Galind looked up, but did not rise from his knee. 'Arthur and Mordred ride towards each other in battle. They will meet soon if they have not met already.'

Guinevere nodded. 'How is he?' she asked with quiet words hard to make out.

Galind shifted uncomfortably. 'I am afraid I do not have the ear of the King, my Queen.'

Guinevere stood silent a moment. She raised her hand to her face. 'This is my fault. All of it.'

Then Galind stood. 'No. Mordred would have made this choice, despite anything … else.'

She looked up. 'You are kind, Galind.'

Christopher inched forward, mesmerised by the people in front of him despite the nagging voice in his head. He was seeing something he had been reading about since he could first read. He knew where he was now. This was the abbey where Guinevere had come after her banishment from court. Where she was banished as Arthur's round table of companions had all but fallen apart, after she and Lancelot had been branded adulterers. This was the last chapter of Arthur's story. It was when the King would die.

'So why are you here, Galind?' Guinevere said.

'We are charged with taking you north, to safety, should the worst happen.'

'Should Mordred win,' Guinevere said flatly.

The knight nodded and bowed his head.

'Arthur sent you on this task?' Guinevere asked.

'He did,' the knight replied.

'He thinks of me even now.' She said it almost to herself, then raised her head proudly. 'Thank you, Galind, but I'm not going to be the cause of any more mistakes. Five of you to escort me is five fewer knights on the battlefield. Go back and fight with him.'

Galind shook his head. 'My Queen …'

'If I am Queen in your heart, Galind, then follow my order.' Guinevere's voice raised a notch. 'Turn around now and ride to him as fast as you can. I don't need or want his protection. Better he protects himself and the kingdom.'

Again Galind tried to speak, but she continued, 'Galind, we can stand out here in the rain for as long as you wish, but I am not going to change my mind.' She stopped for a moment. When she spoke again, her voice had a shaky quality to it. 'If I could, I'd ride into battle with you. Tell him that, will you? Tell him thank you as well. And tell him this; should Mordred win, he won't harm me. He may be a schemer, but he's also a coward. He won't risk the chances of eternal damnation by killing a sister of Christ. I've known him since he was a child and I know what his horrid little mind is capable of. And what it isn't. Besides,' she continued, 'it is not as though I am without protection. The knight that Arthur sent with me is here and looks after me well.'

Galind stood, silently staring at Guinevere.

'I will not change my mind. Do you understand, Galind?' she said.

Finally, Galind nodded. 'Yes.'

'Good. Then go. There isn't time to waste.'

She looked at them a moment more, then turned and walked back through the door. The knights all stood, crowding around Galind and spoke in low voices. Then with another great clatter of armour they turned back and mounted their horses. Once mounted, they spurred the horses and galloped off into the dark.

As the noise of the horses clattered into the distance, Christopher moved around the scrub and took an unsure step towards the doorway ahead. The servant now stood alone, his gaze set off in the other direction, following the path of the horses.

Christopher's mind reeled, struggling to come to terms with what he had seen. If this were real, then the absent gauntlet had not just pulled him somewhere else, it had pulled him some when else!

He glanced the way he had come. Back there was only the lonely path to the beach, with who knew what waiting in the darkness. The idea of other creatures, hungry for his flesh, decided him. He turned back to the abbey.

Whatever was happening, the inside of this place still held the best chance and he needed to be warm, dry and fed. Besides, Christopher considered curiously, perhaps that would be where he could begin to answer the wealth of questions that he had.

'This is madness,' he said to himself, the thought freezing him cold. Was it? A shiver ran down his spine. His legs became suddenly wobbly and he reached out to a branch to steady himself. His worst fear sprang into his mind, consuming him. What if he'd imagined all of this? What did that say about his mind? Was he becoming like Freddie or his mother? 'No.' He pushed the thought away with effort. He was not going to give up to the 'what ifs'. Keep moving. That was the only option.

Whilst he had been deep in thought, the door to the abbey had been pulled closed. Christopher jumped, necessity outweighing any other concerns. He ran forward, across to the thick wood barrier and hammered on it, shouting loudly, 'Hey! Let me in!'

CHAPTER THIRTEEN

The Master Leaves

In the early evening Pope began to set out the talismans. They had arrived with him in a little leather case that looked like it had seen better days. Not the kind of case that anyone would think held such precious items. Pope had placed them in the study when he had followed the Master to see the house. There they remained until he had unpacked.

He had intended to check the food supplies thoroughly and organise everything for the Master's needs first, but then that young woman had knocked at the door. She was only a brat from the village in a cheap blue dress, but she might not be the only visitor looking for the boy. Sighing, Pope postponed his more mundane duties and fetched the little case.

Each talisman was identical, as black as night and shaped in the head of an eagle. The heads all looked upwards with cruel-looking beaks jutting into the air. Where their eyes should be there were deep black holes.

He bustled around the house, looking with a critical eye to see where to place the defences. The doors were the most important. He placed a talisman on either side of the front door, each one's eye sockets suddenly erupting with a slight green glow as it touched the floor. At the back door, out from the staff quarters, he put a single talisman. He placed another at the door to the pantry. In the secret passage below, he placed a further one in front of the door to the chamber, listening quietly for a moment to the quiet mumblings of meditation that came from inside. He walked a good way up the ancient passage and placed another just before the hidden exit.

The talismans were definitely less powerful since he had removed them from Cragtop. They were another part of the soon-to-be-consumed past, but for the moment both he and the Master were sure they would be able to do their job. He turned and walked back to the main part of the house.

He distributed the remaining talismans around the windows of the ground and first floors. Satisfied with his efforts, he returned to the door in front of the chamber.

'Master?' he whispered through. There was no response but the dull mumbling. 'Master, I have deployed the talisman circle. Nothing magical will be able to enter this house without you allowing it.'

The mumbling continued through the wood. Pope shrugged and turned towards the stairs, his mind back on to the matter of provisions.

Sama had changed her dress earlier in the evening. When she came down to join the boisterous celebrations in the bar, Chops looked up from her table and gasped. 'Sama, what on earth are you wearing that old thing for?'

It was true that Sama did have a number of far prettier dresses, but this dull green workday one was loose. Loose was essential to hide the shirt and britches she wore beneath.

Sama was prepared for her aunt's reaction. 'I thought that if I was going to be in the bar tonight, Auntie, that this would be proper. I don't want to get mess on the nice ones.'

Her aunt narrowed her eyes for a moment, then patted a stool next to her. 'You're a strange one, love.'

She said no more, though, accepting the explanation. Her attention was soon back on Stan Neeley. He stood behind the bar. His face was flushed red from whiskey. He had already celebrated his son's joining up with a number of toasts. He had also begun regaling his patrons with bawdy songs.

'Mind you now, Stanley,' Chops called to him as he sang through the colourful chorus of an old army song. 'There's two ladies present here. Something a little less fresh would be in order.'

Stan looked over and nodded dutifully. He switched to a song about a farmer's son and a stubborn barrow that many of the men in the Stumblepot knew. Soon a number of them had joined in.

Sama knew it was just a matter of time until Chops would be persuaded to sing for the men in her surprisingly melodic voice. Once that began, she would hold her audience spellbound for hours.

Then Sama could be away. With any luck, she would have done what she needed to and be back here before Chops had even finished. In the meantime, she sat quietly, clapping along with the music and occasionally fetching her aunt another drink to speed the process.

Jim, Mike, and Joe all stood at the bar. As they were the guests of honour, they were dressed in their Sunday best. Jim and Mike were thoroughly enjoying themselves. They joined in with the songs and gladly accepted the beers they were bought. Joe, however, had not escaped the dark mood that had consumed him earlier.

When Sama returned from Fox Grange, the lads hadn't even noticed that she been away. They had finished boarding up the window by then. Jim had turned his head to concentrating on what they could do to look after Joe's business. In the end, the four of them had walked up to Chops' store and told the little woman their worries.

Chops was always at her best in a crisis. She comforted Joe and told him not to worry about Bailey. She was soon on the telephone asking the operator to connect her to an old friend from her days in the meat markets. Within a short time, she had found a replacement for Bailey. Of course, she was quite happy to look after Joe's house herself until the man arrived.

Joe's mood had lifted slightly then. However, the loss of his friend looked like it weighed heavily on his mind again. Jim and Mike had been keeping an eye on him, making sure his glass was filled or encouraging him to join in with a song. Joe tried to smile and did his best to sing along, but Sama could see that he only did it to make his friends happy.

'Right then, everyone,' Stan Neeley shouted over the end of the latest ditty. 'Now as the owner of this here establishment, and the very proud father of this young fella here.' He cuffed Jim on the shoulder. 'It falls to me to say a few words.'

He continued, 'As we know the lads are off to train. Though there's a good chance this war will be over before they get out there and show the Hun what for.'

Various whistles and hoots came from the assembled men.

'But whether our lads here, or the lads that have already gone, actually go anywhere, isn't important.' He paused and nodded over to the table where Len Archer's dad sat with Dr Conrad. 'What is important, is that wherever they go, they conduct themselves like good English gentlemen and make us proud.'

'Especially with those French girls, eh!' a voice shouted. Next to Sama, Chops quickly glanced across at her, her face going red.

Stan laughed loudly. 'Well, we'll see about that! In the meantime, I ask you to raise a toast. Good luck, good fun, and chase Kaiser Bill all the way back to Germany!'

The crowd lifted their glasses and cheered, Stan Neeley the loudest. His eyes were a little moist, Sama noticed with surprise. For the briefest of moments, he glanced at his son with concern.

At first no one spotted the quiet young woman who had entered the bar and stood shyly at the door. Jim looked over first. The surprised expression on his face was quickly picked up by others who turned to see its cause.

She wore a light yellow dress, almost summery, and a white woollen shawl wrapped around her shoulders. She stared out from under a pretty yellow bonnet, glancing around the pub as her cheeks reddened. She looked most unlike the sort of woman who would come into a public house unaccompanied. Next to her, Sama could feel Chops' sense of disapproval blossoming.

Joe bowled forward. 'Alice!' he said, his eyes wide.

The young woman stepped forward, looked around one more time and swallowed. 'Hello, Joe.'

'What are you doing here?' Joe's mouth hung open.

Alice's face was red. Her voice wavered as she spoke. 'I saw Claire Dunn today. She told me that you were off to training tomorrow.'

'Yes, we are,' Joe said, his eyes never leaving her pretty face.

Alice nodded. 'Well, Joe, I wanted to see you before you go. I wanted to wish you luck, and I wanted … I wanted to take back that thing that I gave you in Henley.'

Mike suddenly spoke, his voice had a note of disapproval in it. 'Thing, Alice? It wasn't a thing.'

Joe placed a hand behind him, catching Mike lightly on the arm. 'Mike.'

'No, you're right Michael,' Alice said, her head bowing. 'It wasn't. It was a feather. It was a white feather, and I should have never given it to you, Joe.'

Alice's eyes were glistening with tears. 'I'm so sorry, Joe.'

Joe smiled at her as kindly as could be. 'It's of no matter, Alice. I'm very pleased to see you. If you'll come in and have a seat, I'd like it if you stayed.' He indicated the table where Chops and Sama sat.

'I will,' she replied, a little smile breaking on her face. 'But please let me have it back, Joe. I can throw it into the fire and show you and all your friends what I think of white feathers, and …' She looked up at him shyly … 'what I think of you.'

'It isn't here,' Joe replied, his face now a beaming smile. 'I put it in my keepsake box at home.'

'What would you do that for?' Alice said, reddening again. 'Come on, Joe, please, let's go and get it.'

She turned and slipped out of the door. Joe stood frowning after her for a moment until Jim sighed and kicked him firmly in the britches. 'Go on, you great idiot.'

Joe grinned again and followed Alice out of the door.

Immediately Chops stood up. 'That won't do at all, a young couple out on their own like that at night. I'll accompany them.'

She almost got to the door before Jim caught her arm. He wheeled her back to the bar. 'Well, tonight we'll pretend that we didn't see, Auntie. You know the day he's had.'

Chops strained towards the door. 'Now Jim, you let me go.'

'Listen to the lad, Violet.' Stan Neeley laughed. 'Come, you sing us a song.'

Before Chops could argue, the men in the bar cheered and drowned out her voice. Jim and Mike sandwiched her in between them on a stool. After a moment, she smiled, defeated. 'All right, all right! Your family will be the death of me, Stan.'

She looked upwards, lost in thought. 'Now let's see …' Then her face broke into a smile and she nodded. She sat a little higher on her stool and began to sing.

Sama slipped into the kitchen at the end of the second song. The little woman had got into the flow of things by then and didn't even look at her as she left. She quietly opened the back door and went outside, closing it just as quietly behind her. She ran to the end of the garden. The shed there was always unlocked. Within, wrapped in a small roll of cloth, were her father's screwdrivers. She pulled off her dress and hid it under a shelf. Then she stuffed the roll of screwdrivers into the back pocket of her britches and hurried out.

As she reached Joe's house, she slowed down. Joe and Alice stood in his front doorway, arms around each other, kissing passionately. Before they noticed her, she ducked into the shadows on the other side of the road. Part of her was most curious. She was tempted to stop and watch, see what all that fuss was about, but there was no time. She sneaked on, careful to remain in the dark so they would not spot her.

It was strange though, Sama thought as she passed the store, she actually did feel like someone was watching her. She stopped at the end of the houses, ducking around a corner. She crouched in the shadows, looking back. There was nothing.

Joe and Alice came through the gate at the end of his house and walked toward the pub, hand in hand. It must have just been her imagination. Sama shrugged continued on her way. She broke into a run as soon as she turned through the path in the woods that reached the top road and Fox Grange.

Sama had never actually broken into a house before. Of course, she was sure that she could do it, but she cursed herself for never having tried at home. It was bound to be something she would have to do at some point. A little practice wouldn't have gone amiss. Still, it was too late to worry about that.

She balanced on Christopher's windowsill. Knocking hadn't worked any better than earlier. She tried to work the longest screwdriver through the draughty space between the top and bottom panes. She grunted quietly as she concentrated.

The problem was finding the little catch. She knew that it was in the centre of the window. If she could use the screwdriver to knock it open, she could then slide the window up. The screwdriver was proving uncooperative. She had to apply quite a lot of force to get it towards the right place. The wood of the window squealed loudly in protest. Sama froze, listening for any noise. Nothing.

Gritting her teeth, she pushed again. No one had come to the window before when she had again tried knocking and surely that had been louder. This time the screwdriver moved. She felt the hard metal of the catch on the other side.

It took a few more minutes to work out how it opened. Finally, Sama realised that it unclasped from the other side. 'Bugger,' she muttered, and pulled the screwdriver out.

She repeated the whole process to the left. This time the catch opened. Sama pulled the window up and stepped into the room.

It was dark, but Sama had prepared for that. From the roll of cloth, she pulled out a candle and lit it with a match. The little flame sputtered and then caught, throwing a dim glow across the room.

Sama gasped. The door was ripped from its hinges completely. It was lying on the floor just ahead. She padded over to it and bent down, lifting the candle close.

It was broken in a number of places. Dents the size of fists were scattered on its surface. The wood was twisted with scratches and gouges that cut deep under the dark varnish.

She turned to the bed. The covers were unmade. The thick blanket, usually tucked so neatly into the bed's corners was in an untidy pile on the floor. It looked as though Christopher had got out of the bed very quickly.

She was worried now. Whatever had happened, Christopher was gone and it didn't look as though he had left happily. Sama checked around the room, but everything else seemed as it was before. His soldiers still fought their eternal battles. The shelves still held his collection of books.

Sama frowned. Christopher had been so convinced that those gypsies could hear him last night. The lads had talked about them while they repaired that window earlier. What if Christopher had been right? Perhaps they had come here and broken in. Perhaps they had caught him and taken him. Sama didn't scare easily, but a shudder at the memories of their strange howling the night before ran through her. He could be in their camp now. A prisoner, desperate for help.

Sama looked around again. There was nothing for it, she would go back to their camp. If Christopher was in trouble, she was going to save him. She blew out the candle and clambered back on to the windowsill. As quietly as she could, she pulled down the window.

She waited for a moment until the ghosts of the candle faded from her vision and she could see out into the night. The tree swayed softly in the breeze. She leapt across then clambered down and dropped the final few feet on to the snow below.

She wouldn't be back at the pub before she was missed. It couldn't be helped. Even if they locked her away, or worse, sent her off to one of the town houses of Henley and put her in service, she would worry about that when it happened. The only thing that mattered was making sure Christopher was safe.

'Well,' Sama said to herself, willing her voice to sound its regular plucky self. 'This is an adventure.'

In the chamber below, Pope was working hard. He had cleared one side of the dark stone room, piling decades old broken furniture and other rubbish into a corner. The stone blocks they had exposed were a dull grey in the dim light of the gas lamp Pope had set up by the door. Pope swept the floor with a large broom. The Master watched impatiently from a corner, dressed in his travelling coat and boots.

The wooden box that had contained the ball of energy that became Winter's Grasp stood clasped shut on a low table. Next to it was another nearly identical box. A little clasp held it closed. On its lid was an intricate silver emblem of a large ornate key surrounded by stars and patterns.

Close by the table a small camp bed had been set up. It was only a few inches from the floor, held up by two metal frames. Christopher lay on the bed, his face white. His eyes were tight shut and he shifted about, occasionally making little moaning noises in fitful sleep.

His clammy arms lay over a thin grey blanket. On his right hand, Winter's Grasp shimmered with a light that at least equalled that of the gas lamp. Minute blue sparks skittered erratically across its surface. Occasionally one would fly off the gauntlet, landing on his body. There it would slowly sink into his skin, gently fading as it did.

Suddenly the boy twisted hard. He groaned. Pope glanced towards him. He had been doing this with annoying regularity. 'The other one didn't make this much racket, sir.'

'Oh, he did,' the Master said, looking at the boy with cold eyes. 'Remember that you didn't join me until far later. By that time I had control of his mind as well as his body.'

Pope nodded. He pushed the brush again, clearing the final dust from the floor.

'He will be calmer then,' the Master said.

Pope placed the broom against the wall and turned back in the dim light. 'Will it take long?'

'Once I have entered, I should be able to find him quite easily,' the Master said. 'Anyone I meet will have no choice but to obey me. They will tell me what I need to know. Anyway, once I am in I will be able to replenish again.' He stopped and smiled at Pope. 'Once I have him I will be in full control.'

'And should I expect any trouble?' Pope asked.

'I won't be gone for long,' the Master replied, coming forward. 'Besides, with any luck, even if we have been discovered, they won't know where we are.' He lifted the second box from its place on the table. 'The sooner this is started, the better.'

The Master flicked the catch open with his thumb and glanced at Pope with a wry smile on his face. Pope shuddered and quickly backed over to the door. The Master laughed.

'Come now, Pope. You've seen the key before,' the taller man said.

Pope nodded and ducked to his knees. Still laughing, the Master opened the box.

The room was immediately drenched in bright blue light. Suddenly every corner was visible. Scores of insects scuttled into nearby nooks to escape the unwelcome exposure. On the bed, Christopher groaned again and began to shake.

The Master's eyes blazed bright blue in the reflection of the light. His face twisted into a hungry leer. He grasped the source of the radiance and dropped the box. Immediately, tendrils of light surrounded his body, crackling and sizzling. His hair rose from his scalp, waving as though it had a mind of its own.

On the bed, Winter's Grasp stirred. At first it was just a little, more as if the boy himself had moved. His hand edged forward, toward the device the Master held. The boy's body shifted strangely, as the gauntlet pulled it to its whims.

The gauntlet lifted into the air, straining to float toward the device. Behind it, the boy's shoulder left the camp bed. His head sagged back at an unusual angle, its weight not yet off the pillow.

The Master turned to the boy and raised his fist before him, his whole arm obscured by blinding blue light. He smiled and his teeth glowed electric blue.

Winter's Grasp leapt higher, pulling the unconscious boy into a sitting position as it strained to reach the object in the Master's hand. The tendrils of light from the object zipped across the space between them, creating a myriad of thin connections between the two objects.

The Master glanced one more time at Pope. His face grinned in triumph. Then he drove his arm forward and the room erupted in blinding white light.

A moment later the room became dark again. Pope realised he had flung his hands over his head. He lowered them, breathing heavily. His heart was pounding in his chest. He could see nothing. The light had temporarily seared his vision to nothing.

Slowly his sight returned. The room was as it had been. The piles of old furniture lay undisturbed. To his left a spider, comfortable once again in the dim gaslight, scuttled across a block of stone in the wall.

The boy was calmer too. He lay in the bed at a strange angle where he had fallen back. On his hand, Winter's Grasp twitched and shimmered with sparks, but even they seemed less than they had been.

Of the Master, however, there was no sign at all.

The Master stepped forward and sucked air into his lungs. Every part of him felt more alive than he had in weeks. Around him the night air seemed to blow in from every direction, rushing to greet him like a loyal dog.

He glanced around. Huge pine trees rose on three sides, bending towards him in the wind as though they were bowing. Their high branches reached down. In his hand, the key crackled and strained to be free of his grasp, but he held on tightly.

It was always the same when the key first brought him through to a new world. Sometimes he could almost swear it was alive. What was the pull of power that it always displayed if not excitement?

He braced himself against the rush of the wind and waited for the object to die down. It only took a few seconds. As its light dimmed, the pull it exerted on his hand diminished. The wind dropped too as if in response. A moment later the trees returned to standing straight as they should, pointing up into the cloudy night sky.

The ground sloped down into a valley. Nestled at the bottom he could see a small cluster of basic hovels. The glow of fires within some escaped through paltry holes that served as windows. Wattle and daub walls held up thatch roofs. In some, single jutting cylinders of clay formed chimneys for the fires below.

The Master smiled to himself. Simple peasants were little use to him, but tonight they would serve his needs perfectly. Pocketing the now silent key in his long coat, he strode forward down the slope towards the houses.

He could hear the laughter as he neared. There were four dwellings immediately in front of him, plus at least another beyond them. He strode to the nearest and pushed open the door.

The laughter had come from a little girl. She sat with dirty, tussled hair on her brother's lap as he bounced a pathetic wooden doll in front of her. At the fire an old woman knelt, stirring something that smelled desperately in need of more ingredients. Beside her a bearded man, her son perhaps, leaned back against a soft pile of cloth and furs. Seated before him, leaning back into his arms, was a thin woman who watched the children with loving eyes.

Their clothes and furniture did nothing to dispel the impression the Master had gotten from outside. Homespun cloth, cut into basic shapes that would do little to protect from cold, covered their bodies. The few pieces of furniture were badly cobbled together from forest scavenges. By the man, an old axe head was roughly fixed to a branch that had been used to replace its original handle.

The Master's sudden entrance ripped them from their quiet contentment. All eyes turned to him with surprise, then a moment later, fear.

'What do you think you're doing?' The man quickly clambered up. His wife reached forward and drew the children to her.

'Before you reach for that axe, I suggest you decide whether it will offer you any protection at all,' the Master said calmly.

The man looked. He squinted, considering the Master, then suddenly his eyes changed. There was still fear, magnified now, but there was more. The man's eyes showed a dreadful recognition. He sat back down, dully and wrapped his arms around the bundle of his family before him.

'Please, we don't have anything,' he said, looking up at the Master with wide eyes.

'You have information,' the Master replied, well used to the fear he saw in front of him. 'Tell me that and I will be satisfied.'

The man nodded and pulled his family tighter to him. The little girl began to cry, pushing her head into her mother's breast.

'This is Britain, yes?' the Master said.

The man frowned. 'It is, sir.'

'And Arthur rules?'

'Arthur is the King.' The man sounded unsure.

The Master raised an eyebrow. 'You do not know?'

'His nephew is trying to take the throne,' the man explained.

The Master laughed. Perfect. The end of the legends. Could there be a darker time to see this world? This would be an ideal womb. 'And where is that throne?'

'Camelot.'

'Yes, yes.' The Master frowned. 'Where is Camelot?'

The man understood. 'To the west, sir. Twenty leagues or more.'

'Thank you.' The Master smiled.

'Will you go, then?' The old woman said quietly, from by the fire.

'Soon, old mother.' The Master glanced at her, the smile never leaving his face. 'There is one thing more I am afraid I will need.'

He looked down at the little girl. Her head was still buried in her mother's chest, and her little body was shaking with terrified sobs. The Master concentrated on her and sucked.

The sensation was not unlike breathing, except it was more like taking a breath with one's soul. As the Master pushed out his aura, the little girl began to shimmer. For a moment, she looked up, her face a picture of pained confusion and then, with a tiny squeal she dissipated into blue light, which burst towards the Master and slammed into his body. He could feel the key dance in his pocket reacting to the sudden rush of power.

Something about the energy that emanated from the younger ones seemed sweeter, more pure. The Master knew that was an illusion. He understood that wherever he took power it was the same, no matter what the source.

One thing that was not illusion, though, was the potency. This energy was so much stronger than that which he had taken from the gypsies and their dying world. He shuddered, his body racked by spasms of pleasure.

The young mother screamed, her eyes wide with horror. The man leapt up, desperate fear in his eyes, and grabbed at his axe.

The Master concentrated again for a moment and the little axe dissolved into blue light before the man's hand had even closed around its handle. The tendrils of light rushed into his body.

He took the boy next, then the two women in quick succession. The younger woman had just time to reach out desperately to her husband before she too became the rush of blue. The man fell to his knees, and closed his eyes, praying to whatever power he imagined might save him.

The Master smiled. Little points of light shone around his teeth. 'That will do you no good.'

The man looked up with hatred and fear. 'Then take me, too. Do not leave me without them.'

'I have no intention of doing that,' the Master replied. Once more, he sucked with his soul and the man disappeared.

Instead of stopping, the Master widened his focus. Suddenly the building itself burst into a million points of light. The energy rushed into his body. He staggered back with the force of it.

He looked up, drunk from the power that coursed through his body. Ahead, people were rushing from the other buildings. Some stared in horror, while others — the more quick witted among them — turned tail and ran as fast as they could into the night.

'That will not help you,' the Master said and stepped towards them, stretching his thoughts to the nearest. A moment later, the valley was ablaze with blue light.

CHAPTER FOURTEEN

The Abbey

The servant pushed hard on Christopher's shoulder. Christopher sank down on to the stone bench. He had been careful to do everything the servant had demanded from the moment he had been allowed in. The man was nervous and not particularly imposing, but he had a dagger. Christopher didn't want to antagonise him.

The man hadn't really wanted to let him in at all, at first. Christopher had cajoled his way with a lie, saying he had a last minute message from Galind. The servant, mostly unconvinced, didn't seem prepared to take the risk of being wrong.

The servant stepped back. A second man, even less imposing than the first, stood slightly further away. He brandished a short, thick log like a club and stared intently, waiting for any sign of mischief.

'Stay there,' the first said. 'Don't you move until I come back, or he'll hit you with that log.'

'I'll stay here,' Christopher said, as respectfully as he could.

The servant nodded at his companion and looked one more time at Christopher with narrowed eyes. Then with obvious relief, he stepped backward, turned and began to walk away with fast little steps.

Christopher glanced around the hall that he had been brought to. It was about fifty or so feet wide and far longer. He was fairly sure this was the hall he had seen from the outside.

Above him, the underside of the roof was a vaulted ceiling made of the same uniform grey stone as the rest of the building. The stone blocks were rough, worked into their shapes with basic tools. This abbey was not supposed to be a place of great beauty. It was practical and solid.

On each side of the hall, about twenty feet apart, tall windows were set back deep in the thick stone walls. Plain glass panes were held in place with simple black lead. The only concession to beauty was the tops of the windows, which rounded up to a point that echoed the shapes in the vaulted ceiling.

Between each window, a plain banner hung illuminated by two flaming torches set in the wall on either side. Each banner was identical. A light blue background with a single large cross in its centre.

Under each was a plain stone bench, exactly the same as the one Christopher sat on. The hard stone seat provided little comfort for a sitter. He turned and glanced behind him. Sure enough, there was a banner hanging down.

As he shifted on the seat, the servant ahead lifted the log he was holding and shook it. Christopher turned back, not wanting to antagonise the man.

To the far end of the hall, the first servant was pulling back a large, surprisingly ornate curtain. Christopher leaned forward slightly and the man before him stepped backwards, lifting the log in a shaking fist. 'Don't you move!' His voice sounded nervous.

Now that Christopher had leaned forward he could just make out the room through the curtain. From what he could see it was a large, very brightly lit chapel. On either side were wooden benches that looked far more inviting than his. On some, nuns were sitting, facing off towards the furthest point of the room. There he could make out an altar, raised on a stone dais and draped with a simple white covering.

The servant moved off to his right along one of the benches, before disappearing out of sight. A few moments later, he reappeared, scurrying towards the hallway.

Behind him, a knight strode into view. He was smaller than the knights Christopher had seen at the entrance, but in all other ways just as imposing. He had a slim, sinewy body robed entirely in a chain mail tunic that ended at his knees. It jangled as he strode forward. Over the chain-mail, he wore a plain white tabard. He wore dark brown trousers that ended in simple boots. On his hands, he wore light padded gloves. One hand rested on the hilt of a sword that swung from a scabbard in his belt. Most imposing of all, his head was completely hidden by a helmet, its visor pulled down.

They reached the end of the benches. The knight pushed past the servant. He quickly outpaced him, marching straight toward Christopher. As he grew nearer, Christopher edged back on the bench. The knight pulled out his sword with a smooth movement of his arm, dropping the point to sway menacingly just above the floor.

Behind the knight and servant two nuns appeared from the chapel. Christopher recognized them both. The older was the abbess he had seen at the gate earlier. Behind her was Guinevere.

She moved with such grace that Christopher found himself unable to stop staring. He was still doing so when he realised that the knight was almost upon him.

'You searched him?' the knight said, muffled beneath his helmet.

'I've only got a log!' the servant with the log replied.

The knight moved forward and grabbed Christopher by his clothes, dragging him up. He slammed him against the wall and lifted the sword to his neck. 'You move, you die. God's house or not.' His voice sounded young.

'No!' The abbess's voice echoed down the corridor.

'Search him,' the knight barked. The servant showed no hesitation now, dropping the log and moving in quickly. He patted Christopher's body, feeling at his pockets and turning them out.

'I'm not dangerous,' Christopher gasped out, pressing his head back against the wall, away from the cold metal blade against his throat.

'Don't speak.' The knight tightened his grip.

The servant continued to search through Christopher's clothes as Guinevere and the abbess reached them. 'Stop!' the abbess cried, wringing her hands. 'We are in a house of God!'

The servant glanced up at the knight. 'Nothing.'

'I will not say again.' The abbess's voice broke with anger. 'In the name of God ...'

Guinevere put her hand on the abbess's arm, cutting her off. Then she walked slowly forward and placed her hand on the edge of the blade by Christopher's throat.

She glanced at the knight. 'Wolf, step back. There is nothing to fear here,' she said.

'My lady, your safety ...'

'Has been well protected, as always,' Guinevere finished. She looked down at the servant and smiled. 'Step back.'

The servant bowed his head and complied immediately. He backed away to join the others by the abbess.

The knight lowered his sword. 'Well, he appears to be harmless,' he said almost petulantly.

Christopher lifted his hand and rubbed at his neck where the sword had been a moment before. 'I said I didn't mean any harm.'

'I decide that,' the knight said, a note of recrimination coming out with the muffled voice.

'I thank you for keeping us safe, Wolf,' Guinevere said, looking at the knight calmly. After a moment, he bent his head and stepped back. Guinevere turned to Christopher and her lips lifted into a small smile. 'Now child, what brings you here in such strange clothes?'

Christopher gazed up into her grey eyes and at once felt calm. Around her eyes, tiny creases from a lifetime of emotion crinkled into a smile that seemed at once friendly and a little sad. She looked no more than forty years old, but something about her seemed wise beyond those years. Around her face, the flecks of white hair he had seen from a distance seemed more pronounced.

Christopher had been hearing stories about Guinevere since as far back as he could remember. Married to King Arthur when she was barely older than a girl, she'd been thrust into the court of Camelot. She had finished growing up in the gaze of hundreds of her subjects, some friends, some with darker designs from the very first. No wonder she had fallen into trouble.

And now she was right in front of him. Whether this was real, a dream, or something worse he wasn't prepared to consider yet. For the moment, he only drank in the calmness she cast out. She met his gaze, quietly waiting for an answer.

'Are you really Queen Guinevere?' Christopher asked, with a breaking voice. 'Is this real?'

Guinevere laughed. Though the sound was warm, there was sadness at its edges. 'I often wish it wasn't, but yes, this is real,' she said. She sat on the bench and looked up at him. Then she patted the place next to her. 'I'm just Sister Gwen now. What's your name?'

'Christopher,' he said, sitting down next to her.

'Well, Christopher,' Guinevere said, a slight smile on her lips. 'Why don't you tell me why you're here?'

He paused for a moment, feeling the day's events bursting to get out of him. Then, because her face was so inviting and because he really couldn't hold them any more, he began to talk.

At first, he tried to keep things to what had happened to him since he had woken. As he talked, Guinevere seemed truly interested. The emotions in Guinevere's face were plain; changing as he told her more. She shuddered when he told her of the creature that had chased him on the stone stairs outside.

Soon, because she was so easy to talk to and without actually realising that he was doing it, Christopher began to tell her more. He told her about the war and his brother and how he had come to be home. He told her about Bailey and the gypsies. He told her about how they had chased him and how they trapped him on the little island of grass. Then he told her about how he had awoken and discovered that he wasn't in his own home any more.

Even though it felt so good to be telling her, Christopher was not so enamoured that he forgot himself entirely. He was careful to leave out some of the details. It seemed easier to say that his home was in a different land. He blurred over Winter's Grasp, its powers and the stories about where it had come from and just described it as a valuable artefact. He left out some of the finer details about the gypsies and a lot of the details about Molly Brodie.

'You poor thing. You have had an adventure, haven't you?' Guinevere smiled down at him when he ran out of steam. 'But so much of your story leaves me intrigued, I don't know where to start.' She paused a moment.

The knight Guinevere called Wolf had been pacing back and forth as Christopher talked, his expression a mystery behind the helmet. Now he stopped and walked quietly over. 'And the message?'

Christopher looked up, frowning.

'The message you said you had from Galind,' the knight expanded.

'I don't have one,' Christopher admitted quietly. 'That was to get in to shelter.'

'I thought as much! My lady, he should be thrown out where he came from.'

'The gauntlet,' Guinevere lifted a hand to silence Wolf without looking at him. 'It's caused you so much trouble, but where is it now?'

'I don't know.' Christopher glanced at the knight, sheepish. For the moment at least he was waiting. 'I haven't seen it since I woke up. I looked for it, but I couldn't find it.'

Behind the knight, the abbess spoke. 'Sister, that is enough.' She snorted. 'We won't entertain these fantasies any more. Especially not when we know what's happening in the world. The boy shall be shown to a bed in one of the outhouses, of course, and we'll feed him. In the morning, he'll go on his way and we will spend the day praying together for peace both here and abroad.'

Guinevere lay a hand on Christopher's knee protectively and glanced at the elder woman. 'Mother, you've shown so much patience today. It will be but a moment more and we'll see the boy housed.'

The abbess went to speak, but closed her mouth and folded her arms instead. Though she might claim to be a simple sister at the abbey now, Christopher could see Guinevere was still a good deal more.

'My lady, this is foolish! He is an urchin in clothes he stole from a merchant from the East,' the knight suddenly burst out. 'He's no more from another country than I am! We should throw him out of the front gate and send him on his way.'

Guinevere looked at the knight, her face sharp. 'Foolish, Wolf?'

The knight was unable to meet her gaze for more than a second. He hung his head. 'I'm sorry, my lady.'

'Sister Gwen,' she corrected. 'Now go and tell Sister Catherine to make up a bed.'

The knight backed away. He turned and disappeared through a small door in the wall a few benches down.

Guinevere turned to Christopher. 'There is more to you than you are saying, isn't there? I don't know how, but I can feel it. It is a most strange feeling.' Her eyes briefly narrowed in thought. 'Tell me, Christopher. You have nothing to fear.'

Again he felt himself drawn to her. The worries of the day all seemed to be unimportant in the light of her calm gaze. There was something more though, something that made him want to risk telling more.

'It's not what Sama would do!' A little voice in the back of his head told him. 'You don't just go about telling all your secrets. Keep watching. Wait.'

Christopher shook the thought away. There was something else about the woman in front of him, more than the calmness. An echo of something deeper.

Christopher suddenly started. His eyes widened. His mother! That's what it was. Far away, and only the slightest hint, but it was there. Something in Guinevere's eyes had reminded him of his mother. No, reminded was the wrong word. It was far more literal than that. How could he have not noticed it before?

He frowned. Was it because it wasn't there before? Suddenly Christopher had the vaguest sense of things somehow shifting around him. He swayed back slightly, glad to be sitting on the cold bench again.

'Christopher, are you all right?' Guinevere reached forward and touched his face, all the while looking down with those calm eyes.

Suddenly from the courtyard outside there were shouts. A moment later there was a loud clatter of hooves on stone.

'What now!' the abbess exclaimed. She motioned the servants to the door. The servant nearest the door pulled it ajar and looked out. 'It's Sir Galind and the others,' he called over his shoulder. 'They've got someone with them.'

He opened the door wider and leaned further out. Suddenly he turned back and stared white-faced at the abbess. 'A knight, Mother Abbess. He looks badly hurt.'

Guinevere stood up and turned away. At her movement, the echoes Christopher had had were gone. The woman was once herself and no more. He let out a breath, suddenly aware he had been holding it. Sweat ran down his body under his clothes.

Wolf reappeared from the side door, alerted by the commotion, and jogged back to where they were. The abbess crossed to the main door. Guinevere stood and walked over to her.

For a moment, Christopher thought that he was forgotten. He stood and made to follow Guinevere towards the door, a myriad of questions blossoming in his mind. Wolf coughed pointedly and lifted his sword to point the tip at him, shaking his helmeted head slowly. Christopher quickly sat down.

'Bring him here,' the abbess called to the men outside. A cold breeze blew through the open door, making the hairs on the back of Christopher's arm stand up.

Guinevere reached the door and stepped outside. 'Oh my!' She turned and touched the servant on the arm. 'Go now and fetch clean linen, blankets.'

'And bring Sister Kyla,' the abbess added. 'Tell her to bring her healing balms.'

The servant nodded and scurried away. Christopher barely had a chance to glance after him before the door filled with knights. Sir Galind and his companions staggered through with an awkward shuffle, supporting another knight, half conscious, between them.

The knight had a deep gash on his head. It bled heavily into long auburn hair that hung lank and unkempt to his shoulders. Another wound somewhere under his breastplate had caused more blood to run down the cuisse plates on his thighs. They reflected through the blood in the torchlight like dull rubies.

'Galind, put him here.' Guinevere indicated the next bench down from Christopher. 'Help is coming.'

At her voice, the wounded knight stirred. 'My Queen? Is that you?' he said in a confused voice. He opened bloodshot eyes and tried to focus on the sound of the voice.

'Claris?' Guinevere's hand shot up to cover her mouth. 'Claris! Why are you not with Arthur?'

They set Claris down on the bench. Galind knelt and began to loosen his armour straps. The wounded knight struggled to raise his head in Guinevere's direction. Then he groaned with the effort and his head fell back.

'He was lashed to his horse.' Galind was still trying to free the armour straps. 'It was pretty crude. It looked like he had done it himself, to stay on.'

Guinevere went closer, her eyes full of tears. 'Is he very badly hurt?'

'We'll know soon enough.' Galind did not look hopeful.

Claris opened his eyes again and looked at Guinevere. 'I found you,' he muttered, his voice mixed relief with pain. He gripped Galind's arm. 'Help me up.'

Galind shook his head. 'Hold still, Claris. Wait until we have looked at your wounds.'

Claris pulled himself forward. 'Don't waste time. They are mortal.' His sentences came in short gasps. 'Help me up.' He fixed Galind with a stare that for the first time since he had come in seemed focused. Galind sighed and put an arm around the wounded man, then pulled him into a sitting position. Claris grunted with the pain.

The abbess dropped down to her knees on his other side, gripping his shoulder and supporting him until the pain passed, muttering a prayer under her breath.

Once the worst of it seemed to subside, Claris looked at Guinevere again. The shock of the pain had made him more alert. 'My Queen, King Arthur sent me. We have lost the war. Mordred is victorious. He is coming this way. We haven't much time.'

Galind gasped. The other knights looked shocked. Wolf stepped closer to the wounded knight, the news making him forget Christopher.

Guinevere lifted a hand, suddenly swaying on her feet. For a moment, it looked as if she might fall, but she steadied herself and looked back down at the wounded knight through tear-filled eyes. 'Where is my husband?'

'I left him with Bediviere,' Claris gasped. 'My Queen, he was severely wounded. Far worse than I. He knew he was dying.'

'No,' the Queen said quietly, turning her head from all of them.

'My Queen, he wanted me to tell you something,' Claris started again with effort.

Guinevere lifted a hand to stop his words. She walked unsteadily to the far wall and leaned against it. For a second, the only noise in the hall was the sound of Claris's laboured breathing. Then Guinevere let out a sob.

It began almost imperceptibly, just a whimper, but once she had let herself go it continued, growing louder until it became a wail, then a scream that echoed through the hall. She lifted her other hand, leaning against the wall as if to ground herself against the force of her grief. The scream went on, a high, tremulous note of pain that only began to crack and break as her breath began to run out. Finally, with no more air in her lungs to use, Guinevere collapsed to the hard rock floor and wrapped her hands over her head, shuddering as she sobbed.

Wolf ran over and then stopped at her side. His shoulders slumped. There was not anything he could do to protect the Queen from this pain. The others seemed too stunned to do anything. No one in the hall moved, silently watching the woman and her grief.

As the minutes ticked by her sobs lessened. The shuddering of her shoulders grew steadily smaller. She closed one hand into a fist. Christopher could see the flesh around her fingertips grow white as she squeezed her hand together. With a shudder she lifted her head.

Wolf bent to the floor and put his arms around her. She grasped him like a woman who had been floating in the sea for hours.

'Let me help you, my Queen,' the knight said too gruffly, as if hiding his lack of experience in such matters.

Christopher looked around. No one else seemed to be going to help. He clambered up, waiting for a voice telling him to stop. When there was none, he bolted forward and grasped the Queen at her other side. Wolf turned his head quickly to face Christopher, but he made no move to attack. 'On three,' he said instead.

Wolf counted in tight, clipped words. Together they raised the Queen back on to her feet. She was so slight.

She lifted her face to look at Christopher. Her eyes were deep and black now, framed with tear-reddened skin. 'Thank you,' she whispered. Then glanced around. The others waited.

She took a long breath that went in shudders and then straightened herself. 'Let me stand, Wolf. I will be able,' she said, her voice unsteady.

Wolf hesitated, but she stepped forward out of their hands anyway and stood on her own feet. She faltered back towards the stricken knight and the others.

Claris was slipping in and out of consciousness. Guinevere bent to him and touched him on his shoulder. He gasped and opened his eyes again. 'The sword, my Queen!' he exclaimed, as though the conversation hadn't had a break.

'My God!' Galind started. 'Excalibur! Mordred has the King's sword!'

Christopher frowned. That could not be right, could it? He knew the stories of King Arthur so well. What happened to Excalibur was one of the most famous of all of them. He frowned. 'No! Bediviere saved it!' He had said it out loud before he realised what he was doing. 'Arthur killed Mordred and Bediviere saved the sword.'

'Be quiet, boy,' Galind barked, looking over. 'We've no time for prattle.'

Claris looked over with wide eyes. 'How did you know Bediviere took the sword? Have you come from the battle?'

Suddenly Galind drew his sword and swung around to Christopher. Two of his knights, their training spurring them to action, took up positions at either side.

'Have you, boy?' Galind said.

'No!' Christopher quavered, wishing he had kept his mouth shut. This wasn't going at all well. 'I came from the beach.'

Before the others could move, Guinevere's voice rang out. 'Wait!'

At her word, Galind stopped and glanced back at her. 'Your Highness?'

'Sister Gwen,' she corrected in a sad voice. 'Let the boy speak, Galind. Without the threat of violence to temper his words.'

Galind nodded and held back. Behind him the other knights edged backwards, though not so far that they couldn't reach him within a couple of bounds, Christopher noted.

Guinevere looked at him. 'Speak, child,' she said. Her eyes were red and wet with tears. 'What do you mean, Christopher?'

All eyes were on him, waiting. His heart beat hard in his chest. There was nothing for it now. He took a deep breath and began. 'By the end of the battle King Arthur was mortally wounded. He rested close by a lake with his last knights. He gave Bediviere Excalibur and told Bediviere to take it to the edge of the lake and to throw it in. Bediviere agreed and took the sword, but when he reached the lake he couldn't do it. He hid the sword in the rushes, then came back and said he had.'

Claris coughed. 'Mordred didn't die. He rides this way. But of the sword, the boy speaks the truth of it.'

From the main door to the hall an older nun appeared, laden with a leather roll that bulged with bottles of medicine. She hurried over to where Claris lay and knelt by his side. She unstopped a small bottle and poured some of its contents on to a white cloth.

'Go on, Christopher,' Guinevere said.

'Arthur asked Bediviere what happened when he threw the sword in. Bediviere said nothing had happened. Arthur knew he was lying. He told him to return to the lake and do as he had promised. Again Bediviere did the same thing. When he came back, Arthur still knew he'd lied.' Christopher continued, his mind going over the legend. His mother had written a story about it; 'In the End a Beginning', and he had read it a score of times.

'The third time Bediviere threw the sword in,' he continued. 'The Lady of the Lake appeared. She caught the sword before it even hit the water. Then she left to take it back to Avalon, where it would be safe until it was needed again.'

'Bediviere said he threw in the sword!' Claris said, with his voice awed. 'He said that from the water a beautiful woman appeared. She caught the sword and then disappeared into the lake. It was only when he told Arthur what had happened, that the King told me I should come to you.'

Claris tried to stand, pushing back the abbess and sister from him. 'Who is this boy? How does he know this?' He reached his feet, going whiter and wincing with the effort. 'None but I and Bediviere were there. I had the fastest horse. No one left the field before us. No one could have reached here.' He stepped forward then clutched his side, gasping in pain. Galind jumped up and grabbed him. Claris face was screwed tight as he rode the wave of agony. He sank backwards into Galind's arms.

Christopher edged back on his seat. They were all looking at him now. The knights' faces were suspicious. Galind's was openly hostile. The nuns didn't look much more sympathetic. Only Guinevere's sad face looked at him gently. Wolf remained inscrutable under his helmet.

'How do you know this, boy?' Galind growled.

Christopher glanced from him to the Queen. She smiled at him through her sadness and nodded. 'Speak, Christopher.'

They were already wary of him. He had told Guinevere most of it anyway. What more was there to lose? They waited. The only sound was that of Claris's laboured breathing.

'I read it,' Christopher said.

'Read it?' Galind scoffed. 'Ridiculous.' He turned to Guinevere. 'This boy could be a spy.'

'No Galind,' Guinevere said quickly. 'There is more to this.'

'Where I come from,' Christopher interrupted, 'stories of King Arthur are famous. They have all been written down many times. All his life and his death.'

'The stories are famous everywhere, boy,' Galind said. 'You're lying.'

'I'm not!' Christopher looked at the Queen again. Her smile had slipped into a frown.

'So you know our future,' Wolf said from behind his helmet. 'Yet you got it wrong that Mordred was dead.'

Mordred still alive? Christopher frowned, considering that again. Arthur and Mordred mortally wounded one another at the end of the final battle. This wasn't right. He stopped himself, but then what was right? 'I did,' he said. 'I don't know why.'

Claris gasped suddenly. 'Guinevere, I have no time.' His words were coming with great effort now. 'Arthur said Mordred would come for the other sword. He said you must save it.'

Guinevere looked from Claris to Christopher and back. Then she nodded. 'Christopher, we will speak more of this, but Claris is right.'

'My husband meant the Sword in the Stone,' Guinevere continued. 'It has been here, in my keeping. If Mordred has victory, he will come for it. If he holds that it will legitimise his claim as much as Excalibur would have.'

'Claris,' she continued. 'How far away is he?'

The knight shook his head, barely able to continue. His words came between gasps now. 'I don't know. They caught me … Beyond the field … Did this. The ride was … Confusing. Wasn't always conscious.' He frowned. 'Little more than an hour.'

Guinevere sighed and reached under her garments. From around her neck she pulled out a small key. Then drew herself up and looked at the people around her. 'Then the war isn't over and we still have much to lose. We'll mourn the King and the others when the time is right.'

'Wolf,' she continued, glancing at her knight. 'Take Galind and go to the stores. Behind the grain, at the back corner you will find a loose stone. Move it out and use this to unlock the front of the box you'll find fixed inside.' She threw the key across to the knight, who caught it deftly. 'In the box you will find the sword. Bring it here.'

Wolf led Galind off down the corridor at a run. Guinevere watched them go silently then turned back to where the abbess and the nun were now trying to patch Claris's broken body.

'Arthur told me once of what should be done with Excalibur,' Guinevere said quietly. 'He said he had told no one else, and he had been told alone by Merlin, when the old man was still with us.'

She turned back to Christopher. 'You could not have known. Not by mundane means.' She fixed him with her gaze again. 'You are not a spy from Mordred are you? This is something else.'

Christopher hesitated. Had the woman seen what he had seen? How could there be a bond? Things were moving so fast. He needed to sit and gather his thoughts, work out what was happening. He'd come here to find his way home and instead he felt further away than ever. 'I'm not a spy. I'm lost and I want to go home.'

From outside there came a shout. 'Torches in the distance!'

The abbess rushed over to the door and glanced out again. 'They are coming. You will need to go quickly.'

The Queen nodded. She looked away from Christopher reluctantly. 'Very well. How quickly before you can get the sisters ready to move?'

The abbess smiled. 'If Mordred finds an empty abbey, how long do you think he will wait before looking for you? We must stay here.'

'Mother, no!' Guinevere's voice shook. 'You don't know what he will do.'

'I will put my faith in God,' the abbess replied evenly. 'We can at least waste his time in looking for you here. What you have brought here is more important than us.'

'I have brought misery here.' Guinevere's voice quavered again. She looked at her feet. A large tear dropped, making little splash marks on the stone floor. 'I always bring misery in the end.'

'This is hardly the end,' the abbess said.

Beside her Claris groaned, his voice tiny and far away. The abbess reached down. He looked up, gasped and his body stiffened. Then he relaxed. The breath escaped his lungs in a slow broken hiss. The older nun who had been tending him shook her head.

'May your soul rest in peace,' the abbess said quietly.

At the end of the corridor, Galind and Wolf reappeared. Wolf carried a long shape wrapped tightly in cloth which was tied with string. They ran down the hall to stop at the Queen.

'Did you hear the call?' Galind said, breathless. 'Lights beyond. They are closer than we thought. We have far less than an hour.'

The Queen nodded. 'That will not be enough time. If we go together, he will catch us.' She looked around. 'Claris's sword. Where is it?'

One of the knights who had appeared with Galind stepped forward. 'I have it here, my Queen.'

'Bring it to me.' Guinevere motioned, 'Wolf, bring that one too.'

The two men moved to the Queen. She took the bundle from Wolf and gently unwrapped it. Inside, a plain, sturdy sword handle stuck out of an ornate scabbard, encrusted with red rubies and gold inlay. The handle looked quite out of place with the scabbard.

Guinevere lifted the scabbard and unsheathed the sword, passing it back to Wolf. The knight took it carefully, cradling it like it was a living thing.

'Galind,' Guinevere said. 'I must ask you to do a difficult task.'

She reached across to the other knight and took Claris's sword, unsheathing it from its scabbard, which she dropped to the floor. 'If we run with the Sword, Mordred will hunt us down and catch us. If he thinks he already has it, we may have time to get it away.'

Guinevere slid Claris's sword into the ornate scabbard and looked down at her handiwork. 'Galind, I need you to take this sword and scabbard. I need you to draw attention away from us and …' Her voice caught. She looked up and stretched the sword and scabbard towards him. 'I need you to be taken with it. With any luck, it will buy us enough time to escape from here.'

Galind barely hesitated. For the briefest of moments a frown of fear passed across his face. Then he looked up at her, his expression tight with control. 'By your word, my Queen.'

He turned to his companions. 'Get supplied. Make it look like we are planning to be on the road for a long time.'

The knights made their way to the door and out into the courtyard beyond. The servants followed. Galind turned back to Guinevere.

'I am so sorry,' she said to him before he could speak.

Galind shook his head. 'God speed to you, my Queen. I am happy to have such an important task to do for you.' He hesitated, then continued. 'Should you see her again, remember me to my wife.'

Guinevere walked forward and hugged the knight. 'I will be glad to.'

Galind closed his eyes, relishing the embrace for a moment. Then he freed himself from her arms and bowed. Without another word, he turned and followed after his men.

'Wolf,' Guinevere said. 'To me.'

Wolf looked at her, ready for orders. He still clutched the sword to his chest reverently.

'You and I shall take the sword and head to the North,' Guinevere continued. 'Quickly, now. We must prepare. We shall go to the village of Bedwell. There are friends there prepared for this. Then we will go our separate ways. I will use our friends to get to a ship and you will take the sword on.'

'No!' Wolf objected, the young voice from inside the helmet sounding suddenly panicked. 'I will stay to protect you.'

'You will do as I command,' Guinevere replied. 'There are many things people will rally around. We cannot not risk two staying together. You'll take the sword to Sir Kay's castle. If he has survived, that is where he will return. If not, it is still where people will gather. He is the rightful heir to the throne. It is the right place to make a stand.'

'The people will rally to you!' Wolf retorted. 'Your safety is paramount.'

'I am a little too blemished to be the best symbol, Wolf.' She smiled thinly. 'If I were not I would hardly be here in the first place, would I? Besides, once I am at sea there will be far more I can do. I will find Lancelot and return with him. Without him and his men, we are lost, no matter who or what we rally around.'

Wolf seemed for a moment like he was about to argue, but instead stayed silent.

Guinevere turned to look at Christopher. 'Will you come with us, Christopher? If you are looking for answers you should go to Kay, too. It is the only haven we will have.'

'Him!' Wolf exclaimed, through his helmet. 'My Queen, we don't know him. He could be a danger to us all. This whole plan is madness.'

'Quickly, Wolf, my mind is made up.' She walked over to the abbess and held her tight in a hug.

Wolf nodded reluctantly and strode over to Christopher. He grabbed Christopher roughly by the arm. 'Just so as we are clear, boy. I don't think you are special, or possessed of anything other than strange clothes and a whining manner. I think you are a liability and I will be watching you wherever we go. Remember that.'

'I didn't say I was coming,' Christopher said, suddenly annoyed at Wolf's gruff way.

The knight's grip tightened painfully on his arm. Christopher nodded vigorously. 'Okay!' He gulped. 'I will.'

The knight looked at him a moment longer, then shook his head and began to pull him along the corridor in the direction of the abbey hall.

The Queen caught up with them as they reached the far end of the abbey. Wolf pulled open a side door that led into a small vestry, with another door on the far wall. As they crossed the vestry, Guinevere touched Wolf's hand where he had a firm grip of Christopher. Reluctantly the knight let go. He opened the door in the wall and looked out.

As Wolf checked outside to make sure the path was clear, Christopher rubbed at his arm, smoothing away the pain from the knight's grip. Wolf glanced back at them and nodded, then walked out into the dark. Guinevere placed a far more gentle hand on Christopher's shoulder and guided him outside.

Her face was lost deep in thought. Her eyes were wet with tears once more. Christopher glanced away quickly, leaving her to her private grief.

There was a smaller gate at the far end of the outer wall. There, two stable hands had prepared a horse and cart. They were packing supplies and blankets into the back. It looked soft and inviting. Another horse was tethered to the back of the cart.

Wolf turned back and stretched out a hand to Guinevere to help her into the cart. She shook her head.

'No, I will take the reins,' the Queen said. 'You will do better on horseback should we find trouble on our way.'

Wolf nodded walked to the front, again stretching out his hand. This time Guinevere took it and allowed him to help her up on to the seat. Satisfied she was settled, he turned back to Christopher. 'You are going in the back,' he commanded. 'There are clothes in there that will make you less conspicuous. Wear them. You'll not bring any attention to us.'

He lifted Christopher into the back of the cart, giving him a push that sent him down on to a furry blanket with a bump. Christopher whipped his head around to stare angrily at the knight. He had already turned away. In his hands was a cloak he must have taken from the cart. He swung it up over his shoulders, covering his chain mail.

There were stables on the right. The knight strode over to them and entered. He re-emerged a few seconds later on another, already saddled horse. He pulled the hood up over his head, hiding the helmet under its folds. That done, he rode around to the front of the cart.

'We will need to move fast for a while. We should get to the edge of the coast by daybreak,' he said to Guinevere.

They set off down a track that stretched away from the abbey, following the side of the cliff before descending inland. The pace was indeed fast and the way steep. For a good forty minutes, Christopher found himself clutching at the sides of the cart to avoid being thrown all over the place. Trying to change into the pile of clothes on the floor of the cart at this speed would be impossible.

Eventually, it felt like they had reached level ground. Wolf spurred his horse to an even faster pace and the Queen pushed the cart horse to keep up. Christopher climbed forward now the going was less bumpy, and climbed out on to the seat next to Guinevere.

She glanced at him quickly, then put her concentration back on the road. 'Christopher, go back. You must change as Wolf asked. Your clothing will attract more attention.'

Christopher sighed. He had so much he wanted to ask, but it was obvious the Queen had to give the cart her full attention. He returned and scrabbled around for the clothes.

He found them at the back of the cart. He pulled off his own jacket, woolly jumper, and under-shirt and tried to put on whatever the clothing in front of him was. After a couple of tries in the dark, he realised that it was going to be impossible without a little light. He opened the rear flap of the cart and looked down. A simple, long sleeved woollen shirt, possibly grey, was in his hands. At least with a little extra light, Christopher was able to work out which hole was which. With a little more struggling, he was able to get the garment over his head.

When he had finished, he glanced out of the back of the cart. In the distance high in the night sky, he could see an intense orange glow, pinpointed against the black horizon.

'I think I can see them,' he called to the Queen. 'I can see the glow of their torches.'

'No, Christopher.' Her voice was strangely flat. 'You would not see torch glow from here.'

Christopher frowned. The glow reached high into the sky, far too bright to be just torches. Suddenly his heart sank. He shuddered. Guinevere was right.

That wasn't torch glow at all. They were burning the abbey.

CHAPTER FIFTEEN

The Cost of the Chase

Sama edged up the last few feet of the slope under the trees on her belly. Her britches were already cold and wet from the ground. Two hundred feet or so to the west the Pickering Tower rose dark into the night sky.

Sama had decided that the best way to reach the gypsy camp undetected was the route that they had returned along the previous night. She peeped over the top of the thick tufts of grass at the edge of the trees. The five caravans still there stood in a rough circle.

'Good,' Sama whispered to herself firmly. It didn't sound quite as convincing as she had intended. A part of her hoped that the caravans would be gone. Now she had no excuse to return to the safety of the Stumblepot.

This time there were no fires in the camp. There was no sign of movement, either. The caravans were just dull, still blocks vaguely picked out against the black beyond by the scant light of a cloud-diffused moon.

There was no light in the caravans themselves, either. There were little windows at their fronts. Sama had noticed them the previous night. Now there was no way to tell the difference between the painted wood of the caravan and the glass of their windows.

Perhaps the camp was deserted. That would be good. Sama could sneak across, give it a once over for clues, and work out what to do from there. Maybe go back to the pub and get Jim.

She had wondered on her climb through the woods whether that would have perhaps been the best idea in the first place. The trees had snagged at her clothes. More than once, when she had to double back because her way was blocked by dense undergrowth, she'd thought about whether she would be better with company. If the gypsies had Christopher, then breaking into their camp meant she could well end up a prisoner herself.

She frowned. If the gypsies were not in their camp, where could they be? On and off throughout her journey here, she had felt that prick of hairs on the back of her neck. Each time it felt like someone was watching her. Yet, as before, when she looked she found no one. She had not seen another soul since Joe and his girl.

Sama lay still for a moment and concentrated on her instincts. Yes, the nagging feeling that there was someone watching her was still there. Perhaps they were back down in the woods. She listened carefully, but all she could hear was the sound of the leaves rustling in the wind. Under that was just silence.

Perhaps the gypsies weren't in the camp because they had been down in the village. What could she do if they had been following her since she left the pub? What if this was all some elaborate trap?

Sama frowned at herself. It wasn't likely. How would they know where she was going, anyway? And wouldn't they leave someone to look after the camp? If they hadn't then they weren't very clever, that was for sure! You didn't leave your castle unguarded. Christopher had told her that one day, using his toy soldiers to demonstrate an assault on a castle from a book he had been reading. She had laughed at him at the time, telling him that he was too old for soldiers now, but she remembered what he had said.

Either way, this wasn't the place she needed to be. If they were in the woods behind her, she would do far better in the open where she could see them arriving. Here they could sneak up on her. Anyway she had to go and check out that camp.

Sama peeked her head over the tufts again. She watched for a moment and then dragged herself forwards. Now her head and shoulders were clear of the trees and she was able to rest on her elbows to get a more assured look. Still there was no movement. A few dull shapes lay by the caravans. She could make out a small heap, perhaps two or three sacks, in the vague shadows of the nearest caravan.

She gritted her teeth and clambered to her feet, crouching just in front of the trees. Then, quick and quiet as a cat, she ran to behind the first caravan. She dropped down in a patch of longer grass poking through the snow by one of the wheels.

Sama decided that the long way around the back of the caravan would be safest getting into the camp. The short way was past the caravan entrance and that didn't seem wise. Sama stalked around the back of the caravan.

Her foot narrowly missed colliding with a metal bucket lying on its side. It lay just below a hook on the back of the caravan from where it should probably be hanging. Her heart missed a beat as she thought of the noise had she kicked it. Resolving to be more careful, she continued to the inner corner of the gypsy caravan. There she dropped back down to her fours, crawling toward the pile of sacks ahead.

Sama realised she was now within the circle of the caravans. Here the moon shadows seemed longer and more pronounced. She glanced at the caravan next to her and a shudder went through her. Up close, she could see the paintings she had seen the previous night weren't paintings at all. They were carvings. The whole side of the caravan was a relief of animals staring down at her. Sama shuddered again. As she moved, their eyes seemed to follow her, silently marking her progress with cold detachment. They looked like they could suddenly leap from their wooden confines and attack, taking great lumps out of her with sharp wooden teeth.

Suddenly from the corner of her eye, something moved. It was out by the edge of the trees where she had sneaked on to the open ground.

There it was again. This time she was watching the exact spot. Something lifted a head and glanced into the camp. It was hard to make out from her current position, but it was definitely there.

She was right. The gypsies had been down in the village, following her all the time. Panic rose in her heart. Which way to go? They could be dotted all around the edge of the field. Whichever way she ran they could be there. Now they had seen her enter their camp they knew she meant them no good.

She scrambled forwards to the bundle of sacks. It was the best hope of cover she had. Perhaps it would give her a place to hide whilst she stole a better look and worked out an escape plan. If they were spread out, at least she would only have to get past one or two. It would pay to see what she could see before she ran blind scared.

The movements stopped. Sama rested an arm on the nearest part of the bundle to look over it.

The bundle moved!

Sama froze, then the smallest moment later looked down. Below her the face of a gypsy looked up into the night sky, its eyes closed, so close that she could feel its breath on her. Sama edged back with horror.

They had called it a gypsy, but immediately Sama understood the only similarity between the horror below her and a real gypsy was the clothing. Its face was ashen grey and twisted. Lines criss-crossed the ghastly skin, so profound at first Sama thought they might be scars. Their pattern told the story of a face that had spent a lifetime in vicious frowns. It was more beast than person. It was covered in light, downy hair that grew thick and black on its eyebrows and chin. On its head, a headscarf partly concealed large hairy ears with low hanging lobes. Each ear was adorned with a dark gold hoop.

The gypsy opened its sallow eyelids. Its eyes were wide and dark, with almost no iris at all. A milky film covered their surface. It was struggling to focus on her. Sama stared down, transfixed with horror.

The creature came to its senses. It thrust a sinewy arm around her and pulled her in tight. It growled, almost as if in pain with the effort. Sama thrashed, struggling to wrench away from the sudden danger. She squealed. The creature's grip slipped a little but held fast enough to keep her trapped.

She caught a stink of dirt and stale sweat, weeks old. She fought to keep from retching, terrified to lose her concentration on escape. The creature howled in a high, mournful voice. It echoed through the camp and into the field beyond.

Sama rolled to her left. The creature clung on, rolling with her until it was on top. She pushed at its body with both hands. They rolled again. She sensed she was on top again, though she was held so tight all she could see was its body.

Suddenly its arm slipped. Sama took her chance. She pulled her head free, gasping for air. They had rolled around to the front of the caravan. Another of the creatures, clothed in tattered rags, staggered on to the first step and stared down at them. Its eyes began to focus on the fight below.

Sama pushed hard against the thing holding her, kicking and punching with all her might. It was no use. The creature still had her. They rolled again. There was an angry scream beyond. The second was fully alert. There was no time.

She was on her back. Suddenly she felt the hard bulge of the screwdrivers in her back pocket. Quick as she could she reached back. She pushed her fingers into the bundle, feeling for the hard wood of a handle.

The creature grew more excited. It shoved its face towards her and snapped at her with sharp inhuman teeth. Sama turned her face away. Its jaw closed on air with a crack. Wet saliva sprayed on to her face. She pushed hard with her arm.

With the other hand, she felt what she was searching for. Her heart leapt with relief. She pulled up and the screwdriver came out in her hand. Without thinking, she stabbed it into the arm of the gypsy-thing holding her. It screeched and its grip loosened. It was enough. Sama twisted and rolled away, springing to her feet.

There were many of them now, appearing from the caravans and rising from the ground. Their movements were still slow and sluggish but were becoming faster as they focused on her.

The creature that had appeared from the first caravan growled and launched itself at her. It stretched long, sharp-nailed fingers towards her. It landed in front of her. Sama threw her arms up. It smashed them out of the way.

Long nails sliced across her cheek. Pain seared into her face, closing one eye. She fell back. Immediately, the creature dived on top of her, a mass of nails and teeth and screeches. Her cheek was wet with blood. The creature reared up, raising an arm to strike again. Sama screamed.

Before it got the chance though, something invisible struck its chest. It flew backwards as a loud bang burst across the field. The other things stopped, briefly distracted by the sound.

Sama took her chance; she launched herself up and sprinted away. She ran the long way across the field, back towards the tower, the image of the other something at the edge where she had entered still in her mind.

Only when she reached the tower did she slow her run for just a moment to look back and see if the gypsies gave pursuit. There was no sign. Sama didn't wait to be sure. She turned straight away and burst into the woods.

Sama ran until she reached the road. She stumbled over exposed roots and low undergrowth, uncaring of the minor injuries when far worse had already seared her soul. Her arm caught on brambles and she fell, tearing her old, favourite jacket. Each time she scrambled up and forced herself on.

She didn't stop once she reached the road. It was only as she rounded the corner by the first large house before Alton and slammed into the vast bulk of Joe Litmus that she stopped. She fell to the ground, panting heavily.

'Sama! There you are.' Jim, next to Joe, was red faced, colour fuelled by beer and anger alike. 'You are for it this time. Chops has got the whole pub out looking for you. You spoiled our bloomin' party!'

They stood with Mike Brophy and Dr Conrad. Both Jim and Mike had bottles of beer in their hands. The doctor carried a small lantern that gleamed and heightened the shadows on their expressions.

'My God, Sama, your cheek!' The anger fell from Jim's face as he saw it.

Sama reached up and felt her cheek. It was slick and wet to the touch. She pulled her hand away. In the night-time light, her fingers were covered with something black. Blood!

Jim bent down next to her. 'Where have you been? What happened?'

Sama struggled for words. Relief at seeing her brother settled heavily on her. She felt her throat constrict with the onset of tears.

Jim lifted her to her feet and bent his head to her level. 'Sama, who did this to you?'

'I went to the gypsy camp to look for Christopher,' Sama began.

Jim lifted himself. 'The gypos? They did this to you?' He turned to the others. 'Bloody gypos! We can't go off and leave them here to do what they want!'

Mike Brophy caught his anger. 'Come on then, Jim! We'll show them they can't attack our folk like this. We'll show them!'

Jim let Sama go and turned to Dr Conrad. 'Will you take my sister back to the Stumblepot? Tell the others we've gone to Pickering Tower to deal with these gypsies.'

'Will you not wait, Jim?' The doctor frowned. 'I can get the others along in a minute. Look what they did to your sister.'

'Exactly! Who knows what else they're up to!' He slurred his words a bit. 'The others can catch us up.' He turned back to Sama. 'Go back with the doctor, Sama. Go back to Dad.'

'Jim, wait!' Sama cried, but he had already taken a few steps away from her.

Jim looked back at Mike and Joe. 'You coming?'

Mike nodded, glancing around for a weapon. 'Course we are, Jim. You can count on us.' He strode over to the gate and pulled hard at a piece of fencing next to it. In a moment, it came off in his hands. He threw it to Jim and pulled off another.

'Jim, don't!' Sama pleaded. 'They're not human!'

Mike Brophy laughed. 'Don't you worry, Sama. They just gave you a fright. They'll drop just like anyone else once they've had a bit of punishment.' To illustrate the point he held his piece of fence like it was a rifle and pretended to fire it.

'Come on, let's go,' Jim said, grim. Without another word, he ran off up the road. Mike nodded and chased after him.

As the road bent out of sight, Mike stopped and turned back. 'Come on, Joe!' he called.

Joe looked to be at a loss. He turned to the doctor. 'You take her back as quick as you can, Doctor. Tell the others to follow us.'

'Joe!' Sama cried desperately at him.

He looked at her and smiled thinly in the darkness. 'Don't worry, Sama. It'll be all right.' With that, he lumbered up the hill after the others.

Dr Conrad stepped over to her and lifted the lantern. 'Hold still, Sama. There's a good girl. Let me take a look at this.'

Sama stood numbly whilst the doctor examined the cuts on her face. Her whole body shook. Fear and exhaustion sent great spasms through her. She struggled to get a breath. The doctor looked into her eyes, worry clearly on his face. 'All right, come on, dear. Let's get you back home.'

He put an arm around her shoulders and began to steer her gently back in the direction of the village. Sama allowed him to pull her along, her steps faltering, and leaned against his reassuring warmth.

'They weren't human, Dr Conrad,' Sama said in a weak voice. She glanced up at him. 'They scared me.'

'Never mind now,' the doctor replied, his voice low and gentle. 'Back to the warmth. That's what you need.'

They reached the next bend. In front of them, the dim glow of the village was starting to show.

Sama struggled to remember what had just happened. In her mind, everything was a mess of claws and teeth and stink. Though their movements had seemed sluggish, certainly not the animal grace that they had shown yesterday, the gypsies had still been deadly and desperate.

Certainly, they would be more than a match for three boys and a couple of fence pieces. She twitched in concern. The lads would not stand a chance against that. She couldn't leave them to rush in without her.

She pulled away from the doctor's arm. 'Wait. I've got to go back.'

The doctor took a step towards her. 'Come on now, Sama. Best thing we can do is get back to the village and send the others to go and join the lads.'

'No! They'll be murdered!'

'As if,' the doctor dismissed, smiling at her in the light of the lantern. 'Three brave British soldiers? Take more than a cowardly group of gypsies to turn them, don't you fear.'

Sama shook her head, stepping away. 'I've got to go back. I'm sorry. Hurry, Doctor. Send the others.'

She turned and broke into a jog. The thought of her brother and her friends taking on those things gave her new stamina. She broke into a run.

'Sama!' the doctor called behind her. 'Come back here!'

The lads had set off at a fast pace, bravado bolstered by alcohol and anger. Sama followed as fast as her tired body would allow. She dodged into the trees and fought her way back up to the Pickering Tower, desperately listening for the sounds of their progress ahead.

When she reached the field again, she spotted them. They were already far across, Jim and Mike at the front with fence pieces held like cudgels. Joe, empty handed, following close behind. There was no way she would reach them before they got to the camp.

Sama picked up her pace and rushed out towards them. She had quite a stitch in her side now. She tried to call out to them, but she didn't have the breath. Her lungs sent sharp pangs of protest.

'You in the camp!' It was Mike's voice, reckless in the distance. 'It's time we had a reckoning here.'

The three figures had slowed to a walk, just outside the camp. Sama felt a blossom of hope. If they stayed where they were and called the gypsies out then she would reach them in time. She would kick up such a fuss that they would have to take her back instead of pressing on.

Then she saw it was no use. The gypsies, still agitated by her earlier invasion, had not retired back to their caravans. They appeared at the sides of the nearest caravan, a heaving mass. It was impossible to distinguish between them.

Mike walked onwards. 'Come on, then! Don't just dawdle by your little wooden boxes! Let's be having you!'

Sama pushed on, more stumble than run now. She was still too far away.

From a few paces behind Mike, Joe called out. 'Mike, wait up. There's something not right. Wait for us!'

Mike changed the grip on his fence piece and raised it higher as if to show his lack of worry. 'Come on, then!' he called.

As if heeding his challenge, the creatures surged forward. Then they were upon him, totally obscuring him from view. He disappeared into the seething, baying horde.

Sama's legs gave way. She fell down hard into the wet, snow-soaked ground. She pulled her head up desperate to see her friends escape.

'Mike!' Joe cried, his voice suddenly reedy and high like she had never heard it before. The huge man lumbered forward.

Part of the mass split off. Three of them hurtled at Jim. He raised his fence piece and met the onslaught with a hard swing. The first dropped. The others leapt over it and closed in.

Sama pushed herself up again and staggered. Her vision was blurring with tears of despair now. She had to keep moving.

Ahead, Joe's massive frame appeared from the mass, dragging Mike back with one hand. In the other, he had managed to pick up the stout piece of wood Mike brought. He swung wildly around with it, keeping the creatures at bay.

'Jim! Jim, what's happening?' Joe shouted, glancing quickly over to where his friend was battling. There was nothing in his voice that reminded Sama of the usual Joe with his quiet good humour. The voice she heard now was disjointed with fear, almost childlike.

Joe threw Mike to the ground behind him and turned back to face the creatures that followed, swinging once again with the fence post. The creatures dodged out of his range. For a moment, they swayed as one, just before him. Joe readied himself for their inevitable attack.

They surged forward at him again. It was so quick.

One of the gypsies, a female, gaunt and sinewy under her light fitting top, burst ahead of the others. She was crouched low, moving on all fours. Seeing her as his first target, Joe swung wide and low with the fence post. At the last moment, she sprang upwards, vaulting the fencepost and gripping on to his shoulder, pulling herself up.

Too late, Joe tried to lift his great hands to ward off the blow, letting go of the fencepost in his horror. The gypsy was already past his guard. She swiped down with sharp nails, passing his face, finding purchase in his neck. Then she vaulted over him, using his shoulder as support and landed heavily on the other side, supporting herself with one sinewy arm.

The other creatures pulled to a halt before the big man, watching. Joe stood for a moment, hands raised to his neck. His head leaned at a strange angle. It was too far over. Sama could hear a wet gurgling coming from his mouth. She reached out, hands clutching towards her friend.

Slowly, ever so slowly, Joe Litmus fell backwards on to the snow and lay still.

The gypsies were moving again, straight over Joe's body towards Mike, who was crawling away. On the other side, Jim had freed himself from the two attacking him. They circled him, toying with him.

There was a movement from the trees to Sama's left. She glanced across. At first, she failed to see what her peripheral vision had noticed.

The only way to describe it was a darkness. It was out from the trees now, a loose mass of impenetrable black, roughly seven feet high and five feet across. In the dim moonlight, it was just possible to make out its edges. They seemed to fade away like the edges of a wispy cloud. Its centre was easier to make out, mainly because its blackness was impossible to see through. The trees at the edge of the field beyond it were hidden. It was barrelling towards the gypsies.

One of the creatures by Jim lunged forward, raking its claws across his stomach. He doubled up, coughing with pain.

As the darkness reached about fifteen feet away, it stopped. At the front of it, there was a sudden bulge. The black around the bulge thinned, becoming almost translucent. There was a shape within it.

A figure appeared. The dark sucked at him as if he was emerging from quicksand. Then it slipped away, letting him free. Sama recognised him immediately.

John Braddock held a pistol in his right hand. Behind Braddock, his wife Makena slipped out through the black. She, too, held a gun, though hers had a longer barrel and seemed to have something sticking out of the top.

197

In her other hand, she held a staff. It caught the moon's weak reflection in its black shiny surface. The blackness held on to the staff for longer than the people. Its trails clung to the length, stretching out like tendrils of glue. Makena wrenched it out with a twist.

It was barely emerged from the mass before the blackness nearest to it was drawn into it. As if it were a drinking straw, the staff sucked the black up into itself. The mass disappeared into the staff so quickly, it was gone before John Braddock raised his pistol to a firing position.

The gypsies nearest to Braddock circled Jim. Jim was on the ground, clutching at his stomach. His head was down and unprotected. One gypsy had his back to the Braddocks, still ducking in and out towards Jim, but yet to go in for the kill. The other, on the far side, looked up at the new threat and roared.

John Braddock fired his pistol. The bullet hit the roaring gypsy in the face, knocking it backwards off its feet.

It never hit the ground.

Sama gasped. As the gypsy's body flew backwards, it burst into thousands of tiny points of bright blue light. Instantly, where the body had been, the cloud of light points flew apart. The gypsy shape disappeared in the vortex of sparks.

One of the lights shot away from the main swirl, flashing across the air. It headed straight towards Sama. She ducked instinctively, but the little light zipped over her head and out into the darkness of the woods beyond. Another few flew past. Then another followed it. Now there were a steady stream of them.

Sama stared at their flight over her head. Despite her anguish, she watched their path, open mouthed. Ahead there were more pistol shots. The stream of light pricks became a torrent. The little lights all flew over her in the same direction, disappearing off into the trees.

Sama looked back to where the Braddocks were. Makena had her gun raised. They had made short work of the gypsies. Only two remained.

One of the two stood over Mike, looking surprised at this sudden turn in fortunes. Makena pointed the pistol at it and fired. She hit it in the stomach. It doubled up and fell to its knees.

It reached forward with its arm, its hand held in a defiant fist. It growled, low and broken with pain. It toppled forward to dissipate into pricks of light before it hit the ground.

For a second, as the pinpricks of light illuminated the ground below them, Sama could see Mike's face. One side was slick with red. His eyes were wide open in horror. Then the lights flew away over her and his expression was lost to the night.

The last gypsy was the female who had leapt at Joe. She backed away from the Braddocks, flicking wary glances at the pistols they held and making little snapping noises that Sama could hear quite distinctly from where she had fallen.

The female looked all around it to search for her own kind, and the truth dawned on her. She lifted her head and howled a long, mournful note into the sky. Then she dropped to her haunches and sprung forwards at the advancing pair.

Both pistols fired. The bullets struck the creature in mid-air. She burst into lights, silhouetting the Braddocks and casting scores of ghosted shadows on to the snow behind them. Then she flew apart as her companions had. The little blue sparks whizzed over Sama's head and were gone.

Ahead Makena was bending down to Mike's body. Sama watched as she lifted the man's head up and poured something into his mouth.

'Hurry,' John Braddock said to his wife. 'The light.'

Makena shook her head. 'Moving too fast. We won't find the source now.' Then she threw a small bottle of something to her husband. John caught in one hand and hurried across to where Jim lay.

Makena moved to Joe. She bent to examine him, still in the dark. Then she raised her head. 'This one is gone.'

The words hit Sama like slaps. She pushed herself up to her feet and began to run once more towards the camp. 'Joe! Oh, Joe!'

John Braddock turned, raising his pistol. Makena lifted her hand. 'John! It's the girl.'

Sama reached the edge of the camp and ran towards Joe. The huge man lay as he had fallen. His head still seemed at a funny angle to his neck. There was a dark pool on the ground around him, almost black against the snow. Was that blood?

Before she could reach him, Makena sprang in front of her. She caught her in her arms. For all her speed, her touch was gentle. She pulled her down to the ground. 'Don't go nearer, sweet. There's nothing you can do.'

Sama looked up at the black woman. 'Is he dead?' she asked in a small voice.

Makena held her tight now. 'I am sorry, Sama.'

Sama screamed. Joe couldn't be dead. Joe was so big and strong. He could lift Jim and Mike at the same time and still be able to walk about. Nothing could kill Joe!

What about Jim and Mike? Sama had been so desperate to check Joe that she hadn't considered the others. A whimper came out of her mouth as she turned to the bodies of the others.

'Calm, Sama. They will be fine.' Makena understood immediately. 'They are just sleeping now. When they wake, they will remember nothing.'

She loosened her grip on Sama. 'I have given them a drink that will make this night a blur and help to dull their pains when they wake.'

Sama looked up at Makena. The older woman smiled back kindly and let her go. Sama sat back on to the cold ground, dumb.

'If you would like, I can give you some too.' Makena lay her hand on Sama's arm. 'Then all the things that you've seen will be dulled. There won't be any nightmares about creatures or fears about what you've seen.' She looked over at Joe. 'There will just be the sadness from losing a friend.'

It was hard to focus on her words with Joe's body just lying there. Nothing that had happened to her compared to the wrenching loss she could feel inside her now. It didn't matter if she was safe or not. Joe, her friend, was gone. Everything else — the gypsies, the blackness that had somehow hidden the Braddocks, the creatures by the edge of the woods — felt lessened.

Sudden understanding pierced her pain. 'It was you!' She snatched her arm away from the Makena's touch. 'You were in the woods. You saved me when I was in here!' Rage boiled inside her. 'Why didn't you help them? Why didn't you save Joe?'

Sama swung a punch at Makena. Before she could connect, strong arms grabbed her from behind. John lifted her from his wife's grasp and pinned her arms by her side. She struggled, kicking back, anger making her desperate to connect with something that would hurt. It was no use.

'Makena, give it to her.' His voice was cold.

Makena pulled the little bottle of liquid she had given Mike from his pocket. She unstopped the cork and lifted the bottle.

'No!' Sama twisted her face away. 'I don't want it! Tell me why!'

Makena grabbed at her face, wrenching it back. Sama kicked out. Makena let go and dodged back out of the way of her legs.

'Why didn't you help?' Sama shouted, kicking out again.

'Calm down,' John Braddock growled in her ear. 'There are things here you can't possibly understand. This will be better for you.'

'No!' Sama didn't want to forget. If she did, she wouldn't remember this or maybe even why she was here. Despite everything, she still hadn't done what she came to. 'I have to find Christopher!'

Makena froze at her words. 'Who is Christopher?'

'Makena, quickly.' John Braddock grabbed at Sama's legs with one hand, trying to pin them too. 'There'll be others on their way.'

'Wait! Sama, tell me who Christopher is.'

'He's my friend and he's gone missing!' Sama could see that the woman was interested. 'He said the gypsies were chasing him, and I have to find him.'

Makena corked the bottle and dropped it into her pocket. 'John, let her down.'

John Braddock held Sama tightly for a moment more. 'Blast!' he swore, then lowered her to the ground. As soon as he released his grip, Sama jumped out of their reach.

'What do you mean, Sama?' There was an edge to Makena's voice now.

'No,' Sama said. 'Why didn't you help them?'

'We didn't want to interfere.' John glanced around the field. Then he shook his head and sighed. 'These creatures were our lead to something else. Now, because of tonight's idiot jaunts, they are gone. So, tell us what you meant. It is important.'

Maybe these people were here for the same reason that she was. Perhaps, they could help. 'I don't want your potion. I don't want to forget.'

Braddock looked at her. His eyes narrowed. He glanced at his wife. Makena nodded slowly at him. Finally, he looked back at Sama. 'Very well. Then you are going to have to trust us.'

'My friend Christopher is missing,' she started. 'I sneaked into his house and his room was all messed up. The door was smashed in. Joe's place was attacked too. Mike said it was the gypsies. So I thought he might be here. That's why I came.'

Makena looked at her husband, an eyebrow raised. John shook his head. 'It's not likely. Check the caravans, in case.'

Makena ran across to the caravans. She jumped up the three steps of the first, disappearing inside. Braddock extended a hand towards Sama.

'You have my word we will not do anything against your will, Sama.' He beckoned her to him. 'Let's go and see if your friend is here.'

The rage had subsided now, just as quickly as it had appeared. Sama felt numb. It was as though she wasn't really here anymore, but rather watching herself through a thick glass window. Dumbly she walked forwards.

'Can't you help Joe?' Sama muttered as they walked on. 'I saw the black cloud you were hidden in. Aren't you magic?'

'It doesn't work that way.' He looked at her with pity. 'Once a person is gone, one cannot bring them back.'

'It's not very good magic then.'

His smile didn't reach his eyes. 'And what do you know of magic, Sama?'

Sama shook her head. Ahead, Makena was entering the third carriage. 'I don't know anything. Christopher is the one to ask about that. He's always reading about it. King Arthur and his knights, that sort of thing.'

'I see,' Braddock said. 'Christopher has a good imagination, then?'

'Yes, he has.' Sama passed Mike, unconscious on the ground. Could they just leave them there? 'His mother was a writer.'

'And when was the last time you saw Christopher?'

Before Sama could answer, Makena gave a shout. She popped her head out of the fourth caravan and beckoned. Braddock grasped Sama's shoulders gently. 'Stay back. Until I see what she's found.'

She watched, disjointed, as Braddock ran over to the caravan. Makena had disappeared inside again. There was a sound of scuffling inside, then Makena appeared with an old man. He leaned heavily on her as she helped him down the steps.

Sama's heart leapt. 'Bailey!'

The old man looked up. His face was gaunt. His eyes darted around. Sama ran towards him. He shrank back, clutching at Makena.

'Bailey! Bailey, where's Christopher?' Sama blurted as she reached them. 'Where is he, Bailey?'

Bailey stared at her as if he didn't know her. Sama went to ask again, but before she could, John Braddock appeared at the top step. In his arms he carried a bundle. From the bottom end of the bundle, two painfully thin legs hung out. Skinny ankles and feet showed bare beneath dirty trousers.

'Christopher!' Sama pushed past Makena and Bailey. She got to John Braddock and reached into the bundle.

'Careful, Sama,' Braddock caught her hand. 'He's fragile.'

He let go. Sama pulled at the cloth around the top of the bundle. Underneath a boy's face looked back. His skin was a milky white as if he hadn't seen the day for a very long time. His eyes had thick black rings underneath them. His lips were parched and dry. His hair was very thin. In fact, in a number of places, large clumps were missing altogether.

Sama frowned. 'That's not Christopher.'

Braddock nodded. 'I thought as much.'

They came down the steps to join the others. The boy shifted, weak in Braddock's arms. The cloth fell open.

Sama gasped. His neck was burned and black. Deep scar tissue ran around his shoulders, down on to his chest. In the centre of his chest, just above the breast bone was a burned imprint of a crucifix. Sama raised her hand to her mouth and looked away.

Makena gently lifted the cloth back over the boy's body. The boy sighed, listless. Then he was still.

Sama turned back to the old man. 'Where is he, Bailey?'

She grabbed his shoulders, shaking him. Then Makena was at her side, gently peeling her hands away. The old man shuddered.

He looked at Sama, old lined eyes full of childlike fear. 'I don't know who you mean.'

'What?' Sama demanded. 'Where's Christopher? If he's not with me or at home then he's usually with you. You've seen enough of him this week. Where is he?' She grabbed him again, angry.

The old man shrank back against her grasp. 'I don't know. I've been here! I've been a prisoner!'

Makena pulled her back, out of reach this time. 'He's telling the truth.'

'What? How can he be?' Sama asked.

The old man scuttled around her and stumbled away. Braddock glanced after him but stood still with the boy in his arms.

'Sama,' he said, his voice firm. 'If your friend was with a man called Bailey these past few days, it wasn't that man.'

Sama frowned. Nothing made sense. 'I don't understand.'

'I think that the Bailey your friend was with was a man in disguise,' Braddock continued. 'A different man entirely. These gypsies were his creatures.'

The old man had reached the edge of the camp. All of a sudden he stopped and stared out into the darkness. 'Joe?' he said.

Braddock ignored Bailey. His eyes were still intent on Sama. 'We need to find your friend. If we don't, he will end up like this poor creature. Burned out and consumed.'

'I don't understand,' Sama repeated. End up like that boy? Her hands began to tremble.

'If we don't find your friend, the man that has him will feed on him. I can't explain how, but you have to trust us. If we don't stop him, Christopher is lost and all this — your friend Joe, everything — will have been pointless.'

Makena touched her on the arm. 'We could have found him if we had been able to follow the lights they made when they disappeared, but events overtook us. Now if we are going to find him, we're going to need your help.'

Sobs echoed across the field. Beyond the camp, Bailey had found Joe's body. His grief grew louder. Beyond, someone shouted in the distance.

'Damn. They're coming already.' Braddock looked at Sama. 'Will you help us?'

She nodded. The pain in Bailey's sobs was scraping against her soul.

'Thank you.' John glanced at his wife. Something passed between them. Then he disappeared off behind the caravan, the boy still in his arms.

Makena moved back too. 'We'll talk in the morning. Now we have to attend to the boy. You must try to convince the others that these were just gypsies. Say they ran away after the fight.' She dropped her hand into her pocket and pulled out the little bottle. 'Here,' she said, 'For the old man. Can you do it?'

Sama looked at the bottle for a moment and then took it. 'Yes,' she said. She turned and walked towards the sobbing man by Joe's body. As she walked, Sama realised for the first time in her life, that there was another side to adventure.

CHAPTER SIXTEEN

The Trouble with Wolf

In the back of the cart, Christopher slept. The cart rocked gently as wheels travelled over soft muddy ground. Its movement was enough to keep his sleep light, always at the edge of wakefulness. There, in that place where his subconscious was more awake than he, Christopher dreamed.

And the Entity followed.

Christopher dreamed of running through a cold, snowy night. Strange beings dipped in and out of the trees, too far away to make out. Beside him, the Entity felt the cold of the snow, the shift of the wind in the trees.

It felt his fear and his sense of helplessness at the creatures beyond. It experienced the things his subconscious mind latched on to and the myriad things that moved just outside his attention. Memories of the way the hard cold ground felt on every part of his feet flashed by so quickly that Christopher would never know they had passed, but the Entity drank it all in.

The Entity no longer felt fear. It was consumed with the urge to create. It had grown used to growing bloated, welcoming it with joy. It filled its consciousness with the knowledge of every one of Christopher's senses. Then, just as it seemed there was no more room, it vomited great bursts of blue energy down into the world below.

As each burst disappeared, the land became larger. Far beyond the cart, out into the sea was a barren nothingness. Suddenly, new land erupted from the waters. High mountains rose up, swirled with icy winds. The winds blew in great clouds laden with snow.

On the land below, long grass that hadn't been there a moment before was assaulted with flurries of snow. Beyond, forests of huge trees bent rebelliously in the gale around them.

In the void, the Entity vomited more energy, its urge to create made strong with the fresh material it fed on. In the snow-covered forests, clearings appeared. Tiny villages grew. In the houses, people pulled their bedclothes tighter to shield out the cold beyond.

At the foot of a mountain a castle erupted upwards, nestling on a high rock edifice. Around it, a city took form. On the broad stone road that led to the castle's outer walls, wind whistled around an alehouse. Inside, drinkers whispered to one another that the storm seemed louder than the previous night's, even though moments earlier they had not been there to whisper.

In the castle, the King of the land sipped a steaming mug of mulled wine and looked out of his great hall window. He smiled to his courtiers and spoke of the time he had been a boy hunting at night in the forests, slipping in and out of the dark.

Christopher dreamed on. He was back at Fox Grange, in his father's study, shouting at the Weasel to listen to him. All the while the unseen creatures were creeping closer outside the window to the constant ticking of the Weasel's pocket watch.

The Entity latched on to the sound of the clock, then fired forth again. All over the world clocks appeared. It didn't notice that the clocks were out of place in the world it had created. It didn't care. Some were huge and made of stone, their great pendulums swung in church towers. Others were tiny and intricate ticking by the side of a person's bed.

So it continued, with each new dream the Entity repainted the world, blurring the edges of Christopher's thoughts, moulding them as best it could to become a living, breathing part of the world.

In dream, Christopher ran on through the night. Just ahead, Freddie stood in an officer's uniform, muddied and bloody. He brandished a pistol out into the dark.

'Freddie!' Christopher called. His brother turned and beckoned.

Christopher ran forward as a massive explosion went off to the left of them.

'Get down!' Freddie cried, reaching for him. Christopher dived to the floor as another explosion went off. This time it was far louder.

He felt the tug of a hand pulling him up. 'All right, old chap?' Freddie was grinning at him. 'That was a bit close, wasn't it?'

'Freddie! You're all right!' Christopher was exultant. 'They called you a coward, but I knew they were wrong!'

Freddie frowned at him. 'Who did? I'll bloody their noses for them.'

Ahead, there were sounds of gunfire. To Christopher it sounded just like the rifles that the officer training corps used at school. He grinned. 'That doesn't sound very scary!'

'No.' Freddie smiled back. 'Now brace yourself! They'll be here in a moment. I must find my men.'

With a final nod, Freddie disappeared around a wall. Christopher looked after him, sorry to see him go. Still, he should do as his brother asked. He glanced around for something to use as a weapon, but there was nothing. There were more sounds of guns ahead. Christopher looked up. In front of him, a ridge obscured his view. He scrambled up the few feet to the top of it and glanced over.

Ahead, hundreds of German soldiers marched forward. Through the smoke of the shells they were little more than strange shadows. Still Christopher knew they were the enemy. Each shadow had a distinctive spike on its helmet.

Shells continued to fall. Blinding flashes lit the landscape, burning a reverse snapshot of the soldiers into Christopher's retina. Deafening explosions cracked. Chunks of earth were blown high into the sky to shower down on to the advancing troops.

Yet no soldiers fell. They grew nearer, becoming more visible against the smoke. They were huge. And there was something about their faces as they were caught in the light of the blasts. Something Christopher couldn't quite make out.

Then one of them saw him. It pointed with an enormous hand, grunting in a low bestial voice. Others began to look where it pointed. Their voices joined its, growling and grunting to one another. A moment later, the first raised a huge rifle. At its end, in place of a bayonet, a long, wide blade was set like the blade of a pole axe.

The soldier fixed Christopher with beady black eyes and fired. Something hard slammed into his shoulder.

Christopher gasped and his eyes burst open. Wolf stood over him. His arm was still tensed from where he had just punched Christopher's shoulder.

'You were making noise. It was distracting,' the knight said and stepped over him. He cocked a leg over the back of the cart and clambered out. 'Anyway, we're here. Get up.'

A few moments later Christopher poked his head out of the cart. He frowned at the early morning light. His dreams had left him with a vague feeling of discomfort, though he remembered nothing of their detail. He climbed down, wiping sleep from his eyes.

The horse that had been tied to the cart had been moved and tethered to a fence post. On the ground next to it, a saddle and riding bags had been placed. Christopher walked around the horse to get a better view of where they were.

207

There was a settlement ahead. It was mostly a cluster of small single storey buildings, with rough stone walls and thatched roofs. They surrounded a larger, sturdier house, fortified with arrow slits on its two floors. Battlements ran along the top of its walls. Christopher squinted up, his eyes still full of sleep. One would get a good view of the surrounding countryside from the top of the building.

Even from ground level, it was easy to get a sense of where they were. The immediate landscape around them was flat. Just beyond the settlement was a crossroads, where the track they had arrived on met another larger highway. Their track passed through the houses and turned off into a copse of trees. The other headed off over a vast plain. Blankets of short grass rocked and jostled against gusts of chilly wind.

Wolf was just ahead with his own horse. He was fixing a loaded riding bag to the battered brown saddle on its back. The horse tossed its head in annoyance at this unwelcome addition, mane catching the wind. Once done, Wolf raised his arm and petted at the horse's neck. Soon she stopped fretting.

Christopher flexed his shoulders, working out a knot that had formed as he had slept. He walked over to Wolf, stumbling on the wet earth. He righted himself just before he knocked into the knight.

Wolf's helmet turned towards him. Christopher strongly suspected the knight was sneering at him from inside. 'Careful, boy. She's unhappy enough without you spooking her.'

'Sorry,' Christopher mumbled. He glanced around. 'Where's the …?'

Before he got a moment to finish the question, Wolf wheeled around and grabbed him by the scruff of his tunic. 'Don't say it!'

Christopher gasped.

The knight leaned in close to him and whispered, 'We're not in the abbey now. Who knows who might be listening?' He relaxed his grip and let Christopher lean back a little. 'Make no mention of anyone's titles.'

He let go and turned back to the horse, pulling a leather bag strap through a buckle on the saddle. Christopher thought for a second, then asked again. 'Where's Gwen?'

Wolf nodded over at the grey house without speaking. Christopher waited, unsure if he should go over there, or if that would elicit another bullying reaction. However, it seemed as if Wolf could not care less. His attention was focused entirely on the horse. Shrugging, Christopher walked away from the knight.

The front door was open. It was a large affair made of thick oak. It was covered with black iron studs and looked as though it could withstand quite a battering when closed. From inside Christopher caught the gentle tone of Guinevere's voice. He glanced back at Wolf. The knight was paying him just as little attention as before. Relieved, Christopher walked in.

The large room was dim. The little light there was, mostly shone from the open door. Faint shafts of light from arrow slits cut through smoky air and made vague lines on the wood floor. A wet fire, the source of the smoke, smouldered weakly in a large fireplace on the far wall. To its left, stone steps climbed upwards to the second floor.

The room was sparse. There was just a wooden table with four chairs around it. A mangy deer hide rug lay before the fireplace.

Guinevere stood with a man and a woman by the table. She turned toward him as he came in. 'Ah, the third member of our little band.' She smiled, though her voice was weary. 'Come in. These are friends.'

The man glanced at Christopher. 'So, boy, you have travelled with interesting company. And now you must say your goodbye to the sister here.'

'Must I?' Christopher felt a lurch of concern. He glanced at Guinevere. 'Can't I go with you?'

She shook her head. 'I wish I had more time to talk with you, Christopher, but no. From here we go on different routes.'

Christopher's shoulders slouched.

'Don't worry. Wolf will take good care of you. I spoke with him whilst you were sleeping,' she said gently, noting his reaction. 'He's saddling a horse for you now. You will ride on as knight and squire. Even in these times, few will question a knight on the road.'

'And Wolf knows to take the back routes where he can,' the man added.

Guinevere walked across to him and laid a hand on his shoulder, steering him around and out of the door. 'See,' she said as they turned back toward the cart. 'He is almost done.'

'I think he hates me,' Christopher said, watching the knight lift a pack up on to the second horse's saddle.

Guinevere smiled. 'No, I doubt that. Wolf is protective with anyone who comes close to me. You will come to know him, I am sure. Then you'll see a far different side to him.'

'I'd rather be with you,' Christopher repeated.

'I can't give you the answers you seek.' Guinevere was firm. 'Where Wolf goes will be the best place to find them.'

Christopher didn't see how he was going to find answers anywhere that would be of use to him, but he recognised her tone. He understood when an adult had decided something that they would not be swayed from.

'Will you be all right?' he asked, accepting his fate.

'I'll be gone from here within the hour. Word has already been sent on, and a ship will be ready.' She glanced down at him. 'Come. Wolf will be keen to get started.'

She took his arm, linking hers through his in a way that quite suddenly reminded him of his mother again, when they would walk through the village on an autumn day. When she was happy and healthy and full of stories for him. Smiling, he strolled with her across towards the knight.

As they reached Wolf, Christopher glanced at the horse. It seemed a lot bigger than it had before he realised he had to get on to it. The feeling of contentment drained away as quickly as it had appeared. The animal stomped a hoof.

'Actually, I haven't ridden before,' Christopher said, trying to sound conversational.

'Wonderful,' Wolf groaned without sympathy. 'Well, you'll have to learn quickly.'

As it turned out, riding a horse was surprisingly easy. It took a few moments to get on to the animal as it kept moving around. Eventually Wolf jerked heavily on its reins and muttered something at it. Once Christopher had gotten into the saddle, though, his feet easily found the stirrups. He took the reins that Wolf offered, feeling them comfortable in his hands.

Wolf vaulted up on to the other horse. He rode it around to face the road that led down towards the copse.

'Go safely and go quickly,' Guinevere said, looking at them. 'It's not a sword you're carrying, it's a symbol. People will come. It will be more important than I, if it gets to the right hands.' She frowned. 'Or the wrong ones.' It was as if she wanted to say more, but then she shook her head and waved them away. 'Go.' Then she turned and walked back toward the grey house.

Wolf spurred his horse and set off at a light trot, seemingly caring nothing for Christopher's lack of experience. Christopher's horse stayed still for a moment then started forward, following the other rider obediently.

For a second, Christopher thought of pulling the reins and jumping down to return to the warm gaze of the Queen. Perhaps he could persuade her that he would be better off with her. He glanced backwards. She had nearly reached the door of the house. She took the last few steps without turning and disappeared inside.

When he turned back, Wolf had already outdistanced him by quite a way across the grassland. If anything, he seemed to be spurring his horse to go even faster. Christopher sighed and dug his heels into his horse's sides. It broke into a trot. Christopher stood in the saddle, balancing his weight against the horse's movements. He frowned to himself, his mind telling him that it really should not be this easy to get a horse do what he wanted for the first time. As soon as he thought it, he felt himself slip to the left in the saddle. He righted himself and carried onwards, now only thinking about the task in hand.

Wolf slowed a mile along the track. The grassland plain stretched out into the distance. A smaller track led to the left, dropping ahead down a slope. As Christopher pulled alongside him, Wolf spoke. 'We cross a bridge soon. Then we can get off the road and travel through the country.'

They rode on in silence, occasionally broken by the sounds of their horses. The knight did not attempt to speak. Christopher thought that was absolutely fine. All the conversation they had so far had involved Wolf threatening him or calling him a liar. Christopher had no wish to start another.

The track continued downhill for another mile, passing from grassland into a wood. Pine trees grew straight and tall, becoming denser as they rode on. Soon they rode in shadow. Christopher caught occasional glimpses of the sky through breaks in the pines. At least here they were sheltered from the wind.

The track bent around behind the trees. As they rounded the corner, it widened and left the woods, crossing a narrow stretch of scrubland. Beyond the bushes and undergrowth, the woods started again, as thick and dense as those they had just left.

Running through the middle of the scrubland was a deep gouge in the land. About fifty feet across, its sides were sheer rock faces that dropped down below Christopher's sight. In front of them was the bridge Wolf had mentioned, crossing the gouge. As soon as he saw it, Christopher frowned.

The bridge was wrong.

Not because it wasn't being a bridge. After all, it was doing exactly what a bridge was supposed to. No, it was wrong because it was a suspension bridge.

Christopher knew he was hardly an expert in bridges. Philip at school was. Philip's father was an engineer. Christopher had spent enough time listening to Philip enthuse about engineering to have some understanding.

The bridge was too clever. That was it. A bridge in the time of King Arthur should be made of stone, held up with simple arches. Perhaps it would be wood and rope, rickety and held together with as much luck as engineering.

It should not be the bridge before him, of that he was sure. A cast iron suspension bridge. Two girders stood at either end. From them, thick steel cables stretched down to take the weight of the carriageway.

'That bridge!' Christopher's eyes went wide.

Wolf glanced at him a moment. 'Yes?' He used what seemed to be his standard voice of annoyance.

The tone made Christopher think better of saying more. He shook his head. 'Nothing.'

Wolf dug his heels into his horse's sides. The horse trotted forward to take the lead. Christopher glanced at Wolf's back and scowled. He really was very rude.

They were almost upon the bridge now. The closer they were, the more out of place it seemed. The four girders were covered in reliefs that had been cast into the metal. All over each column were scenes that seemed like they had come straight out of one of his mother's books. A knight vanquished a dragon. Above, two more knights fought one another in single combat. Each relief was flushed with rust, punctuating the black iron with orange brown. Atop the head of each girder, an iron dragon with wings set to take off, stared menacingly down toward the road. The wingspans of the dragons met on the inner sides making a high arch.

Along the length of the girders, iron rivets were driven into the metal. About three-quarters of the way up each girder, the cables fed through a large opening before descending to the ground away from the bridge. There they were secured somehow within four squat stone outhouses. Each of the cables themselves were made of hundreds of thinner ones twisted tightly together.

'This can only be the last century,' Christopher marvelled as they crossed on to it, only realising he had said it out loud afterwards.

'Don't be stupid, boy,' Wolf muttered over his shoulder. 'The bridge has been here for aeons.'

'Not your last century,' Christopher said. 'My last century. This is a suspension bridge!'

'Yes,' Wolf replied, clearly impatient with this. 'It does indeed "suspend." What of it?'

'It's not right,' Christopher said. 'This sort of bridge shouldn't be here. It doesn't fit. You can't have the means to build this. It's too … modern,' he finished sheepishly.

Wolf looked out from under the helmet. Christopher didn't need to see the knight's face to understand the look of disdain that was underneath.

'Isn't it wrong to you?' he tried again, guessing the response would be negative.

Wolf glanced around the bridge with short sharp jerks of his head. 'It's simply a bridge. So stop your prattle.'

'But it's wrong,' argued Christopher. He might have to travel with the knight, but he did not have to passively accept his dislike.

'Agh! What's wrong is being forced to take you with me.' With that, he kicked into his horse's sides and broke into a gallop. 'Ride!'

'You're an idiot,' Christopher muttered to the knight's disappearing back. Then, without even thinking about what he was doing, he kicked at his own horse and quickly broke into a gallop.

The Master rode through the night, pushing as hard as he could on the sixty league route. Time was so vital when a new child had been pulled under. The sooner he could find Christopher's essence within the world, the sooner he would have complete control.

Once that had happened he would be able to travel across the land at impossible speeds. Until then, he had to content himself using the raw energy to aid his way. With each hour, he felt his impatience growing.

He had found a horse close to the hovels he destroyed. An old nag, it looked at him with tired, watery eyes. He leapt upon it and reached out to touch its skinny neck with the key. As soon as the device had touched the old horse's skin, it blossomed with blue energy.

The Master pushed energy out from himself, guiding it to flow down through the key into the pathetic creature. The results were most satisfying. Within a moment, he was sitting upon a muscle-bound thoroughbred. It snorted impatiently and stamped its hooves in anticipation of the gallop.

The horse set off at a pace that would far outrun any other creature in the world. Though they made better time than he had hoped, it was still an hour after dawn when he dismounted. He sucked back in the remaining energy of the animal, consuming it to nothingness. As the last flickers of blue crackled, he turned to look up the track. There, ahead of him, was Camelot.

The huge castle seemed sad. It rose high from a sea of white early morning mist, the only structure that could be seen for miles. Tall towers with roofs that sloped steeply down reached up, silent sentinels watching the world around them. Flag poles stood unadorned. Where banners would usually hang from windows informing the visitor that this was the seat of a mighty King, there was nothing.

The Castle sat lonely on a twin-summited hill. The keep stood on the higher of the two summits, one side in shadow, its lower storeys obscured by the high outer castle wall that ran around both hills.

On the lower of the two was the gatehouse. The Master headed towards it. He stopped just at the edge of the sea of mist. Wisps flowed around his feet as he strode forwards.

The castle walls were almost as white as the mist around it. In the dawn light they glistened with dew. The Master found himself suddenly mindful of a child's white cheeks, glistening with tears.

It was strangely quiet. Though he could already see men on the walls looking out, keeping watch, he could hear little. The occasional birdsong, made dull through the thick morning mist, rose up to his ears. There were muted clangs of hammering from somewhere within the castle. Beyond that, the silence was funereal. Even when one of the guards spotted him and beckoned to his companions, there was no noise. The man did not shout to bring his fellows over and when they arrived he ducked in close to speak quietly with them, as if to do more would be disrespectful.

A deep moat had been cut into the hill. Where the track met the hill, a drawbridge had been pulled up. The Master glanced down into the black, still water below. There was a flicker of a tail as something passed silently below. Other than that, the water was as still as the castle.

On the walls, more men appeared. Some brandished bows, arrows nocked and pointing at him. Others were talking in voices too quiet to hear, flicking quick glances his way. Mostly they waited to see what he would do. After all, to them he was just one man. Surely he would be no concern.

'Let me in.'

He didn't raise his voice particularly, but it was still clear against the silence. The result was immediate. He knew it would be. At once guards above lowered their weapons. Three disappeared off into the side of the gate tower. There was a squealing of rope pulled taught. The drawbridge began to lower. Ahead, the castle's next defence; a high wood and iron portcullis, began to rise. Behind it, two giant oak doors swung back.

A good company of people had gathered inside the gatehouse. Soldiers and peasants stood side by side as he strolled through to the outer ward. Some stared at him in awe, others bowed their heads. One, a priest, fell to his knees as the Master passed, muttering something reverential. The Master smiled to himself. He knew it was vanity, but the way the peoples of these worlds reacted to him never ceased to be a source of pleasure.

There was more noise now. The nearer he reached to the outer ward, the more he could hear it. The thick outer walls had done a good job of hiding the clamour from outside. He passed through the inner gate and looked out over the grass field.

The outer ward was already busy with activity despite the hour. An army was decamping on the grass. Scores of men toiled together in the cold light. To one side of the tents the Master could see a group of men fixing ropes and horses to three large ballistae. They were so large they looked as if they would only just fit through the gatehouse. Beyond them, a group of foot soldiers had dragged their kit from their tent and were packing it into small cloth backpacks.

Even here the noise was subdued. The men hardly spoke to one another. The melancholy of the castle he had felt outside permeated the outer ward, too. Another group of men pulled down tents, so practiced in their work that no communication passed between them at all.

Within the castle, the track was paved into a road. It passed through the centre of the ward and upwards. The Master strode along it, taking in as much as he could without stopping. As he passed the groups of workers, each within noticed, stopping their activities and staring at him. Some — like the guards in the gatehouse — bowed deeply to him, while others recognised a source of power entirely self-serving and cowered back, seeking to melt away into shadows.

Beyond the grass of the outer ward about twenty houses nestled tightly together along the road, overshadowed by the high castle walls. The Master followed upwards. A few tracks spurred off the road. On each more clusters of houses, often smaller, were packed on either side. The houses on either side of him were neat and clean. A little boy stumbled out of a front door and saw him. The child shrank back against a whitewashed wall and bowed his head.

Toward the top of the road, the houses spread out a little. Two even had small gardens. These would be the dwellings of favoured merchants and courtiers. The Master glanced up at the neatly tiled roof of one of the larger. Terrified eyes stared back down at him from an attic window and almost immediately ducked out of sight.

He glanced through a lower window. A very modern-looking carriage clock ticked on the mantle above the fire grate. He smiled again.

'He's been dreaming,' the Master said happily.

Beyond the houses, the hill dipped into the small valley between the two summits. The road continued on to a bridge that led straight up to the gatehouse of the keep.

The great gateway to the keep itself stood open. A group of civilians scurried out, laden with bundles. They scuttled past two guards standing at the open keep door and headed along the bridge. As they neared the Master they slowed, coming to a stop about twenty feet in front of him. They stood there watching as he passed them without a word. Behind him he heard them pick up their pace again, hurrying even more.

In the courtyard of the keep, any notion that the castle was melancholy and quiet was dispelled. It was full of warriors.

Groups of burly knights stood together, whilst squires scurried around them kitting them out to ride. Other squires worked hard to prepare armour, weapons, and horses.

Beyond them, a group of servants wrestled with a crate of livestock — chickens, from the sound of it — trying to lift it on to an already laden cart. Others were tying two cows to the back of a cart. A cook stood watching with narrowed eyes. It seemed that the knights in the keep would be eating much better than the soldiers below.

A stream of smoke billowed up from a blacksmith's forge. There was a steady clang of hammer hitting armour. A squire came running from the forge. In his hand was a large broadsword. The Master watched as he ran it over to a knight with a red cloak, who took it without a word. The knight strode into a small space where another waited for him and they began to spar. The clangs of their swords mingled with that of the blacksmith's hammer.

The Master stopped and stared. His smile broke into a grin. Beyond the sparring knights was a unit of soldiers quite unlike the rest.

There were about forty. They formed a tight rectangle. The Master turned from the road and strode over to examine them.

Each stood at least six and a half feet. Some reached over seven. They were huge, but their size was the least of their qualities.

Each was dressed in the green-grey greatcoat of a German infantryman. Dark iron buttons ran down their centre to a thick black leather belt. The belt was held with a buckle of the same dark iron. Upon each of their lapels a red rectangle was sewn.

The uniforms stretched tight to their awesome frames. In places on many, the uniform was ripped. Through the rips thick tufts of hair sprouted out. Often the sleeves stopped far short of wrists. Where their forearms showed, they too were covered in thick hair. Each wore a Picklehaulbe helmet covered with dark grey cloth. Atop each helmet a huge steel spike stabbed visciously upwards.

Beneath the helmets, inhuman faces snarled. On each, tiny black pupils surrounded by orange irises stared out from under thick brows. A snout with wide grey nostrils sprouted over a huge mouth. Each mouth was filled with large primitive teeth and surrounded by big pink lips. Their canines were more developed than the teeth around them. They jutted out like daggers. Their skin ranged from almost white to a mottled grey. At once, they seemed to be both boar and baboon and yet neither.

'Remember Belgium,' the Master muttered to himself. They must be! The poster in the street near Henley station. The similarity was too close. The boy must have seen it. This was what his subconscious had provided.

To one side, their commander, the largest of them all, grunted commands at them in a deep growl. The words themselves were impossible to understand. At once, the front line of the formation dropped to its knees and the line behind stepped up. On a second command, the two lines raised their rifles. Each had a long sturdy barrel that stuck out from the thick wood butts. Under the front of the barrel, where a bayonet would be, each had attached a cruel iron pole axe head that reached a foot beyond.

It was a pleasing difference. On the poster there had just been a bayonet. The Master smiled again. They looked as formidable as the steel of their helmets. 'Steel Helms,' he muttered again, thinking of the German. *Stahlhelme.*

The commander barked another order. The soldiers fired their weapons in an ear-splitting crack. People in the courtyard clutched their ears. Others threw themselves to the floor in shock.

At the end of the courtyard, the wall that they were aiming at erupted in a cloud of dust and rubble. The cloud dissipated slowly. There were craters in the wall the size of footballs.

The knight with the red cloak had neither grabbed his ears nor ducked. He stared open-mouthed at the Master. The Master glanced at him. It would be a pleasure to stay and watch the beasts. However, the time for pleasure was later. 'Take me to the King. Now.'

The man lurched away. He was almost comical in his efforts at speed whilst in full armour. The Master followed him, smiling at his efforts. They headed towards the great door of the inner keep.

Until he walked into the central hall, the Master could not be sure who would be wearing the crown. He had a good idea, though. He could have asked, of course, but he was feeling playful, He was looking forward to seeing his suspicion confirmed. Besides, whoever it was would be under his command as soon as he was with them. Once established, his influence would remain even should he later decide to leave.

At the door of the hall, he was sure. In the centre of the vast room, the round table lay broken. It was cracked down the middle in a jagged line. The two huge halves of the table leaned inwards in a 'V'.

Beyond the table, little in the hall had escaped damage. A frenzy of vandalism had been visited on the furniture. Chairs were strewn about the floor, some broken, some simply upended. Along one wall a great tapestry depicting a mighty battle had been half ripped from its hanging. Now one end hung down in a heap. Beneath, a blackened coat of arms lay half in the fireplace. It had recently been doused. The end in the fire still smouldered.

Further on down the hall, a group of men stood in a semicircle watching something beyond. The Master strode towards them, watching their backs. Three were dressed in full armour. The others, a dozen or so more, were dressed in the finery of the nobility. All were men.

A voice rang out from the centre of the semicircle, cold and angry. 'Galind, you have no idea how much pain I can cause you!'

The Master neared them. Through a gap, he could see a young slim man with a jet-black beard in their midst. A golden crown rested on his head. Mordred.

The King continued, 'I will make you tell me where the sword is!'

A voice, racked with pain, struggled to answer. 'You have not yet.'

Mordred raised an arm. 'Cut off another of his toes,' he spat.

The Master had almost reached them now. He raised the key slightly and allowed some of the energy to flow through it, illuminating the space around him with blue light. He lifted his voice, so that they could all hear him, revelling in the drama. 'Stay where you are!'

At the words, some turned to see who called. Eyes widened as they saw him. He pushed through, feeling them almost throwing themselves back to make way for him.

In the centre, two men gripped the shoulders of the kneeling prisoner. The pressure that they were putting on him seemed out of all proportion to what would be needed. The man on his knees looked beaten. From behind him there was a pool of blood. A third captor stood brandishing a long curved blade. It looked sharp enough to quickly cut through a toe.

The Master ignored the torturers and looked straight at Mordred. The young man's face was handsome, but his lips were thin and cruel. He looked back at the Master through bright green eyes.

'What are you seeking?' the Master asked.

'The Sword in the Stone,' Mordred replied immediately. He was not much older than Christopher Flyte. 'It will validate my rule and placate the people.'

'I have something more important to find.'

It was all he needed to say. Their sword would be secondary to his wishes. He could will them to forget it entirely if he wanted, but it didn't always do to force the denizens of the world to drop their own wishes.

'Listen to me,' he continued. 'What you will seek is a boy. The boy is called Christopher. He will be confused, maybe even telling people that he does not belong here. You will put all your resources into finding this boy and catching him. You will tell me anything that you know, and anything that you find, no matter how small, until this boy is found.'

'Master.' The prisoner on the floor, whom Mordred had called Galind, looked up.

The Master turned. 'Yes?'

'I was with a boy called Christopher last night.' Galind was weak. The torture had taken its toll. He gasped in breaths between words against the pain. 'He arrived out of nowhere and dressed in strange clothes.'

The Master started forward, his eyes hungry. 'Tell me everything!'

It was him! From the description that Galind gave, there was no doubt. So the boy was going north. To the same place as the sword Mordred sought.

'It appears our needs are in the same place,' the Master said to Mordred.

It was perfect. If things continued in this vein, there was no reason why he could not be in complete control far in advance of the time-scale he had set himself. Then, back in the world, he would be a force to be reckoned with once again! It was just a case of getting to him.

The Master glanced at Mordred. 'Where are your magicians?'

The young man frowned, confused. 'Master?'

'Your magicians. Your wizards,' the Master snapped, still thinking about the future. 'The ones that make your magic.'

'Forgive me, Master,' Mordred said. 'I don't know what you mean.'

The Master turned to face the King. 'Magicians! Where are they?'

Mordred shook his head. 'There are no magicians, Master.'

It stopped the Master cold.

'What?'

Mordred repeated, 'There are no magicians. The last magician was Merlin, and he died twenty or more years ago.'

'No magicians?' The Master was open-mouthed. 'No magicians at all?'

'No, Master. None.'

The Master swore under his breath. That was inconvenient. He had hoped to quickly take an arsenal of spells from a wizard. As soon as he was able to touch such a man he would immediately be able to absorb all his knowledge. A simple flight spell could have seen him soaring the skies and swooping to catch his prey within the hour. He knew he could not have predicted the exact nature of magic the boy had imagined, but could it really be that Christopher had created a world without any magicians? After the careful grooming he had worked so hard at.

'Damn it!' The idea of a quick conclusion to the plan was beginning to disappear into the distance. He shook his head, forcing himself to move past the irritation. 'Very well. What about Merlin's books? Any artefacts? A wand, perhaps?'

Mordred shook his head. 'You could try in the library,' he said, uncertain.

The Master resisted the urge to blow him out of the nearest window. 'Who are your fastest troops?'

'The beasts,' Mordred said. 'Those in the spike helmets. They need no rest.'

The Master nodded. 'The Stahlhelme.'

'The—?' Mordred raised his eyebrows.

'It doesn't matter,' the Master snapped. 'Send a troop of them north towards this "Kay's" Castle. Tell them to find the boy.'

He turned to Galind and the men holding him. 'Take him, too. Have him describe the boy to them.'

'Master, he may not last,' one of his captors exclaimed.

The Master raised a hand and released a bolt of the raw energy at the prisoner. It struck him and disappeared into his body. Immediately he looked a little stronger, and his breathing became easier.

Mordred fell to his knees. 'Master! That is magic!'

The Master raised his eyes to the heavens and sighed. 'Just show me where the library is.'

It was really only when they stopped and made camp that Christopher finally got a chance to think about the things he had seen. As soon as they had crossed the river, Wolf had taken them on a direct route north. They had ridden cross country through woods and more grass plains. Eventually they reached the edge of an immense forest.

For hours Wolf led them along tiny tracks through the dense foliage. Some tracks were so indistinct that Christopher knew he would struggle to follow them on foot, let alone on horseback. Wolf never wavered. He had maintained a gruelling pace.

They had slowed just once. Deep within the forest they had passed a woodsman's cottage. Two children played outside, giggling and running in circles until they saw the two strangers. They had scurried inside. A squat man had appeared at the door, brandishing an axe in his hand. He had watched silently as they had passed, but made no move that might be considered aggressive. Wolf for his part had guided them in a circle around the property, keeping a respectful distance at all times.

The knight had avoided any further conversation after the bridge. He spoke only when he deemed it entirely necessary to tell Christopher something. Even then, he used as few words as possible.

Now he lay opposite Wolf, wrapped in a blanket by the small, smokeless fire the knight built. He considered the strangeness of his situation. It was like a dream in one way. The way that things he knew shouldn't be in this world had seemed to blur and melt into the land around him. That bridge for example. And later he had seen a man ploughing a field with a plough blade that looked almost exactly like the one he had watched Bailey mending. They had been out of place and yet not.

Christopher frowned to himself. Out of place with what? The world of King Arthur his mother had taught him? The idea that he could be within that world itself was strange enough. The more that Christopher considered it, the more it seemed impossible.

He had noticed oddities in himself, too. It felt as if he was born to ride. The horse, though it could have smelled a little better, responded perfectly to his every command. Surely it wasn't possible to get on to a horse like that and immediately be an expert.

The riding ability hadn't been the first time things had seemed oddly in his favour. Now he thought about it, from almost the moment he had woken up on that mound, he had been finding luck was on his side. The way he had jumped the gully and found perfect footing. He would never have even tried that at home! The way he had found the perfect rock in the dark to topple on to his pursuer. Even the way he had happened upon a place where the most exciting events in this Kingdom had been unfolding. None of it made any sense.

Yet still he was here, he thought yawning. The day's riding had tired him out in a way that he had never experienced. And if this was a dream then he wasn't waking up.

And who sleeps in a dream? Christopher thought to himself, closing his eyes. In his mind, the image of the Queen came into his view, again somehow infused with an essence of his mother. Christopher struggled to hold on to the image against his exhaustion. The urge to let go was overpowering. Quietly, he fell asleep.

When he awoke, hours later, it was still night. The moon was risen high in the sky. It cast a ghostly blue glow on the forest between the dark shadows of the trees. Christopher rubbed his eyes and looked about.

Even in the dark he could see that things again seemed different. The trees, before a mixture of pine and oak, had grown in size, their trunks twisted and gnarled, grasping at the sky. The little camp that Wolf had created seemed even smaller.

The sounds of the night wafted through the camp. A way off something snuffled in the undergrowth, its footfalls cracking over fallen branches and leaves. In the distance, an owl hooted. Christopher glanced across at where Wolf had lain to sleep.

The knight was gone.

Christopher sat up and rubbed his eyes again, suddenly more aware of the snuffling he had heard. The idea of facing whatever it was alone in the dark wasn't a pleasant thought at all. He looked around with a shudder, goose bumps sprouting on his forearms.

Wolf was nowhere to be seen. The horses remained tethered where they had left them. The knight's sleeping bundle lay empty, his helmet and pack lying beside it. Next to that a short bow and quiver of arrows that had been strapped to the side of his horse all day rested on top of his scabbard. The sword inside it was as absent as the knight.

That was a very bad sign. If Wolf had gone somewhere with his sword and had not had the time to grab his other weapons, it could spell trouble. Christopher pushed himself to his feet, glad that he had taken Wolf's advice to sleep with all his clothes on. He held himself very still and listened.

Beyond the snuffing, he thought he could make out the distant sounds of a person. Strains of a voice. He tensed. They almost sounded like wails, carrying back faintly across the camp site. That definitely wasn't at all good. Christopher concentrated on the sound. There it was again.

His heart began to pound in his chest. This was trouble. He glanced again at the knight's possessions and a wild thought came into his mind. Ignoring the warning voice in his mind, he padded over to Wolf's equipment, grabbed the bow and quiver. He slung the quiver over his back and sneaked towards direction of the noise.

Christopher moved quickly, running through the trees, dodging under low branches and jumping over debris on the forest floor. All the while he tried to keep low and quiet. Occasionally he stopped to listen for the cries. Then he adjusted his route towards their direction.

It was nearer now. Ahead, Christopher could see a break in the trees and a large rock beyond. He stopped again, checking his bearings. The noise was certainly ahead.

Suddenly he frowned. Those weren't wails. That was singing!

Admittedly it wasn't very good singing. It was no wonder that he had thought that the sounds were a cry for help. However, now he was closer, he could definitely make out song. The tune carried back to him, sung in a high boyish voice that missed a number of the notes. Christopher winced.

If that was Wolf, Christopher thought as he edged nearer to the end of the line of trees, he was a lot younger than he had seemed. He was possibly younger even than Christopher was. Still, better to be careful. He dropped to a crouch. Ahead, a slight slope blocked his view. He sneaked up it, lying right down just before he reached its top and crawling the last few feet. He peered tentatively over the top.

Below the rock, there was a natural dip in the earth where the trees didn't grow, covered with grass. In the centre, a clear pool reflected the moonlight. At one end a little stream fed the pool, splashing over rocks with a little gurgle. At the other another, wider and flatter, allowed the water to carry on its journey.

Wolf stood in the centre of the pool. He was waist deep in the water, his slim back facing Christopher. On the other side of the pool, Wolf's sword was stuck into the ground. As the moonlight struck it, its long shadow almost looked like a cross.

Wolf dove down under the water, rubbing at his hair with his hands just below the surface. Smiling with relief, Christopher understood. The knight was washing. He might be intimidating when he was in his armour, but he would never get invited to sing at church. Christopher stifled a giggle.

At that moment, the knight burst out of the water. Somehow he had turned when he was below the surface. He pushed up, shaking the water from his hair, facing directly at Christopher.

Christopher gasped and stared. Suddenly the high voice made a great deal more sense. Wolf, from what Christopher found himself unable to take his eyes off, was a woman!

Immediately he looked away, feeling his face reddening with shock. The nearest thing he had seen to a woman unclothed before had been when his mother had taken him to exhibitions of paintings and sculptures in London.

Despite the glow of embarrassment he was feeling, Christopher looked back. His curiosity far outweighed his sense of propriety. He leaned even further forward, still unable to quite believe his eyes.

In his haste he didn't judge his balance. Suddenly, he tumbled forward down the incline and landed in an undignified heap by the pool's edge. A second later, the bow struck him on the head then fell at his side.

Wolf's head snapped to where he had landed. 'What do you think you are doing?' she shouted at him with a voice full of indignation. She wrapped her arms over her chest and sank back a little into the water.

Christopher sat up, feeling his face burning so much now that he was surprised he wasn't glowing. 'I, um … Sorry. I woke up.'

'Evidently.' Wolf glowered. She started to move back across to the far side of the pool, where her clothing lay in a pile by the sword. She kept her legs bent and her torso firmly in the water.

'I couldn't find you,' Christopher explained lamely. 'I came to find you.'

'And you didn't think to simply call?' Wolf said in disdainful tones, continuing towards the edge.

There was a sudden ripple in the water a few feet away from Wolf. Christopher caught it out of the corner of his eye. He glanced across.

Wolf stopped just before the water started to become shallower. 'Well, now you have found me, I am sure you wouldn't mind turning your back so I can reach my clothes.' It wasn't really a request.

The ripple was gone. Sighing, Christopher nodded his head and moved to turn. Suddenly a slight rise in the water appeared, travelling fast, straight towards Wolf. 'Wait …' he started.

'Now!' Wolf barked at him. Then the water around her erupted.

A huge lizard with a mouth full of razor sharp teeth launched out of the water. Wolf just had time to turn and half raise an arm. The lizard reared up so that its head was a good two feet above Wolf, yet its back legs and tail were still submerged. It stretched out muscular arms and crashed down on to the knight. Both Wolf and the lizard disappeared underwater with a splash.

Christopher's eyes widened. The creature had hold of Wolf under the water and was gripping on tight. They thrashed over and over in the water, one moment the lizard's back breaking the surface, the next the woman's.

Instinct took over Christopher. Quick as a flash he grabbed the bow and rolled up on to one knee. He pulled out an arrow from the quiver at his side and strung it into the bow. He pulled it back and stared intently down its shaft.

Again, Wolf broke the surface. Somehow she had managed to free one arm. She was using it to try to pry herself out of the creature's grip, but it was useless. As she crashed down again on the other side, Christopher took aim and let the arrow fly.

The arrow embedded itself in the lizard's head, just behind a small hole to one side that could have been an ear. There was a distinct *thunk* as it slammed into thick bone.

The creature reared up in the water with a great roar of pain. It lifted one massive arm to swat at the place the arrow had struck, breaking its grip on Wolf.

That was all she needed. She ripped free out of its grip. Then she dived across the water, reaching the shallows and threw herself out towards her sword.

Christopher strung another arrow to the bow and fired again. This one struck the lizard through the bottom of its mouth. The arrowhead stuck up, piercing its tongue and making it impossible to shut its jaw.

Wolf strode back into the water, sword in hand. She swung an arc at the creature. The sword sliced into its belly. It doubled up and crashed back into the water. Wolf adjusted her grip on the sword and stabbed down into the pool. The water turned white with the creature's great thrashing. The thrashing slowly grew less. The white foam turned pink with blood. Then all was still. The foam settled on the surface and began to float away in rosy clouds.

Christopher collapsed back down. Blood was pumping fast through his body, each beat thumping in his ears. He waited for the feeling to subside, for his heart to slow. He lay back and stared blankly at the stars above, listening to the sound of Wolf slowly regaining her breath and leaving the pool.

'Those were good shots,' Wolf said later, once they had recovered and made their way back to the camp. Now she lay fully dressed and wrapped in her sleeping blanket, staring up into the sky. 'It would have been difficult to escape without them.'

'Do you mean "thank you"?' Christopher asked, a little irritated. Since Wolf had settled, she had become her usual brusque self again. Christopher could understand she was upset he'd seen her, but that was hardly his fault. If she had the forethought to tell him that she would be leaving the camp for a while, he wouldn't have felt the need to find her.

'No. I just mean it was a good shot,' Wolf replied.

Now he could see she was not that many years older than him it was far easier to ignore her tone.

'How come?' he started. 'How come you're a woman, I mean?'

Wolf remained staring into the sky. 'Because when the Lord blessed my mother with a child, he saw fit to make her female.' She sounded almost frustrated.

'That's not what I mean,' Christopher said. 'How come you're a woman and a knight?'

Now Wolf turned to face him. A strand of the brown hair that she had cropped into one neat length by her neck fell forward over her face. She pushed it back angrily. 'Why? Do you not think I am good enough?'

'I don't think that!' Christopher insisted quickly. This didn't need to turn into an argument. 'You can do everything a knight can. I saw you with that sword earlier.'

His answer seemed to satisfy her. She lay back. 'It was decided when the Queen went into the abbey. The order she joined does not allow men to sleep in the same dwellings as them. The King would not allow her to go unless there was at least one person protecting her. So he sent for me, in secret, and told me that he would get a set of armour made for me and that I was to go with her. From then only the Queen and the abbess knew I was anything other than a knight. Then, in the evening, I could remove my armour and sleep by the Queen without the other sisters being concerned.'

'But where did you come from?' Christopher asked.

'Does that matter? I went to Camelot to pledge my service to the King,' Wolf continued. 'When I got there the knights just laughed at me. Then when I bested a few of them with the sword they stopped laughing. They didn't like that at all. Said it was against God, but they let me help the squires as long as I worked in the kitchens and kept out of their way.'

Wolf stopped suddenly and looked away. It was as if she wanted to avoid going on.

'So what happened then?' Christopher asked, too interested to take the hint.

'Very little.' It was obvious now that she wanted to end the conversation. 'Anyway, we should sleep. It will be daybreak soon enough and we've another hard day ahead of us. Go to sleep, Christopher.'

Christopher blinked. That was the first time that she had used his name. Suddenly a thought occurred to him. 'Wolf, one thing. What is your real name?' He asked.

The woman hesitated, then replied, 'Eleila. Now go to sleep.'

CHAPTER SEVENTEEN

The Beast at Fox Grange

The Master reappeared in the dank cellar so suddenly Pope toppled back off his chair, raising his arms in surprise. He glanced down at the butler with a scowl, then tossed his head impatiently. 'Get up.'

Pope clambered to his feet, brushing himself down. The Master watched with distraction. His mind thought back to the world of Christopher's imagination.

A few little crackles of blue energy still fluttered around his body from his journey back through. One by one they succumbed to the pull of the gauntlet on the boy's hand, arcing across the room to sink into the metal. As each connected with it, the gauntlet pulsed with weak blue light. The boy stirred fitfully, as though somehow aware of the energy passing through him.

'How was it, sir?' Pope asked.

'There have been some setbacks,' the Master muttered.

'Nothing too taxing I hope,' Pope replied. 'Is there anything I can do for you?'

The Master sighed. 'Just leave me with the boy.'

Pope nodded. He stumbled out, still a little shocked, and closed the door gently behind him. The Master sighed again. He crossed the room and sat down on the stool by Christopher.

He glanced down at the boy's face. Already it had begun to take on a sickly pallor, covered with a sheen of sweat. It always happened so quickly once they were under. He looked down at the gauntlet. Soon, once he had gotten the boy completely under his control, it would eat into his flesh, melding itself to his hand to become almost one. It couldn't happen soon enough.

'Nothing!' The Master suddenly shouted at Christopher. 'Not one spell! Not one charm! Nothing!' He turned away from the boy's blank face, seething. 'What child dreams a world with no magic?'

It wasn't a disaster, he told himself, just a situation that needed re-thinking. He had spent hours looking for signs of magic in the library at Camelot. Then he spent hours more searching the castle; every room, every alcove, every secret place, but nothing. As far as he been able to make out, Christopher's world had no magic spells at all.

He reached into his pocket and pulled out a parchment. Opening it revealed a large map; the only thing of real value he had found. At least with this, he would be able to appear roughly where he wanted. There would be no more appearing at random places. No more being forced to travel across the land to the places he wanted to visit. It wasn't the same as being able to move from place to place in an instant — the map might not be entirely accurate — but it was an improvement on hours of riding.

There were other things to his advantage, too, he thought, forcing himself to calm down. He had grilled Mordred for hours, growing more and more agitated. Eventually the new King had fallen to the floor, pleading in a most unkingly way. By that time he was sure he had gotten as much as the King knew.

There were dragons and giants in the highlands. There were mythical creatures in the forests. There were the fearsome shock troops on the castle grounds, too. All of them would certainly be useful in time, but the Master knew how he liked to work. That required spells.

He swore under his breath. How frivolously he had used up the abilities he had retained from the last world. He strained to remember knowledge that he knew was no longer there. He closed his eyes and screwed his face shut, trying to mould himself into the form of Bailey once more. All he succeeded in doing was erupting in a shock wave of blue energy.

It was no use. The boy had created the world now. Its basic rules would not change. Even as the boy dreamed more into it, the absolutes that had been set at its genesis would remain constant.

'Why didn't I tell you story about wizards?' the Master said impatiently. 'Damn you, you mundane little …' He trailed off, thinking.

The trouble with using monsters from a world was that people tended to notice them. Quietly manipulating the odd individual to his needs had kept the Master hidden for a long time. If he had to start threatening people with giants to get them to do his bidding, he would be leaving a trail wherever he went. There were too many eyes out there watching for signs of Artefacts' work. He would not get caught in the middle of a free-for-all. Not now when he had nearly completed a transition unscathed.

'I wish you had been your brother!' the Master spat at Christopher. 'At least his madness would have given me more to work with!'

And suddenly, he had a thought.

Sama sat at her window. Below, Jim walked off down the road, dressed in his Sunday best. Her father and aunt walked alongside him. They walked slowly. Jim's shoulders were slumped.

She yearned to be down there with them. She wanted to hold his hand for as long as possible. To keep him safe until the moment he and Mike joined the train station. There, the volunteers would take the train to Maidenhead and then beyond, to their training camp.

There was no chance of seeing Jim off. She was locked in. The window had been nailed shut late last night. Her father had all but ignored her as he did it.

The only moment that she had with Jim had been just a few minutes before, when he had been let in to kiss her a hasty goodbye. His eyes were red and puffed. He wouldn't look directly at her. She hoped it was because he was trying to hide that he had been crying, rather than because he was blaming her, but there was not enough time to be sure. She thought of Joe's body lying still on the snowy ground. She shuddered with guilt.

'Didn't I tell you your gallivanting would come to no good?' Chops had muttered as she shut the door last night. It had lacked the passion of her normal rebukes and her eyes seemed very far away. Sama thought that was far worse than normal.

What could she say? That she'd seen things that defied belief? Today of all days, they would not listen to her. If she started going on about strange creatures that looked like slavering dogs in gypsies' clothing, she knew she would get a painful clout around the ear, at best. Not that any of it mattered. Christopher was still missing. Joe was still dead.

She had just had time to get over to Bailey where he wailed by the body. She'd forced him to drink the mixture Makena Braddock had passed her. Then she'd hidden the bottle inside her dress before the men from the Stumblepot had reached them.

As the first gasps of realization had erupted into sobs of anger, her father had dragged her away from the camp. He'd entrusted her to a couple of his regulars, demanding they take her back to the pub. They had placed hands on her shoulders, gently but firmly, and walked her home. Sama had dumbly complied. The sudden shock of actual loss erased any wish for more exploration.

There had been no real need for her father to nail shut her window, when he and Jim returned in the early hours. All Sama could think was the way Joe had fallen down, slowly, like a tree being felled, and then lain still. He was so big. She had always thought of him as invincible. He had been so easily beaten in the end. If Joe wasn't invincible, then no one was.

Her family reached the furthest point that she could see and disappeared from view. She sighed and turned away from the window. Who knew when she would see her brother again? Suddenly, Sama felt very alone. In the space of a day she had lost her three closest friends in the village. She glanced at her bed. She could climb under the covers and shut out the world. But with all she had seen, the last thing she wanted was to be on her own. Anyway, whilst nothing could change what had happened to Joe, Christopher was still out there.

Sama tore her eyes away from the bed and stumbled to her door. Along the corridor outside, through a single curtain that did little to muffle sound, were the guest rooms. She took a deep breath and banged loudly on the wood.

'Hello!' she shouted. 'Can you hear me?'

She stopped to listen. Nothing.

She banged and called again. 'Mr Braddock! Can you hear me?'

When she listened this time, she heard footsteps.

'Sama?' The voice came through the door. It was Makena Braddock.

'Yes,' Sama said. 'I'm locked in.'

'Wait.'

There was a click from the lock. The door pushed open and Makena stepped in.

The older woman looked down with such sympathy that before Sama knew it, her vision was blurring with tears. She tottered forward. Makena reached for her, enveloping her in a hug. Huge racking sobs shook through Sama's body. Her legs felt like jelly. No one in her own family had thought to hold her. Perhaps they thought she didn't deserve it. Once the comfort was offered, Sama went to pieces.

Sama suddenly needed to sit, her legs almost giving way underneath her. She collapsed to the floor. Makena held her as she sunk, easing her down gently.

'It wasn't your fault,' Makena kept repeating. Her voice was so soft, close to Sama's ear. 'It wasn't your fault.'

Slowly Sama stopped sobbing. She sucked in a shuddering breath as control began to return. The older woman lifted her hands to Sama's face and turned it up to look into her eyes. 'Sama, I am so sorry about your friend. I wish I could stay here with you, but we won't let him have died for nothing. We'll try to stop anything like that happening again.'

'You can do that?' Sama said hopefully, looking at Makena's bright green eyes.

Makena looked away. 'I cannot be sure and I will not lie, but that is why we are here. We will try.'

'I need to find Christopher,' Sama said. 'I have to get him back before he gets …' At the thought of something happening to Christopher too, Sama found herself at a loss for words.

Makena nodded. 'That is what we plan to do. If you feel able, any more information you can give us may help our chances. It would be most welcome.'

Sama pushed up to her feet. 'I can do that.' She wished her voice didn't sound so small.

'Good girl,' Makena said. 'Come with me.' She led Sama down the corridor and on through to their room.

Doing something immediately felt different. Not better, of course. Sama didn't imagine feeling better ever again. At least taking action made her feel a little less powerless. Doing things and focussing on Christopher, she thought to herself, that was what she should concentrate on. Anything else was too painful.

Like all the rooms in The Stumblepot, the Braddocks' was simple, with white walls. On a plain double bed against the wall, the boy from the gypsy camp shifted weakly, sweating and feverish. At his side, John Braddock leaned over him, mopping his brow. John turned to look at Sama briefly, then returned to his task.

'Is he going to be all right?' Sama asked.

Makena shook her head. 'It is unlikely. His mind is far very away. The damage is too much. We do not think he will return.'

'By the gypsies?' Sama didn't really know what else to call them. 'They did this?'

'In a way,' Makena said. 'They were a part of it, but they were part of something larger. This poor boy was the start of it.'

'I don't understand,' Sama said. 'What were they?'

Braddock reached over and put the cloth by the side of the white enamelled metal basin and jug of water. He stood and walked across to a simple wooden chair by the window. As he sat, he glanced at his wife. Something passed between them. Then he turned and looked out of the window.

'They were nightmares, sweet.' Makena placed a soft hand on Sama's shoulder. 'Made real and brought here as slaves.'

'That's not possible.' Sama crossed her arms tightly over her chest. 'Nightmares are just that, nothing more. They certainly don't kill my friends. And they don't do that,' she finished, pointing towards the boy.

'Yet was last night not a nightmare?' Makena said.

Sama thought about the previous evening. Of course, the woman was right. It had been like a nightmare, but an actual nightmare felt quite different to Sama. The worst that gave you was a funny feeling when you woke.

'No,' she said finally. 'It was like one, but it was real.'

John Braddock turned back from his contemplation of the world beyond the window and nodded.

'So tell me what they were,' Sama demanded again.

Braddock spoke. 'What happened to the man we found?'

'Bailey,' Sama said, frowning. 'I don't know. He was still there when they brought me away.'

'Did you give him the liquid?' Braddock asked, turning back completely now. He leaned forward on the chair, resting his elbows on his knees and interlacing his fingers. Sama noticed his white shirt was hanging out at the waist. John Braddock looked like he had not thought about his own appearance since the night before.

'Yes,' she answered. 'And why did the gypsies have him?'

Braddock nodded, then spoke again, ignoring her question. 'Well, it's probably not important where they have taken him now. I am sure that he will be well looked after. Tell me, Sama, how long has he been in the village?'

Sama soon found that she was answering most of the questions. Each time she tried to ask something, John Braddock would reply with questions for her. Within a few minutes, she had told the Braddocks about how Bailey had arrived a stranger, then began work with Joe.

When she started to talk about how Bailey and Christopher had taken a liking to each other, they both became more animated. She explained how Bailey had spent a lot of time with Christopher when she'd been doing her chores.

They started taking it in turns to question her. They were very interested in what Christopher had said about the old man's stories. They glanced at each other frequently, understanding passing between them that completely escaped Sama.

She tried to ask again about the gypsies. This just took John Braddock down a different line of questioning. Soon she was telling them how Christopher was sure the gypsies could sense him, even though she had thought it impossible.

Then she told them about the mess in his room. That was why she had decided to check the gypsies' camp. Then their questions stopped.

The Braddocks fell silent. John glanced out of the window, his face inscrutable. Makena stared at the floor, frowning. Sama felt frustrated. They had told her nothing, but she had told them everything. She tried to think of a way to get something out of them, but John Braddock's constant stream of questions had left her drained.

Downstairs a door clicked open. Sama jumped. 'They're back! If I'm not in my room, it'll just make things even worse!' She made to go to the door.

'Sama. Wait.' Makena took her hand. She pulled her to sit on the edge of the bed, beside the comatose boy. 'John,' she said, glancing at her husband.

John Braddock went to his coat hanging on the back of the door. He pulled something from one of the huge pockets. Then he slipped out into the corridor.

'What's he going to do?' Sama asked, looking wide-eyed at Makena.

'Nothing that will hurt them,' Makena replied. 'He is just going to make them feel that they don't want to come upstairs to check you for a while.'

Sama frowned. 'I don't understand any of this. Please. Won't you tell me anything?'

Makena glanced at the door, then looked back. 'I cannot tell you much, Sama. I will tell you one thing. I think that your friend Christopher is in danger of ending up like this poor one.' She nodded at the boy on the bed. 'We will try to find him and bring him back before that happens. What you've told us will help. As soon as John is back, he and I will go to see where Christopher lives and see if any of John's little liquids get them to tell us anything else.'

There was a sound of footsteps coming back up the stairs. Makena fell silent, glancing up at the door, waiting for her husband. Sama stared blankly forward. In the far corner of the room a little wooden table stood. There was a small hand-woven square of cloth on it. Upon the cloth was a bible. It was precisely the sort of thing Chops had put in all the rooms. A good example of standards to the Stumblepot's guests. Chops considered it part of her housekeeping duties.

The servants! How could Sama forget? 'Wait, I didn't tell you,' she blurted. 'There's a new housekeeper at Fox Grange. She only started a few weeks ago! Christopher said that she wasn't human or something. He didn't like her one bit!'

John came back in as she began to talk about Molly Brodie. His brow grew more furrowed the more Sama said. As she finished, he spoke to his wife. 'Another manifestation?'

Makena shrugged. 'It may be. It is hard to be sure from the description.'

'Manifestation?' Sama repeated, catching the word. 'What does that mean? Is that what the gypsies are?'

Makena smiled sympathetically at her. 'We will find your friend.'

'No wait!' Sama insisted, pushing up from the bed. 'You think that housekeeper is like the gypsies? She's in Fox Grange!'

What if Christopher was still there, trapped or worse? What if Molly Brodie was like one of those things she had seen last night? Sama felt panic rising in her chest.

Again the image of Joe falling backwards burst into her mind. The gypsy woman had leapt over his body with such agility. There'd been red on her fingertips, Sama remembered. Red blood.

Why hadn't she looked more carefully at Fox Grange last night? She might have found him. She might have gotten him out. Then none of the events by the gypsy camp would have happened. Perhaps Joe would be alive.

'I have to go back!' Sama cried. She bolted toward the door.

'Sama, wait!' Makena said, rising from the bed.

John Braddock leaned forward and reached for her. She ducked under his hand and kicked with all her might at his knee. She made contact. It was like kicking a block of wood and her toes sang out in pain. Still he grunted and stumbled just enough that she could slip out of the door.

She raced along the corridor through the curtain. She jumped down the stairs two at a time, almost falling over herself in her haste.

Her father and Chops sat at the kitchen table, staring blankly forward. Chops raised her head and watched her burst in.

'Sama,' she said, her voice sounding distant, but she didn't make any attempt to stop her.

Then Sama was out of the door and away.

Once the idea had occurred to him, the Master made his preparations quickly. He had rushed to the kitchen, bounding over the weak form of Molly Brodie, who lay curled on the floor in a foetal ball. Pope, who stood at the worktop slicing some ham, jumped and nearly dropped the knife he held. The butler drew in a deep breath to calm himself and put the knife down.

It was the broken housekeeper the Master turned to first. He knelt by her side and rolled her on to her back, demanding she tell him exactly where the old passage beyond the cellar ended. Her answer came in a whisper. She was so weak. Even so, her tone still carried a hint of venom.

Once he knew the answer to his question, he shot a glance at Pope. 'Get the car,' he ordered. 'Take it to the edge of the woods. Park it where the track meets the Remenham road. Then return. Quickly!'

Pope frowned but knew better than to ask why. Immediately he marched off in the direction of Fox Grange's garage. It wasn't long before the Master heard the engine start.

The Master went to the study. The majority of the Flytes' book collection was there. Although he hadn't checked — there'd been no need until now — it was a good bet what he needed would be there.

Freddie was at Hartingdon Hospital. Welstone had been very free with the information once he'd been loosened up. It was over in Oxford somewhere. The address was noted on a scrap of paper on the desk.

The Master smiled. The idea of involving the brother was wild and glorious. He had no real evidence that it would work, but he had always trusted his own instincts. If he was successful, then the possibilities were extreme in the least.

He walked to the bookshelves and began to search. By the time Pope came back ten minutes later, he had found what he was looking for. 'Pratts' South-eastern England for Motorists, Cyclists and Pedestrians.' He handed it to Pope once they were back in the kitchen. As the butler researched the route, the Master explained what they were to do.

'I don't understand, sir,' Pope said, glancing up from the little maps. 'No spells at all? How will this help?'

On the floor, Molly laughed weakly and whispered something too faint to hear.

'All I have is raw power. So that is what I must use,' the Master said evenly. 'The boy's mind was too constrained to create the tools I want. Perhaps his brother's will fare better.'

Pope shook his head. 'Is that even possible?'

'I believe it may be,' the Master answered. 'If it is, I need to try it now before the boy is fully enslaved.' He walked to the entrance to the cellar. 'Make sure the route is quick and direct. The sooner we are there, the better. I'll ready the boy.'

He made his way down to the cellar room. It was easy to move a child in the first few days of a transition. Later, Christopher would become so weak that moving him anywhere could cause a heart attack or a stroke. For the moment his body was as robust as it had been before he had gone under. It did not take the Master long to manoeuvre him into sitting position. He leaned the boy against the wall, ready to be lifted over a shoulder and carried away. It was good he was so slight.

He put the box that had held Winter's Grasp into his rucksack. Then he laid a cloth over it, making sure the box was completely covered. Just to be doubly safe, he put another cloth on top of the first. Next he placed the second box with the key atop that. Last, he did up the strap of the rucksack.

'Sir!' Pope's voice was urgent. Footsteps clattered down the stone stairs outside. His face appeared at the cellar door. 'The talismans are glowing! Someone is coming.'

The Master looked up, surprised. 'So soon? Take the boy. I will follow.'

Pope lifted Christopher on to his shoulder with some effort. Once he had gotten the weight equalled out, he staggered out along the passage. The Master returned to the kitchen.

Molly Brodie looked up weakly at his entrance. He bent to her and lifted her head. She hissed at him with hatred.

'Molly, I have one more task for you,' the Master said.

Her mouth opened and she whispered something. The words could not be made out, but the sentiment was obvious.

'It must be frustrating,' the Master said. 'That just as you feel so much freer from my bond, you find yourself so weak.' He closed his eyes and summoned the power from within him. 'Let us see if we can change that just once more.'

His eyes burst open as he expelled the force, and fed it down into her body. Blue light flowed from his body into hers. As the light diminished, she coughed. The sound was the strongest she had made in days.

The Master sat back and looked at her, regaining his breath. She stared back at him. Her eyes narrowed. She suddenly swung on to her front and pushed herself up.

'Well,' he said, 'you have strength again. How is your will? Should you not attack me as I sit?'

She snarled and started to move toward him. Then she stopped. Her eyes widened. She frowned then looked away.

'The price you pay for a short extension to your existence, I am afraid.' He smiled. 'You are pulled back under my will.'

He walked towards her and gripped her chin with his hand, forcing her to look at him. 'So you will use that strength for me again, Molly. Someone comes. They will get in eventually. When they do, you will fight them until you fall. The longer you can delay them the longer you will live. Do you understand?'

Silently Molly Brodie nodded.

'Good.' The Master smiled and dropped his hand. He looked at her face for a moment. It would be the last time he saw it. Then he nodded and turned away.

'Good bye, Molly.' He began down the stairs again.

The Braddocks caught up with Sama as she crouched in the bushes at the entrance to Fox Grange. Actually, she was glad. As she had raced through the village, the image of the gypsies kept flashing through her mind. If there were similar things in the house, what could she possibly do? She was just one girl.

She'd been worrying about that when John Braddock had suddenly grabbed her arm and pulled her back. He'd hissed a series of expletives at her that she was most impressed with. There were a couple she decided she must remember.

'So what are we going to do?' Sama said as John Braddock's irritation subsided.

'*We* are going to do nothing!' Braddock snapped, letting go of her arm. It didn't seem like he was used to people ignoring his commands, or kicking him in the knee for that matter. 'You are going straight back that way.' He pointed down the road towards the village.

Sama shook her head violently. 'No, I'm not!'

'Wait,' Makena whispered. Both Braddock and Sama looked over at her, their argument forgotten at the urgency in her voice. 'John, I feel something.'

'What?' Braddock asked.

Makena shook her head. 'I need to get closer.' She edged off to the side, lifting her staff in front of her and disappeared into the bushes.

John Braddock scowled at Sama and followed his wife. He called back over his shoulder, 'If you stay with us, you'll be another thing we have to look out for. If your friend is in there, you'll be making our jobs more difficult. You'll make it more dangerous for him.'

He disappeared into the undergrowth. Sama thought for a moment. She'd been helping Christopher out of tight spots since long before these two arrived in the village. She wasn't going to stop now. She shrugged off his words and followed.

Makena stood slightly ahead of her husband in a gap within the bushes. 'Yes. There's power in there.' She put a hand on a tree trunk and leaned against it. 'My head is swimming.'

'How do you know?' Sama asked.

Braddock shot a look at her but said nothing.

'My staff,' Makena said, her eyes closed. 'It makes me sensitive.'

'Makena, hush,' Braddock warned.

Sama tightened her lips. He really didn't want to give anything away to Sama.

'The front entrance looks quite sturdy,' he commented. 'If we try to get in that way, there'll be no hope of surprise. We should find the back door.'

'I can show you,' Sama said.

Braddock turned and sighed with annoyance. 'You don't understand, do you? You're not coming with us.'

'Can you tell us which way to go?' Makena asked, opening her eyes.

'No,' Sama said. 'Let me show you.'

John Braddock stepped towards her with a frown. 'Now listen …'

'Very well,' Makena interrupted, placing a hand on her husband and turning to him. 'She'll follow us anyway, John.'

Braddock stared hard at his wife. She looked in some discomfort.

'John, I need to do something before this gets too much.'

He shrugged in submission. 'It's a bad idea.'

Makena looked back at Sama. 'You will show us. Then you will wait outside the door for us. If you are coming, you must promise.'

'I promise.' Sama used the smile she usually reserved to get around her father.

Makena nodded and gestured forward with her hand.

Sama took them the long way around. They quickly crossed the drive and went past the ruined gatehouse. From there, they stayed at the edge of the property. They followed through the bushes, along a narrow natural passage between the foliage and the wall.

It didn't take long to get around the edge of the garden. Soon they crouched at the side of the house where the driveway split. The smaller of the two tracks curled up to a plain yellow door. Sama pointed at it. 'This is as far as we can go hidden.'

Braddock nodded. 'Both of you stay here.'

'John, wait,' Makena said. She had one hand pressed against the side of her face as if pushing against a powerful headache. 'The power is stronger.'

He looked at his wife. His face twisted with concern. 'The sooner I stop it, the better for you,' he said. 'I'll be careful.' Then he slipped out of cover and ran toward the entrance.

He reached the wall and crouched with his back against it. He edged up, checking that he had not been seen. Once his head was right by the side of the window to the servants' entrance hall, he looked in and scanned the room beyond.

Next to Sama, Makena suddenly sat down. She leaned her back against a tree trunk. 'No, no, no,' she whispered to herself, still holding the side of her head.

'Makena?' Sama scrambled across the short space between them.

'Something is not right,' Makena struggled to get the words out. 'It gets stronger when he is near. Tell him to come away.'

She looked to be in physical pain. Sama jumped up and turned.

Braddock was already reaching for the door handle. Sama opened her mouth to call. His hand touched the handle before a sound came out of her mouth.

It was as if he had been electrocuted. He twisted forward in a spasm of pain. Then his back arched. He collapsed against the door with a dull thud.

To Sama's left, Makena doubled up and slipped sideways from the trunk. She rolled into a ball on the ground, clutching her head. She mouthed a word, 'John!' No sound came out.

Sama looked back to John Braddock. His hand still clutched the door handle. In vain he tried to pull it away. It was like it had been glued there.

Every few seconds he would spasm again as a fresh wave of pain appeared to course through him. He gritted his teeth and on one occasion grunted, but other than that, bore the experience with conditioned silence.

'Traps!' Makena's voice was tight and strained. She reached across to Sama and clutched her arm. 'Help him.'

Sama hesitated, heart suddenly pounding. If something could hurt the two formidable companions she was with, what on earth could she do? 'Sama!' Makena urged again.

Sama burst out of the trees, running to where John Braddock slumped, still held fast. She fixed her attention on his hand. That was obviously the cause of the problem. If she could free him from the handle then perhaps she could drag him back to the trees. Looking at the size of him, neither task seemed likely. Still, she had to try. She took a deep breath and slapped hard at his hand. The hand remained stuck fast.

At least her hand had not become attached too. More confident, she took hold of his hand. She pulled with all her effort. It might as well be stone for all the movement she got. She grunted, then tried again. Exactly the same result.

She took her hands away. She cast her eyes around, desperately hoping to spot something that might help. 'It won't move!' she blurted.

Braddock looked up at her through pain squinted eyes. 'Kick … hand.'

That wouldn't work. She'd felt the grip he had on the door. She frowned. There was nothing within sight that could help either. There was one thing for it. She took a few paces back.

She burst forward and launched herself at his arm with her full body weight, both feet lifting from the ground. Her shoulder hit him just below the wrist. For an instant, the arm stayed solid. A flash of pain broke through Sama's shoulder, as if she had barged a stone wall.

Then the solid wall of his arm gave. His hand wrenched away from the doorway. He fell back. Sama fell with him, landing on his prone body. He coughed out as her weight crushed into his chest.

The pain in her shoulder flashed again as she landed. She rolled off him, on to her back, then over to her other side. She struggled to ignore it. There was no time to lie down until the ache subsided. Who knew what other danger would come whilst they lay in the open?

She clambered to her feet. 'Come on! Get up!' She reached pulled at one of his arms.

To Sama's surprise, Braddock climbed up quickly, shaking his head as if to dispel his own pain. He leaned heavily on her, putting an arm around her shoulders, which sent another jolt through her. She gritted her teeth and began to guide him away. Together they staggered back to the woods. They collapsed to the ground by Makena.

Sama was relieved to see that Makena was recovering too, now that her husband was freed. She watched them slowly pull themselves together, wondering what it was that had affected them so.

Braddock sat up and leaned his back against a tree. 'There'll be traps like that everywhere, I suspect.'

'How come you couldn't feel that before?' Sama asked, now Braddock seemed close to his previous self again.

Makena smiled thinly. 'John doesn't have a staff like mine.'

'We won't be able to get in that way.' John continued, ignoring them.

'But he has something magic, doesn't he?' Sama asked, an idea occurring to her. 'That's why the door hurt him.'

'It seems likely,' Makena said, looking at her husband.

John Braddock looked back at them now. 'We'll need to wait. Contact the others for help.'

'It didn't hurt me!' Sama said. She crawled forward from where she had been sitting until she was in between their line of sight. 'I didn't feel anything.'

Braddock ignored her. 'I'll wait here and watch. You and the girl go back to the inn. Call McCloud.'

'No, wait!' said Sama. She paused and narrowed her eyes. 'It's because I'm not magic! I'm just a girl! It is, isn't it?'

Braddock glanced at her. He sighed. 'I believe so.'

'Then I can get in!' Sama said, surprising herself at her ready acceptance of the events unfolding. 'I can get in and open the door!'

'No,' Braddock said. 'You are completely unprepared for whatever is in there.'

'No I'm not!' Sama said. 'I saw those gypsies, and I've seen you too. I'm not unprepared at all. Besides, how else are you going to get in?'

'We have friends. Once they are here, we'll get in,' Braddock replied.

'You said there wasn't time!' Sama protested. 'I've been getting in and out of this house before you ever came to the village. I can get in through Christopher's window and come down to open that door.'

Makena shrugged and looked at her husband. 'It may work.'

'Or get her killed and trumpet the fact we are out here,' Braddock replied, obviously unhappy.

'John, the traps may have already done that,' Makena answered.

Sama stood up defiantly. 'Mr Braddock, my friend has already been killed. You were there. You didn't help Joe,' she said. 'So if you think I am leaving you to help Christopher without me, you're an idiot!' She took a step towards him, her little hands balling into fists. 'I'll get in a lot more quietly then you banging against that door. Listen Mr. Braddock, I know you don't want me here, but I don't see how you can do this without me. Christopher is my friend, not yours.'

Makena sighed. 'How else do we get in quickly?'

John was silent. He looked from Sama to Makena and back. Then he nodded his head just once, his expression decidedly unhappy.

'All right.' Makena turned to Sama. 'Be careful, and if you see anything that looks dangerous then turn around and come back.'

The window to Christopher's room remained unlocked, unnoticed since the night before. It was easy to slip the frame upwards again and drop through. Sama glanced around for traps, not really sure what it was she was looking for. In any case, there was nothing unusual by the window. She slipped out into the hall, glancing at the damage on the door with a fluttering heart.

She edged down towards the stairs. There was more damage on either side. There were scratches on the walls and large holes where whole lumps of plaster had been gouged out. At the top of the stairs, the carpet had been rucked up into a pile. Sama tiptoed over it and began down the stairs.

There was a click. The dining room door was opening. Sama ducked through the door nearest the top of the stairs; another bedroom. She eased it shut until there was just a crack open. She waited.

Below, footsteps walked to the front door. There was a rattling of the lock. Someone was checking it was locked. The footsteps returned the way they had come. The door into the dining room clicked shut. Sama sighed with relief.

There was a muffled sound behind her. Sama jumped and spun around, her arms already aloft to ward off an attack. None came. She lowered her arms and looked wide-eyed at the source of the sound.

Crawford lay on the double bed against the wall. His back was to her and his hands tied tight behind it. Around the back of his head, Sama could see white cloth tied tight to form a gag. His black morning coat was ripped and dirtied in a number of places. He was missing a shoe.

'Crawford!' Sama hissed. She ran around to the side of the bed. Once she had gestured to keep him quiet, she removed the gag.

'Are you all right?' she whispered, studying his face. There were cuts and bruises all over. One bruise had swelled purple around his left eye, forcing it almost shut.

Crawford nodded. 'I will be when I get my hands on the devils that did this.'

'Well …' Sama started untying the bonds that held his hands. 'There are two people outside that we need to help get in. They're going to help me find Christopher.'

'Where is Master Christopher?' Crawford said, sitting up. He rubbed his wrists where the rope had been.

'We think he's in trouble. Will you help?' Sama answered, already heading towards the door.

Crawford got off the bed and followed her. 'Where are your friends?'

'Out the back,' Sama whispered. 'We need to get the back door open.' She stopped and looked at Crawford. 'There's someone down there.'

'Wait a mo,' Crawford said, then looked around. He slipped over to the fireplace in the wall and reached for an iron poker. He lifted it, testing its weight in his hand. 'Right, Miss. Let's go and let your friends in.'

Sama felt her butterflies ease a little with Crawford at her side. They stole down the stairs into the gloom of the main hallway. All its curtains were still shut, despite the fact it was morning. Part of Sama was glad. A bit of darkness was always good for sneaking about. The trouble was, it was also good for other people.

'Go through that door,' Crawford gestured with the poker. 'It'll take us through fewer rooms than if we go through the dining room.'

Sama looked back to nod to him. Suddenly her eye caught something green and glowing by the side of the front door. She stopped and stared at it. It wasn't possible to make out at a distance. She padded across the hallway.

'Where are you going?' Crawford whispered after her.

Sama raised an arm to tell him to wait. Once she had reached the object, she bent down to look at it. It was an eagle's head made of jet black stone with bright glowing eyes. A glow on the other side of the door caught her attention. Another!

Sama reached down and picked the nearest one up. As soon as she lifted it, the eyes stopped glowing. Across on the other side of the door, the glowing eyes of the second became instantly dimmer. Sama's eyes widened. 'The traps!' she said to herself under her breath.

Now she could get them in. She reached for the handle on the big front door. She turned it, pulling hopefully. The door wouldn't budge. She tried again, pulling harder. Still nothing. It was locked. She wasn't surprised. There was no sign of the key.

She slipped the eagle head into her pocket and turned back to Crawford, motioning to him to continue. He prised open the door he had indicated. In his other hand, he gripped the poker tightly, ready. Once he had looked through, his hand relaxed. Presumably the way was clear.

Sama was willing to bet a month of household chores that when they got to the back door there would be two more of those little eagle heads. If she got them moved, she was sure the Braddocks would get in. She scurried over and slipped through after Crawford.

She was in a passage with long dark velvet curtains, also shut. Crawford was already a good way along it. At the end of the passage were two doors. The one on the left would lead into the dining room. He ignored it and opened the other. It went towards the kitchens. Together they went through, keeping close. The way Crawford brandished that poker was very reassuring.

It was a small storage room. One side of the little room was top to bottom with plain wooden shelves, where the everyday use crockery was stacked neatly. On the other side, two stone steps led down to another door. That would take them to the main servants' hall containing the back door. 'Come on!' Sama whispered, increasing her pace.

'Let me go first,' Crawford said, touching her sleeve. 'Running headlong into trouble won't help anyone, Miss Neeley.' He smiled down at her.

Suddenly, there was a crash behind them. The door burst open, flying off its hinges. It smashed into the wall on the left with a shower of splinters. Sama wheeled around.

Molly Brodie hovered in the space where the door had been, all hair and sinews. Huge membranous wings beat up and down. Their tips scratched at the walls as they beat. Gusts of air blasted into the cramped storeroom with each downward stroke, stinking of sweat and flesh. She opened her mouth in a bloodthirsty screech.

Molly Brodie was anything but human. Christopher had been right. She flexed wings. She flew towards them, talons outstretched.

Crawford screamed and ducked. Sama dropped behind him.

Then the creature was on them. Her wings gathered around them in a putrid, impregnable cocoon.

Sama pushed back desperately, screwing her nose up at the stench. In front of her, Crawford stood, trying to raise the poker.

Molly raked forward with sharp claws. Her banshee scream was deafening in the fleshy tomb.

Crawford cried out in pain and fell. Straight away, he pushed back up, striking forward with the poker. It smashed into the side of the creature's head. It reeled and the screaming stopped for a moment.

Something warm and wet splashed on to Sama's face. Blood. She stared, looking for a way out.

Molly Brodie's wings did not quite reach the stone floor. The way she held them, high and around them, left a gap.

Sama dropped to her knees. The gap was big enough.

In front, Crawford cried out again. The brief moment of respite his attack had given them was over.

A moment of shame passed through Sama's mind. She was leaving Crawford to fight Molly Brodie all alone, but she knew she was of no real help to him like that. She eased herself under the creature's wings and ran. Only once she reached the door did she look back.

The creature wrenched her wings apart, staring after her escaped quarry. She screeched again, her fangs bared.

Crawford struck again, harder. The poker caught her behind her ear. Molly Brodie howled, then lunged for him. He disappeared under her wings. There was a snap. Then a soft gurgling sound.

Sama yanked the door open in front of her. At once, she saw she was right. On either side of the door, was an eagle head with glowing eyes. If she could remove them, she was sure the way would be clear. It sounded so simple in her mind.

Sama sprinted forward, expecting to be grabbed at any second. She fixed her eyes on the little eagle on the left. 'I'm here! Come on!' She shrieked at the top of her voice, hoping the Braddocks remained close enough to hear.

Molly Brodie shot through the door. A triumphant cry erupted from her throat. She flapped her wings, reached Sama in a flash and scraped down with her talons at Sama's back.

The claws ripped through her coat and gouged red lines into her back. Sama screamed and dived to the floor. She scrabbled forward another foot.

It was no use. Molly Brodie clutched at her left ankle. Her claws were like hooks digging into the flesh. Sama's vision blurred with tears. She grasped out, trying to find something to grip on and pull away. They just slapped against the cold hard floor tiles.

The creature turned back towards the heart of the house. Sama was dragged towards the storeroom. She twisted and thrashed, ignoring the pain in her ankle.

It was no use. Molly Brodie had her fast. Soon they would be back in the dark and she would have failed. She stretched down towards her ankle. Perhaps she could prise the talons away one by one.

Her hand brushed her pocket. She felt something hard. The eagle's head statue! With sudden hope, she fished in and pulled it out. She twisted round towards the back door. In the window at the side, she could see John and Makena rushing forward.

She concentrated on the eagle on the left. She judged the angle and ever-increasing distance from her. Then, hoping that her throwing arm wouldn't fail, she launched the eagle in her hand towards it.

The throw was perfect. The eagle's head hit its counterpart dead on. Both smashed into pieces. The one on the other side stopped glowing.

The door crashed open. John and Makena Braddock rushed through. His pistol was ready. He fired.

Molly Brodie was the quickest creature Sama had ever seen. Even as Braddock was squeezing the trigger, she let go of Sama's foot, flexed her wings, and flew towards the new danger. She even managed to veer to the side in the air, soaring out of the path of the bullet.

Her left wing took the hit. The bullet ripped into the bone, sending blood and shards out into the corridor. She crashed to the floor. Her head smashed down on to the stone floor. She arched her back once, grunting. Then she relaxed. She hardly moved at all apart from shallow, rapid breathing

Sama used the wall to lean on as she got to her feet. She stumbled towards Makena. Putting weight on her injured ankle was agony.

Makena reached forward with her left hand. 'Careful, Sama. Quickly!'

Sama kept tight to the other wall as she passed the creature, even though it seemed to have lost all interest in fighting. She reached forward and clutched at Makena's hand. Makena pulled her in behind her protectively. 'You are all right?'

'Mostly,' Sama said. Actually, she wanted to cry, her back and foot hurt so much, but there was no way she was doing that in front of her companions. They still hadn't got Christopher. She wasn't going to give them any excuse to leave her. She glanced at Molly Brodie so Makena wouldn't see the wetness in her eyes. 'You did it.'

Braddock had not lowered his gun. 'Not until it dissipates,' he said.

Suddenly Molly shifted. Braddock stepped forwards, ready to strike again. Molly Brodie raised a hand and spoke. 'You need attack no more. I have carried out my last duty.'

Braddock stopped.

Molly Brodie raised her head and looked at him. 'I was bidden to fight you until I fell. I have fallen. Now he has no hold over me.' Molly's voice sounded calm, resigned. There was nothing of the screaming banshee that Sama had heard before. 'They have gone with the child.'

'Where?' John Braddock said harshly. 'I can make the end quick or slow.'

'Fool,' Molly Brodie replied, staring him down. 'Don't you think I can endure pain? More than you can give out, I promise.'

'Where?' John Braddock repeated. This time his voice was less harsh.

'They have gone to the hospital where the boy's brother is. Hartingdon Hospital. Seek them there.'

'Your master,' Makena said. 'What can you tell us about him?'

No one had noticed Crawford. He had staggered through the storeroom door, the poker clutched in a hand that dripped crimson. Seeing the creature in front of him, he roared and rushed forward.

John Braddock noticed first. He dived forward to reach the butler. Further back, Makena reached for Crawford. Sama froze, watching as the butler stabbed down with the poker with all his weight behind it.

'No!' John Braddock shouted.

Molly Brodie was the last to notice. Once she did, she lifted her head to meet the metal shaft stabbing down at her. At the very last moment, she closed her eyes and smiled.

As the poker did its damage, Molly made no sound. Braddock reached Crawford and forced him back against the wall. It was too late. Molly's head rolled and she sunk down to the floor.

A pinprick of light suddenly popped up from her body then zipped along the corridor and out into the morning. Then another followed. Two more chased after them. Then the whole of Molly's body dissipated into hundreds of tiny blue lights. They disappeared after the first few until where the creature had been there was nothing.

'No,' said John Braddock again. 'Damn it.'

CHAPTER EIGHTEEN

Safety in Numbers

By mid-morning, Christopher and Eleila had left the forest behind. They slogged across high moorland, huddled on their horses against a steady wind-chilled drizzle. Christopher shivered constantly. He wished they still had the comparative dryness of the cart with them.

As they rode, Christopher decided that he understood what was happening to him.

He had been quiet from the moment they awoke. The forest had changed again whilst they slept. However, this time it had not particularly concerned him. He had already started putting his experiences into a kind of perspective.

Eleila — it seemed wrong to continue calling her Wolf — was in a good if determined mood. They made quick work of clearing away the camp. She reminded him that they should appear as knight and squire. He watched her pull on her helmet, then spring up on to her horse. He doubted anyone would have the slightest inkling there was a woman in there.

Christopher had been tempted to talk to her all morning. He was glad that the ride made talking difficult. It gave him the time to really think about things.

The more Christopher thought about everything, the more he was convinced that he understood. It was quite simple really. He was in a coma.

It was a thought that had occurred to him a few times since all this began. Things had just been moving so fast. There'd been so much to take in. He kept being distracted from the thought.

Now he properly thought about it, his first reaction was fear. He recalled memories of his mother lying in her room for hours after she had come home from the increasingly frequent 'treatments' that she had been subjected to. He thought of his desperate attempts to wake her, shaking and shaking at her shoulder with small white fingers. Her eyes had stared so blankly. She had drooled as her head lolled against the side of the chair they had put her in.

He remembered running to his father, begging him to help through desperate sobs. Each time he was told there was nothing to be done. It was the stuff of Christopher's nightmares.

That had been quite different though, he thought to himself, quelling the rising panic. His mother had been ill for a while by then. It had been just one of a series of ongoing turns for the worse.

Christopher hadn't been ill at all. Lonely and unhappy at school maybe, but nothing like that. It wasn't madness, he told himself firmly. If anything, it was sanity.

After all, what was the alternative? To believe that an old storyteller had given him a magic gauntlet that had propelled him through history to a time that never actually was? A time that revolved around his favourite stories, amongst other things. Now that was madness!

If anything, it was like a dream. All right, so it was a very vivid dream, with a lot less confusion than normal. Yet the dream elements were there. There was the way the world around him kept changing. Then there was the way that elements from his own world kept invading, like that bridge or the essence of his mother in Queen Guinevere. It all made perfect sense, he thought, skipping over the nagging doubt about how he could actually go to sleep and dream within a dream.

As Christopher thought things through some more, he began to feel a lot better. If he was right, somewhere he lay unconscious. This was all just in his mind. Didn't that make him quite safe here? Though he did remember one of the boys talking. The boy had told him that if you died in a dream you would die in real life. Christopher thought that was as stupid now as he had then.

One thing that did perturb him was how he had come to be in this state. Perhaps he'd had a blow to the head. He had even seen a similar thing one day in school at games. One of the older boys had received such a blow during rugby. He had been unconscious for at least ten minutes before they could revive him. All right, so this was a good deal longer than ten minutes, but it did make sense.

If it was a coma, Christopher wondered when it began. It seemed obvious that everything he'd experienced from the moment he had woken on that mound was all part of the dream. However, it had to be earlier than that. He thought back past all the strange things that had happened to him.

Surely running from the gypsies must be a dream too. Plus, it was a far-fetched idea to get a magic gauntlet from a handyman who was a wizard. Christopher actually smirked at the thought. Anyway, that had happened afterward.

There was a break in the rain. Eleila reined in her horse and pulled off her helmet. Now they could see a good distance, she was probably confident that she could get it back on before any riders would near them.

Staring at the back of her head, Christopher's heart skipped a beat. 'Of course!' he said to himself. If his mind dreamed up Eleila, then he would likely have been awake when first told about her. It made sense! He thought it unlikely he could conjure her out of thin air. There had to be something, some memory, to spark it.

The little voice in the back of his mind piped up that there was no real reason he wouldn't dream Bailey telling him the story too. He frowned and shook the voice away. There had been enough negatives. Instead he latched on to his idea.

If this were the child from Bailey's story, then he would at least have a point in time to work from. It would be easy enough to find out. Christopher spurred his horse forward. He moved off the path to the slightly longer grass and rode up next to her.

She smiled at him. Her weather-beaten face was slim and she had a strong jawline that made her more handsome than pretty. She would prefer that anyway, Christopher was sure. Her hair, cropped to just below her neck, hung in a centre parting. When she smiled her deep brown eyes crinkled up. She was suddenly much more approachable than when she was Wolf.

'We'll make better time, now we're out in the open,' she said. 'Once we are over the moors we'll go up through Caerbury Forest and then over Drumpeak pass. With luck, we will be at the castle by late morning tomorrow.'

Christopher nodded intent on his questions. 'You must be the only woman who's a knight in the whole kingdom.'

Eleila raised her eyebrows and sighed. 'You're not the first to point that out.' She smiled again, this time her lips thinner.

'Was it the Cornish border you came from?'

She glanced back at the track to him. 'How did you know that?'

'And did your mother die when you were very young?' Christopher continued.

'Yes!' Her eyebrows shot up. 'How did you know that?'

Christopher wasn't ready to be put off his train of thought. 'My mother died when I was young, too.'

It worked, she looked at him with sympathy. 'I am sorry. My mother died when I was born.'

Christopher's heart leapt. He was right! 'And you were brought up by bandits in the forest!'

Eleila pulled on the reins and turned the horse fully to face him. 'No one but the King and Queen knows that! Who have you been talking to?' The smile had left her face now, replaced by confusion.

'No one,' Christopher said. Well, it was nearly true. No one here, at least.

He went on. 'The bandits taught you to hunt and fight like a man. Then, when you got old enough, you left. You yearned for adventure. You went to Camelot.'

'Stop!' Eleila shook her head, her brow knitted.

Her expression made him want to cease his questions. Yet if he was right, she wasn't real. And if she wasn't real he wasn't actually upsetting anyone. A callous wave washed over him. 'Is it true?'

Eleila flicked a leg over her horse and jumped to the ground. She turned her back to him and walked off a few paces, staring out to the moorland.

'Is it true, Eleila?' Christopher asked again. 'Am I right?'

She whirled around and marched straight towards him. Her face was now bright red with high emotion. Before Christopher fully realised what she was doing, she reached up. She grabbed a handful of his cloak, wrenching him from the horse and down to the ground. Then she was on top of him. A dagger appeared in her hand. She held it to his throat.

'Are you a spy?' she spat down at him.

'No!' Christopher blurted. Whether this was a coma-induced fantasy or not, he felt a rush of fear. She had a violent way of expressing her feelings. 'I just knew.'

'You just knew!' Eleila shouted. 'You can't just know!'

She looked down at him, debating what to do next, a dark frown still on her face. Then she snorted, clambered off him and went back to her horse. 'You seem to know too much.'

'So I am right,' Christopher mused aloud. He pushed up to his elbows, considering his what this meant.

'Yes,' she said quietly. 'You are.'

Christopher got to his feet. 'So now what?' he said to himself.

Just because he had a good idea of what was happening now didn't really help. After all, he still existed in this reality. The way to wake himself up could not be less clear.

'No,' Eleila barked suddenly. Her voice was rising again. 'You don't just "know". Tell me how, before I really get angry.'

Christopher sighed. This wasn't going particularly well. Even if this was a dream, he still had to keep her company whilst it lasted. 'You're not going to like it.'

'I already don't.' Eleila's tone was hard.

'No. I can imagine.' Christopher took a deep breath. 'Okay. I think I am unconscious. I think that somehow I got knocked out. I don't know where or when, but I think that's what's happened.'

Eleila was staring at him with an unimpressed scowl.

He continued, lamely. 'And, um, all of this is a dream.'

'What?' Eleila said, frowning. This was clearly not at all what she had expected to hear.

'I'm terribly sorry,' Christopher said, 'but I don't think you are real.'

Eleila stared wide-eyed at him. She seemed lost for words. She opened her mouth to speak, then shut it again. She turned away from him and mounted her horse.

'You are quite the fool, aren't you?' She reached for the reins without looking back at him.

Christopher sighed. 'The thing is, I can't be sure what I've seen that's a dream, or rather, when the dream started. That's why I asked you about your home. You remember I told you about my friend, Bailey?'

'The one who gave you the non-existent magic gauntlet?' Eleila scoffed.

'Um, yes,' Christopher continued. 'Well, one thing I am reasonably sure about is that he told me about you. Well, about your parents, anyway. So I must have been awake then to hear about it. That's why you're in the dream.'

'Oh. Parents now, is it?' Eleila said. She shook her head at him. It was obvious that she had no faith in his explanation. 'I suppose that he told you who my father was.'

'Yes! That was why he was telling me. Your father sent your mother Winter's Grasp to help her protect herself.'

'Ah! I see,' Eleila said. 'Do go on, please. Perhaps you'll be good enough to tell me who my father was then.'

This wasn't going to be good, Christopher realised. 'Yes, I can,' he continued. 'Your father was Sir Lancelot.'

Eleila smirked. 'Sir Lancelot, the most famous knight in the land. Of course.'

'Yes.' Christopher wondered if he could perhaps dream a fair maiden instead. One that was more prone to swooning and believing the first thing that came out of the mouth of a man with a horse.

'Really.' Eleila could not have sounded less impressed. Not like a fair maiden at all.

'It's true!' Christopher said. 'How else would I know? You said that only the King and Queen knew, and you know she didn't tell me!'

Eleila fixed him with a stare. 'You know, Christopher. I don't care what you know or how you know. If you want to think I'm a dream, then you go ahead. This dream has a job to do. Whether you come or not really doesn't matter to me.' She dug her heels into the side of her horse.

Christopher watched her ride away. Then he swore to himself and climbed up on to his horse. Whatever he did next, he might as well go on. At least this part of the fantasy was better than staying around to be caught by Mordred's men. He started after her.

Suddenly, she stopped ahead and spun back in her saddle to face him. 'Don't talk to me again,' she said.

She lifted her helmet and fitted it on to her head, shutting herself away from him. Then she spurred on. She stopped again, a couple paces later. Once more, she turned back. 'You know,' she snapped. 'I was actually starting to like you.'

For the rest of the morning, Christopher thought about his situation. Though he was sure he was right, it really didn't help with deciding how to proceed. He was no closer to waking up. For the time being it seemed like he was trapped here.

The midday sun started to break through the clouds and see off the last remaining drizzle. Eleila, who had been ignoring him completely, pointed down the steady incline to the left of the ridge they climbed. Some miles ahead, Christopher could see the broad expanse of Caerbury Forest. Beyond, the mountain range that they were going to cross was a faint blue grey in the distance.

Eleila pointed at something far closer. Nestled in the valley next to them, a river snaked its way down from the mountains. Clusters of trees were dotted along its bank.

Below them was a larger cluster, a dozen or so trees. Just behind it was a small village. It was the first they had seen in a long while. In the miles of moor they'd travelled across since they last spoke, the largest things they'd passed had been clumps of heather.

Seven little thatched houses stood around a simply built church. The Church itself was not much different, except at one end where it had double doors and a tiny bell tower. From where Christopher rode, the bell didn't look much bigger than a cow bell.

In front of the church was a group of armoured horsemen. They sat on their horses in a rough circle. They chatted quietly to one another. Their voices carried up the slope, almost unnoticeable against the breeze. Four of them were drinking. Soldiers taking a break from their journey.

Behind them were five boys by a little village well; Squires huddled in furs. They attended to a small band of horses. Christopher counted; four powerful war steeds and five smaller ponies. Further away a group of four knights, presumably the riders of the war horses, stood apart, discussing something with heads bowed together.

There was nowhere for Christopher and Eleila to hide. The ridge they were on was in plain sight of all the men and boys below. It was just a matter of time before they were noticed.

'Damn it,' Eleila muttered under her breath. She glanced back at him. Her eyes glinted through her helmet. 'We will carry on along the ridge and hope they don't find us interesting.'

It was not to be. They had only ridden a short distance when they heard a shout of discovery. Christopher looked down at the knights. One of the fully armoured men on foot jumped on to the back of his horse. He dug his heels into his mount and galloped in a straight line up the slope, directly toward them. Seeing him advance, two horsemen broke off from the main group and raced into formation behind him. Eleila looked around, then reached down to her sword with her right hand. It hovered over the hilt, ready to draw should it become necessary. 'This will be nothing. I doubt that they are Mordred's men.' Her voice sounded less sure than her words. 'Don't speak. Don't even look at them. We don't need to be waylaid because of some rubbish you spout.'

Christopher nodded quickly. He looked back at the men. They would be with them very quickly. The knight at the front had drawn his sword. He was standing in his saddle, spurring his horse toward them at full charge.

'Eleila,' Christopher warned. 'I don't think he's coming to talk.'

The knight thundered up the hill. His breastplate caught a shaft of sunlight, glinting dully. He raised the sword higher in the air. He was definitely not preparing for a friendly conversation.

Suddenly, Christopher noticed his other arm. Where his hand should be the gauntlet ended in a ring. The horse's reins were tightly woven through it. It didn't seem to have any effect on his horsemanship. In fact, it was quite the opposite. Christopher hadn't seen a more confident horseman.

'He's only got one hand,' Christopher said, marvelling at the knight's control.

'One hand?' Eleila stammered, her own hand now clutched on the grip of her sword. 'You're sure?'

'Yes. His reins are strung through a ring,' Christopher said.

A one-handed knight. Christopher suddenly understood who it was that rode towards them. Of course! The knight had featured in many of his mother's stories. Who else would it be that he would dream?

'That's Sir Bediviere!' Eleila shouted before he could say it himself. 'Quickly! Dismount!'

She jumped from her horse immediately. She drew her sword and held it, blade down, then plunged it into the soft ground in front of her. She dropped to one knee behind the sword and bent her head forward. Christopher climbed down quickly and dropped to his knee, following her example. He sneaked a glance up, to watch the small party of knights arrive.

They had obviously been on the road for some time. Bediviere's armour was swathed in mud. There was a severe dent on his left shoulder plate. Both of the others were in a similar state, their armour also spattered with mud. One had also lost a greave from his leg.

Bediviere wheeled his horse to a stop. It strained to come to a standstill. Its great iron-shod hooves kicked clods of earth into the air. He leapt down, somehow unwinding the reins from the ring at the end of his arm. He stomped forward, brandishing his sword at them. Once he was just outside striking distance, he stopped.

Behind Bediviere, one of the knights lifted a crossbow. It was a vicious looking thing. Its limb stretched out a foot and a half on either side of its shaft. Any bolt that hit them from such a short range would probably go straight through them, armour or not.

'Who are you?' Bediviere bellowed down at them. 'Reveal yourself, knight.'

Eleila made no move. She just stared down at the ground. 'I can't,' she said. 'We are on a task of great importance. We just want to pass. We are no threat to you.'

Christopher frowned. That made no sense. Guinevere had said people would rally to Kay's castle, so Bediviere was almost certainly going to the same place they were. Anyway, Christopher knew the knight was on the side of right.

'If you will not show yourself, then you will defend yourself,' Bediviere said. He took a step forward.

'Eleila!' Christopher turned to the helmeted girl. 'Don't be stupid.' If this was his fantasy, he wasn't going to let it be any more dangerous than it had to be. More companions would be a good thing.

Eleila said nothing, staying on her knees.

'Sir Bediviere, wait,' Christopher said and jumped up. The knight immediately brought the point of his sword to threaten him. 'Her name is Eleila. She's not a knight, she's a girl.'

Eleila moved, turning her head sharply to face him. From under the helmet, he could imagine her eyes glaring out in anger.

'Well, I mean to say she is a knight, but she's not a man,' he added lamely. Then he hissed across at her. 'Take off the helmet.'

Eleila made a harrumphing sound under the helmet. Bediviere was waiting, but not letting down his guard.

Eleila shot a look over at Christopher again. Then her shoulders sagged. She lifted her hands and took a hold of the helmet. Slowly she pulled it off. Underneath her face was livid.

Behind Bediviere, the knight with the crossbow sniggered. 'Surely it can't be!'

Bediviere narrowed his eyes and motioned with the tip of his sword for them to get up.

'You've come a long way from the kitchens, girl,' the knight with the crossbow continued, his tone more serious. 'Thought you could use these dark times to indulge your fantasy, did you?'

Eleila's voice was defiant. 'King Arthur ordered me.'

'The King is dead,' Bediviere interrupted. 'Speak lies of him again and I'll strike you down as if you are a knight.'

He turned to his companions. 'We'll take them with us. We can't leave them riding around the country, causing trouble. Call the others, then bind them. We'll deal with this foolery when there is more time.'

Bediviere turned back to Eleila. 'Now, get out of that armour and dress yourself in something more seemly for a woman.'

'I will not,' Eleila said. 'I am telling the truth.'

It would go nowhere, Christopher realised. Eleila was too stubborn. If the knights didn't take her at her word, she would suffer in noble silence. She would be far too proud to actually resort to proving it to them. Yet that was exactly what needed to happen. It was up to him.

'Sir Bediviere, wait,' Christopher said. Addressing the knight directly would be more productive than trying to convince Eleila. 'She is telling the truth. The King ordered her to guard Queen Guinevere at her abbey. It had to be her. Men weren't allowed to stay there.'

Bediviere glanced at the boy. He raised an eyebrow but said nothing.

'I was there,' Christopher continued quickly. Behind Bediviere, he could see the rest of the party heading up towards them. If this wasn't resolved before they got here, he knew that he would be tied up and ignored. 'Last night! Sir Galind and Sir Claris arrived and told us what happened. Sir Claris died! Guinevere knew it wasn't safe so we escaped.'

'Be silent, boy.' Bediviere was growing impatient. He glanced back down the hill at the other knights. 'There will be a time when you will be allowed to speak.'

'And I know what you did for the King!' Christopher blurted on, ignoring the knight's command. 'You threw Excalibur back to the Lady of the Lake as King Arthur ordered, even though you didn't want to. It took you three times to do it.'

Bediviere turned back. Now he was listening. His eyes grew wide.

'You didn't tell anyone, did you?' Christopher said, suddenly realising. 'You didn't tell anyone that it took you three times? You were embarrassed, weren't you? It doesn't matter, Sir Bediviere, you did it!'

'Claris told you,' Bediviere said, looking suddenly less bemused.

'Actually, no he didn't, but even if you believe he did, it proves we were with him, doesn't it?' Christopher went on, undaunted. 'And when you were with the King, a boat came, didn't it? A boat with handmaidens upon it, to take the King to Avalon! I'm right, aren't I? Sir Bediviere?'

Bediviere nodded slowly, his mouth set in a grim line. 'They said they would heal the King so that he could fight again, but they were wrong. No man heals from death.'

'It wasn't the only sword,' Christopher continued, his words coming out all in a rush. 'There's the Sword in the Stone, too. If Mordred gets that, then people might think he is supposed to be King. Guinevere gave it to us and told us to take it Sir Kay's castle. She said that would be where people would go. That's where we have to go!'

Bediviere stared at Christopher with a frown, contemplating his words. Then he slowly turned his head back to Eleila. 'The boy speaks the truth?'

Eleila tightened her lips. She shot a look at Christopher, evidently still livid.

'God damn it, girl! Does the boy speak the truth?' Bediviere asked sharply.

'Yes,' Eleila said after a moment. 'The King trusted me to look after his Queen. The Queen trusted me to look after his sword.' Her voice was still tight with affront.

'Bediviere.' The knight with the crossbow called from behind. 'We haven't time for this. Let's tie them up and be done with it.'

The other group of knights reached them. They brought their mounts to a halt behind Bediviere and his companions. The noise of horses snorting and hooves on wet earth mingled with the clang of armour. Suddenly it was quite loud.

Bediviere frowned at the cacophony behind him. He raised a hand without turning around to try to quiet them. When the noise had reduced the barest fraction, he looked back at Eleila. 'Show me the sword.'

Eleila nodded and climbed to her feet. She walked to her horse and reached under the saddlebags, where the sword was concealed. She pulled it free, along with the scabbard, and turned back.

'We hid it in Claris's scabbard,' she said, taking hold of the grip and unsheathing it.

She came forward, flipping the sword so that she was able to present it pommel first to Bediviere. He examined it silently. The knights waited for him to speak.

Bediviere looked down at Eleila with grey eyes. He nodded. 'It is as you say.' He flipped the sword over and handed the pommel back to her. 'We travel to Kay's, as well. Journey with us.'

'Bediviere, what are you saying!' the knight with the crossbow blurted, surprised.

Bediviere turned to him. 'It is the sword.'

'Then we should take it and go to Kay's. We are in a much better position to get it there than this girl and her little friend.'

'Really, Sir Griflet?' Bediviere said. 'You think that you know more than the King? You would undo what he has decreed?'

'Come, Bediviere,' the knight scoffed. 'We have but their word as to how they came by the sword.'

'Can you explain another way?' Bediviere said.

Sir Griflet closed his mouth and looked away.

'Very well,' Bediviere said. He raised his voice so the other men could hear as well. 'They will travel with us. All will give Eleila the accords her armour demands.'

He looked back at Eleila. 'We travel fast, there may be pursuit. We cannot slow because of you or your squire.'

'You won't have to.' Eleila's face was flushed with excitement.

Bediviere nodded. 'Then mount.' He looked over at Christopher again. His expression was bemused, but he said nothing. Then he turned his horse and dug his heels into its side, trotting over to where the others were.

Christopher clambered to his feet. He walked around to the side of his own horse so it was between him and the knights. He reached up to the saddle to pull himself up. Suddenly he was yanked back and spun around.

Eleila had followed him. She gripped his shirt front tightly. Her face was screwed up in anger. 'How dare you!' Drops of her spittle flew into his face. 'This was my task, not anyone else's!'

Christopher felt quite calm. After all, there was no point in being upset by his own imagination. 'Well, now you've got help,' he answered, defiant. 'And it looks like you might have just got accepted by the knight in charge. So why not have a temper tantrum at your squire in front of him? That's bound to make him absolutely sure that he was right to give you that acceptance.'

'You are not my squire.' Her grip on his shirt did not lessen.

'I wouldn't want to be,' Christopher said. 'But if it weren't for me, we'd be tied up right now. So I suggest you let me go, we get on our horses, and we go with them.'

Eleila grunted and let go. She turned her back on him and jumped up on to her horse without another word.

Christopher climbed up on his own horse. He felt quite pleased with himself. If he thought about things and worked out what to do, it seemed that he could make things fall in his favour. He grinned. He would look forward to telling Sama about his strange adventures, when he eventually found a way to wake up.

Feeling better than he had done from the moment he had woken on the hillock, he pulled at his horse's reins and wheeled her around. He dug his heels gently into her sides. She fell into step behind Eleila's horse. They began to head down the hill.

Bediviere rode them hard all day. Christopher found that his new optimism was at odds with the grim spirit of the knights. A knight shot him a suspicious glance. A while later, one of the squires noticed his smile with the same distrust. He forced the smile from his face. Eleila and he probably stood out enough already without making it worse.

Before long he felt the stern mood begin to rub off on him. Though he was sure he was in a dream, it remained so very vivid that it was impossible not to find himself drawn in. Without really thinking, Christopher hunkered down on his horse, observing his companions.

One of them was wounded. He was a slim fellow even in his armour. One of his shoulder plates was missing. His chain mail undercoat was visible and stained bright red with blood. The knight's head would periodically loll to the side and he would sway in his saddle. The potential to fall off snapped him back to attention. His head would straighten up again as he readjusted his position. Each time however, it seemed as if it was taking fractionally more time to recover.

Christopher could see no other obvious wounds, but a number of the knights had dents in their armour. If a blow could do that to metal, Christopher wondered what it could do to flesh beneath.

Despite whatever hurts and tiredness they suffered, the knights stuck with the pace. Not even the squires complained. Christopher soon found that he and Eleila were at the back.

They stopped only once, taking a brief rest for the horses just after they had entered Caerbury Forest. Bediviere led them away from the track through the trees for ten minutes to a secluded glade with a small pool.

The knights dismounted, passing their horses to their squires. The squires immediately saw to the horses with feed and water. Some of the men bent to check and adjust their armour, making the best of whatever they had. Another group of three took saddlebags and, sitting by the edge of the pool, checked the contents, examining the supplies within and reorganising them more equally.

Two of the knights moved to keep watch on the way the party had come, each armed with a crossbow. The wounded knight settled on a log a little further back. Another of his companions pulled a bundle from his mount's saddlebag. He crossed over and began to check his wounds.

Christopher watched, impressed. It was all done so quietly. The men knew what needed doing without being told. Only he and Eleila stood with nothing to do.

He glanced around. Sir Bediviere, Sir Griflet, and one other knight made their way off along a little path that sloped upwards through the trees. Eleila, seeing his glance looked across, too. She frowned, indecisive, then her face set into a determined stare and she went after them. Christopher smiled thinly to himself. Then he too followed, a few paces behind the others.

The path through the trees took them up to a small rocky outcrop a few minutes hard walk away. The knights clambered to the top. They reached the shelter of a weather-worn boulder, a good eight feet high. From there, they were able to get a broad view of the plains they had come through.

Eleila stood behind, unsure for a moment. Mischievously, Christopher pushed the small of her back. She turned around.

'Go on,' he whispered. 'You're a knight, too.'

Eleila narrowed her eyes and tilted her head to the side. 'I thought I was just a dream.'

'Quiet!' Sir Griflet barked, turning with an angry stare. He had removed his helmet. His head was covered in long black hair tied back with a short length of leather cord. He had a full, thick beard.

'I see nothing,' the other knight said, staring out at the way they had ridden.

'We'll stay and watch, anyway,' Bediviere answered quietly. 'Whilst the horses are drinking.'

The three knights stared out into the distance beyond, silently scanning for any sign of movement. Eleila gave Christopher one more glance, then moved forward to stand at their side. None made any comment, merely accepting the extra pair of eyes. It seemed this was a group where you got involved.

Christopher moved up to the other side of the knights. 'Who could be following us?' he said.

Bediviere glanced across at him. There was a look of puzzlement on his face. Christopher was certain it was unusual for a squire to talk to the knights unbidden. For a moment, he expected to be ushered back to the other squires.

Instead, Bediviere spoke. 'Mordred is no fool,' he said. 'He will have a good idea where we will head.'

'So you think his army might be behind us?' Christopher asked, remembering the burning abbey.

'Unlikely. There is a more direct route from Camelot,' Bediviere replied. 'But that's no reason to let our guard down.'

Christopher nodded. He stared out into the moorland below, scanning the terrain for any signs of movement. There seemed to be nothing.

They stayed silently watching for a good five minutes, five pairs of eyes looking out into the distance. Christopher glanced across at Eleila. Her face was flushed again. Next to the knights she suddenly seemed quite young despite her determined expression. She looked up at Bediviere, clearly in awe of the grizzled knight. Then she noticed Christopher watching her and her face reddened even more. She snapped her head forward again to stare out over the moors.

'The horses will be watered,' Griflet said eventually.

Bediviere nodded. 'We'll ride until we reach the tarn atop Drumpeak pass. We can water them again there.'

The knights turned and began to make their way down the ridge. Eleila waited politely until the older knights had started ahead of her. Then she pushed in front of Christopher and began to follow.

A couple of feet down, her foot slipped. She stumbled against the rock, her armour clanging loudly. Sir Griflet looked back with a frown but said nothing. He turned forward again and continued on his way.

Christopher placed his hand under her arm to steady her. Immediately she shook it off. 'I'm fine!' she hissed and pushed away from him. She hurried down the slope, dodging past Sir Griflet to catch up with Bediviere.

Christopher smirked. Just a few hours before, she had been adamant that they should travel alone. Shaking his head, he began down the hill after the others.

Fast and steady, the Stahlhelme ran. They had started running from the moment that King Mordred had given them their orders. Fast and steady, without a moment's rest. They did not have horses that needed to be rested and watered; they did not need to stop for food or sleep. They just had orders.

Find the boy.

They had been told where to find him. The broken knight by their King had described him and his route. From Camelot they had taken the main trade road through to the northern coast, their destination was Drumpeak pass. There they would wait. There they would take him.

They moved as one. Each huge boot step thudding into the ground with a single report, so close was their formation. Each pair of sharp black eyes was fixed ahead, focused purely on the destination and the task. Each enormous snout with tusks sprouting upwards was set in a determined line. Each mighty pair of arms held a vicious gun tight across their body. The pole axe heads on the barrels glinted, clean and polished. Soon they would be marred with blood and dirt.

They passed through villages along the way. Villagers screamed at the sight of them, running from their path. Though it was in their nature to destroy, they thundered on. Though the sounds of screaming innocents brought a desperate taste of blood to their mouths, they kept true to their task.

The slower of the villagers; children, the elderly, a pregnant woman, only just managed to get out of their relentless path. These villagers were tantalizingly close to their reach. It would just take the barest movement to reach them and drag them into their grasp. Still they moved onward.

Only when unfortunate souls failed to get out of the way were they true to their nature. Then they fell upon them, picking them up and raking their bodies with their thickly nailed hands. They ripped the clothes and tore at their skin. They kept them alive for miles as they moved on, tossing them from soldier to soldier in a demonic game of catch. Then finally, they crushed the life from them and tossed them away, leaving their bloody remains in the dirt behind them.

And on the Stahlhelme ran. Fast and steady.

CHAPTER NINETEEN

The Madness

The snow gave way to fat, dirty rain. Sama sat crushed in the tiny back seat of the Braddock's Daimler Tourer. Dark droplets splashed on to the bonnet. They raced through the Oxfordshire countryside with reckless speed. John Braddock's knuckles were white on the steering wheel, but he manoeuvred the car expertly along the country roads.

Sama knew her face was as white as his knuckles. She felt weak and scared. Her movements were shaky. She pushed her hands down by her sides to hide it.

The cuts on her foot were fire-hot where Molly Brodie had mauled her. At least she knew they were only surface wounds. Makena had checked them as soon as they had got to their car. She'd cleaned and dressed them with a small medical kit she had produced from the glove compartment.

The scrape along Sama's shoulder blade was deeper. Makena spent more time looking at that. Eventually, she surmised it wasn't deep enough to need stitches. 'It will hurt, Sama,' she said with a reassuring smile. 'But it is still just a scratch.'

Sama glanced out of the window impatiently. At the edges of the road the snow was brown and mixed with mud. Even the clouds overhead seemed darker than those that had dropped gentle white flurries only a few days before. It was as if the weather understood the adventure she was on had taken a murkier path. Nothing was clean or crisp any more.

Sama shook her head. She had to concentrate on Christopher. He needed her. Nothing else mattered. She closed her eyes. Immediately Molly Brodie, wings spread and claws outstretched, was rushing toward her again with a hideous look of desire on her face. Sama snapped her eyes open. A shudder ran through her body. Before she could stop herself, she gasped.

Makena looked back at her from the front passenger seat. 'All right?'

Sama nodded vigorously. 'How far away are we?'

It wouldn't do to show her companions what she was feeling. Looking at Makena's kind face made her want to blurt her fear out loud. To admit that each time she closed her eyes, terrifying creatures were reaching for her, ready to rip the life from her. No. She had to be strong.

They hadn't said a word of protest when she'd climbed into the back of the car. Her eyes were ablaze with passion. She was ready with a retort should they try to tell her that she could not come with them.

She didn't want to give them an excuse to change their minds now. She had stuck by them. She got them into Fox Grange. She had helped to find out where Christopher had been taken. Whatever lay in wait for them, she intended to be a part of it.

'Not long now, sweet,' Makena answered with a smile that did not hide the concern in her eyes. She turned back to the front of the car, with the barest glance to her husband.

Those creatures scared Sama. The memory of gypsies up close, with their guttural voices, their horrid breath, and their snapping teeth stopped her heart cold. Molly Brodie's wings enveloping her all veins and skin and stink made her want to gag with fear.

Yet, she didn't need to understand how they were there. To question the reasons why they existed didn't cross her mind. She accepted them. Strange creatures were in the world and frankly they terrified her.

That meant there was one thing for it: she had to beat them. Then they wouldn't terrify her. It was that simple. She sat forward in her seat.

'What'll we do when we get there?' She kept her voice steady, directing the question at Makena. Though John Braddock had not been particularly harsh to her since she had knocked his arm from the door handle, he was still far less approachable.

'I don't know,' Makena said without turning around. 'We'll wait and see.'

'And what about the boy we found?' Sama said as the thought popped into her head.

Makena turned back again, this time smiling despite herself. 'So many questions. We have friends that will be on their way to get him now. They'll take good care of him.'

Sama opened open her mouth again, another thought occurring to her.

'And your father,' Makena continued, guessing her next question, 'he will be none the wiser. Nor your aunt. Our friends will clear all traces of us. It will be as though we were never there. They will make it so you will not be missed until you get home.'

Sama wasn't entirely sure she was happy about that. Normally the freedom such a thing would offer would be wonderful. Now a part of her wanted the comfort of Chops and her dad worrying about her.

John Braddock took a hand from the steering wheel and reached into the pocket of his coat. He pulled something out and tossed it back to land on the seat next to her. 'There. You'd best take that.'

Sama looked down. On the seat was a small penknife, folded into an ivory handle. She picked it up dubiously, then she glanced up. 'Is it magic?'

'No Sama, it's not,' Braddock said, his voice sounding amused. 'But it is sharp.'

Makena glanced at her husband. 'Is that wise?'

'It is for defence, not attack, Sama,' Braddock continued. 'You'll still let us lead.'

Sama nodded and looked at the knife. It certainly wasn't for attacking. It wasn't much longer than one of Molly Brodie's claws had been. She didn't imagine it would save her in a desperate situation.

Still, this wasn't about her. This was about Christopher. She had to get him back. If a penknife could help, she'd take it. There would be plenty of time later to return to the boredom of ordinary life that suddenly seemed so appealing. She sat back in her seat and willed her body to calm down, concentrating on the rain spattering the car roof and the wheels sluicing through the wet surface of the road.

The Master wrenched open the door of the Austin Shooting Brake and stepped out on to the wet gravelled drive of Hartingdon Hospital. He reached down to the footwell and picked up the length of strong rope Pope had placed there for him. Then he looked across at the butler, sitting in the driver's seat, and said, 'Bring the boy.'

Christopher lay across the back seat of the car. He was wrapped in a blanket more to keep him under cover than to keep him warm. Pope clambered out and reached into the back. The Master turned towards the dark stone building ahead. Then he strode toward the large square front door.

Hartingdon Hospital was set back from the road, reached by a long straight driveway. It stood tall and sinister, impervious to the onslaught of rain that turned its uniform grey stone walls to charcoal.

The front of the large main building was in shadow. Just a few windows on the ground floor showed any light in them. The other windows were darker still than the walls. Tall black rectangles were divided into smaller panes, with a glint of lead running between them. All the windows were enforced with black iron bars. Any attempt at exit through them would be impossible. The building felt more like a prison than a hospital.

Above the front façade, a clock tower loomed, dominating the rest of the building. The clock face stared down like a single eye on to the courtyard. Its loud, relentless tick was quite distinct against the patter of the rain.

The Master ascended the steps that led to the large main double doors. Above the doors, a carved stone name plaque was set into the wall proclaiming the building simply as 'Hartingdon'. No mention of the fact that this was supposed to be a hospital.

The Master pulled the dull grey chain that hung to one side of the door. Somewhere in the building a bell sounded.

He glanced towards the car. Pope was struggling to lift the boy from the back seat. The rain pelted down on to his shoulders, soaking into the black of his morning coat. The butler staggered upright with Christopher's comatose body against his chest. He staggered across the gravel, pursing his lips upwards to blow water from the tip of his nose.

Pope had just reached the bottom step when the Master heard a click. He turned to the door. A small square had been opened. A chubby woman's face looked out, framed by tightly tied-back red hair, and just visible atop her forehead, the white of a nurse's cap. 'Hello?' she said.

'Thank heavens!' the Master began, his voice suddenly simpering and squeaky, a passable impression of Edwin Welstone. 'Sister, you must help us. My name is Welstone. I am the Flyte family lawyer and guardian. You have our dear Freddie here.'

'Of course. We've spoken on the phone. I'm Sister McCudden.' The nurse's demeanour was at best unfriendly. 'This is somewhat peculiar, Mr. Welstone. You know that we don't allow visits unless arranged and approved in advance.'

'Sister McCudden.' The Master feigned a look of recognition. 'I do understand. I am afraid I did not have the luxury of time. You see Christopher, Freddie's brother, has become ill. Our local doctor is quite unable to find an explanation for such a thing, and … well … Dr Blanchard told me on the phone that I should call on his help at any time.'

'Really, Mr. Welstone, I don't think Dr Blanchard would have meant you should drive over at any time of the day,' the nurse replied, eyes unconvinced. 'This is a special hospital. Our patients need special care.'

The Master tensed and wrapped his fingers around the portal key in his pocket. If he could not convince her to open up, things could become a lot louder than he really wished.

'Sister, I assure you if any other course of action were open to me I would have gladly followed it.' He turned and beckoned Pope forward, pulling the cover away from Christopher's head. The boy's face really was disturbingly pale.

Sister McCudden gasped. Christopher's veins showed blue through his skin, and barely discernibly, an occasional glimmer of blue light seemed to travel along them. The Master pulled the blanket back over the boy's face.

'You undoubtedly know the family history, Sister. His brother isn't the first to suffer mental illness,' the Master continued. 'Dr Blanchard will not just see us. Dr Blanchard will want to see us.'

She looked at him a moment more, then her face disappeared. The door clicked as it was unbolted, then it swung open.

'Come in out of that rain, Mr Welstone,' she said, all brisk efficiency now her decision was made. 'Come through to Dr Blanchard's office.'

The hospital interior was no more inviting than outside. The entrance hall was practical. No consideration given to the impressions of a visitor. Plain red tiles covered the floor. The walls were whitewashed. To one side a set of wooden stairs led up to the first floor. On the other, a dark wood door was just ajar. Above, three bulbs hung down on white painted chains from the high ceiling, casting a harsh clinical light. At the back of the hallway, a corridor led off into darkness.

Sister McCudden, having shut the door, turned to Pope. She moved to lift the blanket over Christopher again.

'Please, Sister,' the Master said quickly, reaching forward to catch her arm. 'The sooner that we are able to see the doctor, the sooner that we will be able to discern what is wrong.'

She snatched her hand away, surprised to be manhandled. The Master stepped forwards. He loomed over her, uncomfortably close.

Sister McCudden backed away, looking a little intimidated. 'Of course, you are right. I'll fetch him straight away for you. This way, please.' She led them through the door to the right.

Dr Blanchard's office was considerably more inviting that anything else they had seen so far. A good quality teak desk dominated the room, silver grey and piled high with papers and books.

'You can put him over there,' Sister McCudden said. She pointed to a leather chaise lounge that was placed in the most open part of the office. Beyond it, a fire blazed in a fireplace.

'Please, take a seat,' she said, once Christopher had been lain down. 'I'll fetch Dr Blanchard now.' She turned and disappeared down the way they had come, her heels click-clicking against the floor.

The Master smiled and pulled the key from his pocket.

At the sound of the click-clicking of Sister McCudden's shoes, Dr Blanchard lifted his head from his thoughts, unconsciously losing the frown from his face. He had been considering Freddie Flyte. It was a subject that always made him frown.

Sister McCudden delivered the news that he had visitors, then left as quickly as she had arrived. He sighed and began his way back to his office, leaning on his walking stick.

It was probably safe to say he had considered Freddie more than he had considered any of his patients. He had known the family through the loss of their mother. How to deal with the young man weighed heavily on his mind.

A temporary insanity in battle that had induced a state of catatonia. That was what the young man's father had written only a week before. Blanchard was not so sure. General Flyte's assumption was born of a father's love. Of course he would not accept that his son could have been a coward.

It was more than that. The alternative meant that it was possible a Flyte could be a coward. The Flytes had been in the British Army for many generations. They had distinguished themselves repeatedly in battle. Their name was well known in military circles. Not just a family's love then, a family's reputation.

Blanchard didn't believe it personally. He firmly believed one didn't see things that turned one mad. He had been working with lunatics for over thirty years. He respected the traditions he had learned on the job. Lunacy was something one was born with. He had met Freddie Flyte on countless occasions before. The boy was not mad.

As far as Blanchard was concerned, Freddie was not suffering from an experience-induced coma. Freddie Flyte had simply run away from the war and been caught in the blast of a shell. He would eventually wake. It was just a matter of time. Then Dr Blanchard already knew what he would recommend; that the officer return to his unit and court martial. What would he say to the father when that fateful day came? It was a question that had kept him awake at night.

Blanchard didn't have a great deal of time for cowards. There were new theories about the insane coming out of Europe. Like most things that came from Europe, they were dubious and a bad influence. Applying such approaches to cases in the army would cause the worst kind of trouble for the Empire. If soldiers were excused for indiscretions or worse, because of claims of madness? It would simply be open to abuse.

The doctor stopped at the entrance to his office, smoothing his grey hair back over his head. Even if there had been anything to the new theories, he knew his duty. There was a war on. It was not time to show any leniency to soldiers running from battle. Examples must be made. He pushed his door open.

At once he felt huge hands grab his lapels. He was lifted from his feet. His walking stick clattered to the floor. Quite suddenly there was grey cloth close to his face. It reached above him and spread wide on either side filling his vision. Curiously there was a dark brass button right in front of his nose. Then his assailant pulled him in close and his face was enveloped in darkness.

There was a sudden, terrible pain in his side. His screamed was muffled in the cloth. The great man holding him squeezed hard, pushing the air from his lungs until there was none to scream with any more. He kicked weakly with his feet. His head swam.

Then the grip eased off. The giant pulled back just enough so he could turn his face sideways and gasp in a breath. Blanchard's mind refocused. He realised he had squeezed his eyes shut against the pain. He flicked them open.

Leaning against the wall, to the side of the giant that held him was a tall, angular man with swept back white hair. The man stared dispassionately at him. 'Excuse the bluntness of my methods, Dr Blanchard. In other circumstances, this would be a markedly more comfortable experience for you, but needs must. Tell me, where is Freddie Flyte?'

'What is this?' Blanchard managed to say, before the grip tightened again and the pain in his side exploded. Something in his body cracked. He heard as well as felt it. Everything went white.

He felt three sharp, hard slaps across his face. He had no idea how much time had passed. The grip had relaxed once more. He forced his eyes open.

'Simply answer the questions, and there will be no more pain,' the man said.

'He's in room B-six,' Blanchard said quickly. He had never experienced real pain before. He knew from its first blossoming that he would do anything to make it stop no matter what the cost or consequences to anyone else. 'It's off Ward B. Please don't hurt me.'

The man in front of him smiled. 'Now, how many are working here?'

'Two tonight,' Blanchard replied. 'Sister McCudden and me.'

'And patients?' the man asked.

'Forty … Ah … Seven,' Blanchard gasped out. 'Please, I'll do anything, let me go.'

From out of sight another voice spoke. 'Master. A car.'

The man in front of him looked over sharply. 'Already? Damn it!' He turned back to face the doctor. 'Where are your keys, man?'

'My pocket,' Blanchard answered immediately, desperate hope in his mind. 'Let me down. I can give them to you.'

The man looked at him for a moment, then raised his eyes to Blanchard's captor. 'Get me the keys. Then he is yours.'

Then Blanchard felt himself lifted higher, suddenly giving him room to see. He looked into the face of the horror that held him and screamed. Dark, soulless black eyes over a huge slavering mouth looked back.

As the beast ripped the pocket of his jacket open, Dr Blanchard had a revelation. It cut through the screams of his terror and pain. Faced with the impossibility in front of him, he realised that he had been wrong. It was possible to see things that could turn a man mad. Then the beast squeezed again. His body let out its final breath; a hideous wet gurgle, and he was able to think no more.

The doctor's death gurgle stopped. Pope shuddered with relief. Fortunately the moment was short lived. The great creature squeezed its arms together, its back obscuring what it was doing. There was a great crack. Pope turned away as the sounds of wet ripping and teeth tearing at flesh began. He struggled to fight the wave of nausea rising from his stomach.

The Master was unperturbed, of course. He marched across to the window to join Pope. 'How many?'

The visitors had climbed out of the car in the courtyard. Three of them. Pope didn't recognise the first two, but from their bearing and the clothes they wore, they were not just simple visitors. The black woman had a light wood staff and pulled a gun from the car. Pope recognised it, a Mauser with a strip clip. The man she was with, an imposing fellow, knelt at the side of the car where a long storage box had been attached to the running board. He opened it and pulled out a rifle. They meant business.

When the third member of their party slipped out of the back seat, the Master laughed. 'The girl from the Stumblepot,' he said. 'She seems to have fallen in with interesting company for a shop girl.'

'You know them?' Pope asked.

'No,' the Master replied. 'But they must be McCloud's. There is no one else close enough to react this fast.'

He turned back to the great soldier behind them. 'Go to the hall. Stop them coming in.'

Dropping its prey with a wet thud, the creature turned to look at them. Its deadly tusks at either side were completely covered in blood and there were smears around its snout. It grunted once and turned to the door.

'Wait,' the Master said. 'Let's not leave this to chance. If they are here, then subtlety is gone. There is no reason to try to get it back.'

He glanced at Pope, pulling the portal key from his pocket. 'Take the keys, go through this place, and open every door that you can. Get the patients into the hallways. I'll be with you in a moment.' Then he lifted the portal key into the air. Pope closed his eyes just in time. The energy burst from the Master's leaving still burned bright through his eyelids. Once it dimmed he opened his eyes, pleased he had not been blinded by the flash.

Pope turned back to the window. The man and woman had started towards the entrance, with the girl following behind. Suddenly, the girl looked across and pointed directly at him.

'Look there! Where the flash came from!' Sama said. It was the man she had seen at the Flyte's house. He peered out through a barred window on the right. 'See him! He was at Christopher's!'

The man ducked into darkness. John Braddock and Makena both looked across, but too late. Braddock glanced at her.

She shrugged. 'He went back.'

'Who?'

'He was dressed like a butler,' Sama said. 'He opened the door instead of Crawford.' The sight of the man sent a wave of adrenaline through her body. Christopher was here! She was filled with the urge to act.

John Braddock nodded at the Flyte car that was parked just ahead of where they had stopped. 'Then they are here. I don't imagine that they will be defenceless.' He turned back to her, bending down close so that his face was on a level with hers. His eyebrows fell into an intense frown and he stared sharply at her. 'Sama, stay behind us.' Little lines around his eyes accentuated into wrinkles. 'At least until we have cleared the way.'

'But what if they have more charms?' Before John or Makena could answer, she rushed forward.

'Sama, wait, dammit!' John Braddock shouted, stumbling forward to try and catch her, but she was already beyond his reach.

'Sama, get back!' Makena echoed her husband's call.

She rushed to the door, grasping the cold metal door handle tightly. 'I can touch it!' she called.

'Sama!' Makena called again. Sama could hear her footsteps running towards her.

Sama pumped at the door handle. Unsurprisingly it held fast, locked from the inside.

Makena reached her side. 'Come away, quickly. Get back from the door!'

Inside another blue flash illuminated the window frame. Thuds and clangs followed.

'Makena!' John Braddock shouted. His voice was full of sudden concern.

Makena grabbed Sama by the shoulders and hauled her backwards with surprising strength. The crashes inside continued.

'To the side!' John Braddock screamed.

Before Makena could pull Sama any other way but back, the door exploded outwards with a crash.

The Stahlhelme that had destroyed the door grunted. It glanced behind. Its companions were at its back. It turned and stepped into the space it had created, filling the doorway with its body. Behind it, slavering and growling, the others jostled at each other with thick muscled trunks of arms, each trying to be the next out of the door.

Further back, another unit charged down the corridor, faithfully following the gaunt figure that had summoned them from the hill on Drumpeak pass only moments before.

There was a scream from the left. A Stahlhelme shot a look across. A woman in a white dress and cap. She threw up her hands in terror. The Stahlhelme unshouldered its rifle and thrust the great pole axe at her, cutting off her scream. It flicked the pole axe up, tossing her over its shoulder just as it had done with the villagers they had toyed with on the march from Camelot.

The wood dust was clearing. The Stahlhelme at the front saw its foes. Two women, one black, one white, sprawled on the ground ahead. Bowled over by the explosion. Struggling to get up. Further back stood a man, legs apart to hold himself steady, a rifle raised to his shoulder. Without a thought, the Stahlhelme raised its own rifle again towards him. The immediate threat.

Before it could get the rifle into position, the man squeezed the trigger of his gun. The muzzle went off with a flash. The bullet hit the Stahlhelme squarely in the forehead and it fell back into the beasts behind it.

The huge beast filling the doorway screamed and fell knocking into several other large shapes behind it. Sama scrambled backwards, pushing at the ground with her feet and elbows, still facing the door. Ahead Makena sprung to hers, lifting her gun.

It was just in time. The first creature John had felled was dissipating into blue sparks and its companions stepped into the breach. One, seeing Makena within reach, swung at her with the pole axe on its rifle barrel.

Makena dodged back. The blade of the axe flashed by just inches from her face. The creature grunted. It wrenched the swing short with muscled arms, turning it to swing back. Before it could, Makena fired her pistol, sending bullet after bullet towards the monster. It dropped the pole axe and collapsed to its knees. Then it toppled forward and dissipated into tiny blue sparks.

'Behind me!' John Braddock shouted, running to his wife. Ahead two more creatures were coming. Sama managed to get to her feet and leapt behind Braddock. Makena slipped in behind him from his other side.

Braddock pulled open his coat. He lifted the coat flaps high to the sides as if they were wings. Sama frowned. He looked like he was an eagle hovering above his prey.

From the other side of him, there was a crack as one of the beast's rifles fired. Somehow though, the sound was muted. The bullet hit John Braddock's coat. He stepped forward with the impact. Then he stepped back again as if the impact had been no more than a slap on the back.

Another explosion came. This time it was even more muted. It was as if they were underwater and the rifle was being fired from far away on the surface.

It was the coat! Sama looked at it. Though John still held it out, the coat was not hanging from his arms. Rather it had taken on a spherical shape, like a great round shield. At its edges, Sama could see a slight shimmering, like the heat shimmer of a summer's day. The shimmer stretched out from the coat, reaching around to John's front and all the way back to the other coat flap. They were completely encircled.

'How long?' Makena asked her husband.

'A short while,' Braddock answered. Beads of sweat were on his forehead. 'It doesn't have much energy left.'

'What about Christopher?' Sama said urgently. 'We're not a lot of help to him in here, are we?'

'You may have noticed,' John said, 'that our new friends here have quite large guns.'

'But we've already stopped two of them!' She poked her head out beyond the cloth of the coat flap. 'There's only two more left, look!' Through the shimmer she could see the two remaining creatures. They had taken up positions by the door.

Both saw her face appear at the side of the coat. They swung their rifles over to point at her. Both barrels exploded as they fired. The bullets struck against the shimmery skin emanating from the coat. Sama could see the little lumps of metal quite distinctly. They flattened against the surface, then dropped to the floor.

Makena pulled her back in. 'Sama, stay down.'

'But we can't stay here!' Sama protested.

'She's right,' Braddock's voice was ragged with effort. 'Be ready.'

Makena nodded. She clambered up into a running position, then looked down at Sama. 'John will turn. They will fire. Then we move. I want you to go to the side of the building and wait until we have dealt with these.'

Sama nodded, getting into a running position herself. Makena looked at Braddock. 'Ready.'

He suddenly turned, stepping around them until he was behind them and the shimmering membrane was between them and the creatures. The creatures, seeing their quarry again, let loose with their rifles. As soon as the bullets fell harmlessly from the shimmer, John Braddock dropped his arms. 'Now!'

Braddock and Makena launched themselves at the creatures. Sama dodged out of the way. On Makena's side the creature was fast. It was sliding the bolt of its rifle to fit another bullet into the chamber. It stopped immediately at the sight of their burst forward, swinging the blade around. Makena ducked underneath it and thrust up with her staff.

The staff smashed it just under the chin. It was not a particularly hard blow, but as it hit something black erupted from its tip. It was almost like ink, yet thicker. In a second it flowed upwards, spreading out over the creature's face, covering its eyes and blinding it.

The one on John's side was faster still. It dodged to the side, out of the way of the hastily fired shot from his rifle, surprisingly nimble. It swung its axe at a twisted angle, catching John a glancing blow on his shoulder. Though it hit the coat, he still cried out, lifted from his feet by the force of the blow.

As he landed, stumbling, the creature saw its chance. It leapt forward on to him. John disappeared under a whirlwind of grey cloth and pounding arms.

The creature Makena had attacked still struggled with the black mask now completely covering its face, stopping it from breathing or seeing. She fired her gun into its body. It slid down to the floor with its hands still clutching its head as it began to turn into sparks.

Makena wheeled around and screeched. It was a high-pitched warbling sound, the likes of which Sama had never heard before. The kind, smiling face that Sama had seen until now was gone. An unforgiving expression of battle replaced it. She lifted her staff high above her head and leapt atop the creature.

Sama tore her attention away from the fight. Makena would make short work of the creature, she was sure. She had to stay focused on Christopher. Ahead, in the broken doorway she could see disappearing sparks of the last creature Makena had dropped.

'Follow the lights to the source,' John had said at the gypsy camp. Sama didn't know what that meant, but she was prepared to take a guess. And if that were the case, then that was where she must go.

At once she was off rushing into the hospital without a glance behind. Ahead the blue sparks disappeared into the distance. Sama raced on after them.

The blue sparks rushed past Pope's head for the third time. Another fallen. That was just one left outside. Whoever those two were with the girl, they would soon be on their way in here.

He pushed the wailing lunatic he had just let out, wishing he would stop moaning and start walking. At the far end of the corridor, others he had let out were milling around one another. Between the cries and the muttering, they were making quite a cacophony. Still, they would only slow things down for a short while. 'Go on!' he hissed violently to the lunatic. 'That way.'

The wild eyed man raised his hands in a gesture of fear. Then he turned and scuttled off the way Pope wanted. Pope returned to the task at hand. He unlocked the last of the cells. Once he had gotten this one out, he could go through to the other wards and lock the main door firmly behind him.

He pulled the cell door open. In the back of the room its occupant cowered against the wall. Pope strode forward and grabbed the man by the scruff of the neck. The man screamed.

'None of that, thank you,' Pope said in his sharp, clipped tones. He cuffed the man on the back of the head, pulled him out into the corridor and threw him toward the others. The man hit the floor and whimpered in a weak voice.

Pope looked at the inmate with hard eyes. 'Go on.'

Suddenly through the patients, blue sparks came flying through the air, dancing around one another in their haste to return to their source. The last of the Stahlhelme was down.

'Oh dear,' Pope said to himself. The idea of taking on the attackers outside held considerably less appeal than bullying a few lunatics. At the near end of the corridor, a few feet away, a section door hung open. It was made of bars, far more at home in prison than a hospital, with a big lock on it. Pope was glad of the hospital's security measures. He ran on and slipped through it, pulling it closed behind him.

He looked down at the bunch of keys he was carrying and picked the most likely one. Unlike the cell keys, numbered most efficiently, the hallway keys had no markings. He would have to find it.

The first he tried stuck fast in the lock, not budging an inch. Pope swore under his breath and fumbled for another.

'Stop right there!'

The voice, a girl's, startled him. Still fumbling with the keys, he looked up.

'Stop!' Sama called again. She struggled through the mess of people milling around the corridor. Ahead, the man behind the door shot a glance at her then looked at the keys he fumbled with.

He took one from the bunch and applied it to the lock. His shoulders fell as it failed. He glanced up again at Sama. Then he looked down at the keys. Sama's heart leapt. He didn't know the key! If she could reach him in time, he wouldn't get the door locked.

Of course, it wasn't that easy. The patients were in her way. A human wall in white cotton pyjamas. Sama frowned and pushed into the crowd.

'Excuse me! Please!' she shouted. She pushed a young man who held his arms close to his chest. He made little rocking movements, staring blankly through her. She had to use both hands to move him to aside.

'They're coming!' an older man with wild brown hair that fell over his eyes squealed, suddenly grabbing at her clothes. He pulled her close to him. He smelled of carbolic soap. 'They're coming to save us all!'

Sama reeled back and knocked his arms away. She stepped on over two more of the inmates. They sat on the floor chattering to one another, entirely lost in their own world.

The man ahead was trying another key. Again it failed in the lock. He looked up at her, eyes wide with concern. He pulled the useless key that he was trying and moved on to the next.

A patient screamed very close to her ear. She dodged past, wincing. The scream left a high-pitched after-whine vibrating in her ear drum. The patient turned away to stare at the wall.

She dropped down and scampered under the legs of a huge man. He was finding great interest in a light bulb, touching it with his fingers then pulling them from the burning heat, before trying again from a different angle.

The last two patients were on either side of the corridor with ample space between them. Sama launched herself forward, pelting past them down the corridor as fast as she could go. She was free.

Ahead, the man's face turned to a look of triumph as he found the right key. It slipped into the lock perfectly. He angled his hand to turn it.

Sama's heart pounded. She wasn't going to get there in time! She was sure that if she didn't, they would lose Christopher again.

The man's face fell. The key was stiff in the lock! He applied both hands, straining to make the key turn. Sama pushed herself faster. Almost there. Just two more steps and she would have him.

The lock clicked shut. His face lifted to look at her with a smug satisfaction. He opened his mouth to speak.

Sama balled her hand into a fist. With all the force of her sprint behind it, she drove it through the space between two bars and punched him full in the face. The punch caught him on the nose. Sama felt it squash beneath her hand and something crack. Whatever he had been about to say came out as a wordless grunt. 'Unurgh!'

He sailed back and landed on the floor with a thud, rolling to the side. Almost immediately, he began to push himself up. He shook his head to try to dispel the pain.

The key was still in the lock. Sama slipped her hand down and pulled it out, then through to her side of the door. She pushed it in.

The man got to his knees. He stared at her, eyes wide. His nose was gushing with blood. He wiped at it, wincing at the pain.

Sama struggled to turn the stiff key, finding herself using both hands as well. The man clambered up and rushed forward. He reached through the bars and swung down with both hands.

Sama was ready. She stepped out of danger, then grabbed one of his flailing hands. She grasped it at the wrist with her left and gripped a finger with her right. Grimly she bent the finger back, ignoring his piercing scream. Only when she felt a crack and the finger gave way did she let it go. The man fell, drawing his broken hand to his body and cupping it with the other. Sama redoubled her efforts to turn the key.

'Sama!' Makena's voice from behind. Sama didn't turn, still struggling with the door.

It was too much for the man ahead. Glancing once down the corridor, he turned tail and fled, calling in an agonized voice. 'Master! Master!'

The key turned in the lock. Sama wrenched open the door and sprinted down the corridor.

'Wait, dammit!' John Braddock's voice rang out behind her. She glanced over her shoulder. Both of them were alive. Makena untouched, ahead of her husband, was moving fast along the corridor. John had a cut across his forehead and his greatcoat was ripped on one side. His arm hung limp, but he was still moving. Sama turned back the way she was going and ran on.

Past the door, the passage came to an intersection with another. Sama didn't hesitate. The little man had run straight on. She followed, passing shut white doors on her left. They were thick wood reinforced by metal plates, with small hinged openings at eye level.

The sudden thud of heavy footsteps sounded. Sama didn't need to wait to see what they belonged to. She doubted it would be anything good. Ahead was another white door, this one slightly ajar. She dived through the door and pressed herself against the wall.

In the corridor, there was the explosion of a huge rifle shot, then the cracks of a pistol and a rifle returning fire. Dark shadows passed the door, once, twice and then a third.

Sama glanced out carefully. Three of the huge creatures had passed her door. They had been close enough to have opened it and spotted her, but they were intent on other things. She shuddered. They had reached the intersection, moving off to either side to use the walls as cover. One fired his rifle down towards the Braddocks.

The creatures had their backs to her. Sama leaned her head out. John and Makena had taken refuge in a room further along. For the moment, they were pinned down. Another of the creatures raised its gun and fired. The walls around the door where the Braddocks were exploded in a cloud of dust. Further down, the patients were screaming. They fell over themselves in their efforts to escape the noise.

Sama frowned, taking in the creatures. Those were German uniforms. Just like the ones that she had seen in the newspapers at the shop before any of this started. She frowned. Surely this couldn't be to do with the War? What on earth would the Germans want with Christopher? It couldn't be, she decided. Besides, no matter what they were wearing, there was no way those beasts were Germans.

John Braddock slipped out of the door he had been in, his rifle in his hands. His left hand, the one that had hung so limply had only a loose grip on the barrel, but at least he was using it. He fired the gun with a loud crack. Two of the beasts dodged back. The third was caught on one side and thrown down the corridor. It howled in pain but didn't dissipate. The others opened up with their rifles. Makena reached out at the last minute and pulled John roughly back through the door.

Sama sighed. There was nothing she could do to fight the creatures. They were huge and armed. She was just a girl with a penknife. The only advantage she had was the fact that she was past them and they didn't know.

She dodged back out of the room. She stole as fast as she could down the way the little man had run. Ahead were double doors, painted the same white as the others. They still swung slightly from the beasts bursting through. Above the door was a sign: 'Ward B.' Another volley of rifle shots exploded behind her. Sama took a deep breath and pushed through.

As the sound of the last volley of shots faded, the Master pulled open a portal. The room erupted in a blaze of blue light. He squinted his eyes against it and stepped into the void.

Immediately he felt a familiar rushing around him. The key was electric in his hand. It desperately wanted to pull him down towards the maelstrom of blue energy so far beyond. To rush him though it until he arrived in the world of Christopher's imagination at its centre. It was something he had grown to love. He closed his eyes, filling his senses with the sensation.

His eyes snapped back open as the strong rope he had tied around his chest, under his arms, pulled tight. The other end was secured to the leg of one of the metal beds in the room beyond. All the furnishings in the ward were bolted to the floor. Though none of the patients that he had seen looked likely to throw furniture about. It was perfect for his needs, so he wasn't complaining.

The rope held him about two feet from the fissure. Blue light crackled around its edges. Beyond, in the real world he could see the ward quite clearly.

Christopher Flyte lay on the bed where he had secured the rope. The boy was angled slightly so that the hand that was enveloped in Winter's Grasp was closer to where the Master was suspended. Pope cowered to the boy's right holding his bleeding nose. On the other side of the room, lying comatose on another hospital bed, oblivious to the noise and light erupting around him was Freddie Flyte.

Freddie Flyte didn't look much better than his brother. Weeks of lying in a coma had turned his skin pallid. His dark hair was plastered to his scalp. On one side of his face, the skin was red and raw. There were still small scabs, the remains of blisters.

Another explosion echoed from outside. Blue sparks whizzed into the room, flying into the artefact on Christopher's hand. Another of the Stahlhelme gone. There was no time left. With one final thought as to the risk he was taking, the Master took a deep breath. He turned and stretched a hand back towards the vortex below.

He sucked towards its essence, just as he did when he consumed that village. In the distance, the maelstrom responded, flashing at this new stimulation.

At first it just felt like a rush of wind blasting into his body. Then he saw it. A stream of blue energy was rushing across the gulf towards his hand, responding to the power of the key holder. It was moving incredibly fast. He barely had time to register it was coming. Then it slammed into his body.

Such energy! Nothing that he had taken from a world before prepared him for the power. It coursed through him, threatening to render him unconscious. If he allowed it to fill him much more, he surely would black out. He gritted his teeth and turned his head back to the fissure.

He thrust his other hand forward towards Freddie Flyte. Then he pushed.

A stream of the bright blue energy blasted forth, flying through the fissure and across the room to consume Freddie. In a moment, Freddie's whole body was swathed in blue light.

The Master was a conduit now. The two streams of energy held him rigid. The force slamming into him from the vortex below pushed him forwards towards the fissure. The rope slackened. He pushed harder to compensate, trying to equal out the streams, so he was expelling as much as he was receiving.

Ahead, Freddie's body arched up. The power was reaching saturation point. Pope scuttled across to the furthest corner of the room and curled into a terrified ball.

Freddie's body lifted clean off the bed. The air around him began to glow. Onwards the Master pushed. Surely there could be no more he could pour into the man ahead.

As if in answer, Freddie's body shifted. Suddenly an explosion of energy from within him flashed off to the side near Christopher. Then a torrent of blue light rushed from his body and slammed into the gauntlet on Christopher's hand.

The Master laughed with teeth that flashed blue. It was going to work!

The Entity felt the laughter as the ripple on a distant pond, tiny and barely noticeable. It was so tired. It had been creating the world almost ceaselessly since the moment it had felt the touch of a new imagination.

It roused. There was something more. It was not just a tiny something at the edge of the void. It had been so focussed inwards that the flow of energy that gushed out into the distance had been unnoticed. Once it had noticed, it turned its attention away from the other below.

Something was drawing it away across the void. The Entity followed the path of its energy, fixing all its consciousness on the stream that was sucked outwards. It followed the path, stretching along its length, curious. At the furthest edge it passed briefly through another being, sucked in and blasted out before it had time to register that surprise.

Then it was outside of itself. It was flowing freely through a place that it recognised with an instinctual love. It moved through air it had not created itself. It sensed the movement and recognised it was in space it had not designed. And it knew that this was what it longed for. This was the truth in which it had created the world below. It had been here before.

This was home.

As quickly as it had experienced the brief bright flower of its past, it was gone. It dropped into something black.

It recognised another consciousness. It was like the one it had so avidly entwined itself around back in the void, another mind with its own set of vivid experience. That was where the similarity stopped. Suddenly, the Entity knew terror.

In the void, once it had started to create, it had danced through the other's mind. It had focussed in on each new experience it found with childlike wonder. Though sometimes the experiences had been dark and scary, it had known that they would not last. The world it had created through them was stern and dangerous, but not without joy and light.

This other wasn't like the one in the void. Before it could stop itself, the Entity was being wrenched through an imagination where everything was night and fear and hate.

It cast about for a way to escape. Now it truly knew pain. Now it understood the things that creatures could do to other creatures. Amidst the panic and fear, a new emotion manifested. Grief.

The stream continued through, sucking it onwards through the black awareness. The Entity folded into itself, trying to escape from the nightmare around it. It was no use. It was relentless. And despite its attempts, the Entity began to fill again.

When it found itself cast from the consciousness back out into the open space beyond it, its terror was so strong that it didn't realise. It was only once it understood that it had returned to the sanctuary of the void that it began to calm.

If only it had returned alone.

It was fat once more. Bloated with experience that it must expel down into the world of its creation. Yet, these experiences were tainted. Blackened horrors that came straight from that other, outer being. The Entity pushed the horrors from itself, down into the void below it.

And the World around Christopher grew once more.

The gaunt man laughed again. Sama cowered back against the door. There was no way to reach Christopher. Not without the man seeing her. She didn't want to begin to think about what the black gash surrounding him was. Whatever he was doing, he was hurting her friends.

At least from her vantage point she was out of his gaze. She looked into the rest of the room. Freddie floated above his bed, blasted by a constant stream of the blue energy from the man's hand. Torrents of blue light, shifting and glowing like rivers caught in moonlight, flared up once more between the Flyte brothers. Was that Winter's Grasp? Whatever was happening, Sama had to stop it. She cast her head about, desperately looking for a way to free Christopher and Freddie from the man.

Sama had no doubt that the man would direct whatever that blue light was right at her if she bowled in and started trying to drag her friends to safety. She swore under her breath. What she needed was a weak point.

Sama went cold. There was a weak point. It wasn't the flow from the man or the flow from Freddie to Christopher.

The weak point was the gaunt man himself.

Sama realised what she needed to do. She gritted her teeth. This was without doubt, the most reckless thing she had ever done. In her mind she could see

Chops with a wagging finger shaking her head vigorously. It was no use though. She had made a promise to herself to find Christopher and save him. That was what she would bloody well do!

'Bugger it!' Sama said and leapt to her feet. She burst around the door, running hard.

The man floating in front of her had just time to turn his head. He looked at her with shocked eyes. Then she leaped head-first into the opening he floated in and locked a hand around his neck. Before he could react she punched him once, twice in the side of the head, hard on his ear. That would really hurt, she grinned to herself.

It was like being in the middle of a storm. They were buffeted here and there. Though she kept focusing on the man she grappled with, she could sense the vastness of the place they hung in. She shook her head. She couldn't think about that now. From the corner of her eye she could see a great blue light. It was all she could do not to turn and look.

To his credit, the man reacted fast. He stopped blasting the blue energy out and grabbed at her arm with both hands, trying to dislodge her grip. Sama smashed her fist into his mouth. He spat blood.

He was strong. Stronger than her. Sama found that she was losing her grip. She stopped punching and grappled at his clothing, grasping something to hold on to. The man sensed his advantage. He punched back at her, catching her in the eye. The pain loosened her grip. She slipped down his body.

If he freed himself from her, she'd fall off into the chaos below. Her heart leapt into her mouth. She clutched again hard on to his coattail just at his waist. Thankfully it held. Now, she was below him, swinging erratically on the coat tail, banging into his legs. He kicked hard at her.

She swung to the side, narrowly avoiding a hard kick to the stomach. Fear made her strong. She pulled herself up his coattail, clambering up on to his back. He reached around behind him, flailing to get another grip on her.

Sama dodged his hands and stuck her head around him. If she could just reach the rope, she could pull herself away from him. Maybe she could get to safety.

Of course! The rope! Sama had the little penknife in her pocket. Why hadn't she thought of it before?

The man was still flailing. She ducked back down. Staying on his back like this was pretty much the hardest place for him to reach her. They buffeted around in the void, at the mercy of the swathes of wild blue energy that gusted around them.

She needed just a moment when he wouldn't grab at her. She changed her grip to his shoulders and brought her knee up as hard as she could into the middle of his back. He coughed violently as the air went out of him. Just for good measure, she kneed him again.

He gasped for air, badly winded. His arms were still flailing, but they had lost any sense of purpose. Sama knew that feeling. It would be all he could do to try and force a breath in. Trying to catch her would be far from his mind. It was now or never.

She scrambled up over his shoulders and pulled herself along the rope length. The blue light fizzed around her as she dragged herself through the blue gash. She dropped on to the floor of the hospital ward again.

Her legs went to jelly. It was all she could do not to collapse down on to the floor there and then. She couldn't. Not yet.

She turned back to the black fissure and pulled the little knife from her pocket. The man had recovered from his winding enough to have realised she'd escaped. He coughed and spluttered ahead of her on the rope. He grabbed forwards towards her, but she was out of his reach.

Sama sliced at the rope with the penknife. John Braddock had been right, it was indeed sharp. The rope, for all its strength, wasn't thick. With her first slice, she was a third of the way through it.

She looked at his face as she sliced again. He was screaming something at her, wild eyes staring up with hatred, but it was lost in the void. Sama grinned at him, just to keep him angry. Then she sliced with the penknife again and the rope was cut. As he fell down into the void, the man's expression changed from anger to surprise.

The fissure disappeared. One moment Sama stared at the man falling away from her, the next she was staring at the white far wall of the ward. She collapsed to the floor, panting heavily. She closed her eyes and laid her face on the cold stone. She could hear the sound of footsteps approaching, running down the corridor. The Braddocks. They had gotten through. They could help her with Christopher.

At the thought of his name, her eyes snapped open. No time to rest. Not yet. With a sigh, Sama pushed herself up on to her feet and stumbled over to her friend's bed.

CHAPTER TWENTY

Almost Stirring

A voice broke through Christopher's sleep. 'Wake up, lads.' Then a hand was at his shoulder shaking him awake. He opened his eyes. Griflet had already stepped over him through the dark to shake another squire awake. 'Look sharp. We ride in ten minutes.'

Christopher sat up and rubbed his eyes. The other boys were struggling to rise, their faces as sleepy as his in the dull glow of a small camp fire. On the other side, the knights that had not been on watch were doing the same. 'How long did we rest?' a little boy who looked no more than about eleven asked in a squeaky voice. 'It feels like it was moments.'

'Long enough, Peter,' an older squire sneered, lengthening the boy's name for effect. 'Long enough for those of us that are used to this, anyway.'

A look of dislike passed over Peter's drawn face. 'I'm not used to this, Thomas,' he quavered.

The older squire, Thomas, pushed himself up. He caught Peter's gaze and sneered again. Then he headed out into the dark.

'I wish we were somewhere warm,' Peter said in a small voice. He sighed and clambered to his feet. Then he stumbled off sleep-stiffened legs, across to one of the knights. He bent to pick up a leg guard and began strapping it to the knight's leg.

Christopher was suddenly aware that he was the only one of the squires that had not started to do something. He glanced across to the left of the fire. Eleila was standing alone, a little way out into the darkness.

He freed himself from the damp blanket and shuffled over to her. The hard ground had made his whole body ache. It hurt to move. But it was obvious from the activity around him that there would be no waiting for an aching boy.

'You slept?' Eleila asked.

'Yes,' Christopher said, rubbing his shoulder. 'Did you?'

'And how do you explain that you slept, even though this is already a dream?' Eleila snapped back at him, ignoring his question.

Christopher sighed. 'I'm sorry. I don't know.'

She grunted and tugged at a strap on her saddle. Her horse snorted in protest and shifted its hooves. Eleila stroked its mane and tickled behind its ear. 'I didn't sleep,' she said. 'I was more use with the guards keeping watch.'

Christopher understood. Eleila's acceptance as an equal was at best fragile, held together by circumstance and a barely confirmed story. She wouldn't let any of the others have reason to question it.

A few feet away, one of the knights called quietly out into the dark, 'Bediviere, it is not as clear as last night. Shall we light the torches?'

Hooves thudded on rocky earth in the darkness. Bediviere appeared at the edge of the camp, already armoured and mounted. 'We cannot afford the risk. We must ride carefully until the morning shows us the way.'

The knight nodded and turned back to his horse. He glanced up into the black sky. 'We will probably be soaked before long.'

The knight was right. After leaving the camp, they climbed into the highest part of the pass, above the cloud line. Strong winds blew thick, sodden swathes of cloud across their path. The moisture soaked into them until the cloth of their clothes grew dark and their armour dripped with little streams.

They occasionally passed dark shapes off the path, in the mist. Lonely trees grew hardy amongst the tufts of mountain grass and heather. Once, they passed an old hut, half fallen down. Its dark slate roof was collapsed down into the walls. Even in the weak morning light the slate had a dull wet shine to it.

The knights rode in silence. The only sounds were those of their journeying, hooves against rock, armour clanking against armour. The horses' deep panting echoed the heavy breaths of the knights themselves.

At the head of the group Bediviere and Griflet led the way. Eleila had again positioned herself behind them. She rode alone. The next pair of knights rode about half a horse's length behind her. Her position in the saddle was stiff and proud. Her head was fixed firmly forward. If she had noticed her companions' refusal to ride by her, she was ignoring it.

Christopher fell in towards the back of the line, where the rest of the squires rode. They too were close-mouthed, taking their lead from their masters.

It was hard going in the dim morning. For the next hour, Christopher found that all he could do was try to keep his horse on the path. He followed close behind the horse in front. Often he had to guide his horse back on to the trail. It was so easy to lose the way.

Once the morning light was strong enough they quickened their pace. It wasn't long before they crossed the top of the pass. Though the mist was still thick, Christopher sensed that they had started to descend. It was just the barest incline at first but within twenty minutes they were coming down at quite an angle.

Soon the countryside around Christopher was easier to make out. Ahead he could see a line of trees. Another forest meant that they would be away from the wind and the wet. The promise of shelter from the elements was very welcome.

Once they were in the protection of the tall pines, Christopher found himself warming a little. The path they followed was very narrow, forcing them to ride single file. The party snaked out into a long line.

There were occasional noises in the undergrowth, as animals were disturbed by their passing. A sudden wet rustling in the trees or a flash of hide bounding away would have one of the knights clutching for their swords before they realised it was nothing and passed on. Even when the sounds were more threatening the knights preferred to pass on. Sometimes swords were even drawn, ready should some creature burst through on to the path intent on protecting itself or its young. Even then though, they didn't veer off the path to look for trouble.

In the forest, the ground beneath the horses' hooves was a mixture of mud and leaves. It was far easier than the rock they had left behind. Ahead, Bediviere raised a hand to signal that the pace should quicken. Christopher spurred his mount forward with a squeeze of his heels.

They rode on as fast as the terrain would allow for another hour. Eventually they came to the edge of the trees. Ahead, Christopher could hear the rush of water. He followed the others out into a clearing.

It was at the top of a high cliff. In a far corner of the trees, a fast flowing stream, the source of the sound, gushed foamy over exposed rocks. Beyond the rocks, the stream cut a narrow groove into the earth then dropped over the edge of the cliff. The path they were on cut across to the stream, then followed along its side. As the stream went over the edge, the path turned sharply to the left and down out of sight.

Bediviere drew to a halt and turned back to the other knights. They pulled their horses into a loose semi-circle around him. The squires stopped behind them.

Eleila had been pushed out to one side. One of the knights, whether consciously or not, moved his horse so she was all but forced out altogether. Eleila's mount stepped backwards and she turned her head, looking for another space in the group.

Christopher rode forward past the other squires and drew up next to her. She frowned at the back of the knight who had blocked her out. Her shoulders slumped a little.

'How are you getting on?' Christopher asked quietly, wondering if the constant snubs were grating on her.

'I am fine and that is not the way that a squire should talk to his knight. Try to follow their example.' She nodded over at the squires.

'Do you really think they accept that I am a squire?' Christopher asked, wondering why his imagination would have conjured up such an antagonistic companion for this dream.

'They probably haven't bothered to give it any thought at all,' Eleila said, staring at him. 'But that's not to say—'

'Quiet!' Ahead, Sir Griflet glanced at them with a frown under his unvisored helmet.

One of the squires, the larger sneering one, sniggered loudly. Christopher looked over. The squire was staring back, a superior smirk on his face.

'And you too, Thomas,' Griflet barked over. 'You should be setting an—'

Suddenly there was an ear-splitting crack that seemed to come from all around them. The very ground shifted under their feet. Some of the horses whinnied, including his own, shifting with fear. Christopher struggled, pulling tightly on the reins trying to stop her wheeling around. 'What was that?' he gasped.

Before anyone could respond, the ground shifted again. This time it was much more violent. The force threw Christopher to the side in his saddle. He gripped hard with his legs to stay on. A rushing sound, like the roar of a mighty wind, filled his senses drowning out the sound of the gushing stream.

Then something slammed into him. It was as solid and hard as a wall, but he could see nothing. The impact knocked him from his horse. Everything was impossibly bright. The world he was in disappeared into pure white. A moment later his vision cleared a little, though the light still filled his senses. It was almost solid, yet he could make out the shapes of the others. Many of them had fallen from their animals, too. Figures were reaching upwards, throwing arms over heads as if to protect themselves from some great force. At the edge of the clearing, the trees swayed violently. No, it was more than that. They were changing shape, growing.

Yet, there was something else twisting through his consciousness. He could still feel the wet grass under his body, but at the same time he had a distinct sense that he was lying somewhere completely different. He frowned and closed his eyes. The feeling grew stronger.

It was not just where he lay. His clothes began to feel different as well. It was as if he were wearing two sets at the same time. The wet, cold ones that he had had on all day and another set. A set of warmer dry clothes. They were light and soft. Here he was both cold and wet and tired on unpleasant wet ground and warm and dry on something much more comfortable.

Then the feeling of what he was lying on suddenly made sense to him. It was a bed!

He opened his eyes. The world around him was still white. The ghosts of the knights still moved through the haze. He went to lift his arm to rub his eyes and perhaps clear his vision.

His arm wouldn't move.

He frowned again and looked down. There! He saw it. It was as if he was looking at two versions of his arm. One was wrapped in the wet cloak he was growing to hate. The other was in one of his grey jumpers from home. And that arm was tied down to a metal bed below it.

Christopher's heart leapt. The question of why he might be tied down flashed through his mind briefly, but disappeared in his excitement. He was waking up! That had to be it. As soon as the idea occurred to him, Christopher concentrated hard on the feeling of being dry and tied down, squinting his eyes against the more vivid reality around him.

It was working. The feeling of being somehow tied down increased and the things in his vision began to shift and swirl. In front of him he suddenly had the sense of high white walls with tall barred windows.

The shapes became more distinct. They were beds. Opposite where he watched from, a man lay strapped down. The man was surrounded by the light, which obscured much of his form.

The light was getting larger both in his mind's eye and in the terrain around him. Eleila was at his side, shaking his shoulders and shouting something. The words were lost in the rushing noise that shut out everything else. It was getting clearer. The man on the bed before him was also strapped down. He appeared to be unconscious. He had twisted to one side. His head lay facing Christopher.

It was Freddie!

Christopher stared with surprise. 'Freddie!' he called. At least he thought he did. The Christopher on the grass cried out. The Christopher on the bed, however, had remained silent, able to do nothing but watch.

Something flashed on the periphery of his vision. Someone running across the room. Christopher strained to move his head on the bed. No matter how hard he tried, there was nothing. Whoever it was on the edge of his sight, they dived forward and disappeared.

Then suddenly the vision was dimming. Christopher's heart lurched. Desperately he tried to keep hold of that other place. His vision began to clear. As the light receded, so too did the feeling of the hard stone floor. The images of walls floated away into nothingness.

'No,' Christopher said, letting his head fall back on to the ground, where it slapped down on to wet earth. He closed his eyes, hopeful that perhaps the act would help to keep his focus. There was nothing. Once again he heard the sounds of movement, armour clanking, horses neighing absently. Behind it, the sound of the waterfall roared steadily in his ears. 'Get up!' Eleila's voice came suddenly from his left. She sounded quite angry. That wasn't how he expected her to sound. Through the light her face had looked terrified. Christopher opened his eyes and looked up at her.

Eleila wasn't kneeling next to him at all. Instead she was still sitting on her horse. She was also very red in the face. Behind her, the other knights and squires were also still mounted. They all glanced at him, some with confusion, and some with mirth. Others, like Eleila, looked angry.

Their expressions didn't hold his attention though. His eyes widened. The whole landscape had changed.

The essential elements that he had seen as they rode from the trees were still there, but it was so transformed it felt like a different place altogether. The grassy cliff top that they had been on was gone completely. Instead, the horses stood on a dirty brown track that picked its way through a sea of mud. Craters dotted the ground. Many were filled with brown water. How deep they were was impossible to tell.

Where the gushing stream had been, a wide river heaved dark water over the edge of the plateau. Indistinguishable shapes polluted the water. Christopher hoped that they were lumps of earth, or perhaps limbs of branches ripped from trees. One floating in the middle of the dirty water looked distinctly like a leg. He looked away quickly.

The tree line on the other side of the river was gone. Instead, the plain of mud continued, dotted with a few blackened stumps. In the distance, the brown of the mud slowly turned to the murky grey of the mountain peaks beyond.

'Get up!' Eleila said again, 'What are you doing?'

Christopher hardly heard her. He twisted and looked behind him.

That way, the path still stretched back into the forest, at least, but the forest was changed almost beyond recognition. The trees were hideous dead things. They twisted into one another, forming an impenetrable wall on either side of the path. They were almost as black as the distant stumps. There were no leaves. There was no sound of animals. There was no movement. The forest was death.

'Get on your horse, boy!' Bediviere's voice carried from the front of the line.

Christopher glanced back at the knights. How were they all on their horses so quickly? At the front of the line, Bediviere continued on his way. Hearing his movement, the knights nearest to him followed. Soon the whole line had turned away from Christopher and followed. All except Eleila.

'Will you get on the horse!' she spat, exasperated. 'If you are trying to make me seem like a fool, you're doing a good job of it.' She glanced over her shoulder at the backs of the other knights. Bediviere had almost disappeared from view, following the path down the side of the cliff. 'They are probably already laughing at my inability to choose a good squire.'

Christopher frowned up at her. 'Eleila, what about this?' He waved towards the river.

Eleila glanced around at the desolate landscape. 'What of it? The terrain will improve when we reach the valley floor.' She shot an irritated look at him, 'All the more reason not to stop for here a rest.'

'But it's changed!' Christopher said. Suddenly it dawned on him. She couldn't see the changes. He clambered up, staring intently at her. 'This was green fields and forest.'

'It's not been like that since before the civil war,' Eleila said.

'It was like it just a second ago,' Christopher protested. He grabbed the reins of her horse. 'Don't you see it?'

'Get off!' Eleila wrenched the reins from his grip. Her horse backed away.

'How can you not see it?' Christopher asked. 'Everything is different!'

'No.' Eleila shook her head. 'Things do not change like that. This is the result of the battles that Arthur fought here. This is the result of war.'

'You're wrong,' Christopher said. Why should she see it? She was part of this dream. She wouldn't remember the rushing. She wouldn't know she had been grabbing at him and screaming. Suddenly Christopher felt very alone.

'Whatever you think you can see or not see,' Eleila snapped, interrupting his thoughts. 'It is of no consequence to me. I have to follow my lady's command. You … You can stay here with your madness for all I care.'

She wheeled her horse around and trotted off in the direction of the others. Christopher watched her pick up her pace, slowing only when she reached the edge and turned to descend the pass. She didn't look back.

He stumbled to his own horse, shaken. There was nothing for it but to follow. He climbed into the saddle and began along the track again.

It must be a dream. Where else did a place that you were in change so completely and so instantly? Besides, he had just almost awakened.

Then what, his mind answered back, had he seen in those phantoms? How had Freddie been there? Had it actually been a dream inside a dream? Why did he not wake up? Tears of frustration stung the bottom of his eyes. He shook them away angrily.

'I'm not wrong,' he insisted to himself. 'I'll wake up soon enough.'

He rode a few paces to the cliff edge. The path turned to hug the side of the cliff. It wound down in sharp zigzags to the valley far below. The others had already dropped down a good way ahead of him. He sighed and began to descend.

'I'm not wrong,' he repeated to himself. His voice seemed small and insignificant against the rush of the waterfall. 'I'm not mad.'

The Stahlhelme had changed.

Twelve of the creatures waited impatiently for their quarry, salivating wildly in anticipation of human flesh. They were taller now. Even the shortest of their number was over eight feet. Their brows had grown thicker. Their eyes had taken on a red, bloody quality. The two teeth of their lower jaw were more like tusks. Their uniforms were more tatters than clothes any more.

The signs of battle were about them. Each sported fearsome wounds. To the front of the throng, one sported a deep gash that ran from under its helmet to the side of its mouth. Part of its lip hung loosely. The gash oozed blood that burst into a squirt each time it growled. To its side, blood and something yellow dripped from a dirty wound in its shoulder. The wound looked old, but still it suppurated.

Another had a wide slash in its stomach. The edges of the slash had been sewn roughly together. Through the gap beneath, its internal organs pumped quite visibly.

Not one had escaped some violation, though their wounds gave them no pain. It was as if the horror of the mutilations was to strike fear into their enemies only. As if to prove it, another missing an arm smashed its blooded stump against a rock beside it in excitement. A bloody stain spattered on to the rock, but the creature didn't flinch.

One pushed forward, its head rising out of the narrow gully they hid within. Its orange eyes squinted as it searched the valley beyond, hunting for distant movement on the descending mountain cliff path. It was not disappointed.

With a roar, it leaned forward. It trained its gaze on the tiny blurs travelling down the winding track. It growled to its nearest companions, who lurched forward too. They stretched grey snouts to sniff at the air and stare wide eyed out at their distant quarry. For one of them, the anticipation seemed too much. It started to lumber forward toward the valley floor.

Behind them, the tallest of the creatures bellowed down at the advancing beast. At the voice of its commander, it stopped in its tracks. Reluctantly, it backed up to the others.

The leader shambled forward, barking out orders in a raw guttural growl. It stabbed its arm up the gorge they hid in, then off towards the right in the direction of the cliff path. Immediately, eight of its companions grunted assent and surged up the slope.

The leader watched them race to the top. They reached it in a couple of minutes and disappeared over the rise. The last of their number glanced back. The beast waved off along the top of the ridge to confirm their actions. Then it too clambered out of sight.

The leader gestured to the remaining three. Growling and jostling amongst each other they reached back to a large bundle. Something wrapped in an oil stained cloth. It took two of them to lift it.

They struggled down the gorge with the bundle, stopping on a small hillock that swelled up on one side. On the flat of its peak, they set the bundle down with effort. The third reached to a thick leather strap that held the bundle together and pulled at the clasp. Its thick fingers struggled for a moment, unsuited for such delicate movements. Its claws kept getting caught in the clasp. One of the carriers growled impatiently at it. Then the clasp was free. The creature pulled the oil stained cloth aside, revealing the shiny black barrel of a machine gun.

It lifted the gun free of the cloth, struggling with the weight. Then it stepped back to allow its companions set up a black steel three pronged stand.

The leader watched the three, saliva pumping into its mouth with anticipation. Then, satisfied with the preparations, it returned to look up the valley once more and watch the steady progress of their quarry.

Christopher's horse picked its way carefully down the path. Once he had caught the others he rode quietly at the back with the other squires. Occasionally they prattled amongst themselves, careful that their volume didn't get loud enough to raise rebuke from their masters.

Eleila rode just behind Griflet and Bediviere again. She had frowned back in his direction and once she had spotted him her face had hardened and she had turned away. She had not looked back again.

The valley floor was growing closer. Like the plateau above, the ground was a crater-scarred plain of mud. On the steep sides of the valley, there were at least patches of grass between rock escarpments. Even there though, the craters continued.

Below them, where the cliff path joined the valley floor, military defences were set out. Christopher stared down at lines of wooden stakes. Each stake had a sharp pointed end that jutted up menacingly. Long lines of vicious barbed wire wrapped around the stakes and stretched between them. Where the line intersected with the craters, the barbed wire was gone as if blown away. In some craters, lengths of it were tangled with mud and remains of vegetation in dark impenetrable clumps.

'What's that for?' Christopher asked the squire next to him, a young lad of no more than about twelve.

The squire frowned and looked downward. 'What?'

'The stakes and the wire,' Christopher replied.

'You really do know nothing,' Thomas, riding just ahead, sneered back over his shoulder. 'They're defences.'

'But against what?' Christopher frowned. 'And what's caused the craters?'

The boy ahead frowned back, struggling with an answer. 'Who knows what goes on out here in these wildernesses? In Camelot, hardly a soul would dare attack, but here there are bandits and who knows what else.'

Peter was just behind Christopher. 'They did attack Camelot though, didn't they?' the younger boy said quietly. 'Or we'd be going home instead of riding through this godless place.'

'Well, we are,' Thomas retorted, 'and that's how it is. So there's no use thinking about it. The men will know what to do.' He stressed the word 'men' and again sneered at Christopher. 'We'll follow them just like we have always done.'

'Into another battle?' Christopher said, surprised at himself for feeling the sting of the obvious slight.

'What kind of squire are you?' Thomas scoffed. 'Following a serving girl who thinks she's a knight? I don't know which one of you is the bigger fool.'

Christopher felt a surge of irritation. 'Perhaps you didn't hear Sir Bediviere. You're supposed to be treating her with the respect that you give all the other knights.'

'Perhaps I didn't.' The corners of Thomas's mouth turned up into a rude smile. 'All I know is I'd be a lot happier if it had been a real knight that had joined us. A knight who had stood with our masters against Sir Mordred.'

Christopher found unexpected hackles rising further. A thought flashed briefly through his mind. Was he just defending a part of his own dream against another part of it? It was so hard not to be drawn in. 'Well, she was trusted enough to be carrying the Sword in the Stone.'

'Is that what it is?' Peter said, coming up next to him, awed. A moment later he sank dejectedly in his seat. 'Then we're really for it.'

'Quiet back there!' Sir Griflet had turned in his saddle. He glared at them through the slit of his visor. The squires immediately turned forwards and fell into silence.

They reached the valley floor ten minutes later. The path passed through a gap in the stake and wire defences. To one side, a wooden gate made of thick planks swung open. On its outward facing side, riveted iron bands held the planks together. Between them spikes stuck out.

Peter looked dejectedly at the defences. 'I wish we could go back to Camelot.'

'Well, we can't,' Thomas retorted again. 'It's not ours anymore.'

'What happens if Sir Kay falls as well?' the young squire asked out loud to no one in particular.

'Then we'll all be subjects of King Mordred,' Thomas replied. 'And he'll probably bring his mother and his aunt down as well.' He glanced back with a cruel glint in his eye. 'And we've all heard the stories of Morgan Le Fay and Morgause.'

'Those stories aren't real. Merlin was the last magician,' Peter said in a small unconvinced voice. 'They wouldn't come.'

'Oh they would,' Thomas said. 'And they'd bring all manner of creatures and beasts with them. There'd be killing and feasting. In fact, I bet the first thing they'd feast on would be weak little squires who weren't brave enough to follow their masters.'

Ahead, Sir Bediviere let out a groan. He wheeled his horse around, spurring heels into its flanks. The horse whinnied and galloped across to the squires.

'Thomas, must you always torment?' Bediviere growled. 'If half the effort you put into that were placed in keeping my sword sharp, I could run you through right now as a punishment.'

'Sorry, Sir Bediviere.' Thomas bowed his head.

'I will have silence from you all,' Bediviere continued. 'Or you'll be joining Thomas mucking out Kay's stables once we have arrived.'

'Sir Bediviere!' Eleila called urgently from the front of the line. 'Something's moving!'

Bediviere scowled one more time at his squire. Then he pulled his horse around and rode back toward the front of the group. He stopped by Eleila. 'Where?'

Eleila pointed into the distance to the far side of the valley ahead. 'Up there. Something glinted.'

'Something glinted?' Sir Griflet spat out. 'We do not have time for—'

'Hold, Griflet.' Bediviere cut him off. He looked out into the distance where Eleila had indicated, frowning.

The others waited silently for him to speak. A couple glanced at Eleila with looks of derision. Another exchanged a smirk with Griflet. Once again, Christopher felt his hackles rise.

Bediviere concentrated for a few moments on the valley ahead. 'You're sure?' he said eventually. 'I see nothing.'

'Come on Bediviere,' Griflet said impatiently before Eleila could speak. 'Are you really going to waste valuable time on her scared imaginings?'

Bediviere ignored the knight. He kept his eyes fixed on Eleila. 'Eleila?'

Eleila rose a little in her saddle, straightening her shoulders against Griflet's words. Her eyes involuntarily flicked at him. She pulled them away to meet Bediviere's steady gaze. 'No, I am not sure, but I'm sure enough to think it's worth checking.'

Griflet snorted back a laugh. Bediviere rolled his eyes at him.

'Let me ride ahead and see,' Eleila said in a voice that struggled to stay steady. 'You can carry on riding. It won't hold you up. If it is nothing, Sir Griflet will be welcome to laugh at me all he wants.' She looked back at Sir Griflet and said sharply. 'At least he'll be alive to do so.'

'So it takes more than Griflet to intimidate you.' Bediviere's face broke into a thin smile. 'But no, what you carry is too precious. Griflet, Jasper, Benton, ride out ahead and scout the valley.'

Eleila sat back on to her horse silently. Christopher could imagine that she was smarting. She'd be trying to think of a good argument to allow her to show her heroism, frustrated at the logic of Bediviere's retort. Again a dry thought pointed out to him that he was believing in the feelings of his own imagination.

Griflet spurred his horse with another derisive snort. He galloped away from the main group. The two other knights followed his example.

'Be ready to charge,' Bediviere said. 'If it is trouble, then we must get through.'

CHAPTER TWENTY-ONE

The Ambush

'Pick up the pace,' Bediviere barked and pushed his horse into a light trot.

They had reached a hundred or so metres into the valley. The group was spread out in a far looser formation than the single file they had descended in. The knights still made up the head of the group. Bediviere was at the front. Eleila was close behind.

She had positioned herself there as soon as Griflet and the other two knights galloped off ahead to investigate. Again, she held her head high. She refused to meet the eyes of any of the others except Bediviere and, somewhat surprisingly, Christopher himself. She glanced back at him, just once. When she caught his eye her defensive expression softened. Christopher smiled back, again feeling the urge to encourage her, even if she was just a figment of his imagination.

Christopher urged his horse forward. It outpaced the two squires next to him by half its length. To his left Peter edged his horse outwards, making more room. The young squire looked up at the bleak slopes that formed the valley walls, his brow knotted with fear. Thomas was on the right. He kicked his horse's sides, overtook then shot a look back at Christopher. 'Ride behind me. Know your place.'

Christopher considered what Thomas would look like if he were suddenly thrown from his horse into the churned up mud all around them. It would be very easy to reach over and grab one of his legs then heave it upward to throw him off balance. He sighed. It would end with Eleila shouting at him for alienating them even further.

Instead, he gritted his teeth and fell into line with Peter. The smaller squire glanced across with a shy smile. 'I'll still ride with you,' he said in a querulous voice.

In the stream gulley, the Stahlhelme manning the machine gun were entirely prepared. The ugly barrel, now fitted to the black metal tripod, jutted out of a thick metal jacket holding water to stop overheating. One of them crouched at the back, great slabs of hands gripping the double handles on the heel of the gun, where the trigger was. A string of saliva dripped from between two tusks.

To its right another had fed the end of a long ammunition belt into a slot in the barrel. To the left the third stood by with a pitcher of cold water to pour into the cooling jacket.

Their leader peered over the ridge. Its breaths came in and out with such force that each one produced a low rumbling growl.

Below, the three knights were almost in line with the gully. A few more seconds and they would be in the sights of the gun. Further back along the valley floor, the larger group had picked up pace too. They were well within the killing zone. The other group of Stahlhelme would be in place behind both parties of knights now. They would be caught quickly.

The leader narrowed its eyes. It stared intently at the larger group, searching out the quarry. The boy must be unharmed. After a moment it shifted, grunting with satisfaction as it spotted him, riding at the back. The leader grunted again, then raised a giant arm to signal to the gun crew behind it to open fire.

Griflet and the others had reached quite a way into the valley. They pulled up close to where Eleila had pointed. The horses took a moment to calm after the gallop. One trotted around in a circle until the knight, Jasper, tugged sharply on the reins and turned the beast to stand next to the others.

They looked up at the side of the valley. The lilt of their conversation carried across the ground, but the words themselves were impossible to make out. Then Griflet turned back to the main party and shrugged.

Thomas flashed a spiteful grin at Christopher. 'At this rate your mistress will be with us squires cleaning boots before the day is out.'

Before Christopher could respond, the other knight with Griflet stood in his saddle. He pointed up the valley slope. He shouted something. Griflet and Jasper turned to follow where he pointed. Griflet swung back around. His hand burst up into the air to wave back, frantic, at them.

The leader of the Stahlhelme dropped its hand. The beast manning the gun squeezed the trigger. The gun leapt into life. Bullet after bullet flew into the valley.

They sliced into Sir Griflet, ripping through his armour like it was paper. He slumped down into his saddle, limp arms dropping. His horse collapsed forward, caught in the same maelstrom of lead. Griflet slid off the saddle and on to the grass.

The beast switched the angle of the gun and squeezed off another hot burst.

301

The ammunition belt chugged through the weapon. Below, Sir Benton was blown from his horse and landed on the ground.

Sir Jasper managed to turn his horse around before he too was caught in the path of the bullets and fell forward. His horse, bewildered but somehow managing to stay out of the danger, galloped up the valley with him slumped on its back.

It all happened so fast. The three knights were gone. Thomas pulled up his horse abruptly in front of Christopher. Christopher's horse bashed into its rear and whinnied.

'What was that?' Peter shouted in terror, pulling up next to Christopher.

There was an explosion behind them. Christopher whipped around in his saddle. On the far side of the valley, eight huge creatures appeared from behind a large outcrop of jagged rocks. Each brandished a great rifle with a vicious axe head at the end of the long barrel.

Atop their ugly heads they wore German Picklehaulbe helmets. They wore grey uniforms. Admittedly the clothes were in tatters, ripped by their giant bodies, but they were unmistakable. Christopher knew he had seen a creature like this before.

'This isn't real,' he said out loud. He shook his head, squeezing his eyes shut to try and clear his mind. How could it be? If he needed any more proof of his dream state, this was it.

That poster. He had seen it outside Henley. The beast in a tattered German uniform, holding the poor defenceless woman symbolising Belgium. He opened his eyes again and looked at the advancing creatures. If anything, they were larger and more fearsome, but there was no mistaking what he saw. The beasts ahead were all born of that creature in the poster.

One of them raised its rifle and fired. For a split second there was a whistle of the bullet speeding through the air, followed by a dull 'whump' as if someone had been punched. Peter swayed in his saddle, then gurgled.

'Christopher.' His voice sounded strange and strangled. Christopher dragged his eyes away from the advancing monstrosities and looked across. He gasped with horror.

There was a hole in Peter's chest. It was about four inches below the left of his collarbone. Peter frowned and looked down at it. He looked up again and mouthed something impossible to make out. Finally, his eyes rolled skywards and he fell across his horse.

Christopher leaned forward to help the boy, but there was another loud report as one of the creatures fired its rifle. Peter's horse started. Without a conscious rider to control it, it bolted off at a gallop. To the left another knight fell from his saddle.

'Ride!' Bediviere shouted with a hoarse desperate voice. Around Christopher, others kicked the sides of their horses, spurring them away from the nightmares.

Thomas wheeled his horse around and galloped back towards the mountain pass. The crack of rifles was regular now. The sound was like fireworks popping in the sky, deafeningly close. Knights and squires fell from horses as bullets struck.

Thomas got about twenty feet. Suddenly he flew off the side of his horse. It was as if he had been swatted by a great fly swat. He angled out four feet before finally hitting the mud and lying still.

'This isn't real,' Christopher insisted to himself again.

The sound of his own voice in his mind was surprisingly calm. Of course! If it wasn't real, which it couldn't be, why be scared? All of a sudden he felt distinct from the drama around him. Everything seemed to slow down.

The riders that hadn't already been felled by the volleys distanced away from him. He considered giving in to the adrenaline he could feel trying to course through him. Instead, he turned the horse around and faced the creatures coming towards him. Unconsciously he cocked his head to one side, his expression quizzical.

He had never dreamed like this before. His dreams were collections of moments filtered through one or two senses at most. Some had been intense. Some had been scary. Nothing had been this vivid or this linear.

Every sense with which he was experiencing the world around him was stimulated. The creatures ahead were perfectly formed, complete in a way he did not remember from other dreams. Their appearance, inspired by something that he only had a short glimpse of. Whilst it had stuck in his mind, how could they be such complete creations? The details on their ragged jackets, insignia and buttons were so well formed. They could not come from memory alone.

Yet it was more than that. They were just one dimension of the scene around. At the same time as he focussed on them, he could feel the cold wind blowing through his already rain dampened clothes. He could hear the whistle of that wind blowing through the valley, between the reports of the guns and the moans of the fallen.

Even his own body was reacting as if it were real. There was a dryness in his throat. His heart pounded with adrenaline-fuelled blood. His stomach danced with fear induced butterflies. Yet his mind remained calm and disjointed. It couldn't be real, despite all the signs.

Someone called his name. He glanced across. Eleila was galloping back toward him. Beyond, Bediviere and the other knights drew close to where Griflet had fallen. The dark base chatter of the machine gun started again, taking the front two down in seconds. The others wheeled away.

Christopher turned back to the creatures. He stared into the face of the nearest, locking gazes with it. Its eyes were blood red, devoid of anything resembling kindness or humanity. They narrowed. It raised its rifle to point straight at him.

Before it could fire, another by its side placed a mighty hand on the gun. It muttered something and gestured at Christopher. The creature nodded. Then it angled the rifle in another direction along the valley. It fired. Behind him, Christopher heard a scream and a thud of another falling from his horse.

Eleila stopped at his side. 'Come on!' She shook him. 'Come on, you fool!'

'It isn't real.' He looked at her. Her face was white with fear. 'They can't hurt me.'

'Well, they can hurt me!' she screamed back at him. 'Please, Christopher, ride!'

She grabbed his reins and spurred her horse towards a small outcrop of rocks about fifteen feet up the slope of their side of the valley. Bediviere and the other survivors raced to the same place. Two more riders had fallen before they reached the outcrop.

Eleila galloped them behind the swathe of rock. The main crag rose nine feet into the air. Behind it they were covered. At one end a smaller boulder had fallen against the main crag. Between the rocks a thin fissure opened into the valley beyond.

Bediviere had dropped to his knees and peered through the slit.

'Crossbows,' he barked.

Eleila jumped from her horse, throwing a furious look at Christopher. She ran to join the others.

Another volley of shots crashed into the front of the crag. Dislodged dirt and rocks showered down into their shelter. Christopher dropped from his horse and walked over.

Only Bediviere and two knights remained. One was tall, with a red tunic. The other wore armour covered in dents and scratches.

'We're trapped!' The knight with the red tunic stared at Bediviere, his face a mask of fear and confusion. 'We can't charge through that. They'll pick us off like the rest.'

'Calm.' Bediviere's brow creased in concentration. 'We take them one by one.' He nodded at the end of the outcrop nearest to the advancing Stahlhelme. 'Position yourselves.'

'What about the ones on the slope?' the knight said.

'Those that advance are the immediate threat. Ready!'

They positioned at points set to lean out. The knight in red clambered to a lip above and crouched.

'On my mark, we aim for the nearest.' Bediviere stuck his head out for the briefest of seconds. He glanced at the others. 'There is one ahead of the others. He is about a furlong away to the left. He will be our first.'

Eleila shot a look at Christopher. 'If you're not going to help, get back!' She pushed him then turned away, facing the fissure.

'Now!' Bediviere swung his crossbow over the rock. To the side, Eleila bent low and pointed the crossbow through the fissure. The others were doing the same.

The machine gun chattered. The rock exploded with mud and stone chips. There was no time. A clang of metal hit metal. The knight in red slumped down from the lip. He landed in a crumpled heap at Christopher's feet.

Only Eleila managed to fire her bolt successfully through the fissure. In the distance, one of the creatures roared.

The knight in shabby armour skipped across and bent to check his fallen companion then shook his head.

'Damn it,' Bediviere said.

Eleila peered out carefully through the fissure. 'They've stopped. Ah, I hit one!' She turned back, a wild grin on her face. 'They're not so casual now.' She looked again. 'They're taking up positions behind the dead.'

'They'll wait us out,' the shabby knight said. 'We can't get away. They know we'll have to try and defend ourselves to escape.'

'We must protect the sword,' Bediviere said grimly. 'If it means that we sacrifice ourselves so that one can escape, then so be it.'

The machine gun chattered again, spraying more earth and rock down on to them. Christopher shook his head, dislodging bits that landed on him. He glanced at the others. Bediviere had begun to speak in low tones, gesticulating with his one arm, but Christopher didn't focus on the words.

That creature had stopped at firing at him. Christopher had felt that before. The creatures recognised him. At least, one had. This was like the gypsies all over again.

What if he just went out there, Christopher thought to himself. He doubted very much that the creatures gave two figs about the sword, none of that was real. But they certainly gave two figs about him. What if he just went out there and confronted them? What if they did kill him? At the very worse that would probably wake him up.

That would wake him up.

Quite suddenly all the fear and horror drained out of his body, leaving it as calm and detached as his mind. The desire to wake up was so strong. Everything else was nothing. Christopher stood. Eleila was listening intently to Bediviere's instructions. He slipped around her. It was just two steps to the open ground.

Christopher took a deep breath and walked out.

In the valley, the Stahlhelme spread themselves out. They lay prone on the ground, behind scant cover of the bodies of horses and men. They were not worried. Their weapons were trained on the rocky outcrop ahead. Any person that tried to fire off another bolt would be dead before they even managed to get their crossbows aimed.

Behind a broken horse, still raggedly clinging on to life, one of the Stahlhelme pulled itself forward. It settled in a better position. Its rifle pointed forward.

Suddenly, its beady blood red eyes caught the barest movement at the side of the rock. Without a moment of hesitation, it fired.

'Christopher!' Eleila screamed, almost as the rifle cracked from out on the valley floor. A hand wrenched him backwards. As he fell, white hot pain ripped across his shoulder.

Next to the Stahlhelme that had fired, a companion roared, recognising the mistake that had been made. It turned its weapon on the first. With equal lack of hesitation, the second squeezed the trigger and shot it full in the face. The first slumped down and lay still.

The second roared loudly. Around it, other Stahlhelme understood the reasons for the summary execution immediately. The boy must not, at any costs, be killed.

Christopher fell to the ground by the fissure. His shoulder felt as though someone was holding a flaming torch to it. He squeezed his eyes shut and clenched his teeth, fighting to control it. Gradually the pain reduced enough that it no longer consumed all his attention. He rolled to his side, wincing, and opened his eyes.

Eleila had dropped to her knees above him.

'Stay down!' Her face was twisted with surprise and anger. 'What do you think you were doing?'

'It isn't real,' Christopher gasped, his voice made hoarse by the wound in his shoulder. He looked at it. The bullet had sliced a good sized gash into his skin. It was bleeding quite a lot. At least it was only a surface wound. 'I didn't think they would fire at me.'

Eleila made a noise of despair. She looked down at him and frowned. Then she slapped him hard on the side of the face.

The smart of the slap was not anywhere as painful as his shoulder, but still his cheek burned red hot. 'Is that real?' she growled.

'You don't understand,' Christopher said, pushing her back.

She brushed his arm away. She hesitated, glancing at his shoulder. Her eyes narrowed. She grabbed at the wound, squeezing it hard. 'Is that real?'

The pain was as if he had been shot again. His body tensed against it. His back arched. He screamed. 'Argh! Yes! Stop!' He twisted away, pulling his shoulder from her grasp.

'Then so is everything, you idiot.' She spat.

After a moment, Christopher scowled through the pain at her. 'It isn't real. It can't be. None of it makes sense. You don't make sense! When the landscape changed, you didn't even notice!'

Bediviere clambered over to them. 'Get him back there. Let me see through.' He gestured to the fissure.

Eleila nodded and grabbed Christopher by the front of his tunic. She dragged him further behind the outcrop. Christopher pulled at her hands angrily.

'Get off!' he gasped.

She dropped her grip and deposited him on to the ground again. He pushed himself up on to his elbows, wincing at the pain in his shoulder. 'Those creatures out there. Their clothes and weapons are from my time, not yours. They're not from King Arthur's time. The only person here that knows about those things is me, so I must have created them as part of my dream!'

Eleila shook her head at him. Her face was so angry, he thought she might hit him again. 'Does it matter?'

'What?'

'Does it matter, you stupid boy?' Eleila said again. 'If you are dreaming?'

Christopher looked blankly at her. The question stopped his train of thought. He hadn't even considered that.

Eleila took his look as reason to continue. 'So what if this is all a dream? You've imagined yourself into a place you know more about than us. You've dreamed creatures that are attacking us. You've dreamed us into danger.' She tossed her head angrily. 'You've even managed to dream a situation where you discovered I wasn't a man and that was certainly exactly what I would expect a stupid boy to be dreaming about! So, perhaps you're right.'

Despite everything, Christopher felt the colour of embarrassment rising on his face.

'They're moving!' Bediviere called from the fissure. He pushed his crossbow to the opening and fired off a bolt.

'Ha!' he said, a moment later. 'One is down.' He glanced back at the two of them. 'Whatever you are doing, stop it. I need you.'

Eleila pulled Christopher up to a sitting position. Their faces were close. 'So if this is a dream, you will wake up when you wake up. Like all dreams. But, if you're wrong and this isn't a dream, I just saved your life.' She shook him. 'Frankly if I were you, I'd be treating this as real just to be on the safe side.' At each shake, the pain in his shoulder burst up again. 'Stop!' he gasped.

She stopped. 'Dream or not, you can still get hurt, Christopher. So I see that you have two choices. You can carry on protesting whilst we fight and die around you, or you can get involved. Either way you are in the same danger.'

She clambered to her feet. 'We need you here now. We must protect the sword.' She turned and reached over to her pack, pulling her short bow and quiver from where it was fastened to the side of her mount and thrust it into his hands. 'Whatever you decide, I won't be jumping out to save you again.' She turned and clambered over to Bediviere.

The pain is his shoulder throbbed in big waves. He felt nauseous. She was right. Nothing that he had done so far had helped him to escape from this.

He looked down at the bow in his hand. The memory of shooting the creature in the lake came to him. The night he had saved her. Colour rose to his face again. Then a second thought. That had been the best shot he had ever made. It had felt good.

She was right. If he was mistaken, if this was all real, then he had just come very close to being killed. He pushed to his feet. Grimacing against the pain in his shoulder, he bent down to pick up the quiver of arrows.

She was right. The only logical thing to do was to behave as if this were all real. Staying passive and removed helped neither him nor the people around him. He could worry about everything else later.

He pulled out an arrow. As he strung it to the bow, he walked across to Eleila and the others. She looked up at him, wary.

'Ok,' he said, returning her gaze. 'I need to help you.'

Bediviere was mid-way through his plan. 'Then you will join Eleila. You will take the sword and ride up out of the valley. Go over the ridge. We will go just before you.'

He pointed to the end of the outcrop. 'We'll exit there and draw their fire away to give you a chance. It will be a slim chance, but it is the best we have.'

'No,' Christopher said quietly. His heart thudded in his chest as a plan formed.

Bediviere frowned at him. 'There is no time to—'

'Listen to me,' Christopher interrupted. 'They don't care about you. They don't care about the sword. They want me.'

'Christopher …' Eleila started.

'No. I've listened and you're right,' Christopher continued, urgent. 'I'm with you now. Now you need to listen to me. I know more than you. I knew about Excalibur. I knew that your father was Sir Lancelot. I also know that no matter how you try to draw fire, their weapons are faster. You'll be dead before we get far enough to escape. The plan won't work.'

'Bediviere,' the knight with the tattered armour said. 'They are moving again.'

'They want me,' Christopher said. 'Alive. I can draw them after me. You'll have easier targets to take down.'

'They just tried to shoot you,' Eleila said.

'They made a mistake. They didn't see it was me. This time I'll make sure I am completely in the open.'

Whatever this was, Christopher was sure of one thing now. Here, luck was on his side. He could shoot better, run faster, dodge quicker than he could on his best days at home. Perhaps it was the dream. It didn't matter.

Christopher took a step back from them. He was standing and they were all on the ground. He would easily be able to leap back if they tried to grab him.

'If I'm wrong, you will simply have one more dead boy in the valley. You, the three best warriors, are left to try your plan.'

'Christopher.' Eleila reached towards him.

Christopher jumped back to the far end of the outcrop. 'Be ready. They will run to catch me. Once they're past, take them down from the cover of the rocks. When the ones on the slope start to come down, that's when you come out to fight. Get in close so they can't use their weapons.'

'Christopher!' Eleila shouted again, her voice high and concerned.

'Can't you be satisfied?' He smiled. 'I'm agreeing with you. I choose you.'

Then he turned back and sprinted out into the valley.

The boy appeared from the side of the rocky outcrop. The leader of the Stahlhelme shuddered with excitement. It barked a low command at the machine gun crew. There was no need. They had recognised the boy too. The gunner pulled its hands back from the trigger.

For a moment, until it was sure, the leader held its breath. The reaction was almost human. It stared at the Stahlhelme in the valley below, silently urging them to recognise the boy as well, to avoid the mistake of their companion and refrain from firing. The fear was misplaced. Below, the other beasts knew immediately that the reason for their ambush had broken cover. They rumbled to their feet and began to give chase, giant legs powering across the expanse of muddy ground, closing the gap with every pace.

There was still a good distance between them and the boy. He ran straight down the valley, along the far side of the valley floor, furthest away from the gun team up on the slope.

As he ran, he jumped, swinging his body around in mid-air. He landed squarely on both feet and lifted the bow, releasing the arrow. It flew high and straight, hitting the foremost Stahlhelme. The beast fell to the ground mid-stride. It clawed at its neck where the shaft protruded.

Then the boy was away again. He ran nimbly between huge craters covering the ground. His feet were steady on the mud-slicked ridges that separated them. In the craters, ominous pools of black water lay, offering danger to any who should fall in. The boy did not. He angled his path and began to sprint towards the centre of the valley.

The Stahlhelme slowed. On the ridges of the craters, their enormous size and lack of agility worked against them.

One mis-stepped. It twisted its great legs in an effort to right itself. It was too late. The Stahlhelme crashed to the ground. Behind it, another, too close, smashed into its prone form, almost somersaulting over it to land on its side in the mud. The momentum of the second sent it rolling down into the crater below.

The leader let out a frustrated howl.

At the sound of the howl, Christopher stopped again. He swung around. The gamble was paying off. They were moving far more slowly now. He pulled another arrow from the quiver, his eyes picking out the one who struggled to rise.

He felt the tension in the string. It forced the blood into his fingertips with a reassuring twinge. He let the arrow fly. It slammed into the creature. The beast dropped back down and was still.

He pulled out another arrow and strung it to the bow, this time choosing one furthest away, still near to the outcrop. Thinning them out there would help Eleila and the others. Whether dream, reality, madness or something else, he had been through it with the people behind that rock. They were his friends. From now on, their well-being was his well-being.

The creature he had aimed at doubled up. The arrow had caught it in a chink just above the left leg plate. It screamed and stumbled.

Suddenly, there was a loud bang. Three feet away from Christopher, the ground burst up in a shower of mud and water. He dodged instinctively.

To the far left one of the creatures had raised its gun and fired close to him. Seeing its companion, another raised its gun and fired, this time to Christopher's right.

He threw himself back and into a crater hole. It was a tactic. They were trying to channel where he went, to pin him down again as they got nearer. There was no immediate danger. They were firing whilst on the move over difficult land. Still, there was a chance of being hit by accident. It would be better to try and stay out of their line of sight for a while.

Christopher turned and ran into the crater, aiming to come up on the other side to the left. There he could sprint away on to the more solid ground at the edge of the valley, leaving many of them floundering through the craters whilst he made good distance again.

He hit the bottom of the crater and his foot sunk straight down. He stepped forward with the other foot to counter his momentum and avoid falling. That foot sunk straight in too.

He tried pull his front leg up. The mud slurped around him, holding fast. He gasped with effort and strained even harder. There was a loud sucking noise. The leg came free.

As soon as his leg was free, all the effort he had been putting into pulling it overbalanced him. He wheeled his arms around, trying keep upright whilst staying on one leg. It was impossible. He sat back in the mud. Now he was caught up to his waist. From above he heard a guttural shriek of triumph.

The leader saw the boy fall and knew he was stuck in the mud. The boy struggled limply. He leaned to one side and tried to slide himself along to a place where it was less sticky and deep.

The other Stahlhelme struggled slowly towards him. There were only two moving now. In the distance, the one who had taken an arrow to the leg was struggling to get up, but seemed unable to put any weight on one side. The other that had slipped down into the crater remained completely out of sight.

Of the two moving, one had a crossbow bolt sticking out of the back of its shoulder and was too far back to be of any immediate use. The nearer one was in a better position, but picking its way gingerly through the craters. It was taking too long. By the time either of them reached the hole, the boy could be up and away again.

It would be faster to reach him from the vantage point that the machine gun nest had been set upon. The leader strode forward, raising its pole axe and roared an order to the gun crew. They stood, lifting their own weapons. The four of them began to run down the slope.

Christopher snapped his head round to the direction of the roar. Four more of the beasts lumbered down towards him. They would reach him in very little time. He cursed. There was nothing for it, he needed to stop them before he worried about moving. He reached back to take another arrow from the quiver.

It was gone!

A terrible emptiness blossomed in the pit of his stomach. Desperate, he cast his eyes around.

He saw the quiver almost immediately, though seeing it didn't make him feel better. It was a few feet away in the deepest part of the mud. Only a few arrows were still in it. The rest were strewn even further away from him. Some floated atop the thicker mud. Some had all but sunk. Christopher stretched towards it. It was too far away. The only way to reach it would be to push on into the deeper mud. Then he would be stuck fast.

It had only been a couple of minutes before he had been telling himself that here he was luckier than he was in his own world. Chiding himself for his arrogance, Christopher slid out into the deeper mud.

From the corner of its beady black eye, the leader noticed movement. It glanced up from the boy floundering in the quagmire below.

Three horses burst from the rock outcrop. The other survivors. They stood high in their saddles, galloping out into the valley floor. The front knight held a large war hammer in his single hand. He charged towards the Stahlhelme struggling through the craters, wheeling across to run down the one with the wounded leg.

It didn't even see him coming. At the last minute, the sounds of hooves registered. It raised a head, only to bring it to the perfect height for the knight's weapon. He struck it with a wide swing and galloped on without even turning to check his work. Behind him, the Stahlhelme dropped into the mud and was still.

The second rider rode straight across to the centre of the valley. This one was smaller. The knight pulled up the horse and took aim with a crossbow at the Stahlhelme with the bolt in its shoulder, then fired.

The Stahlhelme reached up with both arms, stretching behind it to try and reach the centre of its back where the new bolt had lodged. It fell to its knees and keeled over.

The leader roared. The gun crew were so intent on getting down the slope, they didn't notice its roar. It stopped. It lifted its great pole axe.

The third of the knights charged straight towards last remaining Stahlhelme in the valley. The leader stared down the sights of the gun. It held its breath, waiting for the right moment to fire until the rider lifted his sword.

It never had to. Suddenly the knight's horse slammed into the ground, ripped off its feet. It landed heavily, crushing its rider beneath it.

From the crater just to the right, another Stahlhelme appeared. The one that had fallen in. As it clambered out, it let go of the horse's leg it had so forcefully grabbed.

The leader swung his rifle around and fired at the larger of the two remaining knights. The shot missed. It sent a spray of mud up to the knight's left. At the sound of the gun, the smaller knight began to gallop again. Now both knights' horses zig-zagged across the valley, constantly changing direction, leaping over craters and dodging through spaces.

The leader tried to get a bead on the smaller knight. The horse was moving too fast. It would be a lucky shot at best. The leader turned and looked back at the boy. He had managed to manoeuvre himself somehow further into the mud below. The leader grunted and began once again to run down the slope.

The quiver had sunk two-thirds into the mud. There were three arrows in it, almost within Christopher's reach. The mud sucked and slurped around him. He was up to his waist now. Below, through the mud, he could still feel the firm earth, but each painstaking step took him deeper. He stretched as far as he could towards the quiver. Still too far.

He glanced up. The four beasts on the slope were getting closer. They would be in the crater within half a minute.

'Come on!' Christopher gasped at himself. He lunged again. The muscles in his back and arm strained with the effort. The ends of his fingers were so very close now.

The nearest beast roared with elation. It leapt a hillock down to another, dropping a good fifteen feet. It was closing the distance far quicker than Christopher had expected.

He took another step forward. His hand caught the quiver strap and he pulled it towards him. Instead of the quiver just coming to him, however, he had also pulled himself towards the quiver. Now he was in up to his chest.

He pulled again. Now the arm he had reached toward the quiver with was stuck too. He grunted with the effort and strained to free it.

The second beast followed the first, dropping heavily on to the hillock. The third was close behind.

Christopher strained. Suddenly there was give. The sucking sound got louder. His arm began to move.

The third of the beasts dropped down. The first had reached the edge of the crater.

Christopher's arm came free with a final suck. The quiver popped out of the mud and landed just in front of him. He grabbed an arrow, fitted it, took aim, and released.

It smashed into the belly of the beast. At such short range, it pierced the armour easily. The creature dropped like a stone.

The second leapt over its fallen comrade. Christopher pulled the second arrow from the quiver, nocked it and fired, taking the beast in the neck. It fell into the mud, sending an arc of mud and water high into the sky. It floundered around, face down. Instead of freeing itself, it managed to get deeper. It would not escape the mud now.

Christopher pulled out the last arrow. The third beast was at the very edge of the crater. It hesitated for just a moment at the demise of its companions. That was all he needed. He fired the last arrow, catching it in the face. It screamed and clutched at the arrow. Then it sat back on the ground, legs spread out like a toddler, and rolled on to its side.

Ahead there was another thud. The last of the Stahlhelme had leapt from the hillock. It ran the final distance to the crater. It was by far the largest of the beasts. On the arm of its tattered uniform were three stripes. The leader. Christopher searched around desperately for another bolt, but now there was nothing within reach.

The leader reached the edge of the crater.

The boy was defenceless and stuck. The leader glanced to check that its attack would be unencumbered. The two knights on horseback were still a short way off. Between them and the crater there were two of his troops. The knights bore down on the one who had just clambered up. The other was closer and still picked its way through the mud, oblivious.

The knights were close to the Stahlhelme now. It did not fire. The mud must have clogged its rifle. Instead, it lifted its great blade in defence.

The larger of the two knights reached it first and struck down with the war hammer. It parried easily. Then it swung with the butt of the pole axe. It caught the knight's horse on the rump with a jarring blow. The horse stumbled. The knight flew from his saddle.

Quick as a flash the beast moved in and stabbed down with the pole axe. The knight managed to dodge out of the way, but the axe still caught his shoulder.

The other knight moved in on the side. The Stahlhelme was ready. It swung again. This smaller knight ducked low to avoid the swing. The horse wheeled around facing the wrong way. The knight pulled at the reins trying to turn the horse. The Stahlhelme let go of the pole axe. It reached up and pulled the knight from the horse.

The Stahlhelme had both knights occupied. The leader focussed his attention back on the boy stuck in the mud. It stalked forward into the crater. Saliva dripped from its mouth.

Christopher knew he had seconds now. The beast was almost upon him. He looked about again for a weapon. The remaining arrows that hadn't sunk floated tantalisingly a few feet away, beyond his reach.

The beast splashed down through the mud and rushed the last steps to Christopher. All it needed to do was reach over its twitching comrade, face down in the mud. Then it would have him.

Of course! There was an arrow within reach! Christopher desperately dived forward, thrusting his free hand into the mud, to the neck of the face-down beast.

Suddenly there was a great weight on his shoulder. The gash the bullet had caused flared up again. He struggled to concentrate through the pain. The beast had him! There was no time. It began to pull him out of the mud.

There! His fingers found what he was looking for. His hand closed tightly around the submerged bolt in the Stahlhelm's neck. He didn't try to pull it out. He just concentrated on not letting go. Let the leader do all the hard work.

As his body was pulled out of the mud with a wet slurping noise, he kept the grip as hard as he could. For the briefest of seconds, it seemed that the bolt would stay stuck fast. Then he felt a loosening and finally a release. The bolt came free.

The beast drew Christopher up to its eye level. He tucked the hand with the arrow in it behind his back. Its face was vast. Its eyes were so small. It was devoid of anything resembling humanity.

It held Christopher for a moment, sniffing at him. Then it roared in triumph. A blast of putrid breath slammed into Christopher's face. He gagged on it, struggling not to lose concentration.

The creature closed its enormous mouth. It looked sure of its victory now. It turned to clamber away with him. This was the moment. Christopher swung around with his arm and drove the arrow into the beast's beady black left eye.

It screamed. It threw Christopher away from it. He flew through the air. The mud towards the side of the crater was soft enough to break his fall. Thankfully, it was not so soft as to trap him again in its murky grip. He shook off the impact and scrambled to his feet.

He turned back. The beast still thrashed about. It staggered to the far side, all its focus on the wound he had inflicted. The other, face down, had finally stopped moving. Outside the crater, a few yards beyond another Stahlhelme struggled towards him.

His bow. It was still in the mud. Christopher rushed around the side of the crater. He jumped on to the body of the face-down Stahlhelme, using it as a bridge. He reached its upper back, stretched across and picked up the bow.

From the creature's back, he could reach arrows too. He fitted an arrow to the bow and drew a bead on the Stahlhelme outside the crater.

The creature stopped. It stared at Christopher, then stared at the bodies of its companions as if realising its situation for the first time. For a second, its shoulders slumped. Then it opened its mouth and roared a roar of pure malice, and ran straight toward him.

Christopher let the arrow go. It hit the Stahlhelme dead in the centre of its chest as it was mid stride. Its legs buckled and it dropped flat on its face.

Beyond, Eleila and Bediviere circled another of the beasts. Bediviere feinted in with his horse, swinging his war hammer. The beast dodged, growling, unsure where to focus its attention.

Eleila moved back and fitted a bolt to her crossbow. The shot took the creature in the left shoulder. It was enough to distract it. It flinched and reached round with its hand to the source of the sudden pain.

It was all Bediviere needed. He moved in close and swung upwards with his war hammer, smashing the creature in the chest and knocking it to the ground. As it fell he leapt upon it and rained down blow after blow. It was over in seconds.

Christopher clambered out of the crater and ran to his companions. He pointed back into the crater, too tired to speak. Eleila looked over at the last howling creature. Her lips thinned. She fixed a bolt to her crossbow and fired. The howls stopped abruptly.

'Are you all right, boy?' Bediviere was breathless and ragged.

Christopher looked up and waved his hand without really raising it. He suddenly felt the urge to collapse, and sat heavily on the ground. The knight nodded and went back to his own contemplation of the creature lying before him.

Eleila walked over and knelt next to him. 'You did well, Christopher.'

Christopher looked at her. He smiled. 'So did you, for a dream,' he said with a struggle.

Bediviere turned. 'We need to move. There is still a good way to go. We don't know what else is coming for us.' He hobbled back towards his horse.

Eleila stood and reached down a hand to him. 'Come on. He is right.'

Grimly, Christopher reached up and took her hand.

CHAPTER TWENTY-TWO

The Fountains

'Oomph!' Pope grunted. The gag over his mouth made his words impossible to understand. He had been struggling to keep balance all journey. He tried to grasp the door handle with his tightly bound hands, fumbled it and fell. He rolled on to Christopher's lap. The impact did nothing to rouse Christopher. He was as unconscious now as he had been when they found him in the asylum.

Sama leaned around Christopher and pushed Pope back upright. As soon as he was able, Pope shied away from the touch. He mumbled something venomous and shot a look of hatred at her.

Makena drove the Daimler Tourer now. John Braddock sat in the passenger seat in front, bandaging the large gash in his left arm. With Makena driving, it was a task he was trying alone. The results were rudimentary at best.

'Pope,' John snapped. 'Sit still.' He stared over his shoulder at the back seat.

The car wove into the centre of the road, bumping over holes to pass a cart. It was one of the only vehicles they had seen since leaving the asylum. Their speed startled the horse, which reared up as they passed. Sama looked out of the rear window. The cart driver shook an angry fist then wrenched on the reins.

Sama glanced back at Christopher. Her stomach tightened again with worry. It did so each time she looked at him. Most of the time he was quiet. Occasionally he had seemed to stir, a frown forming on his pale, cold face. Then he had quietened again. His breathing was shallow. At least it was steady. Sama pulled him closer to her.

The blanket he was wrapped in fell open. The back of Braddock's seat was suddenly bathed in blue light. Sama looked down. Winter's Grasp pulsed as if it knew it had been exposed. Curious, she reached towards it.

A rough hand snatched her wrist and yanked it back. She looked up. John was glaring at her. 'Please Sama, resist that urge. Let's get him to London.'

Pope muttered something through his gag again. Sama could swear there was amusement in his voice. John cuffed the prisoner with the back of his hand, staring coldly at him. Sama grinned at the butler's discomfort and made a face at him.

'My superiors will do their best for Christopher,' Braddock continued, turning his attention back to Sama. 'Just keep him wrapped up. That's the best thing for him right now.'

Sama considered for a moment then sat back. 'Can't we just take it off?'

'Not without hurting him.' Makena's eyes stayed intent on the road ahead. 'It has attached itself to him. There are ways to remove it safely, but John and I don't know them. You saw the boy at the caravans. If we try to take it off without doing it correctly, that will be dangerous.'

Sama frowned. 'But that was his shoulder! Why would he wear a gauntlet on his shoulder?'

Makena glanced at her husband. Sama looked at her face. She looked somehow guilty. She had just betrayed something.

'What is it?' Sama asked.

'John?' Makena looked back at the road, waiting for her husband to speak.

'Absolutely not,' John muttered.

'Absolutely not, what?' Sama felt a flash of anger burst in her chest. They were definitely keeping something from her. 'If it weren't for me you would still be sitting in the Stumblepot wondering what to do. If I haven't shown you that I can be trusted by now, then you're both blind.'

Makena pulled out on to a larger road. They were passing through a village. 'She makes the point well, John.'

'And who explains to Ward that we suddenly have a seventeen-year-old shop girl as part of our inner circle?' John stared at his wife with a furrowed brow.

'You already did, my love,' she replied. 'Didn't you? I don't imagine you would have left that out when you called him.'

'No good will come of it.'

'We shall see.' Makena glanced back over her shoulder. 'How's that eye?'

'I'll be fine,' Sama said quickly.

Makena laughed. 'You'll be fine? You're quite the warrior, Sama. I don't know if I would have done what you did.'

'So that means you'll tell me?' Sama would not be put off.

'It does. Some, at least,' Makena said. 'John?'

John said nothing for a moment, then twisted around in his seat to face Sama. He winced at the movement.

'It is not always a gauntlet,' he started. 'It isn't even called Winter's Grasp. That's just what it happens to be now.'

Sama frowned. Unconsciously she reached down again to try to get a look at the gauntlet.

John reached forward with his good hand and stopped her. 'It's currently a gauntlet because that is what Christopher wanted it to be.'

'It's one of a set of very special objects, Sama,' Makena interrupted. 'They are very old and they are very dangerous.'

'Dangerous?' Sama drew her hand back a little.

'Most things in the wrong hands are dangerous,' John said. 'These feed on their wearer.'

'How? And why do people put them on?'

'We don't know how for sure,' he continued. 'But the reason they put them on, most of the time, is because they are fooled into it. In Christopher's case, by the man you fought with.'

'Each object is part of a pair, Sama,' Makena said. 'The object and its key. When a child is connected to an object, it feeds on their imagination. It creates a dream world from that imagination. The child becomes trapped in it.

'The person with the key can get into that world, too,' she continued. 'Not just with their mind, though. They can actually get into it.'

'That was where the man was!' Sama's eyes were bright. 'That was an entrance into Christopher's world!'

John smiled thinly. 'I know it sounds exciting, but for Christopher it's probably very frightening.'

Sama stopped. 'Wait! They can bring stuff out too, can't they?' Her eyes darted from John to Makena. 'That's what the gypsies were! And Molly Brodie! And the soldiers at the asylum!'

'There's the root of it.' John nodded. 'The key keepers want power. It always comes down to power.'

Next to her Pope mumbled something venomous through his gag, the lack of words doing nothing to hide the sentiment. To accentuate his intention, he wriggled to leer toward Sama and Christopher.

John reached across with his good arm. He grabbed a handful of Pope's hair. Pope's eyes widened. Braddock shoved hard, smashing Pope's head sideways into the hard wood and metal top of the door.

'I asked you nicely to sit still.'

Pope stayed slumped forward, knocked senseless.

John turned back. 'Better.'

Sama had barely even noticed. Her face was screwed in concentration. 'Follow the source,' she muttered.

John nodded.

'Follow the source!' Sama said again, looking up. 'When one of them dies in our world, they go back to the dream world. That's the blue lights! Follow them and they'll take you to the object!'

'That's right,' Makena said. 'You have it, Sama.'

Sama sat back, speechless. It was a lot to take in and she wasn't really used to having to think this hard. It all made sense, though. She glanced at Christopher, wondering what he had dreamed up. It must be King Arthur and his knights, though that didn't explain the great soldiers they had fought. Still, they had him. Surely it would soon be over.

'So, we've won then?'

'There's rarely winning and losing,' John replied.

'But we've got Christopher,' Sama said. 'We're taking him to get Winter's Grasp removed. So he'll be all right.'

'Sama,' Makena said. 'We need to warn you. The man you fought; the key keeper. He's stalking Christopher through his dream world. If he catches him in there, it will make freeing Christopher here a lot more difficult.'

'What if he has already got him?'

'I don't think he has,' John answered. 'Whatever he was doing back at the asylum, I doubt he has had the time to be in two places at once. With luck, time is on our side.'

Sama looked at them both and nodded. 'Then we have to hurry.' She pulled Christopher close to her and stared out into the dark road ahead.

The Master came to with a head-splitting ache that travelled from the base of his neck up to his right temple. He was lying on his stomach, face in the dirt. He tried a tentative push upwards. As soon as he put strain on his arms, a sledgehammer pounded in his brain. He gasped and lay still until the agony dropped to manageable levels. He opened his left eye and twisted his head to the right. The pain exploded again. He squeezed his eye shut again, waiting for the next respite.

His face was wet. He reached up, taking his time now, and risked a gentle touch to the area. When he moved his fingers back to where he could see, they were red with blood.

That damn girl. He had only been half recovered from the winding she had given him before she cut the rope. He hadn't realised he was falling until it was too late to do anything about it. The energy in the artefact had been terribly disturbed by his actions. The maelstrom had thrown him around like a leaf in a storm.

By the time he recognized he was sucked back into the world of Christopher's imagination, he was falling too fast and too hard towards the earth. He had to brace himself for the inevitable impact.

Now there was more pain. It felt like there were a number of broken ribs. It also felt like something was sticking out of his side. He must deal with his body. Thinking about what had happened could wait.

He breathed in with his essence. A familiar rushing filled his ears. Healing energy flowed into his body, knitting together broken bones, sealing gashes, making him whole once more. The pain ebbed away.

Soon he was able to push himself up on to his elbows. There was no way of telling how long had passed. He looked around.

He was on a battlefield. The detritus of war lay all around. A few feet away, the corpse of a knight lay under his dead horse. To the side of the knight, a foot soldier lay, the knight's sword jammed into him.

The Master clambered carefully to his feet. There had been a major battle here. He was at the top of a long slope. The remains of the battlefield stretched all the way down it to a broad river in the distance. A mess of bodies, armour, and weapons.

The Master gasped in a breath. To one side a large field gun lay on its side with one broken wheel. Beneath it sprawled the bodies of its gun crew. He started towards the weapon.

His foot knocked against something. He looked down. In the mud beneath him, a hand protruded, bloodied and broken. In the hand was a pistol. He bent to the pistol and pried it from the fingers.

The Master recognized it. A Bergmann Bayard. German. It was not something a fifteen-year-old schoolboy would be likely to have run into. However, his brother could easily have seen such a thing at the front.

It had worked! He looked again over at the field gun. The accuracy was far too good for Christopher's subconscious to be its source. Even if the boy had some knowledge from papers or even cadets at his school, this was something else.

He picked up his pace, keen to examine the gun more closely. Now he had seen the changes, they were becoming more apparent everywhere. Among the dead knights lay other bodies in greys and khakis. His efforts in the asylum had paid off.

The asylum! The thought stopped the Master in his tracks. He could examine his successes soon enough. First, he must get back to the boy. He closed his eyes and visualised the asylum.

He pushed forwards out of the world.

In a moment he stood back in the asylum. His body crackled with blue sparks. His vision took a moment to clear. He glanced around the room.

The boy was gone.

'No!'

The bed was there, as was the one upon which Freddie Flyte had lain. Neither was occupied. There was no sign of Pope, either.

'Dammit!' A wave of anger swept through his body as he thought of the girl again. He wished she were here now. He would crush her neck. There was no time for such luxuries.

'Pope! Are you here?' he shouted, bursting through the ward door.

No answer. He sprinted down the corridor towards the exit.

Lunatics still wandered the halls. He dodged through them. A young man with sunken eyes tried to grab at him, muttering something desperate. He punched the man's face, sending him scuttling away.

He reached the office and flashed through. He burst through to the main entrance hall. The main double doors were blown inwards. There was still no sign of his quarry.

In the courtyard, the Flyte family car stood silent. It was the only vehicle there. The Master cursed. He shuffled to the centre of the driveway over thrashed gravel, gouged with tire marks. Other vehicles had been here very recently

They had him. McCloud and his cronies. They had the boy.

The Master screamed at the sky. He clutched at his head. It was all for nothing. The waiting. The planning. The watching. For nothing. His legs collapsed under him. He sat heavily on the ground.

He pulled his hair, using the pain to distract from the feeling of despair. This couldn't be the conclusion to his plans. He had worked too damn hard for this.

If he had just been satisfied, he chided himself. If he had just accepted a world with no magic and disappeared with the boy, they would not have been able to find him. Damn his own ambition. Damn his own greed.

He frowned. There had to be an angle, a trick he could pull. In his pocket the key throbbed, seeming to feel his despair. He slipped his hand inside and drew it out. He looked at it.

They may have the boy, but what could they do? They may be able to save him from the artefact, destroy the world he had created, but what then? Create another? How could they? Whatever they created would be his for the taking. He had the key.

'The game's not lost,' he murmured. After all, the worst that could happen was a stalemate, and he could find a way around that. He looked up. 'The game's not lost.'

He could still bind Christopher in the world. Then they would certainly think twice about trying to free him. Then freedom would mean one thing. Death.

He got to his feet. 'The game is most definitely not lost.' He reached high with the key. In a flash he was gone.

The tourer stopped in a residential street in Knightsbridge. Sama glanced out of the window. They were outside a large, white terraced townhouse. Three steps up to a big black door with an ornate brass knocker in the shape of a lion's head. Black railings and a little gate. On the right of the door was a large window with thick dark drapes, pulled almost shut. A chink of light shone out from a small gap in the curtains.

'Wait here,' John said, climbing out of the passenger side door. He headed up to the entrance and rapped on the knocker.

The street was nearly empty. Sama had never seen such well-to-do looking houses. Cast iron streetlights picked out other smart black fences around immaculate white homes. They had passed through some very busy streets less than a few minutes away, but here all was peaceful.

Some way down, a young mother and her two children came out of a front door, closely followed by a nanny. The children were wrapped against the cold in smart woollen coats, a little boy in blue and a little girl in yellow. Each wore red mittens and hats. The little boy immediately rushed to the nearest pile of snow and grabbed a handful. He turned and fashioned it into a snowball.

His mother raised her hand, wagging it sharply. Crestfallen, the boy dropped his missile and shuffled back to his family. Sama suddenly thought of Chops, her little face red with exasperation at one of Sama's antics. At the thought, her eyes stung. The warmth and safety of the Stumblepot sounded wonderful right now.

'Where are we?' Sama asked, wiping her eyes, angry at herself.

'With friends.' Makena watched the family and their servant start to head off down the road, away from the car. 'Good, they are going the other way.'

The front door opened. Warm light flooded out. John slipped through the crack and disappeared inside. The door shut.

Pope groaned. He'd been silent since John had knocked him unconscious, only recently showing signs of regaining his senses. He was still slumped over to his side of the car. If someone were to walk past, the car would present an unusual sight. If a black woman driving wasn't enough to get them noticed, the funny-looking passengers in the back would be.

The door opened again and John appeared, followed by three burly men. Their clothes were smart and tidy, in perfect keeping with the street. The men in the suits, however, were another matter entirely. Their muscled bodies interfered with the natural cut of the suits, making the cloth hang at odd angles. They looked very uncomfortable in them, restrained by the well-to-do look.

The men were obviously experienced brawlers. If anything, they looked even more menacing than John Braddock could. The suits seemed an attempt to help them blend into their surroundings. To Sama's eye, the attempt was unsuccessful.

The first, wearing a dark suit, reached for the door handle. He pulled it open and offered Sama a huge hand. 'Evenin', miss. Come with me, please. Quick as you can.' Bright blue eyes peered down above a strong broken nose.

'Christopher ...' Sama began.

The man reached down and took Sama's hand. 'Don't you worry yourself about him, miss. We'll bring him too. Inside, where we can help.'

Sama found herself all but wrenched from the car. As she came out, the man put his second hand, surprisingly gentle considering his size, on the small of her back. 'Let me help, miss. I hear you had quite a time of it. Who'd have thought it? Tiny thing like you'

Sama smiled proudly. He was right, she *had* had quite a time of it. Still, they were here and Christopher was with them. She stuck out her chin and gave him her best grin. 'Thanks.'

The man grinned back. A tooth was missing to go with his nose.

Makena had clambered from her own seat and walked around to them. She reached in past Sama and supported Christopher's head. 'Baker. You'll get the car moved?' she said to the man in the dark suit.

Baker nodded. 'We're on it now.'

Sure enough, the other two men had moved to the other side of the car. The one in the pinstripe opened the door where Pope was. The butler, now regaining more sense, cowered away and mumbled something.

'None of that,' Pinstripe said gruffly. He punched down into the seat, catching Pope on the chin. Once again, the butler slumped down.

'All right, Ted,' John murmured. 'Just get him inside.'

Pinstripe reached in and pulled the little man out, cradling him like a child, then turned towards the front door. The other man slipped into the driver's seat. John and Makena eased Christopher out of the car. They followed Sama and Baker up the steps.

Behind the door was a long corridor with a marble floor. The floor was laid in a pattern of deep blue diamonds edged by alternate rectangles of white and beige. The dark curtains visible from the outside hung from ceiling to floor, a blue to match the floor tiles. Sama had little time to take it in. Baker's hand remained firmly behind her back. He kept their pace up. They marched down the corridor, shoes click-clicking on the marble slabs.

Sama glanced around. Down the length of the corridor were large double doors. Each was painted blue to match the floor tiles. On either side of each door were white plaster columns set against the walls.

For the most part, the doors were closed. A man appeared out of one and saw them. He wrenched the door shut behind him before Sama could take a look inside. The man spotted Christopher, now nestled in John Braddock's arms. He opened his mouth, intrigued as they rushed on past. His eyes never left Christopher.

To their right, a short corridor led away to steps downwards. The man in the pinstripe suit carrying Pope turned down the corridor. He flicked a quick nod to John and disappeared.

Finally, they passed an open door. Sama stared inside. The room was a long library with two-storey wooden bookshelves on either side. Sama frowned. The length of the room was far wider than the outside of the house had indicated. It must stretch through a few properties. This was more than just a rich townhouse.

On the floor between the bookshelves were desks, too many to count at a glance. At each, groups of people worked, poring over books and manuscripts. Others scurried from desks to shelves. A couple were up on the second storey of the bookshelves.

Close to the door, a young woman in a plain blue dress stood talking with a short man wearing round glass spectacles. As Sama's group passed she gave a start and gestured at them. The man flicked his head around. Spotting them, he immediately began after them. They passed on. Sama craned her head back around at the door. The man appeared, running lightly to catch them up. The woman he had been speaking with stood at the doorway staring after them. Or rather, Sama could see, she was staring at Christopher.

The man caught up. John glanced at him. 'Levert.'

The man hardly acknowledged him. Instead, he looked down at Christopher in his arms, half walking, half jogging to keep pace with the powerful man.

'Well done, John! Well done!' he enthused. 'You too, Makena.' He looked at Sama for a moment and nodded. 'And this is our newest recruit, is it?'

'Let's not go that far,' John said quickly, but his voice was softer.

Levert touched Christopher's forehead. 'He's cold. We must hurry.'

Ahead was a double door at the end of the corridor. Makena rushed ahead of the others and pushed it open. They hurried through.

Dark, polished wood panelling covered the walls. At the top of each panel was an ornate carving. Each was identical, an intricate relief of a fountain in the shape of a child-like water nymph. From the nymphs, carved water spouted out.

The room felt a little like a chapel to Sama. The wood panels reminded her of where the little choir sat in the Alton church. However, this seemed to be a meeting room. In the centre of the room, a large oval table stood with eight high-backed chairs surrounding it. In the back of each chair was the same wooden carving as the panels. A well-lit fire burned from a fireplace in the wall. In front of it were two leather armchairs. The room extended into darkness beyond.

It was to the armchairs that Baker led Sama. Makena followed.

'Sit down, Miss Neeley,' Baker said. 'Sorry I had to chivvy you along a bit there. Thought it was best to get you into the warm.' He glanced back the way they had come. 'Away from all them prying eyes.'

He eased Sama into a chair, trying quite well to make it look as though it was not compulsory. Once she was sitting, he looked down at her. 'That's a heck of a shiner you're going to have.'

Makena sat in the seat opposite her. She leaned forward. 'Now Sama, we're going to take Christopher downstairs. If you wait here while we help him, I'll have some refreshments brought to you, then later maybe some rest.'

'I'm not staying here!' Sama tried to push herself up out of the chair, straining against Baker's iron grip 'You can't leave me out now. '

'There'll be no 'leaving out', Miss Neeley,' a voice suddenly came from the far end of the room, where the light was dimmest. 'You've earned the right to go with your friend. First however, I'd like to ask you a few questions.'

Sama stared into the gloom. A chubby hand emerged at first, resting heavily on a thick walking cane. It was followed by an almost impossibly broad frame in a red dressing gown. She looked up at the man's face. He was puffing with effort. Sweat ran down his red nose into his thick moustache. He stopped a few feet away, breathing heavily. 'You must excuse me, Miss Neeley. Activity doesn't suit my physique. I'm Ward McCloud.'

Sama stared at the man, determined. 'I won't leave Christopher.'

'I understand,' the fat man said after a moment, 'but if you really want to help him, the more information we have about the man you fought, the better.' He turned to John. 'Pass the boy to Baker. We should begin. Levert, your opinion?'

Levert was dwarfed by Ward McCloud's frame. 'I believe we are in time, though how much is a concern.'

Baker lifted his hand from Sama's shoulder and reached to take Christopher from Braddock.

'Very well, then,' McCloud continued. 'Take him below. See what we can do for him.'

Baker and Levert began to walk towards the dark end of the room. Before Sama could move, John Braddock moved in next to her.

'I wonder,' Makena murmured, her eyes still on Sama. 'John, would you not be better helping get information from that servant, Pope? I'll stay with Sama and Ward. Once we're done, I can take her downstairs.'

'I'm not sure that downstairs is the best idea, Makena,' McCloud said.

'Ward,' John said quietly. 'Sama already knows a great deal more than anyone else. We answered her questions.'

McCloud raised an eyebrow. 'Really? Whose idea was that?' There was a slight edge to his voice.

'It was mine,' Makena answered. 'And I stand by it.'

McCloud looked at her a moment, then shrugged. 'Very well. I am sure you weighed the decision.' He glanced at John. 'Perhaps you should do as your wife says. We will be fine here.'

John nodded. 'I will see you below later.' He turned and left the way they had arrived.

Ward McCloud eased himself into the remaining armchair. It creaked in protest. 'Now Miss Neeley,' he started. 'Please tell me everything that you can about the man you fought.'

The Master appeared in the valley at the second try. His first attempt to jump directly through to the Stahlhelme had ended with him dropping feet first into a water-filled shell hole. He had sworn and immediately jumped back through.

It could only mean one thing if the direct link was broken. The Stahlhelme he had sent were dead. Had there been one alive, he would have appeared by it without effort. The bond he had formed with that one squad meant that he should be able to locate them without any concentration.

The second time he did concentrate, feeling for what remained of their essence. Once he caught what he was looking for, he appeared neatly in the valley.

There had been a significant skirmish. That much was evident. Most of the knights who must have been with the boy were dead. Amongst them were the bodies of his Stahlhelme.

There was no trace of the boy.

The Master gritted his teeth. The boy was not lost. He was traveling north again. Mordred's army did the same. That was where to start.

The Master looked around. To his left, the body of a horse lay crumpled in a heap. He raised his arm and blasted forth blue light. A second later the horse stood full of life and energy, whinnying at him with enthusiasm.

The Master leapt on to the horse's back. He dug his heels into its sides and began to gallop north.

Sama stared at the fountains. 'They're beautiful.'

The hall seemed to have been cut out of the rock. She had no idea how far below the London streets they were. McCloud led the way once he finished questioning her with a 'That will do Miss Neeley.' Without another word, he got up and walked back off into the gloom.

It was Makena who beckoned to her to follow. There was a door in the back of the room. McCloud pushed it open, revealing steps that headed down, lit by gas lights fixed to the wall.

Sama stopped counting steps when she reached fifty. A short time after that the red brick walls stopped. The remainder of the descent was through chiselled stone.

They walked in silence. The events of the day were beginning to catch up with Sama. The bruise over her eye was throbbing with regular rhythm and her lid was almost swollen shut. She was limping too. Her foot was swollen tight in her shoe. With each step raw flesh rubbed against leather. The steps made it worse. At least when they finally reached the great cathedral like hall the way was flat once more.

It was a relief when Makena saw she was struggling and insisted they stopped to rest. McCloud continued on, muttering that time was of the essence. Makena and Sama sat watching the grand stone statues wrapped in silk and spurting water.

'Each represents a child,' Makena replied.

'Like Christopher?' Sama said.

Makena gestured over at a fountain draped in a lilac silk cloth. A steady plume of water shot from its spout. 'That one is for him.'

'It's strong,' Sama noted.

'It is. That is because Christopher is newly taken. He is still strong.' She pointed at another with a black silk. Its fountain was barely more than a trickle. 'The weaker ones are for children that are more … used up'

Sama nodded thoughtfully. 'So each time a child is possessed you set up a fountain here in your temple.'

'We do not set the fountains,' Makena answered. 'We monitor the fountains. They diminish as the children do and replenish when a child is replaced.'

Makena pressed Sama's arm, encouraging her on. 'Come, sweet.'

'I don't understand.' Sama still looked at the fountains

'Neither do I. The fountains have been here long before I was.'

'And the colours? What are they?' Sama asked.

'Now those, we have added,' Makena said. 'Factions. Our research has shown us that some key keepers work together. The blacks represent a group that have joined to gain as much personal power and wealth as possible. We have had some dealings with them. The greens we know less about. They stay out of worldly affairs. The other colours are individuals, working alone as far as we are aware.'

Sama noted Christopher's cloth was pale lilac. 'So he's has been taken in by someone who works alone. Who?'

'We don't know yet.' Makena took her arm now, guiding her onward. 'Over the years, objects and keys have passed from person to person. It is hard to know who is out there. We only know some.'

'So you stay here and watch for changes. Then try to save the child. How long have you been watching?'

'Three years.'

'How many children have you freed?' Sama asked

'Christopher will be my first.' Makena smiled. 'This group started over seventy years ago. In that time we have recovered four objects with their keys.'

Sama frowned. There was something about the word she had used. *Recovered.*

They reached the end of the hallway. To the left was a squat brick building, built up against the side of the hall. It was about thirty feet in length. It had small windows, though why a building would need windows when it was inside was beyond Sama. It actually looked more like a guardhouse than anything else. The windows were wide on the outside, narrowing to small holes. Sama had seen one when Jim had taken her to Windsor once.

At one end, as if to prove the point, another burly looking man stood by the entrance door. He wore a waistcoat over his shirt and over it, a shoulder holster with a formidable looking pistol in it. Sama began to head towards him, her interest aroused.

'This way, Sama.' Makena was opening a door in the wall that she hadn't even noticed.

She sighed and turned back. 'You didn't mention the white drapes back there.'

'No.' Makena sighed. 'I did not. Those are our own children, Sama.'

Sama stopped, horrified. 'Wait! Your children? You don't save them?' She pulled away from Makena. 'You use them, too. After all you've said! Makena, you are just the same.'

Makena shook her head. Her eyes looked sad. 'Not the same, Sama. The children like Christopher are freed. The objects are put to use.'

'So you just dupe other children.'

'No, Sama. The children we work with are fully aware of their situation. They are volunteers.' She held the door open and gestured for Sama to go though. 'Come. I was taking you there to see, anyway.'

Sama looked up with furrowed brows. 'What do you mean volunteers? Who'd want to allow this?'

'They are trained from an early age, Sama. Without them we would have nothing with which to fight the others.' She gestured again for Sama to go through the door. 'Tell me, where did you think I got my staffs from? How do you think John got his coat?'

Sama opened her mouth. No words came out. She couldn't think what to say. It had never occurred to her to think about how Makena and Braddock had come by their tools. She had just accepted them. Actually, she'd been pleased that they had them. That there may be a cost to their existence made her feel suddenly guilty. She walked through the door.

Compared to the dimness of the hall, the room inside was brightly lit. A young woman in a clean nurse's uniform sat at a desk, quietly reading a book. She looked up as they entered. When she saw Makena, she smiled. 'Welcome back.'

Makena nodded. 'Thank you. How are they?'

'The same as before,' the nurse said. 'James perhaps a little weaker, but he is in good spirits. He'll be pleased to see you. They are in the day room.'

'We'll go through,' Makena said, then gestured at Sama. 'This is Sama Neeley, a friend of Christopher Flyte's.'

The nurse smiled at Sama. 'Ward mentioned she would be with you.' She put down her book and picked up a ledger.

As she wrote something in it, Makena led Sama to a second door. It was painted brightly in a cheerful yellow, strangely childlike in this solemn place. Sama glanced at Makena, a question on her lips, but the older woman was already opening the door.

The first thing that Sama noticed was laughter. There were children, giggling with delight. An older, frailer voice laughed with them, then broke up into a cough.

A young girl's voice piped up 'What about my one? Did he look like this?'

'That looks more like a duck with arms!' the older voice croaked with good humour. 'Mandricore wasn't a duck, Elisa!'

The children giggled again.

There were six of them. They sat in a little circle on chairs, around a cushioned recliner that had its back to Sama and Makena. Sama could see the bald head of a man lying on the recliner. Wisps of brown hair were combed across white pasty skin.

Like the first room, it was well lit. Other comfortable chairs were dotted around the room. Each was covered with bright, patterned fabric. On the walls, there hung large, thick-framed paintings. The pictures showed scenes of dashing heroes and heroines beating back their foes.

By the children was a painting that could only be St. George, standing over his vanquished dragon. A few feet along the wall, Robin Hood was firing an arrow off into the distance of Sherwood Forest. On the other side, a pirate stood at the prow of a ship brandishing a cutlass.

Between the paintings, all around the room were bookcases. Gaudy books in a rainbow of colours were stacked on their shelves. On the floor, books lay open where they had been read and discarded.

In one corner, a large wooden box lay brimming with toys. Dolls and bears shared space with toy revolvers and a cowboy's hat. In front of the box, a wooden pirate's cutlass with vivid green sash tied to the hilt, lay flat next to a small squad of toy soldiers. The soldiers brandished rifles at it, as if they fully intended to capture it and set up camp.

On the far side of the room, by one of the tall bookcases, another nurse sat quietly on a chair. From there she could watch the room. She could also glance through a window in the wall, which she frequently did. Sama could not see what it was she looked at.

'Makena!' a little girl cried with delight, her head whipping up and staring across at them. 'We heard you were home!'

The little girl jumped up, dropping a drawing in her hands. She ran across the room and threw herself into Makena's arms. 'Are you staying? Can you play with us?'

'Ho now!' Makena grinned. 'Eliza, can you have grown in these few days? I am sure you were smaller last time I came to see you.'

'No, silly,' Eliza replied. 'People don't grow that quickly!'

Makena hugged the girl tight and then put her down. Eliza grabbed her hand, then pulled her towards the circle of children and the old man. 'Come and see. James is trying to describe what his pet monster looked like. We're trying to draw him.'

Sama followed across the room at a distance, taking everything in. The children shifted, excited, as they drew close.

'And how are they doing, James?' Makena asked. Sama noticed her voice. Her tones were kept upbeat, yet below there was something else. Was it sadness?

'Not very well,' the old man said. His voice was weak. He turned his head with effort. 'I'm not doing a very good job of describing him. We've had a giant duck and a fat dragon and, well, I'm not really sure what the others were.' His sentence finished with another coughing fit that shook his entire body.

The nurse got up and hurried over. She reached the group as James' coughs subsided. 'And you'll need to let them carry on drawing without you soon, James. You look like you need to get some more rest.'

'In a minute though,' the old man pleaded, suddenly sounding quite childlike. 'Makena hasn't tried yet. Let her try, too. Then I can rest.'

Makena turned to the chair and smiled down. 'I am so sorry, James. I cannot stay, but I will be able to spend time with you soon.'

Sama stared at Makena. Her smile had not reached her eyes. In fact, they glistened.

'Do I look so very ill, Makena?' James said, from the recliner.

'No.' Makena shook her head, forcing her smile to be even wider. 'You look as strong as your monster.'

She looked away, unable to meet the old man's gaze. Her eyes alighted on

Sama. She beckoned, looking relieved to see a distraction from the conversation. 'Ah! I have someone for you to meet, children. This is my friend, Sama Neeley. You all know that we have brought a boy called Christopher here, to save him. She has helped to get him here. She's one of us now.'

The children looked across. The little girl, Eliza, clapped her hands together and grinned. 'Hello!' she called.

'Hello,' Sama replied uncertainly. She felt suddenly shy at all the eyes looking at her.

'Can you come over?' James said. 'I can't really turn around to see you.'

Sama nodded and began to walk forward. 'Yes, of course,' she said a moment later, realising he could not see the nod. She came around the recliner, still conscious of the other children watching, and looked down to smile at the old man. Her smile froze on her face.

James' skin was a deathly white and his hair was all but gone, but he was not an old man. He was still a boy, perhaps no older than her. His lips were cracked. His cheeks were drawn and sallow. Great dark rings hung under pale eyes yellowed and milky. Around his forehead, below the wisps of hair was a circle of terribly burned skin, cracked, blistered and blackened, that reached over his ears and behind his head.

Sama drew in a sharp breath. Her entire body felt suddenly cold. Around her, the children were silent, still staring at her, waiting.

Makena broke the silence. 'Sama …'

James raised a hand weakly before she could continue. He looked up and steadily met Sama's horrified gaze.

'Mine was a crown,' he said after a moment. 'I wore it and I rode a monster. I was a prince. I conquered lands and I saved a thousand slaves. I did so many other things.' He glanced at Makena. 'And without me, Makena would not have her staff.'

The atmosphere had changed now. All the toys and paintings couldn't compensate for this. Sama looked away, her eyes suddenly full.

'Don't be sad for me,' the boy whispered. 'I knew what would happen, and I had six years of the best ever adventures I could have. I'm not sad.'

Sama frowned despite herself. 'Six years?' She looked over at Makena, who looked back steadily and soberly. 'Six years? But I thought you said that Christopher didn't have much time.'

'We are not bound,' Eliza said in a flat voice that seemed unsuited to a little girl. It was as if she was reciting something she had been taught. 'When we are tired, we may come home. The unbound return.' She smiled a tiny smile at James. 'So we can come home here.'

'And tell people all about our adventures,' James said, 'so that the friends we met and the things we did don't get lost.'

Eliza jumped up. She was lively again now. How could she be so happy when faced with James' wounds? She grabbed Sama by the hand.

'Look!' She pointed. 'Come see the books!'

She pulled Sama away from the group, towards a bookcase between the nurses' station and the window. Sama dumbly allowed herself to be pulled across.

Eliza dropped her hand as they reached the bookcase. 'See!' She pulled a book from the shelf. The book was red with a name printed on the front in gold letters: *Robert Lloyd*. 'This one is my favourite!'

Eliza pulled open the book and thrust it at Sama. The page had opened to a child's drawing of tall purple men dressed in silver suits. 'These are Venusians!' Eliza exclaimed. 'This boy went to space and these were his friends. I've read loads of these books.'

She looked up at Sama. 'When I go on my trip, I want to go into space. I'm going soon. As soon as your friend is free and his artefact is ready, I'm going! And when I get back, I'll get a book just like James and like all my other friends.' The smile was large on her face, but her eyes were uncertain. They flicked across at the window to their right.

Sama glanced across. In the room beyond the window were six beds. Nurses bustled around them fussing with the patients that lay within. A doctor stood by one bed. He lifted a reedy arm from the bed, checking a pulse. Of the other patients, Sama could see very little.

She didn't need to. She knew exactly what she was seeing. It was too much. She dragged her eyes away, back to the bookshelf, feeling unsteady on her feet.

The little girl was still chatting away to her. Her voice was bright and yet somehow determined. The words no longer registered in Sama's mind. She looked again at the books, bound in every colour imaginable, each with a golden name printed on the spine. The shelves stretched up above her and down below her. There were so many books. Too many to easily count.

Understanding sunk into her. Too many to count. Sama turned away from the little girl and fell to her knees. Then she was violently sick.

CHAPTER TWENTY-THREE

King Kay

At least forty soldiers, if they could be called that, watched Christopher and the others nervously from the battlements. Bows and rifles pointed down at them from all angles, shaking in jittery arms.

'They're just boys!' Eleila said in his ear. She sat behind him, sharing his horse. Her own had collapsed from exhaustion back on the trail. 'Look at them.'

Christopher nodded. She was right. The faces staring down from behind the smooth black crenellations above them were almost all young. Younger even than Christopher. Too young to be standing guard and waiting for an attack. If this was Kay's army, it was a good thing they were behind castle walls.

The gatehouse was four storeys of sheer black granite. It would be impossible to scale those smooth polished walls with anything but the tallest of siege ladders. To even get such a ladder into place would be near-futile. It would need to be carried up the exposed hill below. That would make the carriers a very easy target for anyone with a missile.

The only features in the walls were regular arrow slits running up either side of the central tower. Christopher could see dim movements from within, no doubt more boys with weapons.

From the top of the main tower, two standards hung over the sides, reaching down three storeys. Each was white cloth, vivid against the black stone. A silver ring with a black boar reared up in profile was embroidered on each. Great angry tusks jutted from each boar's lower jaw.

Ahead, the drawbridge opening the route to Kay's austere barbican was drawn shut. Its dark underbelly was exposed, reinforced with rigid steel plates studded into the oak planks.

Eleila stood in the saddle behind him and shouted up at the battlements. 'Open the gate!'

Atop the battlements, some of the young guards flinched, as if the words had been arrows. One scurried across to a companion. They spoke. There was some gesticulating from the first followed by the second shaking his head.

Christopher sighed and watched the first tramp back to his post. The boy lifted his rifle with some effort.

'It's going to take more than that,' Christopher said over his shoulder.

Eleila sat back down again. She grunted with pain. Her hand went to her left hip. When her horse had collapsed on the coastal path they'd been galloping along, she had only just dodged free, but still twisted her leg.

Christopher's horse had taken the ride nearly as badly too. Especially after it had gained a second rider. It swayed and whinnied. It had also started frothing at the mouth now they were stopped. Christopher swung a leg over the horse and dropped to the ground. There was no reason to prolong its pain now they were here.

'Show them the sword,' Bediviere said. His voice was hoarse. He looked like he wasn't doing a great deal better than the animal. Blood flowed from beneath his dented shoulder plate and he was decidedly unsteady in his saddle.

'Sir Bediviere,' Christopher said. 'Take off your helmet. Show them it's you.'

Christopher had been bolder with the knight since the battle. Whether this was a dream or not, some things did seem clear. Here he was strong. Here he was good with a bow. Here — most importantly — he was needed. And no matter what 'here' turned out to be, he had realised he cared about it. The sword, the Queen, Bediviere, Eleila.

'I can't lift my arm, boy. Help me with the helmet.'

When Christopher lifted the helmet from the knight's head, Bediviere screwed his eyes shut. He was obviously in pain. It took him some moments to gather his strength. Finally, he lifted his head.

He bellowed up, pausing for breath between each sentence. 'I am Sir Bediviere, knight of Arthur Pendragon. Riding companion of Sir Kay. We bring the Sword in the Stone, the rightful sword of the King. Open the gate and let us in!' He leaned down against his warhorse.

Eleila pulled the Sword in the Stone from its scabbard and lifted it high into the air so the soldiers atop the battlements could see. Once again, the youngsters shuffled about, seeming at a loss. Some muttered to one another. Still nothing happened.

This was taking too long. It would be a close bet as to whether Bediviere or the horse collapsed first.

Christopher shouted at the soldiers, exasperated. 'If you can't open the gates without permission, go and find someone who can!' He surprised himself with his tone of authority. Two of the boys at the top disappeared back behind the battlements.

Bediviere grunted and climbed down from his horse. He looked back up at Eleila. 'Dismount. Give the horse some rest.'

He led his own mount the last few yards to the edge of the moat. Eleila clambered down, then limped after him. The horse snorted in protest but stumbled along behind her.

When the boys returned, they were accompanied by an older man. His beard was a stark contrast to all the youthful white faces. Perhaps not all the troops inside were so green. The older man stared down. He turned and signalled off behind him. There was a muffled shout from behind the drawbridge.

The drawbridge inched forward towards them with a giant creak. As its tip reached their eye level, Christopher looked inside. A huge portcullis slowly drew up into the roof.

In the entranceway to the barbican, men positioned themselves tight to the walls, brandishing worn weapons at them with tight white hands. Christopher sighed. Though there were some older faces, they were not warriors. At best the men were militia.

Some looked as if they had never even pointed a weapon before. A boy at the front gasped as his spear slipped from shaking hands. He dropped to the ground and snatched it up again, glancing around, red-faced. Another held a rusty battle axe far too high along the shaft, making any swing he should attempt useless.

Their faces were drawn, etched with lines of both worry and exhaustion. Dark rings hung under haunted eyes. The sound of their breathing was ragged with fear.

The drawbridge settled on the ground. There was a thundering of hooves. The militia pressed themselves even tighter to the walls.

A group of mounted knights trotted out from the darkness. The knights rode warhorses in far better condition than their own. There were just a few of them, perhaps two dozen. It was certainly not enough to change the tide of a battle. At least they were well armed. Swords and battle axes were clenched in armoured fists, ready to strike at a moment's notice.

They wore identical helmets with the visors down. Their armour was in pristine condition, dark metal plates mirroring the dark walls of the keep. Each wore a white tabard with the Boar motif embroidered upon it.

The front-most knight pulled up his horse just in front of them. He wheeled it to the side, so that his sword arm faced them. 'Drop all your weapons!' he snarled.

Christopher hesitated. Bediviere, however, unbuckled his sword belt and let it slip to the earth.

He looked across. 'Do as they say.'

Christopher unshouldered his bow and placed it on the ground. He pulled out the sword that he had been carrying since the battle and dropped it next to the bow.

Eleila had not moved. The Sword in the Stone was still brandished in her hand.

'You too,' the knight said, his voice gruff with menace.

'This is the Sword in the Stone.' Eleila drew herself up, shoulders back. 'Pulled from the stone by our greatest King and entrusted to me by Queen Guinevere to pass to his successor. I will not drop it into the dirt like some squire's first weapon.'

'You'll drop it, or we'll drop you,' the knight said evenly. 'Your choice.'

All they needed now, Christopher thought, would be her directing her anger at their potential allies. He shot a look at her. 'Eleila. Do as he says.'

'Bediviere?' an incredulous voice called from the entrance-way. 'By God, it *is* you!'

The knight walking towards them looked like he was not that comfortable dressed for battle. He was tall and slightly overweight. He wore the gleaming armour as if he had been shoehorned into it. Christopher imagined he could hear the creak of leather straps strained to their limit. Judging from the deference the warrior knights showed him, Christopher doubted this was a man in someone else's armour. More likely, he had not had to wear it for a long time.

The knight's long greying hair shone in the mid-afternoon light. He looked well-kept and clean compared to most of the people Christopher had met here. Atop his head was a simple silver band.

Bediviere stepped forward, almost stumbling as the knight reached them. The knight reached forward and caught his arm, steadying him. 'Dear Bediviere. It is good to see you.'

Bediviere pulled back his arm and dropped to his knees. 'My King.'

'My heavens, no.' The knight started.

To the side, Eleila dropped to her knees as well. She thrust the Sword in the Stone up into the air before her. 'King Kay,' she proclaimed. 'This is the Sword in the Stone. Queen Guinevere entrusted it to me to bring to you. Its possession is your right and your proof of monarchy.'

Christopher could hear the relief in her voice. Her arms were shaking. When she was shouting at him or calling him a fool, it was hard to remember she was barely a young woman, untested before the past few days. For all her training and bravado, she was still not much older than him.

Behind Eleila, the knights on horseback dropped their swords and bowed their heads. In the barbican, the militia along the sides of the drawbridge knelt, too.

Christopher was suddenly aware he was the only one not bowing in some way. He went to bend his head. Before he could, Kay caught him with a small, sad smile. 'At least there is one person here who hasn't succumbed to this madness.'

Bediviere looked up, his tired face bemused. 'Your majesty?'

'Oh please, Bediviere! I am many things, but a majesty I am not,' Kay said firmly. 'I've no more right to that damn sword now then I had forty years ago, when I couldn't pull it out of the rock. Look. I am still wearing my seneschal's band, not a crown.'

'Kay, the succession …' Bediviere began.

'Is a conversation for the future.' Kay cut him off, pulling at a shoulder plate where it was digging into his neck. 'We have considerably more pressing matters to worry about. Scouts put Mordred's army no more than an hour's ride. We can discuss how we find a new King if we survive. Now, if you could all please get up we should really get back inside.'

The knights lifted their heads, uncertain. Kay pulled Bediviere to his feet. Then he glanced across at Eleila.

She stayed rigid on her knees, the sword offered out before her. Kay inclined his head to one side. 'Eleila. Or do you prefer 'Wolf'?'

She lifted her head, surprise registering on her face.

Kay smiled his sad smile again. 'There wasn't much my brother didn't tell me, my dear. I may be seen as a glorified quartermaster who enjoys his food and wine a little too much by most, but Arthur listened to me. He chose well when he sent you to Gwen. If she gave you the sword, I am not the man to change that. Bring it and we will find a safe place to put it in.'

He turned to look at Christopher. 'And who might you be?'

'Christopher, Sir Kay,' Christopher said quickly.

'A strange lad,' Bediviere interjected. 'He sees things that he cannot see, but he's good in a fight.'

'He thinks we're all part of his dream,' Eleila blurted out. Christopher stared daggers across at her. He could feel his face growing red. Suddenly all eyes were on him.

'Lovely.' Kay raised a cynical eyebrow. 'Well, we've the rest of the country's refugees here, so why not a dreamer? Perhaps you'll dream us a victory. Come in, all of you.' He gestured to the militia. 'Help Bediviere inside.'

A boy with curly red hair and freckles stumbled forward. His hands shook as he took the knight's arm. An older man who looked like he would be far happier with a kitchen ladle in his hand rather than a short-bow rushed in to join him.

Christopher bent and retrieved his weapons, slipping the sword back into his belt and the bow over his shoulder. Eleila grunted quietly with pain. He glanced over. Walking was obviously an ongoing struggle for her.

'Here, let me help.' He walked across and lifted her arm over his shoulders.

'I don't need any help.' She hissed through her teeth.

Christopher glanced at her, then grinned. 'For once, shut up.'

She resisted for only a moment longer. They limped along, trailing the horse behind them. As they began their way into the castle grounds, another young soldier hurried across to them. He took control of the exhausted beast and led it off ahead.

Eleila turned to Christopher, with an apologetic smile. 'Heavy for a dream, eh?'

Christopher looked at her bright blue eyes and smiled back. 'You know when you smile like that you are quite pretty.'

Eleila's face fell into a frown. 'Pretty!'

She turned her head to the front again, raising it proudly. Then she picked up the pace, forcing herself to use her twisted leg. Christopher grinned to himself and hurried along next to her.

Kay's castle was a flurry of activity. A cluster of houses dotted the open space between outer wall and keep. In front of them were large wicker baskets. Streams of militia ferried missiles over to them. Arrows, crossbow bolts, and bullets were all sorted into individual baskets.

Peasant boys regularly darted into the arsenal. They filled small leather bags with the missiles before running them up to the battlements. There they could be piled at convenient intervals, ready for use.

Christopher and the others continued away from the outer wall between two squat houses. There, a group of women tore strips from huge white cloths. Christopher noticed the Boar motif again. Kay was making bandages from his own banners.

'There was no time to get the women and children to safety?' Bediviere said to Kay, just ahead of them.

'There was. Most refused. Now everyone works.' Kay's voice was flat.

They passed out from the houses and came into an open field, covered with short grass on either side of the track. Christopher could see the inner castle properly now. All of the castle's defences were concentrated in the mighty frontal battlements. Beyond the grassed areas, on either side, the walls tapered down to eight feet in height. A slim walkway ran along their upper parts. Further on they disappeared almost altogether. The back wall of the castle was simply a crenelated wall that could be manned by soldiers standing on the ground.

'What if they come from the rear?' Christopher asked out loud.

'Not possible.' Bediviere glanced back. 'The castle is surrounded by cliffs and sea. The only way to access the castle is from the front.'

Ahead the black keep loomed. Like the main castle, all its defences were at the front. Its rear wall was built close to the cliff edge. On either side of the keep entrance, a black tower rose up. From the battlements atop the keep it would be easy to fire down on those in the field.

On either side of the keep, about twenty feet up, a long bridge jutted out. Each stretched across the field on thick black granite columns, then joined the outer battlements as they reached the same height. A walkway from battlement to keep.

The beginning of each walkway was a drawbridge that could be drawn back to the keep wall should the battlements be overrun.

The field had become a temporary town. Some, mostly soldiers, were lucky enough to have encampments. Torn standards rose by muddied tents. The groups of men by the tents mostly kept to themselves, repairing equipment, discussing plans, resting battle-worn bodies.

Around them were the less fortunate. Peasants huddled together in whatever shelters they had been able to put together. Refugees from the countryside around that had come to the castle with a desperate hope for protection. The ones here in the field were those too old or too young to contribute to the defence effort. Babies cried on grandmothers' knees. Old men stared dim-eyed at the activity around them.

Some of the luckier ones had received charity from the soldier's camps. Here a piece of canvas had been erected with two wooden poles to provide a lean-to. It was full with the desperate. Across from the lean-to, a cart filled with straw had been provided. More sat in it, whilst others sat under it, beneath the wheels.

For the most part, the peasants were just on the open grass with no shelter or comfort. All they could do was wait and try to stay out of the way of their protectors.

Though the field was noisy, there was something missing. Christopher listened to the rowdy neighing of animals and the dull thuds of sacks piled on to others with a frown. He noticed the urgent 'thwack' of arrows and looked across. A soldier trained boys to shoot. They looked as scared as the boys already on the walls. Occasionally there was the crack of a rifle, fired in practice. Though, judging from the infrequency, they were reserving bullets.

Suddenly Christopher realised. Voices! The people in the camps hardly spoke. He let his gaze linger on one of the smaller camps. A young man stood behind another, leaning to bandage a wound on his companion's arm. The wounded man stared out into the middle distance, dull eyes oblivious. The medic seemed only intent on the arm, as if it were an entity in itself and not attached to another living, breathing human.

By one large mud-spattered tent, two cooks doled out ladles of steaming stew. A silent line of waiting militia and peasants stretched back two hundred feet. At least they were being fed. Those already served sat stuffing the food down as if it was the first food they had ever had.

Christopher found himself salivating at the sight of it. He strained his nose and sniffed at the rich smells. They had not eaten since before the fight in the valley. That felt like a lifetime ago.

Eleila smelled the food, too. She closed her eyes and breathed in deeply through her nose. They needed to eat.

'King Kay!' he called ahead to where Kay kept pace with Bedivere.

Kay turned back. 'See? It even sounds ridiculous. Far too many "K"s. "Sir Kay", please.' He noticed Christopher's face. A look of understanding passed across his own. 'Of course. You will eat. We are going to my hall.' He gestured to a young soldier forming part of their guard. 'Go and tell the cooks to fill a bucket. Bring it, and bowls.'

When they reached the keep, Kay led them through to his great hall. A fire burned high and hot in a huge grate. Around the fire, there were piles of cushions. They looked so inviting.

'Rest here, friends,' Kay said. 'I will have my men attend to you.'

Bedivere walked to a chair by a large dining table and sat. Christopher helped Eleila to another.

'Thanks,' she said, once she was settled. 'Now go rest. Take the time whilst we have it.'

He nodded and glanced at the cushions. He could close his eyes, just for a few minutes. It would be wonderful. He stumbled over to them and flopped down gratefully.

He was disturbed a short time later by a hand shaking his shoulder. His eyes sprang open. He pushed back, clutching for his sword. The boy who stared at him looked as shocked as he guessed he must. He almost dropped the steaming bowl of stew in his other hand. Christopher relaxed. 'You were asleep,' the boy apologised.

For the next few minutes Christopher did nothing other than concentrate on the stew before him. The meat was pork, he thought, cooked with big lumps of carrot, turnip, and cabbage. There was something sweet in the meaty sauce, too. Possibly a berry of some sort. It was delicious. Christopher didn't look up again until he had finished the lot.

Bediviere sat at the table. In front of him was a recently finished bowl of stew as well. His armour had been removed. A young man was washing and dressing the wound in his shoulder as he grimaced against the pain. Further back into the hall, Kay talked with two of his guards. There was no sign of Eleila.

Christopher clambered up from the cushions. He stumbled over to the table. 'Hello. How long was I asleep for?'

Bediviere opened one eye and frowned. 'I didn't notice, boy. The food was no more than ten minutes so it could not have been long.'

Christopher glanced around again.

'She is having her leg attended to,' Bediviere said, guessing before he could ask where Eleila was. 'She may be able to do many things like a knight, but stripping to her undergarments in front of the rest of us to be attended to is not one of them.'

'No,' Christopher said, suddenly distracted by the thought of her that night at the pool. 'I suppose not.'

Hearing them talking, Kay dismissed the man and sauntered over to them. 'I hope that is better. Nothing like good food and wine to replenish a man's spirits.' As if to prove the point he reached across the table to where a decanter of red wine was and poured himself a glass.

Bediviere said nothing for a moment. The attendant finished applying an evil-smelling mixture to his wound. He bent his head to the knight. 'If you could just sit forward, my lord, I can bandage your wound. '

Bediviere frowned but sat forward. He looked up at Kay. 'How many are we?'

'There are about eight hundred peasants. Of them, perhaps five hundred we have formed into the militia. Most of them will be seeing their first war. Some can fire an arrow or two. The others will be able to drop things off the battlements. As the days go on, I suspect the ones that learn fast will be the ones that survive.'

'Trained men?' Bediviere asked.

'About two hundred and fifty. But they are either my own men that were too sick or old to go with the bulk of my forces to aid Arthur, or they are the wounded returned.'

'Of knights, we are even fewer,' Kay continued. 'There is my own seneschal guard. You saw most of them at the gates earlier. I kept twenty back when Arthur ordered me to stay here and prepare for a last stand if he fell.' He faltered. 'Never in all my days did I think we would be carrying out that order, Bediviere. Never.' He looked away and was silent.

When he looked back he had regained his composure. 'I would say we have fifty other knights able to ride and fight if needed. To be honest, if we are down to using knights on horseback, then the walls are breached and all is lost, anyway.'

Bediviere nodded. 'Who from the Round Table?'

'Just you and I my friend,' Kay said quietly.

'No one else?' Bediviere stammered. 'No one is come?'

'Some survived the battle, I heard. But none has come here. Perhaps they have decided to slip away. Perhaps they did not survive the aftermath.'

'Sir Galind survived and Sir Claris,' Christopher said suddenly, wanting them to remember he was there. There were things he needed to ask Kay, himself. 'I was with them at the abbey the Queen had been staying in.'

Kay nodded kindly. 'Wolf told me.'

'Wolf.' Bediviere smiled despite himself. 'She prefers the name?'

'She deserves it,' Kay said. 'Either way, our best hope is to keep Mordred and his forces at bay until Lancelot comes.'

'If he comes.'

'He will, Bediviere. The Queen will find him and he will come with an army,' Kay replied. 'Until then we hold here. The castle is strong, and they can only come in one direction.'

'How long can we hold?' Bediviere asked.

'I have stores for three months. With tight rationing, we can stretch it to four.'

Bediviere raised an eyebrow. 'That is impressive for so many extra mouths.'

Kay grinned. 'Always the storekeeper. And you used to laugh at me for it.'

'Sir Kay,' Christopher interrupted. 'May I ask you a question?'

Kay turned his head to Christopher, his perfect hair falling over his collar as he did. 'Speak.'

'I don't know why I'm here,' Christopher began. 'I thought I was dreaming for a long time, but now I don't know. I know this is real. But there are some things that aren't right. Where I come from, I've read stories about you all like it's the past. I've read about how Arthur died and what happened to Excalibur.' He turned to Bediviere. 'And I was right, wasn't I?'

Bediviere nodded, looking thoughtfully at Christopher.

'You've read about this,' Kay sounded bemused. 'How can you read about what has yet to happen?'

'I don't know,' Christopher said. 'I'm sorry.'

'Wait!' Kay said quickly, almost cutting him off in his excitement. 'Have you read what will happen here?'

'No. I'm sorry,' Christopher said. 'What I knew and what has been happening since I've been here are quite different. I don't know why.'

Kay looked away again. 'Well, these are the strangest times of my life. My brother dead and everything he built reduced to the rabble outside on the grass.' He turned back. 'If you could give me a straw, I might just clutch at it, but if you cannot, I don't know what you want from me.'

He looked up at Kay, eyes wide. 'And that's what I mean. The Queen, she said I should come with Eleila ... Wolf, to ask people here. She said someone might know.'

Kay looked at Christopher for a long time before he shook his head. 'Then I'm sorry too, boy. I don't know who you are or why you are here. I fear that you have walked into the dragon's lair. No one will have time for your questions now.' Kay placed a hand on his shoulder. 'I will tell you this, though. Stand with us and when this is done, I will help you find the answers you seek.'

Christopher was not surprised at the answer, but he did surprise himself with his disappointment. Since he had finally accepted that he was actually here, it seemed a part of him had been hoping the Queen was right.

'Sir Bediviere! Sir Kay!' Eleila appeared at the entrance to the hall. She came across, struggling to pull her chain mail coat back on. 'They are here!'

From behind her, a knight appeared and rushed past. 'The girl is right, my lords. The usurper's army arrives.'

'My lords,' the man continued, a tremor in his voice, 'there are thousands of them!'

CHAPTER TWENTY-FOUR

The Killing Zone

There was a hill across from Kay's castle, the last high point before the land sloped down towards the sea. The castle was all but an island. A long spit of land reached out through the sea towards it.

Along its length ran a road. On one side was a sandy beach that at low tide, as now, doubled the width of the land. During high tide, the land and road were barely fifty yards wide.

The beach was well sheltered from the currents of the sea. It would be easy for a friendly ship to moor close to shore. A safe place for allies to land.

Yet, for any foe, there would be no shelter from the castle above. An enemy trying to cross that open stretch of land would be an easy target for the castle defenders, high on their battlements. From there they could rain down arrows and rocks and fire, turning the spit of land into a death zone. Any attack would be a wild, desperate race along the spit, whilst numbers still lasted. It would take a large force to cross the divide with any hope of reaching the battlements.

Mordred's army was such a force.

They had been marching steadily for days. Now the time to kill was upon them. Four thousand strong. A mass of pole axes and pikes, of swords and spears, of longbows and crossbows.

There were the foot soldiers. Seasoned professionals of the standing army. Men for whom, live or die, this was to be just one more battle. Units of pike moved into tight formations and prepared themselves for the long run. They stood calmly in the mass of activity, rationing their words and movements to just the most necessary, conserving their energy for the task ahead.

With them were the recruits. Men press-ganged from farms and villages. They were loud. A forced boisterousness that prepared them for the fight.

Archers checked their bows. Occasionally each would glance up, silently calculating the distance they would need to be along the spit before their weapons began to count.

The King turned in his saddle and barked orders in a high-pitched voice. Messengers scampered around the mound where he had stopped, waiting for him to direct them. Once ordered, they raced off to deliver his words. As each order was relayed, the army positioned itself to attack.

A messenger moved further back through the army, shouting to units of foot soldiers to make way. The soldiers stomped apart to create a channel through their midst, muttering under their breaths to one another.

Through the gap Mordred's knights cantered on their powerful warhorses. Their heads were held high. Bright eyes looked out with arrogance above their bright armour. Their faces were moulded with the zealous expressions of warriors who knew in advance they were on the winning side. The horses snorted and stomped hooves, sensing that soon their capped adrenaline would be released and they would be able to run. The knights took up half position ahead of the foot soldiers, at the vanguard of the attack.

The rhythmic thud of giant boots against hardening mud came from the back of the army. Like a wave, the other men fell silent. It started nearest the sound. Men turned and, realising those behind them had fallen quiet, closed their own mouths. They looked to the rear of the army with awe.

Between the archers and the foot soldiers, the Stahlhelme came.

Mordred surveyed the host around him and nodded with satisfaction. Then he turned to a messenger and nodded. Immediately the short man galloped to the apex of the hill and gestured wildly down to the back of the host. 'Bring them!'

At first there was little more than the sounds of straining. A guttural, angry growl. The squeal of metal rasping against wood. Then slowly from the back of the host four lines of hunchbacked beasts appeared, tusked faces like those of the Stahlhelme, bare to the waist, their bodies a mass of hair and muscle. Over each beast's left shoulder was a great chain they gripped with huge slab-like hands and pulled with muscled arms. Each chain attached to a wheeled carriage behind, two to a carriage.

Upon each carriage lay the source of the weight, an eighty pounder artillery gun, black polished metal gleaming in the daylight, despite the flecks of mud along their barrels from the journey. At one end of each carriage, was an arsenal of artillery stacked and tied in place, ready to be loaded and blasted out across the sky between the hills and the castle.

It took ten minutes of straining and pulling before the beasts finally brought the guns to rest by the archery units. The smaller men flustered and backed away from their giant allies, appearing unwilling to risk standing too close to the monsters, whether on the same side or not. The beasts hardly noticed the men, instead gathering in the chains and placing them beneath the front wheels to form an effective barrier against the carriage rolling forward.

Once each transport team had secured their vehicles, they fell to different tasks, now forming the gunnery team. Some creatures lifted huge shells and moved towards the rear of the great field gun, ready to load it. Others bent over surveying devices, calculating trajectories or measuring wind strength. Others still turned mighty pulleys, pulling dense bands of metal cables taut until they squealed against the strain. Slowly the guns rose into the sky.

Kay was moving before the man had even finished. 'We can see them from the towers. Come!' He bounded up the stairs at the back of the great hall. 'Open the drawbridge to the ramparts!'

Eleila followed immediately. Her limp was considerably less pronounced. Christopher jogged to fall into step with her. 'Your leg?'

'They pulled it about,' she said, glancing again at him. 'Something snapped back into place. It feels better.'

'Good.' He was relieved for her, but if truth be told, his heart was pounding. The man had said 'thousands' of them. Christopher had never seen thousands of people, let alone thousands of people who wanted to attack him.

At the top of the stairs, the guard had opened the side drawbridge. They rushed out on to the wall, crossing the distance to the steps down and the side walls beyond.

As they scaled the ramparts rising to the gatehouse towers, Kay strode forward, shouting out orders to the troops below. 'Leave those now! Get ammunition to the front defence! Boil more oil!'

Bediviere caught them up. The bandage he had been having applied hung unfinished from his shoulder. He had half wrapped a fur around himself. 'Kay, are we ready?' he called out.

'I suspect we will find out,' Kay shouted back without breaking step.

The Gatehouse was ahead, its left-hand tower platform up a short flight of black stone steps. They climbed the steps to the platform, pushing past a disorganised mess of peasants who struggled to deliver more equipment to the warriors beyond.

On the battlements of the tower, every crenellation had soldiers crowding in to observe the army in the distance. To one side, another small group of non-combatants packed baskets of arrows at regular spots on the floor, where they would be easy to reach.

A group of militia stood around a stocky man, their squad leader, Christopher assumed. 'Now lads,' he said, his voice steady. 'There's a lot of the devils, granted, but we know the drill. We're all the way up here and they'll be down in the valley. We'll pick off most of them before they even reach us.' He leaned in. 'I've been put in charge of you lot because I've seen this sort of thing before. They'll come in waves. We'll probably only see one or two today before it gets dark. Then they'll wait until morning.'

Suddenly he noticed the new arrivals behind him. He turned and bent his head. 'My Lords.'

Kay nodded. 'This man is right. Stand steady. They'll get bored of sending men down there to die soon enough. Then it will become a waiting game. We must just hold until then.'

'Ay.' The leader nodded. 'One attack at a time, lads. No more, no less.'

Kay walked to the front of the tower. He looked out between crenellations. Christopher started forward. Before he could slip in, Eleila grabbed him and pulled him back, making way for Bediviere. Christopher shot a look at Eleila, prepared for a sharp comment.

She just looked worried. Her face was white. Her eyes were wide. Christopher understood. She would have never seen as many foes as this either. 'Come on,' he said, taking the arm that had barred him. He led her to the next crenellation. 'We can see from there.'

On the hill opposite them, in the cloud dimmed light, its summit was almost black with men. It was as if a sooty snow had fallen, covering the grass and obscuring it completely. Thousands of men, too small to make out individually, milled around preparing for the attack. The top of the hill undulated and shifted with their movement.

The sheer volume of foes that stretched out before them rendered Christopher's companions silent. Eleila sucked in a sharp intake of breath. Her hand found his shoulder and gripped it tightly.

In the centre, at the front, a section rose taller that the rest, knights on horseback, Christopher thought.

'They are staying out of range.' Eleila broke the silence after a moment. Her hand had remained on his shoulder. He could feel its tremor. The steadiness of her voice was for the benefit of their companions.

'For now,' Kay replied. His voice seemed determinedly positive too. 'They can't do much without getting closer. Then we will have the advantage.'

Christopher stared out at the knights' section. One side of it looked subtly different. Though the figures reached the same height as the men on horseback, they stood on the ground. His heart lurched. He recognised them. He pointed. 'There by the knights at the front.'

By their size, he was sure now. More of the Stahlhelme.

'Yes.' Bediviere had seen them too. 'See there, Kay?' He gestured at the Stahlhelme. 'The same as the ones who attacked us in the valley. They'll be at the vanguard. When they come, tell your men to concentrate on taking them down.'

'Don't worry,' Kay replied. 'We'll take them all.'

Christopher glanced across to the side. The other gatehouse tower rose up to their left. Between the crenellations there he could see other soldiers doing as they did, straining to look out at the distant throng. He glanced back. 'What are they waiting for?'

Finally, the great guns were ready. The leader of the gunner teams shambled to where Mordred sat atop his horse. It growled and gestured back at the weapons.

Mordred smiled a vicious smile. 'Very well. Begin.'

When the noise came, it sounded like a sharp thunderclap. Eleila flinched. Christopher realised he had ducked, too.

Bediviere frowned, 'What was ...?'

The ground in front of the other tower exploded in a shower of rocks and mud. They sprayed up, spattering the gatehouse towers, sending shards of stone to crash against the walls. An arc of dirt and rubble rained down on them. Behind, a man cried out. Christopher turned. One of the militia had been caught by a stone. A gash had opened on his head.

The beast working as the spotter on the first gun crew looked carefully at where the explosion had appeared. It turned, shouted in its guttural voice, gesturing upwards with its hands. The gun crew began to make adjustments with the wheels and pulleys, repositioning the barrels. To the side the second crew was doing the same.

Kay shouted to his men. 'Keep calm. Be ready. If they do that again, use your shields to protect yourselves.'

Christopher was cold all over. The thunder-crack and the explosion. They had artillery! Christopher understood artillery from school. Panic rose in his voice. 'We have to get down from here!'

'Stay calm,' Eleila said to him. 'They can't reach us here.'

'No!' Christopher shouted. 'They can! They are readjusting the trajectory!'

Before he could say any more, the thunderclap sounded again. This time it was followed by an audible whining. It grew closer and wider before he could fully register it.

A moment later the tower to their left exploded.

The Master heard the first explosion from a good distance away. The battle had started, then. He grimaced and squeezed his legs against the horse he was riding. It was already galloping far faster than was natural. Even so, at his touch, its energy-bolstered legs pushed harder still.

The second explosion, a few moments later, worried him. Now he was closer, it sounded surprisingly loud. For a weapon to be making that kind of noise, it would be enormous. It would likely be dealing out considerable damage to the castle. The last thing the Master needed was Christopher getting hurt.

Of course, it was unlikely that anything serious would befall him. The boy had the natural luck of a creator. Most situations would pass him by without more than a scratch, but those guns did sound very big indeed.

At the third explosion, the Master decided enough was enough. He pushed forward on the saddle and sucked in energy from all around him. In a blue flash the horse was gone and he was flying along the ground. He struggled to concentrate. Sucking in a continual stream of energy to fuel his flight as well as trying to steer himself was difficult to say the least. He hated travelling like this. He swerved to the side, narrowly missing a large rock looming into his path.

By the time he had zipped around another, leaving a trail of blue light in his way, he was at the foot of the hill. The back of Mordred's army was ahead of him. He pushed on up towards them, an arc of blue light shooting in a straight line.

He landed in their midst. The light dimmed. The company of foot soldiers around him backed away, soon leaving him in a wide circle.

The attack had not started in earnest yet. The soldiers, those who had not noticed him at least, waited in anticipation, hungry for the order that would begin their charge. In the distance, the castle bled bricks and dust.

Mordred sat stop his horse a short distance ahead by the field guns, surrounded by his generals. He stared up at the smoking barrels with open admiration.

The Master's lips thinned. The castle was crippled. The top of the left gate tower was in ruins, collapsed on to the floor below it. The right had a large hole on one side about halfway up. The gatehouse itself had taken a hit just to the left of the drawbridge. Shaking his head, the Master stretched out his consciousness towards the guns.

There was another ear-splitting explosion from one of the field guns. For a moment it broke the Master's concentration. The base of the left tower ahead collapsed inwards. Great clouds of dust plumed out of the hole.

The other gun cracked. The crews had found their marks now.

Christopher blinked. The concern of the great guns was suddenly erased from his mind. What was that shining blue trail that had suddenly appeared on the hill? He strained forward. It was gone now, as quickly as it had appeared.

Christopher frowned. Something was different. Something was out there that he had the strangest sense was like him. Something from somewhere else.

The whistle of another shell pierced his thoughts. This one was close. He turned to Eleila. 'We ne—'

Then the side of the battlements disintegrated.

'Hold fire!' the Master whispered the command, gripping the key, using its power, willing his words at the batteries. At once, the two crews stopped what they were doing and held still. They would be motionless until he commanded them to action again.

He pushed out his consciousness further to feel the troops about him. They were like hungry dogs, straining at the leash, impatient to get into the fight. The Master smiled and pushed out a thought to them all, *'Be still.'*

As one, the vast throng quieted. Voices raised in bloodlust were muffled as mouths closed. The ring of metal striking metal silenced as men froze in place. Even the knights' horses grew quiet, their excited snorting reduced to the lightest of breaths. Now the hill was silent.

The Master strolled forward to where Mordred and his generals sat, silent on their horses. The only noise was the wind. It blew cold around them. It whistled through the silent hordes. He pulled his collar high against his neck.

The part of the hill where the King and his generals had set up their observation was slightly higher than the ground around it. The Master glanced at Mordred as he reached it. The King looked back down with wide, fearful eyes, but remained still.

The Master looked back at the tower. There was no danger the defenders in the castle would notice the sudden tranquillity in the waiting masses. They had too much of their own to deal with.

The harsh shouts of orders carried across in the wind, high above the spit of land. They mingled with the cries of the wounded. Then he heard a distant squeal.

It was faint at first. He frowned, struggling to pinpoint what it was. It was far ahead, barely audible over the wind and the defender's voices. Then it grew louder, more insistent. The staccato cracks of thousands of tiny wood fibres breaking. The screech of wooden beams straining to support the weight above them that had suddenly increased tenfold.

The Master squinted, straining to see. Ahead dust clouds were caught in fading afternoon light. Through them, he could make out frantic shapes at the top of the left tower, where the battlements had already been all but destroyed. Men clambered, desperate to get to safety before the inevitable happened. The squealing of the wood became a thicker, more final sound. The beams were losing the battle against the impossible load above.

Then the rumbling became a crashing. The left tower melted down into a sea of tumbling rock, mortar, wood, and men. Cries of those falling were drowned out or perhaps cut off. The cloud of dust flew into the sky, caught in the gusts of air, and billowed across the front of the castle walls until they were all but obscured. In a few moments it was over.

For a brief time, the whole landscape was silent, bar for the whistling wind. Then came the first scream for help. Some poor fool realising he wasn't dead. It would be no matter. He would be soon. Other voices joined in. Cries for help were combined with desperate orders. The denizens of the castle were moving fast.

The dust began to clear. It blew out towards the sea. The castle was a shape, then a silhouette. Then, finally, the Master could see its walls again.

Where the left tower had stood, there was now just a huge pile of rubble. Beyond the debris the castle lay open, ready for attack. The Master smiled. It was time.

He reached up to the nearest of Mordred's generals, a tall moustachioed man in a shiny suit of armour and pulled in the essence. The man lurched involuntarily forward from his horse, opening his mouth to cry in alarm, even as he disappeared into a thousand sparks of blue energy.

The energy hurtled into the Master's body, filling him with another hit of power. He leapt into the saddle and stood high in the stirrups. 'Charge!' He dug his heels into the horse and spurred it to a gallop. He pushed out with energy, boosting its gallop. He raced towards the vanguard of the army, trampling the foot soldiers in his way.

There was something pulling Christopher. It tugged at his arm with rapid insistent jerks. He frowned through closed eyes, wishing whoever it was would leave him alone. He felt like he was at the bottom of a very deep well, floating in water that was strangely warm in the blackness. It felt good. Could they not leave him alone?

The tugging persisted. Christopher could hear someone saying his name from what seemed like a long way away. They were shouting it, actually. Sounding pretty desperate about it, too.

He pulled his arm away from whoever was pulling at it. That only seemed to make them more determined to get his attention. Now there were two hands on his shoulders shaking at him. The voice grew louder.

'Christopher! Come on!'

There was nothing for it. They weren't taking no for an answer. Resigned, Christopher struggled to open his eyes, pulling them apart just the barest fraction.

The sense of warm water gushed away as soon as the light hit his eyes. Instead, there was pain. Pain in his head. Pain in his side. He clenched his eyes shut again. Everything swam.

'Christopher! Wake up! We have to move!'

It was Eleila. He pulled his eyes open again. Her face leaned in towards his, pinched and white.

His vision was tinted with red and one eye stung. He reached up and wiped at it. Pain blossomed again. He winced and drew his hand away. There was blood on the fingers. 'What is …?'

'Flesh wound.' Her voice had relaxed the barest amount since he had opened his eyes. 'Come on! The next time we might not be so lucky.'

She pulled him again. This time instead of resisting he struggled up, accepting her help. He winced at the pounding in his head, closing his eyes again. Once it receded to a manageable level he opened them and looked around.

The steps from the battlements were gone. Instead, a rude hole gashed into the side of the tower. To the left of it, the body of the squad leader lay, back twisted at an unnatural angle.

About half of his men were left. The others had disappeared in the explosion. The remaining men had lost any sense of bravery. They struggled to reach the safety of the battlements below, jostling in their haste. They were causing almost as much danger to each other as the shell had. As Christopher focused, one knocked into another. The second lost his grip. He fell through the hole, the cry from his mouth sounding as much affronted as scared until it was cut short on the stone floor below.

Bediviere and Kay had returned to the battlements. Eleila held his arm and gestured at them. 'Can you walk?'

Christopher nodded, gritting his teeth against the fresh fire in his temple. Eleila seemed to be waiting for him to speak, but at the moment talking and moving was too much. She slipped an arm around his waist and they stumbled across.

'They're charging!' Kay shook his head. 'They're coming and we are wide open.'

'Well at least they won't bombard us anymore,' Bediviere replied grimly. 'Get back to the keep. I'll rally the men around the breach.'

Eleila turned, pulling Christopher with her. Together they made their way across to the edge of the hole where the stairs had been. She pointed. 'Look, they're bringing a ladder.' Sure enough, soldiers over at the battlement had arrived with a tall siege ladder and were struggling to get it into place.

Christopher looked down into the void below. The missile had taken out two storeys of the tower, leaving a drop of twenty feet. The bottom was a mess of bodies and rubble.

Eleila pulled him back. 'Careful!'

The sight of the gap and the knowledge that he could have just fallen into it brought on a rush of adrenaline far more effective than Eleila's earlier shaking. He gasped in air and willed the pain in his head to go away. It didn't. At least things felt a little clearer.

'Where's my bow?' It wasn't on his shoulder.

'Don't worry about that.'

Christopher turned back to where he had lain. His bow and quiver were just to the left. He pulled out of Eleila's grasp and staggered towards them.

'Christopher!' she snapped, her voice more concern than anger.

'I'm all right,' Christopher said over his shoulder, finally beginning to compose himself. 'I'm going to need those.'

He bent and grasped the quiver by its strap, slinging it over his shoulder. Then he picked up the bow and slipped that over too.

As he stood to turn back to Eleila, he glanced across at the other tower.

It was gone.

He took an involuntary step forward, eyes wide. Where the battlements between the two towers had met the tower wall there was simply a broken walkway. It jutted out into nothing. Beyond it, the tower had collapsed far below into a mess of rubble.

Militia clambered over the rubble, setting up defensive positions. A mounted knight in the colours of Kay's guards urged them on. More militia and knights appeared from further back in the castle bailey. They emerged from the streets and alleys in groups. Those knights' faces not hidden behind helmets were set. Stony. Determined. They hurried toward the breach, overtaking the militia. The peasants had little of that steel. They struggled to pull on makeshift armour, brandishing second rate weapons for a fight they had not expected to see for weeks, if at all.

Christopher pulled his eyes away from them, ignoring the sinking feeling in his heart. If they could get into place, perhaps there was still a good chance that they could take down the attackers before they reached the breach. He glanced out towards Mordred's army.

There was no way.

The defenders that scaled the rubble below would be no match for the horde that approached. Their way was open. The castle was already lost.

At the head of the army charging towards them, lengthening the distance between themselves and the foot soldiers, Mordred's cavalry bore down on the castle. The thunder of hooves rolled out before them. Afternoon sunlight reflected cold from steel armour. Swords were thrust out. They would be at the breach in less than a minute.

The Stahlhelme ran among them. Though they were on foot, they matched the horses' speed. As they ran they fired indiscriminate blasts from their rifles. At the pace they ran, it was impossible to have any kind of accuracy. So far, none of the bullets had hit anything. Yet each time the crack of a rifle sounded, the defenders dropped to the ground, losing precious moments.

'Christopher!' Eleila shouted behind him. 'Come on!'

The blue light! How could he have forgotten?

Something out there that was like him. At least that was what instinct was telling him. 'Wait!' he called back at her.

Now it was in his mind once again, Christopher felt drawn. He scrambled to the front of the battlements again, slipping his head between crenellations. He looked out, beyond the knights, beyond the Stahlhelme. Almost at once, Christopher noticed the gaunt figure. The blue glow was faint on him, but still distinct against the afternoon light. The pain in Christopher's head dropped away. Instead there was a cold fear, and behind it, there was something more.

The man was riding a little way behind the vanguard but catching up rapidly. He stood in his saddle, his long black coat flapping out behind him. He looked unarmed. Suddenly Christopher understood the other sense he felt behind the fear. Recognition. For the briefest of seconds, Christopher frowned, trying to place him.

The vision.

The man had been in his vision, when he saw Freddie. That was the man that Sama had attacked.

Eleila called out again. Christopher ignored her. He leaned forward and stared out at the man.

He was riding in the saddle like he was very used to riding, but there was something wrong. The horse was moving far too fast to be natural. With each gallop, the horse seemed to glide forward as well. At each of the gallops, the blue light sparkled and diminished.

'Light like the gypsies,' Christopher said to himself.

Eleila grabbed his shoulder, spinning him around. 'Must I carry you across that ladder?' she snapped.

Reluctantly Christopher looked back at the gap. Sure enough, the ladder was in place. Bediviere had already climbed most of the way down and Kay was beginning his descent too.

'I'll be right behind you,' Christopher said urgently to Eleila, desperate to look back at the man again.

From the corner of his eye, Christopher noticed just the slightest prickle of blue light. He whipped his head right to look at where he had just seen it, a stone on the tower's crenellations. When he looked, it was gone.

'You must come now!' Eleila said again. 'We can't get trapped here!'

There was another! Christopher frowned. What was happening?

Eleila was pulling at him. He brushed her hand away and gripped it at the wrist. 'Eleila, listen. There's more to this then you can see. I promise I will be right behind you, but I need to look again. You need to let me.'

Something changed in her expression. He looked into her eyes and for the briefest moment he saw a blue spark flit across the black of her pupil. She blinked and pulled away from his grip. 'Right behind me, all right?'

Christopher nodded. He turned back to the tower wall and looked through. The man was far closer now, almost at the head of the nearest assailants.

Christopher frowned. The recognition was more than just seeing him in the vision. He had recognised him there as well. It had to be from something else.

The overcoat he wore flapped over the horse's hindquarters. It was neither the clothing of a knight nor a commoner. In fact it had a distinctly modern look. The long sleeves dangled over his hands, the one holding the reins and the other. Holding something else. Something blue!

Christopher clutched the stone battlement in front of him. The man's hand was glowing blue. Just like it had in the vision, just like his own hand had when he had put on.

'Winter's Grasp!' Christopher gasped.

'Winter's Grasp!'

The Master had stretched his consciousness out to the countryside around him. He scanned the people and creatures around him. He scanned those ahead and those further on in the castle, hoping to pick up a sign of something out of the norm. It was hard to concentrate on that and stay on the horse too, but now his efforts paid off.

He heard the words quite distinctly over the din of the charging horde. His head shot up and he scanned the castle walls. The boy was close. The boy could see him. And now the connection was almost complete.

The boy thought the key was the gauntlet. It made sense. The Master smiled and fixated on the direction of the voice.

There! A small head with a mop of brown hair leaned out between two crenellations on the remaining tower. Around the top, the battlements shimmered briefly, blue light sparking. The Master nodded. Always at the last, before they were trapped completely, there was that remembered connection with him. It could almost bring them to the brink of wakefulness.

There was no need for pretence now. The prize was so close. Now it was speed that mattered. He tightened his grip on the key and sucked in with all his might.

The horse disappeared. The force of his suction was so strong that two knights he had been alongside dissipated into energy, too. The energy slammed into him.

He flew straight as an arrow up towards the battlements.

CHAPTER TWENTY-FIVE

Back to Reality

'He's stirring!' Sama exclaimed. She shot up from the wooden chair, springing towards where Christopher lay.

Makena grabbed both her arms. 'Sit, Sama.' She pulled her firmly her back down. 'Don't get in their way.'

Sama allowed herself to be reseated. At her left, Makena placed a hand on the top of her leg. John Braddock stood on the other side. He too reached out, putting his hand on her shoulder.

Sama's stomach was still churning from when she had been sick. If she were honest with herself, everything was an effort. Better to conserve strength now rather than struggle away from them. She stared silently at the operating table.

They called it an operating table. To Sama it looked more like an altar. Mr Levert and Ward McCloud had both put on doctors' white coats. Another nurse stood quietly over in the corner, with a hand on Eliza's shoulder. It was as if by wearing the clothes and using mundane terms, the men in the room were taking control. Despite their efforts, the room they were in looked very little like a doctor's room.

The table was a stone plinth. Sama could see its base under the crisp hospital sheet draped over it. A single light hung from above. The bare bulb's glow was dim, as if electricity struggled to reach down to such subterranean depths. The rest of the room was lit by four small oil lamps placed in a square around where Christopher lay.

In the far corner, at the edge of the pool of light, was a freestanding closet made of dark wood. Its large double doors hung open. Inside, wood shelves covered in green felt held a myriad of small devices and artefacts. Ward and Levert scurried back and forth to it, searching its contents and returning with various items.

The walls of the chamber were natural stone, cut back to create an ordered square rectangle, but left unpainted. The only break in the grey rock was the door from which they had entered, behind the nurse and Eliza.

Eliza had started too at the hint of Christopher stirring. She was not looking at Christopher at all. Instead she stared, hardly blinking, at the silver gauntlet on his hand.

Christopher shifted again, this time moaning. Sama's heart leapt. It was the most noise that she had heard from him since they had picked him up at the asylum.

Ward looked across at Levert. 'He is stirring now? What have you changed?'

Levert shook his head, looking down at the book he was holding. 'Nothing. This is the same as was done before, from what they wrote.'

'You're sure?' Ward said.

'As sure as I can be, not having been there.' Levert frowned at the fat man. 'I've read no more accounts than you, Ward. I don't have any secret knowledge.' He looked back at Christopher. 'It seemed straightforward enough.'

Sama turned to Makena. 'He wasn't there the last time? Then how can we be sure this won't hurt Christopher?'

'No one was there last time, Sama,' Makena said. 'It was over thirty years ago. As they say, it was all noted down. Do not fret.'

'Then why are they looking worried?' Sama snapped.

Braddock patted her shoulder, lifting the fingers of the hand that rested on her shoulder and bringing them down in two short restrained raps. 'There are always variables, Sama.'

Makena glanced at her husband and smiled thinly. 'John is not very good at comforting people, Sama. What he means it that it is a good thing to be a little worried. Keeps a person on their toes.'

Makena had been unable to meet Sama's eye since the children's ward. Sama felt alone amongst strangers. It was hard to accept Makena, who had been so kindly, could be part of something that was doing exactly the same to children that had been done to Christopher. It didn't matter whether the children were willing or not. It felt like betrayal.

Sama glanced at Eliza again. The child's eyes blazed blue with reflected light from the gauntlet on Christopher's hand. Her face was a mixture of emotions; fear, excitement, and a childish greed.

Christopher shifted again. He mumbled something impossible to make out. Ward McCloud and Levert exchanged glances, but carried on with their preparations.

From what Sama understood it should be a fairly straightforward process to get Christopher to wake up. Makena had explained that most of what the two men had been doing was to ease Christopher back once he awakened. Well, that and to protect the rest of the complex in case of a problem. Levert and McCloud used item after item from the closet behind them. Occasionally Makena leaned down and whispered to her 'that one will stop fire breaking out' or 'that will stop him feeling pain from his hand'.

Sama was sure these things were important, but when she looked at Christopher, sweating and stirring on the table, she wished they would hurry. It was taking entirely too long.

Once they were finally done, Makena had said waking him up would be the simple act of introducing energy from another artefact — created in a different 'world' — into the one on his hand. That would force the gauntlet to reject anything that was not of itself.

Sama had no questions when Makena had told her. Her mind fixed on something entirely different. With Makena's staff, they could have done that at any time since they found him. When the thought had occurred to her, she had wanted to shout out at them both. Sure, they had said it would be dangerous. She swallowed the anger, knowing they would be able to conjure up a reason for why her friend was still stuck in this coma, looking so very pale and weak, filling her with worry. It always seemed people in charge could find a good reason to tell her why they were doing what they were doing. Even when her instincts told her otherwise.

Again Christopher stirred, bending suddenly and twisting on to his side. Ward leaned over and placed his hands on Christopher's shoulders, shifting him around with some effort to lie him flat on his back again. Sama fidgeted with impatience. When would they be ready?

Christopher's eyes widened. The man flew through the air, straight towards him. His horse and the riders next to him had just vaporized into blue energy sparkling round him as he flew.

Christopher dived away from the battlements. He ripped the bow from his back and pulled an arrow from the quiver with lightning speed. Even so, as he pulled the string back, his body was bathed in blue light.

In front of him, the man floated above the battlements. His eyes stared greedily at Christopher. His face twisted into a hungry smile. The long flaps of his black coat swayed up and down around him, almost as if underwater. Around him, a thousand blue sparks swam in random patterns through the air as if it had become viscous. His white hair floated around his head. Each hair twisted and bent separately like a tiny snake.

Christopher could see now that it was not Winter's Grasp the man wore. Rather, he held something solid and spherical nestled into his palm, glowing blue, mirroring the sparks around it.

'Hello, Christopher.' The man's voice was thick with triumph.

The rest of the world paled back. Christopher still had a sense that he was on the tower, but somehow where the solid stone battlements had become insubstantial. The walls were translucent. They were infused with the same blue light illuminating the man. The solidity they showed seconds earlier seemed an illusion.

The sounds of the battle receded. It was as if Christopher were hearing noises outside from within a shut room. Sounds were thick and dull. The cries of hundreds of men that had filled his ears before, the metal clashes of their weapons, all were now distant.

Christopher gritted his teeth and fought to quell the fear and displacement that threatened to overwhelm him. He loosed his arrow. It flew straight at the man's head. His aim was true. Yet before it reached the man, the arrow burst apart into energy. Then it was gone.

'Be calm, Christopher,' the man entreated with a voice that couldn't entirely mask his own excitement. 'The last days have been frightening, haven't they?'

He floated down in a gentle arc to the flagstones of the tower. His cruel eyes never left Christopher's face. His mouth twisted into a friendly smile. He reached forward. 'Soon you'll be able to rest and forget all this war and fear. I am here to help you, my boy.'

Suddenly, something moved to Christopher's right. Eleila dashed forwards, with her sword raised high. Her face was a grimace of battle. Yet, like the walls around them, she was translucent, incorporeal. Her mouth stretched wide open with a battle cry, teeth bared. Yet her voice sounded small and far away. She looked insignificant.

'Hold,' the man said, glancing at her as if she were a fly. Immediately she stopped, dropping her arm dully.

'Relax, Christopher,' the man whispered back at him. He raised the glowing ball. He smiled again. His eyes still danced with greed. 'I shall make this all better for you, my young friend.' The ball flashed even brighter. Christopher had a sudden sense of the light bursting towards him.

Then everything went black.

Ward screamed. His hands flew from Christopher's body as if it were on fire.

He staggered back and knocked into one of the oil lamps. It teetered dangerously. Ward's back hit the wall. He slid down the stone and was still.

'Ward!' John Braddock rushed across.

Christopher's body spasmed up. His back bent to an unnatural angle. The gauntlet in his hand burst into light, bathing them all in blue. John ducked away instinctively.

'Help him!' Sama jumped to her feet, slipping wide of Makena's hand. If he stayed like that, surely his back would break. She burst forward.

'Sama, wait!' Makena shouted.

Sama dived on to Christopher, pushing him down with her whole body weight. A static charge fizzed around her. The hairs on her arms, legs and neck danced up in a tingling halo.

Christopher's back gave a little. Despite Sama's efforts he was still twisted high from the table. His breathing was ragged.

She screeched back over her shoulder. 'Makena!'

Makena was already coming. She dropped her staff with a clatter and launched herself across at Christopher. She leapt next to Sama, dodging the gauntlet blazing on his hand. With their combined weight, his back sank down until it was no more than an inch above the table.

'What's happening?' Makena shouted at Levert.

Levert stood back, his mouth wide open, staring at the scene in front of him. At the door, the nurse had dropped to her knees and wrapped her arms around Eliza. The little girl seemed the least fazed person in the room, her eyes still intent on the gauntlet.

'Levert!' Makena shouted again. 'What do we do?'

Levert seemed lost to the events in front of him. It was Ward who answered, clambering to his feet with John's aid. 'The binding. It has started!' He staggered forward, 'Levert! Snap out of it, man! We must free the boy now!'

Christopher floated. He wasn't sure if his eyes were open or closed. Everything around him was black. It was as if a thick blanket had enveloped him to hide him from the world. It protected him.

A small part of him worried what was happening. After all, he had just been standing facing what had seemed like a terrifying foe. Now though, he struggled to remember why. The man had said he would help. Perhaps that was what he was doing. It felt like a great weight had been lifted. He drifted, carefree, through ebony syrup.

Vague faces floated through his mind, dim ghosts in the black. A girl's face appeared, just the barest hint of deep grey. Then she was gone. A tall, plain-looking man's face broke into an easy grin, then another girl dressed in armour replaced him. Each sparked vague recognition, but more than that, Christopher could not say.

He struggled to hold on to that recognition. It was too fleeting, too insubstantial. Then as it left, he realised he couldn't think why he had been trying to hold on to it anyway. Finally, what remained of his conscious mind began to float away too, as it did in the last moments before sleep. It lulled him down into the dark.

The Master smiled. The boy's eyes grew dim. He stared out into nothing, a blank smile on his face. Soon this would be over.

The clatter of fighting echoed up from close below. Mordred's troops had reached the breach. They would be making short work of the defenders barring their way.

The armoured girl stood dumb next to Christopher. The Master had seen it once or twice before. Sometimes those imaginings close to a child could carry the same vague resistance as those in the real world. It was just as impotent.

Her audacity amused him. She was nothing. She would simply make good sustenance. He would consume her as soon as the boy was bound.

The Entity was almost gone now. It had fed on thought after thought from the moment the new consciousness had appeared. The vast maelstrom of energy was barely more than the occasional flicker. Instead, a living breathing world existed in its place.

And as the other consciousness grew dark, the Entity's remaining focus blurred away. Final flickers of pure energy began to drift apart, easing into the world it had created.

Soon, once again, the Entity would be dormant. It would live only in the things it had become. There it would remain until the next time. Until the circle began again.

'Come on, Levert!' Ward McCloud shook his companion, making the smaller man's head jolt back and forth. 'Come on!'

As far as Sama could see, Levert was doing anything other than 'coming on'. He hadn't moved at all. He still stared at Christopher, wide mouthed.

McCloud's efforts to jog him to awareness eventually seemed to work. He closed his mouth and frowned. Then he looked around, as if seeing the situation for the first time.

'Levert!' McCloud shouted again.

Christopher's body was pushing Sama and Makena up hard. His body bucked like a colt, threatening to throw them off. Sama gripped his legs tightly. The static tingled all over her body. It was hard to concentrate.

Finally, Levert moved. 'Yes, yes. I'm sorry. You're right, Ward. We need to introduce another power now. Now let me just see, we must be careful not to use too much.'

'Hurry!' Makena gasped, through gritted teeth.

Levert turned back to the closet and began rifling around in it. 'I think I need something other than what I had chosen. That won't work at all now,' he mumbled almost to himself, his voice sounding reedy and scared. 'Yes, yes. I know it's here. Just a moment.'

John Braddock rushed over to him. 'Damn it man, get a grip.'

Levert nodded and carried on rifling through the closet.

Suddenly Christopher sank. The force pushing him up from the table was weaker. The tingling was less too. Sama looked at her arm. Her hairs no longer stood to attention. Now they leaned at an angle away from her arm. It was easier to concentrate, too. Perhaps they were succeeding. Perhaps this was relief.

She glanced at Makena. 'Do you feel—?'

'The power is going out of him!' Makena's face was anything but relieved. 'Ward! The power is going out of him!'

'No, no, no, no, no,' McCloud exclaimed. 'Damn it! We're losing him! Levert!'

Levert showed no sign of finding what he was looking for. McCloud shoved him out of the way. The fat man tore things from the shelves, discarding them with crashes to the floor.

The hairs on her arms were almost flat now. Christopher's back sank to touch the stone table top. Her heart leapt into her mouth. They had not come this far to lose him at this final turn. She cast her eyes about the room.

Makena's staff! It lay where it had fallen on the floor, easy to reach. Sama flung herself at it.

John Braddock was the first to realise what she planned. He shouted. Makena turned her head and twisted her body to drop off Christopher.

Sama turned the staff in her hands. She lifted it like a spear, pointing at the gauntlet. Braddock burst around the side of the table. He dived towards her.

Sama hurled the staff. It smashed into the gauntlet with a loud crack, like a gunshot. An obsidian bolt erupted from the end that struck. It enveloped the gauntlet, then sank into its surface, turning to a green hue as it did so.

John slammed into Sama, knocking the wind from her. Light blazed. Everything was burned out, white. Sama gasped and turned away, clasping her arms over her head.

The energy from the staff was like a squirt of ink in an ocean, almost imperceptible in the void. It flitted around, searching through its new surroundings, then dived down towards the created world below it.

The Entity felt its arrival with a jolt. It wrenched what remained of itself back to awareness. A stain. A contamination within it. Somewhere in the valleys and forests and seas, in the buildings and cities, in the creatures and people, was an energy that should not be there. An alien power.

Instinct consumed the Entity. The urge to expel anything not of itself was suddenly overpowering.

The Master felt something shift. It was so subtle. It took a few moments to catch his attention. When it did, however, he was aware it had been there for some time.

Once he had picked up on it, he grew disconcerted. It was hard to place exactly what it was. Something was just 'off'. It was as though the centre of gravity had been nudged slightly, yet everyone was still trying to stand straight.

He struggled to keep attention on the boy. It would not do to be distracted. It was almost over. The energy would shut him down permanently. He screwed up his eyes to focus, forcing his thoughts to stay with the boy.

The spark from the staff understood it had arrived in a place full of power like itself. Instinctively, it tried to join the larger force. Yet, each time it tried it was rejected.

It floated through a tendril of blue light on its way down toward the world, some last remains of the unrefined void. It lengthened itself, assuming the same shape, and slid into the blue. Immediately the tendril bucked, like the tail of a horse flicking away a fly.

And as the spark tried to join the larger force around it, the Entity felt pain.

The spark flitted away. It slipped down into the world, arriving above a village clinging to the side of a jagged mountain. It rushed towards a church, the largest building near it, and flew through the open door. It tried to attach itself to a chair leg by the entrance, moulding itself into the wood. The leg cracked and broke. The little spark jumped back, startled, then flew out through an open window. It dove down, trying to bury itself and become a part of the earth, but the earth erupted in blue sparks around it.

Each time the little spark attempted to become joined, a shock burst through the Entity. With each spasm the Entity struggled against itself. It fought the instinct to destroy everything it had created, anything to escape the electric convulsions of the spark's touch. It braced itself for the next shock, desperately clinging on to the creations it had made.

Again the spark burst away, flying high into the air. Around it, great winds blew in opposite directions. Even the air molecules strived to get away.

The spark whizzed on, shooting down to dive into an ocean. It hit the water and the sea parted. Monstrous waves crashed out of its way, overturning a ship that sailed too close.

It arrived at a busy port, dropping down into the crowd. It flattened out and tried to meld with a merchant who was calling out his prices to his customers. The man screamed. Blue sparks exploded away from the little green alien, blending themselves into other people and buildings around.

Alone again, the green spark flew on.

Suddenly everything shuddered. It was as if the whole earth had dropped a foot, then popped straight back up again without anything breaking or shifting. Even the air seemed to change.

The Master felt a cold chill run through his body. Something was most definitely wrong.

'No,' he spat through gritted teeth.

They were trying to draw out the boy.

Desperate, the Entity hunted the spark. It was moving so fast. The shocks as it tried to join were so disorientating. It was constantly just ahead of the Entity's attention.

Another spasm hit the Entity. In the western part of the world, a plain of solid power burst from below the ground, returning anything in its way to pure blue energy. Mountains and forests, cities, creatures, and people that had been there just a moment before became a swirling blue vortex.

The Entity was scared now. It was losing the battle with its instinct. The world would be destroyed. In desperation, it gathered the blue vortex, pushed it outwards across the world in all directions.

The wave touched everything created, scanning it, feeling it, confirming its place, searching for anything that should not be there. It spread around the Entity's world, narrowing down the unchecked spaces. Fencing in the little spark.

The spark was oblivious. It continued its journey, trying to meld in with the greater power, unaware of the destruction in its wake.

Suddenly the Entity touched upon other aliens. Not the spark, something else. It took a moment to recognize the consciousness which had fuelled this world's genesis. It felt a protective wave.

It recognised the other being, too. The recognition brought back memories of pain and fear. Memories of being forced from itself. Of being dragged into something beyond its own consciousness.

But its instinct would take no chances now. Whether friend or foe, anything not of itself must be expelled. Once the spark was caught, all would be gone.

The Master felt a tightening of the air around him. He swore under his breath. He would fail. The boy was not yet far enough under to be irretrievable.

The Entity closed in on the little spark as it chased a herd of wild horses across a broad grass plain. Horse after horse burst into blue sparks as it tried to join with them.

The Entity hardened a ball of energy and surrounded the tiny spark. At first the spark flew on, oblivious. Then, it dived down towards another animal.

It hit the wall.

The energy wall did not explode at the impact. The Entity forced its remaining power to keep the spark contained. Each time the spark tried to meld to the inner wall, the Entity held fast, battling to ignore the spasms coursing through it.

Slowly at first, almost gingerly, the Entity began to lift the ball of energy away from the world. Inside, the tiny spark seemed to sense it was being denied what it so desired. It redoubled its efforts, smashing against the walls around it.

The Entity moved the ball faster now, hurling it out into the void. It forced the spark out to its very edges at breakneck speed, steeling itself against the shocks of its touch. And there, finally, at the edges of its existence it forced the spark out into the beyond.

It rested for a moment, pausing with primitive relief. Then its instinct reacted again. Forcing it to turn its attention inwards toward the other aliens within it.

It surged again.

'Think,' the Master said out loud. The boy was still senseless before him. The woman in the armour was still frozen in place.

He glanced at her. Perhaps the energy he could consume from her would clear his mind. The Master pulled in. Her sword, the closest to him, disintegrated into blue sparks from the tip to the cross guard in the blink of an eye.

Instinct overpowered the Entity. It closed the other circle of energy around the two. It wrenched them up from the tower. Everything must be cleansed. Then it rushed both the being and the consciousness out across the void to follow the spark.

The Master screamed, tumbling into the void. A huge thrust of energy rose below him, bouncing him on its tip like a rag doll.

At his side, the boy bounced along, too. The Master struggled to right himself, contorting and turning against the force beneath him. He twisted upright. He grabbed out. He touched the boy's arm.

His hand passed straight through.

'No!' His voice was lost in the maelstrom. The boy was becoming incorporeal. The body he had inhabited in the created world was returning to the energy it was made from. His mind would be free.

The Master grabbed again, this time with the Key itself. Now at least he felt some purchase. The Key latched on to the boy's presence, recognising the source of the world below.

The energy pushed them onwards. The uproar of power threatened to consume his senses utterly. The Master held on to the dissipating form like a drowning man clutching at driftwood.

Only at the very last, when the boy's form was completely gone, did he finally lose control. Then, as the Entity vomited him back out into the real world, he lost consciousness.

Finally, the Entity was calm. The panic and danger were past. Once again, it began to dim. Yet as it faded, it felt the emptiness within itself.

It understood. In its fear, it had expelled the other consciousness. It was suddenly and completely alone. It folded back down into itself, suppressed.

As quickly as the gauntlet had blazed, it dimmed. Sama lifted her arms and looked out. Her pupils took a moment to readjust to the room.

The oil lamps were all extinguished. The single bulb above still cast its inadequate light. Sama could make out the others around the room. Makena, the closest, had been thrown to the floor. She pushed herself up and looked over. 'Sama …' she began, then trailed off, too dazed to complete her thought.

'Sama?' His voice was rough, as if he hadn't used it for days, which of course he hadn't.

Sama's heart leaped. She sprung to her feet, the pains and horrors of the last few hours gone in an instant.

'Christopher!' she squealed and leapt over to the table.

He had pushed himself up on to his elbows. His face was frowning, confused, but already colour was rushing back to his skin.

'Christopher!' she said again, quite lost for anything else to say. She reached to grab him in a hug, then stopped at the last minute, rocking uncertainly on her heels. 'All right?'

Christopher said nothing for a moment. His eyes glazed as he thought about it. Then, he looked back at her and grinned.

That was it. With a squeal, Sama launched herself at Christopher and wrapped her arms around him.

CHAPTER TWENTY-SIX

Genesis

There was paper fluttering all about. Paper and snow. That was the first thing the Master noticed as he opened his eyes. It appeared he had rematerialised in the centre of a pile of old newspapers.

Sheets slowly settled back down to earth. One landed on his head, cold and wet, soaked with snow water that ran down his neck. He flicked it off with a violent jerk of the hand and glanced around.

He was a short way down a dark, narrow alley with high, windowless walls. The walls could be red brick. It was hard to make out in the dull light. Ahead of him was brighter. The orange glow of a streetlamp spewed into the alley's entrance, picking out a wrought iron fence just beyond on one side. Behind him, the way disappeared entirely into gloom.

The Master was glad of that, at least. It would not have done to have appeared somewhere where a crowd would be able to see him. He got to his feet, brushing himself down and ducking out of the way of another floating broadsheet. He glanced down into the blackness of the alley and dismissed it. He would need to find out where he was. For that he would need to see the surroundings properly. The street ahead would offer the best chance.

Already he could hear noises from around the corner. There was a boy's voice calling out the headlines of the newspapers he must be selling. A car horn sounded. A child laughed. As he strained to listen, a couple sauntered past the alley entrance, oblivious to the gaunt figure watching them from the shadows. The man was tall, in a long black overcoat and top hat. The woman, in a warm winter coat, held his arm. They disappeared past the entrance. Then a man dressed in a brown woollen coat, collar turned up against the cold, strode quickly along the opposite way.

The Master pushed back into the shadows. Before he found out where he was, there was something he needed to check. A wave of apprehension washed over him. Maybe this was clutching at the last strings of hope, but admitting defeat would leave him with nothing. Taking in a sharp breath, the Master gripped the key and opened a portal in the shadows.

The alley was suddenly illuminated with bright blue light. The Master swore. He would have to be fast to avoid curious passers-by blundering into the alley. He pushed his upper body through, ignoring the whistling of energy around his ears and stretched out further, through the energy.

The void was all but gone. A weak fog of energy, easy to slip through at will, was all that remained. That was good. If McCloud and his cronies had already passed the artefact to another, this would all be a huge vortex again. The world must still be there!

The Master felt beyond the surface energy, downwards. He held his breath a moment, half expecting to find a rush of energy, pushing him back out. None came. He was unnoticed once more. The Entity was dormant.

The Master allowed himself a small smile of elation, but that was all. There should be no illusions here. His situation was very precarious. Without control of the boy, the world could be lost at any moment.

The Master pushed down to the land itself. Now the void was so insubstantial, it was easy to move the portal onward, directly into the world itself.

A great lake loomed up before him. There, bobbing on the water, was a tiny boat. A lone fisherman hunched down on the single plank bench in the centre, his rod stretched over the side, line hanging in the water. The Master pushed on down until he was leaning through the portal just above the man.

At the last minute, the man sensed something. He turned and looked up. His weathered face twisted into an expression of shock. His mouth hung open under a straggly grey moustache. Perhaps he would have spoken. Before he could, the Master grabbed him by the scruff of the neck and pulled him up into the portal, then on out into the alley. The man fell to the floor and shrank immediately into a foetal ball.

The Master stepped on to his leg in case he suddenly found the strength to up and run. He willed the portal closed. The alley was once again shrouded in shadow.

The Master bent down and wrenched the fisherman up, twisting him around by his coat. He pulled him close until their faces were almost touching. 'Do not speak or move until I return.' Perhaps it was too much, but he would not risk the man managing to get will if a transition began.

The Master let go and stepped back, noting the fisherman remained rooted to the spot. The man grunted, eyes full of fear. His fishing rod was still in his hand. The line hung short, cut off by the closing portal.

Satisfied, the Master walked to the end of the alley. He glanced back once, confirming that the fear-wracked figure was suitably obscured from the street, then turned back.

The street was wide. In the centre, two tram lines ran next to one another. Further down the street, the Master could see a tram moving away from him, its lower level filled to the brim. Only a few passengers braved the winter snow on the upper level.

The way that the tram was going seemed to be the busier end of the street. Light from shop windows spilled out on to wet cobbles. Scores of people milled around laden with parcels ready for the imminent festivities.

On the other side of the street, an old, horse-drawn carriage rolled after the tram towards the bustle. Its occupants were vague shadows on the other side of the glass window, protected against the cold. The driver was tensed against the chill, holding the reins with thickly-mittened hands.

'Latest news from Givenchy!' the newspaper boy's voice called again. 'Read it all here!'

The Master looked around for the source of the sound. He was underneath a streetlamp on the far pavement. He had a pile of papers clutched in one arm, whilst in the other he held one paper aloft. The Master hurried across, jumping over dirty puddles of snow and icy water.

'Paper, sir?' The boy straightened himself in the expectation of a sale.

'No. Information,' the Master said. 'What place is this?'

The boy frowned. 'Beg pardon, sir?'

'Where are we?' the Master barked. 'What city? What town?'

The boy cowered at the sharpness of his voice. 'Why, London, sir! Knightsbridge High Street! Down there's Hyde Park.' He nodded down the street.

Without another word, the Master turned on his heel and strode back towards the alley. London. He scowled. This was what he had feared. They had taken the boy to where McCloud and his minions had their headquarters.

He knew he was close. Though he had never seen the main entrance, he had been in the lair. As a young man, he had been invited twice before they had refused him. Then though, he had been led down through a concealed passageway starting in the cupboard of a nondescript boarding house. There had never been a need to find it, not once he had the artefact. Still, not knowing the way was an inconvenience easily solved.

The effort that he had put into staying with the boy's essence, as they'd been expelled, had paid off. Now that the essence was back with the boy's body. Christopher was whole again. And he was close.

The Master knew what to do now. He ducked back into the darkness. The fisherman stood motionless and terrified. Dispassionate, he gripped the man's neck with both hands. In a single motion, he snapped it.

The fisherman gargled once. He dropped to the ground. The nerves controlling his breathing were broken now. He would suffocate in a very short time.

Sure enough, the man's hold on life started to loosen. His body began to dissipate. The first bright blue sparks burst up from him and flew off towards the street.

The Master didn't wait for the rest. In a shot he was off, sprinting down the alley and out into the street below. He raced after the first sparks. They disappeared off into the distance. It was of no matter. More overtook him, heading the same way, guiding his path. They were heading back to the source.

Sama hopped from one foot to the other, impatient. After their initial greeting, she was pulled away from Christopher so others could get in. The nurse and Levert were giving him a thorough examination, checking every inch for damage. Every few seconds Levert would stop and make a note in his little book.

Ward McCloud, who had already introduced himself to Christopher, was waiting just as impatiently for the examination to finish. He was staring at Levert with scorn. Levert was taking care not to meet his gaze.

All Sama wanted to do, though, was get Christopher away from these people. He was awake now. As far as she could see he was absolutely fine. She was done with cellars and monsters and madhouses. They could get back to Alton and worry about everything else from there. If they would just take the gauntlet — which had become dull and still — from his hand, they could get away.

She stepped forward to say as much and once again Makena's hand touched her shoulder. Makena dropped to her knees and whispered into her ear. 'Just a little more patience, sweet. Then I promise I'll find a place for you and Christopher to spend time catching up.'

Sama frowned and shrugged her shoulder half-heartedly, but then rocked back. There wasn't going to be any advantage in causing a fuss now, there were too many of them.

Christopher was suffering the examination quietly. He glanced across at her and smiled. He seemed surprisingly calm, Sama thought to herself. She had expected him to be scared, angry even, but not calm.

Christopher directed his gaze at Ward McCloud. 'Where are we?'

'This is a hospital.' McCloud's voice was calm and reassuring. He'd been waiting for this question, Sama was sure of it. 'My colleagues brought you here after Miss Neeley raised the alarm.' He gestured to Makena and then to John Braddock.

Christopher glanced over at them, then returned his gaze to Sama with a smile. Sama felt a twinge of guilt at the fluffing of the truth, but stayed quiet.

'What happened to me?' Christopher asked. Sama realised with a start that he was asking her.

'Well, I ...' she began.

'Master Flyte, it's a little difficult to explain,' McCloud interrupted quickly. 'In essence, you were forced into a dream state.'

Christopher nodded. His eyes, Sama noticed with curiosity, looked wistful. 'I thought as much for a while. Then I thought it was real. It seemed so real. Not like an ordinary dream at all.'

'There'll be plenty of time to talk about it and answer all your questions,' McCloud muttered. 'For now we just want to get you checked over and cleaned up. You should take that old gauntlet off.'

Christopher glanced down at the gauntlet. Since he had woken, the gauntlet had been that dull grey. The bright blue light which had shone out of it whilst he was under its spell was gone. Perhaps it would glow again as soon as he took it off. Honestly, Sama didn't care. The sooner that thing was away from him, the better. She glanced at Eliza, who still stood near the door, flanked by John Braddock. Her eyes had not left the gauntlet.

'Funny thing,' Christopher said. 'In my dream I didn't have it. And it was on my hand all the time.'

Suddenly, he frowned. 'So when did I go into the dream then?'

'Eliza,' McCloud said, ignoring the question, 'bring that cloth over, dear, so Christopher can put the gauntlet on it.'

Christopher looked up, the frown never leaving his face. 'Mr. McCloud? When did this all start?'

McCloud gave Christopher his most benevolent smile. 'Please, Christopher. Let us finish this conversation once you are more comfortable. If you'll just take off the ...'

Something slammed against the entrance door with a bang. Sama's heart juddered. By her side Makena gasped. John swung around, his hand balling into a fist.

'John.' Ward was the first to pull himself together. 'See what that was.'

Before John could pull the door open, it creaked on its hinges. From the crack at the bottom, a familiar blue light glared through. Then a stream of blue sparks shot through the crack between the door and the floor. They whizzed across the room and slammed into the gauntlet.

A second later and it was over.

Christopher kicked back with his legs, pushing himself up the table away from Levert, Ward, and the nurse. 'What was that?' he said, his voice sharp.

Ward had momentarily forgotten Christopher. He looked at John. 'You said that there was nothing from the portal here!'

'There wasn't as far as I knew,' John answered, glancing at Makena. 'Certainly nothing that anyone is destroying.'

'It could be something we missed,' Makena said, gripping her staff tightly.

'It could be, or it could be more,' Ward said grimly. 'Go to the main hall. Put the others on alert.'

Sama's pulse leapt. Those sparks meant one thing. Suddenly she was torn between following Makena and John through the door or staying with Christopher. She glanced across at him.

Christopher stared at the gauntlet on his hand, his eyes caught in the dull blue glow that it had started to emit. He spoke urgently but quietly, as if he was speaking to himself. 'What is happening?'

The Master lost the initial sparks as they flew around the corner of a tall townhouse. By the time he had reached the turning, any trace of their onward journey was gone. He ducked into the house's doorway. With only the most perfunctory glance to check he had some privacy, he wrenched open a portal again, grappling to pull out the first living thing he could find.

He pulled out a woman by her hair. She was dressed in the long red dress of a noblewoman. Without even shifting his grip on her hair, he smashed her head into the wall at the side of the doorway with all his might. She didn't have time to make a noise before she was scattering into blue sparks.

He sprinted on down the street, narrowly avoiding crashing into a family who appeared from around another corner, coming in the opposite direction. A small boy giggled and pointed at the sparks as they flew past him. His father snatched him out of the way, just in time to avoid being trampled by the Master's long, lean legs.

The next time he opened a portal, he was mid-stride with the previous sparks still in view. Reaching in with one hand whilst running down the pavement, almost falling with the effort of trying to focus on two places at the same time, he only managed to retrieve a rabbit.

He threw it high into the air ahead of him. The rabbit fell hard to the ground and obliterated in a cloud of blue sparks that hardly lasted at all, seeing him through to the next turn in the street and no further.

The road he turned into was long and straight. He ran up it, scanning both sides for alleys he could hide in to draw out something more substantial. Nothing. He ran a good hundred yards along the pavement before he hesitated. It would not do to go too far in case he was missing something.

The pavement was empty in both directions. That was something. Many of the houses had lights on. Though he couldn't see anyone at the windows, it would only take one person to notice him pull something from the portal and make a phone call. Then the police would be on their way.

The Master shook the thought from his mind. That was the least of his worries. One more time he delved into the portal. This time he took a moment to direct himself properly. He focused his attention and pulled the portal open over Kay's castle.

The battle below was in full swing. Unburdened of his instruction, Mordred's army had gone back to their original goal of taking the castle. The defenders who had grouped around the breach in the outer walls had been cleared away, bar for a scant group on one side. Mordred's army flooded into the breach, spreading out inside the castle walls.

The battle itself was of no interest to him now. He swooped down into the throng of the foot soldiers swarming through the breach. Directly below him, a young lad who had the look of a farm boy about him, all fear and clumsiness cowered behind a cart. A burly looking ruffian armed with a short sword strode up over the rubble towards him. He raised his sword and chopped down at the lad. The farm boy squealed and staggered back. The attacker lifted his sword again.

The Master grabbed the boy and lifted him through the portal, dropping him on to the pavement. The boy coughed once and slumped on to his side. Then he dissipated into sparks.

The Master tensed to run. But instead of flying off down the street, the sparks shot across to an entranceway only a few doors down on the other side. The sparks bunched and danced for a moment at the door, trying to find a way to get through. They bottle-necked around the letterbox, then burst it open and rushed on inside.

The Master grinned, lifted by an almost crazy elation. How very predictable, the main entrance had nothing to distinguish itself from any other home on the street. 'Very well then.'

First he would need some help. Once more the Master pulled open the portal above the battle.

'Christopher, please!' McCloud said, 'The gauntlet. You must remove it.' He edged forward, lifting a hand.

Christopher had pushed back on the table. McCloud drew near. Christopher clambered off the end. He stumbled. Before he could fall, Sama rushed forward. She caught him under the arm, slipping in next to him. Together they backed away to the wall.

'Careful.' Sama could feel him leaning heavily on her. 'You haven't been up in days.'

He glanced at her. 'Sama, what's happening?'

There was no fear in his voice. Sama was surprised. The Christopher that she knew would be most upset by all this, yet he seemed intrigued. Calm.

'I must insist you remove the gauntlet,' McCloud said, closing the gap between them. 'Eliza, please, bring the cloth.'

Christopher steadied himself, taking his weight off her shoulder. 'I'm all right,' he whispered, then turned back to McCloud. 'You're not telling the truth. At least not all of it.'

His voice was growing stronger as he spoke. 'I've seen some very strange things, Mr McCloud. I've been very scared. But I'm not afraid anymore. I want to know what's going on. Until you tell me the truth, I am not giving anything to you.'

He turned to Sama. 'Are you with me?'

Sama felt an enormous wave of pride. 'Bloody hell. 'Course I am!' Then she frowned. This was all well and good, but the sooner he took off the gauntlet, the better. Again, Sama felt torn.

Suddenly McCloud burst forward, his speed surprising given his weight. He clutched Christopher's left arm and yanked him forward. Christopher was nearly wrenched from his feet.

Quick as a flash, Sama slipped around to the fat man's side. She hammered at his belly, raining down blows with both arms.

McCloud didn't even seem to notice. He dragged Christopher back towards the little girl. 'Eliza! The cloth!' he repeated.

He was far more aware of the gauntlet. Even as he tried to pull Christopher back, his eyes were constantly on it. Each time Christopher's right hand was in danger of touching him, he flinched away. Christopher, pulling away hard, hadn't noticed.

Behind McCloud, Levert rounded the table. Sama didn't think it would be possible to hold both men off. There must be a reason the huge man was avoiding the gauntlet. 'Christopher!' she hissed. 'Hit him with Winter's Grasp!'

Christopher didn't hesitate. He swung his arm at McCloud. McCloud tried to dance out of the way again, but now Christopher was actually intending to hit him it was impossible. The gauntlet struck him on the arm.

Winter's Grasp flashed at the impact. McCloud grunted. He lost his grip on Christopher. He jolted backwards away from the touch. Then he fell, rolling on to his back. For a brief moment he struggled on the floor, arms and legs in the air like a beetle.

Christopher feinted forwards, lifting the gauntlet as a threat before him.

McCloud righted himself and sat forward, raising a hand. 'Wait!' He stared at Winter's Grasp, wary. 'All right! Everyone calm down.'

Christopher held his position for a moment, the gauntlet aloft. Sama wondered if he was about to hit the man again for good measure. Instead, he edged backwards to the wall and lowered his fist. 'Don't do that again,' he spat.

'All right, Christopher.' McCloud's voice was resigned. He struggled up to his feet. 'I'll answer your questions. You should know, though, the longer you wear that, the more danger we are all in.'

Another stream of bright blue sparks burst from under the door. They zipped across the room in a line and slammed into the gauntlet. The impact rocked Christopher. Sama thrust her arms behind his back, bracing him until it was over.

The last spark disappeared into the silver. Suddenly the only noise in the room was breathing, McCloud's heavy and fast, Christopher's slowing as he struggled to regain control. She could hear her own too, sucking in oxygen to her thundering heart.

'For a start,' Christopher said, once he had regained his composure. 'What was that?'

'They're sparks from the monsters,' Sama blurted before McCloud could answer. The sooner this was explained, the sooner he would take that thing off.

'What?' Christopher flicked a glance at her, careful not to fully take his attention from the others.

'Your dream. The things that you dream. The gauntlet makes them real. There's a man. He can pull them out of the dream and bring them here and use them to fight with. That's what the gypsies and Molly Brodie were. They were from the dream of the last boy.'

'The last boy?' Christopher frowned. 'How do you know?'

'I met him.' It was all flooding up inside her now. 'You disappeared. That man, he pretended he was Bailey and fooled you. I thought that the gypsies had you, so I went to look. But they weren't gypsies, they were something else. Like wolves! And they had the other boy, the one before you.'

She looked at the gauntlet. 'He was proper sick, Christopher, 'cause he'd worn that too long! And when John and Makena killed the gypsies they turned into sparks and they flew away and went back into the gauntlet. Just like those sparks now. And it's not a gauntlet, either. That's just what you wanted it to be!'

The images were intense now. The gypsies on the ridge, snarling and fighting. Scratching at her and hurting her. Doing far worse if she hadn't escaped and been found by Jim, Mike and Joe.

Oh, God! Joe! How could she tell him about that?

'Sama?' Christopher said. He was looking at her so intently. Sama felt tears stinging her eyes. She couldn't tell him. Not now or here. She turned her face away and stared at the wall.

The Master muttered a single word. The combatants stilled. All across the ruined gatehouse to Kay's castle, their arms dropped to their sides. Enemies stood calmly together, their battle forgotten.

The battle was going the way that he expected. Dotted around his view, two dozen or so Stahlhelme were leading the attack. Around each was a swathe of destruction. Knights and foot soldiers lay dead or dying at their feet. Others had been crawling away, trying to find safety. Instead, they had been finding the swords of Mordred's other troops, close on the heels of the beasts. The new King's army had surged into the castle. The defence was failing.

'To me!' the Master shouted, pointing at each of the Stahlhelme in turn.

As each saw his command, they drove forward, scattering troops in their way with their axes whether friend or foe. In a few moments they were jostling in front of him. Their lust for battle was only tempered by his hold over them. At his word they would once again surrender themselves to the delight of destruction.

The Master pulled the portal gap wider to give them room to enter and ordered them through with a flick of his arm. They thundered through, three at a time.

Heavy boots thudded against the earth with a dull wet clump. Through the portal, the clumping became sharp as they slammed against the cobbles. As the last rushed past him, he muttered again. Released, the armies in the courtyard fell back on one another. The portal slipped closed on the clangs of fresh fighting.

He turned to the horde. They pushed each other, competing for position, staring hungrily at the quiet street before them. He stepped out into the roadway ahead of them and pointed across at the large black door.

'There!' he cried, 'Attack! Destroy everything!'

As one, they groaned. A massed groan of release that became a roar of delight. He dodged out of their way as they rushed forwards.

The front-most Stahlhelme fired at the door without breaking stride. A large hole ripped open in the dark wood, spraying splinters back out into the street. Lead ricocheted against reinforced steel plate. The beast howled with delight and rushed on.

Inspired by their companion, two more, then another, lifted their rifles and fired at the door. One missed, striking the wall to the right, smashing a pane of glass in the window next to it. The others found their mark. Two more holes ripped into the wood.

The first bounded up the steps. It swung its rifle around, chopping heavily at the mutilated door. The axe bit into the steel.

The Master started forward, keeping the bulk of the Stahlhelme between him and the doorway. Three of them had reached the top step. The others crushed together behind them, unable to fit by the door.

The three at the front made short work of it with their axes. The Master was barely across the street before it gave way with a crash.

Lights were coming on in the windows of nearby houses. A man pulled a curtain in the house next door, glancing out with a frown. His face changed to a look of horror as he took in the scene. He ducked back behind the curtain, no doubt intent on raising the alarm. All too soon, the Master knew they would be contending with a battle on two fronts.

Muffled gunshots rang out from inside the building. The foremost Stahlhelme grunted and stumbled, then righted itself. It fired back with a loud report.

'Forward!' the Master cried. The Stahlhelme needed no urging. They were already ducking through the entrance, kicking the broken doors away and taking the fight inside. The Master gritted his teeth and followed.

'Sama, what is it?' Christopher placed his hand on Sama's shoulder. She had not turned back to him. Her body shuddered with sobs. She shook her head, unable to speak.

He frowned. He had never seen Sama like this. Usually she was the strong one. What could have happened to her whilst he had been away?

'Miss Neeley has had quite a time of it working with our agents to get you away from the man responsible for this,' McCloud said as if to answer his unspoken question. He had started to edge forward again, though he still stayed safely out of Christopher's range.

'The sooner that we can get her and you out of danger the better,' he continued, sharp eyes fixed intently on the gauntlet. 'Please don't make our hard work come to nothing. Take it off.'

Christopher looked down. Winter's Grasp was dull grey again. The power it showed moments before gone. 'What will you do with it?'

'Stop it falling into the wrong hands. And use it to protect other children like you.'

Sama's head shot up. 'That's not true! You'll use it! You'll make someone else take it and send them into the dream. You're no better!'

By the nurse, Eliza stamped her little foot. 'Yes we are!' She balled her hands into fists. She looked as determined as Sama usually did. 'We go in willingly!'

Before she could say more, McCloud held up a hand. The little girl fell silent.

'Miss Neeley, I assure you, when there is more time, I'll be delighted to explain the differences between us and less scrupulous key holders,' McCloud snapped at her. 'Now is not that time.'

Levert was edging closer again, too, trying to stay at the side, out of Christopher's vision. Christopher flicked his eyes across at the other man. 'Stay where I can see you, please.' He lifted Winter's Grasp in front of him, stretching the fingers out. Both men stopped.

'Good.' Christopher nodded. 'The first person apart from Sama who comes near me will get another dose of this.' He shook his hand once to accentuate his words.

Feet drummed down the corridor outside. Sama drew close to Christopher. He glanced at her. She wiped at her eyes roughly with a sleeve. Then she raised her fists. 'And these.'

The footsteps halted outside the door. It pushed open. The woman Sama had called Makena slipped through. She looked around the room, calmly assessing the situation.

'Whatever the differences are here, they must be settled.' Her eyes held steady on Christopher. 'We are under attack. The man who did this is here. He's brought more of the beasts with the guns from the asylum.' She glanced at Sama. 'They're bigger this time. And we have few fighters here. John and the others may not hold them for long.'

'Even if they do, he can bring more.' McCloud edged forwards again.

Makena nodded and took a pace further into the room. Straight away, Sama turned to face her, evidently deciding she was the highest threat.

Makena raised her staff. 'Sama, sweet,' she said, her voice soft with regret, 'we need to work together, not against each other. I can knock you both out with this and we can take the device. You know it will be less safe for Christopher to have someone else remove it. Is that what you want?'

Sama spoke out of the side of her mouth. 'Christopher?'

'Stand fast,' Christopher said back. He remembered Bediviere saying the same. The association made him feel secure.

'If you remove the gauntlet, Christopher, it will weaken his hold over them,' McCloud said, then beckoned to Eliza. 'Once the hold is broken, once it cannot feed on you, the world created will be lessened.'

The little girl left the nurse's grip. She stumbled forwards, her eyes still fixated on Winter's Grasp. 'And once I put it on,' she blurted, 'that whole world will be gone!'

Christopher frowned and stared at the girl. Now it was starting to make sense. 'Wait!' A cold feeling washed over him. 'What do you mean?'

Inside, the guards had been quick. Though there had been no warning of the Stahlhelme's approach until bullets hit the front door, they had mobilized immediately. The personnel in the rooms along the main corridor had found themselves herded to evacuate almost as the first explosion was still ringing in their ears.

The guards in each of the rooms knew the drill. They moved to defensive positions along the edges of the corridor, opening out the high doors to the side chambers. Each door, reinforced with steel, was fixed into place with thick bolts driven deep into holes in the tiled floor. Once fixed, the guards took up defensive positions behind the barriers. In the time it took for the Stahlhelme to get through the front door, they had almost completed the defence.

Even if they had completed it, it would not have been enough.

The Stahlhelme came down the corridor like a tidal wave. The front three, fresh from smashing through the door, surged down at a pace that seemed impossible for their size. The wounded one was still ahead of the others, bloodlust outweighing pain. Their companions were a wall of flesh and steel at their backs. They had reached the first door before the first guards had managed to raise their own weapons.

The wounded one veered to the right. It smashed its full body weight against the door. The bolts in the floor bent as if made of tin. They ripped from their fixings with a spray of tile and mortar. The door smashed into the men behind it, knocking them both to land in the corridor beyond. They lay senseless. Then they disappeared under the crushing boots of the attackers.

The other two Stahlhelme fired off shot after shot down the corridor ahead, pinning defenders down, blowing great chunks of masonry from the walls. The corridor was filled with dust.

A few doorways down, a pocket of defenders spoke in sharp urgent tones to one another. Steeling themselves with words of encouragement, they slipped from their cover. They returned fire into the cloud of dust ahead. The gamble worked. From the cloud, bright blue sparks flew past them, down to the artefact far below.

Even as the front line of Stahlhelme fell into sparks, the gap was filled. Bullets slammed into the pocket of guards, dropping three immediately. Two remained, wounded but alive. One fell to a knee. His companion, hit in the arm, tried to drag him back to his feet. Their eyes met. An understanding passed between them. It would be too late. Then the Stahlhelme were upon them and they disappeared.

The beasts lumbered on. They smashed door after door like they were paper, decimating those they found behind. In less than a minute it was over. When it was done, the Stahlhelme stood at the end of the corridor, panting with elation.

The Master hurried through the chaos. He squeezed past them into the wood-clad meeting room. He glanced around. His sharp eyes picked up an area of darkness, far off to the left. It was fractionally darker than the rest of the room. An exit.

'Be still!' he commanded. The Stahlhelme froze, breath held in their great lungs.

Footsteps echoed back up from the darkness. Footsteps moving away and downwards. Footsteps that were nowhere near far enough away to keep safe.

The Master rushed to the exit. Stairs led down. He nodded, knowing what he would find at the stair's conclusion: The Fountain Hall.

'There!' he shouted back at his soldiers. 'On!'

The Stahlhelme gasped in breath again. They hurled themselves towards the door, disappearing downwards in twos through the dank entrance.

From below, the screams started.

'What do you mean?' Christopher repeated, his eyes flicking from the little girl to McCloud. McCloud looked to the floor, a frown on his face. That was confirmation enough.

'If someone else takes this.' Christopher shook Winter's Grasp again. 'The world that I had disappears, doesn't it? And all those people will be gone forever. Is that what will happen?'

Sama turned her head up to him. 'Christopher. I don't know if that's a bad thing. Not if they aren't actually real.'

'You weren't there, Sama,' he snapped back, sharper than he intended. 'I mean, sorry, they were real to me. And if they can be pulled out and brought here, then that makes them real. Doesn't it?'

'But, the gypsies and Molly Brodie were monsters.' Sama's eyes clouded again.

'Not everyone is,' Christopher said back. 'I have friends there.' Back in the world, Eleila and Bediviere were fighting for their lives in a castle already breached. And he had been pulled away. He had left them when they needed him.

'Do not make friends with anyone that you can't say goodbye to,' Eliza suddenly intoned, her eyes leaving Winter's Grasp and looking off into the distance. 'That's "The Sixth Rule of the Journey".'

'Hush Eliza,' McCloud said quickly. 'Christopher. Yes, it's true. I know this is confusing and challenging, but you have to appreciate that everyone that you met, friend or foe was just energy. Just energy moulded into the forms that you imagined.'

There was a distant but clearly audible gunshot from beyond the doorway. McCloud turned his head sharply. 'They are through to the stairs. We wouldn't have heard that if they were at ground level.'

'*They*?' Christopher said. 'Is that the 'just energy' you are talking about?'

'Take off the damn gauntlet, boy!' McCloud finally lost his patience. 'You have no idea what's at stake.'

In Christopher's mind's eye, Eleila's rare grin appeared as she limped along next to him, her arm draped across his shoulder. The Queen's calm touch as she had wished him farewell in her journey to find help. Bediviere's appraising glance after the battle. The fear of the enemy. The pain of his wounds. The ache of the ride. Christopher could still feel that ache.

It was real to him. It wasn't madness. It wasn't anything to fear. It was a power that could make his own imagination real. And now he knew that, he would not just abandon the people inside to be washed away.

'I think I do, Mr McCloud,' Christopher said, narrowing his eyes. 'The answer is no.'

Sama put her hand on his shoulder. 'Christopher, if you don't, I think we're going to get a lot of trouble coming down here pretty soon.' As if to accentuate her words, another gunshot echoed far off through the door.

Christopher nodded. He gripped her around the waist with his free hand. 'I know.'

McCloud sighed, his eyes going cold. 'Very well.' He looked across at the black woman hovering ready at the door. 'Makena.'

Then things happened very fast. Makena raised her staff to strike. To his left, Sama flinched as if she knew what to expect. To his right, the nurse reached forwards, trying to grab Eliza and pull her back from danger. Ahead, Levert sprung back himself, attempting to get out of the way.

Only McCloud stayed still. At the last second the fat man's eyes narrowed, as if he had suddenly had an insight into what Christopher was about to do. By then it was too late.

The first coil of black erupted from Makena's staff. Christopher reached out with Winter's Grasp. He focused his mind on the faces of the friends he had met, the places he had seen and the creatures he had battled. He let the thrills, the fears, and the joys he had felt course through him.

And then, he pulled.

The Entity burst back into its consciousness with an electric jolt of joy. The boy! The creator! All was not lost. That which it had expelled was trying to find it once more.

And suddenly there was a connection again. The Entity opened itself, ready to accept the creator back into the fold. The fear instinct was gone now. The creator was welcome within it.

Yet, as soon as it felt his presence, it recognised something else. He was not yet within it. He was outside. The Entity could almost taste the world beyond.

It remembered being out there, naked and exposed. It remembered being dragged through horrors that had tainted it. And the creator was out there.

It remembered the other man. How at its very edges he had ripped out a fissure. How he had opened the way to that other place. And it understood.

The Entity latched on to the creator's mind, an anchor in this new understanding. It pushed itself outwards, joyful.

In front of Christopher, a tear ripped through the air, exposing a maelstrom of blue light beyond. Christopher grinned even wider. Beside him, Sama gasped. 'Bloody hell!'

Makena's hand dropped. The wisps of night dissipated harmless from the end of the staff. The nurse shrank back against the wall, dragging Eliza with her. Levert ducked down behind the stone dais.

There was a song of recognition in Christopher's ears. No, he thought a moment after he became aware of it. Not a song, and not in his ears in any conventional sense. It was the sound of wind whistling through trees, the pitch of the whistle somehow harmonizing. It was the sound of a storm, the rhythms of the rain and the thunder providing counterpoint percussion to the wind. It was the sound of thousands of voices chattering and laughing, suddenly delighted but not knowing why. It was the sound of determination, armies suddenly finding a fresh focus in the fighting. It was the sound of a rush of blood to the head. It was the sound of joy and it was coming straight through to him, somehow manifesting from the inside.

Makena lifted her staff again, but her face frowned. 'Ward!'

McCloud struggled to speak. 'How can that be?' he spluttered.

Christopher grinned. His head was full of the rush of power and now he knew where it was coming from. He turned to Sama, still clutching at his shoulder. 'Ready?'

Sama's eyes were bright, lit with blue light. She nodded once.

Christopher lifted Winter's Grasp again. He concentrated on the memory of the portal he had seen Sama fighting at in the vision he had on the cliff top, and beyond that, the path back down to Kay's castle. In his mind, the song of joy grew louder, understanding his desire and ready to respond.

'Now!' he cried.

Christopher and Sama jumped through the portal and were gone.

CHAPTER TWENTY-SEVEN

The Courtyard

The Entity knew something was wrong. An all-consuming sense of disquiet filled its remaining consciousness. It struggled for a moment to pinpoint the source of its discomfort. Then, as it understood, the disquiet became panic.

The ornate silver gauntlet on the boy's hand.

The Entity focused on it and knew it at once. It saw it in its true form. Not a gauntlet at all. The container. The place where all its power, all its energy had been confined for millennia. And now instead of containing it, it was here.

The artefact should no more be inside the Entity than a bucket can be within the water it contains. The Entity lurched with fear. It gathered all its remaining consciousness, all its remaining energy, all that it had and plunged down towards the artefact, compressing itself, trying to bury itself back into the safety it knew.

Yet there was no way in. It was too late for that, there was no going back. The Entity struggled on, pushing and pushing, desperate to invade the impassable barrier.

As it pushed against the tiny artefact within it, it latched on to images. Memories of thousands of worlds created like the one it had made from the boy's mind. It struggled through its fear for a moment, trying to understand the source of these memories. They were not from the boy. They were not from some other place.

Then it realised the thoughts it latched on to were in the artefact. The thoughts it latched on to were its own. Then finally, it truly understood.

The Entity let go.

The Energy and the artefact within it exploded in a great blue wave that spread in all directions. It crashed through into the world, washing over the landscape and engulfing everything in its path. And as it did so, it changed the world.

It was a dying act almost human in its nature. An act of legacy. This world would be the last it created. Here, at the last, the dimmest of understandings manifested in its fading consciousness. Understanding of the thousands of times it had created form from itself before. Understanding of the impermanence of the worlds that had been. How easily each new mind had been seduced. How it had destroyed as many times as it had given birth.

So now, it changed *this* world. Everything it encountered, every blade of grass, every particle of air, every beating heart it made real. The great wave moved over the world, taking each element no matter how large or small, and transformed energy into molecule. Everything it touched it gave true existence to. No longer was the world simply the manifestation of a child's imagination made physical, now it was real in the truest sense. Now it was independent. Now it would endure.

As it changed the world, the Entity diminished. Each transformation used up the tiniest spark of the remaining energy until, as the last molecule was formed there was almost nothing left. It was no more than a spark now. It focused back on the boy and his companion falling through the void toward the newly formed world and, with its last efforts, it rushed to join them.

As it reached them it split itself into two minute pinpoints of light, all it needed to accomplish the last two tasks it needed to do. One pinpoint flew up into the path where the boy was falling, solidifying the route between the world he had leapt from and the world below and making it permanent.

The other pinpoint flew to the hand where the artefact had been. The spark flashed once and was gone. In its place, once more the boy was wearing an ornate silver gauntlet.

The Master gasped. His knees buckled. He reached out, hands finding a stone wall. He stumbled in close, leaning against it, then sat on one of the stairs. If he did not sit he might have fallen, crashing down into the Stahlhelme below, even tumbling all the way down to the Fountain Hall.

If his body plunged straight into an icy pool, it would not be as cold as the sudden chill that gripped him. His skin hurt. He struggled to breathe. The cold seemed to be sucking the energy from every part of him. It leached into his bones.

He rolled into the steps, unfeeling of the stone edge that stuck into his spine. For a minute or more, he was lost to the cold.

It was his breath that returned first. His back arched as he sucked in air again. He coughed violently, rolling on to his side, spitting phlegm on to the step. His body shuddered. Still so cold. His skin was covered all over with goose pimples. He could not stop shaking.

The shock receded. Once he stopped coughing, he took another tentative breath. This time his lungs didn't fight him. He rolled back on to his elbows, still shaking.

Something was changed. He rested his head against the cold stone wall, regaining control of himself. He slowly became aware of his surroundings again, the cries of men below, the sounds of gunfire.

Something was gone. He had occasionally felt the tingle when a new child somewhere in the world was attached to an artefact. Then the feeling was warm and pleasant, as if all at once one had stepped into sunlight. This was not that feeling.

A stray gunshot from the next pocket of defenders smashed into the wall next to him. The metal of the bullet shrieked as it ground against stone and sent shards out into the corridor. One shard hit him just above the eye, slicing along his eyebrow. Pain pulled him back into focus.

The Stahlhelme's advance had been unrelenting. Below, they screamed with battle-born rage.

He sat up, then rose carefully to his feet. He staggered down a couple of steps, using the wall to aid him. Whatever had happened, salvation was still below. If he couldn't take the boy, then he must at least retrieve the artefact. He pushed himself away and continued down.

When he reached the Stahlhelme, they had taken up positions on either side of an alcove on the stairs, taking it in turns to lean out and fire volleys down into the dim passage. Fifty paces further down, the defenders had taken similar positions in another alcove.

The Master ducked into the right-hand side, nestling against the wall. The Stahlhelme hadn't noticed him. They were too intent on their quarry. He leaned forward, careful to make sure that he wasn't exposing himself to the rifles below.

His body was still cold, but at least he could move. He pushed himself up again.

'Charge!' he called.

One of the Stahlhelme looked back at him, a momentary expression of rebellion in its eyes. For a moment, he was reminded of Molly Brodie. Something in the eyes.

Was that it? Was he losing his hold over them? If the artefact had been taken, would their free will manifest? It was of no matter. He had never seen a creature manage to escape his hold, even through a transition.

'Charge!' he shouted again.

The Stahlhelme turned back to the passage and growled something to its companions. Three of them moved as one, filling the stairwell side by side and stormed on down. Behind them another three slipped into formation. Two more followed.

They got eight steps down. Below there was a crack, then another. Bullets whizzed past them. There were more cracks. The defenders were firing at will, desperately trying to pick some off before they could reach them.

At the front of the Stahlhelme, one dropped to its knees. It slumped to the side of the passage. Immediately another took its place, closing the gap. They hurtled on down.

The Master followed at a safe distance, still aware that he was unsteady. He reached the one who had been shot. He glanced at it as he passed. A small but deadly hole was in its temple. It stared sightlessly out through its beady black eyes, quite dead. The Master lurched to a stop. Confusion rooted his feet to the stone floor.

If the creature was dead, why was it not dissipating?

The reaction was always immediate once a creature's essence had gone, yet this body remained. He reached to touch it. Quite solid. He bent to examine closer.

Below, the remaining Stahlhelme reached the pocket of defenders. Once they were in close quarters, the men were no match for them. Sudden screams cut off as quickly as they started.

The Master hardly noticed. He pressed its shoulder again and felt it give to his touch as though made of candy floss. Finally it was beginning to shimmer. Small sparks started to float up from the body.

Instead of rushing down through the darkness back to the source, the sparks floated in the air. They danced around, bumping into one another like they were drunken fireflies. The whole passage was filling now, ablaze with blue light. The Master could feel the ends of his hair lifting as if he was surrounded by static electricity.

Then slowly, the sparks began to float away. They floated towards the walls, the floor, the ceiling. They floated towards him. They floated in every direction except down towards the source.

Where each spark touched something solid, it sank into it. Sparks sank into the stone blocks of the steps. They sank into the chiselled rock. And once each had sunk in, the spark was gone. They disappeared into whatever they met, directionless.

As if they had nowhere to return to.

The Master swore. The corridor was dimming once more. Why were they not returning to the source? Fear gripped him. He had to know. He reached into his pocket and clutched at the key.

He wrenched open a portal. The blue light blazed again. He pushed through, ready to duck back again should he see any hint of danger.

The portal opened, just as it had always done. He glanced down. It had opened behind Mordred's army, not far from where he had last appeared to recruit the Stahlhelme. He sighed, relieved. He might not understand what had just happened, but at least his worst fears about the world had not been confirmed.

He glanced back down the corridor. The Stahlhelme thundered down the steps. They had gotten him down this far. Now they were deep below the London streets. If alarms had been raised above, they had been raised already. There was no reason not to flood this place with an army.

He looked back over the battle. There were no more Stahlhelme immediately about him. They must have already got into the courtyard. It wouldn't take long to find them, though. He took a deep breath and dived into the portal.

And found his way was barred.

He hit the barrier just in from the portal. He hadn't even got more than his head and shoulders through before he felt it. Something stopping his entrance. It caught on his face and neck. It felt as though he was trying to push through dense, undergrowth. It gave just a little as he pushed, but stayed impassable.

Yet it didn't affect his perception of the world beyond. He could see everything. The cries of the warriors were tantalisingly clear. He could smell the cordite of the guns. Still, try as he might, he could not push through.

He shoved again. He reached in and tore at the invisible barrier. He could feel it tingling on his hands. No matter how he wrenched at it, it stayed the same. In his way.

From the passageway below, the gunfire started anew. Cursing, he pulled himself all the way back into the corridor and closed the portal. There was no time to worry about it now. He focused on the battle below and banished his worries from his mind. They could not help him. He pushed the key back into his pocket and hurried down the stairs.

At the alcove below, the corpses of defenders lay, broken things where the Stahlhelme had discarded them. The Master bent to the floor by one; the remains of a muscular man in a grey suit. The corpse lay face down. In its right hand was a pistol. The Master reached down and prised the fingers from the weapon.

He lifted it, turning it in his own hand, fitting the grip into his palm. He grimaced with distaste. There was nothing he hated more than the mundane blunt force of a gun. In this world, at least, it would offer no surprises. He placed his finger on the trigger, then rose and started on down again.

Christopher spun, head over heels, twisting and turning, left and right, all the time dragged relentlessly down. Everything was black. He had a sense of Sama at his side, her hand in his.

He couldn't tell how long they seemed to spin and twist on their journey. It could have been seconds or far longer. There was a strange disassociation of time. It was only as he felt them slowing in the blackness that he wondered how long they had been falling. And then, before he really had a chance to think about it, they stopped.

He was aware he was standing. It was no longer black. Though he could see no further in front of him, he was surrounded by a brown-grey haze. He took a breath, then coughed. The haze tasted of dirt. It was dirt! A great cloud of it all around him.

There were noises, too. The clash of steel on steel. A sword fight. The explosion of a rifle. Christopher's heart leapt. A man shouted an order off to the right. He glanced to his side. There was a shape in the dust. A militia man burst past and ran back off into the haze.

A militia man. Christopher grinned. It had worked. They had been brought back.

'Christopher.' Sama's voice at his side.

He turned. 'Sama? Are you all right?'

Sama stared behind them, her eyes as wide as he had ever seen. She didn't seem to hear what he had said. He turned to look in the same direction.

Behind them was a hole. It hung in the air, entirely separate from anything around it. It was four feet wide and five feet tall. Its bottom edge floated a foot from the ground.

Inside, it was entirely black. It was impossible to make out anything in there. Whether it was a yard or a mile deep was a mystery.

Even if the hole had been somewhere that holes were supposed to be, like in a wall or in the ground, it would still have been wrong. Around the edges of it, little blue sparks fizzed and popped.

Christopher peered around the side of the hole. Behind it there was just more dust cloud. Other vague people shapes were moving towards them in it. There certainly wasn't any sort of tunnel stretching off into the distance.

He moved back around to Sama. She was still staring at the hole. Her expression was hard to read. He hoped that the journey hadn't scrambled her brain. 'Sama. Say something.'

'Bloody hell!' she said finally, turning to grin at him. 'That was brilliant!'

Christopher felt the corners of his mouth angle up. He grinned back at her.

'So are we here?' she said. 'Is this where you've been?'

'I think so.' He nodded. He hoped so. If it was, there was no time to be standing around grinning like idiots. They had to find his friends. He took Sama's hand again.

Behind her, a brown shape appeared. Before Christopher could speak, the shape grew more substantial. A man with a dirty brown, tanned leather breastplate clambered over a piece of masonry. In his left hand was a vicious-looking axe, small but deadly. In his right he carried a shield.

'Sama!' He pushed her to the side just as the man raised his axe and swung into the space where she had been. 'Look out!'

Sama stumbled, but caught herself. The man, seeing his first quarry had disappeared out of axe range, narrowed his eyes at Christopher. He backed away, weighing up the idea of rushing the man before he could strike.

Almost as if he had read the thought, the man raised his axe again. Before he could bring it down, Sama sprang at him, keeping low. She shoved him with all her weight towards the black fissure.

The man grunted, stumbling at the entrance to the hole, then fell through. It was as if something had caught him from inside. He was sucked away into the black, becoming a distant dot in seconds. He disappeared from view.

The dust cloud dispersed. Other shapes approached. A huge shadow fell across them.

Instinctively, Christopher ducked. A blade sliced through the air. He scrambled back. The Stahlhelme that owned the blade crashed up on to the mound.

Seeing them both, it roared. Spittle from its hideous mouth showered on to Christopher.

'Run!' he shouted, dodging to the left. Sama dove off to the right. The Stahlhelme hesitated, unsure which way to turn. Then it thundered after Sama.

Christopher could see the other shapes better now. Men. Armed and advancing. None looked like Kay's militia.

The last dust dispersed. On either side dust-shrouded grey edifices became black. The gate house towers. What was left of them, anyway.

The Stahlhelme swung at Sama again. She dodged out of the way and vaulted over a big block of masonry, disappearing behind it.

An arrow whizzed by Christopher's left ear. He looked across at the bowman. A short, ugly boy. He looked barely older than Christopher. Others appeared near the Stahlhelme, brandishing swords. There was no way to get past them and follow Sama.

The boy was stringing another arrow to his bow. The Stahlhelme gave up chasing Sama and turned back. This was not the place to be. Christopher turned and clambered over bits of tumbled wall, hoping the remnants of the settling dust might conceal his escape.

Another arrow clacked against a big stone next to him. The boy appeared to be a useless shot. Still, it would be stupid to test that. Christopher scrambled up a pile of what was once a tower. All about men were clambering over the rubble, heading towards the centre of the castle.

'Come back!' A voice, close behind him. He shot a look. The boy was chasing him, bow now over his shoulder. He brandished a short knife.

Christopher had no intention of going back, not that way at least. He climbed higher. A few feet in front of him a wall rose out of the rubble. The remains of the collapsed tower stretched above him. There was still part of the first floor. It seemed there were enough hand holds in the wall that he could climb. It was either that or turn around.

He jumped for the first handhold, caught it, and pulled himself up, scrambling for footholds with his feet. He found purchase, then stretched to the next hold and slipped his fingers inside.

He clambered from hold to hold, scaling twelve feet of the wall until he pulled himself on to the remains of the first floor. He rolled on to his knees and looked back down over the ledge,

The boy still followed a few feet below, climbing the same handholds with an evil expression on his face. Christopher grimaced. This boy was determined. His knife was back in his belt whilst he climbed. If he got up here, he would be quick to pull it out again.

The boy looked up. His snarl grew more twisted as he saw Christopher looking over. 'Hey! Up here!' he shouted, 'There's one of them here!'

It fell on deaf ears. The Stahlhelme and the other two men had given up on Sama and headed towards the sounds of battle coming from further in the castle. No one else seemed interested in the boy's shouting.

Christopher ducked into the remains of the tower and looked for something to defend himself. A stout piece of wood rested on the remaining floorboards. It was large enough to make a good cudgel. He reached for it, feeling a little better now he had something solid in his hand, and turned back to the edge.

The boy's hand appeared, gripping at the edge of the floor. Christopher hesitated. This wasn't the same as fighting the Stahlhelme. They were monsters. The boy climbing up, much as he might be vicious-looking and ugly, was still just a boy. Christopher didn't particularly want to fight him.

He ran to the edge. 'Stop!' he snarled, hoping the boy would edge back down now he had the wood.

Instead, the boy reached for his knife with his other hand and swung wildly at Christopher's legs. Christopher jumped back. So much for reasoning with him, then.

Still, he didn't want to hurt him. If he could just knock him off the wall. He dodged forward and swung the wood as hard as he could on to the boy's hand. The boy squealed in pain, snatching his hand away.

Realising his mistake too late, the boy scrambled back in vain with crushed fingers. He stared up, wide eyed, at Christopher. Then he fell, twisting in the air, and crashed face-down on to the hard rubble below.

The boy landed with a wet crunch. He lay still. The rock beneath his head slowly turned red. Christopher backed away, feeling sick. The boy hadn't given him an option. He frowned against the guilt, then shook his head. He was here to help his friends. That was what to focus on.

He looked out over the castle grounds, scanning for any sign of Sama, glad to be focusing on something other than the boy below. There was no sign of her. He searched along the wall of the other tower. There was nothing there either. She would be fine, he thought to himself, almost convinced. She would have slipped through anyone stupid enough to try to catch her.

It was obvious the castle was lost. The few of Mordred's troops below him moved slowly through the rubble. They were far from frontline warriors. They casually searched through the fallen, stealing anything convenient.

There were a few pockets of fighting in the village — small groups had barricaded themselves in houses — but for the most part the battle here was done. Beyond the village, Christopher could hear the sounds of the real fighting: Around the keep. That would be where his friends would be making a stand.

The boy had a bow and a knife. Christopher looked down again to where the body lay. It would not be long before someone else took them. The bow was still on the boy's back, arrows in a quiver next to them

There was still no immediate danger. Christopher clambered down.

Sama squeezed under the wheel of the fallen cart, panting heavily and looked out. Finally she had a chance to catch her breath. She had led four would-be assailants a merry dance since dodging from that mound.

The first, the Stahlhelme, gave up on the chase almost as soon as she jumped out of his reach. It made one more half-hearted swing at her, then strode off towards the sounds of battle in the distance.

Sama tried to turn back then and find Christopher, but he had already clambered off the other way. There were men and dust obscuring her view. Before she could find a way around, a pair of them noticed her. They chased across in poorly fitted armour, waving swords in front of them.

However, they were big and Sama was small. She spotted a gap in the wall, a doorway all but filled with rubble, with a little space at its side. Before they could reach her, she slipped through. On the other side, she found herself in a deserted, half destroyed corridor. She ran along it, to the frustrated cries of the men she'd left behind.

Eventually, she reached another doorway that led back out. She ran through, then tried to double back to the mound. The men were still trying to find a way into the hole she had escaped through. So instead, she began a wide circle around them.

The circle took her close to the little wattle-and-daub houses in the courtyard. The end one was ablaze. A rabble of attackers massed, jeering and shooting arrows up at the roof. There, two hapless militias had climbed up to avoid the flames. As she neared, a defender took an arrow to his side with a scream. He fell and landed by her in a heap.

One jeerer came across to be sure the man was dead. When he discovered Sama pulling a short sword from the body, he shouted with delight at finding a foe he could actually fight. He rushed towards her.

He swung his sword. Sama barely had time to lift the blade to catch the blow. The clash of metal on metal jarred her arm all the way to the shoulder. She dropped the sword and fell backwards on to her bottom. This was most certainly not an adventure she was enjoying.

Made bold by her prone form, the man strode forward to deliver a killing blow. Sama kicked up hard, catching him in the groin. His face went red almost immediately and he made a funny, high-pitched whine. Then he fell to his knees, holding his crotch.

Sama jumped up and punched him twice in his face. On the second punch she felt his nose pop satisfyingly under her fist.

There was a shout. A few of the other jeerers had noticed the fight. Five of them broke off from the main group and began toward her. One had a bow. Sama turned and sprinted around the side of the building, away from the houses and towards the louder sounds of battle. There, by the outer wall, she found the broken cart and ducked underneath it.

Her breathing was becoming just a little easier now. In a few moments she would be able to carry on searching for Christopher. She looked out from under the cart. In the distance ahead, the castle keep rose up. It was intact for the moment.

Around the front of the keep, the battle raged. Sama had never seen that many people in one place. It was easily in the thousands. Most of the fighting was out of her sight, hidden by masses of soldiers pressing forward. Mostly what she could see was the soldiers' backs. They jostled with one another to try and get near the action. In the distance she could hear roars of rage, screams of pain, and the clang of weapons.

From what she could see, it was obvious there were far more attackers pushing towards the keep than there must be defenders pushing back. Sama frowned. It looked like an impossible situation.

'There she is!'

Sama turned back. The jeerers, led by the one she had kicked, were racing towards her. An arrow stuck into the spokes of the wagon wheel with a thunk. Sama scrambled backwards, slipping out of the other side of the cart, and sprinted along the outer wall away from the men.

The sound of footsteps was close. She couldn't waste time turning to check. Arrows flew past her, clattering into the wall. She had to get out of the open.

A few feet ahead, another door had been wrenched from its hinges and lay on the earth. Sama made for the opening, keeping her head low. Another arrow whizzed past, this one so close she felt its breeze. She turned sharply, catching the door frame with one hand to swing herself in without losing too much speed and smashed into a swordsman coming the other way.

'What!' he shouted, lifting his sword, bright eyes staring from a blood-covered face. Before he had a chance to swing at her, an arrow buried itself in his chest. He gasped in pain.

Sama grabbed him, pulled him around between her and the mob behind, and then raced on. There were stairs ahead. She rushed up them. Behind her there was a dull thud, then the sounds of feet. The man hadn't slowed them down much. They were close behind her. She gasped for air, pushing on.

She came to a landing. On one side lay an enormous stack of bundled arrows. As she passed, she swung an arm down and grabbed at a bundle. She pulled hard at it, hoping that the whole pile would come down. Nothing. The pile remained intact. She cursed and ran on. She had lost a precious moment. The nearest pursuer grabbed at the back of her shirt. He caught it briefly, but she tore out of his grasp. She spurred on to the next flight of steps, taking them two at a time.

At the top, she had to turn around to race along a short corridor with doors on one side. It ended in another flight of stairs. Above she could see the light of the sky. The battlements. She took the first step.

Then her luck ran out.

The second step was uneven and higher than she expected. Her toes caught on it. She pitched forwards, caught the steps with her hands and pushed up again. If they'd been just a couple of paces further back, she could have recovered, but they were too close. As she pushed up, a hand grabbed the scruff of her shirt and yanked her back.

Her attacker was strong, with a grip impossible to twist out of. He grabbed on to her with his other hand too. She turned and kicked out at him, but he was ready. He turned his own body so her kicks fell against a well-padded leg. He let go with his right hand, balled it into a fist and swung it hard into her face. Her cheek exploded in pain.

'I've got her!' he shouted, raising his fist to strike again.

Sama turned her face, trying to twist away from the next attack. More thudding footsteps came up the corridor. The next blow caught her on the back of the head so hard she bit her tongue, tasting blood.

'Now then,' a gruff voice said. 'I'll show you what happens to peasant girls who kick men between their legs.' The footsteps slowed. Steady, menacing.

Desperate, Sama stared up the steps. At the top a small group of knights were heading past, their backs to the opening. 'Help me!' Sama screamed. 'Help!'

At the back, a knight turned and looked down. A woman, perhaps only a couple of years older than Sama herself. 'Help!' Sama cried again.

She had just enough time to register a puzzled look on the woman's face. Then the strong hands pulled her back down the corridor.

The girl's clothes. There was a flicker of recognition in Eleila's mind. Perhaps it was just the angle, but that shirt the girl was wearing was an unusual cut. A familiar cut.

'Bediviere!' Eleila shouted, not turning to see if he would stop and follow. The girl had disappeared into a crowd of scruffy foot soldiers. Eleila bounded down. Even a poorly armed rabble could be deadly if one were unarmed.

'Hold!' she shouted as she landed on the bottom step. The nearest one to her turned back from where they had pulled the girl. The grin on his face fell. Eleila ran him through with her sword. Now his face was shock.

A second turned as she was pulling her sword from the first. He looked more prepared. A mean looking axe was in his hand.

Before he could swing at her, a crossbow bolt flew over her shoulder and struck him in the head. He arched back.

Bediviere reached her side as the others realised they were under attack. Seeing that they faced two fully armed knights, a good three-quarters of their number ran. Four remained. Eleila glowered at them.

The girl struggled out from between them, almost forgotten in this new danger, and tried to move across to where Eleila and Bediviere stood.

'Not so fast,' one said, grabbing her by the scruff of the neck.

Eleila slammed the nearest hard with her shield, knocking him out of the way. She dodged between the man and the girl and brought her sword down on his arm. The blade chopped clean through. The man screamed, staggering back. His forearm fell to the floor with a thud.

Bediviere struck the one she'd knocked out of the way with the flat of his sword, catching him on the head. The man slumped down. That was enough for remaining two. They turned and ran off down the corridor.

The girl stepped away from the groaning man on the floor, wiping blood from her face. Beneath the mess she had gone quite white. She looked up. 'Thanks,' she said in a small voice.

That was it, Eleila realised. The shirt and trousers the girl was wearing. They reminded her of the clothes Christopher had been wearing that first time she met him.

There'd been no sign of Christopher since the tower. One minute he had been behind her, then he had been gone. She'd clambered back to look over the battlements, terrified that he had fallen, but there had been no sign of him.

Once the fighting started, she'd not had time to consider it. Attackers had already reached the walls through other entrances. Getting up to the battlements had been one long fight. This was the first moment where they hadn't been running or defending themselves.

Eleila looked again at the girl's clothes. 'Have you seen Christopher?'

The girl's eyes widened. 'You know Christopher? I lost him out there.' She grabbed Eleila's arm. 'I'm Sama. I came back with Christopher. We've come to help.'

Eleila raised her eyebrows.

'Wolf. The sword.' Bediviere clasped her shoulder. 'We must get to the keep.'

'I know,' Eleila said over her shoulder. 'Go. I am behind you.' She turned back to Sama. 'Come with us. We'll look for Christopher from the battlements.'

She pushed Sama in front and herded her up the stairs. The girl was breathing heavily but seemed to be regaining her composure already.

'If there is fighting, stay behind me,' Eleila warned gruffly.

Sama glanced up, eyebrows knotted in a frown. 'Not bloody likely.'

Eleila pointed ahead along the battlements. 'That way. Quickly now.'

The girl glanced up at her. 'Okay, but we'll need to stop and look for Christopher.'

Eleila nodded, 'Once we reach the keep.' There was no mistaking this girl. From her attitude, she was definitely from the same place as Christopher.

'The children.' Levert mumbling, rubbing his hands together with short, juddering movements. He stared wide-eyed at the black hole in front of them. 'We must protect the children.'

The man seemed to have gone completely to pieces. Ward glanced away from him, disgusted. Levert had spent too many years with his theories and ideas. Now, the one time when he needed to put them into practice, he had proven to be very short of the mark.

Makena was on her knees, talking softly to Eliza. The little girl seemed almost as stupefied as Levert. Beside them, the nurse was white and drawn.

John looked at Ward, thin-lipped, from beside the wooden door. 'I've started the evacuation. They've been moved out through the back entrance. They'll be in cars and on their way to Lemontrees shortly. You should do the same, Ward. We may be lost here.'

Ward shook his head. 'That's not an option. We need to hold. We can't leave whatever this is.' He gestured at the fissure. 'Where have they reached?'

'We have them held at the entrance to the Fountain Hall,' John replied. 'But they are strong. Anything that we might have had to stop them is out in the field. Makena and I have the only weapons here that might make a difference.'

'Then go.'

John nodded and disappeared out into the hallway. His footsteps echoed as he ran back down to the distant sounds of fighting.

'Makena,' Ward said. 'You too.'

Makena gestured at the little girl. 'You'll get her to the cars?'

A sudden force erupted from the fissure, pushing the air as if a powerful gale had suddenly started to blow at them. Levert staggered back, his hair flying about his head. Eliza screamed and huddled into a corner. Makena stepped backwards towards the door.

Ward's heavy bulk was not moved by the force. He stared into the black void, squinting his eyes against the wind. In the distance a tiny speck appeared. It grew larger by the second, rushing towards them. The room flashed bright white again.

Finally, Ward was thrown back, hitting the hard stone wall. His eyes watered up with the force. Then, as quickly as it had started, it was over.

Ward rubbed his eyes to clear them. Suddenly a shape moved in front of him. An arm raised high, holding something. It flashed down to the left. There was a scream. Then another.

Ward's eyes cleared. In the centre of the room, standing before the fissure, was a man in a dirty leather breastplate. His face was twisted with bewilderment and fear. He bared dirty brown teeth through a grey growth of stubble.

The nurse was sprawled on the floor at his feet. One of her feet jerked erratically.

In the man's hand was an axe, its edge tinged with red. He raised it again, eyes darting left to right, ready to strike.

'Makena!' Ward shouted. She was already ahead of him. Tendrils of black rushed around the end of her staff. She thrust it forward into the man's chest. He screamed and fell back into the void again.

As he fell in, it was as if something invisible grabbed him. The sides of the fissure fizzed with blue sparkles. Some force pulled him off into the distance at a speed far faster than Makena's attack would cause. He flew off into the distance, arms and legs flailing limply.

Ward bent to the nurse. Nothing could be done. He looked at the void and then at Makena. A sinking feeling blossomed inside him.

He sighed. 'If they come from two sides, we are definitely done for.'

Makena closed her eyes.

'We can't fight out there and fight in here.' Ward stood, steeling himself. 'We haven't resources as it is.'

Her eyes remained closed, but she nodded slowly. She knew what he needed to ask. The decision had to be made.

'Go through. Hold the other end if you can. If not, try to block it. Stop anything coming back. With luck the Flyte boy will be there. Use his help if you can.' Ward glanced at Levert. 'If I can get him to make sense I am going to try and seal this end, too. You may not be able to get back. Not this way, anyway.'

Finally, Makena opened her eyes. Her face was set. 'You'll get Eliza to the others?'

Ward found himself struggling to meet her gaze. Who knew what he would be sending her through to? 'Of course,' he said gruffly. 'She is an asset.'

'Good,' she said. 'And tell John …' She frowned for a moment. 'Tell John I'll see him soon.'

She walked forward to the fissure. She didn't look back once. Clutching her staff tightly, she jumped forward into the void. The sides of the fissure fizzed blue.

Ward watched her figure grow smaller until barely a moment later she was a speck in the distance. Then she was gone. He turned to Levert.

'Get up,' he growled. There was no response. He reached forwards and took a grip of the man's lapels. He wrenched Levert to his feet, swinging him round to face him. 'Think! We need to close this off.'

'The children …' Levert still mumbled.

Ward slapped him hard across the face. 'Levert! Listen to me!'

Levert's eyes focused on him. His face was pinched and pasty. If he could have retreated into one of his books and hidden there, Ward imagined he would do it in a heartbeat.

'Levert. We need to stop anything coming through this portal. Can you think of anything that will help?'

Levert shook his head slowly. 'If I can get to the library I can start to research. I am sure there must be something in our books.'

Ward shook him hard. 'The library is likely to be full of dead librarians. You try and get there you'll go the same way. What you have is in this room.'

Levert looked around, his eyes avoiding the fissure as if it were a naked man at a dinner party. He settled on the books they had brought down to free Christopher. 'There may be something in those.' His voice was just a little steadier. 'I should look.'

'Do that,' Ward said. 'Do something. If there's nothing in your books that helps, try some leaps of faith. We may not have a great deal else to go on.' He pushed Levert towards the books.

Levert stumbled forwards and turned back immediately. 'Where are you going?' His voice was tremulous once again. 'I need you to stay and help me.'

'I'll be back momentarily,' Ward said, resisting the urge to shout at the man again. 'I need to take Eliza to the others and make sure they get away. If we do lose this facility today, then they are the future. Their safety is paramount.'

He waddled across to Eliza and bent to draw her up into his arms. 'Come now, my dear. Let's get you away from all of this.'

The little girl shuddered in his arms, wrapping her own arms around his thick neck. As he reached the door, he turned back. Levert had picked up the first book and was rapidly leafing through its contents. Ward sighed and squeezed out into the corridor.

The Master huddled at the entrance way, shielded from the fighting further down the great room by the first of the massive central pillars and watched the Stahlhelme's steady advance. In the passageway, when they'd been forced to file down in threes, their assault had been held back. In the hall of the fountains, they really came into their own.

With the width of the hall to spread through, they were unstoppable. Their rifles blasted out volleys. They separated into two groups, taking it in turn to cover one another's advance.

McCloud's men were continually forced to duck, falling back in crouched groups of threes and fours against the onslaught. In those stolen moments when they had managed to fire back, their shots had been hurried and inaccurate.

Only one of the Stahlhelme had fallen so far, lust for the battle making it move before covering fire had been laid down. It collapsed to the floor with a grunt. The blue sparks it eventually dissipated into had spread up through the great hall, reaching the high cathedral roof, temporarily brightening the hall as if from thousands of blue candles. From that point onwards, the Stahlhelme had been making an excellent job of keeping all the enemy pinned down.

The Fountain Hall was bigger than the Master remembered. But then, when he had seen it at all it had been the briefest of glances from a corridor at the far end. He had never seen the fountains themselves. The circle was much closer to this end of the room. Despite the skirmish ahead, it was hard not to be entranced by the giant statues dominating the room. The twenty-four fountains had been described to him when he was young, but the description didn't really prepare a person for their majesty.

The Master looked back down the hall. The Stahlhelme had managed to get a good third of the way along its length. Their advance had taken them closer to the far wall, the side where the fountains were. It would be safer over on that side, behind them. There was no immediate danger, but anyone who appeared from above would come out too close to him for comfort.

At the next volley, he skirted around the pillar and ran full pelt into the hall. There was a good sixty feet across the centre before he reached the pillar on the other side. As he sprinted, he listened for shouts from the defenders that they may have seen him.

All he heard was the next volley, followed by a scream. Another Stahlhelm's rifle found a target. He ran on, reaching the far pillar some seconds later and diving behind it. Now he was hidden from the passageway entrance and on the right side to advance. He leaned his back against the pillar and sucked in air with deep rapid breaths.

The fountain plinth was close now. He could see them all. The nearest fountain, its flow spurting high into the air, had a black cloth draped over its huge feet. He glanced around, counting the other cloths. Eight black. Six white. Three green. Seven in various colours. He nodded to himself, briefly lost in thought. He had never known the groupings before.

Suddenly he started. His brows knitted together. Something was odd. He looked at the fountains again, standing to see a little more of those most distant. It took him a moment to scan them for what had disquieted him.

It was one of the individual colours. The statue rose, five fountains down on his side, a purple cloth draped over its feet.

There was no flow of water.

The Master's frown grew deeper. The fountains were always supposed to flow. Sometimes they would ebb to almost nothing, he knew, but he was sure they never stopped altogether. He struggled to remember the little he had been told about this room. It had been so long since he had considered it worth musing that the learning was hard to recall. The fountains represented the artefacts. If one was not flowing, wouldn't that mean that an artefact was no longer?

He swore. That couldn't be it. He could still see his world. Even if he couldn't get into it, he could see it.

He glanced around. The Stahlhelme continued their steady advance. He had a brief respite. 'Damn it,' he swore to himself. He had to check again. 'Just for a moment.'

He pulled out the key and ripped open the tiniest opening, willing it to be directly over the castle. Then, he stared through.

He was just over the gatehouse tower, where he had been so close to binding the boy. In the distance, the main fighting had moved to the ground around the keep. Everything was as it had been.

There, towards the back of that battle he spied Mordred's horse and his senior retainers, keeping a safe distance. In the centre of the battle, the remaining Stahlhelme he had not taken were making short work of the militia.

He swore under his breath, wishing that he had brought them all whilst he had been able. Still, it was of no matter now. He needed to get back to the Fountain Hall. That dead fountain could not be anything to do with Christopher or the artefact, after all. He pulled back to leave.

Then something caught his eye at the gatehouse. A flash of light. Those few warriors close to that point fell back, raising their arms to defend themselves against the brightness. The light concealed something. As it dulled, he drew in a shocked breath.

The black woman. McCloud's minion, who had been dogging his steps since Alton, raised herself up from the flash.

The Master stared, wide-eyed. Behind her, something else shimmered. A circle with little blue sparks around its edges. He could see her through its centre, but still, immediately he knew what he was looking at.

'My God,' he said finally. 'There's another entrance.'

And it must be close. That woman had been with the damned girl. They'd got Christopher. They'd brought him to this place. The entrance must be close to the Hall of Fountains. The Master pulled back from the sphere and dropped on to the stone floor by the pillar.

The entrance must be here.

CHAPTER TWENTY-EIGHT

To Save the Sword

As he pulled the bow from the boy, Christopher realised he was wearing Winter's Grasp. He gasped. The silver gauntlet fitted so comfortably to his hand and was so light that, in the chaos since they had appeared, it hadn't occurred to him it was there. In fact, he had actually assumed as soon as he had arrived here, it would be gone. But, as he reached his hand forward to slip the bow from the boy's back, there it was, shimmering silver surface reflecting the siege-damaged walls of the tower above.

For a moment, the bow was forgotten. He lifted his hand closer to examine it. The surface of the gauntlet was etched with intricate patterns that caught tiny sparks of light as he turned it. It was surprisingly light, but it didn't feel in any other way unusual. The sense of power that emanated from it back in the cellar seemed gone. He frowned and flexed his hand.

There was a flash below him. At the entrance to the portal, someone crouched, steadying themselves. Someone else had come through!

The person clambered up, lifting a staff. Christopher stumbled, surprised. Makena. Why had she followed? If it were to take them back, she would find that he was not a willing captive. He reached again for the bow. This time he pulled up the quiver too, swinging it on to his back and nocking an arrow to the bow string.

Makena's appearance had caused more interest than just his. Three straggling foot soldiers mounted the rubble behind her. One held a spear gingerly in front of him. Another advanced with a broken thing that might have once been a pickaxe. The third looked like he was at least used to holding a weapon, his sword well balanced in his hand.

On the other side, a group of men turned from where they'd been rifling through the bodies. One at the front muttered something. They began to move towards her. Ahead a soldier swung his crossbow to point at her.

Christopher angled his bow at the man. Whether she was here to take him back or not, the people he was fighting were about to fight her. That made her his ally, at least temporarily. He loosed the bowstring. The arrow flew straight towards the crossbowman.

It never hit. Makena raised her staff high into the air. A wave of black energy flew out in all directions. It struck the arrow mid-flight, enveloping it in darkness. It caught the three men behind her, knocking them to the floor. It scattered the seven ruffians advancing towards her, lifting two of them off their feet. A clap of thunder rolled across the castle grounds.

Christopher ducked, just too late to fully escape the blast. The force slammed into him. He was blown off his feet. He lifted his arms to protect his fall.

He landed on something soft, though the impact still knocked the breath from his body. He looked and recoiled. He had fallen on the body of the boy whose bow he had taken. Horrified, he scrambled back, then twisted on to his front and got up.

A thought grew bright in his mind. That weapon might well turn the tide of this battle! Ignoring the urge to lie and get his breath back, he stumbled towards the woman, a sudden and fierce hope in his heart.

'There's Christopher, too!' Sama jumped from foot to foot, pointing with one hand and pulling at Eleila with the other. 'Come on, we have to get to them!'

They were a good way from the keep. Since Eleila and Bediviere had brought her up to the battlements, they had managed to move along without any more encounters. They had kept low, moving quietly. Eleila had touched her shoulder, urging her to sneak.

Sama was more than happy to sneak. Besides being good at it, she understood they were just three. The noises from below sounded like many more. Staying quiet to avoid a fight seemed like the best option. Until that is, she noticed the flash of light at the gatehouse.

Eleila was already staring in the direction Sama had pointed, her mouth slightly open. Through the smoke of the burning buildings it was still possible to make out the mound where the portal was. Makena stood atop it, brandishing her staff. One of the men she had felled clambered up to his knees. She gestured with the staff again. A small ball of black, the size of a fist, shot across the space between them and smashed into him. He fell and was still.

Others were circling again. They were keeping a careful distance now. A short way away, a spearman lifted his spear and made to throw it. Before he could, an arrow slammed into him and he fell off to the side. Sama glanced back in the direction of the arrow. Christopher stood, fitting another missile to a bow in his hands.

'Wow!' Sama said. 'When did he learn to do that?'

'The woman.' Bediviere stepped over a body. 'That staff she has. That's magic!'

Eleila nodded. 'Why are they not moving?'

It was true. Christopher clambered up to stand at Makena's side. They scanned the area, covering one another and picking off the occasional assailant who got the stomach to move closer.

'I don't know,' Sama frowned. 'But they can't stay there. Sooner or later they'll get hit with something.' She stepped forward and waved her hands. 'Christopher!' she shouted as loud as she could.

'Quiet girl! Do you want to remind the world we are here?' Bediviere growled.

It was too late. A moment later, a head appeared from the stairwell immediately behind them.

'Damn!' Bediviere spat. He lifted his crossbow and fired a bolt at the soldier.

The soldier disappeared down inside. Before they could move though, two more appeared. They rushed up on to the stone walkway and began towards them. More followed. Suddenly the battlements were getting crowded.

'Bugger! Sorry!' Sama said. 'Too late now. They're coming, so you better get ready for them.'

She turned back to Christopher and Makena, her heart pounding. 'Hey!'

'I cannot, Christopher.' Makena's eyes darted back and forth, scanning for the next sign of movement. Sweat beads ran down the dark skin of her forehead. 'I'm not here to fight your battle. I have to protect the portal.' She shot a look at him. 'None of this is real. Back through there is very real, and in real danger.'

A man's head popped up behind a heap of rubble. Christopher loosed an arrow towards him. The man ducked before the arrow reached him.

'That's what I thought, too.' Christopher pulled another arrow from his quiver. 'I was wrong.'

He glanced around, looking for more potential assailants. Suddenly, out of the corner of his eye, he noticed movement. He glanced up. The figure was immediately recognisable.

'Look! There's Sama!'

Sama was waving at him frantically. She was shouting too, not that he could hear her. By her side, Eleila and Bediviere tensed, preparing to take on a band of soldiers running towards them.

He gasped. 'They're in trouble.'

Makena shot a look over. 'I can't help her. She's too far away. I have to stay by the portal.'

He waved back at Sama. She jumped up and down immediately, doubling her waving. She turned to Eleila and said something. Eleila ignored her, focusing on the men ahead of her.

She pushed Sama back, further out of the way from the advancing soldiers, then stepped towards them, lifting her sword. She caught the first one, blocking his path. Swords clashed against one another, glinting in the distance.

Bediviere struck another with his war hammer. The man fell from the battlements, his arms limp. He disappeared down beyond Christopher's sight.

More were clambering out of the stairwell. They outnumbered his friends three to one. Christopher pulled his bowstring and sent an arrow flying in an arc. It landed amongst the attackers but if it found purchase, he couldn't tell.

Makena looked up at the battlements. 'They won't hold against those numbers for long.' She looked back down, scanning the area. Her face was pinched with torn emotions. She shot a look at Christopher. 'You came to help them. Go!'

On the battlements, Sama bent to the floor and struggled to pick up a sword clearly too heavy for her.

Christopher nodded. Makena was right. If she wouldn't help, he still came here for a reason. He started to run towards the battlements.

Bediviere stepped back again. Sama yelled with frustration. The mass of swordsmen ahead was pushing them back step by step. For every one Eleila or Bediviere killed, another pushed forward to take their place.

Sama could see what the soldiers were doing. In a few paces more they would have forced them to a wider part of the battlements, where they would be no longer forced to fight just two abreast. Then their superior numbers would become a real advantage.

Eleila grunted and stumbled back another step. Sama heaved her sword in between Bediviere and Eleila. It sank into something, catching and nearly twisting out of her hand. She pulled at it, staggering. In front of her companions, another swordsman tumbled to the side and fell from the battlements.

It was no use. Bediviere and Eleila both gave more ground. Sama tried again to find a place to thrust the big sword through, but they were moving too fast. She would probably do more harm than good if she got a thrust wrong.

Suddenly the crenellations to the left were further away. The swordsmen had forced them far enough. Immediately one of them jumped out into the wider space. Now it was three against two.

Sama stumbled over to the left to meet him. He stared down at her, a roar on his lips. He lifted his sword with thick arms covered with coarse red hair, then drove it down. She dropped her own sword and sprang back out of the way. His swing hit the stones where she'd been with a clang.

She saw her chance. Before he could lift the sword, she rushed in, standing on its tip to stop him lifting it. She balled her hand into a fist. If she could break one nose today, she could certainly break another. She punched with all her strength.

The man caught her fist in his free hand, before it reached his face and twisted it violently. Sama screamed, losing her balance. She slammed into the battlement wall. Her head bashed painfully against the stone. Her vision swam. Her foot slipped off the point of his sword.

'*How can he move that so quickly?*' Sama's thought came, disjointed from the danger, even as the sword rose, menacing and close. She pulled back, knowing she should twist out of his way, but his grip was strong and the blow to her head had been hard.

His eyes were so very blue. But his pupils were tiny black dots, pinpricks of anger. He stabbed his sword forwards, catching her on the top of her chest. Sama glanced down. The sword point slipped up and disappeared into her left shoulder. There was an odd gurgling noise. Sama suddenly realised the sound was coming from her. Her legs went to jelly. She slid down to the floor.

Beside her, Eleila shouted out something, but the words were lost to her in a wave of pain and nausea. The man pulled his sword out and drew it up again to swing.

This time Sama knew she would not be able to dodge.

Christopher saw Sama fall as he was halfway across the courtyard. His way had been unbarred. A few arrows had whistled near him, but none so close as to be a concern. All the fighting had moved on from this area to the keep, the gatehouse or the battlements.

From where he was, he saw the look of shock on Sama's face. This wasn't supposed to happen to her. She was the heroine of her stories, getting out of the worst situations by the skin of her teeth.

He felt it as the man raised his sword. A rushing in his ears, a tingling of his skin. A white hot anger that threatened to blot out senses. Anger like the anger he had felt when he beat Daniel Corbyne on the rugby pitch. But there was something more, too.

It all happened in an instant. His anger flowered from deep within. His mind shouted that no one should be allowed to hurt Sama.

His hand inside Winter's Grasp began to tingle.

Suddenly, quite separate from his anguish, he was acutely aware of the gauntlet on his hand. As if it were reminding him it was there. As if it recognised his feelings.

The stories the false Bailey had told him flashed into his head. Then that first time he had tried to use it. The gauntlet wasn't supposed to open worlds. It was meant to help him.

Hoping against hope, Christopher thrust his arm forward towards the battlements and pulled.

Christopher's feet lifted from the ground. He gasped. Eyes wide, he flew up, straight and sure like the arrows he fired. Or rather, the gauntlet flew, carrying him with it. He whistled through the air, hair blown flat to his head.

He was flying! Though it wasn't very controlled. In Winter's Grasp, he balled his hand into a fist, the muscles of his arm protesting against the strain. He hurtled towards the battlements, suddenly wondering how he would stop.

The man just had time to turn his head, distracted from the blow he was about to give by the blur speeding towards him. Then Christopher smashed into him.

The gauntlet struck him under the side of his head. Whether it felt light to wear and looked fragile and delicate, when it hit it was pure steel. The man's head snapped back with a crack, his legs lifted from the floor, the force of the blow knocking him clean over the battlements.

Christopher screwed his eyes shut. There was nothing between him and the hard stone now. The impact would surely break his neck.

Then at the last minute, his velocity slowed. The gauntlet seemed to flip, turning his body so his feet were on the flagstones. He still stumbled as they landed, falling forward and hitting the nearest crenellation with his side. Yet even that was softer than his speed deserved. As though Winter's Grasp had controlled his landing, even as he had made a hash of it.

Christopher turned and scrambled up. Eleila and Bediviere still gave ground. The swordsmen, though their numbers had thinned, were still eight strong and coming on hard.

Christopher thrust out with Winter's Grasp again. This time he reached along the battlements, focusing on a point beyond the swordsmen. He pulled again.

He whizzed along the length of the battlements close to the outer wall, smashing into the men and knocking five over the side. Again, Winter's Grasp slowed him, swinging his feet to a position he could place them on the ground.

It was easier this time. He didn't stumble. Instead, he swung around and pulled the bow over his head. He grabbed an arrow from his quiver and loosed it at the back of the man fighting Bediviere. The man's shoulders arched in pain. Bediviere smashed him with a mailed fist and he fell.

Eleila took on another. She dropped him quickly with a stroke from his hip to his shoulder.

The last man stared dumfounded at the space where his companions had been seconds before. Eleila raised her sword and pushed at him with it. Brought back to his senses, he raised his own and made a half-hearted attempt to fight her. The battle had gone out of him.

Christopher nocked another arrow, training it on the man. Before he could fire, the man turned and ran towards the steps. Christopher lowered the bow, unflexing the string. The man disappeared below.

Sama was white. Far too white. She leaned against the battlements in a half sitting position. The front of her shirt almost entirely red with blood. Christopher forced himself to smile down at her.

She looked up at him with big scared eyes. 'You didn't tell me you could do that,' she said quietly, trying to smile back. Her voice was strained with pain.

Eleila bent down next to them. 'Christopher,' she said, her eyes glancing warily at Winter's Grasp. 'Let me see.'

'Stay still,' Christopher said to Sama, moving off to the side. His hands balled into fists. It couldn't be serious. Not Sama.

Eleila pulled back her shirt. Blood was pumping out of a deep gash in her shoulder in regular waves. It ran down in rivulets and soaked into her clothing.

Eleila pursed her lips. 'There's nothing we can do here. We need to get her to the keep.'

Bediviere leaned over the top of them. 'Moving her will not be good.'

'Well, we have to!' Christopher snapped. He could feel tears of worry stinging his eyes. She was getting paler.

'I'm sorry, boy,' Bediviere said. 'We must save the sword. No one of us is more important than that.'

Eleila looked at him. 'Can you get her away with … that?' She nodded at Winter's Grasp.

Sama smiled. 'If I shouldn't be moved, I don't think going flying would be a

TO SAVE THE SWORD

good idea,' she said in a small voice. 'It does look like it would have been fun, though.'

'Well, we have to do something!' Christopher shouted. 'I can get someone to help, bring them back here.' He looked desperately at Eleila. 'A healer. Where can I find a healer?'

'Stay here with her,' Eleila said gently. 'I'll try and find someone in the keep. I promise.' She rose to go, her face a mask.

'Wait!' Sama whispered. 'Look.'

Eleila turned to where the girl was pointing and gasped. Worry clutched at her heart. She instinctively checked that no one could see her face. The Keep had opened its doors. Someone was coming out.

Fifteen men on horseback galloped out of the Keep's gates, fully armoured and at charging speed. They were formed into a triangle. The knight at the front rode a great warhorse. Swinging his battle axe, he spearheaded the charge. Behind him, two rode with long pikes, held low, ready to strike at the heads of the masses in front of them. Three more rode behind on lighter horses, bows strung with arrows. Four more behind them, swords at the ready. Then came the final five, bringing up the rear.

Kay rode in the centre of the last five, holding The Sword in the Stone aloft. His armour glittered in the cold winter sun. He wore a steel helmet that had a crown built into its design.

'They are trying to charge through.' Bediviere's voice was quiet, resigned. 'They will fail.'

Eleila gripped hard at her sword. The forces ranged outside the Keep against them were still at least a thousand men. Mordred's knights were wheeling in, freeing themselves from the fights they were in. Yet they were still spread across the field of battle.

The Stahlhelme were very few in number. They too were dotted around the field. Perhaps a concerted charge might break through. Surely it had some hope?

Kay's charge broke through the first ranks at full pelt. In seconds they were forty deep into massed throng.

Then Eleila understood.

A Stahlhelme off to the left fired his gun. Two knights at the front, along with their horses and a good few foot soldiers before them, were blown to the side in a spray of red.

Another Stahlhelme rushed in closer, crossing the distance in no time by cleaving a path through friend and foe in its way. Once close, it swung the blade on the barrel of its gun, breaking the pike of another rider in two. It hooked the knight himself on to the end of the blade, then flipped him from his saddle over its head. The knight disappeared into the crowd.

The knights with bows were quick to react, concentrating their arrows on the nearest Stahlhelme. Shafts slammed into him. He went down. Even as he did, another grew near and fired with his rifle.

The charge had been stopped in its tracks. The remaining Stahlhelme waded towards it, clearing paths with their blades. Mordred's knights galloped in. Foot soldiers pressed forward. The route that Kay and his companions had taken was fast becoming the most densely packed on the battle field.

'Clear the path,' Sama's voice whispered from the floor beside her. Eleila looked down.

Christopher knelt by her. 'What?'

'Tell Makena to blow a path through them,' Sama spoke with effort. 'She can do it. Then they can escape.'

'I can't leave you,' Christopher said. His eyes were wet.

Sama reached forward, her hand dropping weakly on to his. 'Listen, stupid. I'm not going to die when things are this exciting.' She coughed suddenly. Her face screwed up with pain.

'Sama ...' he started, his words drying up.

She looked back at him. 'The sooner that this battle is done, the sooner we can find somewhere to rest. Stop being such a baby and go.'

Eleila's heart pounded with a blossom of hope. 'She's right.'

Bediviere pushed to his feet. 'Eleila. Come on!' He ran towards the stairwell.

'Go,' Sama said. 'Both of you.'

Christopher sighed and reached out with the gauntlet, flying in an arrow straight line towards the black woman at the gatehouse.

Eleila glanced at the girl. 'We'll be back,' she said, wondering if that were a lie. Then she turned and ran after Bediviere.

Christopher landed next to Makena, Sama's pinched face still stared at him in his mind's eye, exasperated with him through her pain. She had been trying to help him from the moment she climbed up the tree and jumped into his room. Could that really have only been a few days ago?

'What's happening?' Makena asked. Her eyes still scanned the area for anyone that decided this was a more interesting place to attack.

'Listen to me!' Christopher said. 'Here they don't care about you or that. They are fighting for a sword. The people with the sword are trying to escape. If we help them, the battle will follow wherever they go.'

'I won't risk leaving the portal,' Makena said immediately.

'So you've said.' Christopher was irritated. 'Just listen! They're trying to break through ahead!' He pointed over to the battle by the keep. 'Can you blast a path through to them? Sama said you could!'

Makena looked at him. 'That will bring the whole lot this way.'

Christopher stared straight at her. 'Sama is hurt. She's losing blood. We can't help her whilst this is going on.'

Makena frowned. 'Bad?'

'I think so, yes.' Christopher nodded. He had seen the way Makena had looked at Sama. There was a bond there.

'If I have to I'll bring the whole gatehouse down.'

'I don't care!' he shouted. 'Just help!'

Makena narrowed her eyes and struck out with her staff. A great glut of black energy erupted out, heading straight for the keep. It tore through the armies ahead. It was as though an iron girder had been forced width ways through their numbers. Knight and horse, foot soldier and peasant, all were smashed to the ground. A path about twelve men wide cut into the mass, a good three hundred yards. Around the edges, men dashed away, widening the path further.

It was not quite distant enough though. Still troops blocked Kay's way.

'Again!' Christopher shouted, straining his eyes to see Kay's knights.

Makena sent forth another blast. It slammed down the space the first had gouged and smashed into the warriors beyond.

Now Christopher could see horses wheeling around. There! He spied the flash of Kay's bright armour. The way was free.

'Here!' Makena said, reaching into her pocket and tossing something to Christopher. 'For Sama. Pour the ointment on to the wound. It will help.'

Christopher nodded. 'Thank you!' He turned and reached out with the gauntlet again.

It took a few moments for the knights to break free after the second blast. Of the fifteen, Sama could only count four. Makena's help had come just in time.

Sama lay on the cold flagstones. She slid down as soon as Christopher had flown away. Now her companions had gone to fight she stopped trying so hard to look all right. From their expressions it hadn't been working that well, anyway. She wasn't any use to them now.

That was what hurt the most. The pain she could bear if she stayed very still. She'd felt worse when she had broken her ribs falling out of a tree when she was younger. It was the fact she wasn't able to do anything that really bothered her.

There was a noise. Christopher landed next to her again.

'She said to put this on,' he said awkwardly, showing her a little bottle in his left hand. 'I need to ...'

Sama nodded and he pulled her shirt back. He unstoppered the bottle and moved to pour it over the wound.

'They are away!' Sama smiled as the four knights galloped down the path Makena had cleared, jumping over the bodies of the soldiers in the way. 'It worked.'

As the liquid hit, she gasped out loud. Now that was real pain. The wound burned white hot. She screwed her eyes up against its fire. After a moment the pain ebbed back to something she could deal with. She glanced up at Christopher's face.

'Don't look so worried.' She forced a smile.

His face was nearly as white as she imagined her own to be. She nodded down to the battlefield. 'Look, Christopher.'

Reluctantly, he tore his gaze away. Away from his eyes, her smile fell again. She looked out at the battle too. The four knights were nearly by Makena. At least Christopher's friends would escape.

Then she saw the Stahlhelme.

They very nearly made it. As Eleila burst from the stairwell, running full pelt back towards the gatehouse, eyes searching desperately for a horse, she thought for a moment they would be away before she could join them. They were only a few yards from the mound where the woman stood.

One had fallen before she had reached the bottom of the stairs. Kay and two others had made it. They galloped at full pelt, angling their route to skirt around the side of the mound and into the open fields.

If they did get out there, it would still be a desperate hope they could get past what remained of Mordred's troops beyond. She pushed on. Even when they were gone, she would do her best to slow as many of the inevitable pursuers that would be on their heels.

Then the volley came.

Eleila didn't see from where, only that it came from somewhere back by the keep. There were four loud cracks in such close succession they almost seemed like one.

Eleila knew all three riders were dead before they hit the ground. Kay flew from his horse and landed at the foot of the mound. The Sword in the Stone fell from his hand and clattered over a couple of stones before stopping.

From the mass of attackers a great shout of triumph erupted. Eleila ran on, pushing herself even harder, her eyes fixed on the sword. The sword. She had to get to the sword.

The black woman lifted her staff as Eleila got closer. Her eyes narrowed, ready to attack. 'I'm with Christopher!' Eleila screamed over the noise of the attackers. She chanced a glance to her right. The massed army had turned now. Suddenly it seemed that all of them were running towards the gatehouse.

The black woman was muttering something. Eleila grew closer, only half noticing as she focused on the sword. 'Too many,' the woman was saying. 'It's too many. I have no choice.'

As Eleila reached the mount, the woman stepped away from the strange black hole at its back. She jumped down and headed the way Eleila had come. 'Get back!' she shouted, pushing Eleila.

Eleila pushed the woman's hand away. 'What are you doing?' she shouted. 'The sword!'

'Get back!' the woman cried again. 'I can't save you!'

Eleila ignored her. She bounded up to the sword, then bent and grabbed it. She shot a look forward. Her best chance was to make for the breach in the wall. Perhaps outside, she could find a horse.

Then the world exploded into night.

'She's going to collapse the tower!' Sama grabbed his hand.

Christopher felt the warmth of her hand, small in his. He felt it clench suddenly as the wave of black erupted from Makena's staff. The force smashed into the base of the remaining gatehouse tower. As if in slow motion the tower began to fall.

And Sama let go.

Eleila was framed by the black portal. She thrust the sword above her, impotently warding off the tonnes of rubble that crashed down towards her.

He heard Sama's whisper. Her voice was tiny now against the sounds of destruction. 'Go.'

Then he was flying again, Winter's Grasp stretched out before him.

He hurtled towards Eleila, willing that he would be faster than the falling rubble. He twisted his body to avoid masonry, shooting underneath it. Finally, at the last moment, he felt the solidity of Eleila's body. He gripped tight and continued on, feeling the rush as they burst through the portal entrance and out into the black.

And then they were flying through the tumbling blackness that moved them between worlds.

CHAPTER TWENTY-NINE

The Boy in Winter's Grasp

One moment the girl was standing there, sword held aloft, a last brazen act of bravery before she was crushed by the great blocks. Then there was a streak to Makena's left. Christopher's brown hair. A flash of silver from the gauntlet. And they were gone.

Makena swung her staff up. An umbrella of night flowered above her, deflecting stone blocks as if they were made of leaves. She backed away from the avalanche, watching it cover the portal.

The first stones crashing on to the portal bounced through, hurtling off into the dark. Then two larger pieces landed almost together, catching against one another and toppling into the black circle. The energy of the portal gripped them, pulling them in. Too large to fit at the same time, they were squeezed together, packing into the opening and holding fast. The storm of stone and dust above cascaded down, burying them.

Makena turned back to the keep. The horde ahead of her had frozen, lost in contemplation of the two towers' collapse. Hundreds of eyes looked past her to the great cloud of dust over her shoulders. Defender and attacker stood side by side, mesmerised by the scale of destruction.

As the roar of the collapse faded into echoes, bounced back on the coastal wind, a single cry pierced across the crowd. Atop his horse, to the far eastern side of the battle, a small man — his armour far too clean to have been used in actual combat — stood in his saddle. He screamed again. 'Destroy everything!'

At his words, the attackers remembered their purpose. From the centre of the crowd ahead, an explosion burst. A Stahlhelme firing its rifle. The air again filled with the screams and clangs of battle. The last defenders rallied into pockets of resistance, desperately trying to avoid being hacked away by the superior numbers of the enemy.

Makena gritted her teeth. She moved back to the great cloud of masonry dust and the mountain of rubble it obscured. She had to hold.

'Wait.' A gruff voice sounded at her side. The knight with one arm. 'All is lost. We must be gone.'

Makena glanced at him. 'I defend the portal.'

'That?' The worn knight nodded at the pile. 'You'll last a while, granted, but not that long. Then they will be able to take it apart at their leisure to find the sword. Better to be away and come back with force.'

'It's not the sword I care about,' Makena replied, turning.

'They do,' the knight replied, glancing at the battle. 'And when they have the castle they will be able to dig for it at their leisure. But it won't be fast. Your mountain gives us time.' He loosed a crossbow bolt at a nasty looking ruffian who had moved close to them. The man gurgled and collapsed forward on to the floor.

The knight pulled out his sword and turned to face the rabble. Some charged towards them now.

Makena pushed her staff forwards at them. A black, inky swathe of energy erupted from the end of the staff. It jetted across the courtyard and caught a group of three soldiers. They were blasted to the ground.

'You came back with Christopher,' the knight said flatly, his eyes never leaving the horde ahead. They had slowed now, wary of Makena's staff, but widened out, some running to the right and others to the left to spread out. 'The girl you came with. She needs you now.'

'Sama? Her wound?'

'Serious.' He began to back away. 'Come with me. There will be allies coming. Mordred has a lot of land to occupy and this army will be spread thin. We can take this castle back. Use the time you have given us wisely.' He stopped and looked at her again. 'Or just die.'

She had given them time. She had given time at the other end of the portal. If they won there, they would be able to set defences. If they lost … Well, it wouldn't matter anyway.

Makena sighed. She couldn't stop an army alone. 'Which way?'

It took a moment to recognise the rushing sensation that told Christopher he was being thrust between worlds again. The feeling was so similar to the rush of movement he felt when he used Winter's Grasp that by the time he did understand what was happening they were already zooming along the black tunnel.

As soon as he realised, Christopher twisted his body, gripping Eleila firmly around her waist. She held tight to him. There was something else in her hand, pressed against him, long and hard and cold. The sword.

'Christopher!' Her voice was tiny in the dark.

He couldn't concentrate on her now. They had to go back. In his mind's eye, Sama's pinched white face smiled weakly from where he had left her leaning against the battlements.

He reached with Winter's Grasp and thrust. Thrust back into the path they had come from. Resisting the energy that pulled them down. They began to slow.

Gravity intensified tenfold. The blackness around him began to tinge in grey. He thrust again. Now they began to move against the flow.

Something shot past them. Something heavy. Instinctively he dodged away, but it was already gone. He strained his eyes to see ahead. Futile.

The grey in his eyes was getting worse. His head began to swim. The tunnel felt so heavy. Another something hurtled past.

Something struck his face. It was tiny, but it sliced into his cheek. He ducked his head, squeezing his right arm tight to his ear, Winter's Grasp above him. Eleila pulled herself in closer to him.

It felt like he was trying hold the mountain's weight up with his body. He thrust again. His arm was weak now and he only managed to raise it a few inches above his head.

He was losing consciousness. He was vaguely aware of Eleila's grip around his waist loosening. He struggled to maintain his own grip on her. Her head had lolled against him. The sword slipped from her grasp and dropped down below them.

He banged up against something immobile. Instinctively he grabbed hold of it using it to stop them being dragged down. The gauntlet found purchase almost immediately. He clutched at the solid thing, hanging in the blackness.

Now they weren't moving against it, the pressure became less. Eleila stirred against him. The grey in his own vision began to lift.

'I need both hands,' he said out into the darkness. 'Can you hold on?'

'Yes.' Her voice sounded weak, but she secured her grip again.

He reached forward with his other hand and felt the thing above him. Cold. Its surface was rough, covered with tiny particles. Stone! He understood. The portal. Makena had done her work well.

'Christopher!' Eleila clambered up his body. Her mouth was by his ear. 'The sword!'

'Gone.' Christopher felt around with his free hand. The block ahead filled the portal wherever he could touch. 'It fell.'

'Fell? Where?'

There was no way through. No way to get to Sama. There was no way through. Not here. 'Down there. My world.'

He felt her shift. Her grip loosened. For a second he thought she was slipping. Then he felt her push. It was deliberate!

'What are you doing?' He let go of the rock wall with one hand and grabbed at her. 'Hold on!'

She took her hand from his waist, then gripped the arm he had around her and prised it away from her body. She dropped suddenly. Now she hung from his hand. 'The sword, Christopher. I have no choice.'

Then her grip was gone. She just wasn't there any more. He stared down into the blackness, hoping to see some glint in the gloom. Nothing.

He clutched at the rock barrier above him, renewing his efforts to feel for a way through. His search was desperate now.

The rock was solid. Christopher howled into the darkness. The portal was barred.

He looked away into the blackness, back to his own world. To Eleila and the sword. And then another face came to mind.

A gaunt face with a cruel smile framed by white hair. They'd said he was back there. They'd said he had a portal of his own. Christopher tensed as the answer came to him. If this way was barred, then that way was the only option.

Christopher took a deep breath and released his grip on the rock.

The blood had stopped flowing, at least. Sama pushed herself up into a sitting position, screwing her face up against the pain. Every movement she made felt as if someone was driving a flaming torch into her shoulder. She swallowed hard against the urge to be sick. That wouldn't do. She wouldn't be a burden to anyone.

If she stayed very still, the pain was almost manageable. Whatever had been in the salve Christopher poured on her shoulder, it helped. If she could just stay still.

The battle below had not yet reached back up here. It would not be long. Sama could see the groups of defenders that still fought grew fewer. Already, many of Mordred's men had run out of foes. Rabbles, still high on the adrenaline of the fight, began to circle the remains of the burning houses below. Soon enough some would start to climb the walls.

Then she would have to move. 'Just a few minutes more,' she said out loud, startled to hear how ragged her own voice sounded.

To the seaward side of the castle, close to the keep, a group of men found a cart of arrows. As she watched, one clambered up into it, a flaming torch in his hand. He bent and thrust the torch into the piles. Then he laughed and leapt from the cart.

Flames began to lick out from the arrows. The men gathered behind it and pushed it, rolling it down a slight incline towards a stone outhouse. It trundled at first, then began to roll of its own accord. The men cheered as the cart rolled away. It picked up speed, veering with the incline and rolled on past the outhouse. Then it tumbled over the cliff and down on to the rocks below.

Further across, a larger group had broken through into the keep. The doors had never been properly shut after those knights had made their charge for freedom.

A Stahlhelme led the destruction. Sama saw it reach in through the entrance and grab at something. A screaming woman was flung over the crowd, up and out of the keep, arms flailing. She landed hard in between more fighters. Sama winced, glad to have her view obscured by so many warriors.

Footsteps from the stairwell. Sama tensed. This was it! The horde had returned to the battlements.

She grabbed at a crenellation with her right hand and hauled herself up. The pain was excruciating. Just a few feet away, by a soldier's body, was a short sword. It was much more her size than the beast she had tried to use.

If she could at least get that, she would be able to defend herself. She focused on it, fighting to ignore the pain. Once she had managed to stand, she stumbled forward.

Her legs gave out after the first step. She fell, closer to the sword for all the good it would do. She at least managed to twist to take the brunt of the impact with her right shoulder, but the shock still jarred across her whole body. This time she could not hold back the nausea. She rolled over on her right shoulder to face down and vomited.

This was it, she thought as the shock receded. This would be where she died. No heroic death. No glory that her friends and family would talk about in hushed tones. Just a girl too weak to fight, covered in vomit and blood, all alone and far away from the people she loved. The realisation was suddenly as intense as the pain. Suddenly Sama didn't want adventure anymore.

The footsteps were here now. They stopped at her head. She pushed to look up. If she had to die here she would bloody well look it in the face, even if there would be no one who knew she had.

'Sama.' Makena's voice above her. Sama's heart leapt.

There were hands on her waist, gently turning her, careful to roll her over her right side. Makena's face looked down at her, eyes failing to hide her concern.

Beside her, Bediviere fitted a new bolt to his crossbow. Sama dimly wondered how much harder that must be with only one arm. The gruff knight was practiced though. He glanced across. 'We can follow the battlements and get to the keep from here. The side drawbridge.'

'They've just got into the keep,' Sama whispered up at him. She wasn't sure if he had heard until he spoke.

'No matter. If we are fast they'll still be ransacking the main hall. There's another way out. It leads from the upper levels,' he said, eyes scanning the route ahead. 'But we need to move now.'

'Sama.' Makena spoke softly. 'I can make things easier, but you'll need to use all your strength to move. Can you do it?'

Sama grinned as bravely as she could. 'It hardly hurts,' she lied. 'That potion that Christopher gave me has made it better.'

Makena nodded. 'Well, if anyone can do it, it's you, sweet. Hold still a moment.'

Makena touched the end of the staff to Sama's shoulder as gently as she could. Tendrils of black fluttered out from the staff, wrapping around Sama's shoulder and stretching across her chest. They slipped under her right arm, returning to close on themselves, forming a loose black stocking over her upper body. They constricted around her.

Despite her best effort, Sama cried out.

'Be strong, sweet. It must needs be tight to protect the wound,' Makena said. 'Once it is done you will find moving much easier.'

As the constricting stopped, the fire began to ebb away. Sama lay back and closed her eyes, taking in short, shallow breaths. That was all the tightness of the dressing would allow.

'Now.' Makena placed a hand beneath her right armpit and hauled her into a sitting position. 'We must go.'

The pain had dropped to a constant level, but it was no worse when moving than it was when still. Sama nodded and, with Makena's aid, pushed herself up once again on to weak legs.

'Ok. We can go,' she whispered.

The Master skirted around the column he had been sheltering behind and sprinted full pelt down the hall. The end of the hallway was in sight now. As yet, he had seen no sign of another entrance to a portal.

Ahead, a group of four Stahlhelme had taken cover behind some upturned tables. They fired at will, keeping McCloud's men low and useless. To the left, the other group advanced.

The Master slid to a halt, ducking behind the Stahlhelme. He popped his head up and looked down the hall. At the end was a doorway. The door was closed. Light spilled from its edges, framing it.

'You! Down there!' the Master barked at the nearest beast.

To its credit, it didn't even hesitate. Perhaps he had been wrong when he saw rebellion in the other. It pushed to its feet and lumbered down the hall. The air around the tables filled with cordite as the remaining three fired deafening volleys of covering shots.

The remaining group of McCloud's men had taken up position about thirty feet to the left of the doorway in a narrow brick guardhouse. They were badly outgunned. The guardhouse, whilst holding, had not been built to withstand the power of the Stahlhelme rifles. In a number of places the brickwork had been blown inwards. The guardhouse was covered in holes. With each new volley more holes appeared. Soon the holes would be in men again.

The Stahlhelme he had ordered reached the door. It angled its gun at the lock and blew it in. The door swung open and it disappeared inside.

The other group had reached a column. They dropped flat and began to fire at the guardhouse. The Master smiled and shouted to the three in front of him, 'Forward!'

'Levert!' Christopher shouted at the slight man. 'It's me! Christopher Flyte!'

At their appearance through the portal, Levert had dived to the cupboard, pulling out what looked like a walking stick. Christopher burst across and grabbed the man before he could lift it, slamming him in the chest. He'd seen what that staff of Makena's could do. He wasn't taking any chances.

Levert coughed violently but raised his hand, nodding. 'Christopher? You came back.' He frowned, staring into the void. 'Where's Makena?'

'Back there. She blocked the other end.' The noises of fighting were distinct outside the cellar room. Christopher could hear the sound of distant gunshots.

'Blocked?' Levert said, picking up on his words. 'How?'

'Levert. Listen to me!' Christopher grabbed his starched shirt collar and shook him. 'Who's here?'

Levert stared blankly at him. 'They told me to stay here.'

Eleila bent and picked something from the floor. 'Christopher, look. The sword.'

She lifted it. Its journey through the portal didn't seem to have done it any harm. 'We must go back.' She glanced around the room, eyes uncertain. 'We shouldn't be here.'

'We can't go that way.' Christopher nodded.

Another explosion from outside the door. A rifle boom, sounding like the ones the Stahlhelme used. Christopher let go of Levert's collars, pushing him to one side. Levert scuttled to his cupboard.

'There's another man,' Christopher said, glancing at Eleila. 'He's the key to all this. He has a key that will open the way back for you. I think he's here.'

She frowned. 'Out there? Where the fighting is?'

'I imagine so.'

'Of course. Where else would he be?' Eleila grumbled. She shook her head, then strode towards the door. 'Come on, then.'

He placed a hand on her shoulder. 'Those are the sounds of rifles. You've got a sword.' To make the point, he lifted Winter's Grasp up to their eye level.

Eleila raised an eyebrow. 'And now that makes you in charge, does it?'

'No.' Christopher pushed in front of her, a little more roughly than he had intended. 'But can we agree I might know a bit more about here than you do? Or at least, for once, save the bickering until after the fight?'

'Fine.' She gestured with the sword, thin lipped. 'Be my guest.'

Christopher pulled open the cellar door, ignoring a sudden flare of irritation with her. There really didn't seem to be a single situation where she couldn't find a way to disagree with him. He inched his head out into the corridor.

On one side a dark passage led off into nothingness. He glanced down the other way.

A great hulking shape was advancing, almost filling the corridor. Behind it, light shone, all but obscured by its bulk. The shape grunted and lifted something up. What little light there was caught its end. Black gun metal with a long blade attached.

From the end of the pole axe, a great explosion of fire accompanied the crack of a shot. The corridor wall erupted with stone dust. Christopher ducked back inside the door.

Despite himself, he smiled. ' Stahlhelme.'

Eleila furrowed her eyebrows. 'Well, you seem delighted by that.'

'Don't you see?' he said, pulling the bow from his back. 'That means he must be here.'

He ducked out into the corridor, throwing himself across to the other side. Ahead, the Stahlhelme roared and adjusted its rifle. Before it could fire, Christopher reached out with Winter's Grasp.

He grabbed low, propelling himself like a streak along the corridor, leaning back as he did so to slide down between the feet of the mighty beast. The Stahlhelme towered above him. Its growl sounded almost surprised. It cast its beady eyes left and right searching for the target that had so suddenly slipped from its view.

Christopher fitted an arrow into his bow and fired up, aiming for the exposed stretch of neck just under its chin. The arrow hit true, cutting off the beast's growl instantly. The Stahlhelme tottered, then staggered forwards. For a moment it looked as though it would take another step, but instead its weight pitched forward and it toppled down. Christopher slipped out through its legs, heart pounding with relief.

At the end of the passage was a doorway. The door had been ripped from its hinges, splintering the frame. He jumped to his feet and ran the rest of the way. He rested a hand on the frame, sucking in two sharp breaths, one after the other.

He dared not look back at the creature behind him, dare not contemplate what he had just done or the thought would freeze him to the spot. The tiny voice in the back of his head told him quite plainly this wasn't at all the sort of thing he did. He should wait for Eleila and be far more careful.

'Shut up!' he said to the voice. Listening to it would not help Sama.

The room ahead confused him somewhat. If anything it looked like a children's hospital ward. Not what he was expecting at all. He stepped through. It didn't matter what it was now.

On the other side was another doorway. This one still had a door, though it was wide open and the lock was smashed in.

The gunshots were coming from the room beyond.

There were footsteps behind. 'Christopher!'

He glanced back. Eleila sprinted towards him, the sword in her hand.

'This way!' he shouted over his shoulder and began to run across the room to the open doorway.

The far group of Stahlhelme concentrated their fire. The Master ducked behind the group he was with. This would be the last time they'd need to shelter. They were close enough now. The last defence would be breached.

As if on cue, the far group fired again. The side of the guardhouse collapsed.

The Stahlhelme burst forward. The first reached the breach and ducked inside, firing its rifle. The other three rushed through the hole.

At the other end, McCloud's men burst out of the doorway. They tripped over one another in their haste to escape. Inside echoed with more screams.

'Attack!' the Master shouted.

The Stahlhelme in front of him surged ahead. There were twenty yards to cover. Whether there would be anyone to kill when they got there was debatable.

The Master ducked behind a pillar. Better that his troops should finish them off than get caught in the battle at this final juncture. He popped his head out to watch.

The four erupted from the guardhouse door after the men. The first wheeled his pole axe around with terrifying speed. Two of the men stopped and turned to face him. It was terribly heroic. The Master's mouth curled into a smile. That didn't change how pointless it was.

One wore a three-piece suit. He pointed a short barrelled pistol up at the beast, sheer terror on his face. He squeezed the trigger over and over again, blasting out bullet after bullet. The Stahlhelme was taking no notice at all.

The other, an older man with a tufty brown beard, fired his rifle, missing. He squeezed the trigger again, but nothing came out. Dropping the empty weapon, he fumbled for his own pistol.

The Stahlhelme swung back its pole axe, catching both men. The bearded man took the brunt. The weapon sliced through him as though he were butter. It lodged in the side of the second man. The Stahlhelme growled and kicked the man from the blade into a still heap on the floor.

Other defenders, no more than eight survivors now, raced towards the door in the wall. Three more fell in quick succession, blasted by a volley from the beasts.

Suddenly at the back of the survivors, the Master noticed a familiar face. That moustached man had been dogging his steps since Alton. The man stopped. Now he had space he looked back to the Stahlhelme, then swung his huge coat out behind him. The air around the coat shimmered.

A Stahlhelme fired directly at the man. The bullet glanced off the shimmer around the coat and fell uselessly to the floor. The beast roared and ran on.

The man dropped one hand. The shimmer on that side disappeared. He leaned out and fired shots down the hall.

This was too good an opportunity to miss. The man had been nothing but an irritation since the moment he had appeared. It would be a sweet justice. The Master swung his own pistol up and narrowed in on the man's exposed head.

In the corner of his eye there was a sudden glint of silver. His attention captured, he glanced in the direction of the flash. He gasped.

Christopher Flyte flew towards the Stahlhelme with wide, angry eyes, one hand stretched out in front of him.

The hand was encased in an ornate silver gauntlet.

Christopher smashed into the Stahlhelm's legs. As he'd flown forward, four of them had been in a perfect arc. He focused on their legs, imagining toppling them like dominos.

In the second it took to fly across the distance, they had moved. Only two remained in his arc of attack. He hit the first with Winter's Grasp itself. The gauntlet took most of the impact. There was a sickening crack of bone. The beast screamed and collapsed.

He hit the second. This time the gauntlet spun the creature to the side, into his path. Christopher smashed into its legs with his shoulder. It still toppled downwards, but his shoulder flashed with pain.

He landed in a heap on the flagstones, face down. Ignoring the shock he flipped around on to his back.

The third and fourth had got further than their companions. The third turned back, its face almost a look of shock at its fallen comrades. It stared at Christopher and roared.

He pulled another arrow from the quiver, fixed it to his bow and fired. The arrow struck the thick leather chinstrap of the beast's helmet. Though it passed through, it was slowed enough for the arrowhead to barely enter its flesh. That just made it angry.

It stormed towards Christopher, then lifted a boot and drove it down towards him. He twisted his legs back. The boot smashed the floor with a thud. The Stahlhelme leaned forward and roared again, showering him with spittle. It flipped its rifle around so the pole axe blade faced him.

Behind it, the fourth had turned too. Further back, the one he had hit with his shoulder was struggling to stand.

There was a loud report. A volley of rifles. The roar of the beast in front of him turned into a scream. It arched its back. Little pinpricks of light began to appear all over its body.

Christopher scrambled away. From the side door in the wall, the remaining defenders had turned. They were aiming their weapons again, concentrating their fire on one beast at a time. They fired again. The creature closest to them dropped to its knees, momentarily blocking its companions.

Christopher pulled out another arrow. If he could just kill another then the men at the door had a chance. Ahead, John Braddock pointed at another Stahlhelme. The men turned.

From the corner of his eye, Christopher noticed movement. It was out to the side, away from the action. He glanced across. If the movement were more enemies, then the brief advantage he had created would be lost.

He gasped. Nestled by a pillar to observe the fighting, looking as surprised as Christopher felt he must, was the gaunt man.

They stared at each other.

Christopher's throat constricted with anger. The Stahlhelme were forgotten in an instant. His hand tightened on the bow. He wrenched it up and pointed it at the man.

He wasn't scary now. He wasn't the apparition hovering above him on the battlements, surrounded by a haze of blue. He was just a man, cowering by a pillar until his minions had done his dirty work for him.

Christopher let the arrow fly.

The man was fast. He dived out of the way, rolling on the floor. He righted himself immediately, coming up into a crouch. He stared back at Christopher, his eyes wide.

Those eyes, Christopher thought suddenly. They were so dark. Yet even from this distance there was something recognisable about them. Something behind them. The grey eyes. Sama had told the truth. It had seemed so hard to believe, but then, hadn't everything?

The man behind those eyes was the same man behind Bailey's eyes. 'You!' Christopher accused.

The gaunt man frowned. He sprang to his feet. Then he took off at a sprint into the vast hall beyond.

'No!' Christopher shouted and jumped to his own feet. He lifted Winter's Grasp, ready to grasp out and cover the distance between them. Before he could, he was lifted off his feet and in the air.

For the briefest moment he wondered if this was another effect of Winter's Grasp. Then he felt the hot angry breath of the Stahlhelme.

Makena thrust with her staff. The iron bound door across the little drawbridge shattered into splinters of metal and wood.

Bediviere took the lead. They crossed the drawbridge to the upper level.

Sama reached out to her again, glad of the woman's support. She would not have managed the halting walk along the top of the battlements without the older woman. She gritted her teeth and tried to up her pace, leaning even more heavily on Makena, moaning involuntarily against the effort.

Makena glanced at her. 'Sama?'

Sama shook her head. 'Come on.' She pushed on.

Below, the main hall of the keep was mobbed with looters, elbow to elbow. They ripped fine tapestries from the wall. They rifled through chests. Others flowed in from a side door, laden with silver goblets and plates. In the centre of the room, two men fought over an ornate shield, banging into their companions carelessly in their desire to win the prize for themselves.

Bediviere beckoned, then pointed along the gallery to the far corner. There a stone archway led to a spiral staircase. They sneaked across the gallery.

More of the horde flowed in below. Sama glanced down. The main doors of the keep were open. Any in the crowd who glanced up from their greed would see them.

One head reached high above the others. A Stahlhelme. Denied more fighting it seemed almost placid amongst the frenzy of greed. It appeared to have no interest in the spoils of war. Its tusks dripped with blood. It watched the men with dull eyes.

Until it looked up.

It saw them on the gallery and roared, eyes suddenly bright again. It surged forward, throwing men out of its way in its desire to get to more fighting.

'Makena!' Sama shouted.

Makena thrust Sama ahead of her, sending her sprawling through the archway. The black dressing did nothing to protect her from the impact. Pain shocked through her again.

Had the Stahlhelme simply been a man, perhaps its shout would have been lost in the clamour. Nothing could drown out its blood lust. It raised its rifle and fired towards the upper gallery. Others stopped, looking for its quarry. There were more shouts. Then the thudding of boots.

Makena pulled Sama up again. A voice was in Sama's ear, distant through the pain, words impossible to understand, but sentiment clear: run! Then Sama was stumbling again, up over stone stairs, losing her footing with almost every step

Slowly, at least that was how it seemed, Sama's senses came back. The pain was receding to a manageable level. Now Bediviere was pulling her up the steps. Behind, Makena supported her, an arm back around her waist. Sama concentrated on just lifting each foot high enough to make the next step.

Behind them, the thudding grew louder. Their pursuers were gaining ground.

'I can hold them,' Makena shouted to Bediviere. 'Can you take her?'

Before he could answer, two arrows clacked against the wall by Makena's head. She ducked and pushed Sama harder up the steps.

'Here!' Bediviere kicked open a doorway in the side wall. 'Quick.'

Sama was manhandled through and dropped into a soft armchair. She gasped and clutched at the arm of the chair, fighting the pain of impact.

'The door!' Bediviere shouted at Makena and disappeared out of Sama's vision.

Makena forced the door shut. Behind it was a sizable wooden door beam. She slipped it into place, barring the entrance. 'That won't hold them for long. As soon as the big ones gets here, he'll be able to blow a hole through ...' Makena's eyes went wide.

Despite the pain, Sama tried to twist around to see what she was looking at. Then Makena was at her side, pulling her up. She was swung around and pushed forward.

The room was an ornate bedroom. In the centre of the main wall was an enormous empty fireplace. The whole of its back slid to one side. Behind the panel, a ladder dropped into darkness.

There was a crash on the barred door. Their pursuers had reached the other side.

Bediviere moved off to the far corner. He wrenched open another door. 'That may confuse them.'

He ducked back. 'The door only needs to hold long enough for us to get through here and close it behind us. Down now. This leads to the cliffs.'

The Stahlhelme struggled with the stairs. It wasn't built for small, tight spaces. By the time it reached the doorway leading into the ornate bedroom, the door had already been thoroughly smashed in.

It grunted and squeezed again. One arm was briefly trapped behind it at an awkward angle. Small hands pushed at its rump. It struggled a moment more and then it was through.

It strode into the centre of the room. A door on the far side was open. Its black eyes narrowed. Something felt wrong. The smell it had been chasing since it saw the trio running on the balcony above it didn't go that way.

Three men ducked around it, giving it a deliberately wide berth and disappeared through the open doorway.

The smell was one of pain and blood, of fear and sweat and something else, something like the night. It glanced around, its face forming a bestial version of a frown.

Its attention fixed on the fireplace. That was where the scent went. It growled, raised its great pole axe and began to pound against the back wall of the fireplace.

Another group of men stopped, watching it for a moment, wondering if the great beast had lost what little mind it had. Then what looked to be stone cracked with a small cloud of white plaster. The beast struck again and a small hole appeared.

One of the men gave a shout of triumph and jumped into the fireplace, lifting his sword with both hands and stabbing at the hole the beast had started. A moment later another joined in.

For a short time man and Stahlhelme worked together. Then, once the hole was big enough for the men, they ducked through, disappearing out of sight. The beast grunted and continued in its work, striving to make the hole wide enough for its own considerable body.

The Stahlhelme filled the doorway Christopher had flown through. The men who had slipped through it scattered back. Their guns were next to useless in close quarters against the beasts. As they dived away, the Stahlhelme in the door sliced down along the nearest one's back. The man twisted and fell with a screech.

Eleila sprinted across the room, the Sword in the Stone tight in her hand. Her eyes stayed fixed on the beast as she ran, the barrier to the fight beyond. She gritted her teeth and thrust the sword in front of her.

One of the men — in a long coat with a moustache — turned and started to fire back at the doorway. The Stahlhelme roared with pain. It lifted its mighty arm to shield itself from the barrage of lead.

It struggled to squeeze through the gap. The doorway was just a fraction too small for its frame. It heaved to pull its other shoulder through, grunting with the effort.

Eleila stabbed up into its armpit, plunging the sword as deep as she could manage. The blade disappeared a foot and a half into the beast's flesh. Its roar became a gurgle. Its head dropped. For a moment it stood, held tight in the doorway. Then it began to float away into sparks.

The man with the moustache rushed back to the door. He bellowed at the others. 'Positions!'

Another huge shape rushed towards the doorway. Behind it was another. The moustached man fired his pistol at the head of the first. It slowed, hands reaching for its face. The one behind bashed into it grunting, confused. It shoved the first out of the way.

On the far side were two more. One had its back to them. It was gripping something close to its body. It turned. Christopher was held tight in its arms.

The biggest of the Stahlhelme was behind him. Christopher struggled against its grip. At least whilst it had him in its hands, it couldn't use the rifle. The weapon hung from a strap on its forearm, axe end down.

It was the other Stahlhelme that was the danger. The first, the one that had him, had swung him around to face the second. Christopher twisted in its grip, wriggling his arms. There was the slightest movement on his left arm. Then the beast felt it too. It readjusted its grip. Now there was nothing.

Christopher's heart pounded in his chest. The second was almost smiling. If that bestial face could show emotion, it was triumph. It inched the blade of its pole axe around to him, until the sharp point was just in front of him. It was savouring the kill.

Had that man not wanted him alive? Christopher frowned despite his fear. All that effort to just be killed by these dumb beasts. It made no sense. Shouldn't the man be stopping them? Yet he was running through the hall, along with the only other chance of reaching Sama.

Anger tempered his fear again. He kicked out with his feet impotently. The beast in front was out of his reach. Then it thrust with the blade.

Eleila rushed forward. The beast that held Christopher was oblivious. The gunfire and screams behind her, around the doorway she had slipped through, were doing a good job of masking the clang of her armour.

She swung the sword back. The Stahlhelm's leg was in front of her, thick and meaty. She grunted and smashed the sword into the beast.

Everything happened fast. The Stahlhelme holding him screeched. It lurched to the side. The blade that headed straight towards his face was suddenly sailing past his ear instead. It dug into his captor's shoulder.

The Stahlhelm's grip loosened. Christopher could move his arms just a little. His heart leapt. He thrust down with the gauntlet. It was just a fraction, but it was enough. The force of Winters Grasp drove him down, on to the floor, out of the beast's grasp.

The creature in front grunted, confused. It looked about, searching for him. Christopher balled Winter's Grasp into a fist and thrust up at its face.

He flew up. His fist struck its face. Its bone was hard. There was a loud crack. The bone gave way. His hand sunk into something soft. The beast fell back to the floor. Suddenly he was standing on its chest and it was still.

He swung around, ready to take on the other. There was no need.

Eleila pulled the sword from its chest. It was already dissipating into sparks. Next to it, a smaller shape, its leg, was all but points of light.

'The man!' Christopher swung around, looking up the length of the hall.

Eleila drew up next to him. 'There!' She pointed, even as he spotted the movement. Over on the far side, close to a massive plinth filled with statues, someone scuttled through the shadows.

'Go!' Eleila shouted.

Christopher reached out with Winter's Grasp.

Bediviere led the way until they came to another door. It looked as if it hadn't been opened for a long time. Tendrils of plants grew through gaps in the door planks. Tiny roots embedded themselves into soft, rotted wood. A stout wooden bar held the door in pace. Bediviere lifted the bar, carefully placing his hand at its centre to balance it as he lifted.

Makena set Sama down against the floor. 'Rest a moment, sweet. Let me help him.'

Sama had said nothing. She was looking whiter and whiter by the minute. Makena frowned. She should be lying still, not being forced to make this frenzied escape.

The ointment and the energy poultice would help in any normal situation where she could rest. They would do wonders. They would have her on her feet in a matter of days. However, until they could get her somewhere she could rest, Makena wasn't sure they were doing any good at all.

Makena checked her eyes. She was less alert now. Pain and fatigue would weigh her down.

It was no matter. Worrying about the girl would not help. Action would.

Bediviere struggled to open the door. He thrust against it with his healthy shoulder on the wood. The door held shut. Makena moved next to him.

'Help me. On three,' he said, then started to count.

'Save your strength.' Makena lifted the staff. 'Stand back.'

She smashed the tip of the staff against the door. It blew out, splitting into two, surrounded by an inky black cloud that sailed over the cliff beyond.

She turned and reached to Sama. 'Come.'

Sama raised an arm, half-hearted, and groaned as she was pulled up, but stood on her own feet. She looked at Makena. 'I'm ok. I can do it.'

Makena smiled. The girl had reserves of strength she herself would be proud of.

'Footsteps.' Bediviere picked up his crossbow. 'They come.'

He led them out of the door. The path beyond was no more than five feet wide. It hugged the side of the cliff. They were forty feet below the level of the courtyard, entirely concealed from above.

Stone slabs led steeply down the cliff side in great sea-soaked steps. Makena struggled along, holding Sama up and occasionally throwing glances back the way they came. No pursuers had appeared yet.

They reached an outcrop. Waves smashed against the path, threatening to rip any traveller from it. Ten yards along, a chasm opened to the stormy seas below. A short stone bridge passed over it, dangerously exposed. Beyond, the path became a scored groove in the rock itself. It circled off to the side and out of view.

They hurried to the bridge. An arrow clacked off against the stone as they crossed. Makena turned around. Soldiers surged from the castle exit. Another arrow flew by, caught in the coastal winds and blown off target.

Makena brandished her staff. Its black bolts were not affected by the weather. The first smashed three down into the water. Two more ducked back into the doorway.

At the far side of the bridge Bediviere turned, lifting his crossbow. He shifted, letting Makena and Sama pass him. Makena heard the twang of a bolt being released. The knight swore under his breath.

He caught them up a few paces later. 'Destroy the bridge!' He shouted in her ear.

A loud report echoed behind them. The cliff face to their side exploded into mud. Makena stopped and glanced back.

The Stahlhelme had smashed through the doorway. It raised its rifle to fire again.

'Sama, wait there,' Makena released the girl, guiding her to stagger towards the cliff wall.

Bediviere was putting another bolt on his crossbow in his one-handed style. Makena rushed forward and grabbed his shoulder. 'Get back!'

He ducked against the cliff wall. Makena moved in front of him. The Stahlhelme fired again. Clods of earth and shards of rock flew out at her.

She concentrated on the bridge, focusing the staff. The black energy burst across and smashed into the stonework. It shattered into mortar and slabs. They tumbled away, down into the chasm.

Makena blasted again, this time at the door of the castle itself. The Stahlhelme dived to its left, back into the castle. A soldier next to it, not so agile, screamed and disappeared over the side.

Makena blasted again. The masonry above the door crumbled and fell in. A cloud of dust plumed out around the exit.

She held, heart beating in her chest, then tensed to attack again. Slowly the dust settled.

The doorway was gone completely. In its place was a far larger hole. Big enough that many more enemies could clamber out at once.

A huge shape became distinct against the receding cloud. The Stahlhelme pointed its rifle, searching for foes through the dust. Other shapes hurried out around it.

Makena gritted her teeth and lifted the staff again.

It was like experiencing everything through water, Sama thought to herself. It wasn't that the pain had gotten worse. It was constant. The black bandage was doing its job. What was getting steadily worse was the sense of disorientation.

As they escaped, it was all she could do to hold on to Makena, to put one foot in front of the other.

She leaned against cold cliff face. She was dimly aware of Bediviere and Makena fighting enemies back by the castle. The stone felt nice against her cheek, a counterpoint to the heat that seemed to be running through her body.

There was a dark explosion, then Makena was leaning in toward her, pulling at her arm, encouraging her to get up again.

'I'm ok. I can make it.' She reached for the right words. Makena's face slipped in and out of focus.

A voice. A man's. 'Wait, there's more!'

Makena's face disappeared again. Sama struggled to stay on her feet, swaying back and forth. She persevered. If her friends needed her to go this way, there would be a good reason. She would make it.

Her face was so wet. She wondered if she was underwater. No, she couldn't be. How could she breathe? And wasn't that wind blowing at her, too? Wind didn't blow underwater.

And her feet were stepping forward now. One by one. She wasn't swimming, she was walking. Though it must be through mud or something. Each step grew harder and harder to drag across the earth

Another bang. It seemed far away, but she felt herself jerked to the left. Makena's voice shouted something from the distance. Sama said nothing. Dim irritation flooded through her mind. She was doing it! She was walking. What did they want from her?

She righted herself against the blast. No time to rest, she had to walk. She had no sense of where her friends were now. They must be ahead somewhere. There had been an arm she had leaned on, hadn't there? Or had she imagined that? No matter, it was gone now. She just had to keep putting one foot in front of the other.

There was another deep boom, then another. Where they came from, Sama couldn't say.

Her foot dropped down. Was she on steps now? How had she got to steps? The drop threw her balance and she struggled to get the other foot in front. Someone called her name.

The call of her name. The sudden sense of stumbling. They jolted through her haze.

Her eyes opened. Waves crashed against rocks, hundreds of feet below. She gasped, flailing her arms. Her mind struggled to understand what was happening.

It was too late. Her weight was over the edge. No amount of arm waving would help her now. Then, as she slipped, she understood. She had simply, stupidly, staggered off the path to certain danger. Her mind grasped for a curse at her own foolishness, but the words failed her.

Sama fell towards the crashing waves below.

The Master didn't know where he was running to. For once, there wasn't time for a plan. All he was sure of was that the tide turned. The damn boy! He had almost had the whole of McCloud's forces destroyed.

Gunshots cracked in the distance behind him. They were not the boom of the beasts' rifles. The cracks came from smaller arms. McCloud's men. The Stahlhelme were dying.

He kept to the shadows. Though there was no one here to see him apart from the dead, it was better to be careful.

So close! He'd been so close. If he'd just had a little more time at the asylum or a few more moments on the battlements with the boy, he'd far away by now with a new world in his thrall.

The entrance to the stairs up was just across the way. He veered out of the shadows and sprinted towards it. Who knew what he might find up there, out on the street? Whatever it may be, he was sure he could slip through and disappear off into the night.

Once he was safely away, he could think about things properly. He still had a key. There would be interested parties out there. Parties he could negotiate with. Parties that would help him make it work again.

Then he heard the rush of wind.

The gaunt man turned his head. His eyes grew wide as he saw Christopher flying towards him. He dodged to the side, surprisingly quick, barely avoiding being caught.

Christopher landed just beyond, stumbling. He wheeled around to face the man.

He stood between the man and an archway in the wall. It was obviously where he had been heading. The man hesitated, seemingly unsure whether to turn tail and run or force his way through.

The man's eyes narrowed. He lifted his hand. There was something black in it. A revolver!

Christopher thrust forward, shooting off to the right. A bullet flew past his ear. He landed badly and scrambled up, chest tight with anger.

The man was running towards the archway again. He was not getting away. Christopher would not let it happen. The anger began to rise from his chest. His throat constricted. He ground his teeth together.

That man. If it hadn't been for him, none of this would have happened. Sama wouldn't be hurt somewhere beyond Christopher's reach.

Christopher thrust, angling his arc straight towards the entrance. He flew in front of the man, landing on his feet this time. He spun around and thrust again.

The man's eyes flashed wide. This time there was no chance to dodge, no chance to raise a pistol. Christopher slammed into the man, lifting him from his feet. The two of them flew across the hall.

The force of the boy knocked the wind out of him. He gasped a desperate breath. They were in the air now, a few feet from the ground. The archway with the stairs shrank back into the distance.

The Master twisted in the air, forcing his greater weight around until they were side by side. The landing would still hurt. At least the boy would not be on top.

They hit the stone floor. The impact forced them apart. The Master tumbled over and over. He threw out his arms, stopping himself then twisted on to his front.

They were on the fountain plinth. A giant statue loomed above him, its arc of water squirting high over the black cloth at its feet.

Then the boy slammed into him again.

'Where is it?' Christopher punched down at the man. 'Give me the key!' The gauntlet smashed into his shoulder.

He screeched with pain. Before Christopher could punch again, he kicked up. His left knee smashed into Christopher's guts.

Now they were close, using the gauntlet was far more difficult. The man was like a snake, twisting and dodging the worst of Christopher's blows. He struggled to lift his pistol into the fight. One good shot or one good punch and it would all be over.

The man's face was a grimace. His eyes were narrowed into a protective squint. It was almost as if he were laughing.

Christopher's vision seared to white. Thoughts of the key disappeared. Suddenly he just wanted to hurt the man. He wanted to pound and pound that face until there was nothing left.

A dry voice in the Master's head wondered if the boy understood beating him wasn't going to answer any questions. He didn't seem to care. His eyes had clouded over.

Where was the timid child whom he had met as Bailey? Christopher Flyte had turned out to be quite the wrong type of boy after all. All those months of painstaking research!

The boy punched again. It caught the Master on the mouth. He tasted blood, then shook the pain away. Adrenaline was his painkiller now. This wouldn't do. The boy might have the bloody gauntlet now, but at close quarters the Master was bigger and stronger. He rained blows up, smashing the sides of the boy's head with fist and pistol butt.

The impact of the pistol butt jolted Christopher from his white hot anger. He blinked, suddenly aware he was atop the man. A fist crashed into the other side of his head, knocking him to the side.

The man sensed his brief advantage. He punched again, hitting the same spot.

Christopher saw stars. He felt his weight shift. The man was slipping from under him. Footsteps pelting away.

Eleila kept pace with the others. Four of them ran towards the fountain plinth. Behind them the last of the Stahlhelme was already just a cloud of sparks.

Ahead on the plinth, Christopher struggled up. The gaunt man was a few feet away, running. He disappeared behind a statue.

The man with the moustache raised his pistol. Too late. 'Dammit.'

The Master stopped by the statue and turned back. McCloud's men were still a good distance. He could get across to the door before they arrived. The boy was still the biggest danger.

Christopher had staggered to his feet. His eyes still swam.

The Master lifted the gun. Such a mundane way to end a life. Still, it was the boy's fault that it had come to this.

'You could have had years living in a dream, you little fool,' he muttered.

Christopher looked up. His eyes focused.

The Master squeezed the trigger.

Christopher saw the pistol pointed straight at him. He flung his arm forward. The muzzle flashed as he grasped with the gauntlet, his gaze fixed on the gaunt man's head. He flew forward at the man.

The bullet met him as he flew. There was a sudden pain in his head.

Then everything went dark.

Christopher disappeared behind the statue, his body limp in the air. Eleila stretched her legs even more, her eyes never leaving the plinth. Almost immediately he appeared on the other side.

The gaunt man was with him now. The gauntlet had stuck him full in the face. Both bodies, as limp as one another, sailed over the side of the plinth and down to the floor.

'Christopher!' Eleila screamed. She rushed across last yards, the sword ready in her hand. At her side, the men pulled to a halt, training weapons at the pair on the ground. There was no need.

Both lay as still as the dead.

CHAPTER THIRTY

After the Winter

'Christopher.' A voice. An arm on his shoulder shaking him gently. Pain in his throat. Pain in his side. A throbbing in his head.

Christopher opened his eyes. At least he opened one eye. The other he struggled to open, barely managing a slit. The skin around his eye was fat with blood.

Eleila leaned over him. Behind her stood John Braddock, his face a frown.

'Don't try to move yet,' Eleila said.

John Braddock was talking to a man to his left. Issuing orders in short barked sentences.

'The man!' Christopher said, pushing himself up on to his elbows. The pounding in his head rushed to a crescendo. He slipped back down.

'As usual, you don't listen,' Eleila said. 'Be still. His missile grazed your scalp. You are lucky you are not dead.'

'Lucky!' Christopher wanted to shout at her. 'He was our way back!'

Eleila raised her eyebrows at him. 'Then it is good you stopped him.'

'I did?' Her words hit his heart. Suddenly he felt incredibly tired. He closed his eyes. 'I did.'

Braddock's steps walked across to them. 'Mr. Flyte, you're with us again. I see you come from the same school of foolhardiness as your friend Sama.'

At the sound of her name, Christopher pulled his eyes open once more. 'You have the key? We should go!' He tried to struggle to his elbows again.

Braddock leaned down and put a firm hand on his shoulder. 'There is a lot to talk about. Ward will be along presently.'

'But we must hurry!' Christopher tried to push against the big man's hand. It was useless. It seemed this exhaustion had taken all the strength from him.

'My wife is with Sama, Christopher. I have as much wish as you to get through,' Braddock said, his voice calm. 'But we will wait to hear what McCloud has to say.'

Christopher nodded. A few more minutes would not hurt. He really did feel very tired.

A woman moved in close next to Eleila. She reached forward. There was a cup in her hand. 'Hello, Christopher.' A hand slipped around the back of his head, gently lifting him. 'I've something for you. It will help you heal.'

Christopher opened his mouth and drank.

The Master came to his senses as they dragged him through the day room. It took all his concentration not to cry out with the pain. Everything hurt.

The men, who thought he was still out cold, were not handling him with anything resembling care. His legs dragged along the ground. One of his boots had come off somewhere. They'd removed his coat. The key was gone with it.

He squinted his eyes open, risking a glance around. There was not much to see. Mess mostly. Children's toys. One passed below him as he was dragged on, a furry bear with a bullet-sized hole in its head. Stuffing was strewn all around it.

They took him on, through another door. Now he was in a dark corridor. Grey flagstones covered the floor.

He heard the man's chanting before he saw the blue glow. A steady, rhythmic mantra repeating time and time again. An incantation to raise defences, he had no doubt.

As he was dragged closer the blue glow became distinct. A long rectangle on the floor. He knew that shade of blue. Now was the time to sacrifice the edge. They came up to the door. He lifted his head.

Of course it was a portal. That was obvious. Besides, he had seen the other entrance. It looked just the same. He wished he could leap through and travel back to the relative safety of the other world. They held him too tight. Besides, he was weak now. Better to bide his time. Better to see how things played out.

'Look sharp!' a voice barked by his left ear. 'He's awake!'

They picked up their pace, marching him on before he could get more than another glance through the doorway. He caught a glimpse of the bespectacled man within, thin and white-faced, looking quite out of his depth.

They dragged him down steps and through another door. Then they turned, heading deeper into labyrinthine corridors, moving through chambers, occasionally turning on themselves. Sometimes he stumbled to his feet, scrambling along with them. When he faltered they continued dragging him anyway. Before long, he was sure there would be no way he could find his way back alone.

Finally, they came to the cell. Of course. This journey was always going to end in a cell. They threw him to the floor of the tiny room, slamming the door behind him. He listened as a key turned, then one bolt slipped across, then another.

Their footsteps echoed off into the distance. The Master sat and leaned against the cold stone wall. He shifted, trying to find a part of his back that didn't have a bruise blossoming on it. He licked around his mouth. A tooth was missing at the side. Finally with a sigh, he closed his eyes.

The Master heard the huffing and puffing before he heard the footsteps. He grimaced with recognition, then struggled to his feet. He would be damned if the fat fool would see him sitting on the cell floor. He stumbled over to the door and gripped the handle to steady himself. Then he looked through the barred window and waited.

'Ward,' he said, mustering dry indifference as the outer door opened.

Ward McCloud stopped at his name. A frown passed over his face.

'You got fatter,' the Master said, waiting for the man ahead to show some recognition.

'Barty?' McCloud's frown disappeared. He grinned warmly, as if this were simply the meeting of two old friends. 'You know, I wondered if this was you.' He continued towards the cell door. 'You got a key. I always thought you had it in you.'

'And yet you don't have one.' The Master kept his face neutral. 'Still a glorified clerk.'

'Oh, I did my term.' McCloud refused to let the tone break his smile. 'We stopped them being for life a long time ago. It was felt they had a tendency to corrupt. Then later the committee thought I would serve as a coordinator. It's always suited my talents more than being out in the field. It was your father's idea, actually. A part of his legacy.'

The Master grimaced, feeling his hackles rising at the thought. This was stupid, to let these emotions surface. They were the least of his concerns.

'Is that what this was?' McCloud said. 'Sour grapes? Father denies you your birthright so you plot to bring down his life's work? How did you find another, by the way?'

He wouldn't rise to it he told himself. He smiled. 'No, not at all. It was all about the boy. I wasn't even sure I was here until I saw the fountains.'

'Of course. You never came in by invitation from the front, did you?' McCloud paused, wiping his brow with a handkerchief. 'Remarkable boy, Christopher. He opened a portal without a key. I didn't think that it was possible. How did he do that, do you think?'

'I haven't thought about it.'

'I suppose you haven't really had a chance to.' McCloud smiled and looked at him. He had remarkably bright eyes, even in this dim light. 'Well, you'll have plenty of time now.'

He waved a hand. 'Well, I can't stay, Barty. I simply had to satisfy my curiosity. There'll be lots of time once we've cleared up your mess for you and me to talk. I'll have lots of questions.'

McCloud turned away and stumbled back toward the door. 'Do try and conserve your strength in the meantime. I imagine you'll be keen to try and hold out when we question you. We might as well make a sport of it.'

The Master watched McCloud leave in silence. The door clicked shut behind him. A muttered exchange came back through the wood. Guards. Of course.

It was only once the man's puffing had disappeared off into the dark entirely that the Master sank to the floor again. McCloud may have just been trying to scare him, but that didn't make him wrong. He should conserve his strength.

The Master closed his eyes in the dark once more.

It was two hours before McCloud finally made his way back to the ward. An attack had always been anticipated here. Procedures were in place. The street was now blocked by army trucks in both directions. The soldiers the vehicles contained, looking clean and pressed —and totally inexperienced — had been set to erecting barriers across the street two houses down either way. Others were tasked with evicting the families and their servants from those houses within the barriers, and this itself was causing quite a stir.

The evicted kicked up a great deal of fuss about having to leave their homes so close to Christmas, with no hint as to when they would return. One frustrated man shouted at a raw faced soldier, who stood silently taking the dressing down, red-faced under his khaki cap.

None of the soldiers had been allowed access to the headquarters. The doorway was guarded by five men in dark suits. The men held no weapons, but each had tell-tale bulges at their waists.

McCloud left them to it and walked back through the ruined upper corridor. The bodies had been cleared already. The building would take far longer to restore.

The Fountain Hall was in better condition. Apart from the guardhouse at the end, much of the damage was cosmetic. The order would survive. The order would move on.

Christopher Flyte sat up in bed as he entered. The boy looked better already. Colour had returned to his cheeks. His face was still a mess of bruises, no elixir they had could cure that so quickly, but he was alert. And inevitably full of questions.

'We need to go!' He shouted the words before McCloud reached him. 'Where's his key? We need to get back!'

McCloud raised an arm. 'You need to rest, Christopher. The key is safe, but it is blocked. We tried to open it as soon we had it. Something is stopping us getting through. We need to research it before we can risk using it. The world you created is unlike anything that has come before.'

'But anything could be happening!'

Beside the boy, the girl in the armour shifted, wary. Eleila. That was what they had called her. Her hand gripped the sword. She had refused to give it up, or leave his side. It was a shame. Perhaps separating them would make them both more receptive. For the moment though, allowing them to keep each other's company was keeping them calm. To a point.

'I know you have little reason to trust us right now, Christopher,' McCloud said. 'But Miss Neeley is with Makena. She could not be in better company. They will endure.'

Christopher opened his mouth to protest.

'The point is moot anyway.' McCloud stopped and leaned against the white iron base of the bed. He sighed. 'As I said, the key is blocked. I assure you, when you are rested, you will be included in any plans that we have. You've turned out to be a very unusual boy.'

The boy sighed, then waited, silent.

McCloud nodded and smiled as sympathetic a smile as he could muster. 'Good. Now let me tell you what I suggest. Our other children have been moved. We have a facility named Lemontrees. It is out of London. It is safe. Well, safer than here. We would like to take you there.'

Christopher frowned. He shook his head violently.

'Your brother is there, Christopher,' McCloud said, allowing the words to sink in.

'Freddie?' The boy's face changed. He glanced at Eleila.

She looked back. 'It's your world we are in. I go where you go.'

McCloud pressed on. 'It would be safer for you if you let us take the gauntlet. Then you can concentrate on getting better.'

Christopher's eyes became steel. 'We've been though that, Mr McCloud.

Unless you want me to start flying all over the place in here, you better forget that right away.'

One thing at a time. 'Very well, Christopher. You may keep the gauntlet for now. Your friend may keep her sword. There will be more to say about that later, though.'

Christopher's shoulders relaxed. Once they had him at Lemontrees, there would be plenty of opportunities to relieve them of their possessions, even if it must be by force.

'So, you will come to Lemontrees?'

The boy nodded slowly. 'On one condition.'

McCloud sighed. 'Name it.'

'Take me home first. So I can get clothes for me. And for Freddie.'

The first time Sama woke it was night. She lay on the remains of a castle door, floating on a choppy sea. Her eyes half opened. In the dark, there was no way to tell which way the land was, nor how far she had floated. The only sounds her befuddled ears could hear were the splashes of waves around her.

It was cold. She dimly wondered if it was cold enough to freeze her. The thought didn't particularly concern her. Though she was soaked through and her body still hurt all over, she felt quite calm. Everything still felt distant, as if she were watching herself from far away.

She tried to lift her head. It felt so heavy. It probably wasn't worth the bother anyway. Instead she closed her eyes again. In a moment, she lapsed back into unconsciousness.

The second time she woke, it was with the dawn. The early morning sun blazed across the ocean, shining red through her eyelids, forcing her awake. She squinted against its glare. It felt warm on her face. Pleasant contrast to the soaking clothes on her body.

Now she remembered hitting the water. The sudden splash jolted her. Her body sank deep beneath the waves. She had swum then, pulling upwards with all her remaining strength, ignoring the screaming of her shoulder, striving for the air.

She didn't remember finding the door she was on. Without it, she would have certainly drowned. It was reassuringly solid. Her island in this sea of confusion.

She risked a movement. Careful at first, she manoeuvred her arms to a position where she could push herself up. Gradually she eased on to her elbows, the nerves in her shoulder protesting with each movement. The pain made her want to be sick. She swallowed against the feeling, fighting to stay up. At least the black membrane was still in place. It held tight around her shoulder, impervious to the salty water all around.

She looked around. Nothing. No land in any direction. As far as the eye could see was just ocean.

The effort was getting too much for her. If she didn't rest again, there was a very good chance she would actually be sick. She sank back down on to the door and turned her head away from the sun. Soon, once more, she was unconscious.

She drifted in and out of consciousness for hours. Most of the time she floated along in slumber, oblivious of the water splashing her face, her hand dragging along submerged by her side. When she did come to, it was brief. She was growing weaker.

When she felt the hands on her body, she thought she might be dreaming. She squeezed her eyes tighter, willing herself back into oblivion.

Voices cut through her awareness. Rough, men's voices.

'Careful with her.'

'She looks weak. How long do you think she's been out here?'

Sama felt herself lifted up and rolled on to her back in someone's arms. She groaned as her weight pushed on to her shoulder.

'Careful, I said!' the first voice snapped.

'You be bloody careful.' The second voice was close, just above her head. 'You're not who had to hang over the side.'

There was creaking now. Wood strained against wood. Sama opened her eyes.

A rough ginger beard loomed above her. Below it, a neck with a tattoo. Above the beard, reaching high into the sky was a mast suspending a wind filled sail.

The man carrying her glanced down. His fierce green eyes softened as he noticed she was awake.

'Well now.' His voice was gentler now. 'You're a long way from shore, girly.'

'Where am I?' Sama croaked.

'On "The Abigail." The man smiled. 'Good job too. You don't look like you would have lasted much longer out there. You're safe now.'

Sama closed her eyes. If the man said she was safe, then she was too tired to question it. She was out of the water. Anyone that was helping her could be her friend.

Friends! Sama's eyes snapped back open. Makena and Bediviere on the cliff! 'We have to …' she started, too loud. The effort reduced her to racking coughs.

The man looked down again. 'Calm, girl. Let me get you a place to rest.'

He was walking now. Across the deck, she supposed. All she could see was the man, the mast and the sky.

The coughs subsided. 'We have to get to shore.' This time she managed the whole sentence. 'My friends are in danger.'

'That's not for me to decide,' the man answered. They reached a door, worn wood, crusted with white. 'That's for my lord.'

He glanced over his shoulder. 'You'd better go and fetch him, Billy. If this one has come from shore, he'll want to speak with her.'

'Righty ho.' The other voice came from behind.

Ginger beard barged the door open with a clumsy shoulder. He manhandled Sama through into the darkness. 'There's a bed here. We'll get you warmed up.'

Suddenly he stopped. 'Dammit!' he muttered. Then he looked back to the door. 'Billy! Billy!'

A moment later the door opened a crack. The other man's head popped through. 'What? For pity's sake!'

Ginger beard looked back at him. 'You better fetch her too, Billy. Bring the Queen.'

'This really is the safest way,' the woman said yet again. Her tight smile was still fixed in place. Christopher thought maybe she had been introduced earlier, but he had taken no notice. 'Lemontrees is very well-guarded.'

Christopher looked out of the window. 'And I suppose London was badly guarded, was it?'

Next to him, he felt Eleila's hand on his shoulder, squeezing a warning to stay mute. Christopher let out an exasperated breath of air and sat back into the leather seat.

It was light by the time they pulled off the main road and began along the winding lane down to Alton. They had left London when it was still dark, leaving via a back entrance to an empty street. Just them, the woman, and the driver. McCloud expected they would give no trouble.

Eleila had been jumpy since they had been here. Christopher understood, of course. Everything around her was quite alien. She didn't even have any stories on which to base her understanding. She'd reluctantly agreed to change out of her armour, but she still grasped the Sword in the Stone. It hadn't left her side.

He could see that putting her trust entirely in him had been quite an effort for her. For the most part, she had been staring out of the window taking it all in. She'd calmed a little once they had left London and got out into the country. Occasionally she turned to him, pointing something out and asking for an explanation.

She turned as they drove past the village green. 'This is your home?'

Christopher nodded. 'The village I live in. The house is further out.'

It didn't feel like home now. Home was where the people he cared about were. His brother was at Lemontrees. His father was heavens knew where. The lads would have left for basic training.

They passed along the bottom road. The slope of the green was crisscrossed with thick lines in the snow. Grooves where the village children had played on sleds, the cares of the world safely beyond the boundaries of their lives.

There were no boundaries here for him now. He glanced at the Stumblepot. The curtains were still drawn. It looked sad and lonely. How must Mr Neeley be feeling inside with both his son and daughter gone?

So what if Lemontrees was well guarded? The portal wasn't there. The key wasn't there.

Sama wasn't there.

It was a mistake. Now he was here, in Alton, he knew it. It was good that Freddie was at Lemontrees. That would at least mean he was somewhere safe. But everything that would help them get to Sama was back in London.

The car turned left, up towards the top road. Christopher glanced out of his window towards the river. His eyes rested on Joe's house. The roof was covered with snow.

The last time he had been here, he'd been fooled. The man who claimed to be Bailey hadn't cared anything about him at all. There was no real reason to think that McCloud and his associates cared any more. Why should he and Eleila trust them? They would be better on their own.

They could get back to London and find a way to the portal. He could find his way back to Sama. Eleila could get back to her world. With Winter's Grasp, who could catch them? They weren't captives here. He had listened to other people enough. He had trusted what they told him for the last time.

Besides, Christopher realised, a crafty grin slipping on to his face, it wasn't as if they couldn't get all the resources they might need in London. He wondered how Edwin Welstone would react when he turned up in the gauntlet, accompanied by an angry woman with a sword. That was a reaction he would like to see.

Christopher reached across and touched Eleila's hand. Her eyes narrowed as soon as she saw his expression. She glanced at the two in the front then glanced back. Finally, she nodded. She understood.

The car turned at the top of the road, passing the last houses. They were out in the woods now. Up above them would be the Pickering Tower. Christopher had been sneaking through these woods with Sama since he was small.

He shifted across on the seat, readying the gauntlet.

The driver glanced into his mirror. 'All right back there?'

The woman turned around.

'Now!' Christopher whispered.

Eleila shoved open the door. Christopher wrapped his arm round her. He reached forward with Winter's Grasp and pulled.

Together they flew out from the car into the trees.

Epilogue

The fire had burned low to embers. It was giving off a perfect heat. The old man stirred the bowl steadily. He sniffed, relishing the dark chocolate smells that emanated from within, then lifted the spoon. He touched it to his mouth, wiping a little of the liquid on to lips so thinned by age they were almost gone.

There was no telling exactly how old the man was. His face was a web of lines. They grew deeper as he smiled at the taste of the drink. 'Nice, but far too soon.'

He felt calm. It took a lot to excite him these days. It had as far as he could remember. Not even the icy grip that consumed him a few hours ago raised his heartbeat. He'd waited for the feeling to pass, breathing slowly and regularly. Then he'd clambered up and walked to the little alcove where he kept his key. Everything was as it should be.

He put down the spoon and tottered out towards the mountainside. He had spent much of the previous day chopping and piling wood at the edge of the little Andean cave that had been home for four hundred years or so, ready to keep the fire burning as he made his favourite drink.

He gestured with his hand. Five large logs floated up from the pile and glided over towards him. He turned as they passed him, guiding them on towards the fire, settling them down on to the flames.

'I could have carried those in.' The voice came from below him. He glanced down the path.

The boy was returning. Though to call him 'the boy' had been inaccurate for a very long time. There was probably no more than thirty years age difference between them, but the boy always liked to make out that he was younger and stronger.

'You probably could.' The old man smiled. 'How was the village?'

'Funny you should ask.' He was doing a bad job of pretending he wasn't out of breath. 'It was fine for a while. Then this happened.'

He pulled off his poncho. A thick wool jumper and two undershirts came off too. He dropped them one by one on to the ground. Done, he stood in his trousers and looked up at the old man. 'What do you make of this?'

The artefact he wore had not kept a constant shape for years. It would meld from one item to another as the boy willed it. Sometimes, when he was asleep, it would shift of its own accord.

Now however, it was going crazy. For a moment it was a ring on his hand, then it snaked up his arm, passing through the shape of a snake bracelet the old man vaguely recalled from their Aztec days, before expanding out to form a Spanish Conquistador breastplate. A moment later, it was a headband, then a belt, then a scabbard. On and on it went, never holding one shape for more than a second or two.

'It's becoming a little tiresome.' The boy sighed, looking up. 'Does this mean anything to you?'

The old man nodded. 'Something has changed.'

'Something has changed?' The boy raised an eyebrow. 'Well, whilst I'm sure that's nice, is there any way to stop it? I'll struggle to sleep later with this happening.'

'You may not.' The old man smiled apologetically. He looked off into the distance. 'Finally, it's beginning.'

Acknowledgements

I've been writing this novel for ten years, taking time out from the real world whenever I could and shutting myself away in cottages the length and breadth of the UK. A lot of people have helped me along the way.

Thanks to my readers: Sarah Hill, Josephine Noble, Leigh Perkin and Cat Dunn. You've all been a huge help with the parts you looked at. Particular thanks to Leigh for being my partner in crime on numerous writing trips. Here's to cars crashed, mountains slid down and whiskey consumed. Additional thanks to Simon Woods, Aimee Albiston and Jasper the (idiot) dog for providing extra entertainment on recent escapes.

Thanks also to the owners of the various cottages I have stayed in whilst writing this book. Particularly Mark and family at Blackadon Barns in Devon and Jackie and family down in Porthgwarra, Cornwall. I have very fond memories of both.

Silviu Sadoschi, who has so brilliantly illustrated my front cover and my website, has been a joy to work with. I consider myself very lucky to have found him.

Thanks to my editor, Delena Silverfox for the advice and encouragement she has given me. Thanks too to the editors at Fantastic books for giving it a final 'spruce'.

Finally, thanks to you for getting a copy of the book and reading it. I hope that you enjoyed it. If you did, and you would like to read the sequel in a time period that's less than ten years, please tell your friends. The more people that buy this book, the more time I can devote to writing more for you.

I'd love to hear from you after you finished reading this. You can mail me at john@john-d-scotcher.co.uk or visit my website: www.john-d-scotcher.co.uk.

And PLEASE review the book with your honest opinion on Amazon. The more reviews a book has, the more it features in searches!

John
January 2015